THE YEAR'S BEST

Fantasy and Horror

2007

Also Edited by Ellen Datlow

Blood Is Not Enough

A Whisper of Blood

Endangered Species

The Dark

Inferno (forthcoming)

With Terri Windling

THE ADULT FAIRY TALE SERIES

Snow White, Blood Red

Black Thorn, White Rose

Ruby Slippers, Golden Tears

Black Swan, White Raven

Silver Birch, Blood Moon

Black Heart, Ivory Bones

A Wolf at the Door

Sirens

The Green Man

The Year's Best Fantasy and Horror:
First through Sixteenth Annual Collections

Also Edited by Ellen Datlow and Kelly Link & Gavin J. Grant

The Year's Best Fantasy and Horror:

Eighteenth Annual Collection

Nineteenth Annual Collection

Also by Kelly Link

Stranger Things Happen (collection)

Magic for Beginners (collection)

Trampoline (editor)

THE YEAR'S BEST

Fantasy and Horror

2007

TWENTIETH ANNUAL COLLECTION

Edited by

Ellen Datlow and

Kelly Link & Gavin J. Grant

St. Martin's Griffin ❧ New York

THE YEAR'S BEST FANTASY & HORROR. Copyright © 2007 by James Frenkel & Associates. All rights reserved. Printed in the United States of America. No part of this book may be used or reproduced in any manner whatsoever without written permission except in the case of brief quotations embodied in critical articles or reviews. For information, address St. Martin's Press, 175 Fifth Avenue, New York, N.Y. 10010.

www.stmartins.com

Summation 2006: Fantasy copyright © 2007 by Kelly Link and Gavin J. Grant
Summation 2006: Horror copyright © 2007 by Ellen Datlow
The Year in Media of the Fantastic: 2006 copyright © 2007 by Edward Bryant
Fantasy in Comics and Graphic Novels: 2006 copyright © 2007 by Jeff VanderMeer
Music of the Fantastic: 2006 copyright © 2007 by Charles de Lint

ISBN-13: 978-0-312-36943-9 (hc)
ISBN-10: 0-312-36943-3
ISBN-13: 978-0-312-36942-2 (pbk)
ISBN-10: 0-312-36942-5

OCT 17 2007

First Edition: October 2007

10 9 8 7 6 5 4 3 2 1

Copyright Acknowledgments

For Holly Black

Contents

Acknowledgments

Thanks to the editors, publishers, publicists, authors, artists, and readers who sent us review material and suggestions, but most especially thanks to Terri Windling, Ellen Datlow, Jim Frenkel, Charles Brown, and *Locus*, *Rain Taxi*, and *Publishers Weekly*.

We were grateful for the generous assistance of the following people: Diane Kelly, Jim Cambias, Deb Tomaselli, Jonathan Strahan, Elizabeth LaVelle, Mark & Cindy Ziesing and their essential catalog, Sean Melican, and interns Jedediah Berry and Gwyneth Merner.

Any omissions or mistakes are always, of course, our own.

Because we can only select from what we see, please submit or recommend published fantasy material to the address on this page: www.lcrw.net/yearsbest.

—G.G. & K.D.L.

Thanks to Harlan Ellison, William Smith, Stefan Dziemianowicz. Special thanks to Jim Frenkel, our hardworking packager, and his assistant, Melissa Faliveno, and interns Erik Baxter, Ben Freund, Merrill Hill, Jonathan Gelatt, Mark Kleinhaus, Leslie Matlin, Emma Phillips, Brianna Pintens, and Alan Rubsam.

And always, a very special thanks to Tom Canty for his unflagging visual imagination. Finally, thanks to my coeditors, Kelly Link and Gavin Grant.

I'd like to acknowledge the following magazines and catalogs for invaluable information and descriptions of material I was unable to obtain: *Locus*, *Publishers Weekly*, *Washington Post Book World* Web site, *The New York Times Book Review*, *Hellnotes*, *darkecho*, *Prism* (the quarterly journal of fantasy given with membership to the British Fantasy Society), and *All Hallows*. I'd also like to thank all the magazine editors who made sure I saw their magazines during the year and the publishers who got me review copies in a timely manner.

—E.D.

My thanks to our very talented and hardworking editors, Ellen Datlow, Gavin Grant, and Kelly Link. And to my staff, all of whom Ellen has already mentioned above. The twentieth collection was as much work as the first, though computers have helped us speed certain parts of the process. And thanks as well to our St. Martin's editor, Marc Resnick, and his able assistant, Sarah Lumnah; their help is essential to the success of this enterprise. Also, thanks to the authors and others who have granted permission to reprint works in this volume, and to our intrepid columnists, Ed Bryant, Charles de Lint, and Jeff VanderMeer, for their valuable contributions. And my thanks to Tom Canty, who continues to produce fresh, effective design and imagery.

—J.F.

Summation 2006: Fantasy

Kelly Link and Gavin J. Grant

Welcome to the summation of the year in fantasy for the milestone twentieth annual edition of *The Year's Best Fantasy and Horror*.

This was a good if not particularly remarkable year for fantasy short fiction—although as usual we could happily have filled a tome twice this size with our selections. In both 2005 and again this year, there have been, disappointingly, somewhat fewer than usual anthologies of original fiction but that was counterbalanced by a handful of truly outstanding short story collections. Looking at longer work, a number of the most interesting novels were either the beginnings of new series or the continuations of ongoing series. Perhaps more than the usual number of our favorite books came from the young adult shelves, and our two favorite books of all were a picture book without words and a biography.

In short fiction, there was a good deal of strong journeyman work, and in fact, *Strange Horizons* and the now-defunct small press magazine *Alchemy* provided some of the most innovative short fiction that we saw this year. There was also wonderful work from more established writers, such as Jeffrey Ford, whose novella "Botch Town" from the collection *The Empire of Ice Cream*, although too long to include here, was one of the highlights of the year. M. Rickert's "Journey into the Kingdom" and newer writer Ysabeau Wilce's marvelous "The Lineaments of Gratified Desire" showed the range of styles and genres that *The Magazine of Fantasy & Science Fiction* continues to offer. Literary magazines like *One Story* continue to offer a sampling of fantasy-tinged work.

2006 was the year in which not only did every author have a blog, but every publisher who did not already (such as Eos or the Science Fiction Book Club) began blogging. Already impressive bookstore blogs, such as Powell's, added features, as did genre bookstore bloggers, such as Pandemonium in Cambridge, Massachusetts. A number of authors with similar interests began to blog together. Some of the more enjoyable group blogs we saw included No Fear of the Future (Zoran Živković, Jess Nevins, Stephen Dedman, Chris Nakashima-Brown, and others), Eat Our Brains (Steven Gould, Madeleine E. Robins, Maureen F. McHugh, Bradley Denton, et al.), and the Wyrdsmiths (Eleanor Arnason, Naomi Kritzer, Lyda Morehouse, and others).

We are very much interested in the possibilities that online book search, scan-

ning, and sales offer to readers, authors, and publishers, and found the ongoing positioning between Google, Microsoft, publishers, and libraries to be fascinating. The
production and upkeep of a digital "Library of Alexandria" would seem to be one of
the new Wonders of the World, but no one knows quite how to get there from where
we are today.

Tor continues to publish the most fantasy titles—unless all the titles from the
Penguin imprints (Ace, DAW, Roc, and Firebird) are added up. Tor launches a
number of new fantasy series each year, and in 2006 the best entries came from new
writer Daniel Abraham as well as old hands such as Dave Duncan, Steven Brust,
Kate Elliott, Charles de Lint, and Jane Lindskold. Ace brings out at least one Patricia A. McKillip title every year—this year a wonderful contemporary fantasy—and
has a fine series author in Sarah Monette. Bantam Spectra continues to split its list
between science fiction and fantasy. Among their fantasy titles, books by Lisa Tuttle
and Ellen Kushner stood out. Big books from HarperCollins included novels by
Tim Powers, James Morrow, and collections by Neil Gaiman and Margo Lanagan.
Warner and Little, Brown were bought by Hachette who plan to introduce the Orbit
name over from the U.K. and the Commonwealth. Their biggest book this year was
Jacqueline Carey's first novel in a new Kushiel series. HarperCollins, Harcourt, and
Simon & Schuster published a wealth of young adult and children's titles—of
course this is a boom time for this segment of publishing and anyone seriously interested in locating the most innovative and satisfying fantasy ought to try browsing
in the young adult section of their bookstore. Megan Whalen Turner, Tamora
Pierce, Holly Black, Frances Hardinge, Elizabeth Knox, and Ursula K. Le Guin are
all writers who either already have—or ought to find—a large and enthusiastic readership among adults.

Night Shade Books, increasing both the number of titles in print and their print
runs, is becoming a midsize publisher to be reckoned with, although Jason Williams
and Jeremy Lassen continue to do most of the work. While still publishing horror
and science fiction, in 2006 they also launched a number of significant mixed
genre/fantasy titles, including collections by Kage Baker and Douglas Lain as well
as reprints of Glen Cook's long out-of-print Dread Empire series. Night Shade also
run a popular message board on their Web site that features many authors and editors.

Subterranean Press published high-quality collections by William Browning
Spencer and Jonathan Lethem as well as collectibles by Tim Powers and others.
Subterranean's limited editions are reasonably affordable, and Bill Schafer seems to
announce interesting new projects on an almost weekly schedule.

The Prime/Wildside behemoth added Juno, a paranormal romance line. For
many of their titles it was still hard to tell if a publication date (whether in a catalog,
ad, or on the Web) meant anything. Some books we decided had appeared in 2006,
some not. This year saw the debut of Minsoo Kang and publication of Theodora
Goss's much-anticipated *In the Forest of Forgetting*, as well as anthologies such as
Agog! Ripping Reads, *Mythic*, *Jabberwocky*, and *Eidolon*. Golden Gryphon published Jeffrey Ford's *The Empire of Ice Cream* and M. Rickert's *Map of Dreams*,
while Tachyon had a solid year with collections by Peter S. Beagle and two anthologies: *Feeling Very Strange: The Slipstream Anthology*, edited by James Patrick Kelly
and John Kessel, and the ongoing James Tiptree Award Anthology series (volumes 1
and 2 came out in late 2005 and early 2007).

Dark Horse debuted a varied trade book list under Dark Horse, DH Press, and M

Press, with a couple of excellent Yoshitako Amano art books, a collection by Elizabeth Hand, and some Universal movie monster novels.

Finally, the yearly Clarion Writers' Workshop took place for the last time in East Lansing, Michigan. Under the direction of Kate Wilhelm and a new volunteer board, the workshop moved to a new home at the University of California at San Diego. Workshops like Clarion, Clarion West, Odyssey, and Viable Paradise continue to launch the careers of rising stars such as Christopher Barzak, Marjorie Liu, and Margo Lanagan.

Although we will continue to list the first in new fantasy series, in future years—in order to leave as much room as possible for reprinting our favorite short fiction—we plan to list fewer titles in ongoing series. Readers are encouraged to do some scouting online for books that we have undoubtedly missed, as well as to e-mail us when we seem to have overlooked titles of interest.

Resources

We continue to enthusiastically recommend *Locus* magazine, Mark R. Kelly's excellent and frequently updated *Locus Online*, as well as the LOCUS Index to Science Fiction Awards (www.locusmag.com) for news, reviews, and more on the field. We recommend catalogs from both DreamHaven Books and Mark V. Ziesing Books. Borderlands Books offers an excellent e-mail newsletter. The Speculative Literature Foundation (www.speculativeliterature.org) has become an enormously useful site for readers and writers; the SLF administer the Fountain Award, an annual speculative short story prize. (See the Awards section for the 2006 winner and honorable mentions.) *Rain Taxi Review of Books* unfailingly offers unusual and rewarding recommendations. Books to Watch Out For (www.btwof.com) is three subscription-based monthly e-mail newsletters (lesbian, gay, and women's books). All three include a selection of fantasy titles. *Prism*, the newsletter of the British Fantasy Society, keeps subscribers up-to-date on the U.K. publishing scene. *Chronicle* offers reviews and news, although its schedule became increasingly irregular. Other recommended online resources include (and are obviously not limited to): *Ansible, The Alien Online, The Green Man Review, The Internet Review of Science Fiction, New York Review of Science Fiction, NewPages, RevolutionSF, Rambles, SFSite, Speculations,* and *Tangent.* We were sorry to see Cheryl Morgan's *Emerald City* close up shop.

Disclosure: we are the editors and publishers of Small Beer Press, and the zine *Lady Churchill's Rosebud Wristlet.*

Favorite Books of 2006

Comparing the books on this list isn't really like comparing apples and oranges. It's more like comparing Turkish delight and meerkats. Having said that, two books in particular we recommend to all comers. The first, *The Arrival* (Lothian) by Shaun Tan, is an Australian picture book. (American readers take note: Scholastic will publish it this summer.) *The Arrival,* the story of emigrants leaving war-torn and desolate countries in order to make new lives for themselves in a strange and faraway metropolis, is a wordless dream that will be hauntingly familiar to anyone who has ever traveled, been separated from their families, lived outside of their home country, or been confused about whether an unfamiliar object was edible. Tan's imagination and his illustrations run to outrageous architecture and staggering monsters, as well as intimate snapshots of faces and clouds. The story is moving and hopeful and worth lingering over.

Gordon Van Gelder had been telling us for years about Julie Phillips's biography of writer Alice B. Sheldon and while reading it we learned several important lessons: Julie Phillips could write us traffic tickets and we would enjoy them; and almost as important, always listen to Gordon. The third thing we learned is that Alice Sheldon's life was like no other. (Raised by a socialite-explorer-writer mother, worked for the CIA, invented the pseudonym Tiptree under which she published both her own fiction and also carried on a copious and fascinating series of correspondences with Ursula K. Le Guin and others.) Phillips also vividly captures the world and times in which Sheldon lived and wrote. *James Tiptree, Jr.: The Double Life of Alice B. Sheldon* (St. Martin's Press) is an exhilarating, terrifying page-turner of a biography that deservedly won the National Book Critics Circle Award and is recommended for the shelves of every reader of genre fiction.

Susanna Clarke's short fiction has been collected in *The Ladies of Grace Adieu and Other Stories* (Bloomsbury). This is a particularly lovely edition, and features illustrations by Charles Vess. There is one original story here, as well as old favorites, including the title story. Fans of *Jonathan Strange & Mr. Norrell* will be pleased by what they discover here, but fans of the short story form will be doubly delighted. Like Sylvia Townsend Warner, Susanna Clarke is adept at imbuing her characters and her landscape with a peculiar and formidable kind of magic.

Half Life (HarperCollins) by Shelley Jackson is the picaresque account of a conjoined twin who wishes to cut off the head of her sleeping sister. Like the stories in Jackson's *The Melancholy of Anatomy*, the metaphysical conceits here are more than sustained by the pleasures of the sly, lovely, funhouse strangeness of the prose. Imagine a cross between *Geek Love* and *Tristram Shandy* and you will have a rough idea of what Jackson is up to. One of Kelly's favorite books of the year, this is highly recommended to anyone with siblings, an interest in gender or body politics, or a taste for wordplay.

Readers of this series will already have had a taste of Margo Lanagan's first collection to be published in the U.S., *Black Juice*. This year Eos published Lanagan's earlier collection, *White Time*, while *Red Spikes* (Allen & Unwin) was published in Australia. Confused? Don't be! Rejoice instead, in the fact that wherever you live, there is at least one new Margo Lanagan available this year. From the re-imagining of Wee Willie Winkie ("Winkie," anthologized within by our coeditor) to the historically inspired witchcraft tale "Mouse Maker," Lanagan's stories continue to astonish, disturb, and delight us.

Jeffrey Ford's *The Empire of Ice Cream* (Golden Gryphon), introduced by Jonathan Carroll, would be worth its price if only for the original novella "Botch Town." However, whether or not you've read Ford's "The Weight of Words," "Giant Land," and "The Annals of Eelin-Ok," the stories collected here reward further investigation. Ford is a master of the short story and his manifold talents enlarge and enliven the modes and genres in which he works.

M. Rickert's debut collection, *Map of Dreams* (Golden Gryphon), contains several original stories, including the eponymous short title novel. Rickert dives into the hearts of her characters, shows us how hopeless and muddled they are, and then evokes our sympathy for them. Rickert's work shades more toward dark fantasy and horror, but she draws on fairy tales, myths, and the contemporary landscape and comes away with rich stuff unlike the fiction of anyone else working today.

Theodora Goss's debut collection, *In the Forest of Forgetting* (Prime), includes one recent masterpiece, "The Rose in Twelve Petals," as well as three originals including "Lessons with Miss Gray," whose eponymous protagonist figures in several of these stories. Goss, whose work appears with growing regularity in various *Year's Best* volumes, excels in writing stories that draw on Eastern European traditions, histories, and cultures, and like M. Rickert, her reworkings of fairy tales are expert and refreshing.

Ursula K. Le Guin's *Voices* (Harcourt) takes place in the same world as her young adult novel *Gifts*, and like *Gifts*, Le Guin's latest should appeal to adult readers as well. This series is the mature work of a world-class talent whose excellent and provocative novels regularly manage to be politically thoughtful as well as page-turners. Like the best characters in young adult fiction, Le Guin's narrators compel—it feels significant in more ways than one that this latest novel is called *Voices*.

Megan Whalen Turner has so far written three acclaimed novels about the imaginary kingdoms of Eddis and Attolia, where, as in Greek mythology, gods are as likely to interfere in the lives of humans as not. Most recent is *The King of Attolia* (Greenwillow), full of Dorothy Dunnett–style political intrigue and romantic reversals, and highly recommended to young adult and adult readers alike—although you'll probably want to start with the first of these three novels, Turner's Newbery Honor Book, *The Thief*.

In *The Privilege of the Sword* (Bantam) Ellen Kushner returns to the characters and city of *Swordspoint*. Katherine, at the age of fifteen, is invited to live with a wealthy uncle known as the Mad Duke and discovers, too late, that she is not to attend balls and be educated. Instead she is to be his swordsman. Influenced by Dumas as much as by Georgette Heyer, this latest Riverside novel is something of a departure in tone for Kushner, and it's the kind of book you long to read in one sitting and then immediately pass on to a friend.

In *Three Days to Never* (Morrow), Tim Powers's latest crossover thriller/fantasia, three elements come together in ways that would only ever seem right or inevitable in a Powers novel: a father and daughter begin to read each other's minds; a secret weapon is discovered and then abandoned by Albert Einstein; a videotape at least as chilling as the one featured in *The Ring*. New novels by Powers don't arrive as often as one would like, but in the meantime this one can be read more than once.

The Tourmaline (Tor) by Paul Park picks up where *A Princess of Roumania* left off. Our world is a figment of the imagination and has winked out of existence. The once and future princess, Miranda Popescu, has been separated from her friends as they discover that their Massachusetts identities are being subsumed by their old Roumanian identities. Miranda begins to accept that she may be the White Tyger of national myth. The Baroness, one of the most interesting villains in recent memories, continues to fascinate.

Twenty Epics (All Star Stories), edited by David Moles and Susan Marie Groppi, had a whimsical call for submissions: the shorter the epic, the higher the pay per word. While Christopher Rowe seems to have won that round, standout stories here also include those by Benjamin Rosenbaum, Tim Pratt, Meghan McCarron, Sandra McDonald, and Marcus Ewert who produced an inspired story in the "Choose Your Own Adventure" genre. It was immensely satisfying to read so many epics in miniature. Conan would be proud.

Kathryn Davis's novel *The Thin Place* (Little, Brown) begins when a dead man is revived by one of three schoolgirls. Things get stranger from there. Davis's descriptions—of a small town, its inhabitants, their daily life, and the ways in which the past haunts the present—are both precise and luminous. This is the kind of book where you stop and read sentences out loud to whomever you happen to be sitting next to, just for the pleasure of speaking them out loud.

The Pinhoe Egg (Greenwillow) is the sixth installment in Diana Wynne Jones's Chrestomanci series. It starts off not long after *Charmed Life*—the first book to be published in the series—ended. Confused? Don't worry. New readers will fall right into the story, and longtime fans will find that this is one of Jones's best. As usual, there are wizardly doings, much magic gone haywire, and strong-willed characters who feel much more fully realized (and comfortably familiar) than you usually meet in fantasy. Also of note: Diana Wynne Jones's brilliant, funny, and practical *The Tough Guide to Fantasyland* (Firebird) has been updated and brought back into print: much skewering of the usual unreconstructed fantasy tropes ensues.

Lisey's Story (Scribner) by Stephen King is, like *The Dark Half*, *The Shining*, and *Misery*, not to mention a large number of shorter works, about the process of writing. It's also about marriage, consolation, loss, and yes, about where writers get their ideas. Don't be put off by how long this latest novel by King is, and don't be put off, either, if you think you don't like horror. *Lisey's Story* is as much about the nature of fantasy as anything else, and while there is dark territory here, there's also a great deal of light. This is one of Kelly's favorite books this year.

Naomi Novik's debut historical fantasy *His Majesty's Dragon* (Del Rey) was almost instantly followed by two sequels, *Throne of Jade* and *Black Powder War*. Which came as something of a relief to its many fans—one writer friend confided that waiting for the next volume, he now understood the impulse to write fan fiction. Another friend said that she couldn't help reading it as the utterly satisfying and chaste love story of a man and his dragon. The first book, where a naval captain is introduced to the newly hatched dragon Temeraire, reads like the most delightful mash-up of Anne McCaffrey and Patrick O'Brian imaginable. And even if you've never read McCaffrey or O'Brian, the charms of Temeraire may prove hard to resist.

Chris Adrian is a practicing physician, and *The Children's Hospital* (Mc-Sweeney's), despite the absolute strangeness of its various narrators and the events that occur in its pages, has the texture and authority of real life. Alternately narrated by four angels, the novel follows the fate of the floating hospital of the title, and the children and staff aboard it, the only ones left alive after an apocalyptic flood. Sometimes grim and sometimes absurdly beautiful, there's real genius here.

Salon Fantastique (Thunder's Mouth Press), edited by our coeditor Ellen Datlow and the former editor of this anthology, Terri Windling, was one of our two favorite anthologies this year. The loose theme means that the various stories play off each other in rather less expected ways. Richard Bowes's "Dust Devil in a Quiet Street" continues his hagiography of the denizens of downtown Manhattan (and even sometimes the other boroughs) while Delia Sherman's "La Fée Verte" is a tragic love story set in an earlier century. Paul Di Filippo, Greer Gilman, Jeffrey Ford, and Jedediah Berry, among others, offer excellent work.

Shriek: An Afterword (Tor) by Jeff VanderMeer is a novel-within-a-novel set in the celebrated world of Ambergris. *The Early History of Ambergris by Duncan Shriek* is the occasion for this afterword by his sister, Janice. Nabokovian confusions of the best kind ensue, and the narrative, while never quite proceeding directly from Point A to Point Q, provides a tour of Ambergris and its denizens that will prove both enjoyable and informative enough even for those who have never visited these parts before.

Neil Gaiman's collection *Fragile Things* (Morrow) is the kind of charming miscellany that invites one to read selections at random, rather than straight through. There's some poetry here, as there should be in a miscellany, as well as one original story, "How to Talk to Girls at Parties." Most fans of Gaiman's work will undoubtedly have missed some of the work collected in these pages, but even old favorites are worth a second look. Some of Gaiman's best works as a writer are his short stories, and the standouts here are "Sunbird," "Bitter Grounds," "Forbidden Brides of the Nameless Slaves in the Secret House of the Night of Dread Desire."

Ngugi wa Thiong'o's *Wizard of the Crow* (Pantheon) is a satirical and fantastical antitotalitarian tale of an African dictator's plan to build a new Tower of Babel and what happens in his country as he gets caught up in the idea. Dense, recursive, and quite heavy to haul around, say, on public transportation, you may nevertheless find yourself doing just that.

Gene Wolfe's *Soldier of Sidon* (Tor) is a long-awaited sequel to his two classic novels about Latro, an amnesiac Greek soldier and adventurer and accidental visionary who sees gods and demons without quite realizing what it is that he sees. After all, even his own history and the most familiar of faces are symbols to Latro that must be deciphered over and over. The nature of his hero once again allows Wolfe to put the most unconventional of narrative conceits to good use right from the very beginning: this is a manuscript found in a jar, seeming to be without either a proper beginning or ending. Fragmented, numinous, and quite beautifully illustrated, this latest Wolfe novel makes us hope that there will be future novels about Latro.

Born in Texas, Lisa Tuttle has for many years lived in Scotland. In *The Silver Bough* (Bantam), her second contemporary fantasy set there (after *The Mysteries*), the fate of isthmus town Appleton is in the balance. Fifty years ago the town began to die when the Apple Queen turned down the once-in-a-lifetime golden apple. *The Silver Bough* contains some truly inventive uses of Celtic legends, and several braided narratives in which the various likable protagonists, like the town, find second chances to set their lives aright.

Last year we mentioned Frances Hardinge's young adult novel *Fly by Night*, which is published in the U.S. this year by HarperCollins. Allow us to point you in its direction once more. The first in a trilogy, this book introduces us to the orphan Mosca Mye and her fearsome goose, and the poet-spy Eponymous Clent. Like Joan Aiken's Dido Twite books and Diana Wynne Jones's Spellcoats series, there are innumerable pleasures to be found here. Some readers will delight in Hardinge's evident love of language, while others will be thrilled to discover such a capable and cunning protagonist in Mosca.

Finally, there's *Scott Pilgrim and the Infinite Sadness* (Oni Press) by Bryan Lee O'Malley, the third volume in a manga-influenced, big-hearted Canadian comic that features slacker boy and girl rock-star heroes with rarely used superpowers who live in a world where Amazon delivers via shortcuts through your dreams, and in order to win the girl (literally of your dreams), you may have to conquer seven evil ex-boyfriends in real-life fights that function according to video game rules. This is very funny stuff that ought to find an appreciative audience in genre.

Traditional Fantasy

Sarah Monette's *The Virtu* (Ace) is good enough that readers should really first read *Mélusine*, where Monette introduced Felix Harrowgate and his half-brother, Mildmay the Fox. The brothers, exiled from their home, decide to return and are joined by others, and for a moment the novel looks as if it may veer into standard quest and plot territory. But Monette is ahead of us and keeps the action (and the plot twists) moving along nicely. Like Ellen Kushner or Dumas, this author seems pleasurably intent on providing her readers with courtly intrigue, dialogue sharp as rapiers, and complications both moral and romantic.

Jacqueline Carey launched her second Kushiel trilogy with *Kushiel's Scion* (Warner), an S&M-tinged, epic fantasy bildungsroman featuring Imriel. Carey, after a couple of weaker books, is at the top of her game here and those interested in the darker end of the spectrum (both in fantastic and erotic terms) should investigate at once.

Dave Duncan is a prolific writer who turns out consistently interesting page-turners year after year. *Children of Chaos* (Tor), the first half of a longer novel to be concluded next year, is intense and politically multifaceted, and even better than usual.

The first entry of Kate Elliott's new epic fantasy series Crossroads, *Spirit Gate* (Tor) is one of many recent novels that successfully crosses the lines between adult and young adult fantasy.

Sherwood Smith's *Inda* (DAW) is the first novel set in a richly described world about a prince trained by his brother to be his "Shield Arm," or military champion.

Fortress of Ice (Eos) is the fifth novel in C. J. Cherryh's epic fantasy Fortress series. Like Bujold, Cherryh's work offers interesting characters, strong writing, thoughtful world building, and is always worth investigating. And speaking of Lois McMaster Bujold, she gave us *Beguilement* (Eos), the first of a two-book romantic fantasy, *The Sharing Knife*. A farmer's daughter and a "Malice"-hunter meet under troubling circumstances, only to find that they must each come to terms with the prejudices of each other's peoples. Thoroughly enjoyable, as usual.

R. Garcia y Robertson's quest to return an egg, *Firebird* (Tor), takes place in an alternate historical Russia and may seduce the reader ready for much romance and war even if the characters seem sometimes more archetypes than individuals.

Also noted: Justina Robson's *Living Next Door to the God of Love* (Bantam) is a hard science fiction novel that, late in the book, begins to use the tropes and rhythms of traditional fantasy. Robson is a consistently interesting writer who is well worth following from genre to genre. Sean Williams's *The Crooked Letter* and *The Blood Debt* (Pyr) are the first two (of three) of the Books of the Cataclysm where a personal loss causes the realms of the living and the dead to come together. Complicated and well thought out, this is involving stuff. Sarah Zettel's *Sword of the Deceiver* (Tor) is a strong entry in her Isavalta series, which borrows from Russian, Indian, and Chinese folktales and traditions. New readers can comfortably start the series here. Greg Keyes's third Kingdoms of Thorn and Bone novel, *The Blood Knight* (Del Rey), is, like the previous novels in the series, literary and gripping epic high fantasy. *This Forsaken Earth* (Bantam) by Paul Kearney is one of several novels in The Sea Beggars series. It's well written and somewhat bloody-minded nautical fantasy. *The Gold Falcon* (DAW) by Katharine Kerr is the first novel in The Silver Wyrm, the fourth and final trilogy in the Deverry series. Steven Brust returned to his popular Vlad Taltos series with a sequel to *Issola*, *Dzur* (Tor). This entry offers alternating chapters of more dramatic action with chapters in which the assassin Vlad eats a long-awaited meal. *The Clan Corporate* (Tor) is the third of Charles Stross's Merchant Princes episodes, in which Miriam Beckstein, late of Boston, continues to try to escape her mafialike royal family. There are some echoes of Zelazny and Machiavelli as well as certain thematic elements, oddly enough, of chick lit. Sharon Shinn adds to the Twelve Houses series with *The Thirteenth House* (Ace). The late Chris Bunch's middle and last novels in his Dragonmaster trilogy, *Knighthood of the Dragon* and *The Last Battle* (Roc). Cecilia Dart-Thornton's *The Well of Tears* (Tor), second of the Crowthistle Chronicles; David Drake's *The Fortress of Glass* (Tor) is the first of the Crown of Isles trilogy that promises to conclude the Lord of the Isles series. Night Shade reprinted the first trilogy in Glen Cook's Dread Empire series in one volume, *A Cruel Wind*, with an introduction by Jeff VanderMeer. Lynn Flewelling's *Oracle's Queen* (Bantam Spectra) concludes the trilogy that began very promisingly with *The Bone Doll's Twin*. Ken Scholes's short story *Last Flight of the Goddess* is sweet and sometimes funny and published as a limited edition hardcover by Fairwood Press. Holly Lisle's *Talyn* (Tor) should appeal to readers of Jacqueline Carey and other erotic-tinged epic fantasy novels, as might the second novel in John C. Wright's Chaos series, *Fugitives of Chaos* (Tor), which continues the adventures (tinged, often as not, with sexuality or mild sadism) of five literally otherworldly teenagers as they come into their full powers. Steve Aylett's novella *Fain the Sorcerer* (PS) is published with an introduction by Alan Moore. It hardly fits into this category, yet where would it fit comfortably? In a category by itself. New novelist Joshua Palmatier's first two Throne novels, *The Skewed Throne* and *The Cracked Throne*, were both published this year (DAW); U.K.-author Chaz Brenchley's enjoyable *Bridge of Dreams* (Ace) begins a new series based on the Arabian Nights; Patricia Bray's religious-leaning new series starts with *The First Betrayal* (Bantam); David Keck begins a series with *In the Eye of Heaven* (Tor); Steven Erikson's fourth Malazan novel, *House of Chains* (Tor) was published; David Zindell also launches a new quest series with *The Lightstone* (Tor); Jane Lindskold's fifth Firekeeper novel, *Wolf Hunting* (Tor); Jenna Rhodes begins a new series, The Elven Ways, with *The Four Forges* (DAW); James M. Ward's second Hornbloweresque adventure, *Dragonfrigate Wizard Halcyon Blithe* (Tor), Jack Whyte brought his Camulod series to an end in the ninth volume, *The Eagle* (Forge), and began a somewhat less well received Templar Trilogy with *Knights of the Black and White*.

Finally, although we did not see a copy of P. C. Hodgell's most recent novel of the Kencyrath, *To Ride a Rathorn* (Meisha Merlin), we've been fans of her work since first encountering her characters in *God Stalk*. We'll try to review it next year, but in the meantime readers are encouraged to seek out their own copies.

Contemporary and Urban Fantasy

Patricia A. McKillip's *Solstice Wood* (Ace) is a satisfying gothic romance about returning home and facing the demons long left behind. Sylvia Lynn's return is brought about the old-fashioned way: by an inheritance. Once home, she discovers that her grandmother's circle of sewing friends are witches who have been stitching away to keep the world of magic separate from our own. McKillip, one of our favorite writers, turns in something markedly different from her more recent novels. Although this is a sequel to her earlier novel *Winter Rose*, the jump forward to a contemporary setting offers readers a chance to see McKillip experimenting in terms of style and setting.

Best known for the accompanying Russian blockbuster film, Sergei Lukyanenko's *The Night Watch* (Miramax) is a fast-paced, modernist, good vs. evil, Coyote vs. Roadrunner novel of magic-wielders, vampires, and stranger creatures in contemporary Russia. This is the first of Lukyanenko's more than twenty-five books to appear in English. Undoubtedly the translation by Andrew Bromfield (who has also translated Boris Akunin and Victor Pelevin) adds to the pleasure here.

Charles de Lint's *Widdershins* (Tor) has one of the most striking covers we saw this year. (Never let it be said that we don't judge a book by its cover.) In this latest Newford novel, we are introduced to new characters, but old favorites return as well. The blossoming romantic relationship between Jilly Coppercorn and Geordie Riddell is complicated by a clash between European fairies and Native American earth spirits. By now, readers of De Lint know what to expect—musicians, magic, and urban fantasy at its most enjoyable—but this is a particularly strong entry in the series.

Sam Savage's *Firmin: Adventures of a Metropolitan Lowlife* (Coffee House Press) is the winning and endearingly loopy tale of a mouse who grows up in a bookshop in Boston and then becomes the pet of a science fiction writer.

Ray Bradbury's sequel to *Dandelion Wine*, *Farewell Summer* (Morrow), was apparently written fifty years ago, yet thematically it seems as much an elegy as a coming-of-age story. While there is a good deal of fizzy and lovely Bradbury imagery and language, there are also some rather odd and unintentionally off-putting exchanges between the two protagonists, one at the verge of puberty and the other reaching the end of his life. While *Dandelion Wine* remains a classic, this sequel should be of interest to completists rather than the everyday reader.

David Herter's novella *On the Overgrown Path* (PS), the first of three novellas exploring the history of the Czech Republic, features an unnamed composer and his search for the music of the everyday.

Kate Bernheimer's *The Complete Tales of Merry Gold* (FC2) is the inventive second installment of the Gold family's history that, like companion novel-in-pieces *The Complete Tales of Ketzia Gold*, shreds, rethinks, and reuses German, Yiddish, and Russian fairy tales to tell the contemporary coming-of-age story of its protagonist. Bernheimer, who edits the outstanding *Fairy Tale Review*, not only knows her material, but how to entertainingly subvert it.

Liz Williams's enjoyable second entry in her supernatural dark fantasy Detective Chen series, *The Demon and the City* (Night Shade), should interest fans of crime novels as well.

A. A. Attanasio's lyrical and lovely *Killing with the Edge of the Moon* (Prime) is described as a "graphic novel without illustrations." Attanasio recounts the story of a boy who gets more than he wants in an update of the myth of Orpheus and Eurydice.

Prolific author Elizabeth Bear launches an Arthurian-tinged first fantasy *Blood and Iron* (Roc) in the Promethean Age series. This is a rich if somewhat dense contemporary novel of Faerie and destiny.

Also noted: originally published in 1992 and brought back with an introduction by Neil Gaiman, Martin Millar's *The Good Fairies of New York* (Soft Skull) is an over-the-top and rambunctious tale of a couple of Scottish fairies and their attendant adventures. Kelly McCullough's debut (and start of a series) *WebMage* (Ace) features a hacker child of the fates.

There seemed to be innumerable paranormal romances this year (with plenty more on the horizon). Among the ones that we saw were *Witchling* (Berkley) by Yasmine Galenorn (aka India Ink), in which a bookstore-owning witch has to keep the magic and the human world apart, and Jenn Reese's ass-kicking, smoldering debut novel, *Jade Tiger*, which is one of the first titles from Wildside Press's new Juno paranormal romance focused imprint. Carrie Vaughn's second Kitty novel, *Kitty Goes to Washington* (Warner), is a frothy, entertaining werewolf-disc-jockey-gets-mixed-up-in-politics offering. Fans of Melanie Rawn may welcome the mix of romance, witchcraft, and danger in the urban fantasy novel *Spellbinder* (Tor), although there is an unseemly amount of eyebrow arching, and the love story is never quite as believable or compelling as the details of witchcraft and magic. Violette Malan's *The Mirror Prince* (DAW) is a well-told secret identity tale of a Canadian professor surprised to find he is actually a fairy prince. (Someone somewhere has undoubtedly come up with a catchy nickname for this genre of books, but Kelly refers to them as chick-lit-with-teeth.)

Hal Duncan's *Vellum* (Del Rey) came out in the U.S. We covered the U.K. edition in a previous volume. Of associational interest: Geoff Ryman's *The King's Last Song* (HarperCollins), a dual narrative of twelfth century and present-day Cambodia. Ryman is worth following wherever he goes.

Historical, Alternate History, and Arthurian Fantasy

In James Morrow's excellent and acclaimed *The Last Witchfinder* (Morrow), the only fantastical aspect is a talking book: Newton's *Principia Mathematica* comments on the action as England's Witchfinder General burns his sister-in-law and, after the scandal, leaves the country. Highly recommended.

Morgan Llywelyn gave fans of her novel *Druids* a sequel, *The Greener Shore* (Del Rey). The druids of Gaul, pushed out of their country by invading Romans, reach the Hibernian shores. As they settle, still missing their home, they are intrigued by the spirits of the new land and then saddened as they realize those spirits may have already moved on. Llywelyn's mythic fiction will satisfy those wishing to explore Ireland's prehistory.

Charles R. Saunders heavily revised his 1981 novel *Imaro* in a new edition (Night Shade). Imaro, a Conanesque African hero in an alternate historical fantasy narrative that nevertheless reflects contemporary issues of genocide, race, and still-meaningful tribal conflicts, roams a lushly described alternate Africa, fighting sorcerers, beasts, and men. There are four more volumes promised.

Amanda Hemingway's *The Sword of Straw* (Del Rey) is the second novel in the Sangreal Trilogy, which features boarding schools, alternate worlds in which magic is possible, and young protagonists. Potentially appealing to both adult and young adult fans of Harry Potter.

Following her retelling of *The Iliad* in *Troy*, Adèle Geras reimagines *The Odyssey* in *Ithaka* (Harcourt) from the point of view of one of Penelope's serving girls in a young adult novel that ought to appeal to adult readers.

Richard Calder's *Babylon* (PS) mixes science fiction and mythological elements in a dense, erotic short novel that moves between nineteenth-century London and a parallel dimension Babylon.

Also of note: Judith Lindbergh's *The Thrall's Tale* (Viking) may be of interest to historical fantasy readers. Narrated by three women, it concerns a tumultuous time in Greenland's past as first Vikings, and then Christians arrive. In Jon F. Baxley's *The Blackgloom Bounty* (Five Star), one of Merlin's apprentices is tasked with destroying another. Jules Watson's *The Dawn Stag* (Overlook) is the second book in a historical fantasy series, The Dalriada Trilogy, that draws on Celtic history. Shana Abé's second paranormal romance features people who transform into dragons, *The Dream Thief* (Bantam). Ray Manzarek turned his and Rick Valentine's Southern gothic screenplay into a novel, *Snake Moon* (Night Shade).

Humorous Fantasy

Usual suspects Christopher Moore and Terry Pratchett both had something new for their readers. In *A Dirty Job* (Morrow), a suddenly widowed new father discovers that he is a Death Merchant. Hijinks—most notable involving a goth girl employee who accidentally receives the new Death Merchants job handbook—ensue. Terry Pratchett's newest young adult Tiffany Aching novel, *Wintersmith*, will keep readers happy until there's further Discworld adventures to purchase. (See the Young Adult section for further details.) *Rumo & His Miraculous Adventures* (Overlook), Walter Moers's second Zamonia adventure (after *The 13½ Lives of Captain Bluebear*), is an imaginative, funny, and violent tale of a half deer, half wolf who may be the greatest hero of this world. *In the Company of Ogres* (Tor) follows A. Lee Martinez's previous horror-fun novel *Gil's All Fright Diner* and concerns a soldier who keeps coming back to life after being killed. This is dark—but certainly nowhere near black—humor, marking Martinez as one to watch for fans of Robert Asprin. Radio host Adam Felber's *Schrödinger's Ball* (Random House) is impossible to summarize but hilarious in conceit and execution. If the Free State of Montana and a dead-and-alive rock musician in Boston tickle your interest at all, following up should be an easy choice. For an even lighter note try Azhar Abidi's story of two Brazilian brothers in the eighteenth century who build a flying machine in *Passarola Rising* (Viking).

And keep in mind two graphic novel series: Bryan Lee O'Malley's previously mentioned contemporary magic realism for slackers, following the progress of one Scott Pilgrim; and the cracked, intricate *Dungeon* series (Nantier Beall Minoustchine) from French comic superstars Lewis Trondheim and Joann Sfar and various others.

Fantasy in the Mainstream

Mia Couto's novel *Sleepwalking Land* (Serpent's Tail, translated by David Brookshaw) was originally published in 1992 and deserves a wide readership now that it's finally available here. Recommended not only for the deft handling of the fantastical and the political, but for the writing as well: so clear and easy it is possible to follow the author into the seeming impossibilities of war as easily as seeing the dead walk.

Chris Bachelder's broad literary satire *U.S.!* (Bloomsbury), in which Upton Sinclair comes back from the dead time after time, still calling for industrial action and getting murdered for his views, is highly recommended.

Keith Donohue's acclaimed and memorable debut, *The Stolen Child* (Doubleday), is a literary fantasy narrated in turns by the frozen-in-childhood Henry Day, and the hobgoblin changeling who took his place. This is a haunting and elegiac novel that centers on the loss of childhood and the fading power of enchantment and Faery in the contemporary world.

A confession: we haven't yet cracked *Against the Day* (Penguin) but it looks to offer the usual myriad, perverse charms of a Thomas Pynchon novel.

David Long's *The Inhabited World* (Houghton Mifflin) is a surprisingly joyful story of a postsuicide ghost watching the woman who now lives in his apartment.

In the entertaining middle novella in Jane Stevenson's *Good Women* (Mariner), an English housewife finds herself (in more ways than one) visited by angels.

In Colin Cotterill's third Laotian-based mystery, *Disco for the Departed* (Soho), national coroner Dr. Siri Paiboun once again solves the case with help from the dead.

The Book of Lost Things (Atria) stays close to John Connolly's usual dark territory with fairy tale characters sometimes helping, sometimes hindering a lost boy.

Clifford Chase's *Winkie* (Grove) successfully spoofs the culture of fear with a teddy bear who comes to life and is subsequently interrogated and treated as a potential terrorist.

The Nimrod Flip-Out (Farrar, Straus & Giroux) by Israeli writer Etgar Keret contains thirty quick tales all of which range into and out of the surreal. Translated by Miriam Shlesinger and Sondra Silverston.

Dustin Long's *Icelander* (McSweeney's) is a pocket-sized and beautifully produced mystery novel of the surreal, informed by Icelandic folklore, pulp crime novels, and replete with Nabokovian footnotes and intertextual interruptions.

Lisa Pearl Rosenbaum's *A Day of Small Beginnings* (Little, Brown) opens with a posthumous narration by the ghost of a Polish woman who then watches over generations of a family. History—personal, religious, and political—is at risk, Rosenbaum says, when no one dares to ask questions.

Also noted: Paul Malmont's *The Chinatown Death Cloud Peril* (Simon & Schuster) is a vigorous and pulpy pastiche of the genre it parodies, featuring Lester Dent (writer of Doc Savage) and Walter Gibson (writer of The Shadow) who become involved in a mystery that features a mysterious island, H. P. Lovecraft, E. E. "Doc" Smith, and opium dens. Kate Mosse's *Labyrinth* (Putnam), a Da Vinci Code–esque historical and contemporary Holy Grail–based thriller. Diane Setterfield's *The Thirteenth Tale* (Atria) has a Jane Eyre–like heroine contending with old stories and ghosts. Sherry Austin's *Where the Woodbine Twines* (Overmountain Press) is the story of an old-fashioned southern haunting. Gordon Dahlquist's *The Glass Books of the Dream Eaters* (Bantam) made a splash, although this doorstopper adventure debut would have benefited from losing some weight. Late-night TV host Craig Ferguson offered the surreal and rollicking *Between the Bridge and the River* (Chronicle). Ben Ehrenreich's *The Suitors* (Counterpoint) is a retelling of *The Odyssey*.

First Novels

Daniel Abraham's *A Shadow of Summer* (Tor) is the first of The Long Price Quartet and was one of the most enjoyable renderings of a traditional epic fantasy that we saw last year. Strong characters, diverting plot twists, and a thoroughly worked out magical system unlike anything that we've seen before, where the power of poets and the use of language is a commodity that industry and all other aspects of society are dependent upon. Highly recommended to fans of traditional fantasy series, as well as those who have grown somewhat tired of the usual fare.

Jay Lake's first fantasy novel (following a decent number of collections and a science fiction novel), *Trial of Flowers* (Night Shade), begins a series set in the "City Imperishable," a decadent metropolis where, when the city's ruler goes missing, a group of tortured dwarves plan revolt. Lake is a prodigious talent with a gift for surprising turns of phrase and striking images. The surreal urban landscape offers plenty of space for following novels.

The Orphan's Tales: In the Night Garden (Spectra) by Catherynne M. Valente is a *1001 Nights*–like novel in tales where stories circle, spin off, and always move along a spiral that starts with a girl telling a prince the stories tattooed on her face.

Holly Phillips, already noted for her short fiction and winner of last year's Sunburst Award, turns in debut novel *The Burning Girl* (Prime), a dense melding of parallel worlds and interior landscapes.

Scott Lynch has already received a great deal of praise for his picaresque *The Lies of Locke Lamora* (Spectra), drawing comparisons to the work of both Robert Silverberg and Charles Dickens. There's a great deal of fun to be had here, with much subterfuge, crosses and double crosses, and a fellowship of thieves. The style is chatty—in places distractingly so—which will undoubtedly appeal to as many readers as it puts off.

Poetry

We always find a number of interesting poems in *Mythic Delirium*. The speculative poetry genre continues to produce a number of interesting small magazines including *Dreams and Nightmares* and *Star*Line*, longtime staple *The Magazine of Speculative Poetry*, and literary magazines such as *jubilat*, as well as many of the literary journals noted in the magazine section as well as supplying sites like *Strange Horizons* and *Lone Star Stories* with good work. Sean Wallace's *Jabberwocky* (Prime) continues to be a showcase for poets such as Catherynne M. Valente, Sonya Taaffe, Theodora Goss, and other rising stars.

New online zine *Goblin Fruit* is the latest site to take up the mantle of myth and fantasy-inspired poetry and the three issues put out this year featured work of interest by E. Sedia among others.

Averno (FSG) by Louise Glück retells the story of Persephone in eighteen recursive, brilliant poems and is both a reminder of the power of her poetry and the power of the source myths.

The big news in classics was Robert Fagles's translation of Virgil's *The Aeneid* (Viking). Fagles, following up his recent *Iliad* and *Odyssey*, chose not to translate the epic into any strict structural form, choosing instead to imbue Virgil's work with some of the rhythms and cadences of more recent traditions of poetry.

Ciaran Carson, whose translation of *The Inferno* we enjoyed a couple of years ago, has now tackled Brian Merriman's *Cúirt an Mheán Oíche* as *The Midnight Court* (Wake Forest University Press). This is a bawdy evening's fun—while providing a piece of Irish history for good measure—for any reader.

Malena Mörling's *Astoria* (University of Pittsburgh Press) is a good example of poetry that crosses into the fantastic as if it were part of the natural world.

Fairy tale and mythological characters come to life in Jeannine Hall Gailey's excellent second collection (after her chapbook *Female Comic Book Superheroes*), *Becoming the Villainess* (Steel Toe Books). We selected two poems for reprint and recommend this volume to readers who've enjoyed either strong-willed heroines like Buffy the Vampire Slayer, or Carol Ann Duffy's *The World's Wife*.

We wanted to reprint a poem from Mark Haddon's *The Talking Horse and the Sad Girl and the Village Under the Sea* (Vintage). The success of his novel, *The Curious Incident of the Dog in the Night-Time*, undoubtedly means that Haddon can do what he likes: and happily for us what he likes includes this odd, lovely collection of poetry.

Although we didn't see it this year, Tim Pratt's first poetry collection, *If There Were Wolves* (Prime), seems to have included many original fantasy and dark fantasy poems.

Lidija Dimkovska's first collection in English, *Do Not Awaken Them with Hammers*

(Ugly Duckling, translated by Ljubica Arsovka and Peggy Reid), contained some poems of interest to fans of the fantastic.

The Science Fiction Poetry Association and Prime published *The 2006 Rhysling Anthology: The Best Science Fiction, Fantasy & Horror Poetry of 2005* (edited by Drew Morse) to encourage readers to participate in reading speculative fiction poetry, join the association, and vote for the award.

More from Elsewhere

Entropia: A Collection of Unusually Rare Stamps (Design Studio Press) by Christian Lorenz Scheurer is somewhat similar to projects by Nick Bantock but takes off from the reproduced images of imaginary stamps to tell the story of a fantasy world. The book is beautifully made and the art is comics-influenced.

Tim Powers's *A Soul in a Bottle* (Subterranean, illustrated by J. K. Potter) is a slight, sweet, eerie possible-pasts novella. Powers's other short story chapbook, *The Bible Repairman* (also Subterranean), is about exactly what the title suggests.

Jennifer Calkins's *A Story of Witchery* (Les Figues Press, illustrated by Sarah Lane) is a nicely produced, small press, book-length fairy tale poem of an abandoned girl and her transformation.

Fans of Ellen Klages's short fiction will want to seek out her nonfantastic debut young adult novel, *The Green Glass Sea* (Viking). And we cannot recommend M. T. Anderson's dark historical novel *The Astonishing Life of Octavian Nothing, Traitor to the Nation, Volume 1: The Pox Party* (Candlewick) highly enough. Anderson, the author of several genre-tinged novels, has written a masterpiece with weight and texture of the best kind of fantastic fiction.

Children's/Teen/Young Adult Fantasy

These are great years for writers and readers of young adult fantasy. While books about pirates and spies are growing in popularity, these are still the J. K. Rowling–inspired boom years. This year *Locus* ran a special issue on the subject with short essays by Ursula K. Le Guin, Jonathan Stroud, Garth Nix, and others, and interviews with Scott Westerfeld, Kenneth Oppel, and Holly Black. The issue makes it clear that in the last ten years, while the numbers of new science fiction and horror books for young adults has remained steady, the number of new fantasy titles has more than doubled! Should you be tempted, there are almost enough titles coming out each year to read one per day. We have split these titles into books for older teens, followed by books for younger readers.

D. M. Cornish's engrossing debut, *Monster Blood Tattoo: Foundling* (Putnam), is as richly appurtenanced as a collector's DVD. Illustrated by the author, the novel comes with eight(!) appendices and a variety of maps so that readers (of any age) may spend long hours exploring Cornish's imaginary world. The world is involving, the main character good company, and the monsters are revoltingly interesting. While the end is not quite a cliff-hanger, readers will wish to have a second volume in hand as soon as possible.

As usual, Terry Pratchett's latest Tiffany Aching novel, *Wintersmith* (HarperTempest), fills in just a bit more of the Discworld while keeping readers informed and up-to-date on beloved longtime characters. Here, Tiffany attracts the attention of some dangerous archetypal figures, but the real pleasures are in the scenes where Pratchett's characters just sit around and talk or, even, when they sit around and don't talk. (Inside of the heads of Pratchett's thoughtful witches is a fine place to spend some time.)

Terrier (Random House) by Tamora Pierce is the first of a series about Beka Cooper, and set in Tortall, first introduced in Pierce's beloved Alanna series. Concerning a young girl who becomes a legendary officer of the city watch, this is Kelly's favorite of Pierce's novels so far.

Grace Dugan's debut, *The Silver Road* (Penguin Australia), moves the usual medieval fantasy setting to somewhere in the eastern hemisphere and weaves together a tripartite plot with fearsome and charming results.

In Geraldine McCaughrean's *Peter Pan in Scarlet* (McElderry Books), Wendy and the Lost Boys, now grown-up, must return to Never-Never Land. McCaughrean is a talented writer who, as well as writing her own novels, has turned her hand to many literary projects over the years (including *Stories from Shakespeare*, *Gilgamesh the Hero*, and *One Thousand and One Arabian Nights*) and does a reasonably good job of gently updating parts of the *Peter Pan* story. This authorized sequel to *Peter Pan* doesn't quite provide either the enjoyment of J. M. Barrie's original or McCaughrean's own original work, but it does no damage, either.

Francesca Lia Block's *Psyche in a Dress* (HarperCollins) is a trip through Greek mythology set in the modern day that will have teens and adults running to their D'Aulaires' or Bulfinch.

The Shadow Thieves (Atheneum) by Anne Ursu is a smart and funny contemporary novel that draws on Greek mythology. Auctorial asides and crisp writing make this a fun read for adults as well as young adults. Even better, it appears that there will be further books in this series.

Catherine Fisher's *Darkhenge* (HarperCollins) is a page-turning Celtic-influenced novel infused with dark magic.

Lois Lowry (*The Giver*) produced a delightful and unexpected fantasy, *Gossamer* (Houghton Mifflin), with some very dark edges where dream-givers and nightmares contend for the heart of an abandoned teenager.

Published in Australia, *Maddigan's Fantasia* (HarperCollins) by favorite author Margaret Mahy is about a postapocalyptic traveling circus of magicians, musicians, performers.

Shannon Hale's *River Secrets* (Bloomsbury) is the third in a series of novels that began with *The Goose Girl*. Hale is an expressive and accessible writer full of empathy for her characters and like her other novels, this one is a treat.

The growing friendship between two fifteen-year-old girls is at the heart of Patricia Elliott's gothic fantasy, *Murkmere* (Little, Brown).

David Almond's *Clay* (Delacorte) is a Frankenstein-meets-golem novel where boys in the north of England, scared for their lives, find that there are truly monstrous things out there.

Narrated by Death, the much-acclaimed doorstopper *The Book Thief* (Knopf) by Markus Zusak centers on a young girl who steals books, among other things, in order to survive during the Holocaust.

Matthew Skelton's *Endymion Spring* (Delacorte) splits itself between the fifteenth century and the present day in the tale of a book that contains the whole world's knowledge.

Diane Stanley's *Bella at Midnight* (HarperCollins) is a sparkling fairy tale retelling where our Cinderella (Bella) not only gets to go to the ball (here, a wedding) but also manages to help stop a long-running war.

Neal Shusterman's *Everlost* (Simon & Schuster) is a fast-paced surprisingly adventurous post-life tale of a boy and a girl who meet nine months after death in the titular kids-and-teens-only afterlife.

Susan Cooper's *Victory* (McElderry) is a dual-time fantasy that mixes the story of a present-day girl and a boy in Lord Nelson's navy.

Sean Stewart and Jordan Weisman's latest print project, *Cathy's Book: If Found Call (650) 266-8233* (Running Press), steps into a world next door to ours with a teenager who finds that when her boyfriend dumps her he is not who he seems. The novel comes in a binder with many accompanying documents, as well as usable phone numbers and Web sites that will pull readers into the world of the story.

Helen Dunmore's first in a series, *Ingo* (HarperCollins), starts with a father who dreams of the sea and then disappears and builds two worlds, the world of the children left behind on the Cornwall coast and the world of the Mer people the children come to know. Haunting, engaging: two more books are much to look forward to.

In *Tripping to Somewhere* (Simon Pulse) by Kristopher Reisz two girls run away to find the Witches' Carnival. This is a dark, edgy fantasy that ought to appeal to fans of Holly Black.

Linda Sue Park's *Archer's Quest* (Clarion) is a time travel fantasy about a boy who must help the founder of Korea to return to his own time.

Patricia C. Wrede and Caroline Stevermer's third epistolary alternate history fantasy, *The Mislaid Magician or Ten Years After* (Harcourt), is perhaps slightly less action-packed than previous entries but still a treat.

Nina Kiriki Hoffman's *Spirits That Walk in Shadow* (Viking) is a dark fantasy for older readers that features Jaimie (a minor character from *The Thread That Binds the Bones*) going to college and finding that she needs to rely on her family to help her roommate.

Delia Sherman's *Changeling* (Viking) is geared for a slightly younger set, although adult fans of Sherman's work will enjoy the voice and sly details of life in a fairy-populated New York: a likable scamp of a changeling has to accomplish three tasks to get back into the good books (and under the protection of) the Green Lady of Central Park.

Younger readers will be enthralled and amused by M. T. Anderson's *The Clue of the Linoleum Lederhosen* (Harcourt), the second short story by Anderson published as an illustrated middle-reader.

Kathy Henderson retells one of the oldest narratives known, the Sumerian story of *Lugalbanda: The Boy Who Got Caught Up in a War* (Candlewick, illustrated by Jane Ray). Lugalbanda (who may be Gilgamesh's father) does not have the strength to do what he wants so he petitions the gods for what he needs. This timely translation should be read by adults and children alike, and it may offer an interesting conversation starter on Iraqi culture and history.

The Miraculous Journey of Edward Tulane (Candlewick, illustrated by Bagram Ibatoulline) by Kate DiCamillo is the story of a large china rabbit doll who is forced by circumstances to learn the hardest lesson: to open his heart.

Strange Happenings: Five Tales of Transformation (Harcourt) by Avi is at once intriguing, surprising, and mysterious.

The End (HarperCollins) is the thirteenth and final in Lemony Snicket's A Series of Unfortunate Events wherein some of the Unfortunate Events are tied up while many others are not.

The Secret Order of the Gumm Street Girls (HarperCollins) by Elise Primavera aims for the funny bone with its tale of a group of girls, one of whom inherits a certain pair of ruby red shoes.

Gail Carson Levine is a dependable name in young adult literature. *Fairest* (HarperCollins) follows her successful novel *Ella Enchanted*. Unfortunately the protagonist here is much more passive than the usual heroine in this sort of novel, and the story suffers for it.

The Last Dragon (Miramax, translated by Shaun Whiteside) by Silvana de Mari is a tale full of joy, sacrifice, and destiny.

S. F. Said's second martial arts cat adventure, *The Outlaw Varjak Paw* (David Fickling Books), is as satisfying as the first.

The Beasts of Clawstone Castle (Dutton) is another satisfying Eva Ibbotson tale, this time of a family castle in need of a monetary boost that is supplied by acquiring ghosts and the accompanying tourists.

George R. R. Martin made a successful first foray into children's books with *The Ice Dragon* (Tor Starscape, illustrated by Yvonne Gilbert), a tale of dragons of ice and fire—a story originally published in the anthology *Dragons of Light*.

Julius Lester's *Cupid* (Harcourt) retells the story of Cupid and Psyche.

Kristin Kladstrup's *The Book of Story Beginnings* (Candlewick) is an almost metafictional tale of a series of beginnings that, in the end, add up to an enjoyable quest story.

Also noted: the first part of Elizabeth Knox's Dreamhunter Duet, *The Rainbow Opera*, which we recommended last year, has been published in the U.S. as *Dreamhunter* (Farrar, Straus and Giroux) and we strongly urge readers to track it down, then immediately pick up the fabulous sequel. Set in Tasmania, Donna Jo Napoli's *Ugly* (Hyperion) retells *The Ugly Duckling*. Maureen Johnson's deal-with-the-devil high school entertainment, *Devilish* (Razorbill) was published; Scott Westerfeld brought his Midnighters series to a satisfyingly conclusion with *Blue Noon* (Eos) and bumped his *Peeps*-world along another step with a second book, *The Last Days* (Razorbill). *Magic Lessons* (Razorbill) is the second book in Justine Larbalestier's *Magic or Madness* trilogy in which strong-willed character Reason accepts the existence of magic but fights the seemingly inevitable fatal price. William Nicholson's first in the Noble Warriors series, *Seeker* (Harcourt), plays heavily on religion. T. A. Barron's third Great Tree of Avalon novel, *The Eternal Flame* (Philomel); Herbie Brennan's third Faerie Wars chronicle, *Ruler of the Realm* (Bloomsbury) featuring a heroine named Holly Blue; S. C. Butler's debut *Reiffen's Choice* (Tor) is replete with talking animals, exiled child heirs, and complex mythology; Cat Bordhi's *Treasure Forest* (Ace); Lisa Trumbauer's *A Practical Guide to Dragons* (Mirrorstone); Maureen Doyle McQuerry's *Wolfproof* (Idylls Press, illustrated by John Murphy) is based on early Celtic stories; Veronica Bennett explores Mary Shelley's pre-Frankenstein years in *AngelMonster* (Candlewick). *Fairy Tale Feasts: A Literary Cookbook for Young Readers and Eaters* (Crocodile) by Jane Yolen, with recipes by Heidi Stemple and illustrated by Philippe Beha, is a feast for families with recipes for any time of the day (or year) and folktales for reading time. Harcourt's Odyssey Classics brought back five of P. L. Travers's Mary Poppins books as the stage show continued strong in London, including the long unavailable *Mary Poppins from A to Z*, as well as Alan Garner's historically inspired action adventures, *The Weirdstone of Brisingamen* and *The Moon of Gomrath*. Joseph Helgerson offers a Mississippi fable, *Horns and Wrinkles* (Houghton Mifflin). Kate Coombs considers what happens when a princess refuses to follow her father's wishes in the light confection *The Runaway Princess* (FSG). Cat Weatherill tells the story of a wooden boy who accidentally commits a great crime and runs away hoping to find his true home in *Barkbelly* (Random House). Tobias Druitt's *Corydon and the Island of Monsters* (Knopf) is the first in a new series about the titular hero who was born with one leg shaped like a goat's. Brian Jacques's third Castaways tale, *Voyage of Slaves* (Philomel); *The Man in the Moon-Fixer's Mask* by JonArno Lawson (Boyd's Mill, illustrated by Sherwin Tjia) is a book of nonsense rhymes à la Ogden Nash or Shel Silverstein; *The Little House in the Fairy Wood* by Ethel Cook Eliot is one of many older fairy tales brought back into print by Aegypan; Vera Nazarian's *Mayhem at Grant-Williams High* is one of the first titles from Norilana, a new press specializing in young adult and classic novels.

Single-Author Story Collections

This would have been an astounding year for short story collections if only even half of the following books had appeared. Besides the collections mentioned earlier, readers will want to check out the following.

Elizabeth Hand's *Saffron and Brimstone: Strange Stories* (M Press) adds five short stories to three novellas previously collected in *Bibliomancy*. (The missing novella, *Chip Crockett's Christmas Carol*, originally published on SCI FICTION, was reprinted separately this year by Beccon Press.) Hand's stories manage to be delicate and gritty at one and the same time. These are not exactly optimistic stories, but even the darkest offers a kind of consolation to be found in Hand's exquisite prose. Contains "Kronia" and "Wonderwall," which were included in past volumes of this anthology.

William Browning Spencer's books have been too few and far between, but this year Subterranean published *The Ocean and All Its Devices*, which collects his hilarious and chilling "The Essayist in the Wilderness" (one of Kelly's favorite stories of all time) as well as eight other dark fantasies.

George Saunders's third collection, *In Persuasion Nation* (Riverhead), contains a good selection of stories that begin in absurdity but always reach into the depths of human feelings.

In Douglas Lain's excellent debut collection, *Last Week's Apocalypse* (Night Shade), he translates anger into cutting and chilling, sometimes surrealist tales of people stuck between the government and pop culture.

In Minsoo Kang's reflective and sometimes recursive first collection of fables, *Of Tales and Enigmas* (Prime), he stakes a quiet claim for one corner of the future of fantasy. We included one of his shorter tales in this volume and recommend him to readers of Zoran Živković and Isak Dinesen.

"The Codsman and His Willing Shag" is the title of a sea shanty in the gently haunting story of the same name in Neil Williamson's mixed-genre first collection, *The Ephemera* (Elastic Press). Williamson, who coedited last year's *Nova Scotia: New Scottish Speculative Fiction*, engages Scottish history and cultural mythology and points out the moments of beauty among the daily grime.

Karen Russell's excellent stories are weird in ways that, like the work of George Saunders and Aimee Bender, intersect obliquely with the genre of the fantastic. Her debut collection, *St. Lucy's Home for Girls Raised by Wolves* (Knopf), will carry a frisson of the familiar; summer camps and divorced parents add up to something slightly more spooky than the sum of the parts.

Richard Bowes's *Streetcar Dreams and Other Midnight Fancies* (PS), collects the

World Fantasy Award–winning title novella and five other "orphan" stories that were not included in any of Bowes's other books. Bowes writes gritty (i.e., sex, drugs, and death) fantasy that nevertheless manages to locate the redemptive aspects of the most unhappy lives, and this collection is a must-have for fans and those interested in the fantastic history of New York City.

Master of fantasy Peter S. Beagle's third collection, *The Line Between* (Tachyon), contains stories only from the last half-dozen years or so. Of special note are the Hugo Award–winner "Two Hearts" and an unpublished set of "Four Fables."

Much of Zoran Živković's fiction translated into English is in the enormous collection *Impossible Stories* (PS Publishing, translated by Alice Copple-Tosic). With an introduction by Paul Di Filippo and an afterword by Tamar Yellin, everything is here for either the new or longtime fan of Živković's work. Many of these stories are from *Interzone* and some have already been published in the U.S. in various small press collections, but this omnibus gives substantiality to tales so gentle, taken one by one, that they sometimes seem ready to drift right off the page.

Although a few of the stories are somewhat darker than Kage Baker's usual fare, *Dark Mondays* (Night Shade) is the expected treat for her many fans. More than half of the stories are published here for the first time—including a (short) pirate novel.

Garry Kilworth's *Moby Jack* (PS) is a nicely packaged edition of a cross-genre collection that brings in stories from *Omni* and *Interzone* and others. Kilworth turns his hand to all aspects of the fantastic, and there is some interesting experimental work in here.

Kim Newman's *The Man from the Diogenes Club* (MonkeyBrain) is Richard Jeperson, the man 1970s Scotland Yard turns to when things get a little weird.

Simon Brown's long-awaited *Iliad*-based collection *Troy* (Ticonderoga) included one new story, "The Cup of Nestor," and is a strong introduction for those who may have missed his stories in *Eidolon*, *Aurealis*, and so on.

Ian R. MacLeod's third collection, *Past Magic* (PS), tends toward science fiction but there is enough of MacLeod's lovely, quiet fantasy (including "The Bonny Boy" and "Nina-with-the-Sky-in-Her-Hair" to be worth the time of the reader of this anthology.

Also noted: Roald Dahl, better known for his children's stories, leads us ineluctably down shadowy paths in his *Collected Stories* (Everyman). This was a good year for Gene Wolfe collectors with the publication of two limited edition chapbooks. The first, *Christmas Inn*, was published as a Christmas present for subscribers to PS Publishing's *PostScripts*. The second, *Strange Birds* (DreamHaven), includes two stories, "On a Vacant Face a Bruise" and "Sob in the Silence" (selected by our coeditor), and are part of a series of chapbooks written by authors inspired by the artwork of Lisa Snellings-Clark. Tamar Yellin's mildly fantastic *Kafka in Brontëland* and other stories (Toby Press) contained one new story. A couple of Jonathan Lethem's stories were collected in Subterranean's beautiful *How We Got Insipid*. Ryan Boudinot's *The Littlest Hitler* (Counterpoint) orbits out somewhere among the surreal and absurd but he pins the stories to Earth with his sympathetic characters. Charles Yu's associationally interesting *Third Class Superhero* (Harcourt) where the typographical and structural experiments complement the sometimes surreal stories. Bruce Sterling's *Visionary in Residence* (Thunder's Mouth) contains a couple of high-quality recent fantasies including "The Denial," which was included in last year's volume. Paul Di Filippo's *Shuteye for the Timebroker* (Thunder's Mouth) includes a few over-the-top fantasies. Elizabeth Bear's *The Chains That You Refuse* (Night Shade) is a cross-genre collection from this extremely busy writer. Michael Cadnum's *Can't Catch Me and Other Twice-Told Tales* (Tachyon) are all familiar stories with a contemporary twist. Ben Fountain's first collection, *Brief Encounters with Che Guevara* (Ecco), is well worth seeking out, although with only one fantastic-tinged story (reprinted here), "The Good Ones Are Already Taken." Charles de Lint's *Triskell Tales 2: Six More Years of Chapbooks* (Subterranean) allows De Lint's fans to read his hard-to-find "Christmas card" tales. Don Webb's *When They Came* is the third volume from Henry Wessells's Temporary Culture. As with the previous books, Wessells's own collection and *Arabian Wine* by Gregory Feeley, this is not just a beautifully designed object, but also a well thought out collection. Webb is a master of the secret history and this collection is perfect for those seeking all his secret knowledge in one place. Greg van Eekhout's chapbook *Show and Tell and Other Stories* (Tropism Press) has a basketball fantasy, "Anywhere There's a Game," strong enough to keep nonsports fans reading. Tropism Press's first chapbook, *Tales of the Chinese Zodiac*, is a series of well-written Chinese folktales by Jenn Reese and originally published on *Strange Horizons*. For the chapbook Reese added five pieces including three "forgotten years." Thomas Wiloch's acerbic, wry, and slightly gruesome short-shorts are collected in the chapbook *Screaming in Code* (Naked Snake Press). Mike Resnick's *New Dreams for Old* (Pyr) is mostly science fiction; Lee Battersby's *Through Soft Air* (Prime) generally falls under our coeditor's remit; R. Andrew Heidel's collected collections, *Desperate Moon* (PS); Vera Nazarian, *Salt of the Air* (Prime).

Small Beer Press published Alan DeNiro's debut collection *Skinny Dipping in the Lake of the Dead: Stories* (finalist for the Frank O'Connor International Short Story Award) and the first paperback edition of Howard Waldrop's amazing and long out of print debut *Howard Who?*

Anthologies

Firebirds Rising (Firebird), edited by Sharyn November, is the second anthology featuring (mostly) authors from November's Firebird publishing line, some of whose stories (such as those by Sharon Shinn and Pamela Dean) are set in worlds familiar from their novels. We reprinted Ellen Klages's instant classic of librarians in the wild, "In the House of the Seven Librarians," but also enjoyed stories by Patricia A. McKillip, Emma Bull, Diana Wynne Jones, and Tamora Pierce. *Firebirds Rising* also has a story by Kelly Link.

Eidolon (Prime), edited by Jonathan Strahan and Jeremy G. Byrne, is reborn as an anthology with a lovely Shaun Tan cover and stories from Australians as well as others, including Tim Pratt, Hal Duncan, Lucy Sussex, Holly Phillips, Margo Lanagan, Grace Dugan, Kim Westwood, Deborah Roggie, Jeff VanderMeer, and others. We hope it's the first of many.

ParaSpheres: Extending Beyond the Spheres of Literary and Genre Fiction (Omnidawn), edited by Rusty Morrison and Ken Keegan, was an interesting and impressively large anthology that made a pleasing splash in both genre and literary ponds by pulling together older stories by writers such as Kim Stanley Robinson, Ursula K. Le Guin, and Alasdair Gray, and matching them with new pieces from Maureen N. McLane, Michael Moorcock, Stephen Shugart, Jeff VanderMeer, and others. Morrison and Keegan brought the book to academic and genre conventions and ran successful panels on what genre can bring to the fictional tables, all of which caused much conversation and perhaps inspired more editors and writers to ignore or cross the marketing boundaries that sometimes seem so limiting.

Christopher Barzak, Alan DeNiro, and Kristin Livdahl's fifth annual *Rabid Transit* anthology, *Long Voyages, Great Lies* (Velocity Press), approaches and perhaps surpasses the quality of the previous iterations. Alice Kim's weird science story "The Mom Walk" is a standout, but the other five stories, by F. Brett Cox, Geoffrey H. Goodwin, Meghan McCarron, David J. Schwartz, and Heather Shaw are all deeply imaginative, emotive pieces, and some of the best work we have seen from each of these authors.

The declarative "The" in the title of *Feeling Very Strange: The Slipstream Anthology* (Tachyon), edited by James Patrick Kelly and John Kessel, is deserved: Kelly and Kessel draw widely from within and without the speculative fiction genre to illustrate their view of slipstream, with reprints by Michael Chabon and Ted Chiang among others, and one superbly strange new story by M. Rickert ("You Have Never Been Here"), as well as interstitial material taken from a lively online discussion on the definition of the word.

The sixth entry in the broad-ranging *Polyphony* series provided us with good stories by Tim Pratt, Ray Vukcevich, and Robert Freeman Wexler.

The fourth *Agog! Ripping Reads* (Agog! Press) produced three stories on our Honorable Mention list and a very enjoyable afternoon's reading. This volume is available in the U.S. through Prime Books.

A third Australian anthology, *The Outcast: An Anthology of Exiles and Strangers* (CSFG), edited by Nicole R. Murphy, tends toward science fiction but for those interested in an Antipodean view of strangeness it is worth hunting out.

Those wanting to explore another part of the Commonwealth might enjoy *Mythspring* (Red Deer Press), edited by Julie E. Czerneda and Genevieve Kierans, which has stories based on Canadian songs and poems.

Elemental: The Tsunami Relief Anthology (Tor), edited by Steven Savile and Alethea Kontis, has strong stories by Martha Wells and Sharon Shinn and was a great and worthy idea. It is very heartening to see our genre—from the writers and editors to the publisher and everyone who worked on the book—stand up and be counted and offer a helping hand to those in need.

Jabberwocky 2 (Prime), edited by Sean Wallace, offers a beautiful small annual handful of fiction and poetry that we hope Prime will keep publishing even as their magazine, *Fantasy*, moves from strength to strength.

Cross Plains Universe: Texans Celebrate Robert E. Howard (MonkeyBrain/FACT), edited by Scott A. Cup and Joe R. Lansdale, was produced to coincide with the centenary of R.E.H.'s birth—and the World Fantasy Convention celebrating same. Texans (no matter where they now live) hanging out their shingles here include Howard Waldrop, Brad Denton, Lillian Stewart Carl, and others.

Also of note: the second in Mike Allen's new anthology series, *Mythic,* has work from all the usual Prime Books suspects (Valente, Taaffe, Vanderhooft, YellowBoy) as well as a fun story from rising fantasist and pulp star Cherie Priest. *Alice Redux: New Stories of Alice, Lewis, and Wonderland* (Paycock Press), edited by Richard Peabody, includes many new stories as well as reprints by Steven Milhauser, Robert Coover, Rikki Ducornet, and Angela Carter. *From the Trenches: An Anthology of Speculative War Stories* (Carnifex), edited by Joseph Paul Haines and Samantha Henderson, had interesting stories by Josh Roundtree, Anil Menon, and Mikal Trimm. *In the Dark* (Tightrope Books) edited by Myna Wallin and Halli Villegas.

Of the DAW monthly anthologies, *The Magic Toybox* was the standout. Diane Duane's gods'n'gladiators tale "The Fix" was very much on our short list. *Children of Magic*, edited by Martin H. Greenberg and Kerrie Hughes, included some good work: Nina Kiriki Hoffman's "The Weight of Wishes" and Michele West's "Shahira." *Fantasy Gone Wrong*, edited by Martin H. Greenberg and Brittiany A. Koren, was stronger than *Slipstreams*, which didn't exactly live up to the title.

Magazines and Journals

Our month-to-month favorite genre title continues to be *The Magazine of Fantasy & Science Fiction*—the variety of selections reprinted from this magazine should be self-explanatory. Should you be looking for a gift for yourself or a reader friend, you could hardly do better than a subscription to this redoubtable read. If you like your magazines with more science fiction, then *Asimov's* might be for you. Editor Sheila Williams is making her mark with more guest columns, more reader letters, and a slightly different mix. The Hugo ballot shows that readers are happy to go with her. U.K. mainstay *Interzone* is healthy as a horse and happily publishes stories all over the genre map. Stories by Elizabeth Hopkinson and Sean McMullen shone among the pleasantly biting reviews and columns. Editor Andy Cox says companion dark fantasy magazine *Black Static* is coming soon. *Realms of Fantasy* continues to be a solid bimonthly read and stories by Deborah Roggie, K. D. Wentworth, and Sarah Prineas made us happy to see it in the mailbox.

Alchemy 3 was the last issue of this very high quality annual fiction magazine. We reprinted Frances Hardinge's story and enjoyed the whole magazine more than any other genre magazine we read this year. If someone else were to hire Steve Pasechnick as their fiction editor, they might be onto something good. *Fantasy Magazine* published three of four issues and began to hit its stride. With the hiring of designer and creative director Stephen Segal the magazine perked up its design and began to stand out as its own entity rather than as the younger sibling of *Weird Tales/Absolute Magnitude* that it had resembled. Highlights included stories from old hands (Peter S. Beagle) and new (Stephanie Campisi). *Postscripts* tends toward science fiction by men but usually contains at least something of interest to fantasy readers—this year Michael Swanwick's erotic northern English genre-bender "The Bordello in Faerie" was as close as the magazine came to traditional fantasy. *Subterranean* magazine tended heavily toward science fiction and darker fantasy or horror. After appearing regularly throughout the year editor William Schaffer announced the magazine would migrate online in 2007. The Summer issue of mixed-genre Canadian magazine *On Spec* gave us John Southern Blake's "The Exterminator," a story that we relished and found reminiscent of William Browning Spencer, as well as Dave Whittier's tense topical family tale, "Coming Back from Kabul." In the Winter 2005/2006 issue we particularly enjoyed Leah Bobet's "Metis" and Shawn Peters's "Ticker Hounds." *Weird Tales* threatened to become more regular as its masthead was reorganized once again. A spring redesign should bring it to a new audience.

Tim Pratt and Heather Shaw's *Flytrap* moved from strength to strength in its two issues for the year. The range of fiction is impressive as is the mix of new and familiar writers and men and women. *Shimmer* is an enthusiastic zine with a penchant for elegiac stories and reaching out to new and established writers. We especially enjoyed stories by Angela Slatter and Aliette de Bodard. Venerable zine *Talebones* was reenergized by a huge outpouring of support from readers and writers alike. Their Summer issue was filled with mostly darker stories and showed a move toward more fiction and less nonfiction. *Zahir* showcases consistently well-written (if not always groundbreaking) writing and this year seemed stronger than previous. It was heartening to see a translation (by Lavie Tidhar). *Tales of the Unanticipated*'s twentieth anniversary issue included long stories by Mark Rich and Sarah Monette as well as poetry from Laurel Winter, Bruce Boston, among others. Matt Kressel (et al.) publishes an artful and thoughtful zine, *Sybil's Garage*. This year's highlights included Eric Gregory's "The Redaction of Flight 5766" and poems by Bobbi Sinha-Morey and Ed Lynskey. Fans of recent small press zines are recommended to subscribe. John Klima's *Electric Velocipede* is a new stalwart of the field and featured (among mostly science fiction) poetry from Sonya Taaffe and stories by Tim Akers and Jeffrey Ford. *Full Unit Hookup* produced their annual issue and we particularly enjoyed Erin Keane's poem, "Angels' Share." We saw a number of issues of the Australian magazine *Andromeda Spaceways Inflight Magazine*, of which the best seemed to be No. 25, with challenging stories from Ayne Terceira and Deby Fredericks. We also liked the cleaner redesigned pages. *Not One of Us* continued to publish fantasy with a harder edge as well as an annual themed one-off chapbook. The relatively new zine *Fictitious Force* enthusiastically produced two mixed-genre issues, and we always enjoy *Albedo One*, which sent one issue over from Ireland this year. Small Beer Press published the usual two issues of *Lady Churchill's Rosebud Wristlet* with a spooky collaboration by husband and wife team Cara Spindler and David Erik Nelson "You Were Neither Hot Nor Cold But Lukewarm, and So I Spit You Out" being one of the high points.

Strange Horizons is the grand old dame of online speculative fiction (and reviews, poetry, and articles). Its yearly fundraiser is a community building experience with gifts from many publishers and writers exchanged for the promise of future work from more writers. Leah Bobet, Meghan McCarron, Ursula Pflug, and many others provided fanciful and fabulous stories. Rudy Rucker (*Flurb*), William Sanders (*Helix*), and John Scalzi were just a few of the authors who published fiction (by other writers) on their blogs or started Web zines this year, something we expect to continue as writers trade on their names (Jim Baen, Orson Scott Card) and readers go to "brands" they trust.

Both *Jim Baen's Universe* and *Orson Scott Card's Intergalactic Medicine Show*, start-ups from late 2005, published almost to schedule and, making the writers happy, are paying a decent per-word fee. Making enough money to pay writers (and editors, artists, proofreaders, etc.) is the real challenge for online magazines and we admire Baen's and Card's head-on runs at what is a knotty problem. Other ongoing online magazines we consistently find good fiction in are *Ideomancer*, *Abyss & Apex*, *Æon*, *Son and Foe*, *Susurrus*, *ChiZine*, *The Journal of Mythic Arts*, and—one we very much enjoy—*Lone Star Stories*. There are many more. New online magazines publishing interesting work include *Clarkesworld Magazine* and *Trabuco Road*. We were sad to see the *Fortean Bureau* close.

A Public Space quickly established itself as one of the most broad-minded new literary journals. The first issue included a focus on new Japanese fiction in translation (as well as a story by Kelly Link) and the second issue featured newly translated Russian fiction. David Mitchell's "Acknowledgments" tells a story within an extended set of the eponymous notes and Maile Chapman's "Bit Forgive" is a fantastical ghost story.

There was one annual issue of *The Fairy Tale Review* (the "Green" issue) from which we reprinted Jeanne Marie Beaumont's "Is Rain My Bearskin?" Stories by Wendy Brenner, Jedediah Berry, and Brian Baldi also explored very different and unfamiliar aspects of fairy tales in modern day. The magazine also came with two poems letter-pressed on handmade paper to create an unusual and memorable keepsake.

The Virginia Quarterly Review is one of the most impressive magazines we see. The large page size, the use of color and graphics throughout is eye-opening, and the quality of the fiction is top-notch. In 2006 they published a fiction supplement where writers wrote about other writers, including Jonathan Lethem on Philip K. Dick and Elizabeth Gaffney on Edgar Allan Poe.

Tin House's continued strong design (including a graphic lit issue) and keen-eyed editing kept it at the front of the mainstream lit journals. *The Paris Review* had a James Tate poem we loved, "Police Slumbering."

Since its first issue *Ninth Letter* has been one of our favorite magazines. Its full-size pages give it the feel of an art book or a nineteenth-century magazine. We took one poem, by Josh Bell, from it this year.

One Story continues to publish the fantasy stories in their delightful small chapbook format. Austin Bunn's first published story, "The Ledge," stayed with us all year.

Literary journals that contained a touch of the fantastic included: *The Cincinnati Review* (especially noted: Caitlin Horrock's "Embodied"); *Skidrow Penthouse* (we very much liked Lisa Bellamy's poem "Howling Boy"); *StoryQuarterly*; *The Southern Review*; *Southwest Review*; *The Georgia Review*; *The New Yorker*; *Alaska Quarterly Review*; *The Massachusetts Review*; *Atlanta Review*; *Stand*; *Gargoyle*; *The Kenyon Review*; *Mississippi Review*; *Hobart*; *The Fiddlehead*; *Salmagundi*; *Pindeldyboz*; *DIAGRAM* (from which Caleb Wilson's story came); *Zoetrope: All-Story*; *McSweeney's*; *The Paris Review*; and *Oxford American* (which had one of Kevin Brockmeier's lovely fables).

The New York Review of Science Fiction continues on its merry way covering the field in an enjoyable mix of the formal (academic essays and reviews) and the informal (editorials and pictures of people in the field).

Art and Picture Books

Yoshitaka Amano's *Fairies* (Dark Horse Press) is a lush, dreamy, visual treat somehow reminiscent of the work of both Klimt and Jessie Wilcox Smith. Paired with his second art collection of the year, *The Tale of Genji* (Dark Horse), the reader must be amazed at the breadth of his work.

Maurice Sendak and Arthur Yorinks's pop-up book, *Mommy?* (Scholastic), will amuse readers of all ages—the adults getting a thrill from seeing all their favorite movie monsters while children will enjoy the *Where the Wild Things Are*–like ride.

Continuing the movie monster theme, writer and illustrator Adam Rex, in *Frankenstein Makes a Sandwich* (Harcourt), writes funny poetry about the Creature from the Black Lagoon, Dr. Jekyll, and others.

Wolves (Simon & Schuster) by Emily Gravett is the tale of a rabbit learning a little too much about wolves from a library book that we could imagine reading again and again. Readers be warned: the end is happier for the wolf than the rabbit.

Heinrich Hoffman's *Der Struwwelpeter* gets a new set of clothes in *Struwwelpeter and Other Disturbing Tales for Human Beings* (Fantagraphics), illustrated in flat perspectives and bright colors by Bob Staake.

Richard Michelson's *Oh No, Not Ghosts* (Harcourt, illustrated by Adam McCauley) is a comical story of two children trying to sleep. Not to worry, there's no such thing as . . . wait, what was *that*?

The Magic Horse of Han Gan (Enchanted Lion) by Chen Jiang Hong retells the legend of an artist whose paintings of horses are so lifelike that one of them comes alive.

Spectrum 13: The Best in Contemporary Fantastic Art (Underwood Books), edited by Arnie Fenner and Cathy Fenner, is a pick of the year every year. This is an unmatched resource for anyone interested in the state of fantastic art.

The Adventuress (Abrams) is Audrey Niffenegger's second strange and beautiful visual novel (after *The Three Incestuous Sisters*) and apparently one of her first projects, written and illustrated while she was a student at the Art Institute of Chicago.

R/Evolution: The Art of Jon Foster (Underwood Books) by Jon Foster showcases an up-and-coming artist with book and comic covers and art from other commercial realms. Foster's art is eye-catching and incredibly kinetic.

Nielsen's Fairy Tale Illustrations in Full Color (Dover) by Kay Nielsen has fifty-nine color plates from stories by Hans Christian Andersen, the Brothers Grimm, and others. There's very little text, but the book doesn't pretend to be more than it is: a celebration of Nielsen's art.

James Bama: American Realist (Flesk) by Brian Kane collects his sixty-two(!) Doc Savage cover paintings as well as almost two hundred other illustrations.

The Art of Michael Parkes (Swan King) by Michael Parkes is a luscious production, the richness of the paper matching the visuals.

Carnival of the Animals: Poems Inspired by Saint-Saëns' Music (Candlewick), edited by Judith Chernaik and illustrated by Satoshi Kitamura, joins art, poetry, and music (for the latter two a CD is included with the book).

Cover Story: The Art of John Picacio (MonkeyBrain) is the first collection by an artist who has recently won the Chesley, World Fantasy, and International Horror Guild Awards.

In *Castle Waiting* (Fantagraphics) Linda Medley tells the story of what happens after Sleeping Beauty leaves the castle. Medley's stories—and stories within stories—are perfect to bring readers to both fantasy and graphic novels.

The Art of Wendy Froud (Imaginosis) is a full-color treat for fans of the world-class dollmaker and visual artist.

Roald Dahl's early work *The Gremlins* (Dark Horse), originally published in 1943, is reprinted for the first time. Written as the basis for a film that was never made, this is not as fully worked out or as richly strange as most of Dahl's children's books but very much worth seeing.

Phil Hale's *Sparrow: Phil Hale* (IDW) is a small collection of his work recommended for new fans.

General Nonfiction

Editor of one of Kelly's favorite books, *Dear Genius: The Letters of Ursula Nordstrom*, Leonard S. Marcus has put together another must-have in *The Wand in the Word: Conversations with Writers of Fantasy* (Candlewick). Marcus interviewed Ursula K. Le Guin, Garth Nix, Jane Yolen, and ten other writers about their writing history and habits, as well as provided pictures of the authors and the places in which they work.

Malory: The Knight Who Became King Arthur's Chronicler (HarperCollins) by British historian Christina Hardyment puts together a somewhat plausible case for the life of the man about whom almost nothing is known, other than that he wrote *Le Morte d'Arthur*.

The Magic Circle of Rudolf II: Alchemy and Astrology in Renaissance Prague (Walker) by Peter Marshall will be of interest to those who enjoyed all the John

Dee-themed fantasy of recent years (including novels by Eileen Kernaghan and Liz Williams).

We did not spend much time with Jeff Hoke's *The Museum of Lost Wonder: A Graphic Guide to Reawakening the Human Imagination* (Red Wheel) but for the curious we recommend the Web site (lostwonder.org) that gives a good taste of the "challenges" built into this book.

Polder: A Festschrift for John Clute and Judith Clute (Old Earth Books), edited by Farah Mendlesohn, is a collection of essays, stories, and poems in honor of John and Judith Clute.

Jack Zipes's latest fairy tale study is *Why Fairy Tales Stick: The Evolution and Relevance of a Genre* (Routledge), in which he examines the cultural stickiness of fairy tales and looks into why some are more popular or seen as more relevant than others.

Sadly no one sent us the other project Zipes edited this year: *The Oxford Encyclopedia of Children's Literature*. This one will go on the wish list.

Diana Wynne Jones's hilarious send-up of all things epic fantasy, *The Tough Guide to Fantasyland* (Firebird), was revised and updated. Highly recommended to writers, and readers—those who like fantasy and those who don't.

Myth, Folklore, and Fairy Tales

There are more books published on these topics than we can ever mention, but here are a few that our readers might be partial to: Canongate's comprehensive ongoing series of myth retellings continues with three volumes this year. The first, *Lion's Honey* by acclaimed Israeli novelist David Grossman (translated by Stuart Schoffman), retells the story of Samson. Russian post-modernist Victor Pelevin's *The Helmet of Horror: The Myth of Theseus and the Minotaur* (translated by Andrew Bromfield) is, as expected, a fractured and challenging labyrinth that boots the myth into the modern age. The last title, *Dream Angus: The Celtic God of Dreams* by Alexander McCall Smith, is made up of five fables from the Celtic Eros (that's Angus, not Smith).

Perhaps inspired by Canongate, Penguin has put together an impressive series of Penguin Epics. This year's titles included *The Sunjata Story, The Voyages of Sindbad, The Epic of Gilgamesh, Cupid and Psyche* by Apuleius, *The Abduction of Sita, Exodus, Jason and the Golden Fleece* by Apollonius of Rhodes, *King Arthur's Last Battle* by Thomas Malory, *Odysseus Returns Home* by Homer, and *Sagas and Myths of the Northmen*.

New York Review of Books brought out a couple of beautiful editions of works that have previously been hard to find and that we highly recommend to our readers: Robert Kirk's *The Secret Commonwealth of Elves, Fauns, and Fairies* with a new introduction by Marina Warner and *D'Aulaires' Book of Trolls* by Ingri and Edgar Parin d'Aulaire (the companion volume to their *Book of Norse Myths*).

Marina Warner's *Phantasmagoria: Spirit Visions, Metaphors, and Media into the Twenty-first Century* (Oxford) is a fascinating look at the existence of the human soul and attempts to capture it, from death masks to books and films.

Tales of the Golden Corpse: Tibetan Folk Tales (Interlink) by Sandra Benson is the first complete translation of a series of twenty-five sometimes chilling tales told by a dead body a boy is carrying. The boy, who has killed seven sorcerers while defending his master, is under a ban that forbids him to speak. Yeshi Dorjee learned the tales collected in *The Three Boys and Other Buddhist Folktales from Tibet* (University of Hawaii Press, transcribed and edited by John S. Major) in the monastery where he was raised.

The Man Who Could Fly and Other Stories (University of Oklahoma Press) collects eighteen of Rudolfo A. Anaya's folktales that are never as simple as might first be thought.

In Deborah Grabien's fourth Haunted Ballad mystery, *Cruel Sister* (St. Martin's), actress Penny and musician Ringan must step carefully around the ghosts in case they join them.

The University of Minnesota Press brought back two books into print that we recommend to all our readers: *Tales from Grimm* and *More Tales from Grimm*, translated and illustrated by Wanda Gág.

Ed Greenwood, Jeff Grubb, Lynn Abbey, and Wolfgang Baur take shots at what happened next in *The Further Adventures of Beowulf: Champion of Middle Earth* (Carroll & Graf), edited by Brian M. Thomsen.

JoSelle Vanderhooft explores the story of Rumplestiltskin in her first book, the short novel *The Tale of the Miller's Daughter* (Papaveria Press).

Alessandro Baricco splits readers into lovers and haters by cutting the gods from his sometimes flat *An Iliad* (Knopf, translated by Ann Goldstein, based on Maria Grazia Ciani's Italian translation). As well as removing the gods, Baricco updated the language by removing the rhythms and cadence of the traditional versions.

The Night Life of Trees (Tara) by Durga Bai, Bhajju Shyam, and Ram Singh Urveti is a beautiful book based on the mythological beliefs about trees of the Gond tribe in central India: trees as protective spirits or other, also useful, aspects.

Raouf Mama collects West African trickster tales and sacred tales in *Why Monkeys Live in Trees and Other Stories from Benin* (Curbstone).

Saraya, the Ogre's Daughter: A Palestinian Fairy Tale (Ibis, translated by Peter Theroux) by Emile Habiby is uncategorizable: autobiography, self-mythologizing, fairy tale, and more.

The Story Bag: A Collection of Korean Folktales (Silk Pagoda, translated by Setsu Higashi) collects thirty folktales by So-un Kim.

The Journal of Mythic Arts and the accompanying Endicott Redux Blog are incomparable resources and inspirations here. Many of the writers whose work we love most regularly post essays or reviews of art, music, literature, or link to things that will inevitably be of interest to the writers, readers, or academics. The conversation here is lively. Terri Windling, Midori Snyder, Helen Pilinovsky, and others sift the Web and regularly find its mythic underpinnings.

There were two issues of *Cabinet des Fées*, an online journal edited by Helen Pilinovsky, Catherynne M. Valente, and Erzebet Barthold-YellowBoy of poetry, fiction, and articles, that are also collected in an annual print anthology.

For younger readers, we recommend the following titles. The tall tales in *Porch Lies: Tales of Slicksters, Tricksters, and Other Wily Characters* (Random House) by Patricia C. McKissack and illustrated by André Carrilho will inspire imaginative flights of fancy while Rob Shone and Claudia Saraceni's *Chinese Myths* (Rosen) illustrates a Chinese creation myth, a myth on the origin of the four rivers, and "The Ten Suns," where an archer has to shoot nine suns from the sky so that his people will survive. Michael Cadnum continues his series retelling tales from Ovid in *Nightsong: The Legend of Orpheus and Eurydice* (Scholastic) where he introduces young readers to one of the great love stories and tragedies of all time. Martine Leavitt examines the power of love and the strength a lost young woman can draw from sto-rytelling in a sweet fantasy *Keturah and Lord Death* (Front Street).

Awards

The thirty-second annual World Fantasy Convention was held in Austin, TX. Glen Cook, Dave Duncan, Robin Hobb, Bradley Denton, John Jude Palencar, and Gary Gianni were the guests of honor. The following awards were given out: Life Achievement: John Crowley and Stephen Fabian; Novel: *Kafka on the Shore*, Haruki Murakami (Knopf); Novella: *Voluntary Committal*, Joe Hill (Subterranean Press); Short Story: "CommComm," George Saunders (*The New Yorker*, Aug. 1, 2005); Anthology: *The Fair Folk*, Marvin Kaye, editor (SFBC); Collection: *The Keyhole Opera*, Bruce Holland Rogers (Wheatland Press); Artist: James Jean; Special Award, Professional: Sean Wallace (for Prime Books); Special Award, Nonprofessional: David Howe and Stephen Walker (for Telos Books).

The James Tiptree, Jr. Memorial Award for genre fiction that expands or explores our understanding of gender was awarded to Geoff Ryman for *Air* (St. Martin's Press). The award was presented at WisCon in Madison, WI. The judges also provided an additional short list of books that they found interesting, relevant to the award, and worthy of note: *A Brother's Price*, Wen Spencer (Roc); "Little Faces," Vonda N. McIntyre (*SCI FICTION*, Feb. 23, 2005); *Misfortune*, Wesley Stace (Little, Brown); *Remains*, Mark W. Tiedemann (BenBella); *Willful Creatures*, Aimee Bender (Doubleday); "Wooden Bride," Margo Lanagan (Black Juice).

The International Association for the Fantastic's William L. Crawford Fantasy Award went to Joe Hill for *20th Century Ghosts* (PS Publishing) and the IAFA Distinguished Scholarship Award was given to M. Thomas Inge. The Mythopoeic Award winners were: Adult Literature: Neil Gaiman, *Anansi Boys* (Morrow); Children's Literature: Jonathan Stroud, The Bartimaeus Trilogy: *The Amulet of Samarkand; The Golem's Eye; Ptolemy's Gate* (Hyperion); Scholarship Award in Inklings Studies: Wayne G. Hammond and Christina Scull, *The Lord of the Rings: A Reader's Companion* (Houghton Mifflin); Scholarship Award in General Myth and Fantasy Studies: Jennifer Schacker, *National Dreams: The Remaking of Fairy Tales in Nineteenth-Century England* (University of Pennsylvania Press). The Fountain Award went to Stephanie Harrell's "Girl Reporter" (*One Story*). The Science Fiction Poetry Association 2006 Rhysling Awards: Short Poem: "The Strip Search," Mike Allen (*Strange Horizons*, October 3, 2005); Long Poem: "The Tin Men," Kendall Evans and David C. Kopaska-Merkel (*The Magazine of Speculative Poetry*, 7.1, Winter 2004/05). Mark Kelly's Locus Awards site is indispensable here.

As usual, there were more stories than we had pages for. Here is a list of a few more favorites that we encourage you to seek out:

Austin Bunn, "The Ledge," *One Story* 68
Diane Duane, "The Fix," *The Magic Toybox*
Jeffrey Ford, "Botch Town," *The Empire of Ice Cream*
Elizabeth Hopkinson, "A Short History of the Dream Library," *Interzone* 204
Beth Adele Long, "A Secret Lexicon for the Not-Beautiful," *Alchemy* 3
Meghan McCarron, "The Rider," *Twenty Epics*
Ian McDonald, "The Djinn's Wife," *Asimov's*, July
Patricia A. McKillip, "Jack O'Lantern," *Firebirds Rising* (Firebird)

Sarah Prineas, "Hekaba's Demon," *Lone Star Stories* 14

Becca De La Rosa, "Nine Lives," *Ideomancer,* December

David J. Schwartz, "Grandma Charlie and the Wolves," *Flytrap* 6

Heather Shaw, "Mountain, Man," *Rabid Transit: Long Voyages, Great Lies*

Cara Spindler and David Erik Nelson, "You Were Neither Hot Nor Cold But Lukewarm, and So I Spit You Out," *Lady Churchill's Rosebud Wristlet* 19

James Tate, "Police Slumbering" (poem), *The Paris Review* 177

We keep a small Web page for this book at www.lcrw.net/yearsbest and we encourage e-mail recommendations of works for consideration in next year's volume. However, please check the Summation and Honorable Mention list to see the types of material we are already reading. Thank you and we hope you enjoy the stories collected here as much as we did.

—Kelly Link & Gavin J. Grant
Northampton, Mass.

Summation 2006: Horror

Ellen Datlow

When *The Year's Best Fantasy* was first published in 1988 (that's what the first two volumes were called, despite the fact that half the book has always been horror), we joined Karl Edward Wagner's *Year's Best Horror*—his editorship of that series began in 1980—as the only best of the year books to cover horror. Terri Windling was my coeditor through 2002 and since then Kelly Link and Gavin Grant have become my partners in crime. Through all of this James Frenkel, our packager, has pulled together all the sections of what has grown to be a huge annual project into one cohesive whole. So it's been two decades and this is the twentieth volume.

Now, of course, there has been a flowering of Year's Bests in all three subgenres of fantastic fiction: science fiction, fantasy, and horror.

Short horror fiction is perhaps in a new golden age, with many more excellent stories, novelettes, and novellas being published than one can fit into a mere 125,000 words. Some of the best work of 2006 in novella form were Laird Barron's "Hallucigenia," P. D. Cacek's "Forced Perspective," M. Rickert's "The Christmas Witch," Bradley Denton's "Blackburn and the Blade," Jeffrey Ford's "Botch Town," Joe R. Lansdale's "King of Shadows," Patrick Lestewka's "Imprint," Christopher Golden and James A. Moore's "Bloodstained Oz," and Rosanne Rabinowitz's "In the Pines."

Four Australians (one with two stories included), five Britons (one dead), a Canadian, and eight Americans make this year's horror half more international than it's ever been before.

Where do the stories and poems come from? Five stories and the two poems were first published in single-author collections, three come from anthologies, one from a chapbook, and ten (probably a record) from magazines or literary journals.

Awards

The Bram Stoker Awards for Achievement in Horror are given by the Horror Writers Association. The full membership may recommend in all categories but only active members can vote on the final ballot. The awards for material appearing during 2005 were presented Saturday, June 17, 2006, in Newark, New Jersey, during the Stoker weekend.

2005 Winners for Superior Achievement:

Novel: (Tie) *Creepers* by David Morrell (CDS Books) and *Dread in the Beast* by Charlee Jacob (Necro Publications); First Novel: *Scarecrow Gods* by Weston Ochse (Delirium Books); Long Fiction: "Best New Horror" by Joe Hill (Postscripts); Short Fiction: "We Now Pause for Station Identification" by Gary Braunbeck (Endeavor Press); Anthology: *Dark Delicacies*, edited by Del Howison and Jeff Gelb (Carroll & Graf); Collection: *20th Century Ghosts* by Joe Hill (PS Publishing); Nonfiction: *Horror: Another 100 Best Books*, edited by Stephen Jones and Kim Newman (Carroll & Graf); Poetry: (Tie) *Freakcidents* by Michael A. Arnzen (Shocklines Press) and *Sineater* by Charlee Jacob (Cyber Pulp); Lifetime Achievement Award: Peter Straub; Specialty Press Award: Necessary Evil Press; Richard Laymon President's Award: Lisa Morton.

The International Horror Guild Awards recognize outstanding achievements in the field of horror and dark fantasy. The 2005 awards were presented November 2, 2006, during the World Fantasy Convention in Austin, Texas.

Nominations are derived from recommendations made by the public and the judges' knowledge of the field. Edward Bryant, Stefan R. Dziemianowicz, Ann Kennedy, and Hank Wagner adjudicate.

Chelsea Quinn Yarbro was named the recipient of the Living Legend Award.

Recognized for achievement in the field of horror/dark fantasy during 2005: Novel: *Lunar Park* by Brett Easton Ellis (U.S., Knopf/U.K., Macmillan/Picador); Short Fiction: "There's a Hole in the City" by Richard Bowes (*SCI FICTION*); Mid-Length Fiction: "La Peau Verte" by Caitlín R. Kiernan (*To Charles Fort, with Love*); Long Fiction: *Kiss of the Mudman* by Gary Braunbeck (*Home Before Dark*); Collection: (Single Author) *20th Century Ghosts* by Joe Hill (PS Publishing); Periodical: *Postscripts* (Peter Crowther, Editor/Publisher, PS Publishing); Illustrated Narrative: *Memories* by Enki Bilal (Humanoid/DC); Nonfiction: *Supernatural Literature of the World: An Encyclopedia* (Three Volumes), S. T. Joshi and Stefan Dziemianowicz, editors (Greenwood Press); Art: Clive Barker for Exhibition: *Visions of Heaven and Hell (and Then Some)*, Bert Green Fine Art, Los Angeles, CA.

Notable Novels of 2006

I rarely have time to read novels, so there are not many about which I will say more than a few words. But if one judges the health of a field by the *number* of novels published, there seem to be no fewer horror novels published than in previous years. However, a good chunk of them are now published as mainstream fiction or as the newest "category"—paranormal romance.

Monster Island by David Wellington (Thunder's Mouth Press) is an intelligent, well-told zombie novel about a worldwide epidemic of zombiefication. A former U.N. arms inspector, his daughter having been taken hostage by a Somali warlord who needs AIDS medication to survive, travels with child soldiers to Manhattan in order to get the drugs from the one place he knows still has them—the U.N. But the island is overrun by zombies, and at least two of them have an intelligence that allows them to plan, organize, and control the rest of their mindless compatriots. It's got enough blood and guts for the more bloodthirsty zombie lovers and some intriguing (but not wholly convincing) plot turns to entertain the rest of us.

The Keep by Jennifer Egan (Alfred A. Knopf) is a complex and entertaining contemporary gothic about a wildly successful man who invites his ne'er-do-well cousin—whom he hasn't seen in years—to help renovate a falling-down castle in Eastern Europe that he means to transform into a spiritual retreat. The schlub is lost without his digital connections and feels guilty for a long-ago prank gone wrong played on his now-rich cousin. A mad (and possibly ghostly) baroness protects her ancestral home by whatever means necessary. And then the reader discovers that the tale of the two cousins is actually a story within a larger story.

The Stone Ship by Peter Raftos (University of Hawaii) is an imaginative dark fantasy about a suicidal man saved by a vengeful ghost and the quest the ghost bullies him into performing. The best scene takes place in a library where massacre and mayhem are perpetrated by feral librarians.

Dead Europe by Christos Tsiolkas (Vintage, Australia) is a 2005 title that was recommended by Australian friends. It's an absorbing story about a gay Greco-Australian photographer who, while traveling in Europe, struggles to make sense of the discoveries he makes about his family's—and Europe's—evil past. Although there are ghosts, a curse, a vampire—all done up elegantly, subtly, and frighteningly—the story is more than anything else a metaphor for what cannot be left behind in the homeland.

The Unblemished by Conrad Williams (Earthling Publications) is the author's first out-and-out horror novel, and depicts a nightmarish London filled with human and nonhuman monsters, desperate characters, suspense and terror, and blood and gore done up in a gorgeously literate style that keeps you reading despite events so horrific that you long to turn away. London is the home to an ancient race of insectoid creatures that for a very long time have been planning on a return to power. The ending doesn't come together quite as well as I'd have liked but the book is a very good read.

The Book of Lost Things by John Connolly (Atria) is about a twelve-year-old whose mother dies after a long illness in the mid-1940s. When the boy's father remarries and fathers a new addition to the family, the twelve-year-old, in addition to being grief-stricken, becomes angry and bitter. One night he hears his mother calling to him and wanders into a darkly fantastic realm behind their home. There he encounters people and creatures out of traditional fairy tales turned inside out. What happens to him there and how he grows up makes up the bulk of the rest of this charming, dark novel.

The Keeper by Sarah Langan (Harper Torch) is a promising debut about a dying mill town in Maine and how the rotten underpinnings of its very existence transform a young woman into a monster.

The Exquisite by Laird Hunt (Coffee House Press) is a book to immerse oneself in, as its structure moves fluidly through time with an unreliable narrator who either killed or did not kill someone. A young indigent is embraced by a group of strangers who set up fake murder scenarios for money. The ringleader is a mysterious elderly man who loves herring, and may be somehow related to the cadaver in Rembrandt's famous painting "The Anatomy Lesson." The book is similar in feel to the works of Edward Whittemore and Jack O'Connell.

The Open Curtain by Brian Evenson (Coffee House Press) is about a troubled teenager obsessed with the history of fringe Mormons. Searching for his own identity, he reaches out to his estranged stepbrother and a girl whose family was brutally murdered, setting in motion a disturbing series of events. This one creeps up on the reader and leaves a nasty tingle.

Also noted: *The Loveliest Dead* by Ray Garton (Leisure); *Dusk* by Tim Lebbon (Bantam Spectra); *Full Moon Rising* by Keri Arthur (Bantam); *The Damned* by L. A. Banks (St. Martin's Press); *Deathbringer* by Bryan Smith (Leisure); *Bloodstone* by Nate Kenyon (Five Star); *The Night School* by Michael Paine (Berkley); *Headstone City* by Tom Piccirilli (Bantam Spectra); *Dark Side of the Moon* by Sherrilyn Kenyon (St. Martin's); *Touch the Dark* by Karen Chance (Roc); *18 Seconds* by George D. Shuman (Simon & Schuster); *The Mephisto Club* by Tess Gerritsen (Ballantine); *The Nymphos of Rocky Flats* by Mario Acevedo (HarperCollins/Rayo); *Doppelganger* by David Stahler, Jr. (HarperCollins/Eos); *A House Divided* by Deborah LeBlanc (Leisure); *Crippen* by John Boyne (St. Martin's/Dunne); *Pandora Drive* and *Darkness Wakes* by Tim Waggoner (Leisure); *Broken* by Kelley Armstrong (Bantam); *Offspring* by Liam Jackson (St. Martin's/Dunne); *Touch the Dark* by Karen Chance (Roc); *High Stakes* by Erin McCarthy (Berkley); *Lover Awakened* by J. R. Ward (Signet); *Ghost Road Blues* by Jonathan Maberry (Pinnacle); *The Forsaken* by L. A. Banks (St. Martin's); *I'm the Vampire, That's Why* by Michelle Bardsley (Signet); *The Astonishing Life of Octavian Nothing: Volume 1, The Pox Party* by M. T. Anderson (Candlewick); *Roman Dusk* by Chelsea Quinn Yarbro (Tor); *Wings to the Kingdom* by Cherie Priest (Tor); *Sorcery in Shad* by Brian Lumley (Tor); *Shelter* by L. H. Maynard and M.P.N. Sims (Leisure); *Warrener's Beastie* by William R. Trotter (Carroll & Graf); *Natural Selection* by Dave Freedman (Hyperion); *The Stolen Child* by Keith Donohue (Doubleday); *The Conqueror Worms* by Brian Keene (Leisure); *The Meaning of Night: A Confession* by Michael Cox (Norton); *Cadaver's Ball* by Charles Atkins (Leisure); *When the Dead Cry Out* by Hilary Bonner (Leisure); *Night Wars* by Graham Masterton (Leisure); *Breeding Ground* by Sarah Pinborough (Leisure); *Pressure* by Jeff Strand (Earthling); *World of Hurt* by Brian Hodge (Earthling); *King of Souls* by Brian Knight (Earthling); *Horrorween* by Al Sarrantonio (Leisure); *The Dead Letters* by Tom Piccirilli (Bantam); *Stage Fright* by Michael Paine (Berkley); *Prismatic* by Edwina Grey (Lothian Books); *Carnies* by Martin Livings (Lothian Books); *Bully* by J. F. Gonzales (Midnight Library); *Kindred Spirit* by John Passarella (Pocket Star); *Carved in Bone* by Jefferson Bass (Morrow); *Harvest Moon* by James A. Moore (Cemetery Dance); *The Link* by Richard Matheson (Gauntlet); *Lisey's Story* by Stephen King (Scribner); *Mr. Clarinet* by Nick Stone (Michael Joseph); *Slither* by Edward Lee (Leisure); *Death's Dominion* by Simon Clark (Leisure); *London Under Midnight* by Simon Clark (Severn House); *Dead City* by Joe McKinney (Pinnacle); *Prodigal Blues* by Gary A. Braunbeck (Cemetery Dance); *Summer of the Apocalypse* by James Van Pelt (Fairwood Press); *Heaven's Falling—Redemption* by Garry Charles (Hadesgate Publications); *Tick Hill* by Billy Eakin (Yard Dog Press); *The Myth Hunters* by Christopher Golden (Bantam); *Things from the Past* by Steven Deighan (Hadesgate); *Breath of the Moon* by John Urbancik (Solitude Publications); *The Magic Ring*, a nineteenth-century novel by Baron de la Motte Fouque, edited by Amy H. Sturgis (Valancourt Books); *Monster Nation* by David Wellington (Thunder's Mouth); *The Return of Skeleton Man* by Joseph Bruchac (HarperCollins); *Edgewise* by Graham Masterton (Severn House); *Twilight's Last Gleaming* by Mike Philbin writing as Hertzan Chimera (Chimericana Books); *The Mother* by Brett McBean (Lothian); *Twilight* by William Gay (McAdam/Cage); *Benighted* by Kit Whitfield (Del Rey); *Smonk* by Tom Franklin (Morrow); *The Rutting Season* by Brian Keene (Bloodletting Press); *Mayhem at Grant-Williams High* by Vera Nazarian (Norilana Books); *The Distance Travelled* by Brett Alexander Savory (Necro Publications); *Friends in Dark Places* by

John Bushmore (Sam's Dot Publishing); *Beating Heart* by A. M. Jenkins (HarperTempest); *Grimm Reapings* by R Patrick Gates (Pinnacle); *The Brief History of the Dead* by Kevin Brockmeier (Pantheon); *Traitor to the Blood* by Barb Hendee and J. C. Hendee (Roc); *Pretty Little Devils* by Nancy Holder (Razorbill); *Cell* by Stephen King (Scribner); *Freaks: Alive on the Inside* by Annette Curtis Klause (McElderry); *Criss Cross* by Evie Rhodes (Dafina); *Parasite Eve* by Hideaki Sena (Vertical); *Forever Will You Suffer* by Gary Frank (Medallion Press); *Working for the Devil* by Lilith Saintcrow (Warner); *Awaiting the Moon* by Donna Lea Simpson (Berkley); *Erased* by Nick Gifford (Penguin/Puffin, U.K.); *The Smile of a Ghost* by Phil Rickman (Macmillan, U.K.); *Micah* by Laurell K. Hamilton (Jove); *A Dirty Job* by Christopher Moore (HarperCollins); *Nightlife* by Rob Thurman (Roc); *Boys That Bite* by Mari Mancusi (Berkley); *Dracula: Asylum* by Paul Witcover (DH Press); *Babylon* by Richard Calder (PS Publishing); *Damage* by Lee Thomas (Sarob Press); *Sleeping Policemen* by Dale Bailey and Jack Slay, Jr. (Golden Gryphon); *Harbingers* by F. Paul Wilson (Gauntlet Press); *The Devil You Know* by Mike Carey (Orbit); *The Swarm* by Frank Schatzing (Regan Books); *Fever in the Blood* by Robert Fleming (Dafina/Kensington); *The Crimson Labyrinth* by Yosuke Kishi (Vertical); *Development Hell* by Mick Garris (Cemetery Dance); *Ape's-Face* by Marion Fox (Ash-Tree Press), a novel first published in 1914 and reprinted for the first time; *The White Earth* by Andrew McGahan (Soho); *The Wave* by Walter Mosley (Warner); *The End of Mr. Y* by Scarlett Thomas (Harvest); *Zed* by Elizabeth McClung (Arsenal Pulp); *The One from the Other* by Philip Kerr (Putnam/Marian Wood); *The Road* by Cormac McCarthy (Knopf); *The People of Paper* by Salvador Plascencia (McSweeney's); *Damnation Street* by Andrew Klavan (Harcourt); *The Epicure* by H. R. Howland (Berkley); *Hannibal Rising* by Thomas Harris (Delacorte Press); *The Undying Monster* by Jessie Douglas Kerruish (Ash-Tree), first published in 1922, this new edition has an introduction by Jack Adrian and marvelous jacket art by Jason Van Hollander; *World War Z* by Max Brooks (Crown); *The Glass Books of the Dream Eaters* by Gordon Dahlquist (Bantam); *The Ruins* by Scott Smith (Knopf); *The Lucifer Messiah* by Frank Cavallo (Medallion Press); *The Apocalypse Stone* by Pete Earley (Forge); *The Vision* by Heather Graham (Mira); *Necroscope: The Touch* by Brian Lumley (Tor); *The Pilo Family Circus* by Will Elliott (ABC Books, Australia); *Candles Burning* by Michael McDowell and Tabitha King (Berkley); *Descendant* by Graham Masterton (Severn House); *Danse Macabre* by Laurell K. Hamilton (Berkley); *Walking Lazarus* by T. L. Hines (Bethany House); *Demon Theory* by Stephen Graham Jones (Macadam/Cage); *Boy Heaven* by Laura Kasischke (HarperTempest); *Bound in Flesh* by David Thomas Lord (Kensington); *Relentless* by Robin Parrish (Bethany House); *In the Dark of the Night* by John Saul (Ballantine); *Kitty Goes to Washington* by Carrie Vaughn (Warner); *The Burning* by Bentley Little (Signet); *Finding Satan* by Andrew Neiderman (Pocket Star); *The Harrowing* by Alexandra Sokoloff (St. Martin's); *Renfield: Slave of Dracula* by Barbara Hambly (Berkley); *New Moon* by Stephenie Meyer (Little, Brown); *Mr. Twilight* by Michael Reaves and Maya Kaathryn Bohnhoff (Del Rey); *Dying Words* by Shaun Hutson (Little, Brown, U.K.); *Passionate Thirst* by Cameron Dean (Ballantine); *Cold as Death* by T. J. MacGregor (Pinnacle); *Frankenstein: The Shadow of Frankenstein* by Stefan Petrucha (DH Press); *Greywalker* by Kat Richardson (Roc); *The Secret of Crickley Hall* by James Herbert (Macmillan U.K.); *Mistral's Kiss* by Laurell K. Hamilton (Ballantine); *Brother Odd* by Dean Koontz (Bantam); *Bestiary* by Robert Masello (Berkley); *Surrogate Evil* by David Thurlo and Aimée Thurlo (Forge); *Bottomfeeder* by B. H. Fingerman (M Press); *Rabbit Heart* by Colleen

Hitchcock (Pocket); *No Dominion* by Charlie Huston (Del Rey); *Ju-on* by Kei Ohishi (DH Press), the first English language edition of the novelization of the Japanese horror film and videos, translated by Joe Swift; and *The Wall* by Jeff Long (Atria).

Anthologies

As in the past couple of years, 2006 was a weak year for original horror anthologies, although there were lots of mixed-genre anthologies with some excellent horror stories. Only three stories in this volume were chosen from anthologies, half as many as in 2005.

Lords of the Razor, edited by Bill Sheehan and William Schafer (Subterranean Press), is a very good anthology celebrating Joe R. Lansdale's grisly god of darkness who takes possession of those unlucky enough to become owners of a deadly razor. The best piece is Bradley Denton's new Blackburn novella, but there are other good stories by P. D. Cacek, Lansdale, Hugh B. Cave, Stephen Gallagher, and Christopher Golden. The limited edition is a beauty, with black and gold marbled endpapers, jacket art by Timothy Truman, and interior illustrations by Glenn Chadbourne.

Shrouded by Darkness, edited by Alison L. R. Davies (Telos), is a nontheme horror anthology published to raise money for a U.K. charity on behalf of people with a genetic skin disease. Of the twenty-three stories, nine are original and the best of those are by Paul Finch, Simon Clark, Darren Shan, and a collaboration by Steve Lockley and Paul Lewis. Clive Barker provides an illustration of a cenobite, and the reprints include a varied roster of excellent stories by Christopher Fowler, Justina Robson, Graham Masterton, Neil Gaiman, Ramsey Campbell, Michael Marshall Smith, and Poppy Z. Brite. Simon Clark's story is reprinted herein.

In the Dark: Stories from the Supernatural, edited by Myna Wallin and Halli Villegas (Tightrope Books), is an excellent, mostly mainstream anthology about hauntings and ghosts. Published in Canada, it includes contributions from genre writers Gemma Files, Michael Kelly, and Brett Alexander Savory.

Alone on the Darkside, edited by John Pelan (Roc), is the fifth in this all original, nontheme horror series. Overall it's a very good one, with standouts by Brian Hodge, Paul Finch, Joseph A. Ezzo, Lucy Taylor, d. g. k. Goldberg, and Hank Schwaeble.

Mondo Zombie, edited by John Skipp (Cemetery Dance), is the long-awaited third volume of the series that started the literary, George Romero–inspired flesh-eating zombie craze with *Book of the Dead* back in 1989 and *Still Dead* in 1992. The first two volumes edited by Skipp and his writing partner at that time, Craig Spector, featured all original stories, several of which have become classics. In the interim there has been an explosion of zombie anthologies and movies, so in order to make a mark a story has to be pretty special. *Mondo Zombie* does a respectable job. Despite the unlikelihood that any of this new batch of eighteen originals (out of twenty-seven, total) will become classics, there are some good stories, including what might be one of Robert Bloch's last efforts, plus others by Robert Devereaux, Dana Fredsti, Nancy Kilpatrick, Buddy Martinez, Simon McCaffery, and two collaborations: one by Terry Morgan and Christopher Morgan and the second by Steve Rasnic Tem and Melanie Tem.

Read by Dawn, volume 1, "hosted" by Ramsey Campbell (Bloody Books), is the first of a projected series of annual anthologies from a new imprint of the U.K. publisher Beautiful Books. The first volume has notable stories by Rayne Hall, David Hutchinson, Jeff Jacobson, Michele Lee, Ralph Robert Moore, Lavie Tidhar, and

Ramsey Campbell. Oddly, in addition to providing no bios for the contributors, their names aren't even in the table of contents. Presumably, the latter omission is a production glitch. Campbell introduces the volume and sends it off with a brief endnote.

Dark Arts, edited by John Pelan (Cemetery Dance), is the first official HWA anthology published since 2001. The theme—art and horror—is broader than those of most past volumes, which is a good thing, and the strongest original stories (there are two reprints in the book) are by Charlee Jacob, Michael Kelly, Tim Lebbon, Peadar Ó Guilín, John Pelan, John B. Rosenman, Michelle Scalise, Lorelei Shannon, Steve Rasnic Tem, and a collaboration by Mark McLaughlin and Matt Cardin.

Dead Cat's Traveling Circus of Wonders and Miracle Medicine Show, edited by Gerard Houarner and GAK (Bedlam Press), emanates from a silly joke story published several years ago, and has surprisingly turned into an entertaining anthology series. This newest volume of original tales and poetry and art about a dead cat who has adventures includes some terrific stories by Houarner, Trey Barker, and Jeffrey Thomas, with imaginative artwork by GAK, Alan M. Clark, Chad Savage, and Erik Wilson.

Hardboiled Cthulhu: Two-Fisted Tales of Tentacled Terror, edited by James Ambuehl (Dimension Books, an imprint of Elder Signs Press), is a pretty good anthology (sixteen of the twenty-one stories are original) of stories about private eyes dragged into Lovecraftian horrors. The odd story out is about a barbarian bent on revenge that is neither hard-boiled nor Lovecraftian other than tossing in a couple of elder god names. The editor not only includes a story of his own, but he places it in the first slot, something usually reserved for one of the strongest stories. Some critics see nothing wrong with editors of original anthologies publishing their own work. I do; to me it often indicates a lack of editorial judgment.

Poe's Lighthouse, edited by Christopher Conlon (Cemetery Dance), has the problem that most very narrowly defined theme anthologies have: the least interesting stories are those that stick religiously to the theme. In this case, all the stories must be based in some way on a fragment penned by Edgar Allan Poe. Despite this, there *are* some good stories in the book. In addition to the horror tales, there are two odd sf renderings by William F. Nolan and Paul Di Filippo, respectively.

Another Poe-inspired anthology came out in 2006 and was published by Arkham House: *Evermore*, edited by James Robert Smith and Stephen Mark Rainey. The fifteen stories (all but four original) are lacking the variety in tone and treatment they'd need to make this a truly standout anthology, but there are notable stories by Fred Chappell, Trey R. Barker, Ken Goldman, Charlee Jacob, and F. Gwynplaine MacIntyre.

Shivers IV, edited by Richard Chizmar (Cemetery Dance), is a pretty good entry in this ongoing series of nontheme horror. In this volume there are twenty stories, all but five published for the first time. There's strong work by Gemma Files, Al Sarrantonio, Keith Minnion, Norman Prentiss, Tim Curran, and Stephen Mark Rainey.

Damned Nation, edited by Robert N. Lee and David T. Wilbanks (Hellbound Books Publishing), is a decent all original anthology of twenty-two stories about hell on earth. About one-third of the contributors run far enough with the theme to carve out some new territory. Some of the best stories are by R. W. Day, Gerard Houarner, A. H. Jennings, Paul McMahon, and Norman Prentiss.

Candy in the Dumpster: New and Used Stories, edited by Bill Breedlove (Dark Arts Books), features twelve stories (three each) by Breedlove, John Everson, Jay Bonansinga, and Martin Mundt. A few of the originals are utterly tasteless and utterly hilarious, particularly one each by Martin Mundt and Bill Breedlove.

Masques V, edited by J. N. Williamson and Gary A. Braunbeck (Gauntlet Press), is the last of the Williamson edited series (Braunbeck took over when Williamson died in the middle of the editing process) and has notable stories by Richard Christian Matheson, Ray Bradbury, Tim Waggoner, Judi Rohrig, Gary A. Braunbeck, Poppy Z. Brite, Mort Castle, Ron Horsley, Christopher Conlon, Thomas F. Monteleone, and Tracy Knight.

In Delirium, edited by Brian Keene, was conceived as a thank-you to Shane Ryan Staley (Delirium Books) by the contributors to his horror list. Fourteen of the twenty-two stories are original to the anthology and the best new ones are by Tom Piccirilli and a collaboration by Jeffrey and Scott Thomas. GAK did the jacket art.

Straight to Darkness: Lairs of the Hidden Gods, Volume Three, edited by Asamatsu Ken with an introduction by Robert M. Price (Kurodahan Press), contains seven Lovecraftian stories and novellas by Japanese writers. Collectively, they're an interesting take on the mythos from another culture's point of view. There's also an essay on "Cthulhu metal"—music by Black Sabbath, Blue Öyster Cult, and other bands that were obviously inspired by Lovecraft.

Book of Shadows, Volume One, edited by Angela Challis (Brimstone Press), showcases forty pieces of flash fiction published by *Shadowed Realms*, the only Australian professional dark fiction online magazine, from the Web zine's debut in 2004 through 2005. It also includes four original flash pieces, the best by Mikal Trimm.

Choices, edited by Christopher C. Teague (Pendragon Press), is an anthology of six original novelettes hinging on choices (mostly bad) that a character has made or must make. The book is modeled on the six episodes of the standard U.K. television drama serial. The contributors are Stephen Volk, Eric Brown, Paul Finch, Gary Fry, Andrew Humphrey, and Richard Wright.

Aegri Somnia, edited by Jason Sizemore and Gill Ainsworth (Apex Publications), has twelve original dark stories by an array of writers, both from within and outside of the horror field. The title is Latin for a "sick man's dreams" or "man's darkest nightmares." The strongest stories are by Christopher Rowe, Steven Savile, and Lavie Tidhar. The cover art is by Michel Bielaczyc.

When Graveyards Yawn, edited by Sean Wright (Crowswing), pays homage to August Derleth with new stories about revenge beyond the grave. There are good stories by Gary Fry, Geoffrey Maloney, Michelle Ponto, and David A. Sutton. The attractive cover art is by Gabe Chouinard.

Badass Horror, edited by Michael Stone and Christopher J. Hall (Dybbuk Press), is an anthology of seven stories, six original, and two of those were notable: the ones by Michael Hemmingson and Davin Ireland.

DeathGrip: Exit Laughing, edited by Walt Hicks (Hellbound Books Publishing), has twenty-eight original stories of black humor. Combining humor and horror is a risky enterprise and that even a few of the stories succeed is praiseworthy. the ones stories are by Dennis Lathem, Terry Bramlett, Dayle A. Dermatis, and Mark Zirbel.

Gods and Monsters, edited by Jason Andrew and Michael Dyer (simianpublishing), is a theme anthology about updating myth and monsters, with fourteen stories, nine new. Good stories by Gary McMahon and Michael Nethercott.

Extended Play: The Elastic Book of Music, edited by Gary Couzens (Elastic Press), is a strong, mostly dark anthology of stories connected to music. In between each story is a few pages of commentary by a contemporary songwriter. The stories I liked the best are by Tony Richards, Rosanne Rabinowitz, Marion Arnott, Becky Done, Andrew Humphrey, and Tim Nickels.

Arkham Tales, edited by William Jones (Chaosium), is, according to the editor's introduction, the first anthology in which "... each story ... is realized in Chaosium's adaptation of the cosmic horror sub-genre." In other words, if I understand correctly, each story is inspired directly by an actual aspect of the "Call of Cthulhu" role-playing game published by Chaosium Press. Despite this, the stories *do* stand alone and some do some nice riffs on the mythos, including those by C. J. Henderson, Brian M. Sammons, and John Goodrich.

Night Visions 12, edited by Kealan Patrick Burke (Subterranean), continues the tradition of showcasing three writers, in this case Simon Clark, Mark Morris, and P. D. Cacek. All three writers provide good work; Cacek's novella about an arrogant psychotherapist and one of his patients is the standout. With an introduction by the editor and jacket art by Russell Dickerson.

Dark Doorways: An Anthology of Imaginative Fiction, edited by James Cooper (Prufrock Press), has eighteen stories, all but four original. The strongest originals are by Brandon Alspaugh, Davin Ireland, James Cooper, Steven Pirie, and Paul Edwards.

Tiny Terrors, Volume 1 is the first in a projected series of little books published by Hadesgate, with five short stories and some illustrations. There is no editor credited.

Classic Tales of Horror: Volume One, edited by Adèle Hartley (Bloody Books), is the debut volume of a new series and it includes stories by Jack London, G. K. Chesterton, Mary Shelley, and twelve others.

H. P. Lovecraft's Book of the Supernatural, edited by Stephen Jones (Pegasus Books), is the second volume of classic stories inspired by Lovecraft's recommendations in his famous essay "The Supernatural in Literature." There are twenty stories and an introduction by Jones.

Annual Macabre 2005: Haven't I Read This Before?, edited by Jack Adrian, looks at a number of writers whose work appears either to have been influenced by others, or influenced the work of others. The introduction discusses plagiarism and literary and musical theft. Included are stories by W. W. Jacobs, Andrew Lang, and A. M. Burrage.

Florida Horror: Dark Tales from the Sunshine State, edited by Armand Rosamilia (Carnifex Press), has twelve stories. One, by Lon Prater, is pretty good.

Hell's Hangmen: Horror in the Old West, edited by Ron Shiflet (Tenoka Press), has twenty-two original stories about zombies, evil guns, monstrous cave-dwellers, and other assorted predators in the Old West.

Fear of... (Borderlands Press) is a mini-anthology of four writers: Richard Chizmar, Brian Freeman, Brian Keene, and Thomas F. Monteleone. The book consists of three reprints by Chizmar, two reprints and an original by Freeman, two original stories by Brian Keene, a comic script cowritten by Brian Keene and Tim Lebbon, and a screenplay adapted from a short story by Monteleone.

Ten Plagues: A Collection of Deadly Stories, edited by Ian Donnell Arbuckle and Justin Conwell (Saltboy), doesn't really stick enough to the theme to create a cohesive whole, but there are a few good stories in the book.

Thou Shalt Not ... , edited by Lee Allen Howard (Dark Cloud Press), has thirty-seven stories about breaking the Ten Commandments. The best are by Jennifer Busick, Christopher Fisher, William Jones, and Michelle Mellon.

Lighthouse VI, edited by Paul Calvin Wilson (Calvin House), is being treated as an anthology because it has an ISBN. This volume is the third in a series of Stephen King specials, and includes essays on King's work, in addition to several King-inspired short stories (two, by Stanley Wiater, are reprints). The book also includes interviews with artists Allen Koszowski and Dave Kendall, and Jack Vance.

Tales to Freeze the Blood: More Great Ghost Stories, compiled by R. Chetwynd-Hayes and Stephen Jones (Carroll & Graf), has twenty-four ghost stories culled from earlier anthologies edited by Chetwynd-Hayes. Included are stories by O. Henry, Richard Burton, Emily Brontë, and Steve Rasnic Tem, among others.

Eulogies: A Horror World Yearbook 2005, edited by Nanci Kalanta (Nyx Publications), presents work published in 2005 on the Horror World Web site. It showcases fiction by Jack Ketchum, Elizabeth Massie, Tom Piccirilli, Christopher Golden, and nine other authors plus brief interviews with Tom Piccirilli, F. Paul Wilson, Douglas Clegg, David Morrell, John Skipp, and Christopher Golden.

Northwest Horrors, edited by Jonathan Reitan and James R. Beach (Northwest Writers Professional Press), showcases ten stories by eleven writers residing in the Northwest United States, (three published for the first time) including such authors as Jemiah Jefferson, Elizabeth Engstrom, Bruce Holland Rogers, and Carlton Mellick III, among others.

My Big Fat Supernatural Wedding, edited by P. N. Elrod (St. Martin's), provides proof, for those readers who need it, that not all supernatural fiction is horror. A couple of the nine stories in the original anthology are truly dark, but most are fluff. Fun fluff, but not horrific fluff. I liked the Jim Butcher and the Rachel Caine (the latter a charmer about cursed pirates).

Vegas Bites, edited by L. A. Banks (Parker Publishing/Noire Allure), contains four werewolf romance stories set in a Las Vegas casino run by vampires, werewolves, and other nonhumans.

Chimeraworld #3: Misogynist, Atheist, Terrorist, edited by Mike Philbin (Chimericana Books), is filled with a plethora of tales that go splat and not much else. The best is by Paul Pinn.

Chimeraworld #4: Twenty-three Tales of Traffic Mayhem, edited by Mike Philbin (Chimericana Books), takes J. G. Ballard's *Crash* and Roger Zelazny's sentient car stories a little too much to heart. Most of the cars in these tales have names, and there's an awful lot of human/car love and merging for my taste. But there's one sexy standout by Christina Crooks.

Shadow Regions, edited by César Puch (Surreal Books), is an entertaining non-theme horror anthology of twenty new stories. The strongest are by Bonnie Mercure, David Bell, and Gary A. Braunbeck.

Project Contagion, Volume 1, edited by Dustin La Valley and M. G. Sullivan (lulu.com), has thirteen short shorts, nine original to the anthology.

There has been an explosion of Year's Best anthologies on the sf/f/h scene including Paula Guran's *Best New Paranormal Romance* (Juno); *Horror: The Best of the Year*, edited by John Betancourt and Sean Wallace (Prime); *Science Fiction: The Best of the Year*, edited by Rich Horton (Prime); *Fantasy: The Best of the Year*, edited by Rich Horton (Prime); *Australian Dark Fantasy and Horror*, edited by Angela Challis and Shane Jiraiya Cummings (Brimstone Press); *Science Fiction: The Very Best of 2005*, edited by Jonathan Strahan (Locus Publications); and *Fantasy: The Very Best of 2005*, edited by Jonathan Strahan (Locus Publications). *Year's Best Australian Science Fiction and Fantasy, Volume II*, edited by Bill Congreve and Michelle Marquardt (MirrorDanse Books), includes some darker stories by Lucy Sussex and Stephen Dedman. And of course, among the old-timers are Stephen Jones's *Best New Horror* series (Robinson/Carroll & Graf) and Gardner Dozois's *The Year's Best Science Fiction* (St. Martin's)—among all of the above there is bound to be some overlap (with each other and with *The Year's Best Fantasy and Horror*).

Also, *The Best American Short Stories 2006*, edited by Ann Patchett (Houghton Mifflin), published annually since 1915, has, in its recent past, been more amenable to genre writers and darker stories than previously. In the current volume there are a few notable dark reprints by Donna Tartt, Robert Coover, and others.

Mixed-Genre Anthologies

Eidolon 1, edited by Jonathan Strahan and Jeremy G. Byrne (Prime), is the first of a projected series of original anthologies to be edited by the team that edited the acclaimed Australian magazine of the same name in the 1990s. This first book, with fifteen original stories and two reprints, by Americans, Australians, and one Scot, is heavy on fantasy, with a few dollops of dark fantasy and horror and a wee bit of science fiction. Among the darker stories, the standouts are by Margo Lanagan, Chris Lawson, and Holly Phillips. *The Outcast: The Anthology of Exiles and Strangers*, edited by Nicole R. Murphy, is the seventh anthology of sf/f/h stories published by the Canberra Speculative Fiction Society of Australia. Of the twenty stories, about one-third are dark enough to be considered horror (a few are sf/horror) and the notable ones are by Martin Livings, Richard Harland, Maxine McArthur, Cat Sparks, Kaaron Warren, and Monica Carroll. *Retro Pulp Tales*, edited by Joe R. Lansdale (Subterranean), is a terrifically entertaining original anthology, with everything from westerns and war stories to monster tales, detective and crime fiction, supernatural tales and science fiction, by twelve contemporary writers. The best dark stories are by F. Paul Wilson, Alex Irvine, Stephen Gallagher, Norman Partridge, Kim Newman, Bill Crider, and Al Sarrantonio. *Agog! Ripping Reads*, edited by Cat Sparks (Agog! Press), has a good cross-section of up-and-coming Australian writers of fantastic fiction, with a few American writers thrown into the mix. There were good dark stories by Dirk Flinthart, Paul Haines, David J. Kane, Andrew Macrae, Anna Tambour, and Margo Lanagan, whose "A Pig's Whisper," is reprinted herein. *Tesseracts Ten*, edited by Robert Charles Wilson and Edo Van Belkom (Edge), has a bit of horror, with notable dark tales by Sarah Totton, Greg Bechtel, and Rhea Rose. *Cross Plains Universe: Texans Celebrate Robert E. Howard*, edited by Scott A. Cupp and Joe R. Lansdale (MonkeyBrain Books and F.A.C.T.), is a celebration of the centenary of Howard, and was published for the 2006 World Fantasy Convention in Austin, Texas. The book is filled with a variety of stories, some light, others dark — many taking place in the worlds Howard created. There are notable dark tales by Jessica Reisman, Scott A. Cupp, Lawrence Person, and Howard Waldrop. *The Best of Not One of Us*, edited by John Benson (Prime), collects fifteen stories published during the twenty years of the small press magazine's run so far and includes mixed-genre work by Sonya Taaffe, Gary A. Braunbeck, Wayne Allen Sallee, Jeffrey Thomas, and others. *Jabberwocky*, edited by Sean Wallace, is the second volume of this attractive and quirky perfect-bound anthology with 147 pages of gorgeous prose and poetry, much of it tending toward the dark side. Some of the better known contributors are Catherynne M. Valente, Laurel Winter, Richard Parks, Jane Yolen, Mike Allen, and Theodora Goss. *From the Trenches: An Anthology of Speculative War Stories*, edited by Joseph Paul Haines and Samantha Henderson (Carnifex Press), is dark, as one would expect war stories to be. The stories range from historical to futuristic, and there's even a tale of psychological warfare on an agri-business pig farm. There's notable work by Steve Vernon, Pati Nagle, Amil Menon, and Kameron Hurley. Although *Jigsaw Nation: Science Fiction Stories of Secession*, edited by Edward J. McFadden, 3rd, and E. Sedia (Spyre), is sf, as the title says, there are at least two darker stories by newcomers Darby Harn and Tara Kolden. *The Bizarro Starter Kit* (Bizarro Books) is for those who prefer their fiction surreal, violent, sacrilegious, and/or with minimal concern for plot or story. Ten writers announce their membership in the bizarro brotherhood (there *is* one female) with novellas and short stories. A few hits, a lot of misses. *Philippine Speculative Fiction Volume 2*, edited by Dean Francis Alfar (Kestrel), presents nineteen stories, some of them horror. *Dark Dreams II: Voices from the Other Side*, edited by Brandon Massey (Dafina), has seventeen stories of horror and suspense by black authors including Tananarive Due and L. A. Banks. *The Alpine Fantasy of Victor B and Other Stories*, edited by Jeremy Akerman and Eileen Daly (Serpent's Tail), has original stories by seventeen of Britain's leading artists. There are notable dark ones by David Batchelor and Chris Hammond. *Nebula Awards Showcase 2006*, edited by Gardner Dozois (Roc), collects the winners and some of the stories nominated for the annual award given by the Science Fiction Writers of America. Although concentrating on science fiction and fantasy, there are some darker stories included. *Feeling Very Strange: The Slipstream Anthology*, edited by James Patrick Kelly and John Kessel (Tachyon), attempts to define the term "slipstream," first coined by Bruce Sterling in 1989. Forget the introduction, forget the proclamations, just read the stories, which skip from fantasy, science fiction, and horror—because they're very good. Most of them were originally published in genre publications, and there's one excellent original by M. Rickert. *Ghosts in Baker Street*, edited by Martin H. Greenberg, Jon Lellenberg, and Daniel Stashower (Carroll &Graf), has ten apparent ghost stories for which that supreme rationalist Sherlock Holmes provides nonsupernatural explanations. Also included are two nonfiction essays by Caleb Carr and Barbara Roden. *The British Fantasy Society: A Celebration*, edited by Paul Kane and Marie O'Regan (The British Fantasy Society), is, as suggested by its title, a celebration of the Society. This anthology of science fiction, fantasy, and horror stories is excellent, with six of the twenty stories original to the volume. The best of the originals are by Chaz Brenchley, Mark Chadbourn, and Christopher Fowler.

Collections

The Lost District and Other Stories by Joel Lane (Night Shade), the author's second collection, is filled with exquisitely imagined stories of urban decay and despair. The twenty-four stories (including six published for the first time) are bleak and dark, the language stark, with minimal embellishment. Readers who can handle it are in for a treat.

Basic Black: Tales of Appropriate Fear by Terry Dowling (Cemetery Dance) is Dowling's fifth collection, but only the second (the SFBC published one about fifteen years ago) to be published in the United States. Although some of the stories have already been reprinted in earlier collections, hopefully *Basic Black*'s American publication will bring Dowling a much deserved wider readership. Now if only someone will reprint the book (already out of print in hardcover) as a paperback. Seven of the eighteen stories in the collection were chosen for previous volumes of *YBFH* (one for the fantasy side) and one of the two originals is reprinted herein.

American Morons by Glen Hirshberg (Earthling Publications) is the author's second collection, after Hirshberg's lauded *The Two Sams*. The new book contains seven stories and novelettes, including two previously reprinted in our *Year's Best* anthologies. While this one may not be as dazzling, it clearly demonstrates that Hirshberg continues to entertain and disturb with his marvelous short stories. The three originals are excellent, and I was torn between "Devil's Smile" and "The Muldoon," finally choosing the latter for the current volume.

Unbecoming: and Other Tales of Horror by Mike O'Driscoll (Elastic) is a terrific first collection by this always surprising British creator of obsessed, sometimes scary, but always believable characters who uneasily inhabit the noir cities he envisions. One of the thirteen stories appears for the first time and it's a good one.

Dark Corners by Stephen Volk (Gray Friar Press) is another excellent first collection, this one by the British screenwriter who created *Ghostwatch*, a notorious Halloween hoax for BBC-TV. Volk's fiction has been published in *Postscripts*, *All Hallows*, *Crimewave*, and in various anthologies. Four of the sixteen stories appear for the first time—one is written as a short script—and they are all good. Tim Lebbon provides an introduction, and the author contributes brief story notes. One story, "31/10," is reprinted herein.

Havoc Swims Jaded by David J. Schow (Subterranean), the author's seventh collection of short fiction, showcases thirteen stories by an expert wordsmith. Three of the stories are original to the collection. Schow obviously loves popular culture and writes about pulp monsters, creeps, and ordinary people. The cover and interior art is by Frank Dietz. Also from Subterranean: *Reassuring Tales* by T. E. D. Klein features nine stories and a novella, some previously uncollected. Klein wrote some outstanding stories, one impressive novel, *The Ceremonies* (based on the novella in this collection), and has pretty much stopped writing. Although a couple of the later stories are minor, most pack a nice wallop. The jacket art is by Jason Eckhardt. *Screaming Science Fiction: Horror from Outer Space* by Brian Lumley collects nine sf/h stories plus a new almost twenty-thousand-word novella called "Feasibility Study." Jacket art and interior illustrations are by Bob Eggleton. *Alabaster* by Caitlín R. Kiernan is a collection of five stories about the haunted albino teenager, Dancy Flammarion. Jacket art is by Ted Naifeh.

Birthday by Koji Suzuki (Vertical) features three tales from the famous Japanese Ringu trilogy. I only read the first, and it doesn't really bring much new to the ongoing story. So if you've already seen the movie series, you might want to skip this.

Clinically Dead & Other Tales of the Supernatural by David A. Sutton (Crowswing) is the first collection by Sutton, better known for his multi-award-winning editing than his fiction. But he's been writing and publishing short stories since the 1960s. Ten stories from between 1990 and 2006 are showcased here, including two original tales and a novella. The attractive cover art is by Harry O. Morris. Also from Crowswing comes *The Impelled and Other Head Trips* by Gary Fry, eighteen stories, almost half published for the first time in 2006. Introduction by Ramsey Campbell and an afterword of brief story notes by the author. The excellent cover art and design is by Robert Sammelin.

Bloodlines: Richard Matheson's Dracula, I Am Legend and Other Vampire Stories, edited with preface, introductions, and an appendix by Mark Dawidziak (Gauntlet Press), contains three short stories from the fifties, the entire novel and a screenplay version of *I Am Legend*, plus a *Dracula* treatment and screenplay. Also included are appreciations by various fans and/or friends of Matheson, including Ray Bradbury, John Carpenter, and Rockne S. O'Bannon.

The Man from the Diogenes Club by Kim Newman (MonkeyBrain) is a marvelous book collecting the Richard Jeperson stories and novellas about a secret British law enforcement institution that investigates strange happenings in Newman's entertaining alternate 1970s. There's one original novella.

Unholy Dimensions by Jeffrey Thomas (Mythos Books) has twenty-seven Love-craftian stories, two original, one of which, "The Young of the Old Ones," is very good. The stories were published over a period of about fifteen years and appeared in a variety of small press venues. The stories are nicely illustrated in black and white by Peter A. Worthy.

Thundershowers at Dusk by Christopher Conlon (Rock Village Publishing), the author's excellent second collection (the first was mainstream), contains four contemporary gothic stories and the titular novella. The novella and "Bathing the Bones," the other story published for the first time, are beautifully written and powerful. Gary A. Braunbeck provides an introduction.

Eros Interruptus by P. D. Cacek (Diplodocus Press) is one of two collections published by S. P. Somtow's new press. Showcased here are fifteen of Cacek's erotic horror tales, including the Stoker-winning "Metalica."

Thing of Darkness by G. G. Pendarves (Midnight House 2005) is the first of two projected volumes of the British writer's ghostly tales, originally published in *Weird Tales* during the 1920s and thirties. Edited and with an introduction by Mike Ashley. Also *Darker Tides: The Weird Tales of Eric Frank Russell*, edited by John Pelan and Phil Stephensen-Payne, contains twenty-four stories, including all those in the original collection by the same title published over thirty years ago, and many others written in the same vein.

Punktown: Shades of Grey by Jeffrey Thomas and Scott Thomas (Bedlam Press) is a new, very good collection of Punktown stories, taking place in the future—a mostly ugly urban jungle created by Jeffrey Thomas—in which the denizens just get by (or don't). There are eight stories by Jeffrey Thomas, two original, and seven by Scott Thomas, all original. Not all the pieces are fully realized stories; some are vignettes, but with its aliens and monsters the world of Punktown is one of the best examples of sf horror currently out there.

Destinations Unknown by Gary A. Braunbeck (Cemetery Dance) is a welcome new original collection of two short stories and a novella all centering around the road. The richly detailed novella "The Ballad of Road Mama and Daddy Bliss" creates a new mythology: the road as a god—and the sacrifices it demands. The dust jacket art is by Deena Warner. Also from Cemetery Dance: *Four Octobers* by Rick Hautala featuring four novellas that take place around Halloween, two of them new, both very good. The first original is Bradburyesque (the author dedicates the whole volume to Bradbury) in its depiction of an idyllic childhood marred by a mysterious disappearance and messages from the future. Glenn Chadbourne created the effectively horrific jacket art. *Sinister Purposes* by Gary Raisor dubs itself a "mosaic novel"—that is, a series of novellas strung together in order to create a unified whole—all of them about the evil goings-on in the town of Eden, Georgia. The book has no table of contents, so in that way, it's structured more like a novel. The jacket art is by Keith Minnion and the interior illustrations are by Kariann Childs.

Fine Cuts by Dennis Etchison (PS Publishing) brings together twelve of Etchison's Hollywood stories by a brilliant short story writer who has been far too quiet of late. Two of the twelve were reprinted in earlier editions of this anthology. Introduction by Peter Atkins.

Thirteen Specimens by Jeffrey Thomas (Delirium Books) is a mixed bag of thirteen pieces, all but two original. There are a few brief, entertaining space-fillers, but the strongest stories are the five longer ones, particularly the Punktown novella "Monsters," about a doctor trying to help a female alien who has been punished by her family for having engaged in premarital sex. Also very good are "Close Enough," about aliens who "direct" humans to commit atrocities so that they (the aliens) can voyeuristically view them from afar, and "The Mask Play of Hahoe Byeolsin Exorcism," about a middle-aged man stranded for a few days in Korea who encounters frightening Korean masks.

Geek Poems by Charlee Jacob (Necro Publications) contains seven stories and one novella, all published for the first time, by an intriguing and ambitious writer. The black-and-white interior illustrations and cover art are by Travis Anthony Soumis. Well worth reading.

The Passion Play and Other Ghost Stories by Antony Oldknow (Ash-Tree) is the first collection of stories by a relative newcomer who only began to write his Henry James–inspired ghost stories about eight years ago. Four of the ten stories are original.

Doorways for the Dispossessed by Paul Haines (Prime) is a very strong first collection of twenty dark, edgy stories (two original to the collection) from this relative newcomer, who grew up in New Zealand and now lives in Australia. One of the stories in the book won the *Aurealis* and Ditmar Awards.

The Female of the Species by Joyce Carol Oates (Harcourt) collects recent crime and horror stories about women by this prolific purveyor of dark fiction in multiple genres and the literary mainstream. The nine stories were originally published in magazines ranging from *The Magazine of Fantasy & Science Fiction* and *Ellery Queen's Mystery Magazine* to *The Kenyon Review* and *The Spook*.

Hook House and Other Horrors by Sherry Decker (Silver Lake Publishing), the author's first collection, has eleven stories (one original). Also from Silver Lake comes *Waking Nightmares* by Diana Abbott and Eric S. Brown, a double collection by newcomer Abbott and by Brown, who has been publishing short fiction since 2002. There are twenty-two mostly very brief stories, eight of them reprints by Brown.

Winds of Change by Jason Brannon (Nocturne Press) has three original horror stories: the first about a group of strangers trapped inside a store by a terrifying plague—or something—that turns anyone outside into dust; the second about Lovecraftian creatures who cannot stand the classical music played in a conservatory over their home; and the third about an orphan who uses voodoo to rid the city of evil. Also from Nocturne, *The Commandments* by Angeline Hawkes features ten stories, each based on one of the commandments. A bit more subtlety would have made for some surprises.

When They Came by Don Webb (Temporary Culture) has twenty-three eldritch but rarely scary tales, ten original to the collection, the others published in such magazines as *Realms of Fantasy*, *Weird Tales*, *Interzone*, and *Noctulpa*, and in the anthologies *Forbidden Acts*, *Monsters from Memphis*, and *Crossroads*.

Sheena and Other Gothic Tales by Brian Stableford (Immanion Press) contains ten dark stories, all published between 1990 and 2001, mostly in anthologies. In his fascinating introduction, Stableford designates the stories *contes cruels*, a type of dark fiction that is especially cynical and often ends unhappily.

The Fungal Stain and Other Dreams by W. H. Pugmire (Hippocampus Press) consists of fifteen stories and vignettes on Lovecraftian themes, with some new stories and a few published previously but completely rewritten for the volume. Despite Pugmire's distracting habit of mixing his studied archaic style with anachronistic contemporary terms, his stories often provide unusual and entertaining new variations on the mythos. If only he'd drop the "hey dude" and "wusses" his weird tales would go down a lot smoother.

The Surgeon of Souls by Victor Rousseau (Spectre Library) is a collection of twelve weird stories, most of which were first published in *Weird Tales* during the 1920s. Introduction by Mike Ashley.

All Hallow's Eve: 13 Stories by Vivian Vande Velde (Harcourt) has twelve original Halloween stories for children, a few of which might scare adults.

The Fountain and Other Stories by Cary G. Osborne (Yard Dog Press) has five stories, two original.

Black Pockets and Other Dark Thoughts by George Zebrowski (Golden Gryphon) is the author's first collection showcasing his horror fiction, and includes the powerful titular original novella about a man given a "gift" by his most bitter enemy. The nineteen stories span Zebrowski's entire career, with the earliest published in 1972. The book is introduced by Howard Waldrop and has an afterword by the author about his work and about the individual stories. The jacket painting is by Bob Eggleton.

Wild Things: Four Tales by Douglas Clegg (Cemetery Dance) is a mini-collection about predators, animal and human. Two of the reprints are hard to find, and the two originals are quite good, particularly "The Wolf," in which a hunter takes a young man with him to kill a wolf that is slaughtering sheep. The voice is pitch-perfect. The cover art of this attractive hardcover is by Caniglia.

The Faculty of Terror by John Llewellyn Probert (Gray Friar) has six original horror stories linked by interstitial material to emulate the old British anthology movies. The last two and the finale are the best. With an introduction by Paul Finch.

Twisted Tales by Brandon Massey (Dafina) has fourteen of his original horror stories.

Apple of My Eye by Amy Grech (Two Backed Books) features thirteen horror stories, two original to the collection.

From Tartarus Press: *The Sense of the Past: The Ghostly Stories of Henry James* has seventeen ghost stories, and the unfinished novel *The Sense of the Past*, representing all of James's supernatural fiction. The material dates from the 1870s into the early twentieth century. *The Man Who Could Work Miracles* is a huge book collecting thirty-one supernatural tales by H. G. Wells. Brian Stableford's introduction discusses the stories and their context. The cover illustration is by Mike Kerins. *Father Raven and Other Tales* by A. E. Coppard has thirty-one of the author's fantastical and supernatural stories, and an introduction by Mark Valentine. *The Pale Ape and Other Pulses* by M. P. Shiel, originally published in 1911, features ten stories covering *contes cruels,* crime, and warped romance, published between the 1890s and the first decade of the twentieth century. Brian Stableford wrote the introduction. *The Long Retreating Day: Tales of Twilight and Borderlands* by John Gaskin features ten new stories by an excellent traditionalist whose work creates an eerie atmosphere and is well written and absorbing. The author's first collection, *The Dark Companion,* was published in 2001.

Miniatures Macabre by M. W. Anderson (Naked Snake Press) has twenty-one short-shorts, most of them reprints.

When the Darkness Falls by J. F. Gonzalez (Midnight Library) has fourteen stories, one original, with an introduction and story notes by the author.

Left in the Dark: The Supernatural Tales by John Gordon (Medusa Press) is a collection of thirty stories, one original.

Fiends by Torchlight by Wayne Allen Sallee (Annihilation Press) celebrates the twentieth anniversary of Sallee's first professional publication with twenty-three stories of urban horror from over his career; five stories are new.

Severance by Robert Olen Butler (Chronicle) has sixty-two works, each in the voice of a beheaded, historical figure or mythical creature. Each piece is 240 words, the number of words the author calculates could be spoken before oxygen runs out.

'Nids and Other Stories by Ray Garton (Spiderweb Press) is an all-original collection containing one creepy novella about spiders and four short stories. Nice jacket art by Glenn Chadbourne.

Tarra Khash: Hrossak! and *Sorcery in Shad* by Brian Lumley (Tor) were both originally published by Headline in the U.K. in 1991. They are the second and third (final) volumes in the Tales of the Primal Land, about the barbarian Tarra Khash.

Love Hurts by Barry Hoffman (Edge) is the author's second collection, with seven original short stories.

The Mark of the Beast and Other Fantastical Tales by Rudyard Kipling (Gollancz) is a nice thick volume of forty-nine stories and a poem, edited and with an afterword by Stephen Jones.

Gardens of Fear by Robert E. Howard, edited by Paul Herman (Wildside), contains six stories and one poem. This is volume six in the series *The Weird Works of Robert E. Howard*.

Ash-Tree Press Occult Detectives Library brought out *Shiela Crerar, Psychic Investigator* by Ella Scrymour, edited and with an introduction by Jack Adrian. The book has six stories published between May and October in 1920 by this obscure author. Jason Van Hollander did the jacket art. Also from Ash-Tree: *The Elemental* by Ulric Daubeny, reprinting, for the first time in eighty years, the original 1919 collection of sixteen stories, adding the only other supernatural tale by the author. Introduction by Douglas A. Anderson. The jacket art reproduces the original.

Mixed-Genre Collections

Red Spikes by Margo Lanagan (Allen & Unwin) is this Australian author's third collection, another winning combination of fantasy and dark fantasy, with ten stories published for the first time. She writes of children and their fears, and of how Christian missionaries destroyed Aboriginal families and tried to supplant the old gods of Australia. One of the stories, "Winkie," has been reprinted herein. *Map of Dreams* by M. Rickert (Golden Gryphon) is the eagerly awaited first collection by one of the fantastic genre's rising stars. Her early stories have been mostly published in *The Magazine of Fantasy & Science Fiction*; they are literate, graceful, imaginative, powerful, sometimes extraordinarily dark tales. The title novella is original to the collection. *Fragile Things* by Neil Gaiman (Morrow) is a mixed-genre assemblage of thirty-two stories and poems. Several of the stories are horror or dark fantasy, including the one story original to the collection. *The Empire of Ice Cream* by Jeffrey Ford (Golden Gryphon) is Ford's second collection. He continues to dazzle with his mastery of all he assays. I'm biased, having published many of these stories. The one original, a Bradburyesque novella, "Botch Town" is brilliant in its depiction of a family getting by in the early sixties in suburban America—you can't go wrong with this collection. *Through Soft Air* by Lee Battersby (Prime), the promising Australian writer's first collection, offers twenty-five stories, including one featuring his popular Father Muerte and eight stories original to the collection. *Absolute Uncertainty* by Lucy Sussex (Aqueduct Press) is part of the press's "Conversation Piece" series and has seven stories—three of them original to the collection, by an Australian writer equally adept at the full spectrum of genre fiction. Also included is an interview with the author.

One of the stories, "Frozen Charlottes," was reprinted in this series. *Can't Catch Me and Other Twice-Told Tales* by Michael Cadnum (Tachyon) is full of the author's trademark dark whimsy. Cadnum is better known for his adult and young adult novels, but this first collection of his retold fairy tales showcase his irony. Five of the eighteen stories are original to the collection. The beautiful cover art is by Stephanie Pui-Mun Law. *The Line Between* by Peter S. Beagle (Tachyon) is a welcome collection of recent stories by this great American fantasist. Included among the eight stories are "Two Hearts"—the charming Hugo Award–winning sequel to *The Last Unicorn*—plus two new stories, one a dark tale about the consequences of fooling with magic before you know what you're doing. *Other Edens* by S. P. Somtow (Diplodocus Press) is a collection of five novellas, including the powerful World Fantasy Award–winning "The Bird Catcher" and one original. Introduction by William Hjortsberg (author of *Falling Angel*). *Shuteye for the Timebroker* by Paul Di Filippo (Thunder's Mouth) contains fifteen mostly sf/f stories with a couple of darker tales. Two of the stories are original in this collection. *Urban Fantastic* by Allen Ashley (Crowswing), the author's second collection of twenty stories, is mostly fantasy with the occasional dark bit. *Visionary in Residence* by Bruce Sterling (Thunder's Mouth) showcases thirteen recent stories by the father of cyberpunk. As always with Sterling, some of the tales are dark. *In the Forest of Forgetting* by Theodora Goss (Prime), Goss's first collection, has sixteen stories of fantasy and dark fantasy from 2002–2006—two original to the collection. Goss's fantasy is intelligent and elegantly written. Two of the stories were previously reprinted in our *Year's Best* series. The beautiful jacket art and design are by Virginia Lee and Luis Rodrigues, respectively. *The Chains That You Refuse* by Elizabeth Bear (Night Shade) is a very mixed bag of fantasy, science fiction, and horror. All twenty stories (and one poem) have been published since 2003, and one was reprinted in one of our earlier volumes. The lovely cover art and design are by Samuel Bak and Claudia Noble, respectively. *Dark Mondays* by Kage Baker (Night Shade) has eight stories, four original, and a new short novel about famous buccaneer Captain Henry Morgan. The stories are varied and entertaining. *Strange Candy* by Laurell K. Hamilton (Berkley) is a diverse selection of fantasy and more horror by the creator of the Anita Blake, vampire hunter series. Several of the fourteen stories appear for the first time, and one "Here Be Dragons," about a powerful young sociopath and the therapist brought in to control those powers, is especially good. *Pictures from an Expedition* by Alexander C. Irvine (Night Shade) is the author's second collection. Although better known for his novels *A Scattering of Jades*, *The Narrows*, and *One King, One Soldier*, Irvine has written some fine science fiction and fantasy, much of it dark. *Of Tales and Enigmas* by Minsoo Kang (Prime) is a wonderful collection of fantasy and myth inspired by the author's Korean ancestry. Particularly good are the two ghost stories in the third and last section of the book. *Troy* by Simon Brown (Ticonderoga Publications), the Australian writer's second collection, is inspired by Homer's *Iliad*, although very loosely. The one original, "The Cup of Nestor," is a strong horror story about a young man psychically scarred by war, who is studying a beetle in the Amazon rain forest. *The Ladies of Grace Adieu and Other Stories* by Susanna Clarke (Bloomsbury) is the first collection by the author of the bestselling and highly lauded *Jonathan Strange & Mr Norrell*. The seven reprints and one original comprise all of Clarke's short fiction output. Several of them were included in earlier volumes of this anthology. They're uniformly charming and some of them are dark. The black-and-white Charles Vess interior illustrations beautifully complement each story. *The Ephemera* by Neil Williamson (Elastic) contains sixteen beautifully written stories (one a collaboration) by this Scottish writer published between 1994 and 2006, and one original to this collection. *Ex Cathedra* by Rebecca Maines (Twilight Tales) has eleven sf/f/h tales published in various magazines and anthologies. Four of the stories are original to the collection. *Realm of the Dead* by Uchida Hyakken and translated by Rachel DiNitto (Dalkey Archive) is a dreamlike series of dark, mysterious tales originally published in Japanese in 1922. Interesting if read a few at a time, but tiresome when read all in a row. *Tales of the Chinese Zodiac* by Jenn Reese (Tropism Press) is a chapbook of seventeen tales, a few dark ones about the creatures of the Chinese zodiac. Five of the stories are original to the collection. *Reserved for Travelling Shows* by Trent Jamieson (Prime), the first collection of this Australian writer, has twenty-six science fiction and fantasy stories published in Australian venues between 1994 and 2004 and one original. *At the Molehills of Madness* by Rhys Hughes (Pendragon Press) has twenty-five tales of fantasy, dark fantasy, horror, and just plain weirdness by this prolific Welsh writer, all but three published in the 1990s. A little goes a long way in Martin Mundt's *The Dark Underbelly of Hymns* (Delirium). While some of these twelve tales are horrific, hilariously funny, and in wonderfully bad taste, reading them all in a row becomes dulling overall. The book, with jacket art by Chad Savage, is the seventh in the Delirium Exclusives series, very small limited editions sold only on the publisher's Web site. *Last Week's Apocalypse* by Douglas Lain (Night Shade) is a mix of odd fiction by a promising newcomer. Some of the stories are dark enough to be of interest to readers willing to dip into Lain's weird mind. *Moby Jack and Other Tall Tales* by Garry Kilworth (PS Publishing) showcases twenty-one varied stories, providing an overview of the author's short fantasy and horror output over the past twenty years. Robert Holdstock provides the introduction. *The Butterflies of Memory* by Ian Watson (PS), the author's tenth collection, has seventeen stories and brief story notes. Paul McAuley wrote the introduction. *Streetcar Dreams and Other Midnight Fancies* by Richard Bowes (PS), a powerful collection of six extraordinarily vivid pieces of fantasy fiction, includes the title World Fantasy Award–winning novella, and affords a fine entrée to Bowes's work. With an introduction by Jeffrey Ford. *Corrosion, Book One* by Shane Ryan Staley (Corrosion Press) is a mix of the author's fiction, joke essays, and letters. *The Sense of Falling* by Ezra Pines (Spilt Milk Press) has eleven brief stories, two published for the first time, by a newcomer. Hal Duncan wrote the introduction and Mark Rich illustrated the stories. *Portraits in the Dark* by Nancy O. Greene (iUniverse) is a collection of nine very short stories, two first published in 2006. The stories are a mixed bag, with a couple dark enough to be considered horror. *Saffron and Brimstone* by Elizabeth Hand (M Press) is this genre-straddling author's third collection and while it includes three stories from her previous collection, *Bibliomancy*, there are also four previously uncollected stories and one new one. A few of the stories are horror, others are dark enough to please horror aficionados. *Mortality* by Nicholas Royle (Serpent's Tail) collects stories from 1990 to 2006 and contains mainstream as well as horror, such as the chilling piece "The Churring," the collection's one original, reprinted herein. *Physician to the Universe: The Collected Stories of Clifford Simak: Volume II* (Darkside) is the second of a projected twelve-volume series collecting all the author's short fiction. Although known as a science fiction writer, some of Simak's work is dark enough for horror readers to enjoy. The introduction is by Barry N. Malzberg, and cover art is by Allen Koszowski. *The World, the Flesh, & the Devil: Fantastical Writings: Volume 1* by Gerald Kersh (Ash-Tree) is the first in a projected series of books collecting Kersh's short fiction. He is best known for his novel *Night and the City*, filmed a number of times. I first came across Kersh when I read his tremendously creepy story "Men Without Bones" as a teenager. Most of his work has been out of print for forty years. This long overdue project should change that, bringing Kersh new, appreciative readers. There are twenty-five stories in this volume, edited and introduced by Paul Duncan. The dust jacket painting is by Jason Van Hollander. *The Ocean and All Its Devices* by William Brown Spencer (Subterranean), the second collection by an excellent idiosyncratic writer whose novel *Resumé with Monsters* helped breathe new life into the Cthulhu mythos, contains nine reprints and an introduction by the author. *Two-Handed Engine: The Selected Stories of Henry Kuttner and C. L. Moore*, edited and with an introduction by David Curtis, was originally published in a pricey edition by Centipede Press in 2005 and reprinted by the Science Fiction Book Club in 2006. The book includes thirty-seven stories, including their best-known ones, such as "Shambleau," "The Twonky," and "Mimsy Were the Borogoves," (a film called *The Last Mimzy*, based on this story, was released in early 2007), and more obscure stories as well. *Desperate Moon* by R. Andrew Heidel (PS) is divided into three sections. The first was originally published as a chapbook. The second section has science fiction and wonder tales. The third contains thirteen mostly very brief dark fantasy stories. Harlan Ellison provides the introduction. Prime published two impressive collections by Simon Logan: *Rohypnol Brides* has nine stories and a novella, several original. *Nothing Is Inflammable* has seven stories and a short novel. Four stories and the novella are appearing for the first time. Logan writes really well, and even though his edgy, sometimes futuristic stories are filled with graphic sex and violence, it's always appropriate. Good show. *The Imaginary Lives of Mechanical Men* by Randy F. Nelson (The University of Georgia Press) is a thirteen-story collection published as part of Nelson's prize for winning the Flannery O'Connor Award, which is awarded annually to two short story writers. Some of the stories are dark; one is published for the first time. *Dark Roots* by Cate Kennedy (Scribe, Australia) has fourteen stories, all published previously, by this award-winning Australian. Some are dark, particularly the excellent "Cold Snap." *Flashing the Dark* by Bruce Boston (Sam's Dot) has forty vignettes and short stories. *Collected Stories* by Roald Dahl (Everyman Library) contains all fifty-one of Dahl's stories for adults.

The artists working in the small press toil hard and receive too little credit and money, and I feel it's important to recognize their good work. The following artists created art that I thought especially noteworthy during 2006: Steven Gilberts, Colin Foran, Les Edwards, Allen Koszowski, Russell Morgan, J. K. Potter, Alexander Kruglov, Bob Hobbs, Eric M. Turnmire, Dora Wayland, Susan McKivergan, Chris Nurse, B. A. Bosaiya, Paul Swenson, Paul Lowe, Keith Minnion, Augie Wiedemann, Goran Dacev, David Kendall, James Hannah, Debbie Hughes, Martin Bland, Stefan Olsen, Richard Marchand, Ales Horak, Mike Bohatch, Cameron Gray, Sandro Castelli, Les Petersen, David Gentry, Vincent Chong, Godfrey Blow, Tim Truman, Stephen McSweeny, Mike Dringenberg, HyeJeong Park, Erin and Kelly Carty, Radoslaw Walachnia, Allen Douglas, John Robert Lohmann, H. E. Fassl, Chrissy Ellsworth, Liz Clarke, David Ho, Gregor Scharff, Sheridan Morgan, Carole Humphreys, Sarah Xo, Paul Guinan, Frank Harper, Jim Beveridge, Carlton Mellick III, Timothy Lantz, Hawk Alfredson, Donna Taylor Burgess, Edward Miller, Randy Broecker, Allison Lovelock, Mary Robinette Kowal, Charli Siebert, Chad Savage, Teresa Tunaley, Russell Dickerson, Brian Brennan, and Chris Erkmann.

Magazines, Web Zines, and Newsletters

There's an enormous annual turnover in small press magazines and most rarely last more than a year or two, so it's difficult to recommend buying a subscription to those that haven't proven their longevity. But I urge readers to at least buy single issues of those that sound interesting. The following are, I thought, the best in 2006.

Some of the most important magazines/Web zines are those specializing in news of the field, market reports, and reviews. *The Gila Queen's Guide to Markets*, edited by Kathryn Ptacek, e-mailed to subscribers on a regular basis, is an excellent fount of information for markets in and outside the horror field. Ralan.com is *the* Web site for up-to-date market information. *Locus*, edited by Charles N. Brown, and Locus online, edited by Mark Kelly, specialize in news about the science fiction and fantasy fields, but include a lot of horror coverage as well. The only major professional venues specializing in reviewing short genre fiction are *Tangent Online* (www.tangentonline.com), *The Internet Review of Science Fiction* (www.irosf.com), and *Locus*, but none of them specialize in horror. Most magazines have Web sites with subscription information, eliminating the need to include it here. For those magazines that do *not* have a Web site, I have provided that information:

The Horror Fiction Review, edited by Nick C. Cato, is a quarterly fanzine with interviews and reviews of books, the occasional movie, and magazines. In 2006 there were interviews with T. M. Wright, Simon Clark, James Newman, and Edward Lee, an original piece of fiction per issue, and coverage of horror conventions.

Wormwood, edited by Mark Valentine, is an excellent publication that is brought out twice annually, devoted to discussion of authors, books, and themes in the fields of the fantastic, supernatural, and decadent in literature. It contains essays, articles, short appreciations, new research, and perspectives from new and established writers about acknowledged major authors, lesser-studied writers, and those who are unjustly neglected. *Wormwood* also features the columns "Camera Obscura," surveying recently published but overlooked books, "Late Reviews," reappraising titles from the past, and Brian Stableford's "Decadent World-View." Highly recommended.

Necropsy: The Review of Horror Fiction, edited by June Pulliam, is a Web site with new issues up quarterly (www.lsu.edu/necrofile). The reviewers cover novels, anthologies, and movies and there's also an art and photo gallery.

Studies in Modern Horror: A Scholarly Journal for the Study of Contemporary Weird Fiction, edited by NGChristakos, published one issue in 2006 that was dominated by a lengthy and detailed article about Thomas Ligotti.

Video Watchdog®, a bimonthly edited by Tim Lucas, is one of the most exuberant film magazines around, and is one of my favorites, because I'm usually inspired to watch or rewatch at least one movie they review in every issue. The magazine is invaluable for the connoisseur of trashy, pulp, and horror movies and enjoyable for just about everyone. Among the articles appearing in 2006 were the "Looney Tunes Golden Collection Volume 2" and "Edgar Wallace and the Paternity of King Kong." There were spotlights on the DVDs of the 1933 *King Kong* and a two-parter on the 1950s television series *The Adventures of Superman*. There's also a regular column reprinting Joe Dante's movie reviews from 1969 to 1974, an audio review column by Douglas E. Winter, and a book review column by publisher Tim Lucas.

Fangoria, edited by Anthony Timpone, is the granddaddy of contemporary hor-

ror movie magazines. A monthly, it mostly concentrates on Hollywood horror productions, although it has started to cover independent features as well. The magazine runs regular columns on breaking film news, DVD releases, new video games,
and books. Special effects rule in *Fangoria* and it's the best when it comes to using
the grisliest photographs from the grisliest movies. The magazine sometimes runs
too many pieces on the same movie.

Rue Morgue, edited by Rod Gudino, is a quirky, entertaining monthly. It is
graphic in its coverage of mayhem and perfect for fans of extreme horror. Although
it focuses on movies and video, there are regular columns on books, graphic novels,
and audio. In 2006 there were articles about producer Roger Corman; Czech filmmaker Jan Svankmajer's new movie; Guillermo del Toro and *Pan's Labyrinth*; fifty
essential horror books, contemporary horror literature for children; *The Omen*—the
original, and the most recent remake; horror rap music; profiles of Edogawa Rampo,
the "father of the Japanese mystery story," and Peter Straub.

For those interested in M. R. James there is the *Ghosts & Scholars M. R. James
Newsletter*, a twice-yearly publication, some of which can be read, free, online. For
more information and to subscribe to the print newsletter, go to www.users.global
net.co.uk/~pardos/GS.html.

The Ghost Story Society was formed in 1988 to provide admirers of the classic
ghost story with an outlet for their interest, and membership of the Society now
numbers more than four hundred worldwide. The Society offers members an opportunity to exchange thoughts and ideas through regular publication of its journal,
All Hallows, which averages 140 pages per issue (Number 41 had a whopping two
hundred pages!) and contains articles and letters concerning ghost stories past and
present (more below) at www.ash-tree.bc.ca/GSS.html.

A Ghostly Company, a literary society devoted to the ghost story in all forms,
was created in 2004 to take up the slack left by the Ghost Story Society, which
moved to Canada. It sponsors regular meetings and informal gatherings in the
U.K. (foreign members are welcome). To join and for more information: www
.aghostlycompany.org.uk.

The British Fantasy Society exists to promote and enjoy the genres of fantasy, science fiction, and horror in all its forms. It celebrated its thirtieth anniversary in 2001.
Members receive a copy of every issue of *Prism*, their news magazine; *Dark Horizons*,
their own fiction magazine; all BFS special publications (recent publications include
the 2005 *Fantasy Calendar, Manitou Man, The Age of Chaos, Urban Gothic: La-
cuna and Other Trips*, and *F20: Two*). Visit www.britishfantasysociety.org.uk.

Dissections is a brand-new Web site devoted to horror criticism that debuted January 2007.

Cemetery Dance, edited by Robert Morrish, has lots of book reviews, a regular
column about Stephen King by Bev Vincent, a column by Thomas F. Monteleone,
and in 2006 notable stories by James Ireland Baker, Ed Gorman, Daniel Braum,
Darren Speegle, A. R. Morlan, J. T. Petty, Glen Hirshberg, David Nickle, Peter
Atkins, Tony Richards, Scott Nicholson, and Stephen Graham Jones, the latter two
reprinted herein. Number 56 was a special Glen Hirshberg issue with a new story, an
excerpt from his forthcoming novel, and an interview.

Fantasy Magazine, edited by Sean Wallace and Paul G. Tremblay, has been
giving *Realms of Fantasy* a run for its money since it was launched in 2005. Its fiction is consistently darker and often more quirky than that of *ROF*. Four issues
were published in 2006, and most contained a preponderance of dark fantasy verging on horror, with excellent stories by Theodora Goss, Bruce McAllister, Karen

Anne Mitchell, Wade Ogletree, Margaret Ronald, Lavie Tidhar, Paul G. Tremblay, Richard Parks, Alaya Dawn Johnson, Leslie Claire Walker, and Karina Sumner-Smith. Issue 3 had only a bit, with some good stories by M. E. Palmer, Sandra McDonald, and Peter S. Beagle. The magazine also runs reviews and interviews.

H. P. Lovecraft's Magazine of Horror, edited by Marvin Kaye, brought out one issue, with the spotlight on Brian Lumley. Included in the issue is an interview with Lumley, a bibliographical history, and two stories, one published for the first time, the other a reprint of a very limited edition.

Weird Tales, edited by George H. Scithers, Darrell Schweitzer, and John Gregory Betancourt, published five issues in 2006. Interesting book columns by Scott Connors and Doug Winter. Some good dark stories by Tanith Lee, Terry Sofian, Nina Kiriki Hoffman, Maurice Broaddus, John Shirley, Park Godwin, Stephen Dedman, Gregory Frost, Brian Stableford, and Tina and Tony Rath. The magazine is undergoing a major redesign, beginning with more modern-looking cover art on the October/November issue and with a change of editorship in 2007.

Supernatural Tales, edited by David Longhorn, is an excellent annual published in England. If you enjoy supernatural fiction you can't go wrong with this magazine and *All Hallows*, below. There were strong stories by Helen Grant, Mark Patrick Lynch, Lynda E. Rucker, and Simon Strantzas.

All Hallows, edited by Barbara Roden, is sent to members of the Ghost Story Society and always contains quality fiction, an entertaining regular column by Ramsey Campbell, news updates, obituaries, reviews, and articles about noted ghost-story writers. During 2006 there were notable stories by Peter Bell, Sarah Monette, Stephen Volk, Mark Nicholls, Geoffrey Warburton, and Stephen Benz.

Dark Wisdom: The Magazine of Dark Fiction, edited by William Jones, is a handsome, professional-looking quarterly with literate stories, that—even when not completely surprising—nonetheless entertain. Also book reviews and a movie column. Notable stories and poetry by Marie Brennan, John Shirley, Jay Caselberg, James R. Cain, Simon Wood, Scott Nicholson, Durant Haire, Stephen Mark Rainey, Tyree Campbell, Sandra Fritz, and Terry Bramlett, and the first half of a very good serialized story by Ann K. Schwader.

Bare Bone 9, edited by Kevin L. Donihe, was a solid issue, the only one published in 2006. There was notable fiction and poetry by Paul Finch, Mark Justice, Joy Marchand, Chris Ringler, and Alyssa Sturgill.

Dark Horizons, edited by Marie O'Regan and Jenny Barber, comes free with membership to the British Fantasy Society. Two issues were published in 2006, with a very good new story by Mark Chadbourne, and a charming fantasy by Neil Williamson, interviews with Neil Gaiman and John Connolly, and reviews of books from independent presses, of graphic novels, and of role-playing games. Les Edwards provided the snazzy cover art for one and Ramon Contini did the art for the other.

The Silent Companion: The Fiction Magazine of A Ghostly Company is edited by Clive Ward, with a fiction committee comprised of Bill Read, Jane Read, and Keris McDonald. The first of a proposed annual Christmas compendium came out on the cusp of 2005/2006. In addition to its fiction, there is a brief essay on the ossuary at Kutná Hora, a town outside Prague in the Czech Republic, and several puzzles and quizzes.

Not One of Us, edited by John Benson, keeps chugging along, publishing unusual, often dark fiction. There were two issues out in '06 and a special one-off on the theme of *Change*. The strongest stories and poetry were by Patricia Russo, Erzebet YellowBoy, Karen R. Porter, Jennifer Rachel Baumer, Sonya Taaffe, Elizabeth Barrette, and Jennifer Crow.

ChiZine, the fiction area of the Chiaroscuro Web site, regularly publishes new horror fiction and poetry. *ChiZine* was edited by Brett Alexander Savory, Michael Kelly, and M. Thomas for the first part of 2006. Beginning in April, Hannah Wolf Bowen, Michael Marano, and Gord Zajac took over from Kelly and Thomas. Sandra Kasturi has been the poetry editor from the start. *ChiZine* is a reliable source of entertaining dark fantasy and horror. In 2006 there were very good stories and poems by Leah Bobet, Bruce Boston, Gemma Files, Tristan Davenport, Brenna Yovanoff Graham, Gordon Grice, Samantha Henderson, Vylar Kaftan, Claire Litton, Will McIntosh, and John Park. The Chiaroscuro Web site has reviews, which are updated monthly. The fiction and poetry is updated quarterly.

Horror World, edited by Nanci Kalanta, has been around since 2003, after Kalanta and Ron Dickie took over Andy Fairclough's *Masters of Terror* Web site and renamed it *Horrorworld*. Dickie dropped out in 2005. The site publishes new fiction on a monthly basis, but also has reviews, interviews, an announcements section, runs podcasts, and has a message board. Tim Lebbon's story was the best of the batch in 2006.

Mixed-Genre Magazines

Aurealis, edited by Ben Payne and Robert Hoge, is the premier mixed-genre magazine of Australia. There was an excellent horror story by Lee Battersby and a very good one by Jay Caselberg. The Battersby is reprinted herein. *Andromeda Spaceways Inflight Magazine*, edited by an Australian cooperative, rarely publishes horror. But *Borderlands*, also out of Australia and with its fiction edited by Stephen Dedman, regularly publishes science fiction and horror. The three issues published in 2006 had notable stories by Kaaron Warren, Lily Chrywenstrom, Jarrod Law, Emma Munro, and Shane Jiraiya Cummings. *Subterranean* magazine, edited by William Schafer, is a relatively new professional paying magazine that mixes the genres successfully. The three issues published in 2006 were very good and there were notable dark stories by Norman Partridge, David Prill, Cherie Priest, Neal Barrett, Jr., Jim Grimsley, Stephen Gallagher, and David J. Schow. Dorman T. Shindler supplies a literate, incisive book column. *Albedo One*, edited by John Kenny, Bob Neilson, David Murphy, and Roelof Goudriaan, comes from Ireland and has interviews and book reviews in addition to a wide range of fiction. In 2006 there was an interview with Charles Stross and strong dark stories by Dev Agarwal, David D. Levine, and Julian West. *Alchemy* 3, edited by Steve Pasechnick and with strikingly beautiful James Christensen cover art, published very good dark stories by Theodora Goss, Sonya Taaffe, Timothy Williams, Tara Kolden, Beth Adele Long, and Sarah Monette. *Talebones*, edited by Patrick and Honna Swenson, is a well-produced perfectbound quarterly that showcases science fiction and dark fantasy stories and poetry. During 2006 there were some good dark stories and poetry by James Michael White, Jennifer Rachel Baumer, Melissa Marr, Charles Coleman Finlay, Roger Dutcher, Catherine MacLeod, Mark Rigney, and Joanne Steinwachs. *Electric Velocipede*, edited by John Klima, published its tenth issue in the spring and as always, this attractive boutique zine is a nicely produced package of mixed-genre stories and poems. Some of the darker ones in the issue are by André Oosterman, Jeffrey Ford, Catherynne M. Valente, and Alistair Rennie. *Apex Science Fiction and Horror*, edited by Jason B. Sizemore, mostly publishes science fiction, some of it dark. There were good stories by Steve Parker, Neil Ayres, Marlissa Campbell, M. M. Buckner, Shane Jiraiya Cummings, and a novel by Steve Savile over four issues. They also had interviews with Poppy Z. Brite, Kage Baker, Michael Laimo, Neil Gaiman, Tim Powers, Sherrilyn Kenyon, Kelly Link, and Tom Piccirilli, as well as articles and essays. *Interzone* is the granddaddy of regularly published U.K. sf magazines and its new publisher, Andy Cox, has been doing a great job modernizing its design. The covers and interior artwork were top-notch in 2006, and there were some excellent special features such as an interview with and portfolio of John Picacio's art. The fiction is mostly sf, but as usual there were some good dark stories including those by John Paul Haines, Jay Lake, Elizabeth Bear, Richard Calder, Tim Akers, Karen D. Fishler, and David Mace. *Crimewave 9: Transgressions*, edited by Andy Cox, is by far the most energetic and varied mystery/crime magazine being published. It's an annual, beautifully designed perfect-bound magazine and even though only a few of the stories are ever dark enough to be considered horror, they're usually a good read. In the 2006 issue there were notable darker stories by Daniel Bennett, Scott William Carter, Shelley Costa, and Ian R. Faulkner. *Postscripts*, edited by Peter Crowther and Nick Gevers, put out four solid issues in 2006 with notable dark fiction by Tony Ballantyne, Vaughan Stanger, Mary SanGiovanni, Tony Richards, Scott William Carter, Stephen Volk, T. M. Wright, Conrad Williams, and the first new short fiction by K. W. Jeter in several years, plus interviews with Elizabeth Hand and Howard Waldrop. *The Magazine of Fantasy & Science Fiction*, edited by Gordon Van Gelder, often publishes excellent horror and dark fantasy. In 2006 it had two knockout stories by M. Rickert (one reprinted herein), Gene Wolfe, and Claudia O'Keefe, a terrific novella by Laird Barron, and strong dark stories by Paolo Bacigalupi, Terry Bisson, Amy Sterling Casil, Ef Deal, Carol Emshwiller, Charles Coleman Finlay, C. S. Friedman, Bruce McAllister, Robert Reed, Carrie Richerson, and Jerry Seeger. Under Sheila Williams's editorial reins *Asimov's Science Fiction* magazine published stories that could be considered horror by Carol Emshwiller, David Ira Cleary, Robert Reed, Kristine Kathryn Rusch, Kit Reed, Michael F. Flynn, and Melissa Lee Shaw. *Realms of Fantasy*, edited by Shawna McCarthy, occasionally runs dark fantasy. In 2006 there were notable stories by Scott William Carter, Billy Aul, Leah Bobet, Amanda Downum, Jim C. Hines, Daniel Hood, Devon Monk, Richard Parks, Deborah Roggie, Jena Snyder, and a story by Brett Alexander Savory, reprinted herein. *Zahir: Unforgettable Tales*, edited by Sheryl Tempchin, is a simply but attractively produced tri-annual magazine of sf/f/h. In 2006 it had notable dark fiction by Peter Higgins, Michael Humfrey, Aaron de Long, and a deeply depressing mainstream story by Abigail Padgett. *Phantom*, edited by Nick Mamatas, was a one-shot created by Mamatas and Sean Wallace for the 2006 World Fantasy Convention in Austin, Texas. It had a mixture of the surreal and the dark, with the best darker tales by Sarah Langan and Paul G. Tremblay. Surprisingly, because most of Wallace's Prime projects are very design conscious, the cover was totally nondescript, with an almost invisible pale gray image. *Tales of the Unanticipated*, edited by Eric M. Heideman, celebrates its twentieth anniversary with a "monsters" issue. While there's a good mix of stories and poetry, only one was very scary, the one by Patricia Russo. *Shimmer*, edited by Beth Wodzinski, is an attractive quarterly that occasionally publishes darker fiction. In 2006 there were notable dark stories by Angela Slatter (three by her), Matthew Mantooth, Samantha Henderson, and Tom Pendergrass. *Paradox*, edited by Christopher M. Cevasco, specializes in alternate histories and only occasionally publishes stories dark enough to be called horror. In 2006 there were good dark stories by Danny Adams, Anne Sheldon, and Stephanie Dray. *On Spec*, edited by Diane L. Walton, is the only major Canadian science sf/f/h magazine. It's an attractive, perfect-bound quarterly that sometimes publishes dark fiction. In 2006 there were good stories by John Bowker, Elizabeth Bear, Leah Bobet, Shawn Peters, Douglas Smith, Robert Burke Richardson, and John Southern Blake.

There are other mixed-genre magazines that have dark fiction once in a while, such as *Lady Churchill's Rosebud Wristlet*, Ticonderoga Online (Australian Web site). *Cabinet des Fées: A Fairy Tale Journal*, edited by Helen Pilinovsky, Catherynne M. Valente, and Erzebet Barthold-YellowBoy, is seemingly inspired by Terri Windling and my adult fairy tale anthology series. This first issue has an introduction by Pilinovsky about the commodification of fairy tales, ten pieces of fiction and poetry, and an essay about H. G. Wells. The gorgeous four-color cover art is by Charles Vess and black-and-white interior illustrations are by some of the classic fairy artists. *Mythic*, a new magazine edited by Mike Allen dedicated to fiction and poetry using myth, legends, and fairy tales, published two good-looking issues with notable dark work by Erzebet YellowBoy, Theodora Goss, Catherynne M. Valente, Charles Saplak, Sonya Taaffe, and JoSelle Vanderhooft. *New Genre*, edited by Adam Golaski, includes sf/f/h in its mix and with its fourth issue had two essays disputing Douglas E. Winter's classic essay about horror fiction being defined by the emotion it provokes in the reader. There also were four stories, two notably dark, by Don Tumasonis and Christopher Harman. The Harman is reprinted herein. *Hub*, edited by Lee Harris, is a new, attractively designed mixed-genre magazine from the U.K. It's slick, full cover on heavy paper stock, and comes in an interestingly square shape. It covers films and comics, has book reviews, an article about writers blogging, and ten short stories. Although only James Cooper's dark story impressed me, I'm looking forward to the next issue.

Nonfiction Books

One of the most important nonfiction books published in the field in 2006, and winner of the National Book Critics Circle Award for Biography, is Julie Phillips's amazing, disturbing biography *James Tiptree, Jr.: The Double Life of Alice B. Sheldon* (St. Martin's). Tiptree was the pseudonym dreamed up by Sheldon and her second husband Huntington Sheldon as she began to write a series of brilliant, usually dark short science fiction stories dealing with gender issues, human sexuality, and death in the early–middle 1970s. Her childhood was unusual: at six she accompanied her socialite parents on safaris to Africa where she was carried about "as luggage" and witnessed crucifixions and other torture. Her relationship with her mother was troubled. Through most of her life she was addicted to amphetamines and drank too much. She struggled with depression her whole life, finally succumbing in 1986. *Human Visions: The Talebones Interviews* has thirty-one interviews conducted by Ken Rand over ten years. Most are with sf or fantasy writers, but the writers included who write horror are Tom Piccirilli, K. W. Jeter, Jack Cady, Edward Bryant, Dan Simmons, and Peter Straub. *Cinema Macabre*, edited by Mark Morris (PS), features fifty horror genre professionals writing about their favorite horror movies, approaching from whatever angle they choose. The entertaining result does exactly what this type of book should do — makes the reader search out the movies to watch or watch again. Good show. Very nice jacket art by J. K. Potter. *Icons of Horror and the Supernatural: An Encyclopedia of Our Worst*

Nightmares, edited by S. T. Joshi (Greenwood Press), is a two-volume illustrated set that offers an alphabetically arranged overview of twenty-four of the most significant icons of horror and the supernatural including subjects from the alien to the zombie. The encyclopedia covers a *long* time period, from Homer to Stephen King. *Lynchings in the West, 1850–1935* by Ken Gonzales-Day (Duke University Press) chronicles over 350 instances of lynching in the state of California, mostly perpetrated against Latinos, Native Americans, and Asian Americans, revealing racially motivated lynching to be far more widespread than previously thought. *Insane Passions: Lesbianism and Psychosis in Literature and Film* by Christine E. Coffman (Wesleyan University Press) is an academic study about the roots of the stereotype of lesbian-as-madwoman in theater and movies. *Haunted Homeland* by Michael Norman (Forge) recounts supernatural explorations from around the United States. *The Secret History of Lucifer* by Lynn Picknett (Carroll & Graf) examines the evolution of the notion of Lucifer from origins in earlier characterizations of Pan, reflecting the author's research of ancient heretical Christian and Egyptological texts. *Ghost Hunters: William James and the Search for Scientific Proof of Life After Death* by Deborah Blum (Penguin) is a sympathetic account of James and other respected thinkers of his era who studied and met with spiritualists who claimed they could communicate with the dead. From McFarland: *Cornell Woolrich from Pulp Noir to Film Noir* by Thomas C. Renzi; *Psycho Thrillers: Cinematic Explorations of the Mysteries of the Mind* by William Indick; *The Films of Peter Greenaway: Sex, Death and Provocation* by Douglas Keesey; *Terror on the Air: Horror Radio in America, 1931–1952* by Richard J. Hand; *James Bernard, Composer to Count Dracula: A Critical Biography* by David Huckvale with a foreword by Ingrid Pitt; *The Changing Vampire of Film and Television: A Critical Study of the Growth of a Genre* by Tim Kane; *The Hellraiser Films and Their Legacy* by Paul Kane with a foreword by Doug Bradley; *The Existential Joss Whedon: Evil and Human Freedom in Buffy the Vampire Slayer, Angel, Firefly and Serenity* by J. Michael Richardson and J. Douglas Rabb; *Horror Films of the 1980s* by John Kenneth Muir.

Raised by Wolves: The Turbulent Art and Times of Quentin Tarantino by Jerome Charyn (Thunder's Mouth Press) is a portrait of the artist by an extraordinary novelist and nonfiction writer. *Gospel of the Living Dead: George A. Romero's Visions of Hell on Earth* (Baylor University Press) by Kim Paffenroth, an associate professor of religious studies, provides a detailed and riveting analysis of Romero's zombie films, concentrating on their spiritual subtext. *Thunderstruck* by Erik Larson (Crown) connects wife-murderer Dr. H. H. Crippen and Guglielmo Marconi, inventor of wireless communication, by re-creating the world in which they lived, and showing how Marconi's device brought the news of Crippen's pursuit by the law to the whole world more quickly than ever thought possible. *The Undead and Philosophy: Chicken Soup for the Soulless*, edited by Richard Greene and K. Silem Mohammad (Open Court), is part of the publisher's Popular Culture and Philosophy series. This is a mostly good mixed bag of essays about zombies, vampires, and other soulless creatures. *The Monster in the Mirror: Looking for H. P. Lovecraft* by Robert G. Waugh is a collection of scholarly essays about Lovecraft's writing. Although a bit dry for the casual reader, those interested in Lovecraft's influences and particularly in his story "The Outsider" might consider picking this up. *Collected Essays: Volume 3 Science* by H. P. Lovecraft, edited by S. T. Joshi, is a wonderful book of essays for the layman about the solar system. *Collected Essays: Volume 4*

Travel by H. P. Lovecraft, edited by S. T. Joshi (the latter three titles from Hippocampus Press), is a fascinating trip report by Lovecraft of his travels along the East Coast in the last ten years of his life. *Stephen King: Uncollected, Unpublished* by Rocky Wood with David Rawsthorne and Norma Blackburn (Cemetery Dance) is a thorough and readable look at forty-eight stories never included in a King collection and fifty-one stories that have never been published. *Final Exits: The Illustrated Encyclopedia of How We Die* by Michael Largo (Harper) is very loose in what it includes, i.e., Does cell phone etiquette really cause death? Only if you so annoy someone listening in that they crack a beer bottle over your head. How about playing basketball? Cited is the accidental strangulation of children. It feels like a big reach to me. *Monster Island: The Unauthorized Guide to Japanese Monster Movies* by Jorg Buttgereit (Critical Visions) is an homage to Japanese monster movies, their creators, their stars, and their fans. The book contains film reviews, rare illustrations, and exclusive interviews with filmmakers, special effects wizards, monster-costume makers, and actors, as well as chapters on the changing face of Japanese monsters. *Pretend We're Dead: Capitalist Monsters in American Pop Culture* by Annalee Newitz (Duke University Press) tracks the monsters spawned by capitalism through film and literature, citing the short stories of Asimov and Lovecraft and the novels of William Gibson and Marge Piercy, and movies such as *Modern Times, Donovan's Brain, The Night of the Living Dead, The Silence of the Lambs,* et al. for her argument. Not seen, but seems like fun, despite the iffy premise. *The Aesthetics of Culture in Buffy the Vampire Slayer* by Matthew Pateman (McFarland) examines the cultural commentary running through the popular show that ran for seven seasons. *Bram Stoker and Russophobia: Evidence of the British Fear of Russia in Dracula and The Lady of the Shroud* by Jimmie E. Cain, Jr. (McFarland), with notes, bibliography, and index. *Famous Monster Movie Art of Basil Gogos,* edited by Kerry Gammill and J. David Spurlock (Vanguard Productions); *Roger Corman: Metaphysics on a Shoestring* by Alain Silver and James Ursini (Silman-James Press); *Sweet & Savage: The World through the Shockumentary Film Lens* by Mark Goodall (Headpress), which proclaims itself "the first English-language book devoted exclusively to the Mondo documentary film." *Mondo Cane,* directed by Gualtiero Jacopetti, Franco Prosperi, and Paolo Cavara (1962), made a huge splash with its objective camera roving around the globe filming strange rituals. The "Mondo" series evolved into more sexual, more violent, and more bloody "documentaries" culminating in the *Faces of Death* series. It's an interesting survey of the genre, but it's a shame that the quality of the photo reproduction isn't better. *Running with the Devil: The Best of Hail Saten,* Volume 2 by Brian Keene (Delirium) collects Keene's nonfiction columns, giving the reader a very personal and opinionated glimpse of his writing and personal life. Compulsively readable. *The Freedom of Fantastic Things: Selected Criticism on Clark Ashton Smith,* edited by Scott Connors (Hippocampus Press), includes original and previously published work on Smith by S. T. Joshi, Fred Chappell, Brian Stableford, James Blish, Stefan Dziemianowicz, and others. *The Colony: The Harrowing True Story of the Exiles of Molokai* by John Tayman (Scribner) is about the American leper colony on the Hawaiian island of Molokai that was established in 1866. Not all the people forced into exile there suffered from the disease, and most were not contagious. The book uses historical documents, letters, journals, and hundreds of interviews to tell this tragic story in a novelistic style. *The Gothic Reader: A Critical Anthology,* edited by Martin Myrone with Christopher Frayling (Tate Publishing), is heavy on excerpts from texts from the mid-eighteenth to mid-twentieth centuries and light on real analysis of those texts. *Creepy Crawls: A Horror Fiend's Travel Guide* by Leon Marcelo (Santa Monica Press); *Phantasmagoria* by Marina Warner (Oxford), subtitled *Spirit Visions, Metaphors, and Media into the Twenty-First Century*, probes our preoccupation with the ideas of "spirit, soul, and the supernatural." From wax death masks to Romero's zombies, she's one of the most erudite and entertaining writers about myth, fairy tales, and the modern fantastic today. *The Darkening Garden: A Short Lexicon of Horror* by John Clute (Payseur & Schmidt) is elegantly produced and beautifully illustrated by thirty artists. In it, Clute attempts (in abbreviated entries) to codify horror much as he has done in his *Encyclopedia of Science Fiction* and *Encyclopedia of Fantasy*. It all makes for fascinating reading whether one agrees with him or not. *Lovecraft's New York Circle: The Kalem Club, 1924–1927*, edited by Mara Kirk Hart and S. T. Joshi (Hippocampus Press), collects correspondence by members of the club. *The Transforming Draught: Jekyll and Hyde, Robert Louis Stevenson and the Victorian Alcohol Debate* by Thomas L. Reed, Jr. (McFarland) is a critical examination of the Stevenson story as an allegory of alcoholism. *Monsters: A Celebration of the Classics from Universal Studios* by Ray Milano (Del Rey) takes a look at the making of eight horror films, lavishly illustrated with stills and publicity photos. *Encyclopedia of Fantasy and Horror Fiction* by Don D'Ammassa (Infobase Publishing/Checkmark Books) is a guide to major authors and works. *Charles Addams: A Cartoonist's Life* by Linda H. Davis (Random House) is a biography with notes, index, photos, and cartoons. *On Writing Horror, Revised Edition*, edited by Mort Castle (Writer's Digest), is updated from the 1997 edition sponsored by the HWA and has forty-four essays, twenty-four new, the others revised, about the changing horror field. *Blood and Thunder: The Life and Art of Robert E. Howard* by Mark Finn (MonkeyBrain Books) is a biography with an introduction by Joe R. Lansdale, a bibliography, and an index.

Poetry

MAGAZINES

*Star*Line*, the journal of the Science Fiction Poetry Association, edited by Marge Simon, publishes six issues a year, and although it specializes in sf and fantasy poetry, there are always at least a few darker poems lurking within. During 2006 there were notable dark poems by Jaime Lee Moyer, Mary Lynn Tentchoff, Sonya Taaffe, Catherynne M. Valente, Mikal Trimm, Melissa Marr, Jessica Paige Wick, Charles Gramlich, and Ann K. Schwader. *Poe Little Thing: The Digest of Horrific Poetry*, edited by Donna Taylor Burgess, published two issues in 2006 with good dark poems by Kristine Ong Muslim. *Mythic Delirium*, edited by Mike Allen, brought out two issues in 2006. The dark poems I liked the best were by Julie Shiel and JoSelle Vanderhooft. *The Magazine of Speculative Poetry*, edited by Roger Dutcher, runs sf/f/h poetry and is reliable in its choices. Usually published three times a year, in 2006 only one issue came out, which contained notable darker work by Jennifer Crow and Duane Ackerson. *Dreams and Nightmares*, edited by David C. Kopaska-Merkel, published regularly since January 1986, celebrated its twentieth anniversary with issue seventy-three. There were some good dark poems by Sonya Taaffe, Yoon Ha Lee, and Jessica Langer.

CHAPBOOKS AND COLLECTIONS

If There Were Wolves by Tim Pratt (Prime) has thirty-two poems of fantasy and dark fantasy, eight original to the collection. The cover art—classical and appropriate—is by Richard Hermann Eschke. *Grim Trixter* by Brandy Schwan (Apex) is a debut collection of short horror poems. *A Walberswick Goodnight Story* by Louis de Bernières (Tartarus) is a simple but attractive chapbook of a charming poem of transformation. *The Arkham Alphabet Book* for children by Darrell Schweitzer is a Lovecraftian alphabet reprinted from *Weird Tales*, illustrated by Allen Koszowski.

On Our Way to Battle: Poetry, From the Trenches, edited by Samantha Henderson (Carnifex Press), the companion volume to the prose anthology *From the Trenches*, has some good dark poetry about war by Mikal Trimm, Greg Beatty, and Michael Livingston. *The Troublesome Amputee* by John Edward Lawson (Raw Dog Screaming Press) includes everything from the poet's first poetry chapbook and has more than sixty short poems about various violent impulses. Humor abounds. *Valentine: Short Love Poems* by Corrine De Winter (Black Arrow Press) has thirty-four poems. *From: The Book of the Dead Man* by Marvin Bell (bornmagazine.org/Payseur & Schmidt) has two short poems by a distinguished American poet, illustrated with two beautiful photographs.

Poems That Go Splat by Brian Rosenberger (Naked Snake) has over forty-five brief poems, many of them previously published. *The Lost Poetry of William Hope Hodgson*, edited by Jane Frank (PS & Tartarus Press), was missed when it was published in 2005. The book presents forty-three (more than half those in the collection) previously unpublished poems, many of which use sea imagery and most of which deal with death and dying. The book is a lovely artifact with a photograph of the Aurora Borealis by Hodgson on the cover, purple endpapers, and ribbon bookmark. Many of the poems are morbid, verging on horrific. Two appear herein. *Strange Wisdoms of the Dead* by Mike Allen (Wildside) is an excellent overview of the poet's past ten years of writing sf/f/h poetry, and includes a handful of new works among the reprints. Sam's Dot published the following poetry chapbooks: *A Nameless Place* by Joanne Morcom reprints the poet's haikus, originally published in *Weird Tales* and less known venues; *Oddities* by Aurelio Rico Lopez III and Kristine Ong Muslim features reprinted poems and poetry published for the first time in this dual collection.

Shades Fantastic by Bruce Boston (Gromagon Press) is a new chapbook by one of the premier poets of the sf/f/h field. The book has thirty-seven poems, five published for the first time. The attractive cover and interior art is by Marge Simon.

CHAPBOOKS AND OTHER SMALL PRESS ITEMS

Strange Birds by Gene Wolfe is the first in a projected series of chapbooks inspired by the dark imaginative fantasy work of Lisa Snellings-Clark to be published by Dreamhaven. The first of the two stories in this chapbook is the strange "On a Vacant Face a Bruise," about a runaway who joins a traveling circus. The second, "Sob in the Silence," is more horrific and is reprinted herein. Both stories show Wolfe at his best.

PS Publishing also brought out a chapbook by Wolfe, an odd Christmas ghost story called "Christmas Inn." The cover illustration is by James Hannah. PS also published *The Face of Twilight* by Mark Samuels, a novel about a writer hoping to finally write the novel that will make him famous and the sinister little man with a scarred head who is his neighbor. Mark Morris supplies an introduction and the deliciously grotesque cartoon cover art is by James Hannah. *I Am the Bird* by T. M. Wright is about two men and a parrot living in an apartment and something else—something vile—also living there. Introduction by Ramsey Campbell. Nice cover art by Robert Sammelin.

White Noise Press published a series of signed and numbered limited edition chapbooks including *The Church of Dead Languages*, a Lovecraftian tale by James Newman and Jason Brannon about a mysterious church discovered by some campers in the woods. The cover art is by Keith Minnion; *Funny Stories of Scary Sex*, a "double" with two humorous erotic horror stories by Jeff Strand; *Down in the Boneyard*, by Keith Minnion, featuring four reprints and ten illustrations by the artist. *The Hell Book* by Jason Van Hollander is a lovely chapbook edition of a story originally published in 1991.

Overlook Connection Press brought out an attractive new limited hardcover edition of Jack Ketchum's novel *Offspring*, originally published in 1990 as the sequel to *Off Season*. The dust jacket art is by Neal McPheeters. Also, *The Last Rakosh* by F. Paul Wilson, a Repairman Jack story originally published in Wilson's collection *The Barrens* and later woven into the novel *All the Rage*.

Centipede Press published two beautiful and expensive books in 2006: *Frankenstein*, featuring the wood engravings of Lynd Ward, with an introduction by Patrick McGrath, and *Masters of the Weird Tale: Algernon Blackwood*, a huge collection of Blackwood's weird fiction.

E'Ch Pi El: Chilling Tales of the Cthulhu Mythos from Rainfall Books has three original tales by Kevin L. O'Brien, Robert M. Price, and C. D. Allen.

Carnifex Press: *Then Comes the Child* by Christopher Fulbright and Angeline Hawkes is about what happens when a couple trying desperately to conceive a baby is given a voodoo fetish as a joke gift to help them out. *To the Mountain of the Beast* by Christopher Stires is a western sf horror novella about an alien spaceship that crash-lands in Wyoming. *When Dark Descends* by Charles L. Grant and Thomas F. Monteleone (Borderlands Press) is a terrific-looking hardcover reprint of a collaboration originally published over thirty years ago. Cover photo by Kathi O'Connor, dust jacket design by Mario Martin, Jr. *Rough Cut* by Gary McMahon (Pendragon Press) is a well-told novella about a young man whose mother was a low-level porn star and the discovery of the last film she and her director/lover ever worked on. The story is well written and has some powerful bits, but is a bit chilly for my taste. The good-looking cover art is by Vincent Chong.

The new signature series from Cemetery Dance consists of art-oriented, high-end collectible books, signed and with limited print runs. *Windows* by Ray Garton is the satisfying second novella in the signature series, about a Peeping Tom who sees something he shouldn't, and what ensues. Dust jacket and interior illustrations are by Glenn Chadbourne. *The Baby* by Al Sarrantonio is the third in the signature series, a haunting, moving story taking place in a troubled town where a man's promise to his wife that they'll have a baby, no matter what, brings forth something *special* for Halloween.

Also published by CD: *Weed Species* by Jack Ketchum is about the effect a couple of sadistic murderers have on those around them. Great cover art by Alan M. Clark and interior illustrations by Glenn Chadbourne. The chapbook *Isis* by Douglas Clegg is a self-contained prequel to the author's Harrow books and stories. In the early 1900s a girl and her twin brothers move from the U.S. with their mother to their absentee father's ancestral home in England to care for his raving minister father. The children are warned not to play in the Tombs, a series of underground burial chambers on the property, and are told dire tales about "calling back the dead." Of course, things happen and they transgress. A moving, chilling novelette about the inability of the living to let dead loved ones go. Cover art is by Glenn Chadbourne; *Our Things/The Oilman*, a limited edition promotional paperback double chapbook with original stories by Gary A. Braunbeck and Rick Hautala. The

Braunbeck is a moving one about a bereaved man whose world is mysteriously disappearing. The Hautala is one of his "little brother" tales. *Dark Harvest* by Norman Partridge is a well-written novella of the supernatural about the annual Halloween ritual of a small midwestern town: teenage boys between sixteen and nineteen hunt down the October Boy, a murderous creature that will kill them unless they get him first. *The Colour Out of Darkness* by John Pelan has violence, gore, sex, and Cthulhu and great cover art by Allen Koszowski. *Looking Glass*, illustrated by Alex McVey, is a serial novel written by twelve horror writers including Ray Garton (who started it), Brian Keene, Tim Lebbon, among others. *The Shell Collector* by Christopher Golden, set in Gloucester, Massachusetts, is about a fisherman finding something eerie in his lobster trap and what that something is and does. Glenn Chadbourne did the cover art.

From Earthling Publications: *At the Sign of the Snowman's Skull: Rolling Darkness Rev 2006* is the chapbook that accompanies a group of horror writers who tour the West Coast reading from their work. This one has original stories by Peter Atkins, Glen Hirshberg, Lisa Morton, Clay McLeod Chapman, and Norman Partridge, and a reprint of a story by Dennis Etchison. *Bloodstained Oz* by Christopher Golden and James A. Moore is a wonderfully horrific riff on the *Wizard of Oz* books. The novella takes place in the Kansas of the 1933 dustbowl and begins with tornadoes. But these storms, instead of bringing Dorothy to the wondrous world of Oz, bring vampiric monkeys, vicious dolls, and other monstrous creatures into Kansas, slaughtering everything warm-blooded in their path. The evocative cover and interior art is by Glenn Chadbourne. *King of Souls* by Brian Knight is about four broken-down, bereaved fathers who believe their missing children have been taken prisoner by an unstable recluse. The four storm his junkyard fortress and discover even worse than they feared. Tim Waggoner provides an introduction and Deena Warner the effective cover art and design.

Telos: *More Than Life Itself* by Joseph Nassise is about a father who will do *anything* to save his young daughter, dying of a mysterious disease. *Pretty Young Things* by Dominic McDonagh has sex, blood, and lesbian vampires.

White Tribe by Gene O'Neill (Dimensions Books) is a smoothly written but schematic tale about several groups of people affected by the beast unleashed by a major West Coast earthquake.

Spider on My Tongue by T. M. Wright (Nyx Books) is a novella follow-up to the novel *A Manhattan Ghost Story*.

Mama's Boy by Fran Friel (Insidious Reflections) is a novella about the ongoing therapy sessions between a psychologist and a John Doe in a mental institution.

Necessary Evil Press: *The Familiar Stranger* by Brett McBean is about what happens when an angel whose job is to launder old, filthy souls for recycling to newborns is consumed by curiosity as to what happens to the humans that end up with them. A funny idea with horrific goings-on throughout. *She Loves Monsters* by Simon Clark is about the young, arrogant inheritor of a mansion where a genius filmmaker and his sister live by grace of the narrator's late father. The young man is intent on finding and producing a long-lost masterpiece created by the filmmaker, who suffered a nervous breakdown while editing the film more than a decade earlier. A potent mix of *Throat Sprockets* and *The Ring*, with a hint of *The Magus*. *Take the Long Way Home* by Brian Keene is a road trip (on foot) about three men trying to get home after a mass vanishing. Is it the Rapture? Alien abduction? Scientific experimentation gone mad?

High Ferocity is a sampler of work by seven members of the Dallas/Fort Worth chapter of HWA.

Tales from the Home for Wayward Spirits and Bar-B-Que Grill by Rie Sheridan (Yard Dog Press) is a cute story about a couple of kids and the zombies they meet.

Licker by Michael A. Arnzen (Novello Publishers) is a blackly humorous novelette about a young man who mysteriously develops disgusting pustules on his tongue that when ingested by others make them high. He goes on his first date to a carnival where things really go wrong for him and his date.

Bone Island by John Urbancik is a five-thousand-word story given away with the author's second novel. The cover photograph and design are by Urbancik. It's a ghost story about a callow young man who, over the course of an evening in Key West, becomes a little less callow.

Naked Snake Press: *Love Street and Other Bleedings* by Paul Dracon has four stories by the author, a poorly photocopied cover, no table of contents, and unfortunately some of the ugliest type (double-spaced) that I've seen in a chapbook recently. The production is better for Eric S. Brown's chapbook of "The Queen," a novella about how the survivors of a zombie infestation in the United States cope with their situation. But the red type on gray of the back cover is virtually illegible in most light. *Beyond the Four Walls* by Pamela K. Kinney is a chapbook of four tales. *Beneath Black Boughs My Darlings Slumber* by Cullen Bunn is about a family curse. "El Reptil Rey" by Angeline Hawkes-Craig takes place in 1932, when a woman vacationing in Mexico becomes curious when she learns about a burial crypt with what is purportedly a mummified god. *Screaming in Code* by Thomas Wiloch has thirty-five prose poems and vignettes with photo collage art by the author.

Made Ready & Cupboard Love by Terry Lamsley (Subterranean) is a mini-collection of two novelettes in hardcover, by an exceptional writer who hasn't been heard from in too long a time. "Made Ready" is about a westerner who wanders onto a mysterious island (possibly in Greece) and is chosen for a horrible fate. Lamsley's descriptions of the island and its inhabitants make for an effective story. "Cupboard Love" is about what happens when a couple brings the wife's new best friend on their anniversary vacation. The color jacket art and interior black-and-white illustrations are by Glenn Chadbourne.

Delirium Books initiated its hardcover chapbook line with *Failure* by John Everson, about a wizard seeking power through sex magic who lures three teenagers into his lair. Everson also did the cover artwork. The second is *Imprint*, a powerful novella by Patrick Lestewka about a grief-stricken man who gets himself sentenced to prison in order to revenge himself on his wife's murderer.

Extinction Journals by Jeremy Robert Johnson (Swallowdown Press) is a novella expanded from a story in Johnson's collection *Angel Dust Apocalypse*.

Absinthe by Jack Ketchum and Tim Lebbon (Bloodletting Press) is a two-story chapbook about the exotic hallucinogenic drink that has made a comeback in the past few years. The Ketchum, about a man mistaken for the late Ernest Hemingway, is good, but not horrific. The Lebbon is a nicely told chiller about a woman who bleeds gold. The cover art to this limited edition is by Mike Bohatch. Also from Bloodletting comes *Vessels*, Kealan Patrick Burke's third novella in the series begun with *The Turtle Boy*, about a boy (now a man) who sees the dead. Tim Quinn goes to a remote island off Ireland in order to escape his past. Of course he doesn't. A bit difficult to follow at first if you haven't read the earlier novellas. The book is a good-looking hardcover with black endpapers and cover art by James Higgins.

Art Books and Odds and Ends

Frankenstein Makes a Sandwich by Adam Rex (Harcourt) is a children's book of over twenty incredibly silly but fun illustrated poems, tales, and comic strips about Frankenstein, witches, the Wolfman, the Creature from the Black Lagoon, and other monsters—their eating habits and their problems.

Scary Stories, illustrated by Barry Moser (Chronicle), is for me mostly about the black-and-white illustrations, as I'm a keen Moser fan, but this anthology of twenty horrific stories by such diverse writers as Winston Churchill, Truman Capote, E. Nesbit, Roald Dahl, Margaret Mahy, and Ray Bradbury makes for a nice feast for the young adult and adult. Moser has previously illustrated *Frankenstein, The Wizard of Oz, Moby Dick,* and *Alice in Wonderland.*

The Raven by Edgar Allan Poe with illustrations by Ryan Price (KCP Poetry) is a gorgeously produced book designed by Karen Powers. It has pink endpapers and a translucent overlay with the word "Nevermore" on it that shows the title "The Raven" and bird prints through the overleaf. The sepia-toned, off-kilter illustrations show a bereaved man possibly descending into insanity.

The Magic Bottle, written and illustrated by Camille Rose Garcia (Fantagraphics Books), is about a morose birthday girl who meets a sad turtle on a ruined beach and then discovers a blue octopus in her bedroom. There's a magic bottle, pirates, and all sorts of excitement drawn in Garcia's trademark gothic cartoon style.

Struwwelpeter and Other Disturbing Yet Cautionary Tales by Heinrich Hoffman, adapted and illustrated by Bob Staake (Fantagraphics), is a retelling of the classic children's book of stories about what happens to misbehaving children. It begins with Slovenly Peter, a slob who has no friends, and includes the gruesome story of Conrad the thumb sucker. Nicely bizarre cartoon characters.

Everything That Creeps, the art of Elizabeth McGrath (Last Gasp), showcases the artist's disturbing dolls and mixed media dioramas of grotesquerie. McGrath cites her Catholic upbringing, punk rock, Erté, and Edward Gorey as her influences. Check out her Web site for her toys and dolls: www.elizabethmcgrath.com/homemain.html.

Beauty and the Beast, retold by Max Eilenberg and illustrated by Angela Barrett (Candlewick), has lush, romantic art with some lovely surreal touches such as a candelabra made up of the seven heads of a four-legged critter. The beast is frightening as well as ugly. For those who love the classical tale and are interested in gorgeous illustration.

The Fountain by Darren Aronofsky and Kent Williams is the gorgeous graphic novel version of the mystical love story filmed by Aronofsky. I can't compare the two as I haven't seen the movie but the book looks great.

Cover Story: The Art of John Picacio (MonkeyBrain Books) showcases the work of one of the best young artists working in the field of the fantastic today. His book covers are varied in look and style and use a wide color palette. The book has preliminary sketches, Picacio's commentary providing context for individual pieces, and a new interview with the artist.

Underwood Books published two meticulous and lavish artist portfolios: *Revolution: The Art of Jon Foster,* edited by Cathy Fenner, Arnie Fenner, and Irene Gallo, chock-full of beautiful images in a variety of styles and tones. Included is a profile of Foster by Cathy Fenner and commentary by the artist. *Origins: The Art of John Jude*

Palencar, edited by Cathy and Arnie Fenner, has—in addition to the elegantly sur-real art—an extensive profile of the artist, and a foreword by Christopher Paolini. Also, *Spectrum 13: The Best in Contemporary Fantastic Art*, edited by Cathy Fenner and Arnie Fenner, juried by major fantasy artists, continues to be *the* showcase for the best in genre art—the sheer variety of style and tone and media and subject mat-ter is stunning. Jeffrey Jones is honored as Grand Master, and William Joyce has written an article about Hurricane Katrina's effect on the New Orleans art commu-nity. There is also an overview of the field and a necrology. The jury—all artists themselves—convene and decide on Gold and Silver awards in several categories. This is a book for anyone interested in art of the fantastic, whether dark or light.

The Case of Madeleine Smith, written and illustrated by Rick Geary (NBM Comics Lit), is volume eight in the series A Treasury of Victorian Murder. It is a graphic novel about a scandalous affair between an upper-class Scottish woman and a Frenchman whom she slowly poisons.

The Poison Diaries by the Duchess of Northumberland, with illustrations by Colin Stimpson (Abrams), is a clever gothic fiction supposedly created from the journals of an orphan apprenticed to an evil apothecary. In real life, the Duchess is an expert responsible for growing a "poison garden" in Alnwick Gardens in En-gland, opened in 2004.

The Arrival by Shaun Tan (Lothian) is a stunning wordless story told completely in pictures, following several immigrants on their journey to mysterious new worlds with wonders and monsters lurking at the edges of reality.

Amphigorey Again by Edward Gorey (Harcourt) contains previously uncollected work and two unpublished pieces by the late author/artist/personality: "La Malle Saignante," a bilingual homage to early French serial movies, and "The Izzard Book," an illustrated alphabet of the letter Z. For those not familiar with Gorey's sly, funny, ironic illustrated books, this one's a good start.

American Gothic: The Artwork of Carlos Batts (Scapegoat Publishers) provides an overview of more than fifteen years of photographic and mixed media art by a fear-less artist who often mixes the erotic with the horrific.

Autopsyrotica by Chad Michael Ward (NBM) showcases fetishistic erotic horror and gothic photographic images.

Beasts!: A Pictorial Schedule of Traditional Hidden Creatures from the Interest of 90 Modern Artisans by Jacob Covey (Fantagraphics) is an art book of cryptozoology that both visually and textually is filled with a great sense of humor. Included are the familiar: Baba Yaga, Banshees, and Bigfoot—and mostly the unfamiliar: the Chenoo, "an icy-hearted cannibal known to madly chew off even his own lips."

Magic Land of Toys by Alberto Manguel and photographed by Michel Pintado (The Vendome Press)—over a six-month period seven hundred toys were borrowed from the Musée des Arts Décoratifs in Paris and placed in almost one hundred tableaux created by set designer Jean Haas and his assistant Simon Saulnier to be photographed by Pintado. The text by Manguel comments on toys and their purpose but it's the photographs that make the book. Shame on the publisher for putting only Manguel's name on the cover and title page.

Mommy?, with art by Maurice Sendak, scenario by Arthur Yorinks, and paper en-gineering by Matthew Reinhart (MDC Books/Scholastic), is Sendak's first pop-up book and it's a sweet tale of a child searching for his mom among the monsters in a mysterious house. A young boy goes into a castle and finds lots of monster friends until he comes across his mom.

Alfred Hitchcock: The Master of Suspense pop-up book, paper engineering by

Kees Moerbeek (Simon & Schuster), pays tribute to Hitchcock with scenes from seven of his most famous films. Each one has an extra little pop-up that shows (and tells) where he made his famous cameo in the movie.

The Homecoming by Ray Bradbury and illustrated by Dave McKean (Collins) is a beautifully illustrated edition of a classic charmer by the master dark fantasist.

The Year in Media of the Fantastic: 2006

Edward Bryant

The Big Screen

THE POLITICS OF HORROR — OR VICE VERSA

I'm impressed when work intended as popular entertainment passes the content test. In other words, along with diversion and plot, interesting characters (hopefully), and some visual appeal, is the piece actually *about* something, preferably a reason for being that will provoke me as an audience member?

What I'll optimistically take as a sign of the times and a direction for horror films in the future is 2006's first truly striking fright film, *Hostel*. What a way to kick off January! Writer-director Eli Roth (creator of the visually striking and morally provocative *Cabin Fever*) has filmed a story sufficiently nasty, graphic, and genuinely troubling, it'll linger in your jaded mind and will give you issues to discuss once the lights go up. But is this a good thing? Heck yes. Along with all the Grand Guignol trappings, Roth gives us a provocative political fable that passes the content test—and is sufficiently flashy, in a gut-wrenching way, that maverick A-list director Quentin Tarantino gives *Hostel* his imprimatur in a "Presented By . . ." line.

Jay Hernandez, Derek Richardson, and the engaging Eythor Gudjonsson play young men backpacking on a hedonistic tour through today's Europe. Becalmed on the smoky cultural shoals of Amsterdam, they encounter another young guy who tells them that for even more willing women and ample drugs, they should go east. So they do, winding up in a depressed factory town somewhere in the exurbs of Dubrovnik. They find a hostel that is indeed replete with the touted girls and drugs. But all too soon they—and we—encounter the converted factory that houses a commercial enterprise that furnishes unwilling human victims for moneyed sickos who want to play doctor—and worse, a profitable enterprise that's helping make up for a damaged post-Soviet economy in which everything is for sale and almost nothing has genuine value. It would seem that most of the local community is either passively aware or actively participating in the commercial murder/torture/mutilation biz. Our mostly obnoxious young protagonists either meet or skirt horrific fates that even they do not deserve. One payoff is a disclosure of a rate card that indicates a local victim is worth five thousand dollars American, a European is ten grand, and a genuine American goes for fifteen thousand. Clearly citizens of the world's remaining superpower have finally achieved their true value in the new world economic order. *Hostel*'s an ugly, ugly picture of human nature twisted by economic necessity, but unfortunately it is rooted in reality. To be fair, Eli Roth gives us all a few grace notes to cling to as the closing credits roll.

Hostel is ultimately good but grim.

V for Vendetta is a somewhat more romanticized portrait of a grim world. The Wachowski Brothers and their fellow traveler director James McTeigue based this on the wonderful graphic novel written by Allen Moore and illustrated by David Lloyd. The irascible Moore took his name off the film (he also disavowed the film adaptations of *From Hell* and *The League of Extraordinary Gentlemen*). Because I feel the film *V for Vendetta* possesses considerable virtue, I urge you to check out the graphic novel separately—and to view the movie if you haven't already seen it.

Moore's graphic novel was a scathing indictment of Margaret Thatcher's Britain. The film takes an equally dim view of a near future U.K. as a fascist state. A vile high chancellor (John Hurt) rules Parliament, curfews and managed news are the order of the day, and the streets of London are trod by bully-boy gangs of "black-baggers," ready to pick up any suspicious person and haul them off for interrogation, torture, or worse. After an opening visual lesson about Guy Fawkes, the Gunpowder Plot guy who tried to blow up Parliament four centuries ago, but was caught and executed, we meet innocent Evey Hammond (Natalie Portman), a low-level British Television News drone who presses her luck after curfew and is braced by a quartet of rapacious government security thugs. She's saved by the lethal intervention of one V (Hugo Weaving), a vigilante and rebel who dresses in an unnerving, stylized Guy Fawkes costume and mask. V invites Evey to watch as he blows up the Old Bailey (nicely set off with genuine fireworks). V invites Evey to hang out with him as he embarks upon the next phase of his antigovernment plan, to blast Parliament into gravel. It will be a symbolic act, he explains, to mobilize a people's rebellion against the government.

Naturally, nothing goes that easily. Even though Evey's lost her parents and brother to government atrocity, she's not easily radicalized. But we see the process evolve, along with getting some sense of the earlier horrors that transformed the man who became V into the Edmund Dantes of his time. V is also being pursued by a rumpled Irish chief inspector (Stephen Rea), who seems to be a good guy who just follows too many orders.

Political as it increasingly becomes, this is no romantic adventure à la *Zorro*. We see plenty of desperate courage at work as the film progresses. We also see bitter railing against not only the people who do bad things, but also against those who simply do nothing. This film would probably have been enormously popular in the late sixties.

Eventually Evey goes through a horrendous, morally arguable act of radicalization and it's time for the Fawkesian climax. There are a few lump-in-the-throat moments; the element of political romance remains edgily hard-nosed. In the current political climate, *V for Vendetta* deserves to be widely seen and discussed.

Ditto the tardy French import *District B13*, which was two years delayed when it hit American soil running in the late spring. This near-future action-adventure has a wiry infrastructure of nasty political observation. Paris, 2010: the government, weary of never winning the battle of street-level violence, starts walling off particularly problematic neighborhoods. It's never overtly stated, but the implicit suggestion is that these new ghettos are the perfect way to keep the undesirable immigrant under-class from interacting with the more respectable citizenry. The new microcultures in the segregated districts are drawn right out of the filmic worlds of John Carpenter and George Miller. But the script by Luc Besson and director Pierre Morel affec-tionately honors and builds on its antecedents.

Leïto (David Belle) is a tough guy with honor who's on the run in the first five minutes after ripping off one million euros in heroin from a brutally nutso drug lord named Taha (Bibi Naceri) and destroying it in a bathtub. The drug lord retaliates by kidnapping Leïto's little sister (Dany Verissimo), hooking her on H, and enslaving her as his personal bitch. Leïto's next move is forestalled by a tangle with the cops who are in the process of pulling out of the district and leaving it to complete anar-chy. A few months later, the government loses a neutron bomb (don't ask) that ends up in District B13. Ace undercover cop Damien (Cyril Raffaelli) is assigned to re-cover the bomb, and tricks Leïto, who thinks the mission is to rescue his sister, into accompanying him into B13 as a native guide. All this plot is accomplished with hy-peractive fights, chases, pursuits, sweat, and lots of things that blow up really fine.

This is a live-action Chuck Jones cartoon that works well. It is possessed of a charming goofball quirkiness that doesn't forget humor, whether grim or exuberant. Some of the villains are particularly engaging, regardless of their poor impulse con-trol. The drug lord's jumbo right-hand thug, K2 (which is, after all, the name of the world's most deadly mountain), occasionally leavens his essential viciousness with a wry turn of affect. Drug lord Taha's cocaine-fueled life is played as an odd-couple blending of Al Pacino in *Scarface* and Woody Allen in *Annie Hall*.

Cartoony but earnest, *District B13* takes time for the moral but doesn't belabor its point. The levels of conspiracy on the part of the duplicitous government are not hard to fathom. One of the feds smugly points out that a certain policy ". . . might not be very democratic, but it's effective."

District B13 skates far too quickly over the horrific fate presumably endured by Leïto's abducted sister. But this is the brand of hyperactive melodrama that won't hold up to close scrutiny. It's best to just enjoy the action.

Remakes generally are a bad idea. The poster child for that is Gus Van Sant's shot-for-shot horrible mirror-imaging of *Psycho*. But there are exceptions. Last year's new version of *Dawn of the Dead* carved out some new territory for itself. So did 2006's *The Hills Have Eyes*. When it came time for a remake of his 1977 cult classic of an average American tourist family beset by degenerate cannibals out in the desert, director Wes Craven called upon the French brains behind last year's sus-pense shocker, *High Tension*, Alexandre Aja.

The blending of stock and new footage behind the opening credits confirms what we old-time fans of fifties monster movies knew right along. Just as it engendered giant ants, monstrous scorpions, and so many other ugly and destructive creatures, nuclear testing created populations of cannibalistic mutants in the New Mexico desert. They can't help themselves. They're ugly and hungry, and they devour tox-suited grunts from the Department of Energy with the same gusto as they sample the tourists.

When Dad (Ted Levene) and his family break down on a desert road, what's a poor mutant clan to do? The heirs of the slightly radioactive desert are actually green—nothing should be wasted. The nasty bits from Wes Craven's original are still here, but with added embellishments.

NOW BACK TO YOUR REGULARLY SCHEDULED PROGRAM

The Horrific . . .

Horror and dark fantasy are hardly unique phenomena of the English-speaking world. These days, most of America's knowledge of international horror centers around Japan and other Asian nations from which come a variety of beautifully creepy movies that get remade as generally less creepy Anglo versions. A number of the major Japanese new horror films have been based on written works by Koji Suzuki, appropriately enough a guest of honor at the 2006 World Horror Convention in San Francisco. Several of his books have been published in translation here in the U.S. But a popular Russian novel, *Nochnoi Dozor* by Sergei Lukyanenko, finally crossed the translation barrier to English in the summer. It has also been adapted as a series of three popular films, the first of which, *Night Watch*, finally was released in the U.S. early in 2006. Primarily playing at art houses in its original Russian with English subtitles, *Night Watch* begs to be seen by devotees of the dark fantastic.

The script is by director Timur Bekmambetov and Laeta Kalogridis. The plot, the characters, and their interrelationships, all are stuffed to bursting with details. Suffice it to say that a long, long time ago, the forces of light and darkness, soldiered by supernatural beings called Others, realized that their evenly matched battle could never be decisively won. An uneasy truce brokered by Geser (Vladimir Menshov), the leader of the light Others, and Zavulon (Victor Verzhbitsky), leader of the dark Others, holds for centuries, until the present day. The partisans of light form the Night Watch to keep track of the dark Others, and the dark Others form the Day Watch to keep tabs on the forces of light. But now in contemporary Moscow, one of those pesky predictions about a reincarnated virgin who will give birth to a Chosen One who, once he or she picks a side, will tip the cosmic balance of power. One of the big signs will be a massive space-time vortex opening up.

Okay, that's all background. Enter: a hard-luck psychic named Anton (Konstantin Khabensky), an everyday Joe Vodka–bottle who twelve years before screwed up really badly and ended up as a hapless Other of light drinking blood for life and vodka for oblivion. Much of the background tapestry behind the contemporary sections of *Night Watch* is a fascinating, if depressing, look at post-Soviet Russian urban society—poor, drab, alcohol-sodden. As Anton is called upon to pull himself together and rescue a human child who may very well be the Chosen One, the action ramps up with all manner of exotic Others (shapeshifters, vampires, immortals, psychics, etc.) maneuvering, conspiring, and beating the crap out of each other. A particular high point is when Anton is assigned a helper, a woman who turns out to be a resuscitated were-owl who's been dormant and dusty for eighty years or so. It all finally starts to cohere, but then *Night Watch* ends. One can hope that the other two chapters of this trilogy will appear in a country near you soon. This is rich, fascinating stuff.

Underworld: Evolution unfortunately comes across as something of a *Night Watch*–Lite. The first *Underworld* possessed a cool night-shrouded, rainy, gloomy, Eastern European look to it. Kate Beckinsale as Selene, the rebellious vampire lass, added genuine spirit to the goings-on. Once again the audience is plunked down into the endless and intensely violent feud between the clans of vampires and werewolves who dwell among us unsuspecting mortals. Selene and her hybrid vampire/lycanthrope boyfriend Michael (Scott Speedman) are on the lam after the ultraviolent ending of the first film. Now they come into conflict with the surviving leaders of the creature clans (vampire Tony Curran and werewolf Brian Steele) who seem to be cooking up some kind of nefarious cooperative world-conquering scheme. Bill Nighy, senior vampire patriarch from the first *Underworld*, is sorely missed here. Director Len Wiseman tries to keep the action moving along smartly, but the movie too often seems to be just going through the motions. Kate Beckinsale's newer, more tightly tailored leather jumpsuit cannot by itself carry the film. Also I'm still upset with the series's apparent classist view that the vampires seem to be the white-collar Eloi types, the lycanthropes the blue-collar Morlocks. It's rank stereotyping, I say.

One of the definite highlight horrors of the year is director/writer Neil Marshall's *The Descent*, a 2005 production that finally made it to the U.S. in 2006 for the summer season. It is a sensational thematic bookend to Marshall's *Dog Soldiers* (2002), the sharp, entertaining tale of half a dozen British soldiers stuck in an isolated corner of Scotland, fighting off the local family of Highlands werewolves.

The Descent gives us a half-dozen fit, smart young British women, most of whom have been fooling around in extreme outdoor sports for years. The first scene starts with a white-knuckled rafting sequence, some portentous dialogue clues, and a shocking traffic mishap. Traumatized wife and mom Sarah (Shauna Macdonald) spends the next year recovering from family tragedy and horrific dreams, before being pulled out of her cocoon by her rafting buds who suggest more wilderness therapy, this time caving in the Appalachians. An SUV license plate says North Carolina, but the credits indicate filming was all in the U.K. The women rendezvous and we start to discern the increasingly complicated character interrelationships among the six of them, particularly with their compact and prickly leader Juno (Natalie Mendoza). The descent into the cave starts smoothly enough, but soon veers into jeopardy when a rock slide traps them. Abruptly we learn that arrogant Juno has got them stranded in a newly discovered cavern system that is not mapped at all, and no one knows they are there. With retreat no option, the party has to forge ahead in search of another exit, only to find evidence of century-ago previous explorers, Lascaux-type cave paintings, and skeletal evidence indicating that predators have chowed down on plenty of prey over the years. Before you can say "Ask your local Morlock to lunch," the party is beset by hungry, pasty-white humanoids who look like New World country cousins of Gollum. Blind, their basic hunting sense is batlike hearing. For the female cavers, survival turns desperate and nasty. The film accelerates to the speed of revenge and gains even more darkness and edge. It's a convincingly tough movie, though weakened a bit at the end for an American audience with a boo! scene that can be rationalized but isn't really necessary.

What would Veronica Mars do? Really. One gets so accustomed to Kristen Bell's TV series performance, it's a bit of a shock to see her play a more everyday sort of terribly average young woman in the big-screen *Pulse*, the American remake of the Japanese feature by Kiyoshi Kurosawa. Bell's Mattie Weber is a college student who sees her boyfriend get mysteriously loopy and hang himself with a lamp cord. It seems he's been hacking into a really nasty viral program that allows the life-thirsting dead to cross from the Other Side into our world via cell phones, modems, Wi-Fi, PDAs, or any other of our myriad electronic communications devices. The dead are ill-tempered and hungry; they suck our souls/life force and we start to deteriorate into empty shells that go poof! into ash and blow away. Ah, but the deceased boyfriend apparently developed and then hid a program that can crash the

Program of the Living Dead. Mattie and a new friend (Ian Somerhalder) may be able to save the human world if they can just find the elusive data-stick. Meantime, the city (Bucharest filling in monochromatically for Columbus, Ohio) is becoming rapidly depopulated as the dead feast and mortals turn into ash. Wes Craven collaborated on the script and director Jim Sonzero does a fine job making the film properly grainy and jitter-filled. Visually *Pulse* does a fine job of portraying our mundane existence sinking into apocalypse, but it does *much* better at style over content. It struggles mightily to make a lick of sense and finally wanders away, muttering to itself. Mattie's otherwise intelligent roommate goes down alone into a creepy basement laundry room, then can't resist looking when a dryer abruptly stops, the door pops open, and sodden laundry starts plopping out into the room one garment at a time. Look closer, Izzie! Too bad when a naked bald guy unfolds from the dryer and sucks her soul-energy. Turns out that red utility tape is the key to scrambling the dead's travel frequency when fixed across windows and strung along door frames. So what *would* Veronica Mars have done? Probably spread some red utility tape across the lenses of a few powerful hand-flashes and zapped the shades of any ghost wandering close in search of the snacketeria. But mainly what she would have done is probably not opted to star in this halfhearted remake.

Final Destination 3 reminded us that though the Grim Reaper's attention sometimes briefly wanders, Death really doesn't *ever* take a holiday. The dependable formula used for all three installments of *Final Destination* starts with a small group of attractive teens narrowly avoiding some major disaster because one of their number has a premonitory vision in which he or she sees a terrible fate and has the bejeesus scared out of him or her. That character refuses to board the airliner/drive onto the freeway/get into the roller coaster and convinces others to do the same. Then the disaster happens in reality and Death finagles a terrible ending for each of the unexpected survivors. Each episode is full of ingeniously complicated, Rube Goldbergian scenarios of doom. The team behind *Final Destination* 3 is two talented *X Files* alums, Glenn Morgan and James Wong. This third installment has its share of moments, but as a whole, never has the consistent zest and wit one might have expected.

Hemophages (I guess that pretty much translates as vampires) are the oppressed underclass in *Ultraviolet*. Milla Jovovich plays a supremely gifted revolutionary and rebel squaring off against the übergovernment. Alas, her character's not nearly so tough as her roles in the *Resident Evil* movies; in fact, not even as forceful as Charlize Theron in last year's similar *Æon Flux*. *Ultraviolet* is designed to be a live action Japanese anime. It looks better than it plays.

Silent Hill is yet another film that picks on poor old West Virginia. A couple years ago, *The Mothman Prophecies*, *Cabin Fever*, and *Wrong Turn* tried to remind us that the Mountain State is a verdant wonderland infested with large bugs, exotic diseases, xenophobic natives, and hootin' hollerin' redneck cannibal mutants. Now *Silent Hill*, adapted from the Konami game, proposes to alert us that the titular West Virginia town, its air poisoned by the toxins from an underground coal fire, is also the site of an unending battle between unpleasant witch hunters and the regional emissary of hell. Poor Radha Mitchell (the tough pilot in *Pitch Black*) is the confused mom of a little girl plagued by bad dreams. So Mom researches Silent Hill on the Internet and decides to take her daughter to that abandoned ghost town to confront her nightmares. Bad idea, unsurprisingly. Before you can say "cursed ground" Mom is stranded in the perpetually ash-shrouded town and her little girl has disappeared. She gets some unexpected aid from a tough woman motorcycle cop (Laurie

Holden) who, like the other locals, knows more than she's initially saying. Meantime, the baffled husband (Sean Bean) heads off to Silent Hill in pursuit, only to find himself in a disaster zone somewhat different than the one his wife encountered. *Silent Hill*'s visual look is terrific. The female protagonists find that belowground and inside the abandoned mills, there is a hell created by folks who seem to have looked at some H. R. Giger designs and have been enormously impressed by Clive Barker artwork. Disturbing and even occasionally frightening, the film's visuals occasionally go over the top, as when our heroine's encounter with a blindfolded gaggle of the undead resembles nothing so much as the notorious slow-motion living dead interpretive dance presentation of *Crash* at the Oscars. Sometimes you've just gotta laugh. While Christophe Gans's direction moves everything along handily, Roger Avary's script doesn't always seem to make sense. Tortured plot machinations aside, the film ultimately pays off emotionally with a bitter message about separation and estrangement. I'm not sure it makes sense, but sense doesn't seem to be a major priority of this movie. The final irony is, of course, that *Silent Hill* was actually filmed in Ontario.

Okay, so you could buy DVDs of *Saw*, the remake of *War of the Worlds*, *The Village*, *Dawn of the Dead*, *Brokeback Mountain*, *The Grudge*, *Million Dollar Baby*, and the news footage of President George Bush getting the news about the attack on the World Trade Center while visiting a grade-school class in Florida. Or you can just watch *Scary Movie 4*. The *Scary Movie* franchise has been uneven at best, but when it hits on all cylinders, the humor accelerates like a Looney Tunes character on speed. The old wacky *Airplane* sensibility is in evidence as David Zucker directs from the script by Jim Abrahams and Craig Mazin. The film kicks off with a *Saw* scene played out by the actual Dr. Phil McGraw and Shaquille O'Neal. Then we're introduced to the perfectly perky and vapid ingenue (Anna Faris) who enters into a tortuous flirtation and relationship with the Tom Cruisean character played by Craig Bierko. It takes a beautifully twisted spirit to tie *Saw*'s Jigsaw Killer into the aliens controlling the fearsome tripods of *War of the Worlds*.

If you experience a real sense of déjà vu (or fall asleep) when viewing *An American Haunting*, it's probably because the makers of *Poltergeist*, *The Entity*, *The Haunting*, and any number of other prior melodramas about unholy forces striking honest young citizens through their hormonal levels and emotional wounds knew something of the notorious Bell witch case. Courtney Solomon directed and wrote *An American Haunting* from Brent Monahan's novel *The Bell Witch: An American Haunting*. All this stems from an 1817–18 case in Tennessee in which there was allegedly the only documented case of a spirit killing a human being. Donald Sutherland plays John Bell, a prosperous frontier entrepreneur who runs afoul of a sinister neighbor lady to whom he's charged usurious interest. Sissy Spacek is his wife and Rachel Hurd-Wood plays Betsy, the teenage daughter who gets included in the inevitable curse. Before you can say "call the exorcist," doors are opening and slamming shut by themselves, candles flicker without wind, Betsy's bedcovers slide off without visible help, and then something invisible and bulky settles into bed beside her. Her concerned family does in fact have something of an ad hoc exorcism (which does no good) and then witnesses their daughter suspended miraculously in mid-bedroom while an invisible assailant slaps her silly. They then consult with the local schoolteacher (James D'Arcy, the young studly prof on whom Betsy has a crash), who suggests that maybe the sinister neighbor's black slaves sneaked in and suspended Betsy aloft while an accomplice blistered her cheeks with a peashooter. The parents are skeptical. That's the low point, the moment in which the audience might wonder whether the movie might have been better served by retitling itself *Monty Python and the Bell Witch Project*. But things start getting serious and we can appreciate lots of atmospheric dream-sequence work by the late, great British cinematographer Adrian Biddle. Dark, fog-ridden nineteenth-century Tennessee is played by Romania and Canada. The movie slogs through more poltergeist phenomena, an out-of-left-field black wolf, and a lot of worried looks on the faces of the cast, until plot elements reflect up through time to a clumsy present-day bookend scene intended to give history-haters in the audience a taste of the contemporary world.

Did we need a quite faithful remake of *The Omen*? It opened (ah, those clever, clever marketers) on 6-6-06. The numbers weren't quite on the nose, so it's possible Satan was displeased. A few American law enforcement agencies said they'd be on the lookout on June 6 for the odd loony who might be psyched up for causing apocalyptic mischief. The only demonic hanky-panky I noticed was the country-wide ignoring of the commemoration of D-day. But I may have missed something.

At any rate, we are once again treated to the U.S. ambassador to the Court of Saint James's and his wife Kate (Liev Schreiber and Julia Styles) adopting young orphaned Damien after Kate's baby boy dies during childbirth. No Gregory Peck and Lee Remick they; they seem just kids themselves.

David Seltzer wrote the script for *The Omen*—again. That may be part of the reason why, for better or worse, the remake tills no new ground. The imagery is spiffed up (David Thewliss's version of David Warner's doomed photographer in the original suffers a spectacularly over-the-top and quite gymnastic decapitation) and the fatefully regretful corrupt priest Father Brennan (Pete Postlethwaite) endures the sort of elaborate impalement that would do credit to a *Final Destination* sequel. But mostly Seltzer updates minor things such as letting characters use cell phones. The one truly strange omission is a scene of the Antichrist's adoptive dad Robert Thorne (Schreiber) flying back to London from Israel after discovering the secret of how to kill his demon-spawned boy. Just imagine in the present day *anyone* catching an international flight in Tel Aviv and negotiating airport security while clutching a set of four impressive ceremonial steel knives wrapped in a piece of cloth.

The ooga-booga scary faces appearing in the mirror scenes are all effective, if familiar, and little Damien manages that facial spectrum from impassive to evilly smiling. We can hope that Master Seamus Davey-Fitzpatrick has a more promising film career than did 1976's Harvey Stephens. Does anyone really want their career peak to be a Trivial Pursuit answer?

The biggest treat in *The Omen* is Mia Farrow's gleeful turn as Mrs. Baylock, literally the nanny from hell. She deserves her own reality series. Having now copped two-thirds of the classic horror trifecta with *Rosemary's Baby* and *The Omen* remake, all she needs for history is to be cast in a redo of *The Exorcist*.

The first thing to say about *Feast* is its box-office grosses didn't have much of a chance to shine. Dimension Pictures gave it a two-night (actually at midnight) run in a couple dozen cities around America. The second thing to say is that it doesn't deserve the vilification it received from most quarters. We're not talking *Citizen Kane* here, but the movie was better than some other releases I caught during 2006's lackluster summer season. Recall that *Feast* was the third—and probably last—feature chronicled in cable's *Project Greenlight* series coproduced by Matt Damon and Ben Affleck. *Greenlight*'s premise was to document the process of emerging writers and directors creating a low-budget film that would then be released by Miramax. After the first two projects tanked at the box office, the focus changed to giving corporate sibling Dimension a flick that would finally make money. It's generally hard to lose cash on horror, so that ended up the genre of choice. Fledgling director John Gulager helmed the script by Marcus Dunstan and Patrick Melton. The story is an old and proven one. A group of diverse yahoos is trapped in a remote desert bar while a bunch of ravenous creatures try to break in and eat them. What results is a lot more fun than you might expect; this is assuming you can see the humor in snappy dialogue about an alien's penis getting caught by a slammed door. The director's dad, old pro Clu Gulager, does fine as the grizzled bartender, and punk rocker/monologist Henry Rollins is terrific as a trapped citizen. You might consider this as a double feature with *Slither* for your home DVD night.

And then there was *The Grudge 2*, in which Sarah Michelle Gellar, star of the first remake, gets to perish ignominiously in her hospital room, bedeviled by stringy-haired spirits, little boys who think they're feral cats, and ominous orchestral music. The movie's great, if not wholly successful, conceit is an abrupt experiment to see if Japanese mythic icons of supernatural terror will easily transfer from Tokyo to the inhabitants of a Chicago apartment building. The notion's intriguing, but the battle for cultural transference of horrific imagery may well be lost now that the iconography of a woman's face hiding behind thick strands of cascading dark hair has been co-opted by Garnier Fructis Style anti-humidity hairspray. It's too bad Sarah Michelle Gellar didn't have a bottle in her hospital toiletries bag.

The Fantastical . . .

Arguably the highest-profile fantasy film of the year, and deservedly so, is Guillermo del Toro's *Pan's Labyrinth* with its nearly unanimous critical raves and six Academy Award nominations. This Spanish-language movie, the original title of which was *The Labyrinth of the Faun*, is a magnificently imagined and deeply affecting fairy tale setting the grim reality of the Spanish Civil War in opposition to the Grimm inner life that helps a young girl attempt to withstand the corrosive brutality of mortal violence.

Young Ofelia travels with her pregnant mom to join the older woman's second husband, the commanding officer of a remote Fascist army outpost deep in the forest. The hills are alive with guerrilla fighters, and Captain Vidal's enclave harbors rebel sympathizers. Newly arrived Ofelia discovers that the countryside is dotted with pagan ruins and large and startling walking stick (what we'd call mantises) insects that quickly disclose their alter ego fairy selves to her.

As the jack-booted Captain Vidal rules the local countryside with a brutally heavy hand and an arbitrarily quick pistol, Ofelia's fairy leads the girl to a disreputable-looking faun (Doug Jones) who informs the girl that she's actually a supernatural princess who can regain her elusive magical heritage by completing a three-part quest deep in an ancient labyrinth. It will not be without danger and difficult choices. It's a classic wish-fulfillment fantasy that rapidly leads into direct conflict with the adult world of Ofelia's cruel stepfather and the all-too-graphic realities of war.

Ofelia has a horrific run-in with an eyeless humanoid monster that wears borrowed eyeballs in the palms of its hands, but is the creature any more disturbing than her stepfather who casually beats a suspected rebel nearly to death with a wine bottle before shooting both the young man and his father without a second glance? It's clear that the casual cruelties of the human world are just as disturbing, and probably more so, than the nightmare terrors of the fairy realm. Captain Vidal is a far worse monster than the denizens of Ofelia's magical labyrinth. It's clear that he could make better moral choices if he wished. He doesn't. His vanity and worship of superficial beauty is in acute counterpoint to the superficial ugliness of the faun and the other monsters.

Ultimately the film comes to a powerful and unflinching ending that carries all the impact of classic fairy tales. There is a grace note there for those who wish it, but it's not required. *Pan's Labyrinth* is, I truly believe, bound for classic film status.

Video killed the radio star? Well, not quite; not yet. The fantasy charmer of the year has to be *A Prairie Home Companion*. The new (and unfortunately final) Robert Altman movie is pretty much a collaboration between the legendary director and Garrison Keillor, the creator of National Public Radio's popular live radio vaudeville show. For thirty-three years, *A Prairie Home Companion* has been beamed from the Fitzgerald Theatre in St. Paul (and other venues around the country, when they hit the road each year as is their wont) to an eager audience. Folksy, funny, melodious, and usually quirky, *Companion* has gradually accreted an elaborate mythology about the upper midwestern town of Lake Wobegon. It's a place of bizarre Scandinavian food and dedicated Lutherans, bachelor Norwegian farmers and a joyous American population ever mindful of the doom that lurks around the next corner.

The movie, written by Keillor, is still pure Altman. The powerhouse ensemble cast swirls and merges in endless permutation, conversations graze and overlap, mutating like verbal moiré patterns. With the exception of an epilogue, the film spans one crucial evening, the conceit being that *A Prairie Home Companion*'s longtime radio network has been purchased by a Texas communications mega-corporation and they're going to shut down the show and raze the theatre for a parking lot. The company's hatchet-man (Tommy Lee Jones) is in fact on his way to confirm the end of the program.

It's a melancholy night, but the show must go on. In this parallel worldview of Keillor's real universe, many of the show's fictional characters are very live indeed. Guy Noir (Kevin Kline) is the L.A. hard-boiled detective come upon hard times, who's working as the security guy for the theatre. Woody Harrelson and John C. Reilly are hitting the stage tonight as Dusty and Lefty, the two singing cowpokes with raunchy senses of humor. Also singing tonight are Yolanda and Rhonda (Meryl Streep and Lily Tomlin), the two surviving Johnson Girls. It's pointed out that they're like the Carter family, only not as rich. Yolanda is the ex-flame of the show's host, GK (Keillor himself), and she's still a bit conflicted about the breakup. Lindsay Lohan plays Lola Johnson, her daughter, a bright young lady hanging around backstage, killing time by writing dark poetry about suicide. She gets to belt a sensational vamped version of "Frankie and Johnny." Lohan also gets to prove that yes, as well as being a teen idol, she's a genuine actress as well.

The cast is joined by many of *Companion*'s real-life regulars, such as Rich Dworsky's house band, musicians Robin and Linda Williams, Sue Scott, Jearlyn Steele, and Guy's All-Star Shoe Band.

For my money, the prize is the incandescent blonde drifting around the theatre in a blinding white trenchcoat and a Mount Rushmore T-shirt. Virginia Madsen is the Dangerous Woman, the Angel of Death, the Angel Asphodel. She was also the mortal Lois Peterson, driving to meet her lover for a lakeshore weekend when she started laughing at an absolutely hopeless Keillor penguin joke on the radio. She crashed, died, and has ended up working as an agent for the Almighty. Now she's here on business at the show's final performance.

Director Altman takes Keillor's funny, wry script and melds it with the terrific performances of his cast to form a thoughtful meditation on death and mortality that never wallows in self-pity. Doom may have come for *A Prairie Home Companion* but never defeat.

Equally impressive as a fantasy, but far darker and with nasty sharp edges, is Terry Gilliam's *Tideland*. Gilliam's film, produced by the same maverick bunch that created *Lost in La Mancha*, the 2002 documentary chronicling Gilliam's doomed production of *The Man Who Killed Don Quixote*, hit limited release in the autumn, vilified by such press outlets as *Entertainment Weekly*. Problem is, *Tideland* is a brilliant portrait of the world as seen through a child's eyes, possibly the closest the talented and quirky director has come to creating a perfect film. However ambitious, Gilliam's films usually possess a major flaw or two. *Tideland* does not. All the manifold parts mesh cleanly, picking up momentum until they cascade into the shattering final scenes.

How actually to describe *Tideland*? My first attempt would be via the high concept route: *Finding Neverland* gets mugged by the tag-team assaults of a more malign *Alice in Wonderland* in league with a benign, even sunnily cheerful, *Texas Chainsaw Massacre* (no massacre but all the grotesque ambiance). Or just call it a timeless American Gothic, with talking squirrels.

Extraordinarily talented child actor Jodelle Ferland plays Jeliza-Rose, a young girl being reared in most peculiar circumstances by her drug-addled junky parents (Jeff Bridges and Jennifer Tilly). Rose is a lonely but imaginative little girl, her only friends being Mystique, Baby Blonde, Glitter Gal, and Sateen Lips, four disembodied doll's heads that she sometimes wears on her hands like finger puppets. After Mom dies of a methadone mishap, faded rock-musician Dad decides to take Rose on a loopy cross-country bus ride to her grandmother's country home. Grandma is long dead and the isolated home is an abandoned, decaying shambles rearing like a derelict ship out of a vast sea of swirling grassland. Self-sufficient Rose picks out a room for herself and settles in with her quartet of decapitated pals. Dad promptly overdoses and quietly dies. Rose ekes out a few days nourishment from a jar of peanut butter her dad and she brought on the bus.

Then she discovers she has neighbors. There's the black-clad sister (Janet McTeer) who may also be the Angel of Death who declared the moment of Dad's passing; and there's the retarded, epileptic brother Dickens (Brendan Fletcher) whose manic gait and disfiguring scar declare him a major grotesque. The adult siblings treat Rose to a country feast, help her give Granny's house a top-to-bottom (if haphazard) cleaning, and enlist her help in a down-home taxidermy lesson that helps take care of the growing bad odors that have been emanating from Dad's rocking-chair-ensconced body.

Rose's salvation from wasting away like an Edward Gorey naif provides a short but welcome breathing space. Then things get weirder as the girl dives deeper into the strange blending of her gothic prairie world and her own imagination. There's more Faulknerian taxidermy; the wonderful bottle tree; the daily Amtrak passenger train that retarded Dickens sees as his adversary, a rushing, roaring, murderous great white shark. There's Dickens's elaborate childish mockup of the interior of a submarine. And then there's Rose's groping toward adulthood and relationship as she explores the secret attic filled with her grandma's detritus. What results is a grimly disturbing masterpiece with great visual beauty and just enough grace notes to enable the viewer to survive.

Stranger Than Fiction accomplishes some remarkable goals. First, it functions well on several levels: less ambitious viewers will find a satisfactory romantic comedy; more literate audience members will appreciate both that and the movie's achievement in saying (and demonstrating) quite a lot about the process of creativity and the crafting of fiction. Second, star Will Ferrell reins himself in sufficiently to do an exemplary job portraying a bland, repressed IRS auditor who discovers he's not only the literal protagonist of a novel being written by Emma Thompson, he's also destined for an imminent and dismal death. When it rains, it pours. Ferrell's character is also finding his tidy universe starting to crumble when he meets his next audit target, Maggie Gyllenhaal, a free-spirited bake shop entrepreneur. All will be well if it ends well, but that's ultimately up to the author, and she's inclined to see her protagonist crash and burn. Using a fantasy conceit to say real and valuable things about the creative process works fine here. Also, trying to avoid a serious spoiler here, just remember to pay close attention to Ferrell's wristwatch.

Marvel Comics projects can be such a soap opera! Remember when Bryan Singer was going to direct *X-Men III: The Last Stand*, the final chapter in the *X-Men* trilogy? That relationship ended, Brett Ratner was signed to helm the project, and Singer went to direct *Superman Returns*. What finally hit uncountable multiplex screens is expensive, splashy, slick, and, I fear, boring. Right at the beginning, we get to see cameos of comics writer Chris Claremont mowing his lawn and comics legend Stan Lee watering flowers. Then we're launched into the world of superheroes having to choose sides when the government finds a "cure" for mutant powers. Will the intelligent and humane Professor Xavier (Patrick Stewart) prevail, or will the rebellious mutants organized by Xavier's old friend and implacable foe, Magneto (Ian McKellen), carry the day? Weather goddess Storm (Halle Berry) gets to fly for the first time and she also sports a chic new hairstyle. Mystique (Rebecca Romijn) gets a nude scene. A little later in the film, the "cured" Mystique appears on a background video monitor as she betrays Magneto's secret location. Darned if she doesn't do a spot-on impression of Monica Lewinsky! Jean Grey (Famke Janssen) gets to be reborn as the Dark Phoenix. And in a feat of wasteful psychic engineering, the Golden Gate Bridge is co-opted into a quick and handy bridge between Alcatraz and the mainland. As the mutant armies square off, we get to see lots of Marvel characters wandering on the periphery. Whoopee.

Ultimately, *The Last Stand* is defeated by simple mathematics. In a couple of hours of screen time, there simply is not time and opportunity to grow close to anyone in particular. Wolverine (Hugh Jackman) and Magneto bring themselves to life through sheer brute charisma. Kelsey Grammer attains some interest as the blue-furred Beast, the government's Secretary for Mutant Affairs, primarily for the novelty value. It's Dr. Frasier Crane fitted for a Minnesota winter on a bad morning after.

Finally, one must conclude, sheer quantity cannot substitute for quality. There's far more noise than signal here. The colors are nice and bright, but the human (or mutant) landscape is sterile. This time it was tedium that killed the beast. Word to the eager: stick around for the Easter egg at the end of the final credit crawl.

Marvel Comics fans should also catch *Superman Returns*, the latest revival of the Man of Steel franchise. Brandon Routh looks great as the new avatar of Clark Kent, but the film doesn't do well in terms of sticking in viewer's memory once the lights go up. The special effects are good, but that's just not enough. If the viewer sits there in the center seat, front row, marveling at the counterpoint to *Black Sunday*'s climax posed by Superman arresting the plunge of an airliner as it's about to crash into home plate in a major league ballpark, then the battle's probably over.

So does *Pirates of the Caribbean: Dead Man's Chest* deliver the quota of fun we all expected after fondly enjoying its namesake predecessor? Not quite. It's definitely a worthwhile hoot, if only for Johnny Depp's continuing turn as Captain Jack Sparrow. But it ultimately feels like what it is: an interstitial, middle episode in a very commercial triptych. Still, by all means go to see the physical comedy set-pieces. Don't miss the giant kraken sinking any number of sailing vessels. And marvel at Bill Nighy almost unrecognizable as the shaving-challenged Davy Jones.

M. Night Shyamalan's new supernatural thriller *Lady in the Water* featured a man who finds a water sprite in his building's pool. The film's primary set is a five-story apartment building built from scratch for the shooting. Paul Giamatti's turn as the bemused super who encounters the luminous Bryce Dallas Howard in the pool is well executed, but the writer/director's nomenclature for his mythic story background could use some thoughtful reworking.

Zoom presents us with an academy for juvenile (chronologically, at least) superheroes. Hockey fans should be thrilled since *Zoom* was shot in the now-abandoned Maple Leaf Gardens in Toronto.

So is *The Da Vinci Code* to be classed as fantasy, or is it speculative fiction? Dare one call it horror? Certain souls might defend it as a thinly veiled heretical documentary. By whatever label, it was an adaptation of Dan Brown's bestselling novel that really never had a chance to screen before a completely tabula rasa audience. Thanks to endless publicity, virtually no one was unaware what the plot's basic shtick coiled around. If *The Da Vinci Code* were a murder trial, for an impartial jury the venue would probably have to be transferred to Graustark or Ruritania.

Because of the PR notoriety, I barely skirted dozing through the first third of the film. Instead of being immersed in the plot, I found much more interest in academic Robert Langdon's (Tom Hanks) slide show on symbology. But then things picked up and I realized that Ron Howard's direction and Akiva Goldsman's script were beginning to hook me with an involving philosophical/historical intellectual thriller. Nothing too deep, but at least it wasn't *all* car chases and gun battles. It really would be interesting to look at the population stats and decide that most of modern France is at least a shirttail relation to Jesus Christ his own self.

The cast comports itself well, starting with Tom Hanks in his customary amiable mode. As Sir Leigh, Ian McKellen evokes an even more delicious miscreant than he does as Magneto in the latest *X-Men* movie. Audrey Tautou generates plenty of heat as the big JC's direct descendant. Always a convincing thug, Paul Bettany does his best with the albino, robed, monk-hit man Silas. Jean Reno attempts to evoke some Javertian soul as a hapless French police detective.

Ultimately *The Da Vinci Code* will probably not change anyone's mind about matters theological, but it may stir renewed interest in French vintages for sacramental wine.

Nacho Libre was far better than I'd feared it would be from the trailers. I've liked actor Jack Black ever since I noticed him in an episode of *The X Files*, but *Nacho Libre* didn't look all that prepossessing. I confess that I jumped to conclusions. I should have considered the fact that Jared Hess (*Napoleon Dynamite*) directed from a script by him, his wife Jerusha Hess, and Mike White. Black's turn as a Mexican orphan who grows to adulthood as a friar in a remote monastery, cooking breakfast for kids on a minuscule budget, envying the worldly glamour of *los luchadores*, the masked Mexican wrestlers, flaunts a number of hoary chestnuts of gags as well as the usual tiresome lot of bodily function jokes; but when it catches fire, the film burns with a clear, flickering votive flame that alternates between a goofy, often surreal Mexico of the mind, and a genuinely aware, sad landscape of grinding poverty, foolish authority, and virtually impossible dreams. As Ignacio (Nacho), Black displays expectable manic wackiness as he pursues his dream of donning "stretchy pants" and a fabric mask and becoming a pro wrestler. The unexpected surprise is Mexican actor Héctor Jiménez playing Esqueleto, the tall, cadaverous street person who becomes Nacho's sidekick and tag-team wrestling bro. Scientific rationalist Esqueleto and thoroughly pious Nacho make a pretty good Abbott and Costello. *Nacho Libre* is just off-center enough to be unexpectedly affecting.

Director Michel Gondry's *Eternal Sunshine of the Spotless Mind* is, to me, a modern classic of the fantastic. In *The Science of Sleep* Gondry takes a dreamy look at dreaming itself, through the eyes of Gael Garcia Bernal. Bernal plays Stéphane, whose waking and dreaming lives become increasingly commingled. Visually impressive, the film never digs quite deep enough into the nature of dreaming, and that's frustrating for the viewer.

By now most of you know the background story of *Eragon*—that it was a novel written by teenaged Christopher Paolini, that his family self-published it and pushed it copy by copy until one of novelist Carl Hiaasen's kids discovered it, pushed it on his dad, and the novel wound up at a major publisher. The book became a huge publishing phenomenon. Kids love it; adults aren't so sure, apparently because grown-up readers more readily realize that Paolini's plot and characters are thin versions of all the great fantasy the author read in his earlier years. In *Eragon* a farmboy (Ed Speleers) finds himself the custodian of the last dragon egg. It hatches and we meet the last living dragon (voiced by Rachel Weisz). Turns out that our boy Eragon is the last living dragon rider. It's also Eragon's destiny to lead the rebellion against his kingdom's brutal despot (John Malkovich). This film is not one of Malkovich's finest moments; he eats the scenery atypically without generating much heat. But he's almost balanced by a fine Jeremy Irons playing Brom, Eragon's mentor. While the battle scenes with heir faux Orcs are nothing new, the aerial scenes of a soaring dragon are quite cool. The best visual is that of a dragon hitting the earth in a crash landing, an effect so cool, director Stefen Fangmeier uses it twice.

The Scientifictionesque . . .

Ah, what's summer without an adaptation of another Philip K. Dick novel? 2006 was the time for Richard Linklater's version of *A Scanner Darkly* with a first-rate cast and extraordinarily bizarre animation. Keanu Reeves plays Bob Arctor, apparent screwup Southern California druggie, but also a double-agent informant for a slightly futuristic, extremely high-tech Orange County Sheriff's Department drug unit. Law enforcement employs nearly ubiquitous security scanners to monitor citizen lives indoors and out. They also safeguard anonymity back at headquarters by giving staff and informants scramblesuits, full-body outfits that display constantly changing images. Arctor has become hooked on Substance B, a high-powered illicit drug he's supposed to be tracking down for the law. Winona Ryder plays his damaged platonic girlfriend, Donna, a low-level dealer who has her own tangle of secrets and inner problems. Arctor's household includes whacked-out friends Robert Downey, Jr., and Woody Harrelson, quirkoids all. The main sf device is the scramblesuit, an endlessly mutable visual disguise that would give any self-respecting Predator a raging migraine. One could argue whether director Linklater might have reserved the hyper-realistic animation for the scramblesuits and not used it for the entire picture, but that doesn't detract from the movie's striking appearance. When all is said and done, the characters, plot, social commentary, and paranoia all hang together. There have been a wide spectrum of Philip K. Dick films. This is one of the good ones.

British novelist P. D. James is best known for her tales of mystery and murder. But like Margaret Atwood, Walter Mosley, and many others, she occasionally dips a toe into the murky waters of science fiction. The end of 2006 saw the adaptation of *Children of Men* directed by the esteemed Mexican filmmaker, Alfonso de Cuarón. Set in a near-future U.K., years after the women of our world have all turned infertile and the youngest human is in his late teens, the species is getting majorly depressed. Much of the globe has collapsed into chaos, but the British, with stiff upper lip and plenty of firepower, have closed their borders, are rounding up illegal immigrants, and are keeping the country going. The crunch comes when government and home-country insurgents alike discover the existence of a young, pregnant immigrant woman. Clive Owen's character finds himself conscripted by old friend Julianne Moore to safeguard the expectant mom and shepherd her to the coast where she will be smuggled off to safety. To be candid, the sf element here is merely a convenience to allow the author's cultural observations. What ends up being memorable about the movie is the director's visual imagining of this future England. The climactic scenes of building-to-building street battles in a British city stun the eye. The tension-filled face-off of soldiers, refugees, rebels, and pregnant mom and protector inside a ruined high-rise is unforgettable. It's a remarkable secular translation of the battle between the sacred and the profane.

DO YOU BELIEVE IN MAGIC?

Who is not fascinated by those tricky folks onstage who astonish us with their misdirection and sleight-of-hand and, ultimately, give even the most rational among us a doubtful moment to ponder whether literal magic might actually be afoot? 2006 gave us a fascinating triple feature of legerdemain.

Based on Steven Millhauser's literary tale "Eisenheim the Illusionist," *The Illusionist* presents us with a vintage tale of unlikely young lovers separated by social class, time, and distance, who get a second chance when a mysterious young man (Edward Norton) comes to the city with a fabulous stage magic show. Norton makes the most of a terrific role. Mostly ditto for Paul Giamatti. The plot ultimately does not truly astonish, but it does satisfy.

Truth be told, *The Prestige* is actually a science fiction story. Well, maybe . . . Ambiguity saturates the story and there's ample opportunity for viewers to argue afterward in the lobby whether the plot should be rationalized out of the realm of the fantastic. Working from the novel by Christopher Priest, director Christopher Nolan and his brother Jonathan attempted to make the script as tricky and complicated as Nolan's 2001 success, *Memento*, though with less clear-cut results. *Memento* was a perfectly constructed device; *The Prestige* is not quite so neat and tidy in its structure. Are those top hats and black felines outside real-life genius inventor Nikola Tesla's laboratory above Colorado Springs for real, or are they clever misdirection? Does Tesla's teleporter really do the job, and does it, in the process of instantaneously transporting matter, also duplicate the cargo? The plot gets increasingly complicated as feuding stage magicians Hugh Jackman and Christian Bale, sly manager Michael Caine, and lovely but duplicitous assistant Scarlett Johansson negotiate a murky webwork of scheming and betrayal. It's all quite colorful and tricky, but stimulates as many new questions as it appears to answer.

The Piano Tuner of Earthquakes is not precisely about stage magic, but it certainly does concern itself with a visually spectacular attempt to bewilder the audience. This is the second feature by Stephen and Timothy Quay. They're far better known to moviegoers for their striking body of weird and surreal short films. A

French-German-British coproduction, *The Piano Tuner of Earthquakes* immerses us in a dreamy, misty, sepia wonderland of tenuously intersecting realities. Exquisite young opera singer Malvina, just before her wedding, collapses onstage and dies. Is it murder? Her body is apparently stolen by the obsessed Dr. Droz and perhaps re-animated at the doctor's remote villa. Or maybe Malvina has been re-created as an elaborate singing automaton by Droz, who evidently is a master of robotic wizardry. Expert piano tuner Felisberto is summoned to the villa and commissioned to put a half dozen of Droz's bizarre musical automatons into tiptop shape, as part of the preparation for the doctor's planned "diabolical opera." But what is the real purpose of that performance? Are all six of Droz's peculiar gardeners themselves automatons? And what of the enigmatic and hotly sensual housekeeper? The Quay Brothers' film is a sumptuous feast for the eyes, perhaps less so for the ears and brain. Some of the dialogue is overly arch; the acting is occasionally uninspired, though perhaps deliberately so. Are we to see the characters as suspected automatons and therefore a bit mechanical in their delivery? The film keeps the audience teetering on the edge of *almost* grasping what the hell is going on. Gorgeous but a bit thick; you and I both have known people like that.

CLOSE ENOUGH FOR FOLK MUSIC
These are not exactly sf, fantasy, or horror, but they possess qualities that commend them to your attention.

After becoming a lightning rod for accusations of anti-Semitism, far-right Christian wackdom, and an unseemly love of cinematic brutality, writer/director Mel Gibson prepared *Apocalypto* for release amid choruses of expectant glee and horrified trepidation. Here was a historical film set in a culture and time unfamiliar to most viewers, cast with unknown actors, filmed fully in the Yucatec language with English subtitles, and reputed to be crammed full with hyperviolence. In other words, *Passion of the Christ* without the Christian appeal.

All true, as it turned out. But the good news is that no Jews are injured or insulted in the course of *Apocalypto*. Christians do appear, though briefly, and we never hear a word from them. From a science fiction sensibility, it's not hard to see *Apocalypto* as a cautionary tale of a technologically sophisticated but decadent society that runs roughshod over smaller, more idyllic natural cultures, only to be confronted in turn by a technologically vastly superior alien civilization arriving from a far distance away.

The Proposition is one of the leanest, toughest, most macho, and uncompromising films you could see all year. Essentially it's a period piece, a western set in the 1880s outback of Australia. It's a western that would trigger Sam Peckinpah's and Sergio Leone's drool reflex. It's a violent film, and that violence is extreme but never dwelled upon. That aspect has reminded many beholders of Cormac McCarthy's best-known novel, *Blood Meridian*, something of the Platonic ideal for graphically bloody novels of the West. Still, *The Proposition* is only, at its most extreme, perhaps 10 percent as violent as McCarthy's novel. The proposition of the title is an offer made by a hard-bitten trooper, Captain Stanley (Ray Winstone), to a newly captured renegade, Charlie Burns (Guy Pearce). Stanley has also captured Charlie's younger brother Michael (Richard Wilson), a terrified and apparently retarded teen. Stanley knows that Charlie and Mikey are not the real dangers in the outlaw Burns clan. It's psychotic older brother Arthur (Danny Huston) who's the linchpin. If Charlie will track down and kill Arthur, Stanley offers, he will pardon both Charlie and Mikey. Otherwise Mikey will be hanged this upcoming Christmas Day. It's a terrible bargain, but Stanley believes it is the only way, finally, to bring law and order to the godforsaken backcountry town of Banyon. And then there's the x-factor of John Hurt playing a scarily twisted bounty hunter who makes Boba Fett look like the Lone Ranger. In the meantime, the local community is increasingly incensed by Mikey's presence in the local gaol, since he's suspected of helping murder a local family and of raping the pregnant wife. Lynching's in the wind, abetted by Stanley's otherwise balancing influence, his wife (Emily Watson) who was a friend of the dead mother-to-be. Through Stanley's wife Martha we come to understand that the captain is a decent man forced to make impossibly hard decisions by the exigencies of dwelling in a supremely harsh land. Indeed, Banyon and its people are filmed as a merciless landscape of light and heat and ubiquitous flies. There is a spectacular austere beauty present, the unforgiving presence of death impossible to ignore. John Hillcoat's direction is taut, and the script by Nick Cave is even tighter. An edgy early punk poet, fiction writer, and musician (Nick Cave and the Bad Seeds), Cave doesn't waste a word or image as we see hard whipcord men and women, European and Aboriginal, wrestle with moral dilemmas and survival. *The Proposition* is exhausting to watch, but it amply rewards those who approach it with an open soul.

No matter what the subject matter, it would always be wrong to underestimate the director of *American Psycho*, who won at least two falls out of three. Mary Harron's biopic of America's favorite naughty-but-nice fifties bondage and fetish pinup girl, *The Notorious Bettie Page*, is a pleasurable sight to behold. Appropriately, cinematographer Mott Hupfel shoots this shimmering fifties dream world in black and white. It looks gorgeous, and so does Gretchen Mol as Bettie herself. I don't think this is by any means the entire portrait of one of America's great fantasies, but it hits many of the important points. The supporting cast is solid as well, especially Chris Bauer as B&D shutterbug Irving Klaw and Lili Taylor as his hovering sis, Paula.

New and/or young independent writer/directors seem endlessly fascinated with the noir tradition of shadows, darkness, edges, and a lone guy trudging down a lonely street toward a hard-won goal of shaky honor. *Brick* puts all that into a contemporary high school context and, amazingly, it works. Novice director Rian Johnson went through years of frustration before being able to film *Brick*. Like so many good noir flicks before it, this one starts with a dead body. Flashbacks take us to moping protagonist Brendan (Joseph Gordon-Levitt) getting a mysterious phone call. Before you can say Raymond Chandler, Brendan is sucked into trying to find out who murdered his drug-involved ex-girlfriend. As the local drug lord, Lukas Haas does a more than passable evocation of a Sydney Greenstreet icon. Using exotic metaphor to probe middle-class youthful American pain worked well for Joss Whedon in *Buffy*; it does the same here for Rian Johnson.

Paul McGuigan's *Lucky Number Slevin* and its script by Jason Smilovic are slick, facile, and predictable, while still diverting. The intended surprises occasionally are convoluted enough to catch the audience unaware. In a mythical Manhattan, Ben Kingsley and Morgan Freeman play aging crime bosses glaring at each other from the top floors of their fortified office tower lairs. Josh Hartnett comes to town and is promptly mistaken for a low-life welsher and threatened by both kingpins. To complicate things, Hartnett's character strikes sparks with his new next-door neighbor, Lucy Liu, playing a flaky but earnest coroner. Then, in the tradition of *Sin City*, *Pulp Fiction*, and other noir-ish extravaganzas, Bruce Willis lends his considerable presence to an enigmatic character who's clearly the most lethal hired gun around, but with highly shadowed motives. The body count rises, secrets unwind, vengeance is extracted Ross McDonald–style for long-ago sins, and we learn that Josh Hartnett is far more charismatic than we ever could have guessed from *Pearl Harbor*.

POPCORN WITH DUBIOUS BUTTER SUBSTITUTE

Really, did we need a remake of *The Poseidon Adventure*? Alas, *Poseidon* had no Shelley Winters. But it did borrow some set ideas from L.A.'s Staples Center. It's also a visual feast, though portentously directed by Wolfgang Petersen. If you see some sharp, twisted, metal debris at the bottom of a high, high elevator shaft, you *know* a dispensable character is about to fall screaming to impalement. If you see a shaky improvised catwalk over a patch of bubbling bilge, you can readily guess that some sort of lethal geyser is about to shoot up to parboil an obnoxious character. And so on. The characters almost to every man, woman, and child of them are flat as all get-out. The plot, as a handful of characters attempts to escape through the bowels of a huge cruise ship after it's been capsized by a rogue wave, is about as predictable as the sun rising in the east. But the shattered, upside-down chaos of the liner is fun to watch. Inspiration occasionally strikes with force, as, when we see the ship heel over, spilling the on-deck swimming pools into the sea, an effective coals-to-Newcastle image. You could hope for better emoting from Josh Lucas as the lone-wolf gambler abruptly pressed into service as a reluctant hero, Kurt Russell as a firefighter who was once the mayor of New York, and Emily Rossum as Russell's fairly helpless daughter, but you'd be disappointed. Unsurprisingly, it's a graying Richard Dreyfuss as a depressed gay architect who shows signs of life. At least there isn't a cute little dog on board. The trivia answer you'll want to know: Stacy Ferguson, the front woman for Black Eyed Peas, plays the headline vocalist at *Poseidon*'s big New Year's Eve bash. But if you want to see a more spectacular finish to a loud party, rent the DVD of *Ghost Ship* and hang in there long enough for the snapping steel cable to bifurcate an entire ballroom of unlucky celebrants.

For what it's worth, a pair of spiffy reissues of *The Poseidon Adventure* and *The Towering Inferno*, not exactly coincidentally, were released at the same time as *Poseidon*. Along with remastered views of Fred Astaire, Steve McQueen, and the rest of their merry crews, you get the usual bundle of extras.

Mission: Impossible III, or *M:I III* as the studio marketers shorthanded the latest sequel, is like a very social Scarecrow (as in *Wizard of Oz*)—enormously entertaining but without a brain in its head. Director J. J. Abrams took a break from *Lost* for this. Tom Cruise's character, Ethan Hunt, gets to lead a team against perfectly swinish arms dealer Philip Seymour Hoffman. Team members Ving Rhames, Billy Crudup, and Jonathan Rhys Meyers do their best to exude some presence, but it's a tough job. Besides Hoffman's petulant dialogue, the best lines go to an IMF bureaucrat who may or may not be a mole. Fortunately the story (Ethan's brand-new wife has been kidnapped by the bad guys to help recover a brand-new secret weapon that could destroy the world) barrels along at sufficient speed (the actual theft of the weapon from a glass postmodern office tower even takes place offscreen to keep the plot moving and we've all seen that scene too often anyway, right?), so we don't have time to stop and querulously ask questions such as, hey, you mean there's no reliable cellular reception in downtown Shanghai?

The 1979 version of *When a Stranger Calls* at least had Carol Kane, Charles Durning, Rachel Roberts, and Colleen Dewhurst in the cast. The 2006 remake has Camilla Belle as the babysitter terrified by scary phone calls. It's also got Tommy Flanagan lending his body as the crazed stalker, but it's Lance Henriksen who lends his voice. It's truly a case of an actor phoning in his part. If you got a kick out of the first twenty minutes of *Scream*, then you can skip any version of *Stranger*.

C SPOT RUN—AND SNACK

Sometimes C-movies don't go directly to video. Consider the essentially dreadful, but intermittently amusing, case of Lion's Gate and World Wrestling Entertainment's partnered effort, *See No Evil*, starring pro wrestler Kane (that's Glen Jacobs to us just plain folks) as the eye-gouging bad guy who is unimaginably in need of a good manicure. Those who usually see Kane in heavy paint backing up Undertaker may be astonished to see him here displaying a lot of bare skin, and still looking mighty ugly. Okay, so you've got a coed crew of eight young people from the local county jail who agree to trade three days of community service work for one month off their sentences. Along with a couple of COs, they get packed off to the crumbling old Blackstone Hotel where a nice elderly lady tells them the hotel's to be cleaned up and converted into a homeless shelter. Little do they know . . . Director Gregory Dark isn't big on building up the suspense. It only takes about a minute before annoying minor criminals start getting lunched by a big ugly guy swinging a steel hook on a rusty chain. Turns out that Kane's character collects eyeballs obtained the hard way for reasons that gradually get explained in flashbacks. He's also on something of a spiritual quest. The film looks surprisingly good, doing its best to emulate the yucky indoor grunge of, say, *Saw II*. There's plenty of violence, particularly banging and slamming, hooking and dragging, screaming and pleading. And there are the occasional striking moments: the obnoxious young blonde successfully hides in a hotel room closet until her cell phone goes off and she can't find the mute, an animal rights activist jailed for letting lab animals free ends up dangling like a piñata and getting lunched (literally) by a pack of feral dogs, and there's the Easter egg in which the leader of the hungry dogs lifts his leg on the face of the presumably deceased villain. Michael Myers never had to suffer such indignity. One can imagine wrestling promoter and *See No Evil* executive producer Vince McMahon hosting a private screening of this movie for pro wrestlers. The flow of beer and level of hooting at the end was probably impressive in the extreme. I'm afraid Kane won't get an Oscar nod for this one. But then the movie loses so many of the cast to plot exigencies, the hero (primarily through sheer attrition) turns out to be a thuggish pimp. So I guess there's a moral.

For more of an upscale B-movie feel, one could do worse than watch *Slither*. Writer-director James Gunn knows well the tradition in which he's working. This consciously tacky, occasionally tongue-in-cheek tale of slimy interstellar invasion has its moments. *Firefly* and *Serenity*'s Nathan Fillion plays the local sheriff of a small southern town who's obliged to deal with the unpleasant situation when an obnoxious citizen is attacked and absorbed by a gloppy critter from outer space. Unfortunately there won't be many surprises here for any old-line reader of fifties science fiction. The invader is one of those ambitious protean invaders that intends to eat and incorporate every being on the planet before it burps mightily and heads off through space to another interstellar buffet table. Can the sheriff and his allies stop it, maybe with an enforced South Beach Diet?

As was endlessly trumpeted in journalistic coverage and in a splendid Internet campaign, *Snakes on a Plane* said it all in the title. This is probably the best, most effective title since *Texas Chainsaw Massacre*. In another era, this one could have been titled *Airport 2006*.

Ah, but what about the film itself?

It's an effective B-movie; better than you might think, so long as you put it out of your mind that this one is calculated to be a cult sensation. Just take it for the cheesy amusement it is and shiver deliciously at the use of assorted CGI deadly snakes as a reasonable means for an Asian-American gangster to kill a key witness being escorted by an FBI agent (Samuel L. Jackson) on a sparsely passengered red-eye from Honolulu to Los Angeles. When all serpentine hell breaks loose, he's assisted by plucky flight attendant Julianna Margulies and others. The fun never stops. See horny aspirants to the Seven-Mile-High Club get coitally interrupted by fatal serpents! See an obnoxious tourist discover an all-too-literal trouser snake! See a stuffy dog-hater throw a cute little furball to the python! See the dog-hater himself get swallowed by the python! Don't trouble yourself with the logistics of smuggling a giant constrictor onto an airliner. Come to think of it, don't think too hard about all the snakes being smuggled from California (where the illicit supplier is) to Hawaii. Your brain will hurt if you don't just chill out and pretend this is the in-flight movie you'll never see on a commercial flight. And as a footnote about the relationship between art and life, the end of the year saw a wire service story about a man on a United flight out of Houston who was stung twice by a stowaway scorpion. Can attacks on tourists by digital snakes be far behind?

Fox Atomic is the new studio division taking aim at a demographic you probably don't want to be a part of. Its first release is *Turistas*, something of a lighter spring-break froth drawn from *Hostel* and *Girls Gone Wild*. Imagine a socially conscious Brazilian doctor snatching organs for transplant from pretty young things of both genders. While the movie's a bit lame, the concept is certainly sound . . .

ANIMATION

Ice Age: The Meltdown overcame most of the pitfalls of sequelitis. It's amusing—except when it's not ringing in realistic indications of death, food chain realities, and extinction. Oh, and there's that peculiarly anachronistic Christian fillip there at the end. The effective voices of Denis Leary (Diego the saber-tooth), John Leguizano (Sid the sloth), and Ray Romano (Manny the love-starved mammoth) are joined by Queen Latifah as a hot, reared-by-possums lady mammoth. Then, of course, there's the continuing acorn-obsessive saga of the hyper Scrat. Could this be the perfect kids' movie? You get life lessons with your diverting entertainment. All it needs is Al Gore contributing the voice-over of an omnipotent and omniscient narrator.

Over the Hedge is a clever enough title for this amusing animation about an ecology of feral critters displaced by a huge new suburban development taking over their habitat. Based on the newspaper comic strip by T. Lewis and Michael Fry, this DreamWorks production added a level of trivia to the characters by presenting them with influences from pop culture. RJ the raccoon incorporated bits of Bugs Bunny, Fred Astaire, and Harold Hill (from *The Music Man*); Verne the turtle evokes Jack Lemmon; Sandra Bullock and Jane Russell inform the personality of Stella the skunk.

Cars is a Pixar comedy featuring the eponymous characters that nostalgically evoke the eyeballs-in-the-windshield humanized autos of 1930s cartoons. Superannuated teenage boys (or similarly enthused girls) can identify the bases for characters developed from a 1951 Hudson Hornet, a 2002 Porsche 911, a 1958 Chevy Impala lowrider, and a 1979 Plymouth Superbird.

In *Monster House* three neighborhood kids get to square off with a malign sentient house just down the block. Two boys and a girl—the painless sense of empowerment makes the girl the brains of the outfit. The house of the title is sufficiently an apparent carnivore, it provides a few scary moments.

The computer-generated *Open Season* offers yet another view of a comic outdoors, this time with Martin Lawrence voicing a domestically raised grizzly bear who must take the fish-out-of-water route when he's returned to the forest. Fortunately he receives the advice of Ashton Kutcher tackling the voice of a manic mule deer. Directors Roger Allers and Jill Culton have crafted a simple but pleasant morality tale in which diverse species learn to just get along.

Flushed Away is one terrific underground (literally) fantasy of London. It's also the sad legacy of the ill-fated partnership between DreamWorks and Aardman Animations (the U.K. Claymation masters of Wallace and Gromit). One might be forgiven for suspecting *Flushed Away* would be a compilation of fourth-grade potty humor, but that's not the case. The rat protagonist is a pet rodent (voiced by Hugh Jackman) that manages to get himself flushed down the commode while his human family's on holiday. Our hero finds himself in a subterranean culture ornamented with many droll details. The genuinely wry wit seems far more Aardman than DreamWorks.

THE REAL STUFF

Okay, so Al Gore is *not* the new Rod Serling; but he is pleasingly genial and effective as the narrator of *An Inconvenient Truth,* director Davis Guggenheim's documentary adaptation of the former vice president's book and speeches about global warming and other coming world crises. The knee-jerk naysayers suggest that *An Inconvenient Truth* isn't so much an illuminating documentary about the coming last days of spaceship earth as it is an advance life raft to float a possible 2008 presidential campaign. Some, in fact, view this film as either outright science fiction or as dark fantasy. It's too easy to joke about this production being the result of Al Gore learning about PowerPoint presentations. A more balanced view would suggest that this is sober and provocative of thought if a bit overly careful in its construction.

DVDS

Well worth acquiring is the DVD of Jean-Pierre Jeunet's *Delicatessen* (Miramax), that wackily exuberant 1991 romantic French comedy about postapocalyptic cannibalism. Jeunet followed *Delicatessen* with the equally memorable *City of Lost Children* before following upscale paths to such films as *Amélie* and the fourth *Alien* movie.

Television

Oh, *Hex*! Trust those Brits to breathe life into this series about the contemporary supernatural. It's a coming-of-age saga about a young witch with TK powers. Cassandra—Cassie—(Christine Cole) looks like a younger Peta Wilson and attends a gorgeous old school that looks like Hogwarts without the wizards. Cassie's a tightly wound, lonely young woman whose only friend is her roommate Thelma (Jemima Rooper), a neopunk newly minted, slightly confused lesbian whose moods oscillate seemingly with every change of wind. Unhappy Cassie starts having weird dreams about the weird folk who inhabited the palatial residence three centuries before, recalling flashes of voodoo, slaves, miscegenation, murder, witch hangings, and other mayhem. In the present, she sees visions of an ominously hot gentleman who turns out to be Azazeal (Michael Fassbender), rogue angel and leader of the Nephilim, the fallen angels exiled to the void by God, but who still aspire to stalk the earth and mate with human women.

Indeed, *Hex* matter-of-factly allows the raging hormonal tides of adolescent sexuality and a dollop of eroticism to permeate the plot. Here's a series far edgier than *Charmed*, and similar but perhaps a touch tougher than *Buffy*.

If you like your TV horror with less, um, sensitivity and a bit more testosterone (not to mention more platelets), Spike, the Real Man's Channel, has just the thing. Ripped bleeding copiously from the screaming throat of Marvel Comics, here's *Blade: the Series*. It's a perfect new summer series. Developed and executive-produced by David S. Goyer, the writer of 1998's *Blade*, the first of the Wesley Snipes–starring features, the series has plenty of martial arts fighting and vampire stunting. Rapper Kirk "Sticky" Jones takes over the title role, as the half-vampire, half-human hybrid who controls his bloodlust with an exotic serum and spends his time hunting down and exterminating vamps in Detroit, a seemingly perfect city where large numbers of superhuman monsters could blend in.

As the new Blade, Jones is large and impressively muscled, and can generate a fierce glower. Whether he can equal Wesley Snipes's charisma is still an open issue. His primary local enemies, the powerful vampire House of Cthon, is none-too-subtly headquartered smack in downtown Detroit in a spiffy spotlit Transylvanian castle-influenced skyscraper that looks like it was designed by Michael Graves. There the upscale vampires dress in plenty of leather and, assisted by their ambitious human familiars, busily engage in R&D to stabilize the vampire lifestyle via better living through chemistry.

Open questions for *Blade* include whether the series can come at all close to the striking visuals that lifted the effect of the feature films, and whether the character relationships in the series can jell satisfactorily. Blade's sidekick (Nelson Lee), vampire leader Marcus (Neil Jackson), and the tough ex-vet (Jessica Gower) who is Blade's unpredictable inside woman in the House of Cthon all have promise.

In June, USA Network inaugurated new seasons of *The Dead Zone* and *The 4400*. *The 4400* launched its third season with a two-hour episode that now has the back story, the character relationships, and the general heft to resemble *Battlestar Galactica*. This series is, I think, finally coming into its own. The 4400 abducted (apparently through time, not space) citizens are all back at once and they're all developing wild talents of one sort or another. The U.S. government tried to forestall any threat by giving the 4400 a chemical inhibitor to cancel their paranormal abilities, but that caused no end of bad PR when it turned out to be fatal. Now the 4400s have spread themselves along a political spectrum ranging from being nice and cooperating with the authorities to forming a violent separatist defense league. So are the 4400 *homo superior*? Will they be our partners to help us deal with some upcoming apocalypse? Or will they be our executioners as a species? In any case, the new season for the year brought in a lot more violent chicanery, the prospect of an even more advanced *homo superior*, and new levels of soap-opera plotting.

This fifth season of *The Dead Zone* was announced as the final one. Once again our favorite Stephen King novel–descended psychic Johnny Smith (Anthony Michael Hall) hits the paranormal ground running, tangling with the snakily evil Greg Stillson, corrupt U.S. representative and would-be presidential candidate, just itching to bring about a nuclear apocalypse. As a politico, he's nothing if not ambitious. Last season he killed his father; this year, right off the bat, he again draws on the lethal help of his sinister backer, Mr. X, and stops the heart of his fiancée with deadly snake venom smeared on the post of one of her wedding-present earrings.

ABC's addictive *Lost* cranked through another season, leaving the audience at the end with a few partial answers, but inevitably posing plenty more unanswered questions. Probably the most significant answer was yes, there still is a world outside the mysterious island where our bewildered cast of airline crash survivors are still trying to figure out whether they're marooned in *Survivor, The X Files,* or on *Gilligan's Island.* The weirdest question might well have to do with those pesky Others, the enigmatic, territorial, and homicidal people who live across the island. Just why *do* they dress like hillbillies and put on false beards? Nobody ever does that on *24.*

Medium (NBC) ended its second season in May with a nifty René Echevarria script in which Patricia Arquette's psychic Allison DuBois character is given a chance by her departed grandmother (Ellen Geer) to pursue a different fork in the timestream, an alternate history in which she marries her high school sweetheart and becomes a lawyer. That does not, however, preclude Jake Weber from reappearing as her one true love. As the early dialogue makes abundantly clear, this is an affectionate tip of the topper to *It's a Wonderful Life.* As a product placement bonus, the episode includes music from the Dixie Chicks new album. As it did from the beginning, this series continues to charm with warm, realistic relationships (for once, a TV marriage with kids that actually seems attractive) and just the right intrusion of the paranormal into contemporary reality. Earlier in the season, executive producer Kelsey Grammer did a nice guest-starring role both as the Angel of Death and as a bent insurance agent in an episode called "Death Takes a Policy."

ABC's laudable *Invasion* finished its first season with one of its primary characters accidentally shot and consigned to the risky care of the aliens. Over the hiatus it looked like the rural areas of South Florida would have some real difficulties dealing with the growing number of hybrid humans, alien-impregnated women, crazed normal people going into hyperkinetic survivalist mode, and, of course, the large ensemble cast of two interrelated (by marriage and divorce) families trying to sort things out. But then . . . the dreaded shadow of cancellation descended.

Similarly, the ABC series *Surface,* also about aquatic invaders of earth, sank like a stone after the network pinched off its snorkel.

SciFi added the BBC new incarnation of *Dr. Who* to the powerhouse Friday night lineup. Christopher Eccleston plays the latest avatar of the Doctor with Billie Piper as his sidekick Rose. Even with a higher budget, the present *Dr. Who* does a good job of emulating the tacky feel of the original series' bargain-basement look. Daleks, evil aliens, gene-engineered organisms that rebuild human bodies in order to incorporate grotesque Blitz-era gas masks growing out of their faces, hey, it's all here.

Star Gate SG-1 (SciFi) continued for another season, adding to its attraction by snaffling cast member Ben Browder, formerly the hero of the late but lamented *Farscape.* It will, however, come to a promised mythic climax and ending in the spring of 2007.

SciFi's powerhouse *Battlestar Galactica* added onetime *Xena* heroine Lucy Lawless as a journalist and sneaky Cylon spy for a bunch of episodes as humankind's inimical cyber-enemy occupied the newly discovered habitable planet of New Caprica and set up something a lot like the Vichy Government in World War II France.

Battlestar Galactica will probably never get the increasingly solemn respect given HBO's *The Sopranos,* but the science fiction world will not care. As the episodes roll by, Ron Moore's retooled revival of Glen Larson's old chestnut is a wide-ranging, highly textured, and remarkably nuanced view of a nifty sf universe.

I'd submit that it's a lot like what *Star Trek* should have been, but I'm afraid of the irate villagers circling my home with proton torches and three-tined phasers.

I suspect if you're a fan of professional wrestling, you might have especially enjoyed SciFi's reality series *Who Wants to Be a Superhero?* Comics giant Stan Lee hosted while everyday joes and jills negotiated cockamamie tests in a quest to become recognizable superheroes with their very own comic. The series generated an undeniably tacky charm.

When the WB signed off on Sunday, September 17, it bid farewell by screening the pilots of a quartet of mothballed hits. Along with *Felicity* and *Dawson's Creek*, you could see the pilot of *Angel* and the two-hour pilot for *Buffy the Vampire Slayer*. It was a classy adieu. CW, the brand-new blending of WB and UPN, salvaged *Smallville*, *Supernatural*, and *Veronica Mars* from the wreckage of the two little networks that ultimately couldn't.

IT'S GOOD TO BE THE KING
First there was *Desperation* on ABC. After all, the other networks had to run *something* on April 23 against the *American Idol* final competition, right? Why not director Mick Garris's location-filmed Arizona version of King's novel with Ron Perlman playing the sheriff who would cast a dark shadow even in a Jim Thompson novel.

A midsummer jewel in TNT's programming crown was *Nightmares & Dreamscapes*, eight adaptations of Stephen King short stories drawn from the eponymous story collection. The programs were presented as halves of a two-hour double feature each Wednesday night for four weeks. With first-rate casts and excellent production values, this was a textbook example of the problems of adapting evocative printed-page prose to affecting visual image.

The series led with a Richard Christian Matheson script adapting the "biter bitten" story "Battleground." William Hurt plays an upscale hit man who assassinates a toy company founder only to arrive back at his high-rise San Francisco sanctuary barely ahead of an unsolicited express package from the toy company he just visited. Inside he discovers a set of toy soldiers along with a pair of toy Jeeps, a howitzer, and three miniature Blackhawk helicopters. What follows is a duel between the killer and an animated miniature combat unit. The effects were particularly intriguing since the tiny soldiers looked exactly like the little vinyl guys most of us boys (and admittedly a few girls) used to play with. Script writer Matheson also did a good job of tackling a script completely without dialogue other than a few assorted grunts, pained vocal winces, and cries of testosterone-fueled anger. "Battleground" is not a particularly ambitious story, but this was an entertaining and effective version.

"Crouch End" is a Lovecraftian fantasy about a young American married couple who find themselves stranded in the sinister London neighborhood of the title, a place where reality can wear thin and one sometimes crosses into another plane. Claire Forlani plays the slightly savvier bride who tries her best to cope with potentially fatal strangeness.

TV MOVIES
Competing directly with ABC's *Desperation* was the second half of the NBC disaster sequel, *10.5 Apocalypse*, in which massive earthquakes continue to rock the U.S., and a massive fault line starts running down through the plains states, homing in on a couple of really big nuclear plants near Houston. Beau Bridges is around to lead the country, Kim Delaney's an ace seismologist, and so's her daddy, Frank Langella,

who's stuck in a collapsing Las Vegas hotel, trying to rescue the last surviving show-girls in Sin City. The matte landscape effects are lackluster. Don't bother asking about the writing. The finale is geographically stunning, though. Our president voices platitudes about a divided country still being united, once the Gulf waters drain into the collapsed fault line running down the center of the nation. Apparently no one connected with this disaster studied the Mississippi River in grade school.

SciFi Channel's Saturday night movies were pretty much as cheesy as we viewers have come to expect. But a good example of fragrantly *distinctive* cheese product came from *A.I. Assault*, a melodrama about military technology run amuck. It was a trivia fan's golden opportunity with all manner of *Star Trek* actors and other fellow travelers (George Takei, Robert Picardo, Michael Dorn, Alexandra Paul, Bill Mumy, etc.) providing target practice for a pair of composite alloy brain-boxes on four flexible legs ignoring their sloppy prototype programming (no budget at the Pentagon for Asimovian Laws of Robotics here). Though these contraptions have their clever moments, they also must have learned their marksmanship at the Empire Storm Trooper shooting range, which is often lucky for the hopelessly out-gunned human soldiers. The script by Bill Monroe and director Jay Andrews (Jim Wynorski) provides an odd flash of déjà vu since at least part of it was also used to lay in a plot line for another SciFi feature (I think it was one of the plethora of films about genetically engineered dinosaurs scampering around an isolated Pacific is-land). This may be a popcorn movie, but the popcorn's gone stale.

Or you could catch *Mammoth*. Here's what I think I remember of the plot: a me-teor crashes in rural Louisiana, only it's not so much a meteor (now meteorite) as it is an alien ship. The sole crewmonster has the ability to absorb and *become* the first creature it encounters. Naturally, then, it finds a museum exhibit and becomes a mammoth. Not just *any* mammoth, mind you, but a savage behemoth that's quiet enough to sneak up behind you without the clump of giant feet alerting you. The cast offered some hope: Tom Skerritt as the Local Eccentric Dad and Concerned Citizen; *Firefly*'s Summer Glau as the Girl; Vincent Ventresca as the Young Guy. They all looked uncomfortable. Even the alien reanimated mammoth didn't look totally at home.

SELLING THE IMAGINATION
Ever since Stanley Kubrick's *2001: A Space Odyssey* gave other filmmakers a whole pre-ILM battery of visual tools, some of the most eager grafters of sf/fantasy/horror ef-fects have been the highly motivated denizens of Madison Avenue. By now, nobody blinks twice at half- and full-minute imaginative epics that amuse, provoke, or out-rage the audience. Who can forget last year's Quiznos commercial that featured a feral young yuppy businessman nursing at the teats of a she-wolf? And for a couple of years now, is there any standard horror film that can creep the audience out more effectively than the "Wake up with the king" campaign from Burger King?

THE COMMERCIAL THAT MOST RESEMBLES FRANK ROBINSON'S CLASSIC NOVEL *THE POWER*
Amp'd Mobile's funny but horrifying TV spot themed around "Entertain yourself." A serious, presumably sociopathic young woman says to an elderly man, "Tackle that cake." So he throws himself violently onto a cake, collapsing the whole table in a welter of splinters and frosting. To a young woman: "Bob for fish." The victim does so, doing her enthusiastic best to drown herself in an aquarium. "Ride the pony." Two women spoon into a horsie configuration, one whinnying, the other slapping

the first one's rump as she yanks her mount's hair like reins. "Play with your face!" And a young woman slams her face repeatedly against her piano keyboard. All in all, it's startlingly brutal, amply carrying out the old ad dictum that love it or loathe it, the message should be memorable.

THE MARKETING THAT TIME FORGOT

FedEx manages to compress a funny and affectionate mini-movie of prehistoric life into thirty seconds. First you see a caveman attach a small package to one leg of a pterodactyl. The shipment launches, but is snapped out of the air by a ravenous carnosaur. The cave-boss berates and then fires the cave-staffer for not using FedEx, despite protestations that FedEx hasn't been invented yet. The spot ends with a rip of *Bambi Meets Godzilla*. The wit and the effects carry the message with panache.

MUSIC

Plumb's "Cut" from her third album, *Chaotic Resolve* (Curb). In each album the singer attempts to include at least one new song that very specifically addresses a difficult social problem. This time around, the lyrics candidly and intimately grapple with self-mutilation. Plumb's artfulness here is more gut-wrenching, definitely more affecting than the average horror film.

BOY TOYS, THOUGH GIRLS LIKE 'EM TOO

What, you no longer can afford regular dry-cleaning bills for your life-size soft sculptures of Jack Skellington and Sally? If you don't have room for humongous models of sf movie and television hardware, check out the Titanium Series machine miniatures from Hasbro/Micro Machines/Galoob. Die-cast metal; you can't go wrong, though Hasbro tries to tempt you to spend extra cash by issuing duplicates of some of the craft (the Death Star, Boba Fett's Slave I, the AT-AR walker, for instance) in beautiful but nonrealistic chrome finish. Along with a few dozen *Star Wars* gadgets and warcraft, 2006 introduced some *Battlestar Galactica* ships including a Colonial Viper, Cylon Raider, and the *Galactica* herself (with opening hangar bays), all at about five bucks a pop. Note, though, that while there are still plenty of obscure pieces of *Star Wars* hardware that could be added to the line, the company has started padding things for completists by issuing some of the same vehicles with different paint jobs, and slightly varying the landspeeder so that it carries, variously, Luke, Leia, and an Empire stormtrooper.

A REMINDER OF WHAT NOT TO MISS FROM 2006

Apocalypto (Touchstone)
Battlestar Galactica (SciFi Channel)
Blade (Spike TV)
Children of Men (Universal)
The Descent (Lion's Gate)
Desperation (ABC)
Dexter (Showtime)
District B13 (Magnolia Pictures)
Flushed Away (DreamWorks)
Hex (BBC America)
Heroes (NBC)
Hostel (Lions Gate)

The Illusionist (Yari Releasing)
Masters of Horror (Showtime)
Medium (NBC)
Nightmares & Dreamscapes (TNT)
Night Watch (Fox Searchlight)
Pan's Labyrinth (Picturehouse)
A Prairie Home Companion (Picturehouse)
The Prestige (Touchstone)
The Proposition (First Look Pictures)
Stranger Than Fiction (Columbia Pictures)
Tideland (ThinkFilms)
Veronica Mars (CW)
V for Vendetta (Warner Bros.)

WRAP

In 2007 you can look forward to a vast melange of sequels and spinoffs, ranging from *The Hills Have Eyes 2* to *Spider-Man 3*. The big news, though (in all senses), is the report that Stephen King fan J. J. Abrams (creator of *Lost* and director of the last *Mission: Impossible* feature) has convinced the author to let him tackle a franchise series of features translating King's seven-volume magnum opus, *The Dark Tower*. It could give us all something to look forward to for the next eighteen years or so.

Fantasy in Comics and Graphic Novels: 2006

Jeff VanderMeer

Many comics fans greeted the news that *American Born Chinese* by Gene Luen Yang (First Second Books) had been made a National Book Award finalist (Young People's Literature category) with a great deal of happiness and satisfaction. Certainly, it has to be considered one of the major news developments of the year in comics—and there is no doubt that Yang's work was worthy of the honor. *American Born Chinese* includes an interpretation of the classic Monkey King Chinese fable interwoven with two other contemporary story lines. Dynamic, direct, and complex, *American Born Chinese* shows how fantasy and reality can intersect, comment on one another, and complement each other. At the same time, this was not the best fantasy graphic novel of the year, and would not be emphasized in this summation if not for being a National Book Award finalist.

Several opportunities were lost following the announcement of the National Book Award finalists. I was disappointed that it did not spark a deeper debate over the value of categories or the artistic value of comics in general. No one seemed interested in asking whether Yang's work was singled out as the result of a systematic review of graphic novels—or whether it was unfair that no graphic novels were considered in the adult novel category. And, in terms of genre, hardly anyone really thought of *American Born Chinese* as fantasy, either.

In fact, just as Neil Gaiman's comics nomination for a World Fantasy Award several years ago meant very little, Yang's accomplishment meant very little for the world of comics in general. An arbitrary, ad hoc event, it only underscored the need for a National Book Award category for comics and graphic novels, in both young adult and adult categories. It also generated more publicity for that one particular graphic novel.

More and more, I believe the comics field shares much in common with the fields of science fiction, fantasy, and horror, in that there is a sense of illegitimacy, a sense (even now) of being part of a ghetto or a closed system that only rarely and in random ways receives accolades from the rest of the creative world. The occasional nod in no way indicates a shift in attitude, especially when you consider the National Book

Award is a juried award. This is why *category* and *process* must be revised to be inclusive of an art form that has clearly achieved a maturity and a diversity that should be recognized on a more formal and regular basis.

Process-wise, a much more important event occurred in the comics field, although many industry experts may not have recognized it as such. The addition of *The Best American Comics* to Houghton Mifflin's stable of best-of anthologies in 2006 signaled an important paradigm shift in considering the worth of this art form. Even better, guest editor Harvey Pekar and series editor Anne Elizabeth Moore collected such wonderful fantasists as Kim Deitch and Lynda Barry with no distinction between this work and the more realistic fare.

The Best American Comics also included the work of Rebecca Dart, my favorite personal discovery in 2006. Her wonderfully odd, formally experimental, and yet very satisfying *RabbitHead* may be the most innovative comic of the past few years. This mind-blowing sequence of fantastical adventures begins as one narrative thread and branches out into seven threads before collapsing back in on itself. *RabbitHead* demonstrates a twinned playfulness and seriousness that hooks into your thoughts for days after reading it.

Another highlight, Lynda Barry's comic "The Two Questions" is about what it means to be a creative person, using fantasy as the springboard. The style is deceptively simple and yet each frame is so alive with image and motion that you can study a panel for a long time and not exhaust its richness. The honesty of the questions posed by the narrative captures the reader, while grace notes like a recurring octopus delight for their own sake.

Almost as important as the publication of *The Best American Comics* was the publication of *An Anthology of Graphic Fiction, Cartoons, & True Stories* (Yale University Press), Ivan Brunetti's rambunctious, disorganized, but triumphant overview of the North American comics scene of the past several years, which includes several fantastical offerings. Some of my favorite comics of all time are in this anthology, notably R. Sikoryak's "Good Ol' Gregor Brown" and work from the amazing Jim Woodring, Lynda Barry, Richard Sala, Tony Millionaire, and Bill Griffith, among dozens of others. The best work I hadn't encountered before was the creepy and insanely stippled "Agony" by Mark Beyer, which in part riffs off of the style of Munch's "The Scream." Ignore the nonfiction, which is mediocre, but do buy this for some rich fantastical content.

The publication of both of these books showed that the processes and categorizations that help codify an art form have begun to occur within the comics/graphic novel field.

In applauding two books that place fantastical material in the wider context of comics and graphic novels generally, I do not want to ignore what has become the de facto fantasy sampler of the year, the *Flight* series from Ballantine Books. *Flight: Volume 3* features superlative work from Tony Cliff, Ben Hatke, Kean Soo, Bill Plympton, Michael Gagne, Johane Matte, Israel Sanchez, and several others. Many of the contributors are younger artists or come from Web comics. Some work is serious, some lighthearted, but it is all energetic and intelligent. The *Flight* series not only revitalizes the fantasy genre every year, it is also a good place to find the work of the young turks.

One major footnote to the year in comics: the business relationship between Humanoids Publishing and DC Comics came to an end. Among other things, this unfortunate situation may have deprived us of immediate English translations in 2006 of the latest from genius Enki Bilal, as well as English-language installments of South American visionary Alexandro Jodorowsky's various series.

The Publishing Event of the Year?

It's hard not to fashion my discussion of the year in graphic novels around the release of Alan Moore and Melinda Gebbie's *Lost Girls* (Top Shelf Productions). For me, Alan Moore's *The Watchmen, V for Vendetta,* and *From Hell* form a visceral trilogy of masterpieces created with an uncompromising intelligence and vision. If *Lost Girls* doesn't quite reach that level, it might be because the experiment is so complex and audacious that the goal was impossible.

Moore attempts to create a pornographic cornucopia both salacious and moral, inquisitive yet responsible, using a simple plot: three women staying at a hotel in Austria on the eve of World War I become friends and then lovers. They share the secrets of their dark sexual histories against a backdrop of repression and liberation. Almost every possible form of sexuality is explored, all in the colored pencil textures and pastel hues of Gebbie's artwork. The women are meant to be (the real-life?) Wendy, Dorothy, and Alice from *Peter Pan, The Wizard of Oz,* and *Alice in Wonderland,* respectively. The bizarre coincidence that brought these three women to this particular hotel at the same time is left to the imagination. (In general, Moore's genius in *Lost Girls* is better expressed through the complex erotic set-pieces than through the main narrative.)

Oddly enough, in one sense all three women have been stripped of their fantastical context. There's a suggestion that Alice's mirror talks to her (or she talks to it) and that Lewis Carroll, making an appearance as a pedophile, is inspired by Alice to write his books. But in general Moore presents the pasts of the three women as realistic explanations for the fantasy elements in those works. For example, Dorothy lives through a twister during which she experiences a sexual awakening. When she walks out into the ruined landscape, a damaged road sign now reads "OZ," but she's still in Kansas. Peter Pan is just an androgynous male prostitute and there is no Never-Never Land other than the mental one in which Peter leads Wendy and her brothers into a sexual initiation. I often wondered while reading *Lost Girls* if Moore had so unhinged some characters from their fictional origins that they could no longer function as those characters in any meaningful way. I don't think this is a niggling point, but it will not be an issue for many readers.

As for Gebbie's art, it is supple and ever-changing, whether in the main sequences or where parodying Victorian-era pornography. The softness of the colors makes the sex scenes more human and less mechanistic or harsh. The level of detail in backdrops is precise but not cluttered, with Gebbie able to modulate her effects to convey scenes of unease and horror. Her drawing technique proves better than I would have thought for conveying motion, so that her rendition of a surreal orgy scene during a showing of *The Rites of Spring* might as well *be* in motion.

Lost Girls is a flawed but fascinating phantasmagorical vehicle for sex and ideas about sex that overflows with intelligence and feeling. It uses the farthest reaches of the imagination and the liberating aspect of fantasy as fuel for its narrative. Ultimately, *Lost Girls* rewards a serious (and not so serious) read, but I'm conflicted as to whether or not it belongs beside Moore's best work. Despite my caveats, it still stands as perhaps the most audacious publishing event of 2006.

Other Major Releases

Although everyone's idea of what constitutes a major publishing event will be different, I found six books that, in very different ways, define the contribution of fantasy to the comics field in 2006.

Dungeon, an intricate and stunning fantasy series from Lewis Trondheim and Joann Sfar, continues with a two-part adventure: *Twilight: Dragon Cemetery* and *Twilight: Armageddon* (Nantier Beall Minoustchine Publishing). A lizardlike dust king and his rabbit knight sidekick go forth and encounter monsters, invisible creatures, lost civilizations, and even a protective mother. The books parody heroic fantasy in hilarious fashion while also offering exciting battle scenes, deep and interesting characters, and a complex plot. One scene in particular will make your jaw drop in appreciation of the amazing imagination at play here.

Proving that fantasy doesn't need to be dark to be interesting and important, *Castle Waiting* by Linda Medley (Fantagraphics Books) collects a decade of stories in a sumptuous book replete with marvelous grace notes. Working in retold fairy tale mode, Medley generally focuses on the dynamic between various female characters. The tension and story lines are, unlike most graphic novels, not dependent on unpleasant events or intense action. The style of art takes its cue from late nineteenth-century book illustrators, being less grotesque and more realistic. Iconic imagery adds another level, while several old favorites, such as Rumpelstiltskin, put in an appearance. It's nice to see someone renovating a played-out genre in an original and thoughtful way. Also, as Jane Yolen writes in her excellent introduction, Medley has created an entire self-contained world with this graphic novel.

In a totally different sense, Kim Deitch delights with the deluxe reprint of *Shadowland* (Fantagraphics). The setup sounds like science fiction: aliens crash-landed on Earth a hundred years ago and were found by a boy named Al Ledicker. However, I find it hard to believe anyone could think of this insane medley of circus performers, odd pygmies, flying pigs, and bizarre secrets as anything other than fantasy. Full of sex and violence, rendered in a busy, detailed drawing style, *Shadowland* uses the Ledicker Circus as its major setting while focusing on the early Hollywood star Molly O'Dare and the Grafton Curse. In *Shadowland*, Dietch has rewarded readers by indulging in an adult, sophisticated form of play.

Fables: 1001 Nights of Snowfall (Vertigo), written by Bill Willington with illustrations by, among others, Charles Vess, Brian Bolland, John Bolton, Mark Buckingham, Jill Thompson, Michael Wm. Kaluta, and James Jean, embodies the word "sumptuous." Kaluta and Vess's framing art for "A Most Troublesome Woman" seems both "Sinbad Art Deco" and tongue-in-cheek modern. Conversely, stories like "The Fencing Lesson" update and recombine folktales in interesting and adult ways while using an appropriately photo-realistic approach. The variety of styles and narrative approaches creates a real diversity within the limited fairy tale context. For those who haven't yet read the Fables series, this is an excellent introduction.

Pride of Baghdad by Brian K. Vaughn, with art by Niko Henrichon (Vertigo), has received much positive press for its overtly political story. Based on true events, this graphic novel tells the story of three lions that escaped from the Baghdad Zoo during the initial American occupation of the city in 2002. Vaughn creates vivid action throughout, and the story can at times be poignant. However, the fantasy element—anthropomorphized lions—results in some unintentionally Lion King moments and lends unnecessary melodrama to an already dramatic narrative. In a sense, this is the one fantasy graphic novel published in 2006 that I feel would have been much better without the fantasy element. Still, I include it here for the basic power of the situation and the dynamic artwork.

Finally, *The Ticking* by Renée French (Top Shelf Productions) might be the strangest and yet most compelling fantasy-gothic graphic novel of the year. The story of the deformed Edison Steelhead is told using French's typical shaded/pencil style. Steelhead's strange life is filled at times with despair, sometimes with unexpected beauty. We might as well be looking at our own lives if we were placed in Steelhead's situation. (In a sense, French's tale is the anti-romantic, anti-*Edward Scissorhands*.) Horrific and fantastical in a quiet way, French charts the moments of Steelhead's life with understated emotion. It should be noted that this might be one of French's least disturbing, least confrontational works.

Other Worthy Comics

At first *A.L.I.E.E.E.N.* by Lewis Trondheim (First Second) seems like a cuter version of Jim Woodring's *Frank*, but it soon turns bloody and the cuteness provides a startling counterpoint to the violence. A good parallel would be Vladimir Nabokov's use of vacation guide language to describe a death camp in his novel *Bend Sinister*. Ultimately, though, *A.L.I.E.E.E.N.* conveys a sense of innocent optimism even as, wordlessly, little round bird creatures are being nailed to trees and fuzzy bear creatures brain sad frog creatures with clubs, and yet other strange cuties don the skins of fallen friends to avoid capture and certain death. Each vignette in the book ties in to the next, even though this is not immediately obvious, as an added bonus. *A.L.I.E.E.E.N.* is by turns fun, creepy, and horrific, with a wonderfully clockwork structure.

Billy Hazelnuts by Tony Millionaire (Fantagraphics) reaffirms the mad genius of this prolific creator. Millionaire is a master of the grotesque, usually grafted onto an odd sense of love or empathy. This book is another surreal, absurdist adventure, almost like Sendak on drugs. Hazelnuts, created by rats and at first given dead flies for eyes, goes on a quest to find the missing moon. Along the way, Our Hero battles a steam-driven reptile and much else besides.

The first Hellboy collection since the 2004 movie, *Hellboy: Strange Places* (volume 7) by Mike Mignola (Dark Horse), contains two long, odd tales: "The Third Wish" and "The Island." Both are at first glance more stark than Mignola's usual. At the same time, elements like the giant talking fish in "The Third Wish," no matter how grotesque, are delightful and fun. "The Island" is perhaps the most complex story Mignola has attempted, mixing a secret history of the world with dragons, Crusaders, Lovecraftian flourishes, and, somewhere I'm sure, a kitchen sink. The story is overstuffed, but it is also lively and original. In pushing the boundaries and going for even more esoteric material, Mignola has created something that rewards repeated reading.

B.P.R.D.: The Black Flame by Mike Mignola and John Arcudi, art by Guy Davis (Dark Horse), is the fifth volume of these volumes spun-off from Mignola's *Hellboy*. The Bureau for Paranormal Research and Defense (B.P.R.D.) is made up of some normal people (who usually die, like *Star Trek* extras) and various other odd characters: a firestarter, the spirit of a dead medium in a containment suit, a homunculus, and an amphibian man. In this installment, the B.P.R.D. wages an escalating war against North American toadmen in a series of adventures simultaneously dark and humorous, a Mignola trademark. These spin-offs are almost as interesting as the

Hellboy comics that spawned them. However, *Hellboy: Strange Places* still wins pride of place for creativity and ambition. Toadmen just can't hold a candle to Hellboy's problems, I'm afraid.

The Left Bank Gang by Jason (Fantagraphics) features Ernest Hemingway, F. Scott Fitzgerald, Ezra Pound, and James Joyce as down-and-out cartoonists in animal form. Droll and understated, the book follows their desperate lives in 1920s Paris. Then one day Hemingway suggests pulling a bank heist and everything goes horribly wrong.

The Last Christmas (Image Comics) by Brian Posehn and Gerry Duggan, with art by Rick Remender, might fall into the category of a guilty pleasure. In a postapocalyptic setting, Santa decides the heck with Christmas, then has to get his mojo back. The cruelty and danger of the setting is more than half the fun, sharply rendered by Remender.

Iron West by Doug TenNapel (Image Comics) features dinosaurs, little dialogue, and tons of Wild West adventure, using a bold, dynamic style that carries the reader past any story weaknesses. TenNapel presents the reader with good old-fashioned fun with robots and Sasquatch.

The *Mouse Guard* volumes by David Petersen (Archaia Studio Press) chronicle the adventures and intrigues of twelfth-century mice that act very much like twelfth-century humans. The Mouse Guard of the title serves to protect mice from all kinds of threats. My rule on stories like this is: "Would it be interesting if it were happening to human beings?" Generally, *The Mouse Guard* passes this test.

Polly and the Pirates by Ted Naifeh (Oni Press) is a good-natured adventure featuring one Polly Pringle, who is thankful to be kidnapped by pirates, thus rescuing her from a horrible finishing school. The pirates quickly inform her that her dead mother used to be their leader and that Polly must now take her place. The usual pirate battles and encounters with behemoths of the deep occur, but the story is witty, crisply told, and exciting.

Chickenhare: The House of Klaus by Chris Grine (Dark Horse) has a winter setting, a mad taxidermist, and, of course, Chickenhare and Abe, a companion turtle. To avoid being sold into slavery, they must undertake a long journey that might end in death. Advertised as for "all ages," this graphic novel is indeed for children of a *certain* age, but it's still pretty scary and more likely to be enjoyed by adults, who will enjoy its ghoulish sense of humor.

Enigmatic and original, *Leviathan* by Ian Edginton and D'Israeli (2000 AD) revolves around the mysterious disappearance of a cruise liner carrying more than thirty thousand people. Two decades later, a detective begins to investigate the disappearance. This is a first-rate British graphic novel, well worth seeking out.

Elmer by Gerry Alanguilan (Komikero Publishing/Alamat Comics) has not yet been published in graphic novel form, but is worth mentioning because of the audacious and interesting premise. On an alternative earth, chickens have become as intelligent as humans. Naturally, human beings don't necessarily agree and the comic follows a family of chickens who have to fight for survival. This commentary on equality and discrimination sounds, in summary, ridiculous, but it was clearly one of the more provocative comics of the year.

In addition to the previously mentioned *American Born Chinese*, First Second put out several other graphic novels that one would have to classify as directed at children and young adults primarily, but that also appeal to adults. Several of the best were by Joann Sfar in translations from the French.

Sardine in Outer Space, Vols. 1 and 2, by Emmanuel Guibert and Joann Sfar

(First Second) are unabashed space pirate adventures with lots of humorous touches, all in glorious, eye-popping color. Featuring characters like Doc Hrok, Captain Yellow Shoulder, and, of course, Sardine, these good-natured stories are throwbacks to a more innocent time and function as a kind of homage to old-time space pulp.

Vampire Loves by Joann Sfar (First Second) features lovely illustrations that mix a more fluid Edward Gorey with a more friendly Edvard Munch. Ferdinand is a vampire who bites with only one tooth so he can pass himself off as a mosquito. As one might imagine, he has a lot of trouble with the ladies. In this volume, he has adventures with other vampires, ghosts, a golem, and some tree folk. It's all creepy fun and wonderful to read.

The Lost Colony by Grady Klein (First Second) provides a unique look at nineteenth-century America through the closed system of a mysterious island colony. Featuring Native Americans, immigrants, and even a strange steam-pipey robot, this informal, lively story, the art heavily stylized as counterpoint, serves as a civics lesson and unique narrative at the same time.

Finally, I must mention *Jokes and the Unconscious* by Daphne Gottlieb and Diane DiMassa (Cleis Press), a compelling exploration of grief and melancholy. A teenager named Sasha takes a job at the hospital where her recently deceased father worked as a doctor. In a series of slapstick, darkly funny, disturbing, and often horrifying vignettes, Gottlieb and DiMassa show Sasha dealing with all types of patients and situations. The creators of this tough yet sometimes touching story don't shy away from the gritty details, and the drawing style ranges from deliberately primitive to detailed and precise. Although this collection exists on the edge of fantasy and horror, its surreal structure and hallucinogenic qualities make it of interest to genre readers.

Notable Reprints

Keeping abreast of original comics and graphic novels, let alone reprints, is a daunting job. So this is an admittedly selective and subjective list, focusing on some of my main joys of the year . . .

Moomin: The Complete Tove Jansson Comic Strip (volume 1) from Drawn & Quarterly finally collects the Moomin comics for U.S. readers. For those unfamiliar with Tove Jansson's classic creation, Moomin is a hippopotamus-looking creature who, along with cohorts like giant rats, white finger-looking creatures, and others, has strange and wonderful adventures. Moomin and the other creatures Jansson drew are rendered in an appropriately simple style, while the backgrounds are often nuanced and complex.

First run in the 1950s in the *London Evening News* and syndicated around the world, *Moomin* has a timeless quality. The fantasy element and the emphasis on universal themes like love and friendship—combined with eccentric quests (sometimes including slapstick sequences)—allow modern readers to appreciate these classics all over again. A typical story line might include Moomin having to house unexpected relatives and thus seek out extra money to cover the expense, leading to a series of misadventures from which he emerges unscathed but none the richer.

In less skillful hands, this would be fodder for sticking one's finger down one's throat in revulsion at the treacly whimsy of it all. However, Jansson was a pragmatist and also, if her work is any indication, a wise person. Beneath the gentle surface of

Moomin there is a sly, wicked wit and much nondidactic commentary about the world and people's place in it. Something must also be said about the effortlessness of these comic strips. There isn't a word or image out of place. I cannot think of another comic strip that gives me as much pleasure as this one. There is also something uniquely calming and stress-relieving about reading *Moomin*.

Similarly, it's difficult to be stingy or coldhearted in approaching something like *Big Fat Little Lit*, edited by Art Spiegelman and Françoise Mouly (Penguin Books). The energy involved in this glorious full-color collection acts as something of a caffeine boost while reading it. Reprinting the best of the Little Lit series from *The New York Times*, this explosion of riotous talent includes work by Charles Burns, Neil Gaiman, Kim Deitch, Kaz, David Sedaris, Lemony Snicket, and many others.

Although some of the contents seem as diaphanous as cotton candy and just as filling, even the more ordinary material operates at an uncommon level of sheer glee and manic energy. Think pratfalls, comedy, and bright, vibrant colors. It might get wearing if you read it straight through, but dip in from time to time and you'll be fine.

My favorites included Kaz's "It Was a Dark and Silly Night" and the insane "The Hungry Horse," with its cyclical story line, Art Spiegelman's "Prince Rooster," William Joyce's lovely illustrations for "Humpty Trouble," and a Neil Gaiman/Gahan Wilson collaboration featuring Wilson's frightening/comforting monsters.

Tony Millionaire, one of my favorite creators ever, came out with *Premillennial Maakies* (Fantagraphics), collecting the first five years of the classic cult comic strip. This book reformats the comics into a wonderful wide hardcover to accommodate Maakies madness. For those not familiar with Maakies, it relates the insane adventures of an alcoholic crow in nearly piratical sea adventures. There's more commentary on the absurdity of human nature in one of these strips than in all of reality television.

Dark Horse reissued Paul Chadwick's *Concrete*, featuring a superhero who is basically a walking, talking rock. This series of graphic novels often explores moral or social issues in a fantasy context. Harlan Ellison once called *Concrete* "the best comic being published by anyone, anywhere."

Little Nemo 1905–1914 by Winsor McCay (Taschen Books) gives this classic strip the VIP Taschen treatment. Slumberland has never been as vibrant or respected as in this glorious volume.

A trade paperback reprint of Charles Vess's *The Book of Ballads* (Tor Books) showcases one of this genius-level artist's virtuoso performances. Collaborating with numerous writers, classic ballads are recast and then embellished and enhanced with Vess's work. At times clever and sly, at times earnest and passionate, Vess's illustration style proves fluid, versatile, and deep. This version includes additional ballads.

Finally, I doubt anyone but the most secluded human beings on Earth haven't heard about the Vertigo reissues of Neil Gaiman's Sandman comics, starting with *Absolute Sandman*, Volume 1 (Vertigo), clearly a major publishing event. A potent mix of myth, fantasy, reality, and history, the Sandman series redefined what comics were capable of, in much the same way as the work of Alan Moore. Recolored and more or less "remastered," these new volumes will stand as the ultimate Sandman versions.

Related Materials

A few worthy books from 2006 don't fit into an easy mold, but are definitely worthy of mention.

Rumo by Walter Moers (Overlook Press) isn't really a comic or graphic novel, but this rollicking adventure—half Douglas Adams, half somebody much more surreal and dark—would be much diminished if Moers's darkly whimsical illustrations had been left out. Rumo the Wolperting travels his way through a strange world populated by shark grubs, debonair dinosaurs, robot armies, and scientists with four brains. The opening sequences are as horrific as anything from Stephen King while later scenes will make readers laugh out loud. All of this insanity is anchored by the lovely detail of Moers's many drawings.

The magic of *The Magic Bottle*, written and illustrated by Camille Rose Garcia, (Fantagraphics) comes from the Disney-from-Hell style of the full-color paintings. Sinister and possessing an unexpected depth, the unsettling visuals tend to overwhelm the prose, but who cares? In an alternate universe inhabited by squid and Betty Boop impersonators, Camille Rose Garcia is Queen. This is a lovely, deranged coffee-table book for comics connoisseurs.

Finally, the respected literary magazine *Tin House* (POB 10500, Portland, OR 97296-0500) put out a special Graphic Issue (Issue 29) featuring contributions from Michael Chabon, Dan Chaon, Jonathan Lethem, Zak Smith, Anne Elizabeth Moore, Marjane Satrapi, and Lynda Barry. The issue contains more than eighty images, many of them fantastical, fascinating interviews, comic strips, and essays. The full-color primitive-surreal art of Lynda Barry is particularly wonderful.

Thanks for information, opinions, and advice during the creation of this year's summation to: Jim Frenkel; Andrew Wheeler and his blog The Antick Musings of G.B.H. Hornswoggler; Joe Gordon and his Forbidden Planet blog; and especially the generous Charles Vess, who wrote this summation for many years.

Music of the Fantastic: 2006

Charles de Lint

My album of the year (and I judge that by how I still play it on a weekly basis, months after its initial release) is *The Sky Didn't Fall* (Park), a collaboration between Northumbrian piper and fiddler Kathryn Tickell and harpist Corrina Hewat. The blend of instruments and voices from the Northumbrian and Scottish traditions is sublime, but what really raises the bar for me is "Favourite Place," a collection of reminiscences by Tickell's mother that Tickell narrates over a bed of music.

Often such spoken pieces, while captivating on an initial listen, are what one skips in subsequent listenings as their novelty wears off. But there's something in the combination of spoken voice and music here that has me simply stop whatever I'm doing and pay attention each time the track comes on.

Hewat joined Tickell on a second release this year, *Strange But True* (Park), but here she's only one of many collaborators that include Andy Sheppard on saxophone, Catriona MacDonald on fiddle, and others on various instruments. It's an adventurous album, and fascinating, but while I like all the tracks individually, the disc as a whole doesn't have the flow I normally associate with a Kathryn Tickell album—no real problem in these times, I suppose, with the proliferation of iPods and their shuffle play setting.

I was a little surprised when I considered the other most played discs in my house this year, mostly because my tastes don't always run along the same lines as what the music-buying public as a whole has embraced. Because these discs all had a high profile, I'll be brief in describing them.

The Internet, fueling the interest and success of subsequently released debut albums, made stars of two new artists.

Lily Allen was a MySpace darling, blogging heavily and releasing refreshing mix tapes of her own material blended with songs from those who've influenced her. By the time *Alright, Still* (Regal) came out (with its sweet pop voice and tart, barbed lyrics sung over an infectious bed of ska, hip-hop, and reggae influenced beats), her fans supported her in droves. It was certainly my album of the summer.

Arctic Monkeys took a different route, uploading tracks on the Web with no disc to back them up. But it did mean that from their earliest gigs, the audience was already singing along to Alex Turner's inspired stories of growing up in the Sheffield suburbs. The album, *Whatever People Say That I Am, That's What I'm Not* (Domino), delivered on the promise of their live shows with edgy tunes that ignore the usual pop conventions of verse-chorus-verse, but are eminently hook-laden.

I don't know what happened with Bob Dylan in the past couple of years, but between his vastly entertaining radio show (*Theme Time Radio Hour* on XFM), his interview segments in the Scorsese film (*No Direction Home*, Paramount), numerous books, and a new album (*Modern Times*, Sony), he seems to have reinvented himself once again as an approachable, open artist. Or like the cool uncle who's always pulling out some great old song to play for you. It's true that *Modern Times* owes a heavy debt to the blues and folk music of the thirties and forties, but that doesn't mean it's not a great listen.

And speaking of old uncles, if Dylan's turned into the friendly one, Tom Waits remains the slightly cranky relative who lives out by the railroad tracks, capable of great tenderness, sardonic humor, and more than a touch of the edgy and weird. His latest three-CD set (*Orphans*, Anti-) is an absolute stunner and its "Long Way Home" is my favorite song of the year. I think Norah Jones agrees, since she's been covering it regularly in concert as she tours her own new disc.

Celtic/British Folk

A number of the big guns in Celtic music all had new releases this year.

Lúnasa proved with *Sé* (Compass) that they haven't lost their touch as one of the best and most invigorating interpreters of traditional music, while onetime alumnus Michael McGoldrick continues to break new ground for the Irish flute with his *Wired* (Vertical).

Solas celebrated their ten-year anniversary with *Reunion: A Decade of Solas* (Compass), where they brought together all their members, past and present, for a concert captured on both DVD and CD. Try not to feel a little pang of disappointment that you weren't there when you listen to, or view, the show. But if you prefer studio recordings, Mick McAuley and Winifred Horan took time off from the band to give us *Serenade* (Compass), a lovely blend of fiddle, guitar, and voice.

Flogging Molly also celebrated an anniversary with the raucous *Whiskey on a Sunday* (Side One Dummy Records), again with both a DVD and CD. If you don't know the band, it's where punk and Celtic collide.

Another live DVD/CD combo is Téada's invigorating *Inné Amárach* (Gael Linn). I think all live releases should come in this format. One to take with you in your car or iPod, the other to enjoy in the comfort of your living room.

In November I'm pretty sure I heard a large collective gasp of pleasure from every New Age shop in the world when Loreena McKennitt released her first new album in nine years, *An Ancient Muse* (Quinlan Road). It doesn't break any ground, but it's such a pleasure to hear her voice again, and her distinctive take on world music traditions.

Probably my favorite fiddle album was released late in the year: Matt Pepin's *Pass It Down* (matty-pepin@hotmail.com). It's sweet-but-driving fiddle music at its best, with the highlight being the interplay of Pepin's fiddle with Ian Clarke's guitar on the dreamy "Hambo/Waltz."

If you remember me raving last year about the instrumental prowess of James Stephens, he's back in a new band this year, joining flute- and whistle-player Duncan Gillis, Scottish singer Bobby Watt, and drummer Rob Graves as Écosse.

Their album *The Auld Alliance* (cdbaby.com/cd/ecosse) is a real treat from start to finish.

Young McGill University student Sarah Burnell won the Canadian Folk Music Award for "Young Performer of the Year." If you want to check out what the fuss is all about with this fiddler, give a listen to her delightful debut *Sarah'ndipity* (Sarah-Fiddle).

One of the more innovative albums, while still staying firmly in the tradition, is *Tripswitch* (Compass) with John McSherry on Uillean pipes and flute, and Dónal O'Connor on fiddle. They take their time with the tunes, but the arrangements are muscular and they certainly don't need a vocalist to hold your attention.

If you have an interest in the British folk music tradition but aren't quite sure where to start, you might give *Folk Awards 2006* (PMD) a try. It'll give you a quick overview of some of the stalwarts in the field (Richard Thompson, Kate Rusby, Martin Simpson, Barry Dransfield) and some of the new bright lights (Julie Fowlis, Seth Lakeman, Karine Polwart). It's a mix of instrumental and vocal music, traditional and original, performed by artists nominated for the awards.

Or if you've got Johnny Depp on the brain and you need another pirate fix, try *Rogue's Gallery: Pirate Ballads, Sea Songs & Chanteys* (Anti-), probably one of the best collections of pirate songs around. Okay, maybe the only such collection—but even over two CDs, it never gets boring.

Perennial favorites (at least in this household) Thea Gilmore and K. T. Tunstall both had new discs this year. Gilmore's *Harpo's Ghost* (Sanctuary) is filled with the kind of wonderful stories she's offered upon her previous releases, always moody and intimate. Tunstall's *Acoustic Extravaganza* (Relentless) is a bit of a stop-gap between her hugely successful *Eye to the Telescope* from last year and her next real studio recording. This one was recorded live over a week or so with her band. It's a bit low-key, but perfect for a quiet Sunday afternoon.

Americana

The young turks of bluegrass and old-timey music are still going strong. If anything, they've increased their influence and visibility this year. But at the rate the music business turns over artists, some of these young turks are already becoming the old guard.

The Mammals have kept their familiar sound on *Departure* (Signature Sounds), but now they're including covers of bands like Morphine and Nirvana. The Duhks continue their unique blend of Celtic pop and gospel on *Migration* (Sugar Hill). I love how with an instrumental lineup of cello, banjo, and stand-up bass, Crooked Still still sound like their souls are in the high lonesome hills on *Shaken by a Low Sound* (Signature Records).

Both the Wailin' Jennys (*Firecracker*, Red House) and Be Good Tanyas (*Hello Love*, Nettwerk Records) have new discs this year. I'll admit that I sometimes get confused between which of these two bands I'm listening to, but I never get tired of hearing their harmonies and laidback acoustic interplay.

And speaking of harmonies, the two female vocalists from The Furnace Mountain Band are sublime on *Fly the River* (Shepherd's Ford), while their fiddler has a gorgeous tone.

Adrienne Young & Little Sadie return this year with *The Art of Virtue* (Addie Belle), stringband music with just a whiff of pop in the mix. Jenny Whiteley, on the other hand, shows with *Dear* (Black Hen Music) that you can stay true to your acoustic and bluegrass roots, but still be meaningful to a contemporary audience.

I'm a little in awe of Brock Zeman—not because he's so prolific, because lots of artists are prolific (just consider Ryan Adams with thirty-some new albums available on the Web under various names this past year). No, it's that these story songs of his are so good. It doesn't matter if they're slow heartbreakers or acoustic rave-ups. This year he has a new band, the Dirty Hands, and a terrific new CD, *Welcome Home Ivy Jane* (Busted Flat Records).

Serena Ryder got a record deal with EMI on the strength of her songwriting, so what does she do? She turns in *If Your Memory Serves You Well* (EMI), an album of mostly covers. But it doesn't matter. She's a fine songwriter, but she's a flat-out great singer.

And speaking of albums of cover songs, who would have thought that Bruce Springsteen could do such a fine job on the early Americana songbook with his recent album *We Shall Overcome: The Seeger Sessions* (Sony)? It's a joyous collection of songs, though some of them carry a real lyric bite. The album's good, but from video clips I've seen, this is a lineup you really need to see live if you can.

One of my happiest discoveries from the festival scene last summer was Rachelle van Zanten. Her debut *Back to Francois* (Festival Distribution), showcases her great voice, songwriting, and slide guitar playing.

Norah Jones has flirted with country music on her popular CDs from Blue Note, but the part she plays in the Little Willies self-titled CD (Milking Bull Records) shows she has the chops for a country album proper. And if you live in the New York City area, or plan to visit, you might be able to catch her playing out in her punk persona as a member of El Madmo.

And since we're talking about traveling, let me recommend an art gallery to you if you're ever in Austin, Texas: Yard Dog on Congress Avenue. The last time I was there I got to see a show by Jon Langford and picked up the catalogue for it— *Nashville Radio: Art, Words, and Music* (Verse Chorus Press)—that includes a CD of stripped down songs, *The Nashville Radio Companion Earwig*, that perfectly complement his art. Check out www.yarddog.com for more information on it and other great shows.

I'd never heard of the German acoustic country band Texas Lightning before, but I've been thoroughly enjoying their string band take on old pop classics such as "Like a Virgin," "Walk on the Wild Side," "Norwegian Wood," and so many others. The album's called *Meanwhile, Back at the Golden Ranch* (X-Cell), and if you enjoyed Robinella's bluegrassy take on the song "Fame . . . What a Feeling" (from *No Saint, No Prize*, Sony), you'll probably like this as well.

The two founding members of Calexico used to be the rhythm section for Howe Gelb's Giant Sand. They're a six-piece now and their new CD *Garden Ruin* (Quarter Stick) is a friendly entry into their world of mariachi meets garage band twang meets sensitive singer-songwriter. Meanwhile, Howe Gelb has found himself a new backup group on his latest release *'Sno Angel Like You* (Thrill Jockey) that includes the Ottawa, Canada–based gospel choir Voices of Praise. If you've never tried Gelb before, this wonderful CD is definitely the place to start.

I'd thought we'd lost Linda Ronstadt to big bands and mariachi orchestras, but here she is back with us, this time in the company of Cajun musician Ann Savoy on *Adieu False Heart* (Vanguard) with a stripped-down acoustic sound and an inspired song selection.

I'm running out of room, and there's still a wealth of Americana that I haven't touched on yet, so here are a few quick shout-outs—album titles, but no descriptions—of releases that I know you'll like: Dave Alvin's *West of the West* (Yep Roc Records), Tom Russell's *Love & Fear* and the *Who's Gonna Build Your Wall?* EP (both on Hightone), John Gorka's *Writing in the Margins* (Red House), Neko Case's *Fox Confessor Brings the Flood* (Anti-), Joshua Radin's *We Were Here* (Sony), Wanda Jackson's *I Remember Elvis* (Cleopatra), Todd Snider's *The Devil You Know* (New Door Records), Amy Millan's *Honey from the Tombs* (Access Music), and Janis Ian's *Folk Is the New Black* (Cooking Vinyl).

And last but not least, a couple of discs with direct connections to the genre. Joe Lansdale's daughter Kasey has a terrific debut that came out this year: *No More Rain* (www.kaseylansdale.com). I'm reminded of Tanya Tucker or LeAnn Rimes—not because she sounds like either, but because, like them when they first began to release music, she's a young woman with a very mature voice: deep, rich, and country. Killer album.

And then there's *Some Other Place* (Bagel & Rat) by Whisperado featuring the impeccable guitar playing of Tor Books editor Patrick Nielsen Hayden.

Latin

I don't get to mention a lot of CDs in this column because it's hard to keep up with them all, but also because of the delay in the release of some World music in North America. Here are three discs that came in too late for last year's essay, but you really shouldn't miss them:

My favorite is by the Spanish singer and actress Nieves Rebolledo Vila, better known in musical circles as Bebe. Her debut CD *Pafuera Telarañas* (EMI Spain) is an intoxicating blend of Latin and ska rhythms, DJ scratches and flamenco flourishes, while her vivacious singing ranges from sensual ballads and a capella interludes to raspy rockers and streetwise vocal tricks. It's a busy album at times, but also a slow burner, and a year after I picked up a copy, I have yet to tire of it.

In comparison, Chambao's *Pokito a Poko* (Sony BMG Latin) is a bit calmer, an impeccable fusion of flamenco and chillout, while Si*Sé's *More Shine* (Fuerte Records) has a wonderful romantic vibe on its bed of Latin and soul beats; it's like walking through a northern barrio, but with a hot tropical sun overhead.

This year's releases include Cibelle's *The Shine of Dried Electric Leaves* (Six Degrees) on which the singer continues to be adventurous, with a mix of Portuguese and English lyrics, guests such as Devendra Banhart and Seu George (he of the David Bowie covers fame from the soundtrack to *The Life Aquatic with Steve Zissou*, Hollywood), and even a cover of a Tom Waits song. CéU's self-titled CD (Lcl Records) is rooted in the samba of her native Brazil, but her silky vocals are showcased here on a bed of rhythm that owes as much to dancehall, jazz, and reggae.

There seems to be a growing trend to mixing Latin and Celtic flavors. Salsa Celtica continues to do so with great success on their latest CD *El Camino* (Discos Léon), but my favorite this year was El Sueño de Morfeo's self-titled album (Warner Latina) with its hint of Celtic pipes and fiddles lifting above the Latin grooves.

Their name might translate into "Brown Sugar," but on *Bailando Con Lola* (EMI) Azúcar Moreno's flamenco-tinged pop has too much edge to be dismissed as sweet. Juana Molina has come a long way since her days as a comedic actress on Argentinean TV. Her new album *Son* (Domino) is edgy and unpredictable, but always entertaining.

Lila Downs's *La Cantina* (Narada) is a loving tribute to Mexican *canciones rancheras*, and features a heady mix of heartfelt ballads, *norteño* grooves, spoken verse, and even a rap; Flaco Jiménez guests on accordion. Once you get past the novelty of a flamenco version of "Stairway to Heaven" on Rodrigo y Gabriela's self-titled CD (Ato), you'll find an album of killer Spanish guitar.

Badi Assad's *Wonderland* (Deutsche Grammophon) is an album of mostly cover versions of songs by artists such as Asian Dub Foundation, Eurythmics, and Tori Amos, all held together by a captivating voice and Assad's superb guitar work. Soraya's *Gold* (Hip-O) is a two-CD career retrospective from the late singer that reminds us of just how much she'll be missed.

On her third album, *My Own Way Home* (Rainbow), the Catalan singer Beth offers up mostly English songs, and proves to be a gifted vocalist and songwriter no matter what language she uses.

While Ojos de Brujo's *Techarí* (Six Degrees) flirts with hip-hop and punk rhythms, the band still has its roots in the flamenco tradition and singer Marina Abad's voice continues to soar above the music with the raw fervor of the Gypsies of old. Amparanoia's *La Vida te Da* (Wrasse) features their trademark blend of high energy guitars and Amparo Sánchez's distinctive vocals as the band takes on a blend of rhumba and reggae, spiced with Mexican and West African flourishes.

Los Fabulosos Cadillacs's *Hola Chau* (Sony) features CD and DVD versions of one of the band's last concerts, this one recorded live in the Obras Sanitarias Stadium in Buenos Aires in September of 2000. It's a great collection of their hits that also serves as an excellent introduction to the band.

Maná's *Amar Es Combatir* (Warner Latina) is a swaggering collection of arena-rock. It's the Mexican band's first album in four years, and one of their best. The self-titled CD (Sub Pop) from Brazil's Cansei de Ser Sexy's is a club favorite in the U.K. with its mesmerizing dance rhythms and sensual lyrics. Loe's *Lady Reggaetton* (EMI) with its infectious mix of rap and dancehall proves this popular style has moved beyond its Jamaican origins.

World

Like Björk's *Médulla*, French singer Camille's *Le Fil* (Virgin) is almost entirely put together with vocals, including a soft vocal hum/drone that runs the entire length of the recording (like "the thread" of its title). This is her second solo album, following her stint with Nouvelle Vague on a cover album of bossa nova versions of New Wave songs. And speaking of Björk-influenced artists, Emilie Simon's *Végétal* (Umvd) also fits the bill with its avant-garde arrangements and Simon's adventurous vocal stylings.

I'm not a huge fan of the Putumayo series of compilations, mainly because their choice of material is often too simplistic and they charge way too much for what *are* just compilations. That said, *Putumayo Presents: Paris* is an excellent introduction to the new smoky cabaret revival of French chanson and will undoubtedly have you running off to pick up full-length CDs by many of the artists featured on it.

Algerian singer Nâdiya's self-titled CD (Sony) is a tall cool glass of French R&B with a touch of rap played out over a bed of Euro-tinged rhythms. Also from Algeria, the phenomenal Rachid Taha has a new album, *Diwan 2* (Wrasse), on which he continues to make topical statements, delivered against a backdrop of Arabic rhythms and driving guitars. Think The Clash meets the Middle East.

Leaving the safety of her band Oi Va Voi, Sophie Solomon's violin shines on *Poison Sweet Madeira* (Decca), a heady mix of her native Russian background with everything from Gypsy traditions to North African rhythms. The album features vocals by Richard Hawley, KT Tunstall, and Ralph Fiennes, but Solomon could play on her own without any backing and still shine.

Johnny Clegg's *One Life* (Marabi) is a bit of a return to form for the South African artist with his infectious rhythms and hooks, and a dash of his signature Zulu chanting. Thievery Corporation's *Versions* (Rmxs) features remixes from the band's catalogue that so reinvent some of the material that they could be considered entirely new songs.

While Natacha Atlas's *Mish Maoul* (Beggars UK/Ada) has a very hip, contemporary sound, it's flavored with everything from bossa novas to North African casbah sounds. Atlas is one of the first of the World music divas and she shows no signs of letting go of her crown anytime soon.

Ziggy Marley's *Love Is My Religion* (Xiii Bis) is his second album since leaving the Melody Makers. With simple, heartfelt lyrics, a growing studio acumen, and a willingness to experiment with his beloved reggae, the younger Marley is proving to be as exceptional an artist as was his father.

Ndidi Onukwulu's *No, I Never* (Jericho Beach) is ostensibly blues, but bubbling under those twelve-bars are talking drums and enough juju guitar work to make King Sunny Adé proud. The nine-piece African Guitar Summit features five African guitarists blending soukous and highlife rhythms on their second disc, *African Guitar Summit 2* (CBC).

We lost the African guitarist Ali Farka Touré last year, but his final, posthumous album *Savane* (Nonesuch) is nothing short of a masterpiece.

With the talented Bill Laswell in the producer's chair Matisyahu's *Youth* (Sony) steps beyond the easy description of Hasidic beatbox/reggae to make a seamless meld of Talmudic teachings and Jamaican rhythms.

On *Miero* (Real World), fresh from their stint of producing music for the stage version of *The Lord of the Rings*, Värttinä offers up their tenth album featuring their signature vocal harmonies, blended with accordions, bouzoukis, and yes, even a drum kit. But with this band, you always come back to the voices, and the singing here, in Finnish, is always sublime.

If you're looking for more than an annual fix of the sorts of music discussed above, I'd like to recommend a few Web sites that carry timely reviews and news:

www.frootsmag.com
www.endicott-studio.com
www.pastemusic.com
www.globalrhythm.net
www.greenmanreview.com
www.rambles.net

If you'd like a monthly newsletter of Americana reviews, you should sign up for the Village Records newsletter at www.villagerecords.com. And for one more commercial site that provides excellent band/album information (and is probably the happiest shopping experience you'll have on the Web), point your browser to www.cdbaby.com.

Or if you prefer the written page, check out your local newsstand for copies of *fRoots* (two issues per year carry fabulous CD samplers), *Global Rhythm* (each issue includes a sampler CD), *Songlines* (also has a CD sampler), *Paste* (with CD sampler every issue; sometimes also a DVD sampler), *Sing Out!*, *Riddim* (with CD sampler), *No Depression*, *Rock'n'Reel* (with CD Sampler), and *Dirty Linen*.

While I know there are lots of other great albums out there, I don't have the budget to try everything. But my ears are always open to new sounds. So, if you'd like to bring something to my attention for next year's essay, you can send it to me c/o P.O. Box 9480, Ottawa, ON, Canada K1G 3V2.

Remember to have fun with the music you listen to. And just because someone else likes something you don't, or vice versa, it doesn't mean either of you is wrong. It just means that tastes are different.

Special thanks, once again, to Cat Eldridge of Green Man Review, and Ian and James Boyd of Compact Music, for helping to provide music in preparation of this essay.

Obituaries: 2006

James Frenkel

Each year we include notice of people who contributed to the culture who died in the past year. While we are saddened by their loss and the loss of any new contributions they might have made if they had lived longer, we take this opportunity to celebrate those contributions they did make. The people below all brought something special and unique to their work. Perhaps in reading about them someone will be inspired to his or her own special work.

Jack Williamson, 98, was one of the most legendary science fiction and fantasy writers of our time. His career, which began in 1928 with his first published short story in *Amazing Stories* magazine, continued well into the twenty-first century. He tackled a wide variety of scientific topics in his fiction, including genetic engineering and terraforming (the latter a word he coined). His work spanned the spectrum of imaginative fiction, ranging from the horror of *Darker Than You Think* to fantasy like *Golden Blood*, and science fiction such as *The Humanoids* and *The Legion of Space*. He never stopped adapting to new developments whether they were stylistic, scientific, or logistical. He was active in the field of academic research as well as writing, traveled extensively, and was remarkable for his great range and depth, even well into his nineties.

Born in Arizona in 1908 when it was not quite yet a state, his family settled in Portales, New Mexico, before that was a state, in 1915. He won the Hugo and Nebula Awards for his fiction and also won a Hugo for his memoir, *Wonder's Child: My Life in Science Fiction*. He also was named SFWA Grand Master; was accorded a World Fantasy Life Achievement Award; became an SF Hall of Fame Living Inductee in 1996; was honored with a Bram Stoker Life Achievement Award; and became a World Horror Grandmaster.

Jim Baen, 62, started his publishing career with Ace Books's romance department, moving to edit *Galaxy* in 1973. He returned to Ace where he worked for Tom Doherty, who had invigorated the imprint. In 1980 he joined Doherty's newly founded Tor Books, where he was in charge of their science fiction. In 1983 he founded Baen Books, which specializes in military SF. He has introduced a successful WebScription program, and recently started the online magazine *Jim Baen's Universe*. He was an innovator in many ways, especially in his use of the Internet to promote the books he published; he had an abiding love of the field of science fiction that was obvious to all who knew him.

Octavia E. Butler, 58, was a groundbreaking writer. A self-proclaimed feminist, her work paved the way for women and people of color. She won the PEN Center Lifetime Achievement Award in 2000, won both Hugo and Nebula Awards, her novel *Parable of the Sower* winning the latter award. Most of her work was science fiction, but verged into the fantastic in a novel like *Kindred*. She was the recipient of a MacArthur Fellowship "genius" grant.

John M. "Mike" Ford, 49, was a fiction writer, poet, and game designer who crossed genres from proto-cyberpunk to historical fantasy. His work won him both a World Fantasy Award and a Philip K. Dick Award. He was a regular and popular convention attendee and won Origins Awards for his work on the games *Paranoia* and *GURPS: Infinite World*. His World Fantasy Award–winning novel *The Dragon Waiting* is a great, underappreciated fantasy classic; his *Star Trek* novel, *How Much for Just the Planet?*, stands as perhaps the most entertaining franchise novel ever written. He was plagued by health issues during his entire too-short life.

Charles L. Grant, 64, wrote over one hundred books and almost two hundred short stories, including Nebula winners "A Crowd of Shadows" (1977; also a Hugo nominee) and "A Glow of Candles, a Unicorn's Eye" (1979). "Confess the Seasons" (1982) won him a World Fantasy Award. He received a British Fantasy Lifetime Achievement Award in 1987, the Stoker Lifetime Achievement Award in 2000, was named a World Horror Grandmaster in 2002, and received the International Horror Guild Living Legend Award in 2003. His horror fiction was widely considered among the best in the field for many years.

Tim Hildebrandt, 67, worked with his identical twin brother Greg to illustrate the bestselling *Lord of the Rings* covers and calendars beginning in 1976. This success led to work illustrating covers for books such as Terry Brooks's *The Sword of Shannara*, Anne McCaffrey's *The Ship Who Sang*, and Roger Zelazny's *My Name Is Legion*, but the brothers were best known for producing a popular 1977 movie poster for *Star Wars*. During the eighties the brothers split under financial strain caused by failed bids to interest movie studios in adapting their illustrated fantasy novel *Urshurak*, but they reconciled in the early nineties and collaborated on a number of projects including an updated version of the classic comic strip *Terry and the Pirates*.

Darren McGavin, 83, had hundreds of television, movie, and theatrical credits to his name. Among them was Carl Kolchak, the newspaper reporter in the horror series *Kolchak: The Night Stalker*, said to have inspired *The X Files*, which he also guested on. He won an Emmy for playing Candice Bergen's father in *Murphy Brown*, and played the memorably curmudgeonly father in *A Christmas Story*.

Nigel Kneale, 84, was the screenwriter of the Quatermass serials in the 1950s, which used science fiction, fantasy, and horror tropes to comment on current social issues. He eventually became one of Britain's top screenwriters, producing, among other work, an adaptation of *1984*. **Sid Raymond**, 97, was an actor who worked on a wide range of projects. One of his most well-known creations was the voice of Baby Huey, a cartoon duck. He also provided voices for the magpies in "Heckle and Jeckle." **Peter Boyle**, 71, was a veteran actor of stage and screen. Best known for his role as the father in *Everybody Loves Raymond*, he first reached prominence with his eponymous role in the film *Joe*. Perhaps his most memorable moments were as the monster in *Young Frankenstein*. **Glenn Ford**, 90, was a film actor for more than fifty years. His film credits include *Gilda* (1947), *The Big Heat* (1953), *Blackboard Jungle* (1955), and *Pocketful of Miracles* (1961). In 1978 Ford was cast as Clark Kent's father in *Superman*.

Maureen Stapleton, 80, acted in theater, films, and on television. She won an Academy Award for her fiery performance as the anarchist Emma Goldman in *Reds*. Her film credits also included *Cocoon* (1985) and its sequel. **Joseph Bova**, 81, was an actor whose roles ranged from Prince Dauntless the Drab in the original production of *Once Upon a Mattress* to Shakespeare's *King Richard III*. He was nominated for a 1970 Tony Award for his performance in *The Chinese*, a one-act play by Murray Schisgal. **Dennis Weaver**, 81, acted on stage, television, and the silver screen. He played Deputy Chester Goode, the sidekick of Marshal Matt Dillon on the *Gunsmoke* TV series, and starred in *Gentle Ben*, and *McCloud*, for which he received two Emmy nominations. He also starred in Steven Spielberg's TV film *Duel*. **Al Lewis**, 82, played Grandpa, a vampiric father-in-law to Herman Munster, on the 1960s sitcom *The Munsters*. He also starred in *Car 54, Where Are You?* as Officer Leo Schnauzer and guested on *Taxi*, *Green Acres*, and *Lost in Space*. **Patrick Cranshaw**, 86, was a film and television actor. His credits include *Mars Needs Women*, *Bonnie and Clyde*, *Nightmare Honeymoon*, *Wonder Woman*, *Pee-wee's Big Adventure*, *Quantum Leap*, and *Lois & Clark*. He achieved cult status as elderly fratboy Joseph "Blue" Palasky in *Old School*. **Joan Diener**, 76, was a lush beauty whose show-stopping stage presence and operatic voice made her a favorite in musicals, especially in *Man of La Mancha*.

Stanley Meltzoff, 89, was an artist and the illustrator of sf covers throughout the 1950s. He also had a huge impact on a number of his students including Paul Lehr, John Schoenherr, and Vincent di Fate. **John Stewart**, "in his fifties," was a British illustrator who created portfolios inspired by Stephen King's *The Gunslinger* and Clive Barker's *The Forbidden* respectively for small press magazines like *Whispers* and *Fantasy Tales*. He also illustrated Robert Bloch's Cthulhu Mythos novel *Strange Eons* and Michael Shea's collection *Polyphemus*. **Ronald Clyne**, 80, was commissioned for his first illustration in *Fantastic Stories* in 1930. He had an extremely productive association with Arkham House publishers in the forties and fifties, then moved to more mainstream publishers in the sixties. He was especially proud of his five hundred-plus album covers for Folkways Records.

Alex Toth, 77, was a comics artist. He is most famous for animation designs that created the basis for Hanna-Barbera shows of the sixties and seventies including *Super Friends*, *Johnny Quest*, *Sealab 2020*, *Space Ghost*, and *Birdman*. **Martin Nodell**, 91, was the creator of Green Lantern, a popular comic book that first appeared in 1940. Nodell got the idea of the Green Lantern when he was waiting for a train to arrive and saw the conductor waving a green lantern. **Dave Cockrum**, 63, was a comic book illustrator who helped create the enormously successful comic book *X-Men*. Cockrum worked as an inker for Murphy Anderson on Superman, Batman, and Flash. He then went to work for Marvel where he worked on *The Avengers*, and other books. **Joseph Barbera**, 95, half of the legendary Hanna-Barbera creative team, worked on more than a hundred cartoon series. Under MGM in his early career with William Hanna, he debuted *Tom and Jerry*, a cartoon series that earned fourteen Oscar nominations and seven statuettes. In 1958 *The Huckleberry Hound Show* launched on NBC, earning an Emmy, and spinning off Yogi Bear. *The Flinstones* debuted soon after in 1960, running for six seasons. *Scooby-Doo, Where Are You!*, *The Smurfs*, and *Johnny Quest* are also credited to their collaborative team. He continued to be active in animation up until his death, producing the popular *Powerpuff Girls* and *Dexter's Laboratory* series. **Chris Hayward**, 81, was a writer for the cult-classic *The Rocky and Bullwinkle Show* and also wrote for *The Munsters*.

Aaron Spelling, 83, was an American television producer who created such shows as *Dynasty, Charlie's Angels, 7th Heaven, Beverly Hills 90210*, and *Fantasy Island*. **Van Smith**, 61, was a costume designer and makeup artist solely responsible for the memorable look of Divine, the transvestite star of John Waters's early films. **Joseph Stefano**, 84, wrote the screenplay for the popular, and haunting, Hitchcock film *Psycho* and was the cocreator of the 1960s television show *Outer Limits*. **Akira Ifukube**, 91, was a prolific composer and wrote the score for the celebrated monster movie *Godzilla*. His work was heavily influenced by the culture of the Ainu, the aboriginal people of Hokkaido.

Scott Brazil, 50, was an Emmy-winning producer and director of television shows including *The Shield* and *Hill Street Blues, Nip/Tuck, Grey's Anatomy, Nash Bridges*, and *Buffy the Vampire Slayer*. **Richard Fleischer**, 89, was a film director of such films as *20,000 Leagues Under the Sea, Tora! Tora! Tora!*, and *Fantastic Voyage*. Mr. Fleischer's movies in the 1980s, the remake of *The Jazz Singer* starring Neil Diamond, *Amityville 3-D*, and *Conan the Destroyer*, continued in this vein. **Steven Marshall**, 58, a sound engineer and inventor, developed a process called revectorization to restore decaying soundtracks of old films. He also invented the Marshall Time Modulator, a delay processor that allowed performers to modify or multiply their voices and was used to create the voice of Darth Vader. **Alan Shalleck**, 76, wrote and directed more than one hundred short episodes of the *Curious George* cartoon for the Disney Channel and collaborated with Margret Rey, widow and coauthor to the series' original illustrator H. A. Rey, to create two dozen more *Curious George* books to succeed the original seven. He started his career with *Winky-Dink and You*, an early TV show in which children used a plastic film placed on the television screen to draw along with the action at home. **Val Guest**, 94, was a prolific British filmmaker. He cowrote and directed *The Day the Earth Caught Fire* (1961) and *The Quatermass Xperiment*. **Myron Waldman**, 97, was an animator and illustrator who worked with characters such as Betty Boop, Popeye, Superman, and Casper the Ghost, and *Raggedy Ann and Raggedy Andy*, for the Max Fleischer Studio.

David Gemmell, 57, was the bestselling British author of the Drenai series, the Rigante series, and Sipstrassi series, among other works. The U.K.'s Random House sf and Fantasy imprint was renamed "Legend" after his first novel in the late eighties. **Bob Leman**, 84, worked almost exclusively in the genre of short dark fantasy, publishing nearly all of his fiction in *F&SF*. His Nebula finalist story "Window" was adapted as an episode of the TV series *Night Vision*.

Wilson "Bob" Tucker, 91, published more than twenty books of science fiction and fantasy beginning in the 1940s including the Campbell Award–winning novel *The Year of the Quiet Sun*, but he will perhaps be best remembered as one of the most beloved and visible figures in sf fandom. He published numerous fanzines, beginning with *The Planetoid* in 1932. His work earned him a Retro Hugo for fan writing. His chapbook *The Neo-Fan's Guide to Science Fiction Fandom* (1966) is a classic, and his spurious letter column-debate known as The Great Staple War was a defining moment of early fandom. **Nelson Bond**, 97, was a successful fantasy and science fiction writer in the pulps who also wrote plays and for the screen. Among his works were "Mr. Mergenthwirker's Lobblies," which spawned a radio series and went on to be the first play to ever air on television, the stage adaptation of *Animal Farm*, and the 1957 teleplay "The Night America Trembled," based on Welles's fateful broadcast of H. G. Wells's *War of the Worlds*. **Roderick MacLeish**, 80, wrote the YA fantasy *Prince Ombra* (1982). He also was a longtime broadcast reporter. **John**

Reynolds Gardiner, 61, was best known for his children's books *Stone Fox, Top Secret,* and *General Butterfingers.*

Walter Allner, 97, was the art director of *Fortune* magazine from 1962 to 1974, where he introduced the first computer-generated cover of a magazine (the Fortune 500 issue in 1965). Years before computers revolutionized the rest of graphic design, he worked under the impression that there would soon be an "integration of aesthetics and advanced technology." **Arthur Shimkin**, 84, was the head of the Little Golden Records division of Simon and Schuster. Some of the most popular records that Shimkin produced were the *Sesame Street Fever* record and *Peter and the Wolf.* **Frederick G. Kilgour**, 92, played a major role in the development of the O.C.L.C. (Online Computer Library Center), a computer database of library collections from around the world. The database, which is one of the largest in the world, was made available online in late 2006. **Phyllis Cerf Wagner**, 90, was, in a very accomplished life, an editor at Random House, which her first husband, Bennett Cerf, founded. She worked with Dr. Seuss and with him started Random House's very successful Beginner Books imprint. She went on to write for magazines, and was active in public life.

Charles Newman, 67, was an avant-garde novelist and critic who edited the prestigious literary magazine *TriQuarterly* for more than a decade. Under his stewardship, it became an international journal showcasing the world's most eminent writers, including Jorge Luis Borges, Gabriel García Márquez, Carlos Fuentes, Joyce Carol Oates, Cynthia Ozick, Raymond Carver, Anne Sexton, and W. S. Merwin. He also wrote the novels *White Jazz* (1984) and *The Promisekeeper: A Tephramancy* (1971). **Susan E. Michaud**, 41, helped run Necronomicon Press with her husband from 1983 to 2006. **Albert B. Friedman**, 86, a scholar of medieval ballads, was best known for his anthology *The Viking Book of Folk Ballads of the English-Speaking World.*

George Latshaw, 83, was a highly influential puppeteer. He is best known for his work on the Hollywood musical *Lili* and "Quillow and the Giant," an NBC production that aired in 1963.

John Heath-Stubbs, 88, was a British poet, and a highly respected editor, translator, and critic. He edited the important anthology *Images of Tomorrow* (1953). He wrote poetry that was inspired by mythology, including *Artorias*, an epic Arthurian poem.

Birgit Nilsson, 87, was an accomplished operatic soprano who was best known for her performances in the works of Wagner, redefining the roles of heroines such as Isolde, Sieglinde, and Brunnhilde. **Anna Russell**, 94, the prima donna of operatic parody who claimed to have begun her career as "leading soprano of the Ellis Island Opera Company," said she learned to play the French horn from an article in Encyclopedia Britannica, and who gave indelibly grating performances of a song she identified as Blotz's "Schlumpf" to demonstrate what it is like to sing with "no voice but great art." In her routines, Ms. Russell tapped into a long tradition of deflating the highly formal manners of the concert hall and its devotees, making fun of bad voices and bad teaching, of all pomp and most circumstance. Ms. Russell's most enduring creations were associated with the most cultic portions of the art music repertory—the works of Wagner and those of Gilbert and Sullivan. She was seen on television, Broadway, in film, and on the opera stage, including appearances as the Witch in a New York City Opera production of *Hansel and Gretel.*

THE YEAR'S BEST

Fantasy and Horror

2007

GEOFF RYMAN

Pol Pot's Beautiful Daughter

"Pol Pot's Beautiful Daughter" was originally published in The Magazine of Fantasy & Science Fiction. *Ryman is the author of* Air, 253, Was, *and* The Child Garden. *His most recent book, the historical novel* The King's Last Song, *is—like this story—set in Cambodia. Ryman lives in the United Kingdom.*

—K.L. & G.G.

In Cambodia people are used to ghosts. Ghosts buy newspapers. They own property.

A few years ago, spirits owned a house in Phnom Penh, at the Tra Bek end of Monivong Boulevard. Khmer Rouge had murdered the whole family and there was no one left alive to inherit it. People cycled past the building, leaving it boarded up. Sounds of weeping came from inside.

Then a professional inheritor arrived from America. She'd done her research and could claim to be the last surviving relative of no fewer than three families. She immediately sold the house to a Chinese businessman, who turned the ground floor into a photocopying shop.

The copiers began to print pictures of the original owners.

At first, single black and white photos turned up in the copied dossiers of aid workers or government officials. The father of the murdered family had been a lawyer. He stared fiercely out of the photos as if demanding something. In other photocopies, his beautiful daughters forlornly hugged each other. The background was hazy like fog.

One night the owner heard a noise and trundled downstairs to find all five photocopiers printing one picture after another of faces: young college men, old women, parents with a string of babies, or government soldiers in uniform. He pushed the big green off-buttons. Nothing happened.

He pulled out all the plugs, but the machines kept grinding out face after face. Women in beehive hairdos or clever children with glasses looked wistfully out of the photocopies. They seemed to be dreaming of home in the 1960s, when Phnom Penh was the most beautiful city in Southeast Asia.

News spread. People began to visit the shop to identify lost relatives. Women would cry, "That's my mother! I didn't have a photograph!" They would weep and press the flimsy A4 sheets to their breasts. The paper went limp from tears and humidity as if it too were crying.

Soon, a throng began to gather outside the shop every morning to view the latest batch of faces. In desperation, the owner announced that each morning's harvest would be delivered direct to *The Truth*, a magazine of remembrance.

Then one morning he tried to open the house-door to the shop and found it blocked. He went 'round to the front of the building and rolled open the metal shutters.

The shop was packed from floor to ceiling with photocopies. The ground floor had no windows—the room had been filled from the inside. The owner pulled out a sheet of paper and saw himself on the ground, his head beaten in by a hoe. The same image was on every single page.

He buried the photocopiers and sold the house at once. The new owner liked its haunted reputation; it kept people away. The FOR SALE sign was left hanging from the second floor.

In a sense, the house had been bought by another ghost.

This is a completely untrue story about someone who must exist.

Pol Pot's Only Child, a daughter, was born in 1986. Her name was Sith, and in 2004, she was eighteen years old.

Sith liked air conditioning and luxury automobiles.

Her hair was dressed in cornrows and she had a spiky piercing above one eye. Her jeans were elaborately slashed and embroidered. Her pink T-shirts bore slogans in English: CARE KOOKY. PINKMOLL.

Sith lived like a woman on Thai television, doing as she pleased in lip-gloss and Sunsilked hair. Nine simple rules helped her avoid all unpleasantness.

1. Never think about the past or politics.
2. Ignore ghosts. They cannot hurt you.
3. Do not go to school. Hire tutors. Don't do homework. It is disturbing.
4. Always be driven everywhere in either the Mercedes or the BMW.
5. Avoid all well-dressed Cambodian boys. They are the sons of the estimated 250,000 new generals created by the regime. Their sons can behave with impunity.
6. Avoid all men with potbellies. They eat too well and therefore must be corrupt.
7. Avoid anyone who drives a Toyota Viva or Honda Dream motorcycle.
8. Don't answer letters or phone calls.
9. Never make any friends.

There was also a tenth rule, but that went without saying.

Rotten fruit rinds and black mud never stained Sith's designer sports shoes. Disabled beggars never asked her for alms. Her life began yesterday, which was effectively the same as today.

Every day, her driver took her to the new Soriya Market. It was almost the only place that Sith went. The color of silver, Soriya rose up in many floors to a round glass dome.

Sith preferred the 142nd Street entrance. Its green awning made everyone look as if they were made of jade. The doorway went directly into the ice-cold jewelry rotunda with its floor of polished black and white stone. The individual stalls were hung with glittering necklaces and earrings.

Sith liked tiny shiny things that had no memory. She hated politics. She refused to listen to the news. Pol Pot's beautiful daughter wished the current leadership would behave decently, like her dad always did. To her.

She remembered the sound of her father's gentle voice. She remembered sitting on his lap in a forest enclosure, being bitten by mosquitoes. Memories of malaria had sunk into her very bones. She now associated forests with nausea, fevers, and pain. A flicker of tree-shade on her skin made her want to throw up and the odor of soil or fallen leaves made her gag. She had never been to Angkor Wat. She read nothing.

Sith shopped. Her driver was paid by the government and always carried an AK-47, but his wife, the housekeeper, had no idea who Sith was. The house was full of swept marble, polished teak furniture, iPods, Xboxes, and plasma screens.

Please remember that every word of this story is a lie. Pol Pot was no doubt a dedicated communist who made no money from ruling Cambodia. Nevertheless, a hefty allowance arrived for Sith every month from an account in Switzerland.

Nothing touched Sith, until she fell in love with the salesman at Hello Phones.

Cambodian readers may know that in 2004 there was no mobile phone shop in Soriya Market. However, there was a branch of Hello Phone Cards that had a round blue sales counter with orange trim. This shop looked like that.

Every day Sith bought or exchanged a mobile phone there. She would sit and flick her hair at the salesman.

His name was Dara, which means Star. Dara knew about deals on call prices, sim cards, and the new phones that showed videos. He could get her any call tone she liked.

Talking to Dara broke none of Sith's rules. He wasn't fat, nor was he well dressed, and far from being a teenager, he was a comfortably mature twenty-four years old.

One day, Dara chuckled and said, "As a friend I advise you, you don't need another mobile phone."

Sith wrinkled her nose. "I don't like this one anymore. It's blue. I want something more feminine. But not frilly. And it should have better sound quality."

"Okay, but you could save your money and buy some more nice clothes."

Pol Pot's beautiful daughter lowered her chin, which she knew made her neck look long and graceful. "Do you like my clothes?"

"Why ask me?"

She shrugged. "I don't know. It's good to check out your look."

Dara nodded. "You look cool. What does your sister say?"

Sith let him know she had no family. "Ah," he said and quickly changed the subject. That was terrific. Secrecy and sympathy in one easy movement.

Sith came back the next day and said that she'd decided that the rose-colored phone was too feminine. Dara laughed aloud and his eyes sparkled. Sith had come late in the morning just so that he could ask this question. "Are you hungry? Do you want to meet for lunch?"

Would he think she was cheap if she said yes? Would he say she was snobby if she said no?

"Just so long as we eat in Soriya Market," she said.

She was torn between BBWorld Burgers and Lucky7. BBWorld was big, round, and just two floors down from the dome. Lucky7 Burgers was part of the Lucky Supermarket, such a good store that a tiny jar of Maxwell House cost US$2.40.

They decided on BBWorld. It was full of light and they could see the town spread out through the wide clean windows. Sith sat in silence.

Pol Pot's daughter had nothing to say unless she was buying something.

Or rather she had only one thing to say, but she must never say it.

Dara did all the talking. He talked about how the guys on the third floor could get him a deal on original copies of *Grand Theft Auto*. He hinted that he could get Sith discounts from Bsfashion, the spotlit modern shop one floor down.

Suddenly he stopped. "You don't need to be afraid of me, you know." He said it in a kindly, grownup voice. "I can see, you're a properly brought up girl. I like that. It's nice."

Sith still couldn't find anything to say. She could only nod. She wanted to run away.

"Would you like to go to K-Four?"

K-Four, the big electronics shop, stocked all the reliable brand names: Hitachi, Sony, Panasonic, Philips, or Denon. It was so expensive that almost nobody shopped there, which is why Sith liked it. A crowd of people stood outside and stared through the window at a huge home entertainment center showing a DVD of *Ice Age*. On the screen, a little animal was being chased by a glacier. It was so beautiful!

Sith finally found something to say. "If I had one of those, I would never need to leave the house."

Dara looked at her sideways and decided to laugh.

The next day Sith told him that all the phones she had were too big. Did he have one that she could wear around her neck like jewelry?

This time they went to Lucky7 Burgers, and sat across from the Revlon counter. They watched boys having their hair layered by Revlon's natural beauty specialists.

Dara told her more about himself. His father had died in the wars. His family now lived in the country. Sith's Coca-Cola suddenly tasted of anti-malarial drugs.

"But . . . you don't want to *live* in the country," she said.

"No. I have to live in Phnom Penh to make money. But my folks are good country people. Modest." He smiled, embarrassed.

They'll have hens and a cousin who shimmies up coconut trees. There will be trees all around but no shops anywhere. The earth will smell.

Sith couldn't finish her drink. She sighed and smiled and said abruptly, "I'm sorry. It's been cool. But I have to go." She slunk sideways out of her seat as slowly as molasses.

Walking back into the jewelry rotunda with nothing to do, she realized that Dara would think she didn't like him.

And that made the lower part of her eyes sting.

She went back the next day and didn't even pretend to buy a mobile phone. She told Dara that she'd left so suddenly the day before because she'd remembered a hair appointment.

He said that he could see she took a lot of trouble with her hair. Then he asked her out for a movie that night.

Sith spent all day shopping in K-Four.

They met at six. Dara was so considerate that he didn't even suggest the horror movie. He said he wanted to see *Buffalo Girl Hiding*, a movie about a country girl who lives on a farm. Sith said with great feeling that she would prefer the horror movie.

The cinema on the top floor opened out directly onto the roof of Soriya. Graffiti had been scratched into the green railings. Why would people want to ruin something new and beautiful? Sith put her arm through Dara's and knew that they were now boyfriend and girlfriend.

"Finally," he said.

"Finally what?"

"You've done something."

They leaned on the railings and looked out over other people's apartments. West toward the river was a building with one huge roof terrace. Women met there to gossip. Children were playing toss-the-sandal. From this distance, Sith was enchanted.

"I just love watching the children."

The movie, from Thailand, was about a woman whose face turns blue and spotty and who eats men. The blue woman was yucky, but not as scary as all the badly dubbed voices. The characters sounded possessed. It was as though Thai people had been taken over by the spirits of dead Cambodians.

Whenever Sith got scared, she chuckled.

So she sat chuckling with terror. Dara thought she was laughing at a dumb movie and found such intelligence charming. He started to chuckle too. Sith thought he was as frightened as she was. Together in the dark, they took each other's hands.

Outside afterward, the air hung hot even in the dark and 142nd Street smelled of drains. Sith stood on tiptoe to avoid the oily deposits and cast-off fishbones.

Dara said, "I will drive you home."

"My driver can take us," said Sith, flipping open her Kermit-the-Frog mobile.

Her black Mercedes Benz edged to a halt, crunching old plastic bottles in the gutter. The seats were upholstered with tan leather and the driver was armed.

Dara's jaw dropped. "Who . . . *who* is your father?"

"He's dead."

Dara shook his head. "Who was he?"

Normally Sith used her mother's family name, but that would not answer this question. Flustered, she tried to think of someone who could be her father. She knew of nobody the right age. She remembered something about a politician who had died. His name came to her and she said it in panic. "My father was Kol Vireakboth." Had she got the name right? "Please don't tell anyone."

Dara covered his eyes. "We—my family, my father—we fought for the KPLA."

Sith had to stop herself asking what the KPLA was.

Kol Vireakboth had led a faction in the civil wars. It fought against the Khmer Rouge, the Vietnamese, the King, and corruption. It wanted a new way for Cambodia. Kol Vireakboth was a Cambodian leader who had never told a lie and or accepted a bribe.

Remember that this is an untrue story.

Dara started to back away from the car. "I don't think we should be doing this. I'm just a villager, really."

"That doesn't matter."

His eyes closed. "I would expect nothing less from the daughter of Kol Vireakboth."

Oh for gosh sake, she just picked the man's name out of the air, she didn't need more problems. "Please!" she said.

Dara sighed. "Okay. I said I would see you home safely. I will." Inside the Mercedes, he stroked the tan leather.

When they arrived, he craned his neck to look up at the building. "Which floor are you on?"

"All of them."

Color drained from his face.

"My driver will take you back," she said to Dara. As the car pulled away, she stood outside the closed garage shutters, waving forlornly.

Then Sith panicked. Who was Kol Vireakboth? She went online and Googled. She had to read about the wars. Her skin started to creep. All those different factions swam in her head: ANS, NADK, KPR, and KPNLF. The very names seemed to come at her spoken by forgotten voices.

Soon she had all she could stand. She printed out Vireakboth's picture and decided to have it framed. In case Dara visited.

Kol Vireakboth had a round face and a fatherly smile. His eyes seemed to slant upward toward his nose, looking full of kindly insight. He'd been killed by a car bomb.

All that night, Sith heard whispering.

In the morning, there was another picture of someone else in the tray of her printer.

A long-faced, buck-toothed woman stared out at her in black and white. Sith noted the victim's fashion lapses. The woman's hair was a mess, all frizzy. She should have had it straightened and put in some nice highlights. The woman's eyes drilled into her.

"Can't touch me," said Sith. She left the photo in the tray. She went to see Dara, right away, no breakfast.

His eyes were circled with dark flesh and his blue Hello trousers and shirt were not properly ironed.

"Buy the whole shop," Dara said, looking deranged. "The guys in K-Four just told me some girl in blue jeans walked in yesterday and bought two home theatres. One for the salon, she said, and one for the roof terrace. She paid for both of them in full and had them delivered to the far end of Monivong."

Sith sighed. "I'm sending one back." She hoped that sounded abstemious. "It looked too metallic against my curtains."

Pause.

"She also bought an Aido robot dog for fifteen hundred dollars."

Sith would have preferred that Dara did not know about the dog. It was just a silly toy; it hadn't occured to her that it might cost that much until she saw the bill. "They should not tell everyone about their customers' business or soon they will have no customers."

Dara was looking at her as if thinking: *This is not just a nice sweet girl.*

"I had fun last night," Sith said in a voice as thin as high clouds.

"So did I."

"We don't have to tell anyone about my family. Do we?" Sith was seriously scared of losing him.

"No. But Sith, it's stupid. Your family, my family, we are not equals."

"It doesn't make any difference."

"You lied to me. Your family is not dead. You have famous uncles."

She did indeed—Uncle Ieng Sary, Uncle Khieu Samphan, Uncle Ta Mok. All the Pol Pot clique had been called her uncles.

"I didn't know them that well," she said. That was true, too.

What would she do if she couldn't shop in Soriya Market anymore? What would she do without Dara?

She begged. "I am not a strong person. Sometimes I think I am not a person at all. I'm just a space."

Dara looked suddenly mean. "You're just a credit card." Then his face fell. "I'm sorry. That was an unkind thing to say. You are very young for your age and I'm older than you and I should have treated you with more care."

Sith was desperate. "All my money would be very nice."

"I'm not for sale."

He worked in a shop and would be sending money home to a fatherless family; of course he was for sale!

Sith had a small heart, but a big head for thinking. She knew that she had to do this delicately, like picking a flower, or she would spoil the bloom. "Let's . . . let's just go see a movie?"

After all, she was beautiful and well brought up and she knew her eyes were big and round. Her tiny heart was aching.

This time they saw *Tum Teav*, a remake of an old movie from the 1960s. If movies were not nightmares about ghosts, then they tried to preserve the past. *When*, thought Sith, *will they make a movie about Cambodia's future? Tum Teav* was based on a classic tale of a young monk who falls in love with a properly brought up girl but her mother opposes the match. They commit suicide at the end, bringing a curse on their village. Sith sat through it stony-faced. *I am not going to be a dead heroine in a romance.*

Dara offered to drive her home again and that's when Sith found out that he drove a Honda Dream. He proudly presented to her the gleaming motorcycle of fast young men. Sith felt backed into a corner. She'd already offered to buy him. Showing off her car again might humiliate him.

So she broke rule number seven.

Dara hid her bag in the back and they went soaring down Monivong Boulevard at night, past homeless people, prostitutes, and chefs staggering home after work. It was late in the year, but it started to rain.

Sith loved it, the cool air brushing against her face, the cooler rain clinging to her eyelashes.

She remembered being five years old in the forest and dancing in the monsoon. She encircled Dara's waist to stay on the bike and suddenly found her cheek was pressed up against his back. She giggled in fear, not of the rain, but of what she felt.

He dropped her off at home. Inside, everything was dark except for the flickering green light on her printer. In the tray were two new photographs. One was of a child, a little boy, holding up a school prize certificate. The other was a tough, wise-looking old man, with a string of muscle down either side of his ironic, bitter smile. They looked directly at her.

They know who I am.

As she climbed the stairs to her bedroom, she heard someone sobbing, far away, as if the sound came from next door. She touched the walls of the staircase. They shivered slightly, constricting in time to the cries.

In her bedroom she extracted one of her many iPods from the tangle of wires and listened to *System of a Down*, as loud as she could. It helped her sleep. The sound of nu-metal guitars seemed to come roaring out of her own heart.

She was woken up in the sun-drenched morning by the sound of her doorbell many floors down. She heard the housekeeper Jorani call and the door open. Sith hesitated over choice of jeans and top. By the time she got downstairs she found the driver and the housemaid joking with Dara, giving him tea.

Like the sunshine, Dara seemed to disperse ghosts.

"Hi," he said. "It's my day off. I thought we could go on a motorcycle ride to the country."

But not to the country. Couldn't they just spend the day in Soriya? No, said Dara, there's lots of other places to see in Phnom Penh.

He drove her, twisting through back streets. How did the city get so poor? How did it get so dirty?

They went to a new and modern shop for CDs that was run by a record label. Dara knew all the cool new music, most of it influenced by Khmer-Americans returning from Long Beach and Compton: Sdey, Phnom Penh Bad Boys, Khmer Kid.

Sith bought twenty CDs.

They went to the National Museum and saw the beautiful Buddha-like head of King Jayavarman VII. Dara without thinking ducked and held up his hands in prayer. They had dinner in a French restaurant with candles and wine, and it was just like in a karaoke video, a boy, a girl, and her money all going out together. They saw the show at Sovanna Phum, and there was a wonderful dance piece with sampled 1940s music from an old French movie, with traditional Khmer choreography.

Sith went home, her heart singing, *Dara, Dara, Dara.*

In the bedroom, a mobile phone began to ring, over and over. *Call 1* said the screen, but gave no name or number, so the person was not on Sith's list of contacts.

She turned off the phone. It kept ringing. That's when she knew for certain. ·

She hid the phone in a pillow in the spare bedroom and put another pillow on top of it and then closed the door.

All forty-two of her mobile phones started to ring. They rang from inside closets, or from the bathroom where she had forgotten them. They rang from the roof terrace and even from inside a shoe under her bed.

"I am a very stubborn girl!" she shouted at the spirits. "You do not scare me."

She turned up her iPod and finally slept.

As soon as the sun was up, she roused her driver, slumped deep in his hammock.

"Come on, we're going to Soriya Market," she said.

The driver looked up at her dazed, then remembered to smile and lower his head in respect.

His face fell when she showed up in the garage with all forty-two of her mobile phones in one black bag.

It was too early for Soriya Market to open. They drove in circles with sunrise blazing directly into their eyes. On the streets, men pushed carts like beasts of burden, or carried cascades of belts into the old Central Market. The old market was domed, art deco, the color of vomit, French. Sith never shopped there.

"Maybe you should go visit your Mom," said the driver. "You know, she loves you. Families are there for when you are in trouble."

Sith's mother lived in Thailand and they never spoke. Her mother's family kept asking for favors: money, introductions, or help with getting a job. Sith didn't speak to them any longer.

"My family is only trouble."

The driver shut up and drove.

Finally Soriya opened. Sith went straight to Dara's shop and dumped all the phones on the blue countertop. "Can you take these back?"

"We only do exchanges. I can give a new phone for an old one." Dara looked thoughtful. "Don't worry. Leave them here with me, I'll go sell them to a guy in the old market, and give you your money tomorrow." He smiled in approval. "This is very sensible."

He passed one phone back, the one with video and email. "This is the best one, keep this."

Dara was so competent. Sith wanted to sink down onto him like a pillow and stay there. She sat in the shop all day, watching him work. One of the guys from the games shop upstairs asked, "Who is this beautiful girl?"

Dara answered proudly, "My girlfriend."

Dara drove her back on the Dream and at the door to her house, he chuckled. "I don't want to go." She pressed a finger against his naughty lips, and smiled and spun back inside from happiness.

She was in the ground-floor garage. She heard something like a rat scuttle. In her bag, the telephone rang. Who were these people to importune her, even if they were dead? She wrenched the mobile phone out of her bag and pushed the green button and put the phone to her ear. She waited. There was a sound like wind.

A child spoke to her, his voice clogged as if he was crying. "They tied my thumbs together."

Sith demanded. "How did you get my number?"

"I'm all alone!"

"Then ring somebody else. Someone in your family."

"All my family are dead. I don't know where I am. My name is . . ."

Sith clicked the phone off. She opened the trunk of the car and tossed the phone inside it. Being telephoned by ghosts was so . . . *unmodern.* How could Cambodia become a number one country if its cell phone network was haunted?

She stormed up into the salon. On top of a table, the $1,500, no-mess dog stared at her from out of his packaging. Sith clumped up the stairs onto the roof terrace to sleep as far away as she could from everything in the house.

She woke up in the dark, to hear thumping from downstairs.

The sound was metallic and hollow, as if someone were locked in the car. Sith turned on her iPod. Something was making the sound of the music skip. She fought the tangle of wires, and wrenched out another player, a Xen, but it too skipped, burping the sound of speaking voices into the middle of the music.

Had she heard a ripping sound? She pulled out the earphones, and heard something climbing the stairs.

A sound of light, uneven lolloping. She thought of crippled children. Frost settled over her like a heavy blanket and she could not move.

The robot dog came whirring up onto the terrace. It paused at the top of the stairs, its camera nose pointing at her to see, its useless eyes glowing cherry red.

The robot dog said in a warm, friendly voice, "My name is Phalla. I tried to buy my sister medicine and they killed me for it."

Sith tried to say, "Go away," but her throat wouldn't open.

The dog tilted its head. "No one even knows I'm dead. What will you do for all the people who are not mourned?"

Laughter blurted out of her, and Sith saw it rise up as cold vapor into the air.

"We have no one to invite us to the feast," said the dog.

Sith giggled in terror. "Nothing. I can do nothing!" she said, shaking her head.

"You laugh?" The dog gathered itself and jumped up into the hammock with her. It turned and lifted up its clear plastic tail and laid a genuine turd alongside Sith. Short brown hair was wound up in it, a scalp actually, and a single flat white human tooth smiled out of it.

Sith squawked and overturned both herself and the dog out of the hammock and onto the floor. The dog pushed its nose up against hers and began to sing an old-fashioned children's song about birds.

Something heavy huffed its way up the stairwell toward her. Sith shivered with cold on the floor and could not move. The dog went on singing in a high, sweet voice. A large shadow loomed out over the top of the staircase, and Sith gargled, swallowing laughter, trying to speak.

"There was thumping in the car and no one in it," said the driver.

Sith sagged toward the floor with relief. "The ghosts," she said. "They're back."
She thrust herself to her feet. "We're getting out now. Ring the Hilton. Find out if
they have rooms."

She kicked the toy dog down the stairs ahead of her. "We're moving now!"

Together they all loaded the car, shaking. Once again, the house was left to
ghosts. As they drove, the mobile phone rang over and over inside the trunk.

The new Hilton (which does not exist) rose up by the river across from the Department for Cults and Religious Affairs. Tall and marbled and pristine, it had crystal chandeliers and fountains, and wood and brass handles in the elevators.

In the middle of the night only the Bridal Suite was still available, but it had an
extra parental chamber where the driver and his wife could sleep. High on the
twenty-first floor, the night sparkled with lights and everything was hushed, as far
away from Cambodia as it was possible to get.

Things were quiet after that, for a while.

Every day she and Dara went to movies, or went to a restaurant. They went shopping. She slipped him money and he bought himself a beautiful suit. He said, over
a hamburger at Lucky7, "I've told my mother that I've met a girl."

Sith smiled and thought: and I bet you told her that I'm rich.

"I've decided to live in the Hilton," she told him.

Maybe we could live in the Hilton. A pretty smile could hint at that.

The rainy season ended. The last of the monsoons rose up dark gray with a froth
of white cloud on top, looking exactly like a giant wave about to break.

Dry cooler air arrived.

After work was over Dara convinced her to go for a walk along the river in front of
the Royal Palace. He went to the men's room to change into a new luxury suit and
Sith thought: he's beginning to imagine life with all that money.

As they walked along the river, exposed to all those people, Sith shook inside.
There were teenage boys everywhere. Some of them were in rags, which was reassuring, but some of them were very well dressed indeed, the sons of Impunity who
could do anything. Sith swerved suddenly to avoid even seeing them. But Dara in
his new beige suit looked like one of them, and the generals' sons nodded to him
with quizzical eyebrows, perhaps wondering who he was.

In front of the palace, a pavilion reached out over the water. Next to it a traditional orchestra bashed and wailed out something old fashioned. Hundreds of people
crowded around a tiny wat. Dara shook Sith's wrist and they stood up to see.

People held up bundles of lotus flowers and incense in prayer. They threw the
bundles into the wat. Monks immediately shoveled the joss sticks and flowers out of
the back.

Behind the wat, children wearing T-shirts and shorts black with filth rootled
through the dead flowers, the smoldering incense, and old coconut shells.

Sith asked, "Why do they do that?"

"You are so innocent!" chuckled Dara and shook his head. The evening was blue
and gold. Sith had time to think that she did not want to go back to a hotel and that
the only place she really felt happy was next to Dara. All around that thought was
something dark and tangled.

Dara suggested with affection that they should get married.

It was as if Sith had her answer ready. "No, absolutely not," she said at once.
"How can you ask that? There is not even anyone for you to ask! Have you spoken to
your family about me? Has your family made any checks about my background?"

Which was what she really wanted to know.

Dara shook his head. "I have explained that you are an orphan, but they are not concerned with that. We are modest people. They will be happy if I am happy."

"Of course they won't be! Of course they will need to do checks."

Sith scowled. She saw her way to sudden advantage. "At least they must consult fortunetellers. They are not fools. I can help them. Ask them the names of the fortunetellers they trust."

Dara smiled shyly. "We have no money."

"I will give them money and you can tell them that you pay."

Dara's eyes searched her face. "I don't want that."

"How will we know if it is a good marriage? And your poor mother, how can you ask her to make a decision like this without information? So. You ask your family for the names of good professionals they trust, and I will pay them, and I will go to Prime Minister Hun Sen's own personal fortuneteller, and we can compare results."

Thus she established again both her propriety and her status.

In an old romance, the parents would not approve of the match and the fortuneteller would say that the marriage was ill-omened. Sith left nothing to romance.

She offered the family's fortunetellers whatever they wanted—a car, a farm—and in return demanded a written copy of their judgment. All of them agreed that the portents for the marriage were especially auspicious.

Then she secured an appointment with the Prime Minister's fortuneteller.

Hun Sen's *Kru Taey* was a lady in a black business suit. She had long fingernails like talons, but they were perfectly manicured and frosted white.

She was the kind of fortuneteller who is possessed by someone else's spirit. She sat at a desk and looked at Sith as unblinking as a fish, both her hands steepled together. After the most basic of hellos, she said. "Dollars only. Twenty-five thousand. I need to buy my son an apartment."

"That's a very high fee," said Sith.

"It's not a fee. It is a consideration for giving you the answer you want. My fee is another twenty-five thousand dollars."

They negotiated. Sith liked the Kru Taey's manner. It confirmed everything Sith believed about life.

The fee was reduced somewhat but not the consideration.

"Payment upfront now," the Kru Taey said. She wouldn't take a check. Like only the very best restaurants she accepted foreign credit cards. Sith's Swiss card worked immediately. It had unlimited credit in case she had to leave the country in a hurry.

The Kru Taey said, "I will tell the boy's family that the marriage will be particularly fortunate."

Sith realized that she had not yet said anything about a boy, his family, or a marriage.

The Kru Taey smiled. "I know you are not interested in your real fortune. But to be kind, I will tell you unpaid that this marriage really is particularly well favored. All the other fortunetellers would have said the same thing without being bribed."

The Kru Taey's eyes glinted in the most unpleasant way. "So you needn't have bought them farms or paid me an extra twenty-five thousand dollars."

She looked down at her perfect fingernails. "You will be very happy indeed. But not before your entire life is overturned."

The back of Sith's arms prickled as if from cold. She should have been angry but she could feel herself smiling. Why?

And why waste politeness on the old witch? Sith turned to go without saying good-bye.

"Oh, and about your other problem," said the woman.

Sith turned back and waited.

"Enemies," said the Kru Taey, "can turn out to be friends."

Sith sighed. "What are you talking about?"

The Kru Taey's smile was as wide as a tiger-trap. "The million people your father killed."

Sith went hard. "Not a million," she said. "Somewhere between two hundred and fifty and five hundred thousand."

"Enough," smiled the Kru Taey. "My father was one of them." She smiled for a moment longer. "I will be sure to tell the Prime Minister that you visited me."

Sith snorted as if in scorn. "I will tell him myself."

But she ran back to her car.

That night, Sith looked down on all the lights like diamonds. She settled onto the giant mattress and turned on her iPod.

Someone started to yell at her. She pulled out the earpieces and jumped to the window. It wouldn't open. She shook it and wrenched its frame until it reluctantly slid an inch and she threw the iPod out of the twenty-first-floor window.

She woke up late the next morning, to hear the sound of the TV. She opened up the double doors into the salon and saw Jorani, pressed against the wall.

"The TV . . . ," Jorani said, her eyes wide with terror.

The driver waited by his packed bags. He stood up, looking as mournful as a bloodhound.

On the widescreen TV there was what looked like a pop music karaoke video. Except that the music was very old fashioned. Why would a pop video show a starving man eating raw maize in a field? He glanced over his shoulder in terror as he ate. The glowing singalong words were the song that the dog had sung at the top of the stairs. The starving man looked up at Sith and corn mash rolled out of his mouth.

"It's all like that," said the driver. "I unplugged the set, but it kept playing on every channel." He sompiahed but looked miserable. "My wife wants to leave."

Sith felt shame. It was miserable and dirty, being infested with ghosts. Of course they would want to go.

"It's okay. I can take taxis," she said.

The driver nodded, and went into the next room and whispered to his wife. With little scurrying sounds, they gathered up their things. They sompiahed, and apologized.

The door clicked almost silently behind them.

It will always be like this, thought Sith. Wherever I go. It would be like this with Dara.

The hotel telephone started to ring. Sith left it ringing. She covered the TV with a blanket, but the terrible, tinny old music kept wheedling and rattling its way out at her, and she sat on the edge of her bed, staring into space.

I'll have to leave Cambodia.

At the market, Dara looked even more cheerful than usual. The fortunetellers had pronounced the marriage as very favorable. His mother had invited Sith home for the Pchum Ben festival.

"We can take the bus tomorrow," he said.

"Does it smell? All those people in one place?"

"It smells of air freshener. Then we take a taxi, and then you will have to walk up the track." Dara suddenly doubled up in laughter. "Oh, it will be good for you."

"Will there be dirt?"

"Everywhere! Oh, your dirty Nikes will earn you much merit!"

But at least, thought Sith, there will be no TV or phones.

Two days later, Sith was walking down a dirt track, ducking tree branches. Dust billowed all over her shoes. Dara walked behind her, chuckling, which meant she thought he was scared too.

She heard a strange rattling sound. "What's that noise?"

"It's a goat," he said. "My mother bought it for me in April as a present."

A goat. How could they be any more rural? Sith had never seen a goat. She never even imagined that she would.

Dara explained. "I sell them to the Muslims. It is Agricultural Diversification."

There were trees everywhere, shadows crawling across the ground like snakes. Sith felt sick. *One mosquito,* she promised herself, *just one and I will squeal and run away.*

The house was tiny, on thin twisting stilts. She had pictured a big fine country house standing high over the ground on concrete pillars with a sunburst carving in the gable. The kitchen was a hut that sat directly on the ground, no stilts, and it was made of palm-leaf panels and there was no electricity. The strip light in the ceiling was attached to a car battery and they kept a live fire on top of the concrete table to cook. Everything smelled of burnt fish.

Sith loved it.

Inside the hut, the smoke from the fires kept the mosquitoes away. Dara's mother, Mrs. Non Kunthea, greeted her with a smile. That triggered a respectful sompiah from Sith, the prayer-like gesture leaping out of her unbidden. On the platform table was a plastic sack full of dried prawns.

Without thinking, Sith sat on the table and began to pull the salty prawns out of their shells.

Why am I doing this?

Because it's what I did at home.

Sith suddenly remembered the enclosure in the forest, a circular fenced area. Daddy had slept in one house, and the women in another. Sith would talk to the cooks. For something to do, she would chop vegetables or shell prawns. Then Daddy would come to eat and he'd sit on the platform table and she, little Sith, would sit between his knees.

Dara's older brother Yuth came back for lunch. He was pot-bellied and drove a taxi for a living, and he moved in hard jabs like an angry old man. He reached too far for the rice and Sith could smell his armpits.

"You see how we live," Yuth said to Sith. "This is what we get for having the wrong patron. Sihanouk thought we were anti-monarchist. To Hun Sen, we were the enemy. Remember the Work for Money program?"

No.

"They didn't give any of those jobs to us. We might as well have been the Khmer Rouge!"

The past, thought Sith, *why don't they just let it go? Why do they keep boasting about their old wars?*

Mrs. Non Kunthea chuckled with affection. "My eldest son was born angry," she said. "His slogan is 'ten years is not too late for revenge.'"

Yuth started up again. "They treat that old monster Pol Pot better than they treat us. But then, he was an important person. If you go to his stupa in Anlong Veng, you will see that people leave offerings! They ask him for lottery numbers!"

He crumpled his green, soft, old-fashioned hat back onto his head and said,

"Nice to meet you, Sith. Dara, she's too high class for the likes of you." But he grinned as he said it. He left, swirling disruption in his wake.

The dishes were gathered. Again without thinking, Sith swept up the plastic tub and carried it to the blackened branches. They rested over puddles where the washing-up water drained.

"You shouldn't work," said Dara's mother. "You are a guest."

"I grew up in a refugee camp," said Sith. After all, it was true.

Dara looked at her with a mix of love, pride, and gratitude for the good fortune of a rich wife who works.

And that was the best Sith could hope for. This family would be fine for her.

In the late afternoon, all four brothers came with their wives for the end of Pchum Ben, when the ghosts of the dead can wander the Earth. People scatter rice on the temple floors to feed their families. Some ghosts have small mouths so special rice is used.

Sith never took part in Pchum Ben. How could she go the temple and scatter rice for Pol Pot?

The family settled in the kitchen chatting and joking, and it all passed in a blur for Sith. Everyone else had family they could honor. To Sith's surprise one of the uncles suggested that people should write names of the deceased and burn them, to transfer merit. It was nothing to do with Pchum Ben, but a lovely idea, so all the family wrote down names.

Sith sat with her hands jammed under her arms.

Dara's mother asked, "Isn't there a name you want to write, Sith?"

"No," said Sith in a tiny voice. How could she write the name Pol Pot? He was surely roaming the world let loose from hell. "There is no one."

Dara rubbed her hand. "Yes there is, Sith. A very special name."

"No, there's not."

Dara thought she didn't want them to know her father was Kol Vireakboth. He leant forward and whispered. "I promise. No one will see it."

Sith's breath shook. She took the paper and started to cry.

"Oh," said Dara's mother, stricken with sympathy. "Everyone in this country has a tragedy."

Sith wrote the name Kol Vireakboth.

Dara kept the paper folded and caught Sith's eyes. *You see?* he seemed to say. *I have kept your secret safe.* The paper burned.

Thunder slapped a clear sky about the face. It had been sunny, but now as suddenly as a curtain dropped down over a doorway, rain fell. A wind came from nowhere, tearing away a flap of palm-leaf wall, as if forcing entrance in a fury.

The family whooped and laughed and let the rain drench their shoulders as they stood up to push the wall back down, to keep out the rain.

But Sith knew. Her father's enemy was in the kitchen.

The rain passed; the sun came out. The family chuckled and sat back down around or on the table. They lowered dishes of food and ate, making parcels of rice and fish with their fingers. Sith sat rigidly erect, waiting for misfortune.

What would the spirit of Kol Vireakboth do to Pol Pot's daughter? Would he overturn the table, soiling her with food? Would he send mosquitoes to bite and make her sick? Would he suck away all her good fortune, leaving the marriage blighted, her new family estranged?

Or would a kindly spirit simply wish that the children of all Cambodians could escape, escape the past?

Suddenly, Sith felt at peace. The sunlight and shadows looked new to her and her senses started to work in magic ways.

She smelled a perfume of emotion, sweet and bracing at the same time. The music from a neighbor's cassette player touched her arm gently. Words took the form of sunlight on her skin.

No one is evil, the sunlight said. *But they can be false.*

False, how? Sith asked without speaking, genuinely baffled.

The sunlight smiled with an old man's stained teeth. *You know very well how.*

All the air swelled with the scent of the food, savoring it. The trees sighed with satisfaction.

Life is true. Sith saw steam from the rice curl up into the branches. *Death is false.*

The sunlight stood up to go. It whispered. *Tell him.*

The world faded back to its old self.

That night in a hammock in a room with the other women, Sith suddenly sat bolt upright. Clarity would not let her sleep. She saw that there was no way ahead. She couldn't marry Dara. How could she ask him to marry someone who was harassed by one million dead? How could she explain I am haunted because I am Pol Pot's daughter and I have lied about everything?

The dead would not let her marry; the dead would not let her have joy. So who could Pol Pot's daughter pray to? Where could she go for wisdom?

Loak kru Kol Vireakboth, she said under her breath. *Please show me a way ahead.*

The darkness was sterner than the sunlight.

To be as false as you are, it said, *you first have to lie to yourself.*

What lies had Sith told? She knew the facts. Her father had been the head of a government that tortured and killed hundreds of thousands of people and starved the nation through mismanagement. I know the truth.

I just never think about it.

I've never faced it.

Well, the truth is as dark as I am, and you live in me, the darkness.

She had read books—well, the first chapter of books—and then dropped them as if her fingers were scalded. There was no truth for her in books. The truth ahead of her would be loneliness, dreary adulthood, and penance.

Grow up.

The palm-leaf panels stirred like waiting ghosts.

All through the long bus ride back, she said nothing. Dara went silent too, and hung his head.

In the huge and empty hotel suite, darkness awaited her. She'd had the phone and the TV removed; her footsteps sounded hollow. Jorani and the driver had been her only friends.

The next day she did not go to Soriya Market. She went instead to the torture museum of Tuol Sleng.

A cadre of young motoboys waited outside the hotel in baseball caps and bling. Instead, Sith hailed a sweet-faced older motoboy with a battered, rusty bike.

As they drove she asked him about his family. He lived alone and had no one except for his mother in Kompong Thom.

Outside the gates of Tuol Sleng he said, "This was my old school."

In one wing there were rows of rooms with one iron bed in each with handcuffs and stains on the floor. Photos on the wall showed twisted bodies chained to those same beds as they were found on the day of liberation. In one photograph, a chair was overturned as if in a hurry.

Sith stepped outside and looked instead at a beautiful house over the wall across the street. It was a high white house like her own, with pillars and a roof terrace and bougainvillaea, a modern daughter's house. What do they think when they look out from that roof terrace? How can they live here?

The grass was tended and full of hopping birds. People were painting the shutters of the prison a fresh blue-gray.

In the middle wing, the rooms were galleries of photographed faces. They stared out at her like the faces from her printer. Were some of them the same?

"Who are they?" she found herself asking a Cambodian visitor.

"Their own," the woman replied. "This is where they sent Khmer Rouge cadres who had fallen out of favor. They would not waste such torture on ordinary Cambodians."

Some of the faces were young and beautiful men. Some were children or dignified old women.

The Cambodian lady kept pace with her. Company? Did she guess who Sith was? "They couldn't simply beat party cadres to death. They sent them and their entire families here. The children too, the grandmothers. They had different days of the week for killing children and wives."

An innocent looking man smiled out at the camera as sweetly as her aged motoboy, directly into the camera of his torturers. He seemed to expect kindness from them, and decency. *Comrades,* he seemed to say.

The face in the photograph moved. It smiled more broadly and was about to speak. Sith's eyes darted away. The next face sucked all her breath away.

It was not a stranger. It was Dara, her Dara, in black shirt and black cap. She gasped and looked back at the lady. Her pinched and solemn face nodded up and down. Was she a ghost too?

Sith reeled outside and hid her face and didn't know if she could go on standing. Tears slid down her face and she wanted to be sick and she turned her back so no one could see.

Then she walked to the motoboy, sitting in a shelter. In complete silence, she got on his bike feeling angry at the place, angry at the government for preserving it, angry at the foreigners who visited it like a tourist attraction, angry at everything.

That is not who we are! That is not what I am!

The motoboy slipped onto his bike, and Sith asked him: What happened to your family? It was a cruel question. He had to smile and look cheerful. His father had run a small shop; they went out into the country and never came back. He lived with his brother in a jeum-room, a refugee camp in Thailand. They came back to fight the Vietnamese and his brother was killed.

She was going to tell the motoboy, drive me back to the Hilton, but she felt ashamed. Of what? Just how far was she going to run?

She asked him to take her to the old house on Monivong Boulevard.

As the motorcycle wove through back streets, dodging red-earth ruts and pedestrians, she felt rage at her father. How dare he involve her in something like that! Sith had lived a small life and had no measure of things so she thought: *it's as if someone tinted my hair and it all fell out. It's as if someone pierced my ears and they got infected and my whole ear rotted away.*

She remembered that she had never felt any compassion for her father. She had been twelve years old when he stood trial, old and sick and making such a show of leaning on his stick. Everything he did was a show. She remembered rolling her eyes in constant embarrassment. Oh, he was fine in front of rooms full of adoring students. He could play the *bong thom* with them. They thought he was enlightened. He sounded good, using his false, soft and kindly little voice, as if he was dubbed. He had made Sith recite Verlaine, Rimbaud, and Rilke. He killed thousands for having foreign influences.

I don't know what I did in a previous life to deserve you for a father. But you were not my father in a previous life and you won't be my father in the next. I reject you utterly. I will never burn your name. You can wander hungry out of hell every year for all eternity. I will pray to keep you in hell.

I am not your daughter!

If you were false, I have to be true.

Her old house looked abandoned in the stark afternoon light, closed and innocent. At the doorstep she turned and thrust a fistful of dollars into the motoboy's hand. She couldn't think straight; she couldn't even see straight, her vision blurred.

Back inside, she calmly put down her teddy-bear rucksack and walked upstairs to her office. Aido the robot dog whirred his way toward her. She had broken his back leg kicking him downstairs. He limped, whimpering like a dog, and lowered his head to have it stroked.

To her relief, there was only one picture waiting for her in the tray of the printer.

Kol Vireakboth looked out at her, middle-aged, handsome, worn, wise. Pity and kindness glowed in his eyes.

The land line began to ring.

"*Youl prom,*" she told the ghosts. Agreed.

She picked up the receiver and waited.

A man spoke. "My name was Yin Bora." His voice bubbled up brokenly as if from underwater.

A light blinked in the printer. A photograph slid out quickly. A young student stared out at her looking happy at a family feast. He had a Beatle haircut and a striped shirt.

"That's me," said the voice on the phone. "I played football."

Sith coughed. "What do you want me to do?"

"Write my name," said the ghost.

"Please hold the line," said Sith, in a hypnotized voice. She fumbled for a pen, and then wrote on the photograph *Yin Bora, footballer.* He looked so sweet and happy. "You have no one to mourn you," she realized.

"None of us have anyone left alive to mourn us," said the ghost.

Then there was a terrible sound down the telephone, as if a thousand voices moaned at once.

Sith involuntarily dropped the receiver into place. She listened to her heart thump and thought about what was needed. She fed the printer with the last of her paper. Immediately it began to roll out more photos, and the land line rang again.

She went outside and found the motoboy, waiting patiently for her. She asked him to go and buy two reams of copying paper. At the last moment she added pens and writing paper and matches. He bowed and smiled and bowed again, pleased to have found a patron.

She went back inside, and with just a tremor in her hand picked up the phone.

For the next half hour, she talked to the dead, and found photographs and wrote down names. A woman mourned her children. Sith found photos of them all, and united them, father, mother, three children, uncles, aunts, cousins and grandparents, taping their pictures to her wall. The idea of uniting families appealed. She began to stick the other photos onto her wall.

Someone called from outside and there on her doorstep was the motoboy, balancing paper and pens. "I bought you some soup." The broth came in neatly tied bags and was full of rice and prawns. She thanked him and paid him well and he beamed at her and bowed again and again.

All afternoon, the pictures kept coming. Darkness fell, the phone rang, the names were written, until Sith's hand, which was unused to writing anything, ached.

The doorbell rang, and on the doorstep, the motoboy sompiahed. "Excuse me, Lady, it is very late. I am worried for you. Can I get you dinner?"

Sith had to smile. He sounded motherly in his concern. They are so good at building a relationship with you, until you cannot do without them. In the old days she would have sent him away with a few rude words. Now she sent him away with an order.

And wrote.

And when he came back, the aged motoboy looked so happy. "I bought you fruit as well, Lady," he said, and added, shyly. "You do not need to pay me for that."

Something seemed to bump under Sith, as if she was on a motorcycle, and she heard herself say, "Come inside. Have some food too."

The motoboy sompiahed in gratitude and as soon as he entered, the phone stopped ringing.

They sat on the floor. He arched his neck and looked around at the walls.

"Are all these people your family?" he asked.

She whispered. "No. They're ghosts who no one mourns."

"Why do they come to you?" His mouth fell open in wonder.

"Because my father was Pol Pot," said Sith, without thinking.

The motoboy sompiahed. "Ah." He chewed and swallowed and arched his head back again. "That must be a terrible thing. Everybody hates you."

Sith had noticed that wherever she sat in the room, the eyes in the photographs were directly on her. "I haven't done anything," said Sith.

"You're doing something now," said the motoboy. He nodded and stood up, sighing with satisfaction. Life was good with a full stomach and a patron. "If you need me, Lady, I will be outside."

Photo after photo, name after name.

Youk Achariya: touring dancer
Proeung Chhay: school superintendent
Sar Kothida child, aged 7, died of "swelling disease"
Sar Makara, her mother, nurse
Nath Mittapheap, civil servant, from family of farmers
Chor Monirath: wife of award-winning engineer
Yin Sokunthea: Khmer Rouge commune leader

She looked at the faces and realized. *Dara, I'm doing this for Dara.*

The City around her went quiet and she became aware that it was now very late indeed. Perhaps she should just make sure the motoboy had gone home.

He was still waiting outside.

"It's okay. You can go home. Where do you live?"

He waved cheerfully north. "Oh, on Monivong, like you." He grinned at the absurdity of the comparison.

A new idea took sudden form. Sith said, "Tomorrow, can you come early, with a big feast? Fish and rice and greens and pork: curries and stir-fries and kebabs." She paid him handsomely, and finally asked him his name. His name meant Golden.

"Good night, Sovann."

For the rest of the night she worked quickly like an answering service. This is like a cleaning of the house before a festival, she thought. The voices of the dead became ordinary, familiar. Why are people afraid of the dead? The dead can't hurt you. The dead want what you want: justice.

The wall of faces became a staircase and a garage and a kitchen of faces, all named. She had found Jorani's colored yarn, and linked family members into trees.

She wrote until the electric lights looked discolored, like a headache. She asked the ghosts, "Please can I sleep now?" The phones fell silent and Sith slumped with relief onto the polished marble floor.

She woke up dazed, still on the marble floor. Sunlight flooded the room. The faces in the photographs no longer looked swollen and bruised. Their faces were not accusing or mournful. They smiled down on her. She was among friends.

With a whine, the printer started to print; the phone started to ring. Her doorbell chimed, and there was Sovann, white cardboard boxes piled up on the back of his motorcycle. He wore the same shirt as yesterday, a cheap blue copy of a Lacoste. A seam had parted under the arm. He only has one shirt, Sith realized. She imagined him washing it in a basin every night.

Sith and Sovann moved the big tables to the front windows. Sith took out her expensive tablecloths for the first time, and the bronze platters. The feast was laid out as if at New Year. Sovann had bought more paper and pens. He knew what they were for. "I can help, Lady."

He was old enough to have lived in a country with schools, and he could write in a beautiful, old-fashioned hand. Together he and Sith spelled out the names of the dead and burned them.

"I want to write the names of my family too," he said. He burnt them weeping.

The delicious vapors rose. The air was full of the sound of breathing in. Loose papers stirred with the breeze. The ash filled the basins, but even after working all day, Sith and the motoboy had only honored half the names.

"Good night, Sovann," she told him.

"You have transferred a lot of merit," said Sovann, but only to be polite.

If I have any merit to transfer, thought Sith.

He left and the printers started, and the phone. She worked all night, and only stopped because the second ream of paper ran out.

The last picture printed was of Kol Vireakboth.

Dara, she promised herself. *Dara next.*

In the morning, she called him. "Can we meet at lunchtime for another walk by the river?"

Sith waited on top of the marble wall and watched an old man fish in the Tonlé Sap river and found that she loved her country. She loved its tough, smiling, uncomplaining people, who had never offered her harm, after all the harm her family had done them. Do you know you have the daughter of the monster sitting here among you?

Suddenly all Sith wanted was to be one of them. The monks in the pavilion, the white-shirted functionaries scurrying somewhere, the lazy bones dangling their legs, the young men who dress like American rappers and sold something dubious, drugs, or sex.

She saw Dara sauntering toward her. He wore his new shirt, and smiled at her but he didn't look relaxed. It had been two days since they'd met. He knew something was wrong, that she had something to tell him. He had bought them lunch in a little cardboard box. Maybe for the last time, thought Sith.

They exchanged greetings, almost like cousins. He sat next to her and smiled and Sith giggled in terror at what she was about to do.

Dara asked, "What's funny?"

She couldn't stop giggling. "Nothing is funny. Nothing." She sighed in order to stop and terror tickled her and she spurted out laughter again. "I lied to you. Kol Vireakboth is not my father. Another politician was my father. Someone you've heard of. . . ."

The whole thing was so terrifying and absurd that the laughter squeezed her like a fist and she couldn't talk. She laughed and wept at the same time. Dara stared.

"My father was Saloth Sar. That was his real name." She couldn't make herself say it. She could tell a motoboy, but not Dara? She forced herself onward. "My father was Pol Pot."

Nothing happened.

Sitting next to her, Dara went completely still. People strolled past; boats bobbed on their moorings.

After a time Dara said, "I know what you are doing."

That didn't make sense. "Doing? What do you mean?"

Dara looked sour and angry. "Yeah, yeah, yeah, yeah." He sat, looking away from her. Sith's laughter had finally shuddered to a halt. She sat peering at him, waiting. "I told you my family were modest," he said quietly.

"Your family are lovely!" Sith exclaimed.

His jaw thrust out. "They had questions about you too, you know."

"I don't understand."

He rolled his eyes. He looked back 'round at her. "There are easier ways to break up with someone."

He jerked himself to his feet and strode away with swift determination, leaving her sitting on the wall.

Here on the riverfront, everyone was equal. The teenage boys lounged on the wall; poor mothers herded children; the foreigners walked briskly, trying to look as if they didn't carry moneybelts. Three fat teenage girls nearly swerved into a cripple in a pedal chair and collapsed against each other with raucous laughter.

Sith did not know what to do. She could not move. Despair humbled her, made her hang her head.

I've lost him.

The sunlight seemed to settle next to her, washing up from its reflection on the wake of some passing boat.

No you haven't.

The river water smelled of kindly concern. The sounds of traffic throbbed with forbearance.

Not yet.

There is no forgiveness in Cambodia. But there are continual miracles of compassion and acceptance.

Sith appreciated for just a moment the miracles. The motoboy buying her soup. She decided to trust herself to the miracles.

Sith talked to the sunlight without making a sound. *Grandfather Vireakboth. Thank you. You have told me all I need to know.*

Sith stood up and from nowhere, the motoboy was there. He drove her to the Hello Phone shop.

Dara would not look at her. He bustled back and forth behind the counter, though there was nothing for him to do. Sith talked to him like a customer. "I want to buy a mobile phone," she said, but he would not answer. "There is someone I need to talk to."

Another customer came in. She was a beautiful daughter too, and he served her, making a great show of being polite. He complimented her on her appearance. "Really, you look cool." The girl looked pleased. Dara's eyes darted in Sith's direction.

Sith waited in the chair. This was home for her now. Dara ignored her. She picked up her phone and dialed his number. He put it to his ear and said, "Go home."

"You are my home," she said.

His thumb jabbed the C button.

She waited. Shadows lengthened.

"We're closing," he said, standing by the door without looking at her.

Shamefaced, Sith ducked away from him, through the door.

Outside Soriya, the motoboy played dice with his fellows. He stood up. "They say I am very lucky to have Pol Pot's daughter as a client."

There was no discretion in Cambodia, either. Everyone will know now, Sith realized.

At home, the piles of printed paper still waited for her. Sith ate the old, cold food. It tasted flat, all its savor sucked away. The phones began to ring. She fell asleep with the receiver propped against her ear.

The next day, Sith went back to Soriya with a box of the printed papers.

She dropped the box onto the blue plastic counter of Hello Phones.

"Because I am Pol Pot's daughter," she told Dara, holding out a sheaf of pictures toward him. "All the unmourned victims of my father are printing their pictures on my printer. Here. Look. These are the pictures of people who lost so many loved ones there is no one to remember them."

She found her cheeks were shaking and that she could not hold the sheaf of paper. It tumbled from her hands, but she stood back, arms folded.

Dara, quiet and solemn, knelt and picked up the papers. He looked at some of the faces. Sith pushed a softly crumpled green card at him. Her family ID card.

He read it. Carefully, with the greatest respect, he put the photographs on the countertop along with the ID card.

"Go home, Sith," he said, but not unkindly.

"I said," she had begun to speak with vehemence but could not continue. "I told you. My home is where you are."

"I believe you," he said, looking at his feet.

"Then. . . ." Sith had no words.

"It can never be, Sith," he said. He gathered up the sheaf of photocopying paper. "What will you do with these?"

Something made her say, "What will *you* do with them?"

His face was crossed with puzzlement.

"It's your country too. What will you do with them? Oh, I know, you're such a poor boy from a poor family, who could expect anything from you? Well, you have your whole family and many people have no one. And you can buy new shirts and some people only have one."

Dara held out both hands and laughed. "Sith?" *You, Sith are accusing me of being selfish?*

"You own them too." Sith pointed to the papers, to the faces. "You think the dead don't try to talk to you, too?"

Their eyes latched. She told him what he could do. "I think you should make an exhibition. I think Hello Phones should sponsor it. You tell them that. You tell them Pol Pot's daughter wishes to make amends and has chosen them. Tell them the dead speak to me on their mobile phones."

She spun on her heel and walked out. She left the photographs with him.

That night she and the motoboy had another feast and burned the last of the un-mourned names. There were many thousands.

The next day she went back to Hello Phones.

"I lied about something else," she told Dara. She took out all the reports from the fortunetellers. She told him what Hun Sen's fortuneteller had told her. "The marriage is particularly well favored."

"Is that true?" He looked wistful.

"You should not believe anything I say. Not until I have earned your trust. Go consult the fortunetellers for yourself. This time you pay."

His face went still and his eyes focused somewhere far beneath the floor. Then he looked up, directly into her eyes. "I will do that."

For the first time in her life Sith wanted to laugh for something other than fear. She wanted to laugh for joy.

"Can we go to lunch at Lucky7?" she asked.

"Sure," he said.

All the telephones in the shop, all of them, hundreds all at once began to sing.

A waterfall of trills and warbles and buzzes, snatches of old songs or latest chart hits. Dara stood dumbfounded. Finally he picked one up and held it to his ear.

"It's for you," he said and held out the phone for her.

There was no name or number on the screen.

Congratulations, dear daughter, said a warm kind voice.

"Who is this?" Sith asked. The options were severely limited.

Your new father, said Kol Vireakboth. The sound of wind. *I adopt you.*

A thousand thousand voices said at once, *We adopt you.*

In Cambodia, you share your house with ghosts in the way you share it with dust. You hear the dead shuffling alongside your own footsteps. You can sweep, but the sound does not go away.

On the Tra Bek end of Monivong there is a house whose owner has given it over to ghosts. You can try to close the front door. But the next day you will find it hanging open. Indeed you can try, as the neighbors did, to nail the door shut. It opens again.

By day, there is always a queue of five or six people wanting to go in, or hanging back, out of fear. Outside are offerings of lotus or coconuts with embedded joss sticks.

The walls and floors and ceilings are covered with photographs. The salon, the kitchen, the stairs, the office, the empty bedrooms, are covered with photographs of Chinese-Khmers at weddings, Khmer civil servants on picnics, Chams outside their mosques, Vietnamese holding up prize catches of fish; little boys going to school in shorts; cyclopousse drivers in front of their odd, old-fashioned pedaled vehicles; wives in stalls stirring soup. All of them are happy and joyful, and the background is Phnom Penh when it was the most beautiful city in Southeast Asia.

All the photographs have names written on them in old-fashioned handwriting.

On the table is a printout of thousands of names on slips of paper. Next to the table are matches and basins of ash and water. The implication is plain. Burn the names and transfer merit to the unmourned dead.

Next to that is a small printed sign that says in English HELLO.

Every Pchum Ben, those names are delivered to temples throughout the city. Gold foil is pressed onto each slip of paper, and attached to it is a parcel of sticky rice. At 8 A.M. food is delivered for the monks, steaming rice and fish, along with bolts of new cloth. At 10 A.M. more food is delivered, for the disabled and the poor.

And most mornings a beautiful daughter of Cambodia is seen walking beside the confluence of the Tonlé Sap and Mekong rivers. Like Cambodia, she plainly loves all things modern. She dresses in the latest fashion. Cambodian R&B whispers in her ear. She pauses in front of each new waterfront construction whether built by improvised scaffolding or erected with cranes. She buys noodles from the grumpy vendors with their tiny stoves. She carries a book or sits on the low marble wall to write letters and look at the boats, the monsoon clouds, and the dop-dops. She talks to the reflected sunlight on the river and calls it Father.

NIK HOUSER

First Kisses from Beyond the Grave

Nik Houser graduated from Wesleyan University where he received the Dorchester Prize for fiction. He lives in Northern California where he is at work on two novels.

"First Kisses from Beyond the Grave," Houser's first published story, originally appeared in Gargoyle 51.

—E.D.

My mother says I'm handsome. I believe her. It's something she's always said and it's always done me, more or less, the same amount of good.

"You're so lucky to be so smart and handsome!" she hollered from the porch as I waited for the bus to my new school. I remember the air was drastically cool for the tail end of summer, but I didn't want to go back in that house for a jacket and risk a second hug, a second kiss goodbye. I'd lost track of how many times Mom had said, "Don't worry, you'll make friends in no time!" but I could stand no more of those either. It was one of her favorite phrases, as though the clay of creation was mine to shape and mold into a brand-new clique of ostracized freaks with whom I had nothing in common save the fact that the social trapeze had snapped between our fingers somewhere between our eleventh and twelfth years.

So I stood at the curb, freezing like an idiot. I looked back at my mom standing in the open doorway, unwavering optimism painted over her face in great broad strokes. One of her legs hovered at a forty-five-degree angle from the other, so that Mouselini, our cat, wouldn't bolt out the door.

I smiled thinly, then looked back across the street where my best friend Art White snickered as he waited for our bus. At the sight of him, my head snapped back like a spider had swung in front of my face. I squished my eyes shut, then opened them, like a cartoon, which is what I must have looked like to the casual passerby, staring in astonishment as I was at the empty sidewalk across the street where my dead friend had stood only a moment before.

The morning after Art let all his blood run down the bathtub drain (rumor has it his mom kept running into the bathroom with cups, pitchers, and ice cube trays, trying to save some of it, some of him, before it all got away), the school bus stopped in front of his house. For years it had always stopped in front of his house and I'd always crossed the street to get on, just as I did that morning. Like always, I lurched to the back row of seats and propped myself against the window, reflexively leaving room for my pal, though I knew he would not be joining me.

The bus driver idled in front of Art's house. An uncomfortable silence fell over the crowded transport, something my English teacher Ms. Crane might refer to as a "pregnant pause." The driver was the only one on board who didn't already know. Everybody else had seen it on the news the previous night, had spread word via email and cell phones, text messages for the dead. Ask not for whom the cell tones, the cell tones for thee.

Gus the Bus looked up at me through the broad rearview mirror.

"I'm only waitin' another minute."

A month later, when I got the notice in the mail which informed me that I would be spending my latter three years of high school away from the boys and girls I had grown to love and loathe respectively, my mother was as positive as ever. It was June by then. School was out and Art was in the ground, missing his finals by a week.

"What a great opportunity!" Mom said when I was done reading the letter aloud at the dinner table. "You can meet new people and . . ." I glared at her across the table as she struggled to maintain her unwavering optimism ". . . make new friends."

"You said the same thing to your cousin when he was sent to Riker's Island," Pop reminded her, looking over his glasses at the seven o'clock news on mute. My old man was nearsighted, but he loved the condescending erudition of looking over his tortoise-shell rims at whatever questionable piece of Creation happened to fall under his scrutiny.

"And he was so smart and handsome, too," Mom replied absently.

When the ghost of Art White had come and gone, I pulled the Notice of School District Transfer out of my pocket. It read like a draft notice, or one of those letters you get with a folded American flag to inform you that your child has been killed in action:

> Dear Mr. Henry,
> As superintendent of the Northside Public School District, it is my responsibility to inform you that as of September 1st, 2004, in an effort to further integrate our public schools, your street address will no longer be included in our district's educational zone roster and will henceforth be transferred to the Middle Plain School District. I apologize for any inconvenience this may cause.
> Sincerely,
> J. R. Sneider, Jr.
> Superintendent, Northside Public School District

No sooner had I finished reading my own death sentence than the familiar, noisome expulsion of school bus air brakes sounded off at the far end of my street. I looked up for the bus, but saw nothing—only the familiar line of SUVs parked along the curbs and in driveways. A stiff breeze picked up and made me shiver with cold for the first time since last April when the previous winter exhaled its death rattle. Or maybe it was the sudden silence that ran that chill up my spine. The street was dead quiet, a far cry from the familiar din of leaf-blowers, garbage trucks, and protein shake blenders that usually accompanied Monday mornings on our fair boulev—

CREEEEEE-SWOOSH!

The door to the school bus swung open in front of me, coming within an inch of my face and exhaling a cloud of dusty, tomb-like air.

Startled by its sudden appearance, I backpedaled on the wet grass, tripped on a sprinkler, and fell flat on my back.

I lay there for a second, staring up at the overcast sky, trying to breathe. It had been a long time since I'd had the wind knocked out of me, and for a second I thought I was dying. At last the airlock in my chest opened up and I sat bolt upright, panting, and stared up at the great black school bus humming cantankerously in front of my house like a hearse built for group rates.

Where the fuck did that come from?

I looked up through the open door, at the driver staring ahead at the road, black jeans and a gray hooded sweatshirt draped over his wire-hanger frame. The sweatshirt's hood covered his eyes as he slowly turned his head toward me. The rest of his body remained frozen in place, both hands glued to the steering wheel.

I stood up, grabbed my sprinkler-soaked backpack, and looked back at my house, an are-you-seeing-what-I'm-seeing? face pointed at the empty doorway. Mom was gone. Only Mouselini stood on the front step, eyes wide and tail shocked-up, a tremulous rumble sounding from the depths of his twelve-year-old gut like a drawstring dolly that's been buried alive.

Behind me, the bus's engine revved, once. I turned and started up its steps, heard the door close behind me while the driver's hands remained on the wheel. At the top step I paused and stared down at my chauffeur, at the empty black space where the shade of his hood covered his eyes.

"Morning." I slipped on the thin, polite smile I saved for teachers, strangers, extended family.

I looked back at the empty bus. The seats and windows were in decent condition, but dusty and tired-looking, as though the great vehicle had only just been called back into service after decades of neglect.

"First to get on, last to get off, I guess." Again that thin smile, more for myself than the driver now.

The driver turned his pale, expressionless face back to the road as the houses, cars, and trees began to slip slowly past the windows. The bus betrayed no perceptible shudder or lurch when we pulled away from my home, as though we remained still while the stage set of the neighborhood was drawn back to the flies.

When I first received the notice of transfer, I thought my folks were responsible. I wasn't exactly inconsolable after Art leapfrogged over his elders into the Great Beyond, but I wasn't the same either. I lost weight, stopped sleeping, stopped jerking off. I think the fact that I put down my penis worried the 'rents more than putting down my fork. They'd read that loss of libido was a common part of the grieving process for any close friend or relative. But they also knew that he was my *only* close friend, and that I was dreading the fall. More than any summer before, the phonetics of the forthcoming season sounded to me, and to them, like some dramatic plunge I was about to take, a forty-foot dive into a glass of water.

Mom and Pop were both teachers at my school. Having them with me at home, with their lingering smells of chalk dust and textbooks, the tiny snowflakes of spiral-bound notebook paper torn from its binding caught unmelting in the hems of their clothes, was like bringing the funeral home with me. It was because of this that I started to wonder if maybe the transfer wouldn't be so bad.

Strangely enough, however, it was when I suggested this very notion, and the uncharacteristically positive outlook inherent therein, that my folks started worrying, in earnest, about my mental well-being.

As the bus drove on, the sky grew dark. My surroundings grew increasingly unfamiliar as we passed into a stretch of suburbs which had taken an early turn toward fall and even winter. On the street below, the bus's enormous tires scattered decay-colored leaves across sidewalks that crumbled into the road like rows of rotting teeth. It soon became apparent that we would be making no other stops.

Jesus Christ, I thought as we passed into the overcast farmlands beyond the city — a bleak stretch of wild, untended wheat interrupted only by the occasional skeleton of a burned-out barn, *I've been transferred to Deliverance High.* The sky was nearly black. The sight of it took me back to the tornado drills we practiced on days like this in the second grade, when we would duck under our desks with our thickest textbooks held tight over our heads, a mere three hundred pages of long division standing between us and total, whirling annihilation.

Eventually, the rolling fields gave way to a vast stretch of incinerated woodlands — black, emaciated cedars reaching out to the day-for-night sky like the arms of the damned on Judgment Day. I opened my mouth to holler down the row of seats, to casually inquire about the fire which had apparently torn through this area. But when I opened my mouth, the nervous vacuum inside me would let no words escape. I looked up at the mirror suspended above the driver, at the yawning sweatshirt hood which now absorbed his features entirely, then at the massive fog bank rushing toward us as we began to accelerate.

The landscape was quickly erased by the fog, as though we'd traveled beyond the borders of Nature's grand composition and were barreling toward the edge of God's very canvas. I closed my eyes, felt the bus shimmy and shake as it continued to accelerate. Every bump in the road felt like the one that would dislodge a wheel, every turn was the road ending at a thousand-foot cliff.

"Please, God," I muttered to myself, a knee-jerk theological reaction. "Please."

The word itself was the prayer, not so much asking for a safe arrival, but to simply let me *keep* everything that I had and was, to finish the things I'd planned to do. The bus shook and shivered, tires screaming against the road. All my blood pressed against the surface of my skin in a centrifuge of fear. Everything that had ever happened to me: birth, laughter, friends, growing up, jerking off, Christmas, was boiled down to one word —

"PLEASE!" I screamed, my cry punctuated by the sound of the bus's door folding into itself as we came to a gentle stop. We were there.

I marched down the aisle on wobbly sea legs, bracing myself on the rubbery, crimson seatbacks. When I came to the driver I stopped to say something nasty, or sarcastic, or grateful, but when I saw his hands gripping the wheel, knuckles pressed against their gloved surfaces like only bone hid beneath, I thought better of it and climbed down the stairs to the curb.

"A fucking cemetery?" I asked myself aloud.

I surveyed the endless rows of tombstones to which I'd been delivered. No school. No students. Nothing but graves, trees, hills, fog.

I turned around to get back on the bus and ask the driver wh —

The bus was gone.

I looked down either side of the empty road, swallowed entirely by mist after ten yards in either direction. The driver had taken off as silently as he had arrived at my house that morning.

"Great. So what the fuck am I supposed to do now?"

As if in response, a lone crow cackled down at me from a nearby tree and took off over the stones. I watched him glide, then turn to croak at me again. A third time I watched him cruise out a dozen yards, double back, and let out another sonorous cackle.

"I'm already looking back at this and wondering what the fuck I was thinking," I said. I hopped the low wooden fence and followed the old black bird into the cemetery.

Most of the headstones were for people who'd died before I was born. Some dated within the year. Covered with moss and undergrowth, the sweat stains of finality and neglect, grave markers of every size and shape, from hand-carved mausoleums to wooden planks nailed together in cross formation, covered the surrounding hills in rows so crooked the caretaker had to be either cross-eyed, blind, or both.

When the old crow and I crested the last hill I looked back at the boneyard, at so many stones like goose bumps running up the spine of some tired leviathan.

I turned around to see where the crow had led me—a vista no less gloomy and depressing than the graveyard.

My new school was flat and broad and as featureless as it was silent. With a resigned sigh, I crossed a field of knee-high weeds, at either end of which stood a tall, crooked football goal, and hiked up the parking circle to the empty campus. The building itself was gray and unremarkable. The front door was unlocked. Inside, the lights were out. The only light came from the windows that lined a hallway to my right. The other side of the hall was lined with blue lockers, with the occasional break where a classroom door could be found. The tiled floor was white and clean. I started walking to see if anyone was home. All in all, it looked like your basic high school on a still, overcast Sunday afternoon. It was, however, Monday morning, and by now I was more annoyed than intimidated. I could be at my old school now, getting depressed, getting bored, getting horny. But instead I found myself wandering the empty halls of a forei—

What the fuck was that?

I whirled around, heart suddenly racing, more nervous than I'd let myself believe, and spied a tall locker door hanging halfway open a few yards away.

Whatever.

I turned back to where I was headed an—

"Who the fuck is there?!" I shouted, spinning around when the locker slammed shut behind me, its flat echo continuing past me down the hall.

"WHO—"

The locker creaked halfway open, slowly.

Someone's in there.

I took a step back with one foot, a step forward with the other, half brave and half smart. The front foot won. Slowly, I made my way toward the locker, sliding along the windows that lined the opposite wall to try and get a peek around the open door. The combination latch was missing. Only two rough screw holes remained where the lock had been torn off. I opened my mouth to say something to whoever was inside, some idle threat, but the vacuum inside my stomach had started up again, so that all I could manage was to slowly reach out, curl my fingers around the rusty locker door, and—

BA-RIIIING!!! went the homeroom bell. I jumped, slipped, cracked my head on the floor.

I stared up at the ceiling. The homeroom bell rang in my ears, bounced off the tile under my head. My first reaction was to panic that I was late, but once the combination of shock, terror, and pain had ebbed to a dull throb between my ears, I asked myself, "Late for what?" I didn't expect an answer.

Then the sounds came.

Something stirred outside.

I stood up and looked out the window at the hideous, skinless face staring in at me.

"Late," moaned the walking corpse on the opposite side of the glass. He looked about my age, his face puffed out in gaseous boils of decomposition. The flesh of his jaw hung loose, exposing a bloated green tongue laminated in pus and mud. He wore blue jeans and a varsity letterman's jacket. A backpack hung from his right shoulder. Dirt littered his unkempt hair, filled the spaces between his teeth.

I didn't even know I was screaming. The sound of my terror echoed down the hall, harmonizing with the great earthy rumble rising up from the ground outside as the tiled floor beneath my feet began to quake. Scared beyond coordination, I stumbled back on stilted legs and crashed into the wall of lockers behind me. My eyes stayed glued to the window, growing ever wider. Scores of rotten, worm-riddled bodies staggered from the cemetery beyond the football field, dusting the consecrated earth from their team jackets and cheerleader uniforms as they stalked en masse toward the school. No sooner had the first of the walking dead reached the parking lot than a ghostly white school bus pulled into the parking circle and expulsed a swarm of iridescent vapors who drifted toward the school dragging their souls and sack lunches behind them.

Thisisadreamthisisadreamthisisafuckingnightmare, I chanted in my head, pinching myself over and over until a trail of stinging, bloody fingernail marks lit up my arm like Christmas tree lights.

"You'll want to get those looked at." A voice from inside the locker behind me.

Again I shrieked, turned around, staggered into the middle of the hallway, surrounded by drifting, translucent ghouls from the white school bus. Twenty yards to my left, the front doors of the school opened, admitting the horde of teenage undead as they made their way inside like a river of coagulating blood. I looked back at the talking locker, which was now open. A tall, pale kid stepped out from within. He stretched out his folded arms and yawned, exposing two rows of healthy white razor-sharp teeth.

"Hey, watch it!" warned a female voice. The tall boy's clothes wavered in an unseen breeze.

"Fuckin' vapors." A second kid emerged from the next locker down, his face as gaunt and bloodless as his neighbor's. Beside him, one of the walking dead from outside bumped into a locker and fiddled clumsily with its combination.

"Next one down, you *moron!*" hollered a voice from inside the locker. The zombie moaned, lurched one step to the left, opened his locker, and pulled out a spiral notebook riddled with teeth marks.

"Hey!" yelled the voice from the locker. "That bonehead locked me in, you guys!"

The two boys in front of me snickered.

"You guys suck!" The voice banged on the inside of the locker.

"Yeah," the tall one chuckled. "That's kind of our thing."

The two vampiric jocks stalked down the hall, laughing wildly. By now the hall was swarming with rotten, lurching corpses, pale red-eyed kids staring ravenously at the cuts on my arms, and a gaggle of ghostly, transparent figures drifting over and through the meandering rabble. Wolf-men, swamp things, and hellhounds ambled to and fro, chatting briefly with each other as they parted ways to head to class.

"Come on, you guys!" pleaded the voice from inside the locker. "Lemme out!"

By the time the second bell rang, I was on my feet and the rest of the hall was empty. Well beyond shock, my heartbeat returned to normal. Calmly, I surveyed my surroundings. The occasional puddle of blood and ectoplasm notwithstanding, the loose bits of paper and scattered contraband cigarette butts at my feet gave the impression of a typical, harried Monday morning at Average Joe High School, USA.

"Hey," came the sad voice from the locker in front of me.

I turned to look at the three dark slats at the top of the locker door.

"Hey, new kid, lemme out or I'll suck the jelly from your eyeballs."

I stood there, staring blankly at the locker, slightly perplexed and, perhaps as a result of previous exposure to the relentless bullying I'd witnessed at my old high school, slightly amused. He clearly wasn't one of them. Just trying to fit in.

"Please?" the voice said, pitiful now, drained of all pretense of malice or ferocity.

I stepped up to the locker and tapped the combination lock. I always felt sorry for geeks and nerds, always helped them pick up their books while they dug wedgies out of their lower intestines.

"What's your combination?" I asked the locker.

"Six . . . six . . . five," the voice muttered hollowly.

At last the locker opened and out spilled the lanky, woe-begotten creature inside.

"You'd think with all the brains they ate, those fucking zombies would be like, geniuses, right?"

The kid bent down, dusted himself off. His voice sounded familiar. At first I was unsure. It sounded deeper and farther away than when I'd last heard it, a certain knowledge of things beyond haunting its cadence. But the sarcasm was unmistakable, and when he finally straightened himself up and showed me his bloodless, trademark smirk, all doubt vanished.

"Art?" I gasped, dropping my backpack into a splat of green, luminous jelly at my feet. I looked down at the long, deep canyons he'd cut into his arms only three months before. "Is that you?"

"Holy shit, man," my friend laughed, dead eyes wide with friendly astonishment. He leaned forward, pressed his cold, stiff chest against mine and hugged me. "Welcome to Purgatory High!"

"English, History, Health, Woodshop, Geometry, P.E.?"

Behind the registrar's desk, a skeleton in a moth-bitten sky blue pantsuit stared blankly up at me through a pair of faded pink reading glasses as I read my schedule aloud. Behind me, Art sat reading an old newspaper.

"Would you look at that," he muttered to himself. "Ollie North sold guns to Iran. Wait a minute . . ." He flipped over the newspaper, examined the date, then shrugged. "News to me," he obliged, and continued reading.

"Is that it?" I looked up from my schedule to the registrar, at the heavy layer of foundation mortared evenly across the surface of her skull, punctuated by two slashes of red-light-red lipstick, explosions of rouge, and neon-blue eye shadow, all watched over by a magnificent, Babel Tower beehive hairdo. A regular Bloomingdale's Day of the Dead Special.

"Is there a problem?" the secretary asked. Her rusty screen-door voice rose up from the center of her rib cage and escaped through two empty eye sockets adorned by a set of outrageously long false eyelashes.

"What do dead people need Geometry for?"

"You're not dead."

"I know. And yet I find myself asking the same question. I mean, come on, Health? You don't *have* health. You're dead!"

"This is Middle Plain High, young man. *Purgatory High*, if you will. *Good* little boys and girls, who die the *right* way, aren't sent here."

"Wait a minute. You mean I got transferred to like, Juvenile Hall for the Damned?" I threw up my hands. "That's great! Fantastic! Whatever. Doesn't matter." I leaned on the counter. "The point is I'm, you know, *alive*. Right? So obviously there's been a mistake. I shouldn't be here."

"That's what they all say."

By the time we got back to first period, Homeroom was over and English class had begun.

"Ah, Mr. Henry, welcome to our class." Mr. Marley stood in front of the blackboard, dressed in a turn-of-the-century waistcoat, dusty gray pantaloons and a powdered wig lying limp over his scalp, as though it had been ridiculed and debased by larger, more imposing wigs until all sense of pride or decorum had been wrung from its monochrome curls. Draped across the pedagogue's chest, over his arms, and around his legs was a seemingly endless length of rusty chains from which a series of padlocks and strong boxes rattled and clanged with his every movement.

I stood at the head of the class, staring at the erudite, emaciated apparition. He returned my gaze with polite impatience, no doubt accustomed to new students gawking at him.

"Chains you forged in life?" I asked casually.

He nodded like I'd asked if he'd gotten a haircut.

"Okey-dokey," I replied and turned to search for an empty seat.

As Mr. Marley began the lecture, I surveyed my classmates from the back row. I watched a gargoyle pass notes to a drowned drama queen covered over with seaweed and bright patches of dried brine. A studious nerd, the noose with which he'd hung himself still hanging around his neck, took notes while a bright red she-devil in a cheerleader's uniform giggled behind him.

Not much different than a regular high school, Art scribbled on a scrap of paper and passed to me. *Right?*

In the exact moment I finished reading the note, an anonymous spitball slammed into the five-inch-tall aborted fetus taking notes in front of me. He was dressed in a tiny basketball jersey and warm-up pants.

"What up, nigga'?!" the tiny voice hollered up at me, mistaking me for the perpetrator of the spitball. "You got a muthafuckin' problem!? You wanna piece a'this, son?!"

"No thanks," I said in the distracted fashion that warded off most every gangster and jock at my old school. I jotted down my response to Art's note: *Not as such*.

History class, as it turned out, was History of Everything. Purgatory High, apparently, had dug its foundations outside of the conventional space-time continuum, and could look at the history of the universe from a fairly objective vantage.

"Dude." Art put a hand on my shoulder, "I don't think it's a good idea for you to go in there."

"You mean about me gaining potentially hazardous foreknowledge of mankind's future which I could use to alter the course of human events?"

"Huh? No, I mean I got this joint from Lenny Baker and we should go smoke it."

"Nah, I'll pass, this whole day's been like one long, bad trip anyway."

"Suit yourself."

Over the next forty-five minutes I learned that (a) I would never be famous, (b) mankind would never be conquered by super-intelligent robots of our own design, and (c) ipso facto, my lifelong ambition of being the leader of the human resistance against their titanium-plated tyranny would never be fulfilled.

Such is life.

Next was Health Class.

On my way into the classroom, Missy Nefertiti, a hot little mummified number shrinkwrapped in a layer of Egyptian cotton no thicker than an anorexic neutrino, stumbled behind me in the hallway, spilling the contents of her purse at my feet.

"Thanks," she said absently as I knelt to help her.

I picked up a small, pearly jar which contained her brain, then another for her liver, and a third for her lungs.

"Where's the one for your heart?" I asked as we stood up together.

"No room," she replied. "I'd have to carry a bigger purse."

Five minutes into Health Class Ms. Tenenbaum-Forrester, a decomposing zombie, announced that this week would be Sexual Education and Awareness Week. It was at this point that I raised my hand, looked into my teacher's deflated, rotten-tomato eyes, and respectfully asked to be excused.

Lunch was no better.

"You gonna eat those brains?" Art asked from across our table. Roland, the gangster fetus from first period, sat to my left, poised on Missy Nefertiti's lap and free-styling to all who would listen, most notably, her big round gazungas.

"Ask George." I pointed to the towering zombie in a Middle Plain High basketball jersey sitting beside me. "They're his anyway."

Without a word, Art reached over the table and speared a forkful of gray matter from my tray.

"So what do you think so far, man?" He gestured at our surroundings with his fork.

I turned around, glanced back at the lunch line where a tall vampire dressed in fishnet tights and a Joy Division T-shirt leaned over the serving area and sank his teeth into the lunch lady's neck. I looked back at my friend sucking the dendrites from an oblongata kabob.

"I think you should chew with your mouth closed."

That afternoon, when the last horn of the apocalypse rang out the end of the school day, Art and I wandered back through the cemetery as our fellow students made their way to their graves, loaded up with that night's homework.

"Hey, Art," I said. "I've been meaning to—"

"Think fast!" interrupted a distant voice.

I turned around in time to throw up my hands and block a dive-bombing football before it spread my nose over my face like a warm pad of butter.

"Sorry about that, new guy!" From the direction of the dive-bombing pigskin, a burly, middle-aged man as wide as he was tall, dressed in a shimmering red leotard, hurdled a nearby tombstone and landed in front of us.

"You teach my gym class." I spoke to his huge, waxed handlebar mustache.

"That's right," the strong man agreed. "I was watching you today. You looked good. You've got good moves."

"I sat in a tree while everyone else ran around the track."

"Yeah, well, you've got to be in good shape to climb trees, right?"

"I was smoking two cigarettes at once."

"And *that's* the kind of go-getter attitude we need on our football roster, son! That little sneak attack earlier was my subtle way of testing potential new recruits!"

"There's a football team here?"

"Of course!"

"Do you get hoarse very often?"

"Excuse me?"

"Nothing. Besides, I didn't even catch the ball."

"But you managed to block it, which is better than most, let me tell you. So whad'ya say, son?"

"Um, no thanks. I'm not really what you'd call a team player."

There was a pause here, where I could almost hear the magnetic tape inside the coach's head reach the end of its reel and start rewinding itself for the next recruit.

"Well hey, no hard feelings!" he said and patted me on the back. He scanned the horizon and found his mark.

"Hey, DeMarco! Think fast!"

We turned and kept walking.

"Isn't Tim DeMarco deaf?" Art asked.

I shrugged, stared at my feet. We walked in silence for a time, weaving around the tombstones. Angels etched in granite stared up at us from stones marking the graves of children. Dead leaves pressed into the ground underfoot.

"I dunno," Art said at last.

"Huh?" I looked up at my friend.

"I don't know why I did it." My friend stared down at the dark little rivers running up the topography of his forearms, the barren, tilled flesh. "You know how, like, when you're trying to do something that takes a long time, like fixing something, or balancing something, and after a bunch of tries you finally just throw it at the wall because you're so frustrated? I don't know—that was how I felt about pretty much everything, I guess. I just sort of threw my life at the wall. I was tired of trying to fix it. Of course, it was only after I showed up here that I realized it wasn't *broken* to start with, just not *finished* yet. I dunno. That's what the school counselor told me. I guess that makes sense."

I didn't know what to say. It had been a long summer, during which I'd developed a staggering resentment for my best pal and his cowardly exit. I was angry at how selfish he could be, leaving me alone with this fucked-up world.

At last we came upon the road which had led me from my front door to Death's . door that morning. The sky was overcast and still, as it had been all day.

"I was pretty mad," I said at last, staring down at the uneven pavement.

Art let out a long breath, like he'd been holding it in for a while.

"I'm sorry, man," he said. He looked wistfully up at the treetops across the street. "If I could change anything . . . If I could go back and change *anything* I'd *ever* done, or left *undone* . . . I'd have felt up Suzie Newman at the Freshman Home-coming Dance."

I laughed and punched his shoulder as hard as I could, heard something crack under the putty-like flesh.

"Had I but known she'd become the biggest slut in our fucking class!" he entreated the clouds overhead, throwing his head back melodramatically and clenching his fists until the squeal of air brakes snatched the laughter out of our throats and tossed it on the ground like so much loaded dice.

We stood at the edge of the road, staring up at the hooded driver and his great black bus idling restlessly.

"Well, uh," Art backed away slowly. His eyes never left the driver. "I'll see you tomorrow man."

"Dude, wait!" I jogged a couple of steps to where my friend stood poised to sprint back through the boneyard. "You should come back with me," I whispered, and reached out for his shoulder. No sooner had my hand touched him then a bolt of lightning screamed out of the sky and seized my forearm in a cataclysmic Indian burn. The shock of the bolt knocked me back six feet through the dazzling, electrified air. I landed at the edge of the road, the wind knocked out of me, head buzzing like a pressure cooker full of hornets. I stood up slowly, gasping, reaching for the stars that swirled around my smoking head. By the time the Big Bang orbiting my head had dissipated in the encroaching dusk, my friend was gone.

I looked down at my arm, which was turning green, then up at the sky. Broad, rumbling thunderheads stared back at me like a reproachful parent. I remembered my uncle telling me about the time he was struck by lightning during his barnstorming days. He said it was like "God put a hand on my shoulder." He also said it "hurt like a motherfucker."

I craned my neck for a last glance at my friend, but there was no one, not even a crow.

"See you tomorrow," I said to cemetery, the vast stone harvest.

My only assignment that night was to memorize a poem of my choice, which I did, while nursing my fried appendage back to life and listening to my folks converse politely about their student, Ginger Banks, who had been brutally slain at school that afternoon. The cadence of John Donne bounced around my brain, playing tag with phrases like "teeth marks," "massive trauma," and "still at large."

Once my homework was done I could eat, as had been the rule of my family since my first day of kindergarten. The table was set with the summer dishes, though the brisk, teasing breath of fall could be felt in the breeze coming through the propped kitchen door. Autumn was my season—so haughty, yet sexy, it always reminded me of an aloof librarian with a brain full of Hawthorne and rabid, sexual fantasies.

Both my parents had a habit of reading at the table. You could always tell what kind of mood they were in by what they were reading. Grading papers meant they didn't want to talk. A newspaper meant they wanted to talk, but not about themselves, that the outside world would do just fine. A novel meant they were feeling romantic, while poetry meant I was going to sleep in the garage if I didn't want to lie awake to the sound of groans, spanking noises, and all manner of nauseating aural hullabaloo. Dr. Mengele, for all his crimes against nature and man, unknowingly left one form of torture untapped throughout his long years of evil: the sound of your own parents talking dirty to each other.

When I sat down at the table that night, I saw a folded *New York Times* beside my mother's plate, and a book of two thousand crossword puzzles adorning my father's place setting. I was safe. The table was set with two polite candles, three steaming chicken potpies, a bowl of green beans, and news of a bloodbath.

"I don't know what this world is coming to," my mother said, one hand on her paper, the other around her fork. "That poor girl."

"Didn't you used to have a crush on her, Zack?" My father glanced over the rim of his glasses at my blurred visage.

I shrugged and blew on a spoonful of thick, under-salted chowder. My mother was allergic to salt.

I thought about Ginger Banks, about her fiery red hair, and the first time I'd ever whacked off. She was the one I'd thought about on that distant autumn afternoon not so dissimilar from the evening we were presently enjoying. I'd always imagined her pubic hair as a tiny, quivering lick of flame where her warm, rosy thighs came together. I remember ejaculating far less than I thought I would.

"And in the women's lavatory of all places," my mother continued.

I held my spoon in front of my mouth, stared down at its congealing contents while my mother described the state in which Ginger Banks had been found—her head bashed in, with little bits of bone and brains scattered across the floor like the dashed dreams of every boy who'd ever dreamed of standing below her in a pep rally "cheeramid."

"Bruce Salinger is beside himself," my mother informed us. "I understand they had quite a thing."

"I thought she was dating George Dickson."

"Hmm, not sure. She could have been dating them both, for all I know, and for all either of them would care."

"She took quite a reputation with her when she went. Ms. Knotsworth was talking about it in the lounge."

"Speaking of the lounge, that new boy Pennybaum wandered in today while I was pouring myself a cup of java. What an odd young man, so pale and quiet. I think he was rather shaken up about what happened to poor Ginger. He was just wandering around in a daze. When I asked him what was the matter, all he could say was 'Brains.'"

"I think he's from Slovenia. Or is it Pennsylvania? Some vania or another. Which reminds me, your Aunt Ruth from Fairbanks called."

"Now why would Pennsylvania remind you of Fairbanks?"

"Oh, I don't know, it's just one of those things. Actually, I think I was at the supermarket today and I saw this can of tuna from Fairbanks right next to . . ."

Listening to my folks, I felt my appetite burn up and vanish, like my stomach was made of bright, flashing magnesium. I couldn't eat, but couldn't excuse myself from a full plate. So I sat there and watched my parents eat, in awe of these dull, lifeless creatures.

"I'm a nobody.

"Who are you?

"Are you a nobody too?"

"So let me get this straight," Art whispered from his desk. At the front of the class, Missy Nefertiti recited Emily Dickinson with all the passion and understanding of an empty Gucci shoebox. Tucked under her arm was a pearly, hand-carved jar adorned with the head of Anubis, in which she kept her brain. "You're saying that if *you* were the one that found Ginger Banks's corpse, you *wouldn't* sneak a peek before you called the cops? I'm sorry—which one of us is dead again?"

"All I'm saying is that it would depend on how gross she was," I hushed back. "I mean, her freakin' head was bashed in."

"So," Art replied. "You've *seen* her *head*."

Missy Nefertiti finished her poem and took her seat in front of Art.

"I heard she was already dead by the time they found her," Art informed me as I stood to walk to the front of the class, "before her last rites could be performed. Her soul's lost, dude! She's totally transferring here!"

I stood before my classmates, scanned their eyes, horns, and globules of proto-plasm. I thought about Ginger Banks, and about her transferring to our school. I thought about cold pussy.

·"Death be not proud," I began.

"Mr. Henry," the skeletal registrar addressed me as I waited to see Principal Grimm, "it appears that you were just dying to come back and see us."

"Was that supposed to be funny?" I asked from my chair.

"Do I look like I know funny?"

I glared at the tacky, painted skull glaring back at me with all the knowledge of the grave, then at the great wigwam of coiled, purple locks festooned on top of it.

"So, care to explain why you're here?"

I thought back to Mr. Marley interrupting my poem, waving his iron-clad arms in embarrassed indignation. As I'd gone back to my desk to collect my things, Roland the gangster fetus had offered me his condolences.

"Shit, son," he'd said, holding up a tiny fist for my fist to bump. "Grimm's secre-tary is scary, yo. They call 'er the muthafuckin' Clown of Dachau. Good luck."

At first I'd felt apprehensive about seeing the principal on my second day of school. But when an aborted fetus feels sorry for you, you have nowhere to go but up.

"So," I asked the neon skull to pass the time, "how did you die?"

There was a moment's pause, statistically long enough for someone to die in a car accident.

"A fanatical cultist blew himself up in the drive-thru where I worked. He was protesting the Korean War. He wasn't even Korean."

I paused a moment to reflect on the suddenness of it all, at having no time to say goodbye, to leave so many things left undone.

"Did you have to wear roller skates at work?"

"Yes."

"Mr. Henry, we have a problem."

Principal Grimm sat behind his tidy, faux-wood desk in a brown suit with a green tie. The pinstripes of his suit were the same width as the wood grain running along his desk. My first impression was that he was growing out of his furniture.

"You know, sir," I began casually, with just a hint of condescension. I've always found the best way to deal with authority figures is to talk to them like they're deliv-ering your pizza. "I'm sorry if the poem offended anyone. I thought it was apropos."

Of course I knew perfectly well that my poem might offend the teacher. That was the point—the point of the poem and of high school in general, it seemed: Four years of sailing as fast as we could toward the edge of the earth to see if it was round.

"There's no need for an insincere apology, Mr. Henry. That's not what I need from you." Mr. Grimm gripped the surface of his desk and wheeled his rolling chair around to my side as all sense of subtle mockery was wrung from my guts like a sponge full of blood. I stared down his lower half, or lack thereof: His brown blazer ended in a bloody tangle of bone, sinew, and strips of torn flesh. Averting my gaze to let the nausea pass, I looked up at the surfboard mounted on the wall behind him. An elliptical path of two-hundred-some-odd teeth marks ran up the middle of the board where a massive chunk was missing. "You see, the same clerical error which was responsible for your transfer here, transferred one of our students to your old school, and apparently, there's been some sort of incident."

I recalled poor Ginger Banks and her bashed-in brains.

"Is she coming here?" I asked, perhaps a little too eagerly.

"Excuse me?"

"Ginger Banks. Is she transferring here, now that she's, you know, dead?"

Mr. Grimm's face looked somewhere far off, as though called by a bell only his ears could hear.

"I really couldn't say," he began tentatively. "What I can say is this: you can't go back to your old school while Mr. Pennybaum is enrolled there. However, if he were to somehow meet an untimely *end* in your world, perhaps through the sudden rupture of his cranial cavity, you would be able to resume your place at your former alma mater."

"You're saying I have to kill this guy to go back to my old school?"

"Well, technically, he can't be *killed*, per se, because he already died. He's un-dead. A zombie, in the popular nomenclature."

"You want me to *kill* this guy?"

Mr. Grimm sighed and wiped a layer of ectoplasm from his perspiring brow.

"As of . . ." Mr. Grimm looked at his watch, held up an index finger. He opened his mouth, made ready to bring his hand down, then paused, and spoke quietly to his watch. "*What are you waiting fo*—NOW! Paul Pennybaum has killed three more of your former classmates."

"So you want me to stop him before he kills again."

"Mr. Henry, with deaths so sudden, the victims are bound to end up here. If this continues, our student-to-teacher ratio will be drastically upset. We're underfunded as it is. Lockers, desks, and food will start to run low."

I looked up at a corkboard mounted under the surfboard. This month's cafeteria menu was pinned to it by a single black thumbtack. I perused today's menu.

"So you want me to stop him before you run out of meatloaf?"

A long pause. Long enough for someone to realize that someone else has loved them all along.

"Yes," the principal nodded, rolled back behind his desk. His stomach rumbled. Behind the desk a dripping noise pricked the momentary silence. "That sounds about right."

When I left Mr. Grimm's office she was there, standing in profile, looking down at her new class schedule, just as I had done nearly twenty-four hours earlier, with equal amounts of disbelief and anger. I imagine it sucks finding out you're dead, especially when you were so popular. Ginger Banks was tiny, pale, her head shaved where they'd cleaned up the wound for her autopsy. She wore the cheerleader's uniform in which she'd died. Long, dark blood stains ran down the back of her white top.

I approached and opened my mouth to say something clever or sarcastic to the secretary to show Ginger how funny I was, how alive and breathing I was. But when I got close and felt all the boy in me flare up my front in a wave of campfire warmth, the speech centers of my brain stalled out. I tried to talk, to say something casual yet enigmatic. But I couldn't form a coherent sound, frozen in a mute, awkward panic, mouth open and eyes wide, like a wax museum dummy getting molested by a lonely security guard.

I came to my senses when she turned toward me and reflexively drew a wave of nonexistent hair behind her ear. She'd been crying. Watercolor veins of tear-diluted eye shadow ran down her cheeks. I closed my mouth, kept staring.

I love watching people cry. Maybe I shouldn't, but I do, and I've done nothing to change.

Still, I wanted to say something nice, something cool yet empathetic. But the problem was that I'm none of those things, really. Well, maybe I'm nice, but I'm too selfish to call myself a nice *person* and still be honest. Either way, I wanted to make her feel better about being dead. But how?

Say something, I thought to myself. *Make it good. Show some insight into the human condition that will lessen the blow of eternity rolling out before her.*

"Hey, at least now you can eat all you want and never get fat."

"Excuse me?" Ginger sniffed, wiped her nose on her bare forearm.

Oh God, just keep going you idiot. Don't stop till you can end on something good.

"Uh . . . you'll never get a pimple again?" *Never mind. Stop now.* "And you can smoke all you want."

"Who *are* you?" she asked.

"Plus, you died when you were still totally hot." *Please stop. For you own good.* "Just let that little nugget sink in."

For the love all that's holy . . . STOP!

She paused. Let it all sink in. More mad. Less sad. I have that effect on women.

"What are you, kidding?" she replied. "I'm freakin' *bald* you moron!"

From behind the counter, Ms. Needlemeyer, the Clown of Dachau, cleared her throat.

"Mr. Henry—"

I held up a single index finger, finally feeling the residual ire of Principal Grimm's admission that my transfer here had been a clerical error.

"Can it rollerball," I snapped, still locking eyes with Ginger, who flinched a little and smiled. Now that I'd made a complete fool of myself and had no chance of her being attracted to me, I could actually relax, be myself, and say something interesting. "Look Ginger, the most popular kid in school is an aborted fetus. I think bald's gonna work."

"Are you like, *retarded* or something?" Missy Nefertiti asked. Roland sat on her lap, leaning back against her tightly wrapped midriff. Missy took a jiggly bite of blood-flavored Jell-O.

"No doubt, son," Roland concurred. "You gotta be outta your goddamn mind."

"Whatever," I said absently. Across the cafeteria, Ginger ate alone at her table. "She looks alive."

"She dead, son," Roland said.

"So are you."

"But you're *not*," Art chimed in. "There are like, *laws* against that shit. Not like, *don't smoke pot laws*, but, you know, *real* ones."

I thought back to the previous day, to the lightning that had struck me when I suggested Art return with me to the land of the living. My arm was still a faded shade of aquamarine, and twitched when I tried to make a fist. What would become of my soul if I made it with Ginger Banks? Would it turn blue and feel fuzzy for a week? I could live with that.

"There's more than one high school for people like us, dude."

I glanced up at Art.

"What do you mean?"

"I mean stick around for the football game after school."

"*Football game?* Who the hell are we playing?"

Roland, Art, and Missy exchanged a look. Across the cafeteria, a pair of she-devils from the Spirit Squad sat down at Ginger's table and said something that made her smile.

"Why isn't anybody cheering?"

"What's the point?" Art asked. "It won't make any difference."

Even the cheerleaders sat on the sidelines watching the slaughter in total silence.

"The sun ain't even set yet, son."

I looked down at Roland sitting between me and Missy on the decrepit wooden bleacher. All around us the students and faculty made polite conversation in the packed stands, rarely watching the game as our hometown boys, the Middle Plain Lost Souls, were taken to school by the Inferno High Horsemen. Our players, a group of small, unassuming squirts with all the fighting spirit of a euthanized tree sloth were squaring off against the greatest generals of Satan's Legions. On the opposing sidelines, the Dark One himself sat in the bleachers, a great swirling mass of flame and agony contained in an old ratty letterman's jacket.

The grassy plain before us looked like a minefield in which every bomb had been detonated, so many times had our poor, brave lads been driven face-first into the sod. The score was thirty-six to zero. The opposing team had already rushed five hundred yards. A buzzer rang out to end the first quarter as the surrounding hills slurped down the last rays of sunlight. I edged my way to the stairs and stepped down to the sidelines where Ginger sat with the Spirit Squad.

"Hey, Zack!" She waved me over and scooched to make room for me on the bench. That one gesture made my heart beat so fast that every Christmas morning, every birthday I'd ever had, was instantly put to shame and forgotten. My whole life added up to that little space on the bench next to her teeny-tiny skirt.

"This is Misty and Twisty." Ginger waved to the two devils I'd seen in the cafeteria. The twins gave an upward half-nod that meant they'd seen me before, had scraped me off their shoe, and kept walking.

"Can you believe this game?" Ginger said.

"Yeah, I know. Why aren't you guys cheering?"

From the other side of the bench, Misty and Twisty sighed and rolled their eyes.

Ginger shrugged and bunched up her shoulders in a chilly gesture, leaning into me. She rubbed her hands up and down my bicep for warmth. Casually, I looked over my shoulder at Art, who studiously ignored me as the moon slowly hoisted itself over the field and the buzzer for the second quarter sounded.

"Come on, Ginger." Misty and Twisty stood with the rest of the squad and led Ginger before the crowd. I suddenly noticed that I was the only spectator still sitting. The entire crowd began to stamp and holler. The cheerleaders twirled and spun and ground their palms into their hips, spinning their heads around 360 degrees, whipping their hair in every direction. Too bad the crowd wasn't looking at them. All eyes were on the field as the home team broke their huddle, newly transformed into a raving band of howling wolflike demons. Matted black fur bristled through every seam in their uniforms. They howled up at the full moon blazing down on them.

The Middle Plain Lost Souls scored seven touchdowns in six minutes, plus seven two-point conversions, chewing their way through the opposing line until Inferno High didn't have enough players on the field to continue.

Ginger never stopped looking at me while she cheered. When it was all over I sought her out before the lightless vacuum of victory and popularity sucked her down for the rest of the evening. Misty and Twisty glared at me, my social ostracism forming a hideous, invisible hunch on my back which only they could see.

"Hey, can I walk you to your grave?"

Ginger stood at the stands, smiling broadly, out of breath. The air must have been gloriously thin at the top of a cheeramid. I imagined that when it dispersed and Ginger fell from the top and was caught, it must have been like the whole world was reaching out for you, wanting to make sure you're safe.

"Sure." Ginger's dead, glassy eyes caught the light of the full moon and swallowed it. Behind her, the other cheerleaders scratched behind the victorious players' ears. The crowd began to disperse.

As we left the field, Ginger put her arm around mine and put her head on my shoulder. I felt her cheek muscles tense with a smile.

"You're so warm," she said.

I looked back at the stands, at my friends studiously ignoring me, at Principal Grimm shaking his head. Across the field, someone else watched me. Though I didn't dare look back, I could feel a dark smile fix on me from the opposing sidelines, as the visiting team was carried off the field in defeat.

"I'm surprised you remember me, from when you were alive."

Ginger and I walked side by side through the rows of tombstones, fingers intertwined.

"Of course I remember you. Just 'cause you weren't popular doesn't mean you weren't cute." Ginger spoke to the moon, to the dead leaves at her feet.

"But I'm still not popular."

"So what?"

"So why do you like me?"

"Does it matter?"

"Not in the slightest. Just wondering why aren't you ignoring me now?"

"I don't know. Maybe vampires and ghosts don't have like, pheromones or something. And besides, you're *way* cuter than an aborted fetus."

"Awe shucks," I replied. "You're too good to me."

"You ain't seen nothin' yet, honey."

I could tell she'd said it before, with other guys, and that she recycled the phrase because she knew it was sexy. And it was sexy.

For a second, before her cold, dead tongue slid between my teeth, I thought, *maybe this isn't a good idea. What about the rules of Heaven and Earth?* But then my hand slid under her shirt, cupped her firm, icy breast, and I didn't care.

Let me tell you something you already know:

A polite girl or woman, with whom you've never spoken of sex, suddenly telling you where to go, grabbing your hand, and sliding it between her legs, admitting that she wants to feel good—in the years after that night, such a thing wouldn't seem like a big deal. Grown women can talk about what they want, what they need from you. But in high school, when girls are supposed to be ladies instead of human beings, hearing such things from a total hottie like Ginger Banks, when all I'd dared to dream of was first base and a decent view of second, was like looking for trace elements of fossilized bacteria on Mars and finding the Miss Hawaiian Tropic competition camped out at your landing site.

Her skin was achingly cold.

"You're freezing," I said.

"I get goose bumps all the time."

She stood there with her top off while we kissed. She kept her skirt on, her socks and shoes too. Half-dressed like that, that strange combination of nudity and modesty, was an intoxicating cocktail of dream life and daily life. I'd only ever seen one or the other. In movies, they always cut from the kissing to the sex montage. In pornos, "actors" peeled off their own clothes like layers of useless, dead skin. But when Ginger lay back on a patch of hallowed earth overrun with clover, grabbed my hips, and guided me into her hidden, frozen pussy, it was as though we'd fallen into the crack between fantasy and reality, into that twilight of sensuality which you can visit once, the first time, but only in dreams thereafter.

Plus, I'd always thought people called out each other's names when they did it. I've since learned that this is seldom the case. I've also learned that people seldom even think of each other when they're fucking each other. But back then, that night, I could only think of Ginger—and not even all of her, just her breasts, or her eyes, or how we tried to keep it in when we turned over so she could be on top. One thing at a time. I didn't even know my name.

She came when I came, *because* I came, I would later find out. Apparently, what I left in her was hot and anxious and she had only the chill of death to fill her insides the rest of the time. I haven't made many women cum since then.

"It's so weird just sitting here," she remarked afterwards, propped against the base of a towering, angelic grave marker. "I used to have to, you know, button up while my boyfriend defrosted the windshield so he could drop me off before curfew." She sighed. "It's so weird being dead. You know?"

"Not really."

"You will."

"Thanks."

She smiled at me, straightened her clothes, and reached back to try and tuck her buzzed-off hair behind her ears.

"I heard your hair keeps growing after you die," she said. "I hope it's true. You know—" She sounded serious all of a sudden (something else I would have to get used to, and dread—a woman getting a serious tone after a sound shag). "How do you know, for sure, that you shouldn't be here?"

"What do you mean?"

"I mean, think about it," she said.

But I didn't have to. Already my heart started rattling in my chest like a punching bag. She meant *how did I know I wasn't dead*. Did I know?

I started talking fast. More to myself than the dead girl scrutinizing my dazed expression.

"But I've gone home to my house and seen my parents and—"

"Did they talk to you? Did they acknowledge you?"

"No, but they usually don't. They—"

I stopped when I saw it. By the light of a lightning flash, I saw it staring back at me, unassuming, defiant, smug.

"Ohmigodimdead." I knelt in front of my grave, stared down at my name and the date underneath. July fourth. I died on Independence Day. I thought back to a firecracker nearly going off in my hand. It must have gone off too soon. I must have bled to death.

"I'm dead?" The world went quiet. Long enough for a light to turn red too soon. The cool earth snuck up and cold-cocked me from behind. I was on the ground.

Somewhere beneath me, I was *in* the ground. The transfer wasn't a mistake. I was supposed to be here in the land of the dead, haunting my parents at night, unable to let g—

"PSYYYYYYYYYCH!"

The call resounded through the boneyard. Disoriented from my fall, I tried to stand, tried to use my own tombstone for balance as it crumbled into a lumpy mass of gray, standard-issue, sophomore Art Class self-hardening clay and I fell into it on my way back to Earth.

From behind the nearest mausoleum, Art, Roland, and Missy Nefertiti leapt into the moonlight, the surprise causing my heart, my still-beating, magnificent, most all-important muscle to batter against its calcium housing, threatening to stop, but persevering nonetheless.

"Sha-ZAAM, son!" Roland called out, laughing hysterically before Missy nearly squashed him as she doubled over in hysterics.

"You guys are so fucking dead!" I swore to Art as he helped me to my feet. Had they been there listening to us the whole time? Did I care? No! I was alive! I was laid! It was funny, too—I'd equated those two states of being for so long, now that I got both at once, they seemed completely different.

I grinned at the smug bastard, punched him in the shoulder as hard as I could, which wasn't very hard. "You are so *fucking* DEAD!"

"I know."

Nobody parties like the dead. The damned have rhythm. The entire school celebrated our victory in the cemetery that night, stamping their feet, howling at the moon loud enough to wake the dead and serve them up a tall one from the keg.

Ginger stayed close to me, getting drunk and clingy as the night spiraled down into the rosy abyss of bad breath and good vibes. Living in Limbo, a place to which God apparently turned a blind eye, was like your folks going away for the weekend and leaving the keys in the ignition and the liquor cabinet unlocked. The idea of bashing Paul Pennybaum's skull in was as distant and meaningless as Monday morning seen from the observation deck of Friday night.

"Listen!" Ginger said to me over the music sometime after midnight. She was sweaty from dancing and talked right into my face with a boozy lack of depth perception. "I don't want you to think I'm a slut or anything because we fucked!"

"But *aren't* you kind of a slut?!" I howled and lit a cigarette.

"Well, yeah, but I don't want you to think of me that way!"

"I don't!"

"Good!" she proclaimed, then climbed on top of a broad, flat grave marker, took off her shirt, and started to dance. It was at that moment that I knew I was falling in love.

Just before dawn, things started to slow down, and my new girlfriend started to cry.

"I was sooooooo fucking popular!" she lamented, tears streaming down her face. The moon was down and all was dark. All around us, drunken kids and bilious abominations stumbled back to their graves. "I was about to get my *license!* And just 'cause that dumb-ass zombie ate my brains I wound up here. I should *totally* be in *Heaven!*"

"At least you didn't wind up in Hell."

"My cell phone doesn't get *any* reception here!" she shouted to the black sky. "I *am* in Hell!"

She sobbed. I held her close. Her nipples were hard under her shirt. Her tears were cold.

"What the fuck is a *last rite* anyway? Is that like, the directions to Heaven? They couldn't give me directions before I died, so I got lost and ended up here? I don't even believe in God!"

I struggled to find the right thing to say that would either make her feel better or at least make her stop crying.

"Yeah, but, you know, *He* believes in *you*."

"Really?" she asked, teary-eyed and hopeful. "You think so?"

"Um . . . not really. Sorry. I just said that to make you feel better. I stopped believing in God before I stopped believing in Santa Claus."

In the next plot down, Brutus Forte, our school's star quarterback, slid down into his grave, drunk with victory, beer, adoration of the masses. Peering over the lip of his grave, I watched him fluff up the dirt where his head would rest, then reach up to the surface, and in a single, sweeping motion draw a pile of loose earth on top of him as he fell back, already sound asleep before his head touched the cool, wormy terra firma.

"Do you love me?"

"Huh?" I turned back to Ginger. She propped herself against a headstone, watching me like a mirror while she wiped away her smeared eye shadow. Dead leaves clung to her scalp and clothes. The last of the alcohol had left her body, leaving her more sober than she was before she started drinking, the way you get when you've stayed up late enough for the booze to find its way back out, temporarily flushing out the drunkenness of everyday self-denial.

"I know they want you to kill Paul Pennybaum," she continued. "If you do, you won't ever come back."

"Well, I could come back," I swallowed. "I mean . . . I'd have to do it like Art di—"

"But you wouldn't." She looked up at the moon, saw herself in it, pursed her lips, drew a finger around them to erase a smudge. "You're not that kind of person."

"What do you mean?"

"You're the kind of person that makes good decisions. That's why girls don't like you—as more than a friend I mean." She sighed, eyes focused on a leaf stuck in the front clasp of her bra. "You'll never break my heart," she said. She sounded a little surprised, and a little disappointed.

She looked up at me, caught my expression.

"I'm not stupid," she replied to my thoughts. "Girls understand boys. It's just that most of the time, we don't have to, or we don't want to."

"I don't wanna kill Paul. I want to keep coming to see you."

"Then *don't* kill him," she pleaded softly. "He'll probably get killed some other way, anyway. People die all the time. Look at *me*."

A cold wind rustled through the cemetery, a parent checking up on their child after lights-out. It found us and we huddled together. Ginger's skin made me even colder, but I didn't want to let go.

"I should get to bed," she said at last, and lowered herself into the empty grave beside us. Once in, she paused and peered up at me. Her head just barely came up above ground level. "Will you tuck me in?"

"Sure," I replied, and got down on my knees. As I worked the dirt into her grave, I thought about the times my father would wake me up and tell me I was having a nightmare. I never remembered having a bad dream, but I believed him and felt better with him there.

"When you're done," Ginger said before I covered her face, "you have to go."

"What do you mean?"

"You can't spend the night here, or you can never leave again."

"How do you know?"

"I don't know, I just know. It's just one of the rules. Your parents are probably worried sick."

"But I wan—"

"Nobody worries about me anymore," she interrupted.

She leaned forward, crawled her fingers through the hair on the back of my head, kissed me, then fell back to the dark earth, the dirt around her body caving in as she fell. Behind me, I could already hear the black bus idling at the side of the road.

"Where have you been?"

"Have you been drinking?"

"We've been so worried!"

"You have no idea!"

It's funny how quickly relief can turn to anger. It's like we keep both emotions spring-loaded inside the same little tin can inside our chests and when we let one feeling out, the other must inevitably follow.

"Did you drive drunk?" my father demanded to know, rubbing the sleep from his eyes. "Who have you been out with?"

"Zombies."

"Zombies? What is that, some kind of gang?" The old man inquired, exasperated from running every drug overdose and child-kidnapping scenario imaginable through his head while waiting to hear my key in the door. "Are you in a fucking gang now?"

My father rarely cussed at me. It was one of those rare glimpses I ever caught of his non-father personality. I rarely liked what I saw.

"Oh my God." My mother sat down at the table, her face in her hands. She looked up at her jailbird son. "Are you dealing drugs?"

I wanted to tell them to get real, to remember that the best lessons they ever learned was from the mistakes they made, that the first step in becoming your own person is to make a conscious decision *not* to become your parents.

But I didn't know how to say all that, to articulate what I would only learn years later when I yelled at my own kids, because the only way to grow old is to forget what it's like to be young. And besides, they didn't *deserve* a response, or so I believed. They'd never been this mad before, never talked to me like this. It made all their love, all their kind words and tender moments seem totally and unforgivably conditional.

"Yeah," I replied coldly. If they needed to blame everything on changes in the world outside, instead of changes in their son, I wouldn't stand in their way. "That's it." I started up to my room, spoke over my shoulder, let my words tumble down the stairs behind me. "The big bad wolf made me do it."

"That must be his supplier," I heard my father explain to my mother. "They all have nicknames. It's all—"

The door SLAMMED! on his words, caught them and held them like fingers in a car door.

I collapsed on my bed, listened to my parents fighting downstairs, turned on the ten o'clock news. Channel 4 was running an exposé on the deaths at my old high school. A young, statuesque, serious-minded telejournalist reported that students were living in a state of mourning, that grief had struck the school "like a brick through a stained-glass window." As she said this, a man with a clipboard stepped behind her, into frame, and waved off the mob of students mooning the camera and flashing middle fingers and gang signs.

"Excuse me, young man." The reporter snared a passerby and aimed the camera at him. It was Paul Pennybaum, lurching to class. Flies orbited his tilted head, alighting on his rotten fruit face and taking off again. His clothes were tattered and sullied from his time in the grave. His eyes looked at the world like a retarded monkey would look at a banana painted on a brick wall.

"Young man," the reporter began again, "how does it feel going to school under the shadow of Death?"

"Brains," Paul droned, with great effort, as he stared straight through the reporter.

"Yes," the reporter responded, "the victims have all suffered severe trauma to their craniums. How does that make you feel?"

"Feel . . . dead."

The reporter turned back to the camera.

"As you can see, some of the students here already consider themselves future victims. Back to you, Bob and Alice."

I changed the channel, tried to pick up some scrambled porn, but nothing was on. So I sat there in the dark, weighing the gravity of so much death against the weight of Ginger's body on top of mine. I supposed it was partially my fault. If I whacked Paul, got rid of him somehow, the killing would stop. But I would never see Ginger again. Thus, the combination of my lust for her and my loathing for my former classmates was enough to persuade me, before I whacked off and fell asleep, that most of them were better off dead anyway. Paul Pennybaum was by no means the only zombie at San Los Pleasovale High.

By the following Saturday, five more students and three teachers were dead at school. My parents spoke as though I was one of them. Good riddance. And don't give me that look, either. How many times have you looked around a room and, however fleetingly, wished half of them would just disappear?

At the table that morning, my father spoke of days gone by, when he and I would barbecue burgers in the backyard and play catch. My mother made no reply. Tears welled up in her eyes as she hid them behind that day's crossword. Sitting between them at the table, I wanted to remind my father that he was a vegetarian, and that we had played catch once. Neither of us liked it. We both hated sports. And while I couldn't claim to like the jocks at my school, I couldn't blame them for being what they were. After all, if I had the choice between being a moderately clever writer, amusing himself alone at his computer, or being a Neanderthal in a football jersey at a blowjob buffet (or so I have to imagine them), I'd have to think about it.

Leaning over his bowl of cereal, my father flipped to the business section, exposing the front page to the rest of the table. The headline read that both the FBI and the Centers for Disease Control and Prevention had been called in to investigate the series of deaths at my old high school.

I got up to leave when I heard my bus arrive to take me to the Homecoming pep rally and game. We'd been prepping for it all week—hanging streamers in the hallways at school, pinning up signs so parents and alums wouldn't get lost when they arrived for the game from their various planes of existence. I'd stayed late every day to help decorate and then fuck my girlfriend. Every day was Christmas. Then I would come home and see my parents asleep on the couch, in the armchair, at the kitchen table, dreaming in uncomfortable positions. First I'd be mad. Then I'd be sorry. Then I'd go to sleep feeling mad that they made me feel sorry.

I paused for a second at the door, looked back at my parents looking down at their papers and plates, not so much looking at these items of interest as not looking at me.

For all they know, I am in a gang. This could be the last time they see me, and they don't care. They wouldn't care if I was next.

Going out the door, I thought about what Ginger said every night when I tucked her into her grave and I always asked to stay a little longer. *If you stay*, she'd invariably warn me, *you can never go home.*

I thought about that as I got onto the bus, and about how little home felt like home anymore.

Well, maybe I will be next.

As we pulled away, I looked back at the house I'd grown up in. It felt like I hadn't been there in years, as though it had been sold long ago and that I'd only just returned for nostalgia's sake, but had changed my mind when I drew close, and decided to keep driving.

"Where are they?"

"They'll be here."

The air was cold and electrified, the sky black. It was two minutes till game time and the opposing team still had yet to show, as had their fans. The bleachers opposite ours were bare, the sidelines equally so.

"If they don't show, do they forfeit?"

"They'll show."

I sat in the top row of bleachers with Art and Roland.

"I need a smoke," Roland said. He and Art, along with the rest of the hushed crowd, watched the field intently. The players on our side had already made their big entrance and were sitting on their benches, waiting and watching the field. "Wish I could hold a cigarette."

That afternoon, the pep rally had proceeded as all such events do—cheering, clapping, yelling, clapping some more and yelling louder, followed by more cheering, and, time permitting, more yelling and clapping. All throughout, however, there had been something in the air between the fans and the players, something in their distant smiles that made our good wishes sound almost mournful—some unacknowledged dread, as though our boys were going off to war, that we might not ever see them again.

"But if they don't show up," I repeated.

"They'll show up."

My breath came out as a fog. Nobody else's did.

"But if they d—"

A sound rang out from On High—a lone trumpet echoing down from the cloud cover. I looked up at the sky, as did everyone, and felt fear choke my heart. The horn sounded once more, like a distant cavalry charge. As it did so, a solitary ray of golden light, no wider than a child's arm, pierced the clouds and focused on the fifty-yard line. A third time the trumpet sounded. My breath caught in my throat. I wanted to hide, to cover my face, so terrible was this sound that said *your dreams are over*, a sound that told you, convinced you, that *everything you thought you would become you will never become; all the plans you have laid for yourself, will never come to pass.* It was the bang of an unseen gun pointed at your heart. It was the sound of The End.

The fourth time the horn sounded it was joined by a chorus of bellicose brass, horns of war that wrung all will to resist from my body as the tiny spotlight that shone down on our home field widened suddenly, split the sky like a knife ripping open a wound, flooding the terrain with a rapturous, unflinching blaze as a host of seraphim in gold and white football jerseys poured down from the break in the clouds and stormed the field, a beautiful, thunderous stampede of infallible athletic ability with the greatest record of any school in the history of the universe. These were our opponents. This was Paradise High.

"We have to fight *Heaven* in our Homecoming Game?" I asked, totally flabbergasted. Across the field, a glowing body of halos and white robes filled the opposing stands.

"They've never been defeated," Art said and bit into a corndog.

"Why am I not surprised?"

"It ain't that bad, son," Roland offered. "It's like, this one doesn't count, you know?"

"Doesn't count?"

"Yeah, you know," Art said. "They can't be beat. Nobody's ever even scored on these guys. When God's sitting in the other team's bleachers, the bookies take the day off."

"Is that Genghis Khan looking through their playbook?"

"He's their head coach."

"But wasn't he, like, a bloodthirsty conqueror?"

"And a strategic genius."

"But wasn't he, like, a *bloodthirsty conqueror?*"

"Did the first-string linebackers at Harvard score 1600s on their SATs?" Roland asked.

I stared blankly down at the fetus.

"I don't *think* so," he answered as the whistle rang out for the kickoff.

I left when the scorekeeper lost count. The hometown crowd hadn't made a peep for the better part of three quarters. Whether we were too sorry to cheer for Middle Plain or too guilty to root against Heaven I couldn't say, but I supposed it didn't matter. My mind hadn't been on the game anyway.

I wandered back to the cemetery. Every grave was empty. Everyone had shown up to see their team get clobbered. I wondered why.

"You know, you're quite a unique young man."

I whirled around, surprised. I was going to school in the land of the dead, but a strange voice in the middle of a cemetery was still mildly alarming.

Ms. Needlemeyer, the Clown of Dachau, leaned against the wall of a mausoleum, trying to light a cigarette without the ability to inhale.

"Excuse me?" I asked.

"You're a very unique young man," she reiterated. "You are, after all, the only one who's ever been unhappy."

"Wha . . . huh? I don't get it."

"That's what you want to hear, isn't it?"

I stopped, looked at her with her painted skull and fallen stockings. She looked like a hooker who'd died propped against a lamppost and no one had noticed while she wasted away to nothing but bleached bones and a low-cut dress.

"No," I replied, softly.

"Here," she held out the as-yet unlit cigarette. "Little help?"

I plopped down on the tombstone beside her, lit her cigarette, handed it back.

"So what *do* you want to hear?"

I thought about that question, tried to look past the immediate thoughts of fame, money, sex. I thought about Ginger, and my 'rents. Most of all I thought about how everyone on the planet seemed to kind of suck, in a general way, while I, clearly the only one who didn't suck, seemed to be the only one that was unhappy.

"I want someone to tell me it's going to be alright."

A dry chuckle sounded in Ms. Needlemeyer's throat, the sound of drumsticks on a pelvic snare drum.

"What?" I asked.

"You, young man, are the only person that can honestly say that to yourself. That's what growing up is, hon." She held the cigarette between her bare teeth, let the smoke float up into her eye cavities in a dead French inhale. "Becoming that person."

Mercifully, across the churchyard and over the last hill, the final whistle of the game blew. We turned and watched the sky tear open behind the school. The angels flew home quickly, whooping and hollering and cheering like a parade.

"Everybody always wants to be somewhere else," Needlemeyer noted. "Always making plans to be somewhere they'd rather be. I don't imagine it's any different in Heaven. I'd just like to know where they'd rather be."

I looked at the painted bag of bones, at the dirt caked on my shoes.

I had to keep my distance from Ginger at the Homecoming Dance. No one but our inner circle of friends knew how serious things had gotten between us and no one else *could* know, or there would be hell to pay. Literally. So I stood against the wall with Art while Roland danced on Missy's outstretched palm and Ginger boogied beside them. After a few songs he came back to catch his breath. Missy went to the bathroom with Ginger.

"What the dilly, son?" Roland asked. He sounded like a winded rubber squeaker toy. "You upset about the game? Don't let it get to you, bro. We *always* lose Homecoming."

"Huh?" I looked up from my feet. "Oh. Nah, I don't care about that shit."

"Then what's up?" Art asked.

"Nothing."

"Yeah, right."

"You love her?" Roland asked.

On the dance floor, Misty and Twisty and everybody else danced. Everyone danced differently. I wondered what it had been like, years ago, when nobody danced alone. You found a partner or you waited for one, looking for someone to ask.

"I don't know," I replied.

"That means *no*, son. When it comes to love, anything but *yes* means *no*."

I watched Ginger and Missy come out of the bathroom. Ginger looked for me across the dance floor, found me. I met her gaze, held it as I walked out to the dance floor and took her hand for a slow song.

"What are you doing?" she asked.

I made no response. We fit our bodies together and started to move.

"I think I love you," Ginger said after the first refrain.

She said it the way everybody says it the first time, when what they really mean is *I think I want to tell you I love you.* She looked at me, wanting me to say it back. I wanted to say it back, but I couldn't speak. All the blood in my body reversed its flow.

I felt like I did in the cemetery, when Art, Roland, and Missy had played the prank on me, convincing me that I'd been dead the whole time.

"Aren't you gonna say it too?"

There was a pause between songs, long enough for someone to bet it all and lose; long enough for a plane to make an emergency landing; long enough for the next song to load, and begin.

"I, I—"

"I mean, if this isn't love, what is?" she asked, needing me to have the answer.

Again I found no words. I couldn't speak to her. Couldn't look at her.

"What are you thinking about?" she pleaded softly. She pressed her head against my chest, let the familiar cold of her tears soak through my shirt.

"Nothing," I replied, the old conversational parachute that worked more like an anvil tied to a ripcord.

"Please tell me."

I looked down at her, and for the first and probably last time, spoke with absolute honesty to a woman who I cared about:

I'd been thinking about my mother, about a certain Christmas morning when I was seven years old. It was our hardest holiday together. My father had been laid off before the previous semester had begun and it had plunged him into a crisis of being from which it seemed he might never emerge. He slept most of the day and haunted our house at night while we slept. Once, when I couldn't sleep, I'd gone down for a drink of water and found the old man standing in front of the open refrigerator, talking to the appliance's innards like a door-to-door salesman might present his product on some anonymous stoop, trying his damnedest to get his foot in the door. He'd sold vacuums door-to-door one summer when he was nineteen to save for the down payment on a car. He was brushing up the old pitch. I didn't know this at the time.

Months later, when Christmas came, my mother picked out my presents, spent hours poring over the discount bins at Toys "R" Us and JCPenney's looking for toys I might like that wouldn't break the bank. When the morning of December 25th finally came around, I found her asleep on the couch. She'd waited until late to bring out the toys and had fallen asleep wrapping them. When I saw what Santa had brought, I cried. I said they were stupid. I said they were awful.

Like everyone, I've done some shitty things in my life. I've hurt good people, most of the time without meaning to. And I've forgiven myself for those misdeeds, because like everyone, I convince myself that the things I do, I do because I must. But I've never forgiven myself for what I said that morning.

My mother had tried to explain, rapidly wiping tears from her eyes before I could see them. She said that there must have been a mix-up. Santa, she explained, had confused our house with someone else's. She said she was surprised it didn't happen more often. But all I could do was cry and whine and complain about how good I'd been all year.

"I know, sweety," she sniffed, comforting me, hugging me. "You've been so good. We'll write Santa a letter. We'll write him a letter and he'll clear everything up. You just have to give it a little time to get there."

By the following Christmas, I didn't believe in Santa Claus. Yet to this day, my mom still writes "From Santa" on a couple of presents every year.

"I don't get it," Ginger replied when I finished telling the story.

"That's what I think love is."

"But it's such a sad story," she explained. "What does that have to do with me?"

"I love you."

"I love you, too."

The second slow song ended. The DJ came on to announce that the next song would be the final slow number of the evening. I'd reason, years later, that neither of us really *loved* each other then. I'd also figure that it didn't really matter.

"I love this song," she said. It was a song about dreams, about having a nightmare that the singer's true love had died. "You know, I've never had a nightmare since I've been here. I don't think I've had a single dream."

I looked down at her, at the people staring at us with attraction and disgust.

"I love you," I said again, to the whiskers on her head.

"I love you too," she said as I pulled away, turned around, and began to run.

I found Paul in the gymnasium, trying to dribble a basketball and failing. As I approached, I watched him pick up a ball with both hands and drop it. He swatted at the bouncing thing and missed, waited for it to settle at his feet, then picked it up again. I looked at the floor around him, at the equipment he'd dragged from storage: dodge balls, footballs, soccer balls and nets, tennis rackets, swim caps, and racing hurdles. He was wearing a gym uniform. The shirt was inside-out. I picked up a metal baseball bat, felt the weight. I watched him pick up the basketball again. Outside, moonlight streamed in through the high windows. I held the bat over my shoulder, stood like a major leaguer. I thought about Ginger. I thought about Art's blood in his mom's ice cube trays. I thought about Christmas, and swung the bat.

They were asleep when I got home. The TV was on and the color bars watched over them silently. My father sat at the end of the couch with my mother sprawled out on the adjoining cushions, her head on Pop's lap. The old man's brow was creased, his throat moving and sounding, talking to someone in his dreams. His head ticked to the left and he spoke again, in his throat. His mouth opened suddenly, breathing in.

"Hey," I said quietly. I put a bloody hand on his twitching shoulder. "I'm home."

CHRISTOPHER HARMAN

The Last to Be Found

Christopher Harman lives in Preston, Lancashire. Most of his working life has been spent with the Lancashire public library service and he currently works in a hundred-year-old Carnegie building on the Fylde coast. His stories have been published in All Hallows, Ghosts and Scholars, Supernatural Tales, Dark Horizons, Enigmatic Electronic, Kimota, New Genre, and the Ash-Tree Press anthology Acquainted with the Night. Two stories have previously been reprinted in The Year's Best Fantasy and Horror. A new story is due to appear in Postscripts.

Supernatural horror comprises most of his reading, and he also enjoys some SF and fantasy. His other main interest is classical music, particularly the various fantastical, grotesque, and exotic works of the early twentieth century. Occasionally, he takes to nearby hills.

One of his favorite films is Dead of Night, and he thinks the house party segment may have been at the back of his mind when he wrote "The Last to Be Found," which was first published in New Genre, issue 4.

–E.D.

As Peter Meltish drove up to the house he thought it deserved ghosts, though he doubted Bob Parrish's testimony would sway the matter one way or the other. A sudden shiver wasn't just an anticipation of the cold he'd be stepping into outside the car. Did the house appear as forbidding and prisonlike in the daylight? Small dark-filled windows were embedded in a black facade that soared to a jagged line of gables around a tall thin chimney stack. A house as black as the churning mix of night and cloud.

Meltish parked by Jennifer's Honda, glad that she'd arrived before him. She was his essential go-between on his mission tonight. He got out, shoved his hands into the pockets of his suit jacket that the wind wanted to take from him. Sounds from the salt marshes beyond an enormous unkempt hedge, gull cries lamenting his arrival, the hiss of wind through marram grass, the smack and slosh of water in mud channels. Thinking the outdoors was more bothersome than anything the house might have to offer, Meltish pressed the bell push. He peered through the small smoked-glass panes of the front door into a hallway meagerly lit by thin right angles of light escaping around a door at the back of the house. A bulky round-shouldered individual mystifyingly failed to turn and acknowledge his arrival. Light spilled as the inner door opened and another figure was coming forward; a disturbing spindliness became attractively boyish. Jennifer reached for the latch.

In her jeans and gray woolen tank top, Jennifer appeared to have dressed down for the occasion, as if, half the gathering comprising family members, no serious effort was required. The stubbornly motionless figure turned out to be a loaded coat stand. Around the high ceiling, streamers rustled, holly gleamed. Meltish was apologizing for his lateness, blaming the maze of roads in and out of the nearby village of Longton, when Jennifer, uninterested in his excuses, broke in, her voice low, excited, "He's here."

An apprehension more intense than his usual diffidence engulfed Meltish and was as quickly gone as Jennifer ushered him into the dining room at the back of the house. Slightly breathless, and with her words having to negotiate her abundantly toothed grin, Jennifer introduced Meltish as her "ghost-hunter friend." Overstating the case, she was patronizing him in the nicest possible way, and he was prepared to play along with it. Smiling the sociable smile he hadn't employed for quite some time, Meltish said, "Civil servant, actually." There, his sober and quotidian credentials established and surely reinforced by his best brown suit and gray hair combed to a semblance of neatness. "Local historian in the evenings. Weekends I'm struggling to finish a book on haunted houses of Lancashire and Cheshire."

Polite murmurs of interest out of the way, Jennifer introduced the others. The man who'd spared Meltish a glance and continued to pour into a half dozen or so wineglasses was Ted Biddulph, Jennifer's brother, a local head teacher. He was a dry-looking, fiftyish stick of a man, bulked out in a very new-looking sweater with a portcullis design on the front. His wife Phyllis was his physical opposite, her roundedness enclosed in a tentlike garment. She was sawing grimly through the remains of what must have been a monstrous Christmas turkey. Ted and Phyllis both seemed to be taking the evening very seriously. Ian and Claire were friends of theirs. Claire was mousy, her penciled eyebrows permanently raised. Ian had a twist of black hair and a mouth constantly open and on the verge of smiling.

At the head of the table was Bob Parrish, the "man of the hour" as far as Meltish was concerned. He was large, his knife and fork gripped in ham fists. He wore a tight, dusty-looking black suit jacket over an open-necked pink shirt. His long, lank dark hair looked like it was used to being tied back in a ponytail. There were dark rings under his eyes. After he'd nodded minimally at Meltish, his doughy face had resumed a dour preoccupied expression.

"Speaking of ghosts, Jennifer, I read your article in the *Southport Herald*," Ian said. His eyes flickered wickedly toward the others, as if this were her guilty secret. It was a long way from that. Jennifer's speciality was rooting out local oddities and strange phenomena and the "characters" invariably associated with them.

Meltish enjoyed his and Jennifer's double act as they interrupted and corrected each other's recollections of their night-long vigil in a tiny terrace house in Southport several miles away down the coast. That had been three weeks ago. The elderly owners had been in no doubt the place was haunted. The mysterious stain on the wall Meltish had had to admit hadn't *felt* damp. Knockings at 3 A.M. Water pipes? Meltish's voiced doubts had been an affront. Nobody takes baths at *this* hour, the old man had argued. And on one side the house was empty, on the other the owner worked nights. There was no denying the quarter-inch swing of a ceiling lampshade in the living room. Well—I can't *feel* a draft, Meltish had said tactfully. And the cold patch over the window ledge at dawn? Final proof for the old woman. Meltish had refrained from pointing out that cold air sank.

The listeners around the table commiserated—all except Bob who, Meltish noticed, had barely been listening. His gaze had dreamed in the long smoking flames of the table candelabra, wandered to their vague doubles in the deeply polished wood paneling.

"I made a little go a long way in that article," Jennifer admitted. "And there wasn't much for Peter to put in his book." On the night, she'd concealed her disappointment behind that trademark smile and an expression of intense interest that must have had the elderly couple (and there'd been many before them and no doubt there'd be many to come) thinking they were fascinating, funny, charming. They'd reflected Meltish's reserve back at him, no doubt sensing his skepticism.

Meltish couldn't help but sound magisterial as he addressed the gathering. "There needs to be some explanation for a haunting in the first place. Failing that I like to hear reports of ghosts behaving interestingly—if not atrociously. The odd damp patch, the occasional mysterious tapping, just won't do."

Meltish hoped there would be further collaborations with Jennifer, of one kind or another, but the Southport escapade had depressed him. And even the neo-Gothic mansion before that had failed to be more than a sad inert pile despite reports of a ghostly ex-butler. Over coffee and a croissant in a café on the Southport promenade the next morning, he'd confessed his interest in ghosts, and their supposed habitats, was on the wane. Before it disappeared completely, Jennifer had suggested he should meet her cousin Bob. He and his parents had emigrated to Australia when he was seven, shortly after being the focus of a strange set of circumstances in the house that had been in the Biddulph family for three generations and had finally passed onto Jennifer's brother Ted following a complex inheritance deal. Jennifer had been enticingly coy, refusing to be drawn further other than to inform Meltish that Bob was now a successful artist and illustrator. Meltish could hear it all from Bob himself who was on vacation in Europe and would be staying with the Biddulphs over Christmas in the house he hadn't seen in thirty years. Jennifer had telephoned Meltish a week later with the date and time of the dinner party. After an infinitesimal hesitation, Meltish had accepted the invitation and then mulled over his decision. He hated social gatherings, but at least there'd be a point to the evening. It wouldn't consist of interminable, inconsequential chatter on subjects in which he'd struggle to shine, with people he'd nothing in common with.

But now with the meal coming to an end the subject of ghosts had only been touched on—and not at all by the man whose input Meltish was here to listen to. On a smattering of other subjects, Bob had stirred himself to contribute, in terms embarrassingly intense, his laughter disproportionate to whatever instigated it. Meltish didn't think it was for him to direct the conversation toward Bob's experiences in the house in which they now sat. Was the event a sensitive area—perhaps taboo? The usually forthright Jennifer was signally failing to tackle him over it. Now she was seeking to draw him out on a recent exhibition of his work in Melbourne. Not entirely helpfully, from the look on Bob's face, she told everybody Bob had brought some pictures over from Australia. Bob seemed to grasp at Ian's mercenary inquiry regarding the financial rewards in book and magazine illustration. While they were discussing that, timid Claire sprang the question on Meltish that he'd fielded many times with a range of replies.

So, again, did he believe in ghosts? The attention of everyone fell on him, and the evening was on course again. As a hedging answer formed in his head, the mouse-like Claire added a supplementary: "Do you think there are any here?" She hugged herself; her eyebrows nearly touched her hairline. Meltish wondered how her expression would configure if she ever encountered an apparition herself.

"Claire," Ian said through a wince, as if he'd had to warn her about this kind of thing before.

"Who knows," Meltish said. "Perhaps every house has its ghosts, and for the most part they're as unaware of us as we are of them." His faintly awkward smile conveyed what a flight of fancy *that* had been. "In any case I've never seen one, though I wouldn't deny the possibility that one or more has seen me."

"If there were any here," Phyllis said with a forthright sniff, checking what was left of the tarry Christmas pudding on their plates, "they'd have made themselves known to Ted and me by now."

They wouldn't dare not to, Meltish thought. Bravely the guests declined her offer of seconds.

"There are weirder happenings than ghosts, aren't there, Bob?" There had been gentle encouragement in Jennifer's voice. In the silence, Meltish hardly dared to breathe.

Bob squirmed in his chair. "Ah," he said, looking cornered, a grimace showing his lower teeth. Meltish struggled to maintain an expression of mild inquiry. Knowing, stoical glances were exchanged between Ted and Phyllis. Claire and Ian, realizing they were in the dark, pestered, learned from Jennifer it had all happened in this very house. More insistence from them before Bob relented.

"'Weird' just about sums it up," he said in his mild antipodean drawl. He cast his gaze forlornly around the paneled walls of the room as if wishing he were in the company of their mute dim reflections. He took a breath, expelled it in a sharp gasp. "I was about seven. I remember it all like it was yesterday—last night even. In fact last night I dreamed the whole thing again." Another pause in which he seemed to be gathering his thoughts and not liking too much what he was gathering.

Speaking a little wearily, Ted suggested they adjourn to the living room. There, Jennifer directed Bob to a winged chair by a bronze and enamel gas fire. The rest settled in armchairs and a sofa. Around them, dark scuffed furnishings included a grandfather clock—thankfully silent. There was a Christmas tree in one corner that appeared to issue from the high cornice like a jeweled black waterfall. Meltish was aware of a silence in the rest of the house. Ted and Phyllis's teenaged children were out at parties for the evening, so the telling wouldn't be spoiled by extraneous noises. Outside, wind blustered and pellets of rain hit the windows.

"Go on, Bob," Jennifer said. She'd sat cross-legged on the floor at Bob's feet. "You never know, Peter might have an angle on it." She narrowed one eye at Meltish, as if to say, Here's the treat I promised you.

Bob began diffidently. "It was around this time of year, two or three days after Christmas. Grandma . . . *our* grandma"—he nodded toward Jennifer and Ted—"owned the house at that time. It had been noisier that evening with several families present. Outside it was a cold night, calm. There was a full moon.

"After the evening meal, the adults remained in the dining room and we children were left to our own devices. Things were a bit mad at first until some leader emerged among us—some hulking teenage brute called, let me see . . . yeah, Ted." There was laughter, quickly stifled.

"Anyway, he started organizing us. We played blindman's bluff first, and then someone suggested hide and seek.

"I was one of the younger ones. The teenagers were as good as adults to me. Ted began counting, and giggling figures darted off like minnows in a stream. Curtains breathed out and in and were silent. In the hallway someone smaller than I squeezed into an oak chest. Someone else disappeared into the cubbyhole beneath the stairs. A wicker basket snickered around muffled voices. Others had fled to the kitchen and conservatory and beyond.

"I was left alone in the hallway beneath the spaced out stare of a stag's head. I didn't need to think hard for very long. I hadn't noticed anyone venture upstairs. If there had been any orders not to—I hadn't heard them. So up I went. At the top of the stairs, I peered down into the hallway through the stair rods. The laughter and talk of the adults faded to a few giggles, then nothing. There wasn't time for me to wonder what they were doing as Ted's counting continued inexorably. It had begun to sound like a countdown to the end of the world—but I suppose I *was* an imaginative child.

"There were several closed doors in the shadows away from the landing light. I thought for a moment before deciding that the bedrooms would be definitely out-of-bounds. Besides, I might find somewhere better at the top of another staircase I'd spied. Though the higher landing was lit by a bare bulb, I still had misgivings about heading up there, but hearing Ted shout, 'Coming ready or not!' spurred me on and up I went. Like many a timid child, I had a stubborn streak.

"The tight staircase creaked like the plastic molds in boxes of chocolates. I expected Ted to come pounding after me, but he didn't. At the top I found two doors facing each other. One door was locked, the other ajar. This one wouldn't open many more inches when I pushed because of obstructions on the other side, but I managed to squeeze through.

"Moonlight poured through a small window onto several lifetimes of abandoned junk. There was a rocking horse, a crib stuffed with dolls, a tottering pile of comics I'd have devoured in other circumstances. A cluster of golf clubs poked from a leather sheaf. There was a bed with a trough down the center as if an invisible body lay in it. At the far side of the room was a huge wardrobe. A perfect hiding place, but the bottomless crevasses of shadow between the junk seethed with little monsters. I wasn't daft enough to struggle past it all to hide in a dark wardrobe in a moonlit room. A child with a fraction of the imagination I had at that time wouldn't have. I was already uneasy. Sensibly enough, I reached for the light switch just inside the door.

"With the room bathed in electric light, a little of my confidence returned—but not much. Everything was so much more present. Things eyed me—the rocking horse with its drugged human-looking eyes, the dolls in the crib. Even the golf clubs appeared to be blind eyeless muzzles considering this interloper. I'd left the door open a couple of inches and was glad I had. The rocking horse began a squeaking metallic canter as I squeezed between it and the bed. I froze hearing shouts and giggles below. The wardrobe was beginning to seem a haven to secure as soon as possible. It became monolithic as I approached it. Each door was inlaid with a haphazard pattern of small, roughly rectangular varnished woods. It was like looking down from a great height onto tiny fields. Pulling open the right-hand door, I felt like a giant lifting up a slab of the Earth's crust.

"Long garments hung inside—dressing gowns, ancient-looking coats, stained mackintoshes. I stepped inside and crouched among them, finding the physical contact comforting. They were like partners, silently supportive, hiding me and muffling the sound of my breathing. I'd disturbed unused coat hangers, and for a moment they clinked against each other like wind chimes.

"I pulled the door back—but carefully. I had a heart-jolting vision of one Robert Parrish found weeks later, mummified. Prescient in a way . . . I left a gap of an inch or two. I waited. I was certain I'd be the last to be found. I'd be the winner. The center of attention for a change.

"There were faint sounds below as one by one the other children were caught by the silent shark Ted. Then there was a commotion, nothing to do with hide and seek. Adult voices, one or two upset, others concerned, trying to ease things. I was puzzled in the moment before a door closed, sounding as if it were in a deep pit. Silence again, I couldn't hear any of the children either. But the intense quiet didn't last. I heard pipes knocking, a floorboard somewhere below snapped, a scrabbling could have been tiny rodent feet. There was a massive wheeze like a vast rib cage filling. Still I couldn't hear anyone. I had the strangest notion the house had dispensed with its occupants.

"But then I heard the stairs. Wood joints clicking rapidly—or was I hearing the quick hard impact of little steps? The latter, I decided as they stopped—and it was as if all the sounds had been sucked out of the house again. I had the odd feeling I wouldn't be capable of making a sound myself if I'd tried. Worse than the silence was the low snigger that abruptly broke it. I'd no choice but to picture a child as excited as I had been. The light yet hard, slightly echoing footfall was rising higher—chuckles, grunts—as if the climb were an effort. Then with a burst of startling speed it reached the attic landing. Who was this? I couldn't match the throaty chuckle with any child I'd met that evening, though I was convinced it was searching for a hiding place.

"Stay away from here, I thought with faltering bravado. This place is taken.

"I could sense it thinking—unless its silence was to enable it to hear Ted prowling about downstairs, which I certainly couldn't. At a click of a switch I realized the landing light had been turned off. While that was upsetting me, there was another click and the room dropped into a pit of darkness. I bit back a cry of fear.

"My eyes adjusted to the moonlight. Through the gap I saw shadows more solid-seeming than the objects casting them. Steps pattered forward on the hollow-sounding floorboards. It was not only a braver child than I making its way forward without hesitation, but nimble with it, as if the room had become mysteriously cleared of clutter.

"Then I heard piercing metallic squeals, and I realized it was jumping up and down on the bed—its insane chuckles amazingly sustained as if it didn't need to take a breath. It seemed hide and seek was forgotten—for the moment at least. That suited me fine. Attracting attention to itself would ensure its capture first. I only needed to keep motionless, which I did.

"But Ted failed to burst through the door to investigate the rhythmic tortured creaks from the bed. They ceased suddenly, as did the bizarre chuckling. I somehow knew the child was looking in the wardrobe's direction. I thought, No—this is *my* place. It hopped off the bed. Now through the gap between the doors I could see its shadow cast onto the white back wall. I was puzzled as well as scared.

"The child wore some kind of hat; it seemed like a crown at first except there were only two points and these seemed to droop or curl. Now I think in terms of the cap and bells worn by medieval jesters—that's when I'm not thinking of the curling horns of a ram. I trembled. Surely it was just another child, perhaps from Longton, the nearby village, or from one of the farms. A tiny gate-crasher, way off the mark in its fancy dress. Now its elongated shadow, arms reaching, was creeping along the wall in my direction. I shrank back behind the long coats. I tried to convince myself that should it pull open the doors, of the two of us, it was in for the bigger shock.

"Then what I'd dreaded happened. The wardrobe doors whined. Cold moonlight seeped between the coats. Telling myself it was another child, and there was more than enough room, didn't work. Even the coats seemed to crowd around me—not so much protectors as prison guards intent on keeping me where I was crouched.

"Fear is where it all ended—in any event it was sufficiently intense to prompt a—I don't know—prolonged faint? A self-protective sleep? I suppose it was one way of escaping the situation. The next thing I know I'm crawling out of the wardrobe into wintery sunshine slanting into the room."

Bob blinked at his listeners as if emerging into the light at that very moment. Ian and Claire looked at each other, then at Bob as if to say, And? Bob looked a little shamefaced—a "that's all folks" shrug.

"Quite a tale," Ian said, adding with a smirk, "but I think you should work on the ending."

Jennifer glowered, pointedly not looking at him. "It's not a tale—it's the truth, and Bob had been missing nearly twelve hours. How do you explain that?"

Ian made a mock-chastened expression. Bob examined the backs and palms of his large hands. "I was examined by a local doctor but there was nothing wrong—no concussion or anything from a bang on the head."

Meltish learned from Jennifer that everyone had gone through the house from top to bottom. The police had been called and they'd searched the immediate vicinity of the house and then, armed with powerful floodlights, a wide area of the mud-flats and gullies flanking the estuary.

"And then the next morning he appears without a care in the world asking 'Have I won?'" Ted chuckled, eyeing his cousin and shaking his head with schoolmasterly affection.

"That's what I *said*?" Bob asked doubtfully. Jennifer was looking at Meltish expectantly. Ian took her lead. "Come on, Mr. Ghost Hunter," he said, grinning insufferably, glancing at the others for support.

"Ghosts don't seem to be the issue here," Meltish said, feeling Jennifer had lured him on false pretenses, though he'd have to admit Bob's story had been worth the hearing. "Am I to take it you were in the wardrobe all that time and nobody thought to look in it?"

Meltish was given to understand in no uncertain terms that it *had* been checked. "But not thoroughly enough," Ted conceded. "The best explanation is that Bob was asleep and the coats fell off the hangers and onto him, concealing him. Bob was a lot smaller then."

Smiles slipped as Bob failed to add his own. He ran a hand through his lank hair.

"This child that joined you—" Meltish wasn't sure how to complete the question, and Bob was no help. He frowned, head on one side as if listening for sounds beyond the confines of the living room.

"A ghost do you think?" Claire's mouth gaped. There were groans and laughter. Bob looked startled, then smiled wanly, patently clueless as to the cause of the hilarity.

"He or she was never identified," Jennifer said. "After Bob turned up again we were all questioned but none of us had gone up to the attic floor—"

"Nobody *admitted* to going up there, Jennifer," Ted broke in. "But I suspect one of the invited children did. When the crisis ended, the child may have felt guilt by association and kept quiet. Even so, I'm sure if they had seen Bob they'd have spoken up."

Plausible, Meltish reflected, but what kind of child turns off the lights and trampolines on a bed in a darkened attic room? Opening the wardrobe doors, fear may have dawned and it had retreated elsewhere. Had Bob reared up at him out of the darkness, screams would surely have shook the house; the mystery over before it had begun.

"Of course, Bob could have dreamed his little friend," Ted said, his shrewd gaze taking Bob in, perhaps the clincher as far as he was concerned. Surely that had occurred to Bob before, yet he seemed to consider the possibility now as if for the first time.

Ted brought an end to the topic with a loudly expelled breath and a resounding slap of his hands against his knees. "Time for more drinks I think." He rose from his chair, shielded his mouth from Bob, and stage-whispered, "Bob looks like he needs one."

Bob dragged his gaze up from the flames in the gas fire. Ted's proposal registered. He got up, stopped Phyllis who'd been struggling up from her chair, telling her it was about time he "earned his keep."

"Oh, I think you've done that," Jennifer said, stretching contentedly, watching Bob follow Ted out of the room. Meltish wondered if she'd noticed that having relived that ancient episode, in his own words before a captive audience, Bob's demeanor hadn't lightened. Had a perennial disquiet at the affair been attenuated by his reacquaintance with the house? Still, it appeared that as far as Jennifer was concerned the evening had run according to plan—Bob had told his story and Meltish had heard it.

She said, "If all that doesn't revive your interest in the supernatural, Peter, I don't know what will— Oh, Bob?"

Bob reappeared. "The *photographs*," Jennifer half whispered, communicating enthusiasm with her eyes. Emanating troubled indifference, Bob left the room. A door opened in the hall, sounds of rummaging, and Bob was back again handing a plastic-wrapped package to Jennifer, which she in turn passed to Meltish.

Opening the package, Meltish expected Bob's pictures to be mildly more diverting than the jaw-breaking tedium of colleagues' holiday snaps. Should he make his excuses and leave fairly soon? His disillusion with all things pertaining to the spectral hadn't significantly altered. Bob's experiences, intriguing as they were and whatever the truth of them, were a world away from clanking chains and Roman soldiers walking through walls. But Bob being haunted didn't mean the house was. And there had been no hint from Mr. and Mrs. Biddulph of any further sightings of Bob's co-participant in hide and seek.

Meltish had extracted a batch of photographs out of the package that had turned out to be a folded-over, grubby supermarket shopping bag. Jennifer had her chin on the armrest of his chair, watching for his reaction. In the background, Phyllis, Ian, and Claire were discussing the triumphs and disasters of various teenaged children. Jennifer informed Meltish how Bob used a piece of computer software to combine and manipulate photographic images. He hardly heard her.

Here were images at once mundane and utterly strange. House interiors seen from unexpected angles, anything but a human view. Here was an armchair set against an unevenly plastered wall that was simultaneously a white winter sky dotted with tiny shapes, birds—or insects. Here in the highly polished depths of a kitchen floor dark figures stood, staring raptly up at a doglike mass of shadow gnawing a bone. Attic rafters curved like a saurian rib cage seen from the inside. A group of figures, winged or cloaked with shadow, huddled around a blaze of light that appeared to be an upturned tasseled center lamp shade sprouting from the "floor," as above them, hanging from the "ceiling," a family gathered around the bright glow of a television. On a vast gray expanse beneath floorboards, prone figures blanketed with dust stared upward. The wood grain of a tabletop outlined a man-shape—concentrically enclosed by his winding tail. There was a wardrobe, doors open; pressed among shroudlike garments inside, almost camouflaged by them, something not unlike a moth hung.

Some of the pictures were copies from illustrations and book covers; others were photographs of images attached to various gallery walls. Included in the latter was a picture depicting a jumble of darkened rooms and staircases; below it was a block of words he had to squint to read:

> I used to dream of strange personages—beneath the floorboards, in wall cavities and attics and other spaces you wouldn't find if you dismantled a house brick by brick. I dreamed of running through these anomalous spaces, hiding where I could. They searched for me—or pretended to. I was always found. I dreamed of discussions, arguments. Should they let me go? They always did—after all—I was only a child. And if I hadn't been what would have happened? Would I have never awoken?

"They make me think of interiors seen by a ghost who's forgotten what rooms and fixtures and fittings are for," Jennifer said, more charmed than disturbed, to Meltish's disappointment.

Ted came in with a tray loaded with cups and jugs. "Bob's bringing the food—though I shouldn't think anyone needs much." Slight reproof in the glance he shot at Meltish and the pictures in Meltish's hands, his hopes of the evening taking a more festive course, for the moment at least, dashed.

A cry, so faint it had to have originated in Meltish's own head but hadn't because everyone else had heard it. Seagull, Phyllis said. Or a drunk, Ted added. They come out of the Sea Lights pub half a mile down the coast and get totally lost. Phew, Claire said, relieved, wafting her face with a hand. Meltish thought it had come from inside, a sound reaching from one end of a house to another rather like . . . "Bob said something about a cry, a commotion—before the little chap joined him."

"Oh, *that*," Jennifer said, with a dismissive flick of her hand. "It was one of the women guests. Tired and emotional, as they say. Typical grown-ups, letting the side down. Booze and card games while the kids are otherwise engaged. Mum said a friend got tearful about something and nothing."

"Actually it wasn't quite like that." Ted stared hard at the cups and saucers he'd suddenly ceased transferring from the tray to the coffee table. Pedantry was almost certainly his weakness; he'd spoken too soon and nobody, least of all Meltish, was going to pretend he hadn't.

"Ah—the plot thickens," Ian said, chortling. Meltish wished Jennifer would slap him down again with the kind of look she'd already shown tonight she was capable of. Ted glanced warily at the door. "If Bob's parents ever put him in the picture, he's not told me." He looked at Jennifer as if weighing up whether to go on. "I'm not sure it'd be wise to tell him—he's obviously too imaginative for his own good. He had a restless night last night. Phyllis and I heard him creeping about. I only found out the truth from Dad not long before he died. We were talking about the famous occasion. Dad mentioned it in passing. He seemed surprised I didn't already know—"

"Ted!" Jennifer cried, impatient and rattled by his prevarication. It seemed she hadn't expected any revelations from this quarter and looked like she'd every intention of taking Ted to task for keeping his own sister, a journalist no less, in the dark on a matter as close to them both as this. But that would be later.

"Yes, come on, Ted," Phyllis said, her voice calm, just a little deadly. That Ted's wife was equally at a loss was more serious. Poor Ted, beset by wife and sister. There was a space in Meltish's racing thoughts to appreciate the fact he had neither.

"I'll be quick, he'll be back in a minute," Ted said. He took a breath; this seemed to be a "now or never" moment. "While we played hide and seek our elders were happily playing card games. That was until Gran got out this Ouija board. Since Granddad died she'd visited a medium, attended a couple of séances. Mum and Dad hoped it was a phase that would wear off with time. Anyway, they indulged her on this particular evening—unwisely as it turned out."

Meltish was alert. Ted was looking distinctly uncomfortable.

"Anyway, someone played a joke. The culprit never owned up. An unpleasant trick considering Grandma's sensitivities. Though I can sympathize with anyone who thought the occult needed debunking. Well, someone, or so Dad claimed, had made the glass spell out the words 'under the table.'" Suffering a little, Ted pressed the bridge of his thin nose with a thumb and forefinger. "Presumably it was the same individual who blew out the candles. Yes—they'd gone that far. Apparently in the darkness things got out of hand."

"And did anyone?" Meltish asked.

"Did anyone what?" Ted said witheringly.

"Before the candles went out, did anyone look under the table?"

Ted sighed at the ludicrousness of what he had to report. "Yes—our grandmother did, apparently."

"Dare I ask . . . ?"

"Later, when she'd calmed down, she said she thought she saw a child." Ted spoke quickly, determined to get the distasteful nonsense he'd found himself obliged to impart out of the way as soon as possible. "There hadn't been, of course. All the children were accounted for, once they'd been prized out of their hiding places—none of which, incidentally, had been in the dining room. Only Bob proved elusive." He folded his arms, face closed, refusing eye contact.

"She may have thought they'd released something," Meltish said, wonderingly.

"Yes, well, that's what *you* may think," Ted said, looking at Meltish over invisible half-moon glasses.

"That's what anyone might think," Jennifer said, touchy on Meltish's behalf. No telling if Claire's and Ian's uneasy laughter was a response to the tense atmosphere or Meltish's spirit-summoning theory. Cups of coffee and tea steamed untouched.

"I wonder where Bob's got to," Ted said, bleakly bright. He got up and left the room. Ian asked to see the photographs and Meltish handed them over saying, "Bob has quite a talent"—a bit of conversational noise. He wished Bob would hurry back so he could probe him, not that it required much insight to divine the source of his inspiration.

"He has quite a following 'down under,'" Phyllis said, and that was hardly a recommendation from the tone of her voice. Incomprehension, almost distaste, on Ian's features as he examined the photographs, passing them to Claire without lingering on anything. Phyllis's voice took on a gossiping tone. "Of course it all came in the nick of time." Meltish responded with monosyllables when Jennifer decided at that moment to tell him about her meeting with some UFO gazers in the heart of the Trough of Bowland the previous weekend. He was more intent on Phyllis getting into her stride on the subject of Bob. Started off so well. Top-notch degree, job in publishing. Marries a lovely girl by all accounts. Then throws it all away. Drink, we hear. Loses job, loses lovely wife. *Such* a worry for his parents.

"Reading between the lines," Phyllis's voice dropped, "we think he had a break-down." With that out of the way, she directed her voice at its normal volume toward the open door into the hallway as if suspecting Bob of eavesdropping nearby. "Then we hear he's producing these—well—*unusual* pictures. *And* being paid over the odds for them." She brushed imaginary crumbs off her lap. Ian and Claire took in her haughty "I'm saying nothing more, though I *could*" face.

"They don't make a lot of sense to me, but I hear a lot of this modern stuff isn't meant to," Ian said, taking Claire's share of the photographs off her. He'd seen enough and decided that she had too.

Ted was back. "Must have gone upstairs," he said, following his apparently fruit-less search of the ground floor. "Bob?" he called up, his voice amplified in the stair-well.

"Perhaps he's having a lie down," Claire said. "It was a big dinner."

"He only played with his food," Phyllis said, listening to her husband's slippered feet slapping on the wooden stair treads.

"It's a big house; perhaps he's got lost," Ian quipped. Jennifer ostentatiously be-gan to flip through *Home and Garden* magazine but soon began to listen hard with the rest of them.

Five minutes later, Ted was with them again, frowning. "Not upstairs," he said, adding in an undertone to Jennifer, "He wouldn't, would he?"

"Wouldn't what?" she replied sharply, the final magazine pages whipped over be-fore she tossed it aside. Reenact a decades-old scenario was what her brother meant, and she knew it. "Course he wouldn't."

Though Bob hadn't seemed the type, nor on tonight's evidence in the mood, to put into action such a crass prank, Jennifer's confidence seemed misplaced to Meltish. There had been a child, a thirty-year gap leavened by a handful of biogra phical facts. He returns, large, untidy; somber and nervous by turns. Was there a flip side of playfulness?

Plainly unimpressed by Ted's efforts, and muttering that Bob had to be *some-where*, Phyllis left the room. Ted, puffing out his cheeks, followed; Jennifer too. There was a low-voiced family conference in the hallway. Ted said Bob's hire car hadn't gone from the drive and he was going to check the front and back gardens. The front door opened, and Meltish felt the periphery of a large body of cold air en-ter the house. From the window came the slight sound of glass bending—as if hands were pressing against it. Phyllis and Jennifer went upstairs calling.

Not being invited to help in the search and sensing it would be inappropriate to offer at this stage, Meltish, with a sense of frustration and unease, remained in the living room with Ian and Claire. Could Bob have gone for a walk down the lane? Claire wondered. It's pitch-black down there, Ian said. And dangerous if he got onto the salt marshes. Meltish went to the window and lifted a curtain. The wind blew beads of rain into spectral patterns on the glass.

Jennifer came back, big-eyed, followed by Phyllis. The rooms had been checked again, not forgetting the ones on the attic floor, Phyllis informed them. Meltish felt a heightened awareness of his surroundings—the sofa, armchairs, sideboard, china cabinet, bookshelves, the television, the Christmas tree—shadows between them too black. An oppressively overfurnished room, suddenly redolent of an attic. The influence of Bob's chilly anecdote, his weird pictures at work? Now Meltish's com-panions in the room were like familiar words that stared at too long become strange, exotic. Claire's eyes and mouth were too thoroughly rodentlike. Ian's face looked carved. Phyllis in her chair was like a loaf rising in an oven. Jennifer was like a doll with real teeth and eyes. Meltish shook off the nightmarish fantasy. Here were ordinary people mulling worriedly over a mystery in their midst. Taking no part was why Meltish heard first.

"Listen," he said in a penetrating whisper. Patterings—rain? Let it be rain, he thought. Anxious talk burbled on. "Quiet!" he demanded, none too quietly. Silence now. Everyone listened. Everything seemed to listen. The bluster of wind and rain, ever-present during the evening, had ended. Silence outside now as if the house were contained in a greater dwelling.

The quiet didn't persist. From outside the room but inside the house a chorus of moans rose and fell. Everyone looked at the door, open a few inches. Nobody went to close it. Now a succession of anguished creaks were descending through the house. Nobody's going to join us, Meltish insisted to himself. Perhaps the wooden joints of the staircase were reacting as warm air met the cold entering from outside. A draft swung the door wide. Flames in the gas fire flittered. The Christmas tree shuddered as if coming to life again. The others were all standing now and appeared to be growing out of the chasms of shadow between the furnishings. Then a wind found its way into the house, pulled the door back through ninety degrees with a hideous strength to slam thunderously.

"Ted should have closed the front door after him," Phyllis said, starting to move toward the door, her fingers twitching at her throat.

"I'll do it," Meltish said. He hesitated at the living-room door; it seemed to lean, daring him to open it on whatever was outside. He strained his hearing. Were those voices—in an excited whispered discussion about what to do next? Flappings—a telephone book riffled by a strong draft? He'd spent eighteen months asking questions and receiving unsatisfactory answers. He felt exhilaration, his senses merging in a dull thunder. An answer—if he had that, nothing else would matter.

The handle was turning down in tiny incremental jerks. He'd help things along. He reached with his hand, was struck by its trembling. He grabbed the handle, jerked it down, and pulled.

Ted stumbled forward nearly into Meltish's arms. Surprise and fierceness in his face, not quite saying, "What do you think you're playing at?" The others considered Meltish oddly, as if his door-opening flourish had been a vulgar lapse—this being no occasion for melodramatics. It was as if the tangible supernatural dread of a moment ago had never been. Meltish felt cheated, dismayed. He went into the hallway; no pinched diaphanous faces stared down at him through the stair rods.

"Nothing?" Jennifer asked. No, Meltish nearly answered, but she was speaking to Ted, who wondered aloud if he should call the police. And the minute they get here Bob'll materialize grinning all over his face, Ian said, grinning stiffly as if to illustrate his point. Not for long he won't, Phyllis said, darkly. Give it . . . ten minutes, Ted, Jennifer advised. What do you think, Peter?

Meltish spoke back into the room. "Sounds sensible." More than he felt himself to be. He deserved to be ignored by the others continuing their perplexed discussion.

That other whispered debate must have been in roughly equal parts his overworked imagination and the influx of cold air. Unearthing Bob would make things feel real again. First he had to be found. The others hadn't searched carefully enough—and there was a precedent for that in this house. He'd start at the top of the house and methodically work his way down.

Meltish climbed the stairs. He was soon at the top of the house, somehow a lesser dwelling than the towering edifice evoked in Bob's tale. Bob was in neither of the two attic rooms; one a small office with a computer and box files, the other filled with new generations of junk. There were no golf clubs like eyeless heads, no bed with a trough down it, no sinister rocking horse—the almost obligatory prop in lonely attics in creepy tales. Something calculated in Bob's eerie list. Had he honed his story during previous tellings? Now his whole account seemed a little too "finished," worked at. True events, at least as far as hide and seek, the wardrobe, and possibly the mysterious child were concerned, but lately elaborated into an entertaining party piece. Ideal for Christmas, though Ian had been spot on with that "weak ending" gibe. On reflection, that sleep, that prolonged unconsciousness, that mini-death, wouldn't do at all. But until the denouement, the tale had been chilling enough to prepare the ground for the moment things began to mirror his tale. Meltish despised himself a little for his jitters, his seeping dread, his seeing his companions in grotesque terms, as when overfamiliar words suddenly seem strange and new.

On the floor below, Meltish searched the bedrooms. Bob's whole demeanor, dour and animated by turns, could have been an act. Could Jennifer have been in collaboration with him, Meltish the primary and guileless beneficiary? A moment earlier had it been Bob and Ted plotting in the hallway? But that was really stretching credibility; Ted was far too humorless and sensible to support antics such as this. There were no unholy alliances. Bob was controlling the situation. When was he going to bring it all to a conclusion? If he was sufficiently deluded to expect applause and not rotten tomatoes he was surely in for a rude awakening. Bob was an attention seeker. Hiding, enjoying the sense of chaos and bafflement—now as then. Attending his own funeral, feeling alive in his absence.

In a small spartanly furnished room at the back of the house Meltish's head swam, vertigo as he looked down a precipice of three decades. He sat on the bed and stared.

From its intricate inlay of different woods Meltish was sure this was the same wardrobe Bob had hidden in. It was forbidding and indefinably fantastical—like a portal to another world.

Meltish got up and went to the wardrobe. He discovered, with something like surprise, that it was solid, occupying real space. He could pull both doors wide on their rusty hinges. Still the object seemed outside time. His "Bob? You there?" was deadened by the row of hanging garments. No "Fooled you!" face grinned back at him. But the wardrobe exuded significance; he wasn't about to walk away from it yet.

He reached an arm between colorless and unidentifiable hanging items of clothing; the back panel, sealed in darkness, eluded his reaching fingers. He stepped inside, the floor seemed sturdy enough to support his weight. He pushed between the softly brushing whispers of the garments until he was behind them in a space more than adequate to take him. He'd heard of film stars' walk-in wardrobes; this seemed to be trying to be one. And still with his arms extended the back of the wardrobe was unseen and out of reach in the gloom ensured by the wall of fabric. Bob wasn't here—that was obvious—but Meltish was for, for sins. And how ridiculous. Absurd to find himself playing Sherlock Holmes in what was a scene in a bedroom farce in which he was the only player and nobody was laughing. Time to be out now. He turned on the spot. Darker, no doubt about it. No bands of light that had been above and below the barrier of clothing. Someone, some officious switcher-offer, had turned out the lights in the room beyond. Come on, Meltish, he thought, the sense of direction he shouldn't require in the interior of a wardrobe, for God's sake, gone. Turning, turning, walking now, dwarfed and shaking in a cavernous nothingness into which his calming mantras fled. No—he refused to stand for this. He wasn't a child, he could think, couldn't he? Fear wouldn't let him, even though he sensed it had deigned as yet to reveal only a part of itself, teasing for the moment, but readying itself to flood every inch of him and obliterate everything he'd ever thought or felt. He floated. Crying out, he heard nothing.

One sensation was allowed him—a pressure, a roughness, as if a small dry hand found its way into his. Better than nothing—a thought amid a swirl of terror. He no longer felt bodiless. Now fractured light ahead, a thin broken column of it. Enough for him to resume his true existence again as Peter Meltish, with a half-seen past and a future that for a spell the darkness had threatened to deny him. That hand that had seemed to lead him—mind-manufactured company he no longer needed. He ran to the column of faint blue light, heard his voice cry out as he hit the slabs of dark to each side of it, casting them away.

He stumbled into the room. Yes, someone, perhaps Bob himself, *had* switched out the light. His waking nightmare was subsiding, his mind healing itself efficiently of that infantile panic. Bob had even more to answer for now. Outside, odd light, luminous thick snakes of mist quickly slithering.

Leaving the room, he glimpsed in the dressing-table mirror a ghost moving away too—himself, hair metallic, face gray as dawn. On the landing, he listened. Silence thicker than air filled the house. He looked up the narrow dark throat of the staircase leading to the top floor, listened for a moment, then descended the stairs.

The hallway was unlit save for the fitful livid white light coming through the panes of the front door. The oak chest was like a sarcophagus. Something was wrong with the oval hallway mirror, his reflection indiscernible in its fogged surface. The coat stand, stripped of its load, looked skeletal. That meant they must have all left the house to search for Bob, seeing fit to turn out all the lights first rather than let the house serve as a beacon in the night. All? Two or more remained—he could hear their murmurs coming from behind the closed door to the living room. Yet they failed to dispel his uneasy bafflement. The light didn't come on when he flicked the hallway switch. He went to stand before the living-room door. Now he heard sounds in addition to the murmurs; chirrupings, low whistles, chuckles—as if their owners were hiding, unable to maintain in their excitement a total silence. Or had the TV been left on, burbling to itself in the darkness?

He became aware of another sound behind him, muffled, almost like, but surely not, whimpering. He turned and faced the door beneath the stairs. Whoever produced the sound was easier to face than the people in the living room. He opened the door.

A confined space—as if a cluttered attic, contracting in the meantime, had fallen to the ground floor. Discernible as if in murky waters—a vacuum cleaner, a broom, mop and bucket, a heap of dry and laceless shoes, shelves of polish and cleaning fluids. Overalls and housecoats hanging from hooks.

Crisscrossed by the broom and floor mop a sheeted ghost at the back; an in-out movement where its mouth should be. Paint-stained. An edge clutched by a large white-knuckled hand. Below, telltale feet in large brown shoes. Jennifer and Ted would kick themselves for not thinking to investigate this place.

"Bob? It's me, Peter—Peter Meltish." The circumstances seemed to demand the reassuring familiarity of first names. But it felt wrong, fake—but everything felt wrong, even the shoes he stood in, the brown suit tightening around his shoulders, the house itself, grayer with the strange sounds from the living room he was convinced were intended for him to hear.

The shuddering shoulders eased a little. "Go away," Bob's voice rasped. "Find your own place." Stepping somewhat gingerly inside, Meltish reached, placed a hand on Bob's shoulder. It was shaken off violently as if it were the clutch of insect legs. He seemed to be trying to make his considerable bulk smaller.

This was no act. He seemed to be undergoing some breakdown. Meltish should never have doubted him. Recounting his experiences in the place where they had occurred was asking for trouble. Helping Ted, finding himself briefly alone in the kitchen, had something, a new recollection perhaps, tempted Bob to explore the house anew? Rational objectivity had been disrupted by . . . what? Had the years telescoped to a timeless moment of terror? Had he found himself in another house, sounds behind doors frightening, threatening? Meltish could empathize. His own apprehension was growing at the bizarre array of sounds from the living room. It had to be a TV program—as if this were any kind of time for watching television.

"There's nothing to fear, Bob," Meltish said, alarmed at the lack of conviction in his voice. "They're all waiting for you in the living room."

"I *know* who's in the living room—" A bottomless regret in his squeezed-tight voice. A shuddering, despairing sigh.

Meltish recognized he wasn't up to the job of bringing to his senses a man who'd become a frightened child again. He needed backup. This was more Jennifer and Ted's problem than his, but he felt an extreme reluctance to ask for help from the people in the living room.

"Go away. Close the door," Bob's voice hissed. The door into the living room was forbidding, ovoid featureless faces swam in the swirl of the wood grain. Behind him, the door beneath the stairs slammed shut.

If he dithered any longer he'd be as wretched as poor Bob. His apprehension was growing—a sick "butterflies" sensation—more than butterflies—moths, wriggling things—God knows what else.

He knocked. Three knocks, so unintentionally loud he might have had iron-shod knuckles. And why should he have seen fit to knock at all? He hardly needed an invitation to cross the threshold of the living room to rejoin people whom he'd left what only *seemed* like hours ago. The sounds, like electronically distorted cries of unidentifiable wildlife, ceased. Television—volume turned down or the set switched off. So they'd heard his knocking—couldn't have failed to, and would be justifiably alarmed by it. He turned down the door handle and pushed.

They sat in darkness around the white fiercely hissing flames of the gas fire. The restless white light beyond the uncurtained window failed to penetrate into the room. The words stopped inside him that would have made the dark head shapes turn and respond and so cease to be too large or too small, with here an ear stretched to a point, there a lengthy rope of nose wriggle like a worm on a hook. A fanlike whirring behind one figure, a blurring at its back, like dragonfly wings. There were others not quite concealed between the furnishings.

And there was a small child playing perilously close to the white flames of the gas fire. It had belatedly noticed the intent staring of its elders who had finally deigned to notice the shaking Meltish. Its head was black against the flames. It had some kind of party hat on with drooping appendages like curving horns.

Meltish closed the door. The butterflies crawling now, a sluggish mass of fear trapped inside him.

He entered the dining room. On the long rectangular table was an upturned glass at the center point of a large circle of tiny Scrabble letters like bits of polished bone. Had the "Ouija board" that other Christmas been a makeshift affair like this?

Were these in fact the selfsame items once more set up in order to make amends for the damage done then? Perhaps here was the means by which he could summon back the house in which he truly belonged, where the living fretted over a double disappearance.

Meltish sat at the table. The letters and glass were in place for his use. He clung to the belief that someone was mindful of his best interests in this dark place in which the thinness of a wall was all that separated him from an amalgam of noises that outdid nature at its cruelest and most alien.

He placed the quaking fingers of his right hand on the glass. It immediately began to move—to the "R" then the "U." It didn't linger "N" at any of the letters, moving without "H" hesitation through the central axis in great "I" sweeping "D" curves. After touching "E" it went to the center and stayed there.

Meltish stood, upsetting the chair. RUN HIDE. Had he unconsciously been making evident to himself what he had to do? The noises in the living room— chitterings, slitherings, buzzings—moving up a gear seemed to confirm that. Waves of shudders inside him were like soundless laughter—his body might have been preparing itself to sprout wings for flight. Perhaps it already knew what was to follow. Soon enough Meltish did. From the creaturely sounds in the room next door a voice had emerged. Each utterance was a single unintelligible word like a knife slash through fabric so that Meltish didn't immediately realize the voice was counting. And there was a ragged regularity in the chaotic sounds surrounding it. So they *too* were counting. *Not fair*, Meltish wailed inside himself. It shouldn't be like this. One counts, the *rest* hide.

But he prayed for the counting not to stop as he ran up innumerable flights of dimly perceived stairs and through an endless succession of rooms that offered only shadows in which to hide. Soon the rooms had gone and running was like treading black water.

Then the counting, which had never significantly diminished in volume, as if despite his efforts he'd put no significant distance between himself and it, stopped. A listening silence. Don't let it end, Meltish begged the deity he'd long derided. His fervent wish was ignored. No windows in the dark, no walls. A house without boundaries to seek out. Nevertheless Meltish had to run, or at least believed he was running, in the house not seen only heard—adding its creaks and sighs to the myriad cries and shrieks and exultant bellows of its inhabitants, as they passed rapidly through it.

Fourteen Experiments in Postal Delivery

John Schoffstall's fiction has been published in Fortean Bureau, Lady Churchill's Rosebud Wristlet, *and* Asimov's. *He was a Writers of the Future contest winner and attended the Clarion Writers' Workshop in 2004. He works nights, and lives on Hong Kong time in the Philadelphia suburbs. "Fourteen Experiments in Postal Delivery," a surreal and delightful epistolary tale, was published in the June 5 issue of the online magazine* Strange Horizons.

—K.L. & G.G.

Christopher:

I got your voice mail. You ask, why do I hate you? Have you forgotten? Perhaps you have had an alcoholic blackout.

You got drunk. You hit on my sister Heather, at my party, in my apartment. You then threw up on Heather while humping her on my bed.

You now have the temerity to forget all about this. You have not made a good faith effort to apologize to my sister, or to me, and I'm the one who had to clean your Seagram's-7-Coca-Cola-and-pasta-puttanesca vomit off Heather while she was having hysterics. Also, every time I see my sister I can't help thinking about your dick in her cooter, which chills the warm feelings Nature intended siblings to have for one another.

Do not call me again. I will delete, unheard, all further messages from you.

Hating you,

Jessica

Christopher:

I received a letter from you today, expressing contrition for your past bad behavior and requesting a reconciliation with me. It was written in blue felt-tip pen, with big blurry spots that I think you intended to be taken as the marks of tears. However, when I burned the letter those spots did not produce the characteristic yellow flame that indicates the presence of sodium. I conclude that you made those stains with water drops, or some other aqueous liquid. Definitely not tears. Therefore, I am unconvinced of your sorrow, but reassured as to your guile, insincerity, and general incompetence.

Still hating you,
Jessica
P.S.: All further tear-stained letters will go directly into the In-Sink-Erator.

Christopher:
I have received a dozen red roses, or rather what was left of them after having transited the U.S. Postal Service from the Village to the East Side. You had tied them together with twine, and pasted postage and an address label directly on the stems. Most of the petals were gone, the rest were mangled. There were a few buds on the stems, and I have placed them in water in a vase.

I have also received a magnum of Moët, empty, again with Priority Mail postage and an address label pasted directly on the bottle.

I realize that these are traditional gestures of male romantic affection, and express a desire for forgiveness. They are not nearly enough. You are trying to melt the glacier of my anger with the Bic lighter of your contrition. You are attempting to scale Everest while wearing sling-backs. Give it up, Christopher. Your cause is hopeless.

The letter carrier who delivered the roses and Moët bottle was cheerful. He had alcohol on his breath. He reminded me that it is Postal Service policy that all packages must be wrapped.

Hating you as always,
Jessica

Christopher:
I received a notice from the Lenox Hill Post Office that a package was waiting. When I got there, I found you had mailed me a ski, affixing the label and postage to the ski itself with transparent tape.

It's one of the pair of skis I left in your studio after we went to Vermont last winter, isn't it? We had a lovely time. That was before I discovered you were hateful.

The postal worker at the pickup window was unhappy about the ski. He said that the originating post office should have refused to accept it. He reminded me that packages must be wrapped.

Waiting for the other ski to drop,
Jessica

Christopher:
Today I received your letter with an invitation to your gallery showing a week from Saturday. No fucking way. Just send me my ski.

Don't forget I hate you,
Jessica

Christopher:
I received a slip in my mailbox, informing me that the mail carrier had left a package on the street. By the time I arrived home after work, the package had disrupted foot and vehicular traffic for several hours. It's *Kuro 19*, isn't it? I saw pictures in the *Times* when it was installed at MoMA, although that series tends to run together, and I honestly couldn't tell *Kuro 17* from *Kuro 24*.

It reminded me of why Schneeberg in the *New Yorker* called you a "positive space Louise Nevelson." I also think I'm seeing references to Rodin's *Gates of Hell*. By the way, did I tell you that Lou wants me to edit Schneeberg's second volume of collected criticism? I've been hip-deep in classical and medieval for years, and it might be interesting to do something with modern sensibilities.

Kuro 19 is thirteen feet tall, and will not fit into my apartment. However, my landlord has agreed to exhibit it in the courtyard at the center of my building. One of the crane operators who helped move *Kuro 19* off the street chipped some paint off the plinth at its bottom right corner as he was moving it, and I bit his head off. Not literally.

You might want to get some flat black exterior paint and touch up the chipped place, it distracts from the effect of the piece. However, if you get anywhere near my apartment I'm calling 911.

I still remember how irritated you were with that Schneeberg review. And how you brushed me off rather than tell me why. It's because he compared you to a woman, isn't it? And even though I know you love Nevelson's work, you couldn't stand being compared to her, because she's a chick. Honestly, Chris, you're so twelve years old sometimes. Why didn't I realize that before? I always made excuses for you, even in my own mind. Hating you is good. It brings clarity.

The mail carrier who delivered *Kuro 19* said it should never have been accepted for mailing. It is over the Postal Service's weight and size limits. He also reminded me that packages must be wrapped.

Where's my ski?

Jessica

Christopher:

I received today an inflatable love doll with an address label and postage taped to its arm. It was recognizably dressed in Heather's clothing, but had a photographic print of my face pasted to its head.

I called Heather, and she confirmed that she had given you some of her clothing for this purpose. I am disturbed that she would even speak to you, since she's the one you hurt the most. Or at least that's what I thought. It's always been one of Heather's weaknesses that she can't hold a grudge. She just doesn't care deeply enough. She never has. I can't believe she has forgiven you already. Are you still shtupping her?

The doll is enigmatic. I have placed it on the Le Corbusier chair in the living room, the one everyone refuses to sit on. I wish you had signed it, because then I would be able to sell it, although thematically it doesn't fit easily into the rest of your oeuvre.

Still waiting for that other ski,

Jessica

Christopher:

I received notice of attempted package delivery today. It was too big for me to pick up at the post office, so they left it in the vacant lot on York where that brownstone used to be, the one the homeless got into and stripped.

I thought that was odd, so I walked down there. I found that you had sent me Harold Angel's Bar. It looked exactly as I remember it, when we left Chapel Hill six years ago.

I don't know quite what to say. Maybe something like "You can't go home again" would be appropriate. Or, more simply, "Grow up." Still, the feelings aroused in my breast when I saw the gold-leaf angel on the window, the one that Rod Wrenn from Carrboro made for Harold in 1996 just before his accident, and when I peeked in the window and saw Joy tending bar, and Harold greeting people and working the register—I would be lying to you if I said I felt nothing.

I felt nothing.

I'll go down there tonight after dinner and say hello to everyone. Don't come. Don't even think about it.

No ski yet.

Jessica

Cristohpher:

Hereld's angle was nice. egveryone was nice. I clried on herald. He was sad we slpit up. I was ssad too. Jo9y swaid she'd talk to you and fix things up and i siad aI'd lkkilll her if she did that. hehe.

tHERE WAS A GUY PLAYIHJG A GUITAR IN THE BADK JUST LIKE WE USDE TO LISTEN TO oops cap loc anyway there are a lot of new pop;e who come nhow nowadays and i got to talk to some of them before i got tooooooo drunk and i was kinda sad we left chapel hill becuase life used to be more fun. not that i'mj uynyhappy now, just saying. i meand i was satified with you as you are whichw as a mistake becdaut you 're a shitl. you dcheated on me and i didnt' say ainything at least you did once that i know of with that chick owh came to your amsters's thesis exhibition at the Ackland. and poly amoery isz fine i'm opehn minded about stuff like atha but it has to be two way if you know waht i mean.

i hoped you'd grow up anhd mature becaust you're a fuckijng great sculpute even if yo think you are but fuck if i want to be with somjeone who is stilll 12 yeras old at age 31. the wordl iss full of aritstic genouses genious gieniousus how elver you spell it whyo are totlt shitgs lik e jackson poloock who drank like a fish that was a pun or tenesee williams whosde lifw was one catamite afrer another once he got famous and rich and his playw3riting went to hell. i'sll even spot you thye occasional catamkite but nnot my ficjking sister. fand you drink to much and i kdon't want to make making hyou A NO CODE in some hospital ER atfer an auto accident like theyd id to poor Rod Wrenn. and i kdnon twant you to get dylan thomas's liver.

andn it sn 't bnecause I vloe you becaus e don't i hate yhou hate hat e3hate you.

so i me et this cute gguy who was impressed i edit for sim ona schuster and had read books i edityed and i thought about blwoing him in the bathroom but i'm no togoin got tell you whether i did or not.

fuck yuo, you skiinapper

Jess

Christopher:

Thank you for mailing me the Motrin. It helped a little.

Jessica

Christopher:

I HAVE HAD IT WITH YOUR PLAYING GAMES WITH THAT DAMNED SKI. I CANNOT LIVE WITH ONE SKI IN MY House. IT'S EITHER TWO SKIS OR NONE.

Hating you all over again,

Jessica

Christopher:

Today you sent me Saturday. The postman had me sign for it, and departed in good spirits. He must not work weekends. I was headed out to the office, of course, expecting it to be Thursday—which generally follows a Wednesday—but when I realized it was Saturday I turned around, changed clothes, and called up Ruth Jacoby to see if she wanted to do some shopping and have lunch.

We went to Christian Louboutin and got new sandals which you wouldn't deign to notice or comment on if you saw me in them, which you won't. Then we ate a shiitake risotto with pancetta at the East River Café, and Ruth told me to forgive you.

Suppose I did. What would you have to do in return, Christopher?

Nothing. That's the deal killer, Christopher. All you have to do is make promises, to do better the next time. Promises are nothing, they disappear into the air as soon as they are uttered. Maybe you'll sleep with my sister again, next week, whenever I make you angry about something, or even just when you've had too much to drink. And in return, Ruth says I should forgive you. I have to open my heart and rip out a piece, and hand it to you. No. I won't. It's too much to ask, Christopher, it's not a fair trade.

Forgiveness is difficult in a post-Christian world.

Tomorrow is Friday, so I still have one more day at the office before the weekend, but it was thoughtful of you to send me Saturday early. I hope the rest of the city enjoyed it, too. I'd like to think I am accusing you unfairly of not paying attention to my shoes, but I don't think I am. I would like to think that an artist would be more sensitive to such things than the common joe, but maybe not. Well, actually, definitely not. Randall Jarrell—that's a poet, Chris—once ate dinner with Willem de Kooning, and do you know how he described him afterward? "A barbarian," he said. De Kooning was a barbarian. Chris, I'm just fed up with the constant piss and shit of loving a barbarian. I mean, what kind of man reads comic books at age 31? Yes, I've read your Scott McCloud book, and I still think it's all *petitio principii* reasoning, and I don't buy it.

I've put the ski under the bed where I don't have to look at it. Maybe I'll forget it's there.

Jessica

Christopher:

I received a package from you today, labeled as "Human Male Generative Organs." The postal clerk informed me that it was against regulations to send human body parts through the mail, but that the Postal Service was making an exception in this case, because they thought the contents might be of sentimental value.

Inside the package I found your cock and balls, cushioned in white foam peanuts in a Reebok box. As I lifted it up, your cock stiffened in my hand. I teased it a little, because it reminded me of the good times you and I once had. The skin was as velvety as I remembered. While touching it, and remembering things, I found I had become slightly achy in the bits, and I wondered whether having sex with your cock alone would be considered intercourse, or merely masturbation. I think that would depend on whether your cock was still part of you, partaking of your essence, *homoousios*, or a separate being, of separate essence, merely similar to you, *homoiousios*, the latter possibility bearing obvious similarities to doctrine advanced by Arius of Alexandria, which was ultimately condemned as heretical by the Council of Nicaea (325 AD). While I was still pondering this delicate issue, your cock erupted its own warm and sticky metaphysics all over my hands.

I have washed off your parts, dried them, and put them in the drawer with your copies of *Maxim* and the PlayStation 2 you left in my apartment. Do you need them back soon? I don't know whether you are dating other women, but if you are, you obviously aren't getting past the preliminaries as long as I have your stuff.

I guess this is your way of telling me that you aren't still boinking Heather. It does confirm that your intentions toward me have a certain *gravitas*, and I appreciate that, although I hold with the Council of Nicaea, and am definitely not ready to fuck you, or even just your dick, at this time.

Jessica

Dear Chris:

This morning you mailed me Spain.

No, no, no, no, no, no. No.

It's way too much. It's not fair to the Spaniards. It confuses world geography (which has been an awful mess since the dissolution of the Soviet Union anyway) if we now have Spain floating off Long Island. It leaves the French with no place to take their holidays except to crowd into Italy, which would make August on the Tyrrhenian coast even more intolerable than it is already.

Just no, for so many reasons. It was a sweet thought, and the imagination and extravagance of it are among your redeeming qualities—but it's not practical. I hope you understand.

I know you'd give me Spain if you could. Or wealth beyond the dreams of avarice. Or the moon, the sun, and the stars. That's not the problem between us.

I refused the package at the post office window. They'll just have to send it back.

Jessica

Chris:

This morning I found waiting for me at the Lenox Hill Post Office a man astride a horse, his walet lay biforn hym in his lappe, bretful of pardoun, comen from Rome al hoot. A voys he hadde as smal as hath a goot. No berd hadde he, ne nevere sholde have; as smothe it was as it were late shave. I trowe he were a geldyng or a mare.

He also had a bunch of crap with him that he said was the veil of the Virgin, and pieces of the True Cross, and some body part of St. Peter, knucklebones or something equally disgusting. He started in on whether any womman, be she yong or old that hath ymaked hir housbonde cokewold, which is just insulting, seeing as how you're the one with the zipper problem. I gave him your address, and sent him clip-clopping off across Manhattan toward the Village.

Try again. You're not understanding the forgiveness thing.

The postal window clerk was irate, claimed that the transportation of livestock was contrary to USPS regulations, and referred me to the Domestic Mail Manual, Standard 601, Section 9.3.6, "Warm-Blooded Animals." He said you were abusing the services of the United States Postal Service, and the USPS Board of Governors had you on their watch list.

Be careful, my onetime love.

Regards,

Jessica

Dear Chris:

Heather came to my apartment late last night. I wasn't going to let her in, because, you know, she still hadn't apologized. But I could see through the fish-eye in the door that she was dressed in a black ninja costume, and was carrying a round metal can with a very tiny opening, some towels, and a coil of rope.

I admit, my curiosity got the better of me. I said, "Who are you supposed to be?"

She pointed to the love doll you sent me. "Who do you think that is supposed to be?"

"I don't know. It's creepy."

She rolled her eyes. "While you're thinking," she said, "put on something black and come with me. We're going to burgle the Lenox Hill Post Office. Chris sent you something, but it was intercepted by the postal inspectors. It'll be shipped back to the Prado soon, so we have to get to it first."

"Heather," I said, "you can't burgle the post office."

"Sure I can. I have ether, rope, and an attitude."

Heather is adorable when she's determined. I hate her for it.

"You don't have an attitude," I said. "You've never needed an attitude."

At night a deserted loading dock is like the nave of a ruined cathedral open to the moon: lifeless geometric surfaces lit by halogen floods, depthless black shadows. We hid in the dark below the post office docks until a truck backed in. Heather dowsed a towel with ether, and told me to turn my head away and hold my breath when I stuck it over the face of the truck driver. She held his arms and legs until he stopped struggling.

We undressed him, tied and gagged him with the rope, and dragged him into the back of the truck. Heather honked the truck's horn until a postal worker came out onto the loading dock, and we did him, too. Their clothes fit us adequately, although the pants were a little tight across the hips, and Heather had to roll up her trouser legs. My guy had a ring of keys.

"What are we looking for?" I asked.

"Hieronymus Bosch's *The Garden of Earthly Delights*," Heather said.

The uniforms proved adequate disguise: the few half-asleep postal workers present at that hour ignored us. We finally found the Bosch in a locked room in the back, surrounded by confiscated cases of firearms, counterfeit watches, and rugs from countries accused of human rights violations.

"I'll bet you think Bosch is creepy, too," Heather said.

"Yes," I said.

Heather and I removed our clothes, because in the Garden of Delights nakedness is the rule, and wandered through the garden in the center panel of the triptych. The grass was soft and coldly damp on our bare feet, and a scent of cherries and strawberries pervaded the air. Annoying bagpipe music played.

Heather stretched, inhaling deeply and rising up on her tiptoes. "Lots of cute guys here," she said. "See anyone you'd like to prong?"

One man was tongue-kissing a large puffin. Another dallied with two women in a red tepee that unaccountably sprouted pollard branches from its side. Others, with bored expressions, copulated with women white or Nubian while riding giant boars around a circular track. All were pale and vegetal as the roots of mandrakes pulled from the ground. "No," I said.

"Very well," Heather said. "Let's see what Hell has to offer."

In the triptych panel on the right, satanic mills released roaring jets of steam and spattered the dark clouds with light. A sow in a nun's wimple pressed her affections upon a reluctant man. A man with a flute in his rectum groaned. He carried a giant trumpet on his back.

A white, ferretlike creature with the wings of a moth, about the size of a Great Dane, approached, embraced me, and attempted to penetrate my sex with its furry member. I pushed it away. A hawk-headed twenty-foot-tall demon swept me up in its claws and shoved me into its mouth entire. I passed through its stomach and intestines and out its anus, and tumbled to the ground at its feet. I stood up and cleaned myself as best I could.

"Damnation not doing it for you either?" Heather asked. Something halfway between a periwinkle and a hedgehog jammed an immense corkscrew through her chest and cranked it around enthusiastically.

"I can't take Bosch seriously," I said. "We're moderns. Bosch is merely quaint. His paradise isn't alluring, his Hell isn't frightening."

"So what kind of Hell would frighten you?" Heather asked. I was silent. "How about what you have now?" she asked. "Why can't you make up with Chris? He loves you, and you love him, I think. What the fuck is your problem?"

"What's yours?" I said. "You still haven't apologized to me for fucking him, and right now I don't fucking care that he was drunk and threw up on you, *I'm* the one who needs the apology. You seem to be just fine with that behavior."

"And I'm not going to give you an apology," Heather said. "Even though I really want to. I'm not going to because you, Jess, need practice in forgiveness. It's something you are almost unable to do, and I'm exercising your moral capacity for it. Consider it a sisterly gift. It's hard on me, you know, because my natural instinct is to apologize, but I'm not going to do it this time because I love you."

"I'm not going to forgive him, or you, as long as you're the ones who screwed up," I said. "And take that damned corkscrew out of your chest while I'm talking to you." I pushed the periwinkle-hedgehog thing out of the way with my foot, and pulled the corkscrew out of her, dragging bits of muscle and viscera with it.

"Do you want to know why he came on to me?" Heather said. "Let me tell you. He didn't want me. He wanted you. He wanted to love you, but he couldn't, because you are a cold, judgmental, perfectionist bitch. He was drunk, and he picked me, just so he could pretend it was you, because he was so sick of failing to be perfect enough for you." Blood poured from the hole in her chest and ran down in sheets over her stomach and legs. She glanced around, found a demon trudging along on some demonic errand, carrying a knife as long as Heather was tall. She punched the demon in the face and grabbed the knife in both hands, then drove its blade into my chest. .

With a grunt, she forced it downward, splitting me from throat to pubes. She pushed me to the ground, dug her hands into the opening, and pulled apart my chest. My ribs shrieked and cracked. She reached into my body and pulled up huge dripping handfuls of intestines, liver, lungs, kidneys, ovaries. "Look at all this crap," she panted. "Just look at it. Disgusting, oozy, icky, filled with shit and urine and slime. Look at all this crap inside you, Jess. How can you be such a perfectionist? How can you not forgive, roll the dice, and take your chances, like everyone else in the fucking world? How dare you demand perfection in others when you lack it yourself? How dare you? How dare you?"

We took a cab home. I dropped Heather off at her apartment and went on to mine. We didn't talk much.

It was late. I was tired and achy, and thought I'd take a bath before going to bed. I lay in the hot soapy water for about ten minutes. Then I got up, threw on a robe, and fetched your cock and balls out of the drawer. I took them back into the tub with me, played with them for a while, then used them in their accustomed offices. It felt good. We had fun together, didn't we?

Why is it so hard to forgive?

In the morning I unlock my door. I wrap myself in brown paper and two-inch-wide clear packaging tape approved by the USPS. At the usual time of mail delivery there is a knock. Twenty letter carriers and ten window clerks, male and female, march in. They bring in you, Christopher, wrapped as I am, and place us together on my bed. I can feel the contours of your body, and sense the warmth of it, but cannot touch it. While the postal workers stand at attention, Heather arrives, dressed in a short-sleeve powder-blue shirt with the USPS logo, gray polyester culottes, and sensible black walking shoes. She carries a pair of scissors.

"Should I unwrap you both?" Heather asks. "My advice is, 'Yes.'"

I say to you, "You're never going to remember to send me the other ski, are you?" I see movement within the wrapping paper, but I can't tell whether you are nodding or shaking your head.

I ask Heather to cut us out of the wrapping paper enough so that I can give you a kiss. And maybe a little more.

Love,
Jessica

JEANNINE HALL GAILEY

Becoming the Villainess

Persephone and the Prince Meet over Drinks

Last year we recommended Jeannine Hall Gailey's chapbook Female Comic Book Superheroes, *calling it "funny and opinionated spins and retellings of the eponymous heroes and their complicated lives." Her new book,* Becoming the Villainess, *from which these two poems were taken, is even better. Reminiscent of Carol Ann Duffy's* The World's Wife, *the poems here are wicked, mythic retellings and original takes on familiar characters. Gailey's poems have appeared in* The Iowa Review, The Columbia Poetry Review, *and* Verse Daily, *among others. She lives in the Seattle area with her husband.*
—K.L. & G.G.

Becoming the Villainess

A girl—lovelocked, alone—wanders into a forest
where lions and wolves lie in wait.
The girl feeds them caramels from the pockets of her paper dress.
They follow like dogs.

Each day she weaves for twelve brothers, twelve golden shirts
twelve pairs of slippers, twelve sets of golden mail.
She sleeps under olive trees, praying for rescue.
In her dreams doves fly in circles, crying out her name.

For a hundred years she is turned into a golden bird,
hung in a cage in a witch's castle. Her brothers
are all turned to stone. She cannot save them,
no matter how many witches she burns.

She weeps tears that cannot be heard
but turn to rubies when they hit the ground.
She lifted her hand against the light
and it became a feathered wing.

She learns the songs of mockingbirds, parakeets, pheasants.
She wanders into the forest more herself.
She speaks of her twelve stone brothers.
There is a dragon curled around eggs. There is a princess

who is also a white cat, and a tiny dog
she carries in a walnut shell.
She befriends a reindeer who speaks wisdom.
They are all in her corner. It seems unlikely now

that she will ever return home, remember what
it was like, her mother and father, the promises.
She will adopt a new costume,
set up shop in a witch's castle,

perhaps lure young princes and princesses
to herself, to cure what ails her—
her loneliness, her grandeur,
the way her heart has become a stone.

Persephone and the Prince Meet over Drinks

At first I thought, Daddy?
squinting in the shadows when I saw his face,
alone at the bar.
So many similarities to the picture
mother keeps on the mantel,
that squared jaw, those cold grey eyes.

His ravishing grin drew me in,
the way he treated me like a grown-up.
He bought me cocktails, whispers
of pomegranate in the bottom of the glass.
(How many is this? Four? Five? Six?)
I laughed and laughed, though he wasn't joking.

And so what if, at the end of this story,
with a ring on my finger and a castle
to boot, you find out that my prince
is prince of nothing but darkness?
I knew what I was doing.
I was prepared for a long dance with death.

JEFFREY FORD

The Night Whiskey

Jeffrey Ford's most recent books are the Edgar Award–winning novel, The Girl in the Glass, *and a second story collection,* The Empire of Ice Cream— *which also contained one of our favorite long stories of the year, "Botch Town." He has won the Nebula, Fountain, and World Fantasy Awards, as well as the Grand Prix de l'Imaginaire. Ford reports he is working on both a new novel,* The Shadow Year, *as well as a third collection, titled* The Night Whiskey. *He lives in New Jersey and teaches Composition and Literature at Brookdale Community College. "The Night Whiskey" was originally published in Ellen Datlow and Terri Windling's anthology* Salon Fantastique.*

—K.L. & G.G.

All summer long, on Wednesday and Friday evenings after my job at the gas station, I practiced with old man Witzer looking over my shoulder. When I'd send a dummy toppling perfectly onto the pile of mattresses in the bed of his pick-up, he'd wheeze like it was his last breath (I think he was laughing), and pat me on the back, but when they fell awkwardly or hit the metal side of the truck bed or went really awry and ended sprawled on the ground, he'd spit tobacco and say either one of two things—"That there's a cracked melon" or "Get me a wet-vac." He was a patient teacher, never rushed, never raising his voice or showing the least exasperation in the face of my errors. After we'd felled the last of the eight dummies we'd earlier placed in the lower branches of the trees on the edge of town, he'd open a little cooler he kept in the cab of his truck and fetch a beer for himself and one for me. "You did good today, boy," he'd say, no matter if I did or not, and we'd sit in the truck with the windows open, pretty much in silence, and watch the fireflies signal in the gathering dark.

As the old man had said, "There's an art to dropping drunks." The main tools of the trade were a set of three long bamboo poles—a ten-foot, a fifteen-foot, and a twenty-foot. They had rubber balls attached at one end that were wrapped in chamois cloth and tied tight with a leather lanyard. These poles were called "prods." Choosing the right prod, considering how high the branches were that the drunk had nestled upon, was crucial. Too short a one would cause you to go on tiptoes and lose accuracy, while the excess length of too long a one would get in the way and throw you off balance. The first step was always to take a few minutes and carefully assess the situation. You had to ask yourself, "How might this body fall if I were to prod the shoulders first or the back or the left leg?" The old man had taught me that generally there was a kind of physics to it but that sometimes intuition had to override logic. "Don't think of them as falling but think of them as flying," said Witzer, and only when I was actually out there under the trees and trying to hit the mark in the center of the pick-up bed did I know what he meant. "You ultimately want them to fall, turn in the air, and land flat on the back," he'd told me. "That's a ten pointer." There were other important aspects of the job as well. The positioning of the truck was crucial as was the manner with which you woke them after they had safely landed. Calling them back by shouting in their ears would leave them dazed for a week, but, as the natives had done, breaking a thin twig a few inches from the ear worked like a charm—a gentle reminder that life was waiting to be lived.

When his longtime fellow harvester, Mr. Bo Elliott, passed on, the town council had left it to Witzer to find a replacement. It had been his determination to pick someone young, and so he came to the high school and carefully observed each of us fifteen students in the graduating class. It was a wonder he could see anything through the thick, scratched lenses of his glasses and those perpetually squinted eyes, but after long deliberation, which involved the rubbing of his stubbled chin and the scratching of his fallow scalp, he singled me out for the honor. An honor it was too as he'd told me, "You know that because you don't get paid anything for it." He assured me that I had the talent hidden inside of me, that he'd seen it like an aura of pink light, and that he'd help me develop it over the summer. To be an apprentice in the Drunk Harvest was a kind of exalted position for one as young as me, and it brought me some special credit with my friends and neighbors, because it meant that I was being initiated into an ancient tradition that went back further than the time when our ancestors settled that remote piece of country. My father beamed with pride, my mother got teary eyed, my girlfriend, Darlene, let me get to third base and part way home.

Our town was one of those places you pass but never stop in while on vacation to some National Park; out in the sticks, up in the mountains—places where the population is rendered in three figures on a board by the side of the road; the first numeral no more than a four and the last with a hand painted slash through it and replaced with one of lesser value beneath. The people there were pretty much like people everywhere, only the remoteness of the locale had insulated us against the relentless tide of change and the judgment of the wider world. We had radios and televisions and telephones, and as these things came in, what they brought us lured a few of our number away. But for those who stayed in Gatchfield, progress moved like a tortoise dragging a ball and chain. The old ways hung on with more tenacity than Relletta Clome, who was 110 years old and had died and been revived by doctor Kvench eight times in ten years. We had our little ways and customs that were like the exotic beasts of Tasmania, isolated in their evolution to become completely singular. The strangest of these traditions was the Drunk Harvest.

The Harvest centered on an odd little berry that, as far as I know, grows nowhere else in the world. The natives had called it *vachimi atatsi*, but because of its shiny black hue and the nature of its growth, the settlers had renamed it the deathberry. It didn't grow in the meadows or swamps as do blueberries and blackberries, no, this berry grew only out of the partially decayed carcasses of animals left to lie where they'd fallen. If you were out hunting in the woods and you came across say, a dead deer, which had not been touched by coyotes or wolves, you could be certain that that deceased creature would eventually sprout a small hedge from its rotted gut before autumn and that the long thin branches would be thick with juicy black berries. The predators knew somehow that these fallen beasts had the seeds of the berry bush within them, because although it went against their nature not to devour a fallen creature, they wouldn't go near these particular carcasses. It wasn't just wild creatures either, even livestock fallen dead in the field and left untouched could be counted on to serve as host for this parasitic plant. Instances of this weren't common but I'd seen it first-hand a couple of times in my youth—a rotting body, head maybe already turning to skull, and out of the belly like a green explosion, this wild spray of long thin branches tipped with atoms of black like tiny marbles, bobbing in the breeze. It was a frightening sight to behold for the first time, and as I overheard Lester Bildab, a man who foraged for the deathberry, tell my father once, "No matter how many times I see it, I still get a little chill in the backbone."

Lester and his son, a dim-witted boy in my class at school, Lester II, would go out at the start of each August across the fields and through the woods and swamps searching for fallen creatures hosting the hideous flora. Bildab had learned from his father about gathering the fruit, as Bildab's father had learned from his father, and so on all the way back to the settlers and the natives from whom *they'd* learned. You can't eat the berries; they'll make you violently ill. But you can ferment them and make a drink, like a thick black brandy that had come to be called *Night Whiskey* and supposedly had the sweetest taste on earth. I didn't know the process, as only a select few did, but from berry to glass I knew it took about a month. Lester and his son would gather them and usually come up with three good-size grocery sacs full. Then they'd take them over to The Blind Ghost Bar and Grill and sell them to Mr. and Mrs. Bocean, who knew the process for making the liquor and kept the recipe in a little safe with a combination lock. That recipe was given to our forefathers as a gift by the natives, who, two years after giving it, with no provocation and having gotten along peacefully with the settlers, vanished without a trace, leaving behind an empty village on an island out in the swamp . . . or so the story goes.

The celebration that involved this drink took place at The Blind Ghost on the last Saturday night in September. It was usually for adults only, and so the first chance I ever got to witness it was the year I was made an apprentice to old man Witzer. The only two younger people at the event that year were me and Lester II. Bildab's boy had been attending since he was ten, and some speculated that having witnessed the thing and been around the berries so long was what had turned him simple, but I knew young Lester in school before that and he was no ball of fire then either. Of the adults that participated, only eight actually partook of the Night Whiskey. Reed and Samantha Bocean took turns each year, one joining in the drinking while the other watched the bar, and then there were seven others, picked by lottery, who got to taste the sweetest thing on earth. Sheriff Jolle did the honors picking the names of the winners from a hat at the event and was barred from participating by a town ordinance that went way back. Those who didn't drink the Night Whiskey drank conventional alcohol, and there were local musicians there and dancing. From the snatches of conversation about the celebrations that adults would let slip out, I'd had an idea it was a raucous time.

This native drink, black as a crow wing and slow to pour as cough syrup, had some strange properties. A year's batch was enough to fill only half of an old quart gin bottle that Samantha Bocean had tricked out with a hand-made label showing a deer skull with berries for eyes, and so it was portioned out sparingly. Each participant got no more than about three-quarters of a shot glass of it, but that was enough. Even with just these few sips it was wildly intoxicating, so that the drinkers became immediately drunk, their inebriation growing as the night went on although they'd finish off their allotted pittance within the first hour of the celebration. "Blind drunk," was the phrase used to describe how the drinkers of it would end the night.

Then came the weird part, for usually around two A.M. all eight of them, all at once, got to their feet, stumbled out the door, lurched down the front steps of the bar, and meandered off into the dark, groping and weaving like namesakes of the establishment they had just left. It was a peculiar phenomenon of the drink that it made those who imbibed it search for a resting place in the lower branches of a tree. Even though they were pie-eyed drunk, somehow, and no one knew why, they'd manage to shimmy up a trunk and settle themselves down across a few choice branches. It was a law that if you tried to stop them or disturb them it would be cause for arrest. So when the drinkers of the Night Whiskey left the bar, no one followed. The next day, they'd be found fast asleep in mid-air, only a few precarious branches between them and gravity. That's where old man Witzer and I came in. At first light, we were to make our rounds in his truck with the poles bungeed on top, partaking of what was known as The Drunk Harvest.

Dangerous? You bet, but there was a reason for it. I told you about the weird part, but even though this next part gives a justification of sorts, it's even weirder. When the natives gave the berry and the recipe for the Night Whiskey to our forefathers, they considered it a gift of a most divine nature, because after the dark drink was ingested and the drinker had climbed aloft, sleep would invariably bring him or her to some realm between that of dream and the sweet hereafter. In this limbo they'd come face to face with their relatives and loved ones who'd passed on. That's right. It never failed. As best as I can remember him having told it, here's my own father's recollection of the experience from the year he won the lottery:

"I found myself out in the swamp at night with no memory of how I'd gotten there or what reason I had for being there. I tried to find a marker—a fallen tree or a certain turn in the path, to find my way back to town. The moon was bright, and as I stepped into a clearing, I saw a single figure standing there stark naked. I drew closer and said hello, even though I wanted to run. I saw it was an old fellow, and when he heard me approaching, he looked up and right there I knew it was my uncle Fic. 'What are you doing out here without your clothes,' I said to him as I approached. 'Don't you remember, Joe,' he said, smiling. 'I'm passed on.' And then it struck me and made my hair stand on end. But Uncle Fic, who'd died at the age of ninety-eight when I was only fourteen, told me not to be afraid. He told me a good many things, explained a good many things, told me not to fear death. I asked him about my ma and pa, and he said they were together as always and having a good time. I bid him to say hello to them for me, and he said he would. Then he turned and started to walk away but stepped on a twig, and that sound brought me awake, and I was lying in the back of Witzer's pickup, staring into the jowly, pitted face of Bo Elliott."

My father was no liar, and to prove to my mother and me that he was telling the truth, he told us that Uncle Fic had told him where to find a tie pin he'd been given as a commemoration of his twenty-fifth year at the feed store but had subsequently lost. He then walked right over to a tea pot shaped like an orange that my mother kept on a shelf in our living room, opened it, reached in, and pulled out the pin. The only question my father was left with about the whole strange episode was, "Out of all my dead relations, why Uncle Fic?"

Stories like the one my father told my mother and me abound. Early on, back in the 1700's, they were written down by those who could write. These rotting manuscripts were kept for a long time in the Gatchfield library—an old shoe repair store with book shelves—in a glass case. Sometimes the dead who showed up in the Night Whiskey dreams offered premonitions, sometimes they told who a thief was when something had gone missing. And supposedly it was the way Jolle had solved the Latchey murder, on a tip given to Mrs. Windom by her great aunt, dead 10 years. Knowing that our ancestors were keeping an eye on things and didn't mind singing out about the untoward once a year usually convinced the citizens of Gatchfield to walk the straight and narrow. We kept it to ourselves, though, and never breathed a word of it to outsiders as if their rightful skepticism would ruin the power of the ceremony. As for those who'd left town, it was never a worry that they'd tell anyone, because, seriously, who'd have believed them?

On a Wednesday evening, the second week in September, while sitting in the pickup truck, drinking a beer, old man Witzer said, "I think you got it, boy. No more practice now. Too much and we'll overdo it." I simply nodded, but in the following weeks leading up to the end of the month celebration, I was a wreck, envisioning the body of one of my friends or neighbors sprawled broken on the ground next to the bed of the truck. At night I'd have a recurring dream of prodding a body out of an oak, seeing it fall in slow motion, and then all would go black and I'd just hear this dull crack, what I assumed to be the drunk's head slamming the side of the pickup bed. I'd wake and sit up straight, shivering. Each time this happened, I tried to remember to see who it was in my dream, because it always seemed to be the same person. Two nights before the celebration, I saw a tattoo of a coiled cobra on the fellow's bicep as he fell and knew it was Henry Grass. I thought of telling Witzer, but I didn't want to seem a scared kid.

The night of the celebration came and after sundown my mother and father and I left the house and strolled down the street to The Blind Ghost. People were already starting to arrive and from inside I could hear the band tuning up fiddles and banjos. Samantha Bocean had made the place up for the event—black crepe paper draped here and there and wrapped around the support beams. Hanging from the ceiling on various lengths of fishing line were the skulls of all manner of local animals: coyote, deer, beaver, squirrel, and a giant black bear skull suspended over the center table where the lottery winners were to sit and take their drink. I was standing on the threshold, taking all this in, feeling the same kind of enchantment as when a kid and Mrs. Musfin would do up the three classrooms of the school house for Christmas, when my father leaned over to me and whispered, "You're on your own tonight, Ernest. You want to drink, drink. You want to dance, dance." I looked at him and he smiled, nodded, and winked. I then looked to my mother and she merely shrugged, as if to say, "That's the nature of the beast."

Old man Witzer was there at the bar, and he called me over and handed me a cold beer. Two other of the town's oldest men were with him, his chess playing buddies, and he put his arm around my shoulders and introduced them to me. "This is a good boy," he said, patting my back. "He's doing Bo Elliott proud out there under the trees." The two friends of his nodded and smiled at me, the most notice I'd gotten from either of them my entire life. And then the band launched into a reel, and everyone turned to watch them play. Two choruses went by and I saw my mother and father and some of the other couples move out onto the small dance floor. I had another beer and looked around.

About four songs later, Sheriff Jolle appeared in the doorway to the bar and the music stopped mid-tune.

"OK," he said, hitching his pants up over his gut and removing his black, wide brimmed hat, "time to get the lottery started." He moved to the center of the bar where the Night Whiskey drinkers table was set up and took a seat. "Everybody drop your lottery tickets into the hat and make it snappy." I'd guessed that this year it was

Samantha Bocean who was going to drink her own concoction since Reed stayed behind the bar and she moved over and took a seat across from Jolle. After the last of the tickets had been deposited into the hat, the sheriff pushed it away from him into the middle of the table. He then called for a whiskey neat, and Reed was there with it in a flash. In one swift gulp, he drained the glass, banged it onto the table top and said, "I'm ready." My girlfriend Darlene's step-mom came up from behind him with a black scarf and tied it around his eyes for a blindfold. Reaching into the hat, he ran his fingers through the lottery tickets, mixing them around, and then started drawing them out one by one and stacking them in a neat pile in front of him on the table. When he had the seven, he stopped and pulled off the blindfold. He then read the names in a loud voice and everyone kept quiet till he was finished — Becca Staney, Stan Joss, Pete Hesiant, Berta Hull, Moses T. Remarque, Ronald White, and Henry Grass. The room exploded with applause and screams. The winners smiled, dazed by having won, as their friends and family gathered round them and slapped them on the back, hugged them, shoved drinks into their hands. I was overwhelmed by the moment, caught up in it and grinning, until I looked over at Witzer and saw him jotting the names down in a little notebook he'd refer to tomorrow when we made our rounds. Only then did it come to me that one of the names was none other than *Henry Grass*, and I felt my stomach tighten in a knot.

Each of the winners eventually sat down at the center table. Jolle got up and gave his seat to Reed Bocean, who brought with him from behind the bar the bottle of Night Whiskey and a tray of eight shot glasses. Like the true barman he was, he poured all eight without lifting the bottle once, all to the exact same level. One by one they were handed around the table. When each of the winners had one before him or her, the barkeep smiled and said, "Drink up." Some went for it like it was a draught from the fountain of youth, some snuck up on it with trembling hand. Berta Hull, a middle-aged mother of five with horse teeth and short red hair, took a sip and declared, "Oh my, it's so lovely." Ronald White, the brother of one of the men I worked with at the gas station, took his up and dashed it off in one shot. He wiped his mouth on his sleeve and laughed like a maniac, drunk already. Reed went back to the bar. The band started up again and the celebration came to life like a wild animal in too small a cage.

I wandered around the bar, nodding to the folks I knew, half taken by my new celebrity as a participant in the Drunk Harvest and half preoccupied watching Henry Grass. He was a young guy, only 25, with a crew cut and a square jaw, dressed in the camouflage sleeveless T-shirt he wore in my recurring dream. With the way he stared at the shot glass in front of him through his little circular glasses, you'd have thought he was staring into the eyes of a king cobra. He had a reputation as a gentle, studious soul, although he was most likely the strongest man in town — the rare instance of an outsider who'd made a place for himself in Gatchfield. The books he read were all about UFOs and The Bermuda Triangle, Chariots of the Gods; stuff my father proclaimed to be "dyed in the wool hooey." He worked with the horses over at the Haber family farm, and lived in a trailer out by the old Civil War shot tower, across the meadow and through the woods. I stopped for a moment to talk to Lester II, who mumbled to me around the hard boiled eggs he was shoving into his mouth one after another, and when I looked back to Henry, he'd finished off the shot glass and left the table.

I overheard snatches of conversation, and much of it was commentary on why it was a lucky thing that so and so had won the lottery this year. Someone mentioned the fact that poor Pete Hesiant's beautiful young wife, Lonette, had passed away from leukemia just at the end of the spring, and another mentioned that Moses had always wanted a shot at the Night Whiskey but had never gotten the chance, and how he'd soon be too old to participate as his arthritis had recently given him the devil of a time. Everybody was pulling for Berta Hull, who was raising those five children on her own, and Becca was a favorite because she was the town midwife. The same such stuff was said about Ron White and Stan Joss.

In addition to the well-wishes for the lottery winners, I stood for a long time next to a table where Sheriff Jolle, my father and mother, and Dr. Kvench sat and listened to the doctor, a spry little man with a gray goatee, who was by then fairly well along in his cups, as were his listeners, myself included, spout his theory as to why the drinkers took to the trees. He explained it, amidst a barrage of hiccups, as a product of evolution. His theory was that the deathberry plant had at one time grown everywhere on earth, and that early man partook of some form of the Night Whiskey at the dawn of time. Because the world was teeming with night predators then, and because early man was just recently descended from the treetops, those who became drunk automatically knew, as a means of self-preservation, to climb up into the trees and sleep so as not to become a repast for a saber-toothed tiger or some other onerous creature. Dr. Kvench, citing Carl Jung, believed that the imperative to get off the ground after drinking the Night Whiskey had remained in the collective unconscious and was passed down through the ages. "Everybody in the world probably still has the unconscious command that would kick in if they were to drink the dark stuff, but since the berry doesn't grow anywhere but here now, we're the only ones that see this effect." The doctor nodded, hiccupped twice, and then got up to fetch a glass of water. When he left the table Jolle looked over at my mother, and she and he and my father broke up laughing. "I'm glad he's better at pushing pills than concocting theories," said the Sheriff, drying his eyes with his thumbs.

At about midnight, I was reaching for yet another beer, which Reed had placed on the bar, when my grasp was interrupted by a viselike grip on my wrist. I looked up and saw that it was Witzer. He said nothing to me but simply shook his head, and I knew he was telling me to lay off so as to be fresh for the harvest in the morning. I nodded. He smiled, patted my shoulder, and turned away. Somewhere around two A.M., the lottery winners, so incredibly drunk that even in my intoxicated state it seemed impossible they could still walk, stopped dancing, drinking, whatever, and headed for the door. The music abruptly ceased. It suddenly became so silent we could hear the wind blowing out on the street. The sounds of them stumbling across the wooden porch of the bar and then the steps creaking, the screen door banging shut, filled me with a sense of awe and visions of them groping through the night. I tried to picture Berta Hull climbing a tree, but I just couldn't get there, and the doctor's theory seemed to make some sense to me.

I left before my parents did. Witzer drove me home and before I got out of the cab, he handed me a small bottle.

"Take three good chugs," he said.

"What is it?" I asked.

"An herb mix," he said. "It'll clear your head and have you ready for the morning."

I took the first sip of it and the taste was bitter as could be. "Good god," I said, grimacing.

Witzer wheezed. "Two more," he said.

I did as I was told, got out of the truck, and bid him good night. I didn't remember undressing or getting into bed, and luckily I was too drunk to dream. It seemed as if I'd only closed my eyes when my father's voice woke me, saying, "The old man's out in the truck, waiting on you." I leaped out of bed and dressed, and when I finally knew what was going on, I was surprised I felt as well and refreshed as I did. "Do good, Ernest," said my father from the kitchen. "Wait," my mother called. A moment later she came out of their bedroom, wrapping a robe around her. She gave me a hug and a kiss, and then said, "Hurry." It was brisk outside, and the early morning light gave proof that the day would be a clear one. The truck sat at the curb, the prods strapped to the top. Witzer sat in the cab, drinking a cup of coffee from the delicatessen. When I got in beside him, he handed me a cup and an egg sandwich on a hard roll wrapped in white paper. "We're off," he said. I cleared the sleep out of my eyes as he pulled away from the curb.

Our journey took us down the main street of town and then through the alley next to the Sheriff's office. This gave way to another small tree lined street we turned right on. As we headed away from the center of town, we passed Darlene's house, and I wondered what she'd done the previous night while I'd been at the celebration. I had a memory of the last time we were together. She was sitting naked against the wall of the abandoned barn by the edge of the swamp. Her blonde hair and face were aglow, illuminated by a beam of light that shone through a hole in the roof. She had the longest legs and her skin was pale and smooth. Taking a drag from her cigarette, she said, "Ernest, we gotta get out this town." She'd laid out for me her plan of escape, her desire to go to some city where civilization was in full swing. I just nodded, reluctant to be too enthusiastic. She was adventurous and I was a homebody, but I did care deeply for her. She tossed her cigarette, put out her arms and opened her legs, and then Witzer said, "Keep your eyes peeled now, boy," and her image melted away.

We were moving slowly along a dirt road, both of us looking up at the lower branches of the trees. The old man saw the first one. I didn't see her till he applied the brakes. He took a little notebook and stub of a pencil out of his shirt pocket. "Samantha Bocean," he whispered and put a check next to her name. We got out of the cab, and I helped him unlatch the prods and lay them on the ground beside the truck. She was resting across three branches in a magnolia tree, not too far from the ground. One arm and her long gray hair hung down, and she was turned so I could see her sleeping face.

"Get the ten," said Witzer, as he walked over to stand directly beneath her.

I did as I was told and then joined him.

"What d'ya say?" he asked. "Looks like this one's gonna be a peach."

"Well, I'm thinking if I get it on her left thigh and push her forward fast enough she'll flip as she falls and land perfectly."

Witzer said nothing but left me standing there and went and got in the truck. He started it up and drove it around to park so that the bed was precisely where we hoped she would land. He put it in park and left it running, and then got out and came and stood beside me. "Take a few deep breaths," he said. "And then let her fly."

I thought I'd be more nervous, but the training the old man had given me took hold and I knew exactly what to do. I aimed the prod and rested it gently on the top of her leg. Just as he'd told me, a real body was going to offer a little more resistance than one of the dummies, and I was ready for that. I took three big breaths and then shoved. She rolled slightly, and then tumbled forward, ass over head, landing with a thump on the mattresses, facing the morning sky. Witzer wheezed to beat the band, and said, "That's a solid ten." I was ecstatic.

The old man broke a twig next to Samantha's left ear and instantly her eyelids fluttered. Eventually she opened her eyes and smiled.

"How was your visit?" asked Witzer.

"I'll never get tired of that," she said. "It was wonderful."

We chatted with her for a few minutes, filling her in on how the party had gone at The Blind Ghost after she'd left. She didn't divulge to us what passed relative she'd met with, and we didn't ask. As my mentor had told me when I started, "There's a kind of etiquette to this. When in doubt, Silence is your best friend."

Samantha started walking back toward the center of town, and we loaded the prods onto the truck again. In no time, we were on our way, searching for the next sleeper. Luck was with us, for we found four in a row, fairly close by each other, Stan Joss, Moses T. Remarque, Berta Hull, and Becca Staney. All of them had chosen easy to get to perches in the lower branches of ancient oaks, and we dropped them, one, two, three, four, easy as could be. I never had to reach for anything longer than the 10, and the old man proved a genius at placing the truck just so. When each came around at the insistence of the snapping twig, they were cordial and seemed pleased with their experience. Moses even gave us a ten dollar tip for dropping him into the truck. Becca told us that she'd spoken to her mother, whom she'd missed terribly since the woman's death two years earlier. Even though they'd been blind drunk the night before, amazingly none of them appeared to be hung over, and each walked away with a perceptible spring in his or her step, even Moses, though he was still slightly bent at the waist by the arthritis.

Witzer said, "Knock on wood, of course, but this is the easiest year I can remember. The year your daddy won, we had to ride around for four solid hours before we found him out by the swamp." We found Ron White only a short piece up the road from where we'd found the cluster of four, and he was an easy job. I didn't get him to land on his back. He fell face first, not a desirable drop, but he came to none the worse for wear. After Ron, we had to ride for quite a while, heading out toward the edge of the swamp. I knew the only two left were Pete Hesiant and Henry Grass, and the thought of Henry started to get me nervous again. I was reluctant to show my fear, not wanting the old man to lose faith in me, but as we drove slowly along, I finally told Witzer about my recurring dream.

When I was done recounting what I thought was a premonition, Witzer sat in silence for a few moments and then said, "I'm glad you told me."

"I'll bet it's really nothing," I said.

"Henry's a big fellow," he said. "Why should you have all the fun. I'll drop him." And with this, the matter was settled. I realized I should have told him weeks ago when I first started having the dreams.

"Easy, boy," said Witzer with a wheeze and waved his hand as if wiping away my cares. "You've got years of this to go. You can't manage everything on the first harvest."

We searched everywhere for Pete and Henry—all along the road to the swamp, on the trails that ran through the woods, out along the meadow by the shot tower and Henry's own trailer. With the dilapidated wooden structure of the tower still in sight, we finally found Henry.

"Thar she blows," said Witzer, and he stopped the truck.

"Where?" I said, getting out of the truck, and the old man pointed straight up.

Over our heads, in a tall pine, Henry lay face down, his arms and legs spread so that they kept him up while the rest of his body was suspended over nothing. His head hung down as if in shame or utter defeat. He looked in a way like he was crucified, and I didn't like the look of that at all.

"Get me the 20," said Witzer, "and then pull the truck up."

I undid the prods from the roof, laid the other two on the ground by the side of the path, and ran the 20 over to the old man. By the time I went back to the truck, got it going, and turned it toward the drop spot, Witzer had the long pole in two hands and was sizing up the situation. As I pulled closer, he let the pole down and then waved me forward while eyeing back and forth, Henry and then the bed. He directed me to cut the wheel this way and that, reverse two feet, and then he gave me the thumbs up. I turned off the truck and got out.

"OK," he said. "This is gonna be a tricky one." He lifted the prod up and up and rested the soft end against Henry's chest. "You're gonna have to help me here. We're gonna push straight up on his chest so that his arms flop down and clear the branches, and then as we let him down we're gonna slide the pole, catch him at the belt buckle and give him a good nudge there to flip him as he falls."

I looked up at where Henry was, and then I just stared at Witzer.

"Wake up, boy!" he shouted.

I came to and grabbed the prod where his hands weren't.

"On three," he said. He counted off and then we pushed. Henry was heavy as ten sacks of rocks. "We got him," cried Witzer, "now slide it." I did and only then did I look up. "Push," the old man said. We gave it one more shove and Henry went into a swan dive, flipping like an Olympic athlete off the high board. When I saw him in mid-fall, my knees went weak and the air left me. He landed on his back with a loud thud directly in the middle of the mattresses, dust from the old cushions roiling up around him.

We woke Henry easily enough, sent him on his way to town, and were back in the truck. For the first time that morning I breathed a sigh of relief. "Easiest harvest I've ever been part of," said Witzer. We headed further down the path toward the swamp, scanning the branches for Pete Hesiant. Sure enough, in the same right manner with which everything else had fallen into place we found him curled up on his side in the branches of an enormous maple tree. With the first cursory glance at him, the old man determined that Pete would require no more than a 10. After we got the prods off the truck and positioned it under our last drop, Witzer insisted that I take him down. "One more to keep your skill up through the rest of the year," he said.

It was a simple job. Pete had found a nice perch with three thick branches beneath him. As I said, he was curled up on his side, and I couldn't see him all too well, so I just nudged his upper back and he rolled over like a small boulder. The drop was precise, and he hit the center of the mattresses, but the instant he was in the bed of the pickup, I knew something was wrong. He'd fallen too quickly for me to register it sooner, but as he lay there, I now noticed that there was someone else with him. Witzer literally jumped to the side of the truck bed and stared in.

"What in fuck's name," said the old man. "Is that a kid he's got with him?"

I saw the other body there, naked, in Pete's arms. There was long blond hair, that much was sure. It could have been a kid, but I thought I saw in the jumble, a full size female breast.

Witzer reached into the truck bed, grabbed Pete by the shoulder and rolled him away from the other form. Then the two of us stood there in stunned silence. The thing that lay there wasn't a woman or a child but both and neither. The body was twisted and deformed, the size of an eight year old but with all the characteristics of maturity, if you know what I mean. And that face . . . lumpen and distorted, brow bulging and from the left temple to the chin erupted in a range of discolored ridges.

"Is that Lonette?" I whispered, afraid the thing would awaken.

"She's dead, ain't she?" said Witzer in as low a voice, and his Adam's apple bobbed.

We both knew she was, but there she or some twisted copy of her lay. The old man took a handkerchief from his back pocket and brought it up to his mouth. He closed his eyes and leaned against the side of the truck. A bird flew by low overhead. The sun shone and leaves fell in the woods on both sides of the path.

Needless to say, when we moved again, we weren't breaking any twigs. Witzer told me to leave the prods and get in the truck. He started it up, and we drove slowly, like about fifteen miles an hour, into the center of town. We drove in complete silence. The place was quiet as a ghost town, no doubt everyone sleeping off the celebration, but we saw that Sheriff Jolle's cruiser was in front of the bunker-like concrete building that was the police station. The old man parked and went in. As he and the sheriff appeared at the door, I got out of the truck cab and joined them.

"What are you talking about?" Jolle said as they passed me and headed for the truck bed. I followed behind them.

"Shhh," said Witzer. When they finally were looking down at the sleeping couple, Pete and whatever that Lonette thing was, he added, "That's what I'm fucking talking about." He pointed his crooked old finger and his hand was obviously trembling.

Jolle's jaw dropped open after the second or two it took to sink in. "I never . . . ," said the Sheriff, and that's all he said for a long while.

Witzer whispered, "Pete brought her back with him."

"What kind of crazy shit is this?" asked Jolle and he turned quickly and looked at me as if I had an answer. Then he looked back at Witzer. "What the hell happened? Did he dig her up?"

"She's alive," said the old man. "You can see her breathing, but she got bunched up or something in the transfer from there to here."

"Bunched up," said Jolle. "There to here? What in Christ's name . . ." He shook his head and removed his shades. Then he turned to me again and said, "Boy, go get Doc Kvench."

In calling the doctor, I didn't know what to tell him, so I just said there was an emergency over at the Sheriff's office and that he was needed. I didn't stick around and wait for him, because I had to keep moving. To stop would mean I'd have to think too deeply about the return of Lonette Hesiant. By the time I got back to the truck, Henry Grass had also joined Jolle and Witzer, having walked into town to get something to eat after his dream ordeal of the night before. As I drew close to them, I heard Henry saying, "She's come from another dimension. I've read about things like this. And from what I experienced last night, talking to my dead brother, I can tell you that place seems real enough for this to happen."

Jolle looked away from Henry at me as I approached, and then his gaze shifted over my head and he must have caught sight of the doctor. "God job," said the Sheriff and put his hand on my shoulder as I leaned forward to catch my breath.

"Hey, doc," he said as Kvench drew close, "you got a theory about this?"

The doctor stepped up to the truck bed and, clearing the sleep from his eyes, looked down at where the sheriff was pointing. Doctor Kvench had seen it all in his years in Gatchfield—birth, death, blood, body rot, but the instant he laid his eyes on the new Lonette, the color drained out of him, and he grimaced like he'd just taken a big swig of Witzer's herb mix. The effect on him was dramatic, and Henry stepped up next to him and held him up with one big tattooed arm across his back. Kvench brushed Henry off and turned away from the truck. I thought for a second that he was going to puke.

We waited for his diagnosis. Finally he turned back and said, "Where did it come from?"

"It fell out of the tree with Pete this morning," said Witzer.

"I signed the death certificate for that girl five months ago," said the doctor.

"She's come from another dimension . . ." said Henry, launching into one of his Bermuda Triangle explanations, but Jolle held a hand up to silence him. Nobody spoke then and the Sheriff started pacing back and forth, looking into the sky and then at the ground. It was obvious that he was having some kind of silent argument with himself, cause every few seconds he'd either nod or shake his head. Finally, he put his open palms to his face for a moment, rubbed his forehead and cleared his eyes. Then he turned to us.

"Look, here's what we're gonna do. I decided. We're going to get Pete out of that truck without waking him and put him on the cot in the station. Will he stay asleep if we move him?" he asked Witzer.

The old man nodded. "As long as you don't shout his name or break a twig near his ear, he should keep sleeping till we wake him."

"OK," continued Jolle. "We get Pete out of the truck, and then we drive that thing out into the woods, we shoot it and bury it."

Everybody looked around at everybody else. The doctor said, "I don't know if I can be part of that."

"You're gonna be part of it," said Jolle, "or right this second you're taking full responsibility for its care. And I mean full responsibility."

"It's alive, though," said Kvench.

"But it's a mistake," said the sheriff, "either of nature or God or whatever."

"Doc, I agree with Jolle," said Witzer, "I never seen anything that felt so wrong to me than what I'm looking at in the back of that truck."

"You want to nurse that thing until it dies on its own?" Jolle said to the doctor. "Think of what it'll do to Pete to have to deal with it."

Kvench looked down and shook his head. Eventually he whispered, "You're right."

"Boy?" Jolle said to me.

My mouth was dry and my head was swimming a little. I nodded.

"Good," said the sheriff. Henry added that he was in. It was decided that we all participate and share in the act of disposing of it. Henry and the sheriff gently lifted Pete out of the truck and took him into the station house. When they appeared back outside, Jolle told Witzer and me to drive out to the woods in the truck and that he and Henry and Kvench would follow in his cruiser.

For the first few minutes of the drive out, Witzer said nothing. We passed Pete Hesiant's small yellow house and upon seeing it I immediately started thinking about Lonette, and how beautiful she'd been. She and Pete had only been in their early 30's, a very handsome couple. He was thin and gangly and had been a star basketball player for Gatchfield, but never tall enough to turn his skill into a college scholarship. They'd been high school sweethearts. He finally found work as a municipal handy man, and had that good natured youth-going-to-seed personality of the washed up, once lauded athlete.

Lonette had worked the cash register at the grocery. I remembered her passing by our front porch on the way to work the evening shift one afternoon, and I overheard her talking to my mother about how she and Pete had decided to try to start a family. I'm sure I wasn't supposed to be privy to this conversation, but whenever she passed in front of our house, I tried to make it a point of being near a window. I heard every word through the screen. The very next week, though, I learned that she had some kind of disease. That was three years ago. She slowly grew more haggard through the following seasons. Pete tried to take care of her on his own, but I don't think it had gone all too well. At her funeral, Henry had to hold him back from climbing into the grave after her.

"Is this murder?" I asked Witzer after he'd turned onto the dirt path and headed out toward the woods.

He looked over at me and said nothing for a second. "I don't know, Ernest," he said. "Can you murder someone who's already dead? Can you murder a dream? What would you have us do?" He didn't ask the last question angrily but as if he was really looking for another plan than Jolle's.

I shook my head.

"I'll never see things the same again," he said. "I keep thinking I'm gonna wake up any minute now."

We drove on for another half mile and then he pulled the truck off the path and under a cluster of oak. As we got out of the cab, the Sheriff parked next to us. Henry, the doctor, and Jolle got out of the cruiser, and all five of us gathered at the back of the pickup. It fell to Witzer and me to get her out of the truck and lay her on the ground some feet away. "Careful," whispered the old man, as he leaned over the wall of the bed and slipped his arms under her. I took the legs, and when I touched her skin a shiver went through me. Her body was heavier than I thought, and her sex was staring me right in the face, covered with short hair thick as twine. She was breathing lightly, obviously sleeping, and her pupils moved rapidly beneath her closed lids like she was dreaming. She had a powerful aroma, flowers and candy, sweet to the point of sickening.

We got her on the ground without waking her, and the instant I let go of her legs, I stepped outside the circle of men. "Stand back," said Jolle. The others moved away. He pulled his gun out of its holster with his left hand and made the sign of the cross with his right. Leaning down, he put the gun near her left temple, and then cocked the hammer back. The hammer clicked into place with the sound of a breaking twig and right then her eyes shot open. Four grown men jumped backward in unison. "Good lord," said Witzer. "Do it," said Kvench. I looked to Jolle and he was staring down at her as if in a trance. Her eyes had no color. They were wide and shifting back and forth. She started taking deep raspy breaths and then sat straight up. A low mewing noise came from her chest, the sound of a cat or a scared child. Then she started talking backwards talk, some foreign language never heard on earth before, babbling frantically and drooling.

Jolle fired. The bullet caught her in the side of the head and threw her onto her right shoulder. The side of her face, including her ear, blew off, and this black stuff, not blood, splattered all over, flecks of it staining Jolle's pants and shirt and face. The side of her head was smoking. She lay there writhing in what looked like a pool of oil, and he shot her again and again, emptying the gun into her. The sight of it brought me to my knees, and I puked. When I looked up, she'd stopped moving. Tears were streaming down Witzer's face. Kvench was shaking. Henry looked as if he'd been turned to stone. Jolle's finger kept pulling the trigger, but there were no rounds left.

After Henry tamped down the last shovelful of dirt on her grave, Jolle made us swear never to say a word to anyone about what had happened. I pledged that oath as did the others. Witzer took me home, no doubt having silently decided I shouldn't be there when they woke Pete. When I got to the house, I went straight to bed and slept for an entire day, only getting up in time to get to the gas station for work the next morning. The only dream I had was an infuriating and frustrating one of Lester II, eating hard boiled eggs and explaining it all to me but in backwards talk and gibberish so I couldn't make out any of it. Carrying the memory of that Drunk Harvest miracle around with me was like constantly having a big black bubble of night afloat in the middle of my waking thoughts. As autumn came on and passed and then winter bore down on Gatchfield, the insidious strength of it never diminished. It made me quiet and moody, and my relationship with Darlene suffered.

I kept my distance from the other four conspirators. It went so far as we tried not to even recognize each others' presence when we passed on the street. Only Witzer still waved at me from his pick up when he'd drive by, and if I was the attendant when he came into the station for gas, he'd say, "How are you, boy?" I'd nod and that would be it. Around Christmastime I'd heard from my father that Pete Hesiant had lost his mind, and was unable to go to work, would break down crying at a moment's notice, couldn't sleep, and was being treated by Kvench with all manner of pills.

Things didn't get any better come spring. Pete shot the side of his head off with a pistol. Mrs. Marfish, who'd gone to bring him a pie she'd baked to cheer him up, discovered him lying dead in a pool of blood on the back porch of the little yellow house. Then Sheriff Jolle took ill and was so bad off with whatever he had, he couldn't get out of bed. He deputized Reed Boccan, the barkeep and the most sensible man in town, to look after Gatchfield in his absence. Reed did a good job as Sheriff and Samantha double timed it at The Blind Ghost—both solid citizens.

In the early days of May, I burned my hand badly at work on a hot car engine and my boss drove me over to Kvench's office to get it looked after. While I was in his treatment room with him, and he was wrapping my hand in gauze, he leaned close to me and whispered, "I think I know what happened." I didn't even make a face, but stared ahead at the eye chart on the wall, not really wanting to hear anything about the incident. "Gatchfield's so isolated that change couldn't get in from the outside, so Nature sent it from within," he said. "Mutation. From the dream." I looked at him. He was nodding, but I saw that his goatee had gone squirrely, there was this over-eager gleam in his eyes, and his breath smelled like medicine. I knew right then he'd been more than sampling his own pills. I couldn't get out of there fast enough.

June came, and it was a week away from the day that Witzer and I were to begin practicing for the Drunk Harvest again. I dreaded the thought of it to the point where I was having a hard time eating or sleeping. After work one evening, as I was walking home, the old man pulled up next to me in his pick-up truck. He stopped and opened the window. I was going to keep walking, but he called, "Boy, get in. Take a ride with me."

I made the mistake of looking over at him. "It's important," he said. I got in the cab and we drove slowly off down the street.

I blurted out that I didn't think I'd be able to manage the Harvest and how screwed up the thought of it was making me, but he held his hand up and said, "Shh, shh, I know." I quieted down and waited for him to talk. A few seconds passed and then he said, "I've been to see Jolle. You haven't seen him have you?"

I shook my head.

"He's a gonner for sure. He's got some kind of belly rot, and, I swear to you he's got a deathberry bush growing out of his insides . . . while he's still alive, no less. Doc Kvench just keeps feeding him pills, but he'd be better off taking a hedge clipper to him."

"Are you serious?" I said.

"Boy, I'm dead serious." Before I could respond, he said, "Now look, when the time for the celebration comes around, we're all going to have to participate in it as if nothing had happened. We made our oath to the Sheriff. That's bad enough, but what happens when somebody's dead relative tells them in a Night Whiskey dream what we did, what happened with Lonette?"

I was trembling and couldn't bring myself to speak.

"Tomorrow night—are you listening to me?—tomorrow night I'm leaving my truck unlocked with the keys in the ignition. You come to my place and take it and get the fuck out of Gatchfield."

I hadn't noticed but we were now parked in front of my house. He leaned across me and opened my door. "Get as far away as you can, boy," he said. The next day, I called in sick to work, withdrew all my savings from the bank, and talked to Darlene. That night, good to his word, the keys were in the old pickup. I noticed there was a new used truck parked next to the old one on his lot to cover when the one we took went missing. I'd left my parents a letter about how Darlene and I had decided to elope, and that they weren't to worry. I'd call them.

We fled to the biggest brightest city we could find, and the rush and maddening business of the place, the distance from home, our combined struggle to survive at first and then make our way was a curative better than any pill the doctor could have prescribed. Every day there was change and progress and crazy news on the television, and these things served to shrink the black bubble in my thoughts. Still to this day, though, so many years later, there's always an evening near the end of September when I sit down to a Night Whiskey, so to speak, and Gatchfield comes back to me in my dreams like some lost relative I'm both terrified to behold and want nothing more than to put my arms around and never let go.

ELLEN KLAGES

In the House of the Seven Librarians

Ellen Klages's story to warm the hearts of bibliophiles everywhere, "In the House of the Seven Librarians," was published in Sharyn November's second Firebirds anthology, Firebirds Rising. *Klages's first novel,* The Green Glass Sea, *won the Scott O'Dell Award for Historical Fiction. Her short fiction has been published in a number of magazines and anthologies, including* Infinite Matrix, The Coyote Road, Strange Horizons, *and* Black Gate. *Her story "Basement Magic" (from* The Magazine of Fantasy & Science Fiction) *was a Nebula Award winner. Klages lives in San Francisco.*
—K.L. & G.G.

Once upon a time, the Carnegie Library sat on a wooded bluff on the east side of town: red brick and fieldstone, with turrets and broad windows facing the trees. Inside, green glass-shaded lamps cast warm yellow light onto oak tables ringed with spindle-backed chairs.

Books filled the dark shelves that stretched high up toward the pressed-tin ceiling. The floors were wood, except in the foyer, where they were pale beige marble. The loudest sounds were the ticking of the clock and the quiet, rhythmic *thwack* of a rubber stamp on a pasteboard card.

It was a cozy, orderly place.

Through twelve presidents and two world wars, the elms and maples grew tall outside the deep bay windows. Children leaped from *Peter Pan* to *Oliver Twist* and off to college, replaced at Story Hour by their younger brothers, cousins, daughters.

Then the library board—men in suits, serious men, men of money—met and cast their votes for progress. A new library, with fluorescent lights, much better for the children's eyes. Picture windows, automated systems, ergonomic plastic chairs. The town approved the levy, and the new library was built across town, convenient to the community center and the mall.

Some books were boxed and trundled down Broad Street, many others stamped DISCARD and left where they were, for a book sale in the fall. Interns from the university used the latest technology to transfer the cumbersome old card file and all the records onto floppy disks and microfiche. Progress, progress, progress.

The Ralph P. Mossberger Library (named after the local philanthropist and car dealer who had written the largest check) opened on a drizzly morning in late April.

Everyone attended the ribbon-cutting ceremony and stayed for the speeches, because there would be cake after.

Everyone except the seven librarians from the Carnegie Library on the bluff across town.

Quietly, without a fuss (they were librarians, after all), while the town looked toward the future, they bought supplies: loose tea and English biscuits, packets of Bird's pudding and cans of beef barley soup. They rearranged some of the shelves, brought in a few comfortable armchairs, nice china and teapots, a couch, towels for the shower, and some small braided rugs.

Then they locked the door behind them.

Each morning they woke and went about their chores. They shelved and stamped and cataloged, and in the evenings, every night, they read by lamplight.

Perhaps, for a while, some citizens remembered the old library, with the warm nostalgia of a favorite childhood toy that had disappeared one summer, never seen again. Others assumed it had been torn down long ago.

And so a year went by, then two, or perhaps a great many more. Inside, time had ceased to matter. Grass and brambles grew thick and tall around the fieldstone steps, and trees arched overhead as the forest folded itself around them like a cloak.

Inside, the seven librarians lived, quiet and content.

Until the day they found the baby.

Librarians are guardians of books. They guide others along their paths, offering keys to help unlock the doors of knowledge. But these seven had become a closed circle, no one to guide, no new minds to open onto worlds of possibility. They kept themselves busy, tidying orderly shelves and mending barely frayed bindings with stiff netting and glue, and began to bicker among themselves.

Ruth and Edith had been up half the night, arguing about whether or not subway tokens (of which there were half a dozen in the Lost and Found box) could be used to cast the *I Ching*. And so Blythe was on the stepstool in the 299s, reshelving the volume of hexagrams, when she heard the knock.

Odd, she thought. It's been some time since we've had visitors.

She tugged futilely at her shapeless cardigan as she clambered off the stool and trotted to the front door, where she stopped abruptly, her hand to her mouth in surprise.

A wicker basket, its contents covered with a red-checked cloth, as if for a picnic, lay in the wooden box beneath the Book Return chute. A small, cream-colored envelope poked out from one side.

"How nice!" Blythe said aloud, clapping her hands. She thought of fried chicken and potato salad—of which she was awfully fond—a Mason jar of lemonade, perhaps even a cherry pie? She lifted the basket by its round-arched handle. Heavy, for a picnic. But then, there *were* seven of them. Although Olive just ate like a bird, these days.

She turned and set it on top of the Circulation Desk, pulling the envelope free.

"What's *that*?" Marian asked, her lips in their accustomed moue of displeasure, as if the basket were an agent of chaos, existing solely to disrupt the tidy array of rubber stamps and file boxes that were her domain.

"A present," said Blythe. "I think it might be lunch."

Marian frowned. "For you?"

"I don't know yet. There's a note . . ." Blythe held up the envelope and peered at it. "No," she said. "It's addressed to 'The Librarians. Overdue Books Department.'"

"Well, that would be me," Marian said curtly. She was the youngest, and wore trouser suits with silk T-shirts. She had once been blond. She reached across the counter, plucked the envelope from Blythe's plump fingers, and sliced it open with a filigreed brass stiletto.

"Hmph," she said after she'd scanned the contents.

"It *is* lunch, isn't it?" asked Blythe.

"Hardly." Marian began to read aloud:

> This is overdue. Quite a bit, I'm afraid. I apologize. We moved to Topeka when I was very small, and Mother accidentally packed it up with the linens. I have traveled a long way to return it, and I know the fine must be large, but I have no money. As it is a book of fairy tales, I thought payment of a first-born child would be acceptable. I always loved the library. I'm sure she'll be happy there.

Blythe lifted the edge of the cloth. "Oh, my stars!"

A baby girl with a shock of wire-stiff black hair stared up at her, green eyes wide and curious. She was contentedly chewing on the corner of a blue book, half as big as she was. *Fairy Tales of the Brothers Grimm.*

"The Rackham illustrations," Blythe said as she eased the book away from the baby. "That's a lovely edition."

"But when was it checked out?" Marian demanded.

Blythe opened the cover and pulled the ruled card from the inside pocket: "October seventeenth, 1938," she said, shaking her head. "Goodness, at two cents a day, that's . . ." She shook her head again. Blythe had never been good with figures.

They made a crib for her in the bottom drawer of a file cabinet, displacing acquisition orders, zoning permits, and the instructions for the mimeograph, which they rarely used.

Ruth consulted Dr. Spock. Edith read Piaget. The two of them peered from text to infant and back again for a good long while before deciding that she was probably about nine months old. They sighed. Too young to read.

So they fed her cream and let her gum on biscuits, and each of the seven cooed and clucked and tickled her pink toes when they thought the others weren't looking. Harriet had been the oldest of nine girls, and knew more about babies than she really cared to. She washed and changed the diapers that had been tucked into the basket, and read *Goodnight Moon* and *Pat the Bunny* to the little girl, whom she called Polly—short for Polyhymnia, the muse of oratory and sacred song.

Blythe called her Bitsy, and Li'l Precious.

Marian called her "the foundling," or "That Child You Took In," but did her share of cooing and clucking, just the same.

When the child began to walk, Dorothy blocked the staircase with stacks of Comptons, which she felt was an inferior encyclopedia, and let her pull herself up on the bottom drawers of the card catalog. Anyone looking up Zithers or Zippers (*see* "Slide Fasteners") soon found many of the cards fused together with grape jam. When she began to talk, they made a little bed nook next to the fireplace in the Children's Room.

It was high time for Olive to begin the child's education.

Olive had been the children's librarian since before recorded time, or so it seemed. No one knew how old she was, but she vaguely remembered waving to President Coolidge. She still had all of her marbles, though every one of them was a bit odd and rolled asymmetrically.

She slept on a daybed behind a reference shelf that held *My First Encyclopedia* and *The Wonder Book of Trees*, among others. Across the room, the child's first "big-girl bed" was yellow, with decals of a fairy and a horse on the headboard, and a rocket ship at the foot, because they weren't sure about her preferences.

At the beginning of her career, Olive had been an ordinary-sized librarian, but by the time she began the child's lessons, she was not much taller than her toddling charge. Not from osteoporosis or dowager's hump or other old-lady maladies, but because she had tired of stooping over tiny chairs and bending to knee-high shelves. She had been a grown-*up* for so long that when the library closed, she had decided it was time to grow *down* again, and was finding that much more comfortable.

She had a remarkably cozy lap for a woman her size.

The child quickly learned her alphabet, all the shapes and colors, the names of zoo animals, and fourteen different kinds of dinosaurs, all of whom were dead.

By the time she was four, or thereabouts, she could sound out the letters for simple words—*cup* and *lamp* and *stairs*. And that's how she came to name herself.

Olive had fallen asleep over *Make Way for Ducklings*, and all the other librarians were busy somewhere else. The child was bored. She tiptoed out of the Children's Room, hugging the shadows of the walls and shelves, crawling by the base of the Circulation Desk so that Marian wouldn't see her, and made her way to the alcove that held the Card Catalog. The heart of the library. Her favorite, most forbidden place to play.

Usually she crawled underneath and tucked herself into the corner formed of oak cabinet, marble floor, and plaster walls. It was a fine place to play Hide-and-Seek, even if it was mostly just Hide. The corner was a cave, a bunk on a pirate ship, a cupboard in a magic wardrobe.

But that afternoon she looked at the white cards on the fronts of the drawers, and her eyes widened in recognition. Letters! In her very own alphabet. Did they spell words? Maybe the drawers were all *full* of words, a huge wooden box of words. The idea almost made her dizzy.

She walked to the other end of the cabinet and looked up, tilting her neck back until it crackled. Four drawers from top to bottom. Five drawers across. She sighed. She was only tall enough to reach the bottom row of drawers. She traced a gentle finger around the little brass frames, then very carefully pulled out the white cards inside and laid them on the floor in a neat row:

She squatted over them, her tongue sticking out of the corner of her mouth in concentration, and tried to read.

"Sound it out." She could almost hear Olive's voice, soft and patient. She took a deep breath.

"Duh-in-s—" and then she stopped, because the last card had too many letters, and she didn't know any words that had Xs in them. Well, xylophone. But the X was in the front, and that wasn't the same. She tried anyway. "Duh-ins-zzzigh," and frowned.

She squatted lower, so low she could feel cold marble under her cotton pants, and put her hand on top of the last card. One finger covered the X and her pinkie covered the Z (another letter that was useless for spelling ordinary things). That left Y. Y at the end was good. funnY. happY.

"Duh-ins-see," she said slowly. "Dinsy."

That felt very good to say, hard and soft sounds and hissing Ss mixing in her mouth, so she said it again, louder, which made her laugh, so she said it again, very loud: "DINSY!"

There is nothing quite like a loud voice in a library to get a lot of attention very fast. Within a minute, all seven of the librarians stood in the doorway of the alcove.

"What on earth?" said Harriet.

"*Now* what have you . . ." said Marian.

"What have you spelled, dear?" asked Olive in her soft little voice.

"I made it myself," the girl replied.

"Just gibberish," murmured Edith, though not unkindly. "It doesn't mean a thing."

The child shook her head. "Does so. Olive," she said, pointing to Olive. "Do'thy, Edith, Harwiet, Bithe, Ruth." She paused and rolled her eyes. "Mawian," she added, a little less cheerfully. Then she pointed to herself. "And Dinsy."

"Oh, now, Polly," said Harriet.

"Dinsy," said Dinsy.

"Bitsy?" Blythe tried hopefully.

"*Dinsy*," said Dinsy.

And that was that.

At three every afternoon, Dinsy and Olive made a two-person circle on the braided rug in front of the bay window, and had Story Time. Sometimes Olive read aloud from *Beezus and Ramona* and *Half Magic*, and sometimes Dinsy read to Olive *The King's Stilts*, and *In the Night Kitchen*, and *Winnie-the-Pooh*. Dinsy liked that one especially, and took it to bed with her so many times that Edith had to repair the binding. Twice.

That was when Dinsy first wished upon the Library.

A note about the Library:

Knowledge is not static; information must flow in order to live. Every so often one of the librarians would discover a new addition. *Harry Potter and the Sorcerer's Stone* appeared one rainy afternoon, *Rowling* shelved neatly between *Rodgers* and *Saint-Exupéry*, as if it had always been there. Blythe found a book of Thich Nhat Hanh's writings in the 294s one day while she was dusting, and Feynman's lectures on physics showed up on Dorothy's shelving cart after she'd gone to make a cup of tea.

It didn't happen often; the Library was selective about what it chose to add, rejecting flash-in-the-pan best-sellers, sifting for the long haul, looking for those voices that would stand the test of time next to Dickens and Tolkien, Woolf and Gould.

The librarians took care of the books, and the Library watched over them in return.

It occasionally left treats: a bowl of ripe tangerines on the Formica counter of the Common Room; a gold foil box of chocolate creams; seven small, stemmed glasses of sherry on the table one teatime. Their biscuit tin remained full, the cream in the Wedgwood jug stayed fresh, and the ink pad didn't dry out. Even the little pencils stayed needle sharp, never whittling down to finger-cramping nubs.

Some days the Library even hid Dinsy, when she had made a mess and didn't want to be found, or when one of the librarians was in a dark mood. It rearranged itself, just a bit, so that in her wanderings she would find a new alcove or cubbyhole, and once a secret passage that led to a previously unknown balcony overlooking the Reading Room. When she went back a week later, she found only blank wall.

And so it was, one night when she was sixish, that Dinsy first asked the Library for a boon. Lying in her tiny yellow bed, the fraying *Pooh* under her pillow, she wished for a bear to cuddle. Books were small comfort once the lights were out, and their hard, sharp corners made them awkward companions under the covers. She lay with one arm crooked around a soft, imaginary bear, and wished and wished until her eyelids fluttered into sleep.

The next morning, while they were all having tea and toast with jam, Blythe came into the Common Room with a quizzical look on her face and her hands behind her back.

"The strangest thing," she said. "On my way up here I glanced over at the Lost and Found. Couldn't tell you why. Nothing lost in ages. But this must have caught my eye."

She held out a small brown bear, one shoebutton eye missing, bits of fur gone from its belly, as if it had been loved almost to pieces.

"It seems to be yours," she said with a smile, turning up one padded foot, where DINSY was written in faded laundry-marker black.

Dinsy wrapped her whole self around the cotton-stuffed body and skipped for the rest of the morning. Later, after Olive gave her a snack—cocoa and a Lorna Doone—Dinsy cupped her hand and blew a kiss to the oak woodwork.

"Thank you," she whispered, and put half her cookie in a crack between two tiles on the Children's Room fireplace when Olive wasn't looking.

Dinsy and Olive had a lovely time. One week they were pirates, raiding the Common Room for booty (and raisins). The next they were princesses, trapped in the turret with *At the Back of the North Wind*, and the week after that they were knights in shining armor, rescuing damsels in distress, a game Dinsy especially savored because it annoyed Marian to be rescued.

But the year she turned seven and a half, Dinsy stopped reading stories. Quite abruptly, on an afternoon that Olive said later had really *felt* like a Thursday.

"Stories are for babies," Dinsy said. "I want to read about *real* people." Olive smiled a sad smile and pointed toward the far wall, because Dinsy was not the first child to make that same pronouncement, and she had known this phase would come.

After that, Dinsy devoured biographies, starting with the orange ones, the Childhoods of Famous Americans: *Thomas Edison, Young Inventor*. She worked her way from Abigail Adams to John Peter Zenger, all along the west side of the Children's Room, until one day she went around the corner, where Science and History began.

She stood in the doorway, looking at the rows of grown-up books, when she felt Olive's hand on her shoulder.

"Do you think maybe it's time you moved across the hall?" Olive asked softly.

Dinsy bit her lip, then nodded. "I can come back to visit, can't I? When I want to read stories again?"

"For as long as you like, dear. Anytime at all."

So Dorothy came and gathered up the bear and the pillow and the yellow tooth-brush. Dinsy kissed Olive on her papery cheek and, holding Blythe's hand, moved across the hall, to the room where all the books had numbers.

Blythe was plump and freckled and frizzled. She always looked a little flushed, as if she had just that moment dropped what she was doing to rush over and greet you. She wore rumpled tweed skirts and a shapeless cardigan whose original color was impossible to guess. She had bright, dark eyes like a spaniel's, which Dinsy thought was appropriate, because Blythe *lived* to fetch books. She wore a locket with a small rotogravure picture of Melvil Dewey and kept a variety of sweets—sour balls and mints and Necco wafers—in her desk drawer.

Dinsy had always liked her.

She was not as sure about Dorothy.

Over *her* desk, Dorothy had a small framed medal on a royal-blue ribbon, won for "Excellence in Classification Studies." She could operate the ancient black Remington typewriter with brisk efficiency, and even, on occasion, coax chalky gray prints out of the wheezing old copy machine.

She was a tall, rawboned woman with steely blue eyes, good posture, and even better penmanship. Dinsy was a little frightened of her, at first, because she seemed so stern, and because she looked like magazine pictures of the Wicked Witch of the West, or at least Margaret Hamilton.

But that didn't last long.

"You should be very careful not to slip on the floor in here," Dorothy said on their first morning. "Do you know why?"

Dinsy shook her head.

"Because now you're in the non*friction* room!" Dorothy's angular face cracked into a wide grin.

Dinsy groaned. "Okay," she said after a minute. "How do you file marshmallows?"

Dorothy cocked her head. "Shoot."

"By the *Gooey* Decimal System!"

Dinsy heard Blythe tsk-tsk, but Dorothy laughed out loud, and from then on they were fast friends.

The three of them used the large, sunny room as an arena for endless games of I Spy and Twenty Questions as Dinsy learned her way around the shelves. In the evenings, after supper, they played Authors and Scrabble, and (once) tried to keep a running rummy score in Base Eight.

Dinsy sat at the court of Napoleon, roamed the jungles near Timbuktu, and was a frequent guest at the Round Table. She knew all the kings of England and the difference between a pergola and a folly. She knew the names of 112 breeds of sheep, and loved to say "Barbados Blackbelly" over and over, although it was difficult to work into conversations. When she affectionately, if misguidedly, referred to Blythe as a "Persian Fat-Rumped," she was sent to bed without supper.

A note about time:

Time had become quite flexible inside the library. (This is true of most places with interesting books. Sit down to read for twenty minutes, and suddenly it's dark, with no clue as to where the hours have gone.)

As a consequence, no one was really sure about the day of the week, and there was frequent disagreement about the month and year. As the keeper of the date stamp at the front desk, Marian was the arbiter of such things. (But she often had a cocktail after dinner, and many mornings she couldn't recall if she'd already turned the little wheel, or how often it had slipped her mind, so she frequently set it a day or two ahead—or back three—just to make up.)

One afternoon, on a visit to Olive and the Children's Room, Dinsy looked up from *Little Town on the Prairie* and said, "When's my birthday?"

Olive thought for a moment. Because of the irregularities of time, holidays were celebrated a bit haphazardly. "I'm not sure, dear. Why do you ask?"

"Laura's going to a birthday party, in this book," she said, holding it up. "And it's fun. So I thought maybe I could have one."

"I think that would be lovely," Olive agreed. "We'll talk to the others at supper."

"Your birthday?" said Harriet as she set the table a few hours later. "Let me see." She began to count on her fingers. "You arrived in April, according to Marian's stamp, and you were about nine months old, so—" She pursed her lips as she ticked off the months. "You must have been born in July!"

"But when's my birth*day?*" Dinsy asked impatiently.

"Not sure," said Edith as she ladled out the soup.

"No way to tell," Olive agreed.

"How does July fifth sound?" offered Blythe, as if it were a point of order to be voted on. Blythe counted best by fives.

"Fourth," said Dorothy. "Independence Day. Easy to remember?"

Dinsy shrugged. "Okay." It hadn't seemed so complicated in the Little House book. "When is that? Is it soon?"

"Probably." Ruth nodded.

So a few weeks later, the librarians threw her a birthday party.

Harriet baked a spice cake with pink frosting, and wrote DINSY on top in red licorice laces, dotting the *I* with a lemon drop (which was rather stale). The others gave her gifts that were thoughtful and mostly handmade:

> A set of Dewey Decimal flash cards from Blythe.
> A book of logic puzzles (stamped DISCARD more than a dozen times, so Dinsy could write in it) from Dorothy.
> A lumpy orange-and-green cardigan Ruth knitted for her.
> A snow globe from the 1939 World's Fair from Olive.
> A flashlight from Edith, so that Dinsy could find her way around at night and not knock over the wastebasket again.
> A set of paper finger puppets, made from blank card pockets, hand-painted by Marian. (They were literary figures, of course, all of them necessarily stout and squarish—Nero Wolfe and Friar Tuck, Santa Claus, and Gertrude Stein.)

But her favorite gift was the second boon she'd wished upon the Library: a box of crayons. (She had grown very tired of drawing gray pictures with the little pencils.) It had produced Crayola crayons, in the familiar yellow-and-green box, labeled LIBRARY

PACK. Inside were the colors of Dinsy's world: Reference Maroon, Brown Leather, Peplum Beige, Reader's Guide Green, World Book Red, Card Catalog Cream, Date Stamp Purple, and Palatino Black.

It was a very special birthday, that fourth of July. Although Dinsy wondered about Marian's calculations. As Harriet cut the first piece of cake that evening, she remarked that it was snowing rather heavily outside, which everyone agreed was lovely, but quite unusual for that time of year.

Dinsy soon learned all the planets, and many of their moons. (She referred to herself as Umbriel for an entire month.) She puffed up her cheeks and blew onto stacks of scrap paper. "Sirocco," she'd whisper. "Chinook. Mistral. Willy-Willy," and rated her attempts on the Beaufort scale. Dorothy put a halt to it after Hurricane Dinsy reshuffled a rather elaborate game of Patience.

She dipped into fractals here, double dactyls there. When she tired of a subject—or found it just didn't suit her—Blythe or Dorothy would smile and proffer the hat. It was a deep green felt that held one thousand slips of paper, numbered 001 to 999. Dinsy'd scrunch her eyes closed, pick one, and, like a scavenger hunt, spend the morning (or the next three weeks) at the shelves indicated.

Pangolins lived at 599 (point 31), and Pancakes at 641. Pencils were at 674 but Pens were a shelf away at 681, and Ink was across the aisle at 667. (Dinsy thought that was stupid, because you had to *use* them together.) Pluto the planet was at 523, but Pluto the Disney dog was at 791 (point 453), near Rock and Roll and Kazoos.

It was all very useful information. But in Dinsy's opinion, things could be a little *too* organized.

The first time she straightened up the Common Room without anyone asking, she was very pleased with herself. She had lined up everyone's teacup in a neat row on the shelf, with all the handles curving the same way, and arranged the spices in the little wooden rack: ANISE, BAY LEAVES, CHIVES, DILL WEED, PEPPERCORNS, SALT, SESAME SEEDS, SUGAR.

"Look," she said when Blythe came in to refresh her tea, "Order out of chaos." It was one of Blythe's favorite mottoes.

Blythe smiled and looked over at the spice rack. Then her smile faded and she shook her head.

"Is something wrong?" Dinsy asked. She had hoped for a compliment.

"Well, you used the alphabet," said Blythe, sighing. "I suppose it's not your fault. You were with Olive for a good many years. But you're a big girl now. You should learn the *proper* order." She picked up the salt container. "We'll start with Salt." She wrote the word on the little chalkboard hanging by the icebox, followed by the number 553.632. "Five-five-three-point-six-three-two. Because—?"

Dinsy thought for a moment. "Earth Sciences."

"Ex-actly." Blythe beamed. "Because salt is a mineral. But, now, chives. Chives are a garden crop, so they're . . ."

Dinsy bit her lip in concentration. "Six-thirty-something."

"Very good." Blythe smiled again and chalked CHIVES 635.26 on the board. "So you see, Chives should always be shelved *after* Salt, dear."

Blythe turned and began to rearrange the eight ceramic jars. Behind her back, Dinsy silently rolled her eyes.

Edith appeared in the doorway.

"Oh, not again," she said. "No wonder I can't find a thing in this kitchen. Blythe, I've *told* you. *Bay Leaf* comes first. QK-four-nine—" She had worked at the university when she was younger.

"Library of Congress, my fanny," said Blythe, not quite under her breath. "We're not *that* kind of library."

"It's no excuse for imprecision," Edith replied. They each grabbed a jar and stared at each other.

Dinsy tiptoed away and hid in the 814s, where she read "Jabberwocky" until the coast was clear.

But the kitchen remained a taxonomic battleground. At least once a week, Dinsy was amused by the indignant sputtering of someone who had just spooned dill weed, not sugar, into a cup of Earl Grey tea.

Once she knew her way around, Dinsy was free to roam the library as she chose.

"Anywhere?" she asked Blythe.

"Anywhere you like, my sweet. Except the Stacks. You're not quite old enough for the Stacks."

Dinsy frowned. "I am *so*," she muttered. But the Stacks were locked, and there wasn't much she could do.

Some days she sat with Olive in the Children's Room, revisiting old friends, or explored the maze of the Main Room. Other days she spent in the Reference Room, where Ruth and Harriet guarded the big important books that no one could ever, ever check out—not even when the library had been open.

Ruth and Harriet were like a set of salt-and-pepper shakers from two different yard sales. Harriet had faded orange hair and a sharp, kind face. Small and pinched and pointed, a decade or two away from wizened. She had violet eyes and a mischievous, conspiratorial smile and wore rimless octagonal glasses, like stop signs. Dinsy had never seen an actual stop sign, but she'd looked at pictures.

Ruth was Chinese. She wore wool jumpers in neon plaids and had cat's-eye glasses on a beaded chain around her neck. She never put them all the way on, just lifted them to her eyes and peered through them without opening the bows.

"Life is a treasure hunt," said Harriet.

"Knowledge is power," said Ruth. "Knowing where to look is half the battle."

"Half the fun," added Harriet. Ruth almost never got the last word.

They introduced Dinsy to dictionaries and almanacs, encyclopedias and compendiums. They had been native guides through the country of the Dry Tomes for many years, but they agreed that Dinsy delved unusually deep.

"Would you like to take a break, love?" Ruth asked one afternoon. "It's nearly time for tea."

"I *am* fatigued," Dinsy replied, looking up from *Roget*. "Fagged out, weary, a bit spent. Tea would be pleasant, agreeable—"

"I'll put the kettle on," sighed Ruth.

Dinsy read *Bartlett's* as if it were a catalog of conversations, spouting lines from Tennyson, Mark Twain, and Dale Carnegie until even Harriet put her hands over her ears and began to hum "Stairway to Heaven."

One or two evenings a month, usually after Blythe had remarked, "Well, she's a spirited girl," for the third time, they all took the night off, "For Library business." Olive or Dorothy would tuck Dinsy in early and read from one of her favorites while Ruth made her a bedtime treat—a cup of spiced tea that tasted a little like cherries and a little like varnish, and which Dinsy somehow never remembered finishing.

A list (written in diverse hands), tacked to the wall of the Common Room.

10 THINGS TO REMEMBER WHEN YOU LIVE IN A LIBRARY
1. We do not play shuffleboard on the Reading Room table.
2. Books should not have "dog's ears." Bookmarks make lovely presents.
3. Do not write in books. Even in pencil. Puzzle collections and connect-the-dots are books.
4. The shelving cart is not a scooter.
5. Library paste is not food.
    [Marginal note in a child's hand:
    True. It tastes like Cream of Wrong Soup.]
6. Do not use the date stamp to mark your banana.
7. Shelves are not monkey bars.
8. Do not play 982-pickup with the P-Q drawer (or any other).
9. The dumbwaiter is only for books. It is not a carnival ride.
10. Do not drop volumes of the Britannica off the stairs to hear the echo.

They were an odd, but contented family. There were rules, to be sure, but Dinsy never lacked for attention. With seven mothers, there was always someone to talk with, a hankie for tears, a lap or a shoulder to share a story.

Most evenings, when Dorothy had made a fire in the Reading Room and the wooden shelves gleamed in the flickering light, they would all sit in companionable silence. Ruth knitted, Harriet muttered over an acrostic, Edith stirred the cocoa so it wouldn't get a skin. Dinsy sat on the rug, her back against the knees of whoever was her favorite that week, and felt safe and warm and loved. "God's in his heaven, all's right with the world," as Blythe would say.

But as she watched the moon peep in and out of the clouds through the leaded-glass panes of the tall windows, Dinsy often wondered what it would be like to see the whole sky, all around her.

First Olive and then Dorothy had been in charge of Dinsy's thick dark hair, trimming it with the mending shears every few weeks when it began to obscure her eyes. But a few years into her second decade at the library, Dinsy began cutting it herself, leaving it as wild and spiky as the brambles outside the front door.

That was not the only change.

"We haven't seen her at breakfast in weeks," Harriet said as she buttered a scone one morning.

"Months. And all she reads is Salinger. Or Sylvia Plath," complained Dorothy. "I wouldn't mind that so much, but she just leaves them on the table for *me* to reshelve."

"It's not as bad as what she did to Olive," Marian said. "*The Golden Compass* appeared last week, and she thought Dinsy would enjoy it. But not only did she turn up her nose, she had the gall to say to Olive, 'Leave me alone. I can find my own books.' Imagine. Poor Olive was beside herself."

"She used to be such a sweet child." Blythe sighed. "What are we going to do?"

"Now, now. She's just that age," Edith said calmly. "She's not really a child any-more. She needs some privacy, and some responsibility. I have an idea."

And so it was that Dinsy got her own room—with a door that *shut*—in a corner of the second floor. It had been a tiny cubbyhole of an office, but it had a set of slender curved stairs, wrought iron worked with lilies and twigs, which led up to the turret between the red-tiled eaves.

The round tower was just wide enough for Dinsy's bed, with windows all around. There had once been a view of the town, but now trees and ivy allowed only jigsaw puzzle–shaped puddles of light to dapple the wooden floor. At night the puddles were luminous blue splotches of moonlight that hinted of magic beyond her reach.

On the desk in the room below, centered in a pool of yellow lamplight, Edith had left a note: "Come visit me. There's mending to be done," and a worn brass key on a wooden paddle, stenciled with the single word: STACKS.

The Stacks were in the basement, behind a locked gate at the foot of the metal spiral staircase that descended from the 600s. They had always reminded Dinsy of the steps down to the dungeon in *The King's Stilts*. Darkness below hinted at danger, but adventure. Terra Incognita.

Dinsy didn't use her key the first day, or the second. Mending? Boring. But the af-ternoon of the third day, she ventured down the spiral stairs. She had been as far as the gate before, many times, because it was forbidden, to peer through the metal mesh at the dimly lighted shelves and imagine what treasures might be hidden there.

She had thought that the Stacks would be damp and cold, strewn with odd bits of discarded library flotsam. Instead they were cool and dry, and smelled very different from upstairs. Dustier, with hints of mold and the tang of very old leather, an un-dertone of vinegar stored in an old shoe.

Unlike the main floor, with its polished wood and airy high ceilings, the Stacks were a low, cramped warren of gunmetal gray shelves that ran floor to ceiling in nar-row aisles. Seven levels twisted behind the west wall of the library like a secret labyrinth that stretched from below the ground to up under the eaves of the roof. Floor and steps were translucent glass brick and six-foot ceilings strung with pipes and ducts were lit by single caged bulbs, two to an aisle.

It was a windowless fortress of books. Upstairs the shelves were mosaics of all colors and sizes, but the Stacks were filled with geometric monochrome blocks of subdued colors: eight dozen forest-green bound volumes of *Ladies' Home Journal* filled five rows of shelves, followed by an equally large block of identical dark red *LIFE*s.

Dinsy felt like she was in another world. She was not lost, but for the first time in her life, she was not easily found, and that suited her. She could sit, invisible, and lis-ten to the sounds of library life going on around her. From Level Three she could hear Ruth humming in the Reference Room on the other side of the wall. Four feet away, and it felt like miles. She wandered and browsed for a month before she pre-sented herself at Edith's office.

A frosted glass pane in the dark wood door said MENDING ROOM in chipping gold letters. The door was open a few inches, and Dinsy could see a long workbench strewn with sewn folios and bits of leather bindings, spools of thread and bottles of thick beige glue.

"I gather you're finding your way around," Edith said, without turning in her chair. "I haven't had to send out a search party."

"Pretty much," Dinsy replied. "I've been reading old magazines." She flopped into a chair to the left of the door.

"One of my favorite things," Edith agreed. "It's like time travel." Edith was a tall, solid woman with long graying hair that she wove into elaborate buns and twisted braids, secured with number-two pencils and a single tortoiseshell comb. She wore blue jeans and vests in brightly muted colors—pale teal and lavender and dusky rose—with a strand of lapis lazuli beads cut in rough ovals.

Edith repaired damaged books, a job that was less demanding now that nothing left the building. But some of the bound volumes of journals and abstracts and magazines went back as far as 1870, and their leather bindings were crumbling into dust. The first year, Dinsy's job was to go through the aisles, level by level, and find the volumes that needed the most help. Edith gave her a clipboard and told her to check in now and then.

Dinsy learned how to take apart old books and put them back together again. Her first mending project was the tattered 1877 volume of *American Naturalist*, with its articles on "Educated Fleas" and "Barnacles" and "The Cricket as Thermometer." She sewed pages into signatures, trimmed leather and marbleized paper. Edith let her make whatever she wanted out of the scraps, and that year Dinsy gave everyone miniature replicas of their favorite volumes for Christmas.

She liked the craft, liked doing something with her hands. It took patience and concentration, and that was oddly soothing. After supper, she and Edith often sat and talked for hours, late into the night, mugs of cocoa on their workbenches, the rest of the library dark and silent above them.

"What's it like outside?" Dinsy asked one night while she was waiting for some glue to dry.

Edith was silent for a long time, long enough that Dinsy wondered if she'd spoken too softly, and was about to repeat the question, when Edith replied.

"Chaos."

That was not anything Dinsy had expected. "What do you mean?"

"It's noisy. It's crowded. Everything's always changing, and not in any way you can predict."

"That sounds kind of exciting," Dinsy said.

"Hmm." Edith thought for a moment. "Yes, I suppose it could be."

Dinsy mulled that over and fiddled with a scrap of leather, twisting it in her fingers before she spoke again. "Do you ever miss it?"

Edith turned on her stool and looked at Dinsy. "Not often," she said slowly. "Not as often as I'd thought. But then I'm awfully fond of order. Fonder than most, I suppose. This is a better fit."

Dinsy nodded and took a sip of her cocoa.

A few months later, she asked the Library for a third and final boon.

The evening that everything changed, Dinsy sat in the armchair in her room, reading Trollope's *Can You Forgive Her?* (for the third time), imagining what it would be like to talk to Glencora, when a tentative knock sounded at the door.

"Dinsy? Dinsy?" said a tiny familiar voice. "It's Olive, dear."

Dinsy slid her READ! bookmark into chapter 14 and closed the book. "It's open," she called.

Olive padded in wearing a red flannel robe, her feet in worn carpet slippers. Dinsy expected her to proffer a book, but instead Olive said, "I'd like you to come with me, dear." Her blue eyes shone with excitement.

"What for?" They had all done a nice reading of *As You Like It* a few days before, but Dinsy didn't remember any plans for that night. Maybe Olive just wanted company.

Dinsy had been meaning to spend an evening in the Children's Room, but hadn't made it down there in months.

But Olive surprised her. "It's Library business," she said, waggling her finger, but smiling.

Now, that was intriguing. For years, whenever the Librarians wanted an evening to themselves, they'd disappear down into the Stacks after supper, and would never tell her why. "It's Library business," was all they ever said. When she was younger, Dinsy had tried to follow them, but it's hard to sneak in a quiet place. She was always caught and given that awful cherry tea. The next thing she knew it was morning.

"Library business?" Dinsy said slowly. "And I'm invited?"

"Yes, dear. You're practically all grown up now. It's high time you joined us."

"Great." Dinsy shrugged, as if it were no big deal, trying to hide her excitement. And maybe it wasn't a big deal. Maybe it was a meeting of the rules committee, or plans for moving the 340s to the other side of the window again. But what if it *was* something special . . . ? That was both exciting and a little scary.

She wiggled her feet into her own slippers and stood up. Olive barely came to her knees. Dinsy touched the old woman's white hair affectionately, remembering when she used to snuggle into that soft lap. Such a long time ago.

A library at night is a still but resonant place. The only lights were the sconces along the walls, and Dinsy could hear the faint echo of each footfall on the stairs down to the foyer. They walked through the shadows of the shelves in the Main Room, back to the 600s, and down the metal stairs to the Stacks, footsteps ringing hollowly.

The lower level was dark except for a single caged bulb above the rows of *National Geographics*, their yellow bindings pale against the gloom. Olive turned to the left.

"Where are we going?" Dinsy asked. It was so odd to be down there with Olive.

"You'll see," Olive said. Dinsy could practically feel her smiling in the dark. "You'll see."

She led Dinsy down an aisle of boring municipal reports and stopped at the far end, in front of the door to the janitorial closet set into the stone wall. She pulled a long, old-fashioned brass key from the pocket of her robe and handed it to Dinsy.

"You open it, dear. The keyhole's a bit high for me."

Dinsy stared at the key, at the door, back at the key. She'd been fantasizing about "Library Business" since she was little, imagining all sorts of scenarios, none of them involving cleaning supplies. A monthly poker game. A secret tunnel into town, where they all went dancing, like the twelve princesses. Or a book group, reading forbidden texts. And now they were inviting her in? What a letdown if it was just maintenance.

She put the key in the lock. "Funny," she said as she turned it. "I've always wondered what went on when you—" Her voice caught in her throat. The door opened, not onto the closet of mops and pails and bottles of Pine-Sol she expected, but onto a small room, paneled in wood the color of ancient honey. An Oriental rug in rich, deep reds lay on the parquet floor, and the room shone with the light of dozens of candles. There were no shelves, no books, just a small fireplace at one end where a log crackled in the hearth.

"Surprise," said Olive softly. She gently tugged Dinsy inside.

All the others were waiting, dressed in flowing robes of different colors. Each of them stood in front of a Craftsman rocker, dark wood covered in soft brown leather.

Edith stepped forward and took Dinsy's hand. She gave it a gentle squeeze and said, under her breath, "Don't worry." Then she winked and led Dinsy to an empty rocker. "Stand here," she said, and returned to her own seat.

Stunned, Dinsy stood, her mouth open, her feelings a kaleidoscope.

"Welcome, dear one," said Dorothy. "We'd like you to join us." Her face was serious, but her eyes were bright, as if she was about to tell a really awful riddle and couldn't wait for the reaction.

Dinsy started. That was almost word for word what Olive had said, and it made her nervous. She wasn't sure what was coming, and was even less sure that she was ready.

"Introductions first." Dorothy closed her eyes and intoned, "I am Lexica. I serve the Library." She bowed her head once and sat down.

Dinsy stared, her eyes wide and her mind reeling as each of the librarians repeated what was obviously a familiar rite.

"I am Juvenilia," said Olive with a twinkle. "I serve the Library."

"Incunabula," said Edith.

"Sapientia," said Harriet.

"Ephemera," said Marian.

"Marginalia," said Ruth.

"Melvilia," said Blythe, smiling at Dinsy. "And I, too, serve the Library."

And then they were all seated, and all looking up at Dinsy.

"How old are you now, my sweet?" asked Harriet.

Dinsy frowned. It wasn't as easy a question as it sounded. "Seventeen," she said after a few seconds. "Or close enough."

"No longer a child." Harriet nodded. There was a touch of sadness in her voice. "That is why we are here tonight. To ask you to join us."

There was something so solemn in Harriet's voice that it made Dinsy's stomach knot up. "I don't understand," she said slowly. "What do you mean? I've been here my whole life. Practically."

Dorothy shook her head. "You have been *in* the Library, but not *of* the Library. Think of it as an apprenticeship. We have nothing more to teach you. So we're asking if you'll take a Library name and truly become one of us. There have always been seven to serve the Library."

Dinsy looked around the room. "Won't I be the eighth?" she asked. She was curious, but she was also stalling for time.

"No, dear," said Olive. "You'll be taking my place. I'm retiring. I can barely reach the second shelves these days, and soon I'll be no bigger than the dictionary. I'm going to put my feet up and sit by the fire and take it easy. I've earned it," she said with a decisive nod.

"Here, here," said Blythe. "And well done, too."

There was a murmur of assent around the room.

Dinsy took a deep breath, and then another. She looked around the room at the eager faces of the seven librarians, the only mothers she had ever known. She loved them all, and was about to disappoint them, because she had a secret of her own. She closed her eyes so she wouldn't see their faces, not at first.

"I can't take your place, Olive," she said quietly, and heard the tremor in her own voice as she fought back tears.

All around her the librarians clucked in surprise. Ruth recovered first. "Well, of course not. No one's asking you to *replace* Olive, we're merely—"

"I can't join you," Dinsy repeated. Her voice was just as quiet, but it was stronger. "Not now."

"But why *not*, sweetie?" That was Blythe, who sounded as if she were about to cry herself.

"Fireworks," said Dinsy after a moment. She opened her eyes. "Six-sixty-two-point-one." She smiled at Blythe. "I know everything about them. But I've never *seen* any." She looked from face to face again.

"I've never petted a dog or ridden a bicycle or watched the sun rise over the ocean," she said, her voice gaining courage. "I want to feel the wind and eat an ice-cream cone at a carnival. I want to smell jasmine on a spring night and hear an orchestra. I want—" She faltered, and then continued, "I want the chance to dance with a boy."

She turned to Dorothy. "You said you have nothing left to teach me. Maybe that's true. I've learned from each of you that there's nothing in the world I can't discover and explore for myself in these books. Except the world," she added in a whisper. She felt her eyes fill with tears. "You chose the Library. I can't do that without knowing what else there might be."

"You're *leaving*?" Ruth asked in a choked voice.

Dinsy bit her lip and nodded. "I'm, well, I've—" She'd been practicing these words for days, but they were so much harder than she'd thought. She looked down at her hands.

And then Marian rescued her.

"Dinsy's going to college," she said. "Just like I did. And you, and you, and you." She pointed a finger at each of the women in the room. "We were girls before we were librarians, remember? It's her turn now."

"But how—?" asked Edith.

"Where did—?" stammered Harriet.

"I wished on the Library," said Dinsy. "And it left an application in the *Unabridged*. Marian helped me fill it out."

"I *am* in charge of circulation," said Marian. "What comes in, what goes out. We found her acceptance letter in the book return last week."

"But you had no transcripts," said Dorothy practically. "Where did you tell them you'd gone to school?"

Dinsy smiled. "That was Marian's idea. We told them I was home-schooled, raised by feral librarians."

And so it was that on a bright September morning, for the first time in ages, the heavy oak door of the Carnegie Library swung open. Everyone stood in the doorway, blinking in the sunlight.

"Promise you'll write," said Blythe, tucking a packet of sweets into the basket on Dinsy's arm.

The others nodded. "Yes, do."

"I'll try," she said. "But you never know how long *any*thing will take around here." She tried to make a joke of it, but she was holding back tears and her heart was hammering a mile a minute.

"You will come back, won't you? I can't put off my retirement forever." Olive was perched on top of the Circulation Desk.

"To visit, yes." Dinsy leaned over and kissed her cheek. "I promise. But to serve? I don't know. I have no idea what I'm going to find out there." She looked out into the forest that surrounded the library. "I don't even know if I'll be able to get back in, through all that."

"Take this. It will always get you in," said Marian. She handed Dinsy a small stiff pasteboard card with a metal plate in one corner, embossed with her name: DINSY CARNEGIE.

"What is it?" asked Dinsy.

"Your library card."

There were hugs all around, and tears and good-byes. But in the end, the seven librarians stood back and watched her go.

Dinsy stepped out into the world as she had come—with a wicker basket and a book of fairy tales, full of hopes and dreams.

SARAH MONETTE

Drowning Palmer

Sarah Monette grew up in Oak Ridge, Tennessee, one of the three secret cities of the Manhattan Project. Having completed her Ph.D. in English literature, she now lives and writes in a 101-year-old house in the Upper Midwest. She has had two novels published by Ace Books, Mélusine *and* The Virtu. *Her short fiction has appeared in many places, including* Strange Horizons, Alchemy, *and* Lady Churchill's Rosebud Wristlet. *Her Kyle Murchison Booth stories, of which "Drowning Palmer" is one, were recently collected in* The Bone Key *from Prime Books. Visit her online at* www.sarah monette.com.

"Drowning Palmer" was originally published in All Hallows 41.

—E.D.

I had made the mistake of admitting I had been at school with John Pelham Ratcliffe. Ratcliffe was now an archaeologist of considerable repute—although I remembered him as a pensive, unpleasant boy given to picking his nose in public—and Dr. Starkweather, in consequence of a number of Ratcliffe's recent publications, had become determined to lure him away from the Midwestern museum which currently funded his excavations in Greece and the Levant. Our Persian collection was (Dr. Starkweather felt and said, often and loudly) criminally inadequate, and Ratcliffe was just the man to redress the imbalance. Also, I believe there was a long-standing rivalry with the director of that Midwestern museum, but that was not a matter into which I cared to inquire.

Dr. Starkweather seized on the fact that I had known Ratcliffe fifteen years before, ignoring all my protests, caveats, and disclaimers, and insisted that I was the perfect person to approach Ratcliffe on the Parrington's behalf. I said (truthfully) that I was sure Ratcliffe would not remember me; Dr. Starkweather countered with the blood-chillingly logical proposal that I should reintroduce myself to him in a context that would remind him naturally of my identity. When I objected that I did not think any such context existed, he glared at me for several unnerving moments and said, "You knew him at school. Which school?"

"Brockstone."

"Private school, isn't it? Wealthy, upper-crust?"

"Er, fairly, I suppose."

"Then you have reunions, don't you?"

"Er, yes . . . that is, I've never been to one—"

"When's the next one?"

"I don't know."

"Can you find out?"

". . . Yes."

"Well, then!" he said triumphantly.

"But what if . . . what if Ratcliffe isn't there?"

"Then you write and say how sorry you are to have missed him at the reunion and so on."

"Can't I . . . can't I do that *without* going?"

His glare became alarmingly thoughtful. "Mr. Booth, sometimes I wonder if you are as dedicated to your work as you say you are."

"Dr. Starkweather, I . . . I assure you . . ."

"Well, then," he said with sinister emphasis, and I said, "Yes, Dr. Starkweather," as if he had been Brockstone School's formidable headmaster, Dr. Grisamore.

And that was how I came to attend the fifteen-year reunion of my class of Brockstone Scholars.

Brockstone School was founded in the mid-nineteenth century by a group of well-to-do English recusants who wished their sons to be educated as proper gentlemen. I do not know why they chose to come to America, nor why they chose to settle in this part of the country, but I have always suspected the influence of *The Dial* and the more impassioned writings of Emerson.

The school itself was never Catholic, and it quickly attracted those families in the surrounding area—such as my father's—who did not wish to demean themselves by competing with the Boston Brahmins. Within a generation, Brockstone had become the school of the Twenty—the city's elite—and their satellites and clients; some of the boys with whom I was at school had grandfathers who had been in the first graduating class.

Especially since the war, Brockstone had taken to having its reunions in batches, to try to mitigate the melancholy sparsity of its alumni population. Therefore, my fifteen-year reunion was being held concurrently with twelve-, thirteen-, fourteen-, and sixteen-year reunions. The train to Bourne was full of men about my age, all peering nervously into each others' faces, trying to determine whether this gentleman in coat and tie was a former dearest friend or someone with whom they had sworn undying enmity. I barricaded myself behind my research and prayed not to be noticed at all.

The reunion was an all-weekend affair, beginning on Friday and ending Sunday. I had suggested to Dr. Starkweather that surely I needed go down only for one day—an afternoon perhaps—and had been withered by his incredulous reaction. Thus I was doomed to follow the ordained schedule: a reminder in its own right of the past, when every aspect of my existence at school had been regimented by bells, dictated by the schedule written out in Mrs. Grisamore's beautiful copperplate. The schedule of events for the reunion was typed, on a sheet of paper that had been crisp and white before my nervous fidgeting had crumpled it, smearing the ink and creasing the lines.

Friday's schedule began with a Welcome Dinner. Saturday was full of ceremonies and speeches, while the highlight of Sunday seemed to be the baseball game between the graduating class and the alumni. I would let Dr. Starkweather fire me before I participated in that event. But the rest of it was drearily inescapable. I wondered, with a fresh chill, if the sports master, Mr. North, was still there to accuse me of lacking "spirit."

I am thirty-three, I said to myself. But somehow fifteen seemed closer and more real.

The station at Bourne did not help, being crowded and sooty and horrendously loud, just as I remembered it being. The fact that the people jostling me were grown men instead of adolescent boys helped less than one might expect. Some of them were reverting to adolescence there on the platform, bawling each others' school nicknames and obsolete shibboleths across the crowd. I wished I had had the wit to fall down the Parrington's main staircase and break my leg. Or my neck.

The school omnibus at least was new, a motorized vehicle instead of the old horse-drawn wagon. I boarded reluctantly; each passing moment, each step I took toward Brockstone School, made it increasingly likely that one of my fellow alumni would, in the manner of Sherlock Holmes, deduce my identity. And the barricade of books and papers which worked so well on a train was not feasible on an omnibus. I sat and suffered and waited for discovery.

It did not come, although I was aware of the puzzled glances of my fellow passengers. I recognized several of them: Horace Webster, Charles Cressingham, Albert Vanbeek, Robert Claudel. But I had had no friends at Brockstone School, and none of my cautiously non-hostile acquaintances were on the omnibus. I did not feel brave enough to make overtures to men who had called me half-wit, coward, freak, twenty years ago. I was afraid their opinions would not have changed.

The typed schedule also informed us alumni of where we were to sleep. We were being housed in the student dormitories, which seemed in my current overwrought state an unnecessary piece of cruelty. I was only grateful I had not been given my own old room, but I supposed that refinement was beyond even Brockstone's institutional sadism.

I found—and was filled by the discovery with something akin to despair—that I remembered the route to the dormitories with perfect clarity. Leaving my increasingly raucous fellow alumni in the vast formal entry-hall of the main building, known always and forever as the School, I started up the stairs, wondering in some remote corner of my mind if this was what it felt like to cross the Bridge of Sighs on the way to one's execution.

The only mercy was that we were not housed in the juniors' dormitories—although I learned later that groups of alumni could and did request them—but were extended the same privilege we had been extended as upperclassmen. Each of us was granted a separate room. The room I had been assigned for this purgatorial weekend was not even on the same hallway as the room I had occupied as a student. So much of my attention was consumed with being grateful for that, and in the remembered relief of acquiring a private room in the first place, that I had the door of my temporary sanctuary open before I fully took in what I had seen on the card of the door next to mine.

I froze, like one of the victims of the Gorgon Medusa, then slowly, stiffly, forced myself to step back for another look. Neatly typed, the name JOHN PELHAM RATCLIFFE stared me blandly in the face.

For a wild moment, it seemed to me as if the authorities of Brockstone School must have entered into some dark-purposed conspiracy with Dr. Starkweather. But rationality returned with the realization that, while I would put nothing past Brockstone itself, Dr. Starkweather was the last man in the world one could plausibly cast as a Machiavel; his idea of subtlety was to send me to talk to Ratcliffe. This was merely the malignant hand of coincidence.

And just when, by these reflections, I had succeeded in calming my pounding heart and was on the point of retreating into my assigned room, the door at which I was staring opened, and John Pelham Ratcliffe emerged, so abruptly and with such velocity that we only narrowly averted a collision.

He had changed remarkably. Where I remembered a weedy, sniffling rat of a boy, here was a small, spare, dry man, with fierce bright round eyes like those of a hunting hawk. Even if it had not been necessary, I suspect I would have gone back a pace.

"I beg your pardon," he said, and even his voice did not match my memories, although that was more a matter of his decisively brisk speech than of the inevitable shift in timbre. "Mr. . . ." He frowned up at me—nearly a foot, for I am six-three, and he could not have been more than five-five.

". . . Booth," I said. "Kyle Murchison Booth. We, er . . . we were the same year."

"Ah, yes," he said, without enthusiasm. His memories of me were clearly no kinder than were my memories of him.

I should have left it there. I knew it, and yet, as if in a bad dream, I heard my voice continuing, "I, er, I work for the Parrington now."

"The museum?"

"Yes. And the director, Dr. Starkweather . . . he wanted me to ask you . . ."

"Yes?" Ratcliffe said, one eyebrow sardonically raised. He knew what I was going to say, and we both knew what his answer was going to be, and still I bleated on, "Ask you if perhaps you, er, you might be interested in . . . that is, he admires your work very much and . . ."

Ratcliffe stood there, watching me twist and thrash; I had not hated him when we were boys, but for a moment I hated him then, and from the depths of that hatred managed finally to spit it out: "If you would care to be funded by the Parrington on your next expedition?"

"No, thank you," said Ratcliffe, turned on his heel, and walked away.

I stood and watched him go, my face burning, my hands clenching and unclenching uselessly at my sides.

If there had been an evening train back from Bourne, I would have taken it. There was not, and the sordid, brute fact of the matter was that I was hungry. *Ergo*, I attended the Welcome Dinner.

It was three hours of unrelieved misery. I saw one person I knew—aside from Ratcliffe and his slight sardonic smirk—and that was Barnabas Wilcox, a bully I had feared and loathed. He was an overweight, inarticulate businessman now. He mumbled some vague greeting and thereafter left me strictly alone. Otherwise, it was a sea of half-familiar faces, voices whose adult timbre I could not retranspose into their childish ranges. The men to either side of me were two years younger than myself and close friends; they talked across me all through dinner. I kept my eyes on my plate and said nothing to no one, escaping upstairs to bed at the earliest possible opportunity. It was all too vividly like my memories of my first day at Brockstone, except that then I had been in a room with five other boys, and had not even had the dubious solace of solitude.

I was exhausted; I changed into my pajamas and lay down on the bed—narrow and not quite long enough, so that I ended up curled awkwardly, like one of the strange creatures drawn in the margins of medieval manuscripts. And yet, despite the discomfort, I fell asleep almost before I could wonder whether I would be woken by a muscle cramp in the small, dark hours of the morning.

———

I was not surprised to find myself dreaming about the school. I was a little surprised, at first, to find myself dreaming about the swimming pool, which I had always avoided to the greatest extent possible, but then I realized that in my dream I was not myself, and dismissed the matter from my consideration.

In the dream, in which I was not myself, I was running through the pavilion which housed the swimming pool, a monstrous mid-Victorian edifice like the spawn of a cathedral and a greenhouse and having the worst characteristics of both. Behind me, there were voices yelling, and I knew they were the voices of the boys chasing me. At first I thought they were yelling, "Pelham! We're gonna getcha, Pelham!" and almost woke myself with my frantic assertions that I was *not* Ratcliffe, and would not be for love, money, or ten pounds of tea. But before I succeeded in disrupting the dream sufficiently to escape it, I realized they were yelling "Palmer!" not "Pelham!" and I ceased struggling. It was, after all, only a dream, and I did not care if I was someone else, as long as it was someone I did not know.

And a moment later, it was too late; running, as Palmer, I glanced over my shoulder, a quick terrified glimpse of the boys following, dark horrible figures like demons, and looked back barely in time to prevent myself running straight into the water.

For a moment I teetered on the edge of the pool, arms windmilling, and then a pair of hands shoved suddenly and hard against my shoulder blades, and I fell.

The water was tepid, brackish; I surfaced, gasping, and instinctively thrashed away from the boys now standing in a solemn row along the side of the pool. There were six of them; the only names I knew were those of the two largest, the ringleaders: Grimes and Carleton. I hated and feared them both.

The light was thick, slow, syrupy with late afternoon. It was a Sunday, the one day when the swimming pool was not in use for lessons or coaching or races between years to build "spirit." There would be no one in earshot, except the six boys standing and watching.

I know how to swim. I am as ungainly and awkward in the water as I am on land, but I can swim. But in the dream, as Palmer, I could not. I splashed and floundered; the pool was a uniform ten feet deep from end to end, the bottom far below the reach of my heavy schoolboy shoes. I begged the boys to help me; they stood and watched, and the looks on their faces were terrible: solemn and exalted and inhuman, as perfectly inhuman as the faces of owls. Not one of them moved.

I tired rapidly. My clothes were heavy; I had already been near exhaustion from the blind, terrified run that had ended with me in this dark pool. And I was panicking, thrashing more and more frantically, going under and getting great mouthfuls of water in my open, screaming mouth.

And the boys on the side of the pool stood and watched. Once they laughed, and their laughter was as cruel and remote as their faces; it might have been the laughter of hyenas. Their laughter rang in my ears, even after they stopped. It was still echoing when I went under for the last time, felt mouth and throat and lungs and body fill with water, and sank slowly toward the bottom of the pool, still staring upwards at the dim, dusty light and the black wavering shapes of the boys.

I woke myself by the brutal expedient of falling out of bed, tangled in sheets and blanket and catching myself a tremendous crack on the hip as I hit the floor. I did not even notice for several minutes; hyperventilating, half-hysterical, I curled myself into an awkward knot, both hands clenched in my hair and my face pressed into my knees, every atom of control I possessed channeled into the fierce and frantic effort not to make a noise loud enough to be heard from the hall or the next room. I do not know how long I stayed that way; when I finally calmed enough to notice my throbbing hip, to raise my head, the sun was rising.

Slowly, grimly, one shattered piece at a time, I assembled my armor to face the day. More than ever, I wished I could simply leave, but now, entirely regardless of Dr. Starkweather, I could not. That scene in the pavilion had been real. I knew that as clearly as I knew my own name, as profoundly as I felt the throbbing pain in my hip. That boy Palmer had truly drowned, and his death had truly been watched by six of his so-called peers. I discovered that I remembered two names and paused, knowing the ephemerality of dreams, to write them in my pocket notebook: Grimes, Carleton.

I bathed, shaved, dressed. The bathroom mirror told me I was bloodlessly pale, and there was a jitter in my hands that I could not quell, but I did not expect anyone at Brockstone School would look at me too carefully. They never had before.

But on the way back to my room, for the second time in as many days, I came within an inch of colliding with Ratcliffe, and this time when he frowned up at me, he said, "You look dreadful. What's wrong?"

"Nothing," I said and tried to sidestep, but he sidestepped with me.

"You look like you've been dragged through Hell's own bramble bushes backwards. Is it the reunion? I know it's a bit of a pain, but—"

"No, nothing like that. Please."

I sidestepped again, and he sidestepped with me; for a moment I wavered perilously between laughter—even John Pelham Ratcliffe was not at his most formidable in a ratty old bathrobe, armed with a sponge bag and toiletries kit—and tears of pure frustration. Then he said, "Look. I came by car. Let me get washed up, and I'll drive you into Bourne where we can get decent coffee, and you can tell me about it."

"But we can't," I said. "The . . . the schedule . . ."

"To hell with the schedule. What are they going to do? Expel us?"

This time I did laugh, although the noise was choked and strange.

"Will you wait?" Ratcliffe said.

"Yes. But . . . why?"

His mouth quirked sardonically. "In celebration of the fact that we are no longer fourteen." And with that, he stepped neatly around me and headed for the bathrooms.

Ratcliffe knew, he said cheerfully, exactly where we ought to go. He guided his car—as sleek, stream-lined, and impressive as he was himself, if considerably larger—to Bourne's only hotel, a rickety old monster called the St. James which had seen the temporary housing of the families of Brockstone scholars for three generations now. The St. James's restaurant was open for breakfast, and the smell of coffee was entirely ambrosial, even to me. I do not normally drink coffee, but Ratcliffe said firmly that I needed it, and I was past the point of arguing with him.

I startled myself by being ravenously hungry, and Ratcliffe let me eat in peace, himself absently consuming a vast quantity of food while discoursing, freely, learnedly, and frequently scurrilously on his excavations in Asia Minor. But when we were both replete, he beckoned the waitress over to refill our coffee cups and said, "Now. Tell me why you were in the hall this morning at six a.m., fully dressed and looking like Banquo's ghost after a hard night's haunting."

I had had the whole meal to work out my answer. "I am sorry to have disturbed you, but it was just a nightmare. I am prone to them."

"Are you?" He gave me a strange look. "What was your nightmare about?"

"Why do you care?" The next moment I was apologizing in a welter of mortification, but he waved me to silence much as he had waved the waitress over to refill our coffee cups.

"Call it guilt," he said and then laughed at the expression on my face. "The fact that I would no more work for a Napoleonic egomaniac like Emerson Starkweather than I would paint my face bright green and propose marriage to a Bactrian camel is no reason to be rude to you. It's just that, for a moment—" He spread his hands in a gesture of rueful helplessness. "For a moment, I was fourteen again. I want to make amends."

"But, Dr. Ratcliffe—"

"Please. 'Ratcliffe' is fine. Or my friends call me Ratty, if you can bring yourself to it."

"It was just a dream," I said doggedly.

"Not by the expression on your face this morning. And I've never quite understood dismissing things as 'just' dreams. Why should that make them any less important?" He paused, then asked in a voice unexpectedly warm with sympathy, "Was it about the school?"

I found myself telling him the whole thing, with details and names and even, because he listened with such attention and concern, my belief that I had dreamed about something that had really happened. I did not mention my falling out of bed.

He was silent for a long time when I had finished, and I finally asked timidly, "You do . . . you do believe me, don't you?"

"Oh, yes," he said, as if the matter hardly warranted discussion. I must have looked startled, for he said, "Archaeology is a strange field, and Asia Minor an even stranger place. I have a colleague who has dreamed of the fall of Troy once a year for the past thirty years. Always on the same date and always the same dream. He doesn't excavate in Troy—never has—and says there isn't a power on Earth that could make him. He dreams, you see, that he is one of the women."

We were silent for a moment, watching the bright play of sunlight on the tableware; then Ratcliffe said briskly, "So I don't see any inherent implausibility in the idea that you dreamed about a real murder."

"Murder?" I said, although that was how I characterized it to myself.

"They pushed him in, and they didn't drag him out. Murder by omission is murder nonetheless. It was the swimming pool, for goodness sakes! It isn't as if there's an undertow."

"Yes," I said. "I mean, no."

"You know," said Ratcliffe, "there's a master at the school named Carleton."

"There is?"

"He wasn't there in our time. But they needed a new Mathematics master a few years ago, and he took the position. My friends who are active in the Alumni Council tell me that Old Boys often do."

"He was a student?"

"Forty years ago, yes. You didn't know about him, did you?"

"No. I don't . . . that is, I haven't been . . ."

"And that makes this a very interesting coincidence. I think we might proceed with forging our own agenda by calling to have a small chat with Mr. Carleton."

I followed helplessly in Ratcliffe's wake, like a sailboat caught by an ocean-liner — or perhaps, given the disparity in our heights, an ocean-liner caught by a sailboat. It was a little after nine when we returned to the school. Ratcliffe marched briskly and decisively through the grounds and the buildings and the carefully organized schedule, waving aside all efforts to intercept or deflect him, until he found the office of Mr. Frederick Carleton, M.A., Brockstone's Master of Mathematics.

The odds were extremely good that Mr. Carleton, like Ratcliffe and I, was supposed to be out somewhere participating in the reunion festivities, but when Ratcliffe rapped smartly on the door, an irritable voice from within demanded, "What in the name of God is it now?"

Ratcliffe chose to interpret that as meaning "Come in," and opened the door. "Mr. Carleton," he said, "we were wondering if you could spare us a few minutes of your time."

Frederick Carleton was a short, owl-like man, stocky body, round eyes, upstanding tufts of hair, and all. He was seated on the floor amid a jumbled confusion of file boxes, folders, textbooks, and papers; either he was genuinely in the middle of a massive organizational endeavor, or he had hit upon that as the most inarguable excuse he could provide for avoiding the reunion.

He looked from Ratcliffe to me, clearly trying to deduce a context in which we might both fit. He said, "If this is about the baseball game —"

Heroically, Ratcliffe turned a laugh into a cough. "No, nothing of the sort. We wanted to ask you about a boy named Palmer."

"No Palmer in any of my classes. If you're concerned about his progress, I suggest you go talk to —"

"Not one of your students," Ratcliffe interrupted, mild but inexorable. "One of your classmates."

Carleton stared at him blankly, as if Ratcliffe were some strange beast he had never before seen or imagined. "One of my *classmates* . . . Here! What is this all about?" Truculently, he came to his feet.

Ratcliffe glanced at me; clearly his ingenuity had not extended to concocting a plausible reason for our query. And I saw unspoken in his face: *After all, it was your dream.*

"Er," I said. I could think of no convincing lie, and I could tell that the truth would not help us; I said, "You needn't talk to us if you don't want to."

Ratcliffe's glare became positively agonized, but Carleton, deprived of an adversary, deflated like a collapsing tent. "No, no," he said, and now that he did not sound pugnacious, he sounded merely tired and much more like a man of nearly sixty. "There's no reason not to tell you about Palmer, though I can't imagine what good it will do you. Please, sit down."

Despite the chaos of the floor, it took only a few moments to clear two chairs. Ratcliffe and I sat down. Carleton retreated behind his desk and became pedantic.

"I assume," he said, "it is the safety of the swimming pool that concerns you?"

"Among other things," Ratcliffe said.

"Well, on that score I can reassure you. Stuart Palmer drowned because he was violating school rules. The boys are strictly forbidden to enter the pavilion unless escorted by a master."

Ratcliffe and I exchanged a look, both of us remembering how frequently — and how easily—that rule had been flouted in our school days, particularly by upper-classmen, and Ratcliffe said, "Suppose you simply tell us what happened."

"I can only tell you the events as they were reconstructed at the inquest," Carleton said stiffly.

"Of course," Ratcliffe murmured, as smooth and gracious as any prosecuting attorney.

I startled myself by asking, "Was Palmer of your year?"

"No. A year ahead," Carleton said with a slight resurgence of his customary glower. "You want the story or not? I have other things to do, you understand . . ."

"We are listening," Ratcliffe said.

"It was a Sunday," said Carleton, bringing out a pipe and beginning the slow, in-effectual search for tobacco pouch and matches so characteristic of pipe smokers, particularly when they want to buy time. I winced—I hate pipe smoke—but held my tongue. I did not want to derail Carleton's story, fiction though Ratcliffe and I both already suspected it was going to be.

"Then, as now," Carleton continued, "the pavilion is closed on Sundays, so there were no witnesses to say how Palmer got in there in the first place."

I remembered my dream: the pounding footsteps, the baying pursuers.

"Somehow or another he came to fall in. Probably skylarking about." He paused and added heavily, "Palmer was a facetious child. And since there was no one within earshot and since Palmer could not swim, he drowned. I pray God it was quick."

You know exactly how long it took, I thought. You stood there and watched. But still I did not speak.

"He was missed at the roll-call for dinner. It took some time to determine that he was not in the School, and longer still to find him. By then he had been dead several hours. That's the story, gentlemen. A pointless, senseless, stupid tragedy. Boys are frequently thoughtless. It is only by God's mercy that the consequences are generally less final."

It was a chilling way to view the subject, even without my deep-seated conviction that Carleton was lying. But he had finally gotten his pipe to draw and was rapidly barricading himself behind a wall of smoke. It was clear we would get no more out of him. Ratcliffe thanked him for his time and we made our departure.

At the door, I paused and turned back. "Mr. Carleton, did you have a brother?"

"A brother?" He stared at me through his veiling pipe smoke, his owl-eyes round and blank. "I did have an elder brother, but he's been dead for thirty years. Why do you ask?"

"No reason," I said. "Thank you." And I shut the door.

Ratcliffe all but pounced on me. "What did you think?"

"One of us must be lying. Or . . . or deranged."

We started back the way we had come.

"Of course he was lying," Ratcliffe said impatiently. "But do you think he was the boy who was in your dream?"

"I . . . I don't think so. That is, I'm not sure. He *did* have an older brother, so—"

"Did he?" Ratcliffe said, and I imagined he got that same bright intentness in his eyes when he was fitting fragments into a reconstruction of a vase or an inscription. "Let's go look for Carleton Major."

I realized after a moment that I had stopped walking and had to trot to catch up with him. "Look for . . . what do you mean?"

He grinned at me, delighted with himself. "I'm willing to bet the pictures that adorned the library in our day are still there. Come on."

The library was—in a grandiose phrase I remembered hearing the current head-master use in his speech the night before—the memory of the school. It was the repository of all the artifacts and memorabilia that such a school inevitably generates, including photographs and daguerreotypes commemorating every imaginable event, going all the way back to the school's founding. The first headmaster had been a fanatic and a pioneer of photography.

It took some searching to find what we wanted, the cleverly paired group portraits of each class, entering and graduating, each portrait with its carefully written label. We started at the beginning and worked forward, staring at row after row of round, alien faces.

The faces from my dream jumped out at me unexpectedly, even though I had been looking for them. "There," I said, my voice an uneven croak. "This boy and the one next to him. Carleton and Grimes."

Ratcliffe craned to look at them. "Nasty, smirking pair of codfish. Yes, here we are. 'V. Carleton' and 'N. Grimes.'"

He did not sound at all surprised, and I said before I could stop myself, "You believed me."

"Of course I believed you."

"Why?"

"Because you obviously weren't lying."

"But . . . I, er . . ."

He took pity on me. "Peter Ludgate—do you remember him?"

"The artist?" He, too, had been a member of our class, a shy, dreamy-eyed boy as awkward and silent as myself. We had frequently been in the library at the same time, peacefully unspeaking for hours, until either someone else came in or the librarian made us leave.

"Yes. His wife's always after him to come to these things—potential patrons and so on. Peter came once. After the first night, he insisted on leaving by the earliest possible train, and he hasn't been back since, despite everything Eleanor can say to him. He won't talk about why, but the image of the drowned child has become a recurrent theme in his work."

"You seriously think . . ."

"I think the coincidence is suggestive. And I don't think it's coincidence. Now, do you recognize any of these other horrid specimens?"

I looked again at Grimes and Carleton's year, and then at the three years following. "There's Mr. Carleton," I said after a moment. He was as owl-eyed and scowling a child as he was an adult. "And I think . . ." I pointed to another boy in the younger Carleton's year, and then two in the year behind V. Carleton and N. Grimes. "I think these are the others."

"Six of them," Ratcliffe said and sighed. "Like many predators, boys hunt in packs." He found their names and noted them down on the back of an envelope. In the meantime, I found myself, without wanting to, searching for Stuart Palmer. I did not know what he had looked like, so had to scan the list of names the year before Mr. Carleton's for "S. Palmer," and then count over in the row of blank-faced first year boys until I found him. He was a thin, ferret-faced child, his mouth hanging slightly open; I could almost imagine the adenoidal wheeze of his breathing. In my head, I heard the terrified, panting sobs of the last breaths he had ever taken.

Ratcliffe said, startling me out of my morbid contemplation, "I think we've learned about all we can here. Booth?"

". . . Yes. Yes, of course."

"Don't brood," Ratcliffe said, almost gently.

"I, er . . . that is, no."

"Good." He led the way out of the library, talking briskly and cheerfully over his shoulder as he went. "It shouldn't take more than a few minutes to find out if any of these boys are listed in the alumni records. Then we can—"

He pushed open the library doors, straight into cries of "Ratty!" "Where have you been?" "Come on! Lunch!"

Ratcliffe twisted around to look for me, but his friends were boisterous and had clearly been indulging in pre-luncheon cocktails. All he managed was the single word "Later!" before he was swept out of sight.

I walked alone to the dining hall, where in the teeming confusion I found myself wedged in next to Barnabas Wilcox, a fate which in my 'teens I would have considered worse than death. Now it was merely strange and insuperably awkward. Wilcox attempted to make polite adult conversation, asking me about my work, but after a brief, limping exchange, it was clear that without hatred we had nothing in common, and he turned his attention to his other neighbor. I ate silently and quickly and thought bleakly of Ratcliffe's remark that boys hunted in packs. That was how Palmer had seen his pursuers, his murderers, and I had a faint nagging feeling that if I could follow that thought far enough, it could make clear to me some of the things about which Carleton had been lying. But every time I tried, I came back to Palmer's last, dark, wavering view of the boys who had watched him die, and I could go no farther.

By the time I was finished eating, the conversation at the table had turned to the infamous and scandalous among our fellow alumni. I did not wish to listen to gossip, and they were all as enthralled as Scheherazade's sultan. I got up quietly and left.

I had somehow lost my typewritten schedule and, emboldened by Ratcliffe's example, I did not care. I had never played truant as a child; it was in some strange way exhilarating now to cut behind the school chapel and walk across the quadrangle, knowing that wherever I was supposed to be and whatever I was supposed to be doing, it was not here and it was not this.

I wandered in pleasant aimlessness for some time, enjoying the Brockstone campus as I never had as a child, glorying in my much-belated delinquency. But eventually—and, I suppose, inevitably—I found myself outside the swimming pavilion.

It had been refurbished since my graduation: a new coat of paint, dazzlingly white in the summer sunshine, modern and well-hung doors. But the changes were not enough to free it from the dark tints of my dream.

I should have turned away, gone back to the School and the safety of the schedule. But instead I walked up and tried the doors. They were unlocked, and I slipped into the pavilion.

It was dark inside, and the air was heavy with water. I should have left, and I knew it, but I crossed the atrium, cut through the students' changing room—the same dull tile in desperate need of regrouting that I remembered—and emerged into the great echoing vault that housed the swimming pool itself.

There were electric lights now. I pressed the switch and watched them flare into life along the walls. The pool lay blue and serene, as if it were as natural as a lake. In the glare of electricity, it looked nothing like the pool I remembered, nothing like the pool in my dream.

I suppose it was that which made me foolhardy enough to advance to the edge of the pool. I stood and looked at the water and waited madly to hear voices yelling behind me, to feel myself suddenly propelled by nothing into the water. I felt recklessly defiant, as if I had drunk champagne instead of water with lunch, and ready to face down any number of bullying ghosts.

They did not come, of course, and I was about to turn away and forsake my foolishness when I realized something *was* happening. At first it was just a disturbance in the water, an isolated eddy. But as I watched, it increased in size and intensity until there was a great cloudy roiling in the middle of the pool. And from it, with a frantic splash and a half-choked scream, emerged a boy's head and flailing arms.

A voice beside me called, "What's the matter, Palmer? Can't you swim?" and laughter, like the cries of hyenas, echoed through the pavilion.

Without turning my head, I knew the voice had been Grimes's. But the laughter had been everyone's, even my own. I wondered if I was going insane; inside my head I could hear myself screaming like poor Palmer—and surely whatever he had deserved it had not been this—but it was as if that screaming voice had been locked in a cellar. The denizens of the house could hear it, but they did not care.

And then, suddenly—so suddenly that I staggered and almost fell into the pool after all—it was gone. The turbulence, the drowning boy, the pack of predators along the side . . . the pack of which I had been a member.

I left the pavilion through the faculty changing room, taking no chances with what might be lingering, haunting, on the student side.

I walked for hours after that, though I have only the barest memory of where I went. I was horrified—mesmerized—by what had happened in the pavilion, but I realized very quickly after the initial shock had worn off, that as with my dream, there was a significant sense in which I had not been myself. I did not know what Grimes had sounded like; I had no idea whether Palmer had "deserved" anything or not, although I was inclined to doubt it. Those thoughts, and that strange, hysterical entrancement, had belonged to someone else, someone I was now willing to wager was Frederick Carleton. I had neither proof nor explanation, only that mad inner surety that I suspect is characteristic of all those who hear voices in an empty room, whether those voices be spectral or merely delusional.

As the shadows began to lengthen toward dusk, I realized I needed to talk to Ratcliffe. I had the knowledge, but I did not know what, if anything, I ought to do about it. It was certainly pointless to attempt to try Carleton for Stuart Palmer's murder when the evidence was only my dreams and megrims. And remembering what it had felt like to be Carleton, even briefly, I did not think that cold, blind, judicial Justice could make sense of Palmer's death.

But beyond that I could not go. I was too close, caught in the oscillation of terror between Palmer and Carleton, both of whom were drowning, albeit in water only one of them would die of.

I walked back to the School and straight into the convivial press of cocktail hour. Noise and light and the heat of crowding bodies struck me together like a stunning blow. If it had not been for my need to talk to Ratcliffe, I would have turned tail and fled. But I knew better than to imagine I could face the rising night of Brockstone without some kind of human contact and support, so I fought my way grimly through the throng, and at last ran Ratcliffe to earth in one of the window embrasures. Surrounded by his friends.

I pulled up short, cursing myself for an idiot. I had come so completely to think of Ratcliffe as an ally that I had forgotten he was not like me. He was not here under duress. He had been remarkably patient, giving up half his Saturday to my disordered imaginings, and I had no right to expect any more of him or to attempt to drag him away from his friends.

I was about to turn away when the image of Palmer's flailing hands burned across my mind like a comet. I wondered if Carleton was haunted by that same image and imagined what it would be like to be presented with that every time I closed my eyes, every night for the next forty years.

The ancient Greeks had a word, καθαποις the exact translation of which is still hotly debated among classicists. At that moment it seemed to me no more elusive or troublesome than the word "justice." I was not sure if either could be achieved. But I understood now why the Grail Knights had continued with their quest, even knowing it was hopeless, doomed, futile. Some things demand that you search for them, even though you will not find them.

It was a pretty flight of fancy, imagining myself as a Grail Knight, but not enough to disguise the iron-cold meaning beneath it: I still had to talk to Ratcliffe.

I had been in this situation a thousand times. I could feel it ahead of me like the steps of a ritual: my advance, clumsier and more ungainly than ever; the polite, mocking silence as they waited for me to speak; my voice, stammering incoherencies; a pause, like the moment before the marksman fires; and then the dismissal, cool and stinging, leaving me with nothing to do except stumble away again, praying that they would contain their laughter until I was out of earshot. That was how it always went.

I took a deep breath in a vain effort to steady myself and started forward.

Ratcliffe looked up at my approach and, unbelievably, smiled and rose to greet me. "Booth! Where have you been?"

". . . I, er . . ."

"Charlie, you remember Booth, don't you? Mr. Booth, Mr. Cressingham. Mr. Cressingham, Mr. Booth."

Mechanically, I shook hands with Charles Cressingham, who looked as if he had swallowed a live spider. "Ratcliffe, I need to talk to you."

"Do you?" His bright eyes summed me up, seeming to recognize that indeed I did. "All right. Excuse us a moment, gentlemen, if you would." And he steered me away through the crowd, leaving his friends goggling after us like a collection of frogs.

Once out of the atrium, Ratcliffe simply picked the nearest classroom. When we were in school, it had been the domain of the terrifying Herr Brueckner, who taught history and German. Now Ratcliffe propped himself against the desk with insouciant *lèse-majesté,* and waved at me to speak.

I told him as quickly and clearly as I could of what had befallen me in the swimming pavilion. I fear I was neither particularly clear nor particularly quick, but he heard me out in patient silence. When I had at last stammered to a halt, he considered a moment longer and then said, "What do you wish to do?"

"What do *I* wish to do?"

"Is it such an odd question? They are your dreams, your visions. Surely the decision must be yours, as well."

"But I don't *know* what to do!" I cried and realized too late that it had become a wail.

"Well, let us consider your options. You can do nothing—"

"No. I can't."

"There. You see? Or you can go to the police." His quirked eyebrows and ironic tone indicated that he knew the feckless lunacy of that idea as well as I did. "Or you could, I don't know, hire a medium to speak to the departed spirit of Stuart Palmer. Or," and he raised one finger for emphasis, "you could talk to Frederick Carleton again."

"But—"

"You said you *were* him in your second vision. And he is both alive and here, as the other members of that group are not—least of all Stuart Palmer, God rest his soul. I agree that this is not a situation covered by the etiquette manuals and it is difficult to know how to proceed, but if there are any indications at all to be gleaned, they are pointing you at Frederick Carleton."

"Yes," I agreed dismally.

"Look. Come and have dinner, and then afterwards we can go up and beard the lion in his den."

"We?"

"Good Lord, yes! You don't think I'd bow out *now*, do you?"

"I didn't . . . that is . . ."

"I'll come with you," Ratcliffe said. "Now come and eat."

Dinner was surprisingly pleasant. Ratcliffe's friends did not know what to make of his sponsorship of me, but he said something about archaeology and museums, and they fell over themselves in their anxiety not to learn anything more. When none of them was watching, Ratcliffe winked at me.

I was left politely alone—which is a very different thing from being ignored. They looked at me if their remarks were generally addressed, including me in the social life of the table, but they did not demand a response or ask me questions. They seemed like a litter of half-grown puppies, good-natured, clumsy, and anxious to please, and I found it difficult to remember that they were all within a year or two of my own age. I realized somewhere in the salad course that they valued Ratcliffe's good opinion very highly. I listened attentively to their conversation and remembered not a word of it five minutes after we had risen from the table.

They were headed in pursuit of after-dinner drinks, and Ratcliffe had some difficulty in extracting himself from their conviviality. But he persevered and in the end prevailed, and he and I made our way to the masters' wing. We did not speak; Ratcliffe seemed to understand that I could not speak lightly, as his friends did, and that the subject of our excursion was something about which I was on the verge of being unable to speak at all.

As he had that morning, he led me with assurance. My perplexity must have shown on my face, for he grinned as he opened the door at the top of the fourth staircase we had climbed and said, "My father's on the Board, but he sends me to be his proxy if I happen to be in the country for the annual meeting. I try not to be, but I've still been taken over the school in loving, excruciating detail three times in the last ten years. I know where *everything* is."

"Is that why you're so . . . concerned?"

"No, not a bit of it. Can't resist a mystery, that's all. And here we are." He knocked with brisk authority on Frederick Carleton's door.

The door was opened remarkably quickly, almost as if Carleton had been waiting for us. He was still fully dressed, even down to the undisturbed knot in his tie.

"What do you want?" he said, words and scowl hostile, but his voice was tired.

"May we come in?" Ratcliffe said.

"I suppose." Carleton stood aside.

It was the first time I had ever been inside a master's chambers. Though far larger than any living space I had had as a student, Carleton's rooms were dark and depressing, and the oppressive woodwork made me not at all certain that the masters had gotten the better end of the deal.

Carleton slumped into a battered armchair and waved an apathetic hand at the Chesterfield, which itself had seen better days. Ratcliffe and I sat down, and Carleton repeated dully, "What do you want?"

Ratcliffe looked at me, and I realized, my heart sinking, that he was right. He had played my Virgil all day, but he could not take this final step for me.

"Er," I said. "Mr. Carleton, I need to tell you about a dream I had last night, and something that happened to me this afternoon."

He sat, inert as stone, while I fumbled and stammered my way through a description of what I had witnessed from two angles; when I had finished, he said, still in that flat, monotonous voice, "What do you want me to do?"

"Beg pardon?"

That seemed to rouse him; there was more than a hint of a defiant snarl in his voice when he said, "What do you want me to *do*? Turn myself in to the police? Write a confession to the headmaster? Take flowers to Palmer's wretched grave? *What*? What can I possibly do that will make the slightest difference?"

"Tell me what happened."

"I beg your pardon," he said with a savage parody of courtesy. "I thought that was what you had just told me."

"No," I said. "The rest of it."

For the first time, Carleton looked frightened. "I don't know what you mean," he said, but he and I both knew he was lying.

"Tell me *how* it happened. Tell me what Grimes and your brother wanted. I know you didn't want Palmer to die."

"No," he said slowly. "No, I didn't. Not really." He sat up straighter, as if he had come to a decision and in so doing had been relieved of a burden. When he spoke again, his voice was quicker, sharper. I imagined that was what he sounded like when he was teaching.

"You have to understand that none of us liked Palmer. Things would never have gone even half as far as they did if Palmer hadn't been what he was."

"Which was?" Ratcliffe asked.

"I have boys like him in my classes now," Carleton said, so distantly that if he had not been answering Ratcliffe's question, I would have thought he had not heard it. "Smart boys, sharp boys, but they won't learn the rules. Can't keep their mouths shut. Can't see that it all applies to *them*."

"Oh," I said involuntarily. There had been boys like that in my year; though none of them had been as relentless as Barnabas Wilcox, they had been among my most inventive tormentors—when they were not being tormented by other boys themselves.

Carleton nodded at me. "Palmer was a natural target. And Victor was looking for one."

"Your brother?"

"Yes. My elder brother, Victor, and his dear friend Norman Grimes." Carleton's face twisted, and it was a moment before he continued: "I don't know how much of it was deliberate—by which I mean I don't know how much they intended, and how much of it they simply let happen. Victor and I never talked about it, and I was grateful when he died because it meant I never had to ask."

He stood up abruptly. "I need a drink. If you want to get me fired, go ahead and tell Jernigan. That'll get me fired faster than you can say *Mene, Mene, Tekel, Upharsin.*"

Ratcliffe and I looked at each other and said nothing as Carleton disappeared into what was presumably his bedroom. He returned with a tumbler three-quarters full of scotch, sat down, and took a large gulp. Then he continued with his story.

"Palmer had crossed Victor. I don't know how. We younger boys didn't ask questions—we knew what the rules were if we wanted to be 'friends' with Victor and Grimes." He invested the word *friends* with heavy sarcasm; what he really meant, of course, was *slaves.* "It was worst for Teddy Thorpe and me; we were only allowed to be part of the pack because I was Victor's younger brother and Teddy was my best friend."

" 'Pack'?" Ratcliffe said.

"I've never been able to think of a better word," Carleton said. "We weren't a group of friends. We were like a pack of wolves. Or jackals. Victor was the leader, and Grimes was his lieutenant, and the other four of us skirmished and suffered and cowered and crawled behind them. It gave me and Teddy cachet with the other first years, and kept us both from being trampled underfoot. I know now that it wasn't worth it, but I didn't know that when I was eleven. At least, not before Palmer."

He took another mouthful of scotch. "Grimes's father was a devoted follower of the philosophy of Herbert Spencer."

"Social Darwinism," Ratcliffe said grimly.

"Exactly. I don't know how much of what Grimes said was what his father actually believed and how much of it was his misunderstanding . . . never having had the misfortune of meeting Grimes Senior I can happily form no opinion of his intellectual capacity. But Grimes had taken it to mean that bullying wasn't bullying; it was admirable work done in the name of advancing the species. Come to think of it, I don't know if Grimes actually believed that himself, or if he just found it convenient. I don't know if Victor believed it either, but he certainly liked it. That's what they used to shout when they had us ganging up, six on one, on some poor boy who'd gotten better marks than Grimes or made Victor look stupid in Latin: 'Survival of the fittest!'"

"Palmer," Ratcliffe said.

"Yes, Palmer. He had crossed Victor. I don't know what he did. All I know is that that Sunday, Victor and Grimes told us we were going out to 'get' Palmer." He sighed heavily, sinking deeper into his chair. "He ran. That was his first mistake. They tell you never to run away from wild animals, and I know why. Because the longer we chased him, the more serious it got. I don't think I can explain it properly, although goodness knows I've made this speech in my head several thousand times since then. But, at first, we were just going to beat him up, or tear his clothes off and make him walk back to the School naked, or something like that. Some stupid humiliation, the sort that gets served out a dozen times a day in any school you care to name. But he ran. And we chased him, and well, after you've been chasing after someone for half-an-hour, you can't just punch him and yell 'Tag you're it!' and run away. Whatever you do has to be worth the effort he's put into trying to escape it. Do you see?"

I am not sure either of us did, but Carleton was no longer paying any particular attention to us. He paused only long enough to drink some more scotch. His words were coming faster now, as if the story was developing some inner urgency of its own. "You know what happened. We chased him into the pavilion; someone shoved him into the pool. And I know it sounds nonsensical, but I can't tell you which one of us it was. I don't *think* it was me, but some days I'm not even sure of that. And then we all stood there and watched him drown."

The silence was heavy and brackish, like the water in my dream. Carleton finished his scotch and said, "I can't explain it. Except that I knew then and know now, as clearly as I will ever know anything, that if any of us—Wrexton, Griffith, Teddy, me—if any of us had tried to help Palmer, or tried to run for help, Victor and Grimes would have thrown *us* in. If they'd had to, they would have held us under. And they didn't have to because we were . . . we were caught. Not by them, or not exactly. By something . . ." He made a despairing gesture with his hands. "Something deeper, darker. Something worse than those two stupid sixteen-year-old boys—although they were bad enough, and I did not weep at Victor's funeral. We watched Palmer drown and we laughed."

He looked at his glass, as if surprised to discover it held no more scotch. "Afterwards, when we'd left the pavilion, Victor and Grimes told us not to say anything. We didn't, and it never occurred to any of the masters, or the coroner, or *anyone*, that we might have had something to do with it. I don't believe it ever crossed anyone's mind that it might not have been an accident."

He stood up, and Ratcliffe and I stood up with him. "Swimming was made compulsory the next year," Carleton said, setting his glass down on the mantelpiece and beginning to herd us, like a surly old collie with two stupid sheep, towards the door. "Every day for six years, I had to swim in that pool and not think about Palmer drowning. When I had nightmares—and both Teddy and I did, although I don't know about the others—I had to lie there, sleepless and sweating until dawn, and not make a sound, waiting for Palmer's cold, wet, dead hand to touch my face. I know that I am damned. I have been damned since I was eleven years old, and Hell has not waited for my death. What more do you want of me?"

"We want nothing of you," I said.

He stopped where he was, staring at us. Ratcliffe opened the door and waved me through. In the hall, I turned. Ratcliffe was still standing in the doorway, looking at Carleton, who was still staring at us as if had never seen anything so strange in all his life. Ratcliffe said levelly, "Despair is also a mortal sin," and came out, shutting the door behind him.

In unspoken accord, we said nothing as we retraced our route through the masters' wing. On the other side of the enormous double doors, Ratcliffe looked at me and said, "Are you going to be able to sleep tonight?"

"No," I said, startled into honesty.

"Neither am I. If I drive you back to the city, will you promise never to tell Starkweather?"

"I promise."

"Good. Let's get out of here."

Scarcely half-an-hour later, we departed from Brockstone School; Ratcliffe had left a glib, facilely apologetic explanation with one of his many friends. The moon, almost at the full, was hanging in the sky like a lamp set to guide lost travelers. Ratcliffe said nothing until we had passed the school gates; then he said abruptly, "Will you go back?"

"No."

"No," he echoed. He drove silently and extremely fast for three-quarters of an hour, then asked, just as abruptly, "Do you think you'll have that dream again?"

"No," I said. "I think . . . I think it belongs to the school. I think that's why Carleton had to go back. He's the only one left, you know."

"He is? Did you look at the alumni records?"

"No. I looked at the five black-bordered photographs on his wall."

Silence caught us then, and held us, through the hours of darkness as Ratcliffe drove toward the city and the moon.

Landfill

Joyce Carol Oates is one of the most prolific and respected writers in the United States today. Her fiction spans an enormous range of styles and subjects, and has appeared in many diverse venues. Her keen interest in the gothic and psychological horror has spurred her to write dark suspense novels under the name Rosamond Smith, and to have written enough stories in the genre to have published five collections of dark fiction, the most recent The Female of the Species: Tales of Mystery and Suspense, *and to edit* American Gothic Tales. *Her short novel* Zombie *won the Bram Stoker Award, and she has been honored by the Horror Writers Association with a Life Achievement Award.*

Her most recent novels, under the name Lauren Kelly, are Missing Mom, The Stolen Heart, *and* Blood Mask. *Oates has been living in Princeton, New Jersey, since 1978, where she teaches creative writing. She and her husband Raymond J. Smith run the small press and literary magazine* The Ontario Review. *"Landfill" was originally published in the October 9 issue of* The New Yorker.

—E.D.

Tioga County landfill is where Hector, Jr., is found. Or his "remains"—battered and badly decomposed, his mouth filled with trash. He couldn't have protested if he'd been alive, buried, as he was, in rubble and raw garbage. Overhead are shrieking birds; in the vast landfill, dump trucks and bulldozers and a search team from the Tioga County Sheriff's Department in protective uniforms. For three weeks, Hector's disappearance was in all the newspapers and on TV. Most of his teeth are broken at the roots, but those which remain are sufficient to identify Hector Campos, Jr., of Southfield, Michigan. Nineteen years old, a freshman engineering student at Michigan State University at Grand Rapids, reported missing by his dormitory roommates in the late afternoon of Monday, March 27th, but said to have last been seen around 2 A.M. Saturday, March 25th, in the parking lot behind the Phi Epsilon fraternity house, on Pitt Avenue. And now, in the early morning of April 17th, Mrs. Campos answers the phone on the first ring. These terrible weeks that her son has been missing, Mrs. Campos has answered the phone many times and made many calls, as her husband has made many calls, and now the call from the Tioga County Sheriff's Department they have been dreading. *Mrs. Campos? Are you seated? Is your husband there?*

Mrs. Campos is not seated but standing, barefoot and only partly clothed, shivering, with matted hair and glazed eyes, her mouth tasting of scum from the hateful medication that has not yet helped her to sleep. Mr. Campos, hurriedly descending the stairs in rumpled boxer shorts and a sweated-through undershirt, says, "Irene, what is it? Who is it?" and rudely pries her icy fingers off the receiver. The Tioga County landfill, approximately eighty miles from the Campos home: how soon can Mr. and Mrs. Campos drive to the morgue to corroborate the identification?

Of course, the body has "badly decomposed," so Mr. Campos views it alone, through a plate-glass partition, while Mrs. Campos waits in another room. *Remains!* What is this strange, unfathomable word? Mrs. Campos whispers it aloud: "remains." She seems to have stumbled into a rest room, white tiled walls, door locked behind her, and the light switch triggering a fierce overhead fan that blows freezing antiseptic air: the stark settings to which, on a weekday at 10 A.M., emergency brings us. Why is Irene Campos here? Why has this happened? Is this a public rest room? Where?

Elsewhere, Mr. Campos observes the body laid upon a table beneath glaring lights, most of it shielded by a sheet so that only the head, or what remains of the head, is exposed. How is it possible that these "remains" are Hector, Jr., who once was a hundred and seventy-five pounds of solid flesh, who was, like his father, slightly soft at the waist, short-legged, with thick thighs, a wrestler's build (though Hector, Jr., who'd wrestled for Southfield High in his senior year, had not made the wrestling team at Grand Rapids)? What now remains of Hector, Jr., could not weigh more than ninety pounds, yet his father recognizes him at once, the shock of it like an electric current piercing his heart: the battered and mutilated and partially eaten-away face, the empty eye sockets. Oh, God, it is Hector, his son.

Mr. Campos can barely murmur "Yes," turns away quivering with pain. "Yes, that is Hector, Jr." Mr. Campos will never be the same again—now that he's a man who has lost his son, his soul cauterized, telling his anxious wife, "Don't ask, don't speak to me, please," even as she loses control. "Are you sure it's our son, I want to see him, what if there's a mistake, a tragic mistake, you know you make mistakes, why would Hector be in that terrible place, how has this happened, how has God let this happen, I want to see our son."

Hector, Jr. Called by school friends Heck or Scoot. Within the Campos family, sometimes called Junior (which he hated, as soon as he was old enough to register the insult) and sometimes Little Guy (until the age of twelve, when Hector, Jr., was no longer what one would call "little"), more often simply Hector. At Grand Rapids, Hector, Jr., was called Hector by his professors, Scoot by his fellow-pledges at Phi Epsilon, and Campos by the older Phi Epsilons he so admired and wished to emulate. *Campos was a good guy, great sense of humor, terrific Phi Ep spirit. Of the pledges, Campos was, like, the most loyal. Seems like a tragedy, a weird accident, what happened to him, but it didn't happen at the frat house, that's for sure.*

On the Hill, partying begins Thursday night. Mostly, you blow off your Friday classes, which for Scoot Campos were classes he'd got into the habit of cutting, anyway: Intro Electrical Engineering, taught by a foreigner (Indian? Pakistani? whatever) who spoke a rapid, heavily accented English that baffled and offended the sensitive ears of certain Michigan-born students, including Hector Campos, Jr., whose midterm exam was returned to him with the blunt red numeral 71; and Intro Computer Technology, in which, though the course was taught by a Caucasian American male who spoke crisp English, he was pulling a C, C-minus. *Probably, yes, Scoot had been drinking that night, maybe more than he could handle, not in the dorm here but over at the frat house. Most weekends he'd come back to the dorm pretty wasted, and, yes, that was kind of a problem for us. But basically Scoot was a good kid. Just maybe in over his head a little. Freshman engineering can be tough if you don't have the math, and even if you do.*

His roommates in Brest Hall reported him missing late Monday afternoon. They guessed something might be wrong, called the frat house, but there was no answer. Scoot's things were exactly as he'd left them sometime Saturday afternoon, and it wasn't like Scoot to stay over at the frat house on a Sunday night, or through Monday. He was only a pledge and didn't have a bed there, and he'd missed four Monday classes.

Weeks later, Mr. and Mrs. Campos are signing forms in the Tioga County Morgue, as through the twenty-two years of their marriage they have signed so many forms—mortgage papers, home-owner's insurance, life insurance, medical insurance, their son's college-loan application at Midland Michigan Bank. Hector Campos, Sr., one of the most reliably high-performing salespersons at Southfield Chrysler, at least until recently, has often lain sleepless in his king-size bed in the gleaming-white, aluminum-sided Colonial at 23 Quail Circle, Whispering Woods Estates of Southfield, his thoughts racing like panicked ants, his head ringing with the crazed demand for money, always more money. Apart from the sum quoted by the university admissions office for tuition, there was room and board, textbooks, "fees" for fraternity rush, for fraternity pledging, a startlingly high fee (payable in advance, Hector, Jr., said) for fraternity initiation in May. "Send the check to me, Dad. Make it out to Phi Epsilon Fraternity, Inc., and send it to me, Dad. Please!"

Mrs. Campos, lonely since Hector, Jr., left for college, took up the campaign, excited and reproachful. She pleaded and argued on Hector's behalf. "If you refuse Hector you will shame him in the eyes of his friends, you will break his heart. This fraternity—Pi Episom, Pi Epsilom?—this fraternity means more to him than anything else in his life right now. If you refuse him he will never forgive you, and I will never forgive you."

Only when Mrs. Campos threatened to borrow the fifteen hundred dollars from her parents did Mr. Campos give in, disgusted, defeated—as so often through the years, if a man wishes to preserve his marriage, he gives in. *Married for love—does that mean for life? Can love prevail through life?*

Now, in the chilled antiseptic air of the Tioga County medical examiner's office, Mr. and Mrs. Campos are co-signing documents in triplicate that will release the "remains" of Hector Campos, Jr., for burial (in St. Joseph's Cemetery, Southfield) after the medical examiner has filed his final report. The police investigation has yet to determine whether Hector died in the early hours of March 25th in the steep-sided Dumpster behind the Phi Epsilon frat house—where investigators found stains and swaths of blood, as if made by wildly thrashing bloody wings—or whether he died as many as forty-eight hours later, after lying unconscious, possibly comatose from brain injuries, until Monday morning, and then being hauled away unseen beneath mounds of trash, cans, bottles, Styrofoam and cardboard packages, rancid raw garbage, stained and filthy clothing, and paper towels soaked in vomit, urine, even feces. At approximately 6:45 A.M. on March 27th, he was dumped into the rear of a thunderous Tioga County Sanitation Department truck and hauled sixteen miles north of the city to the Packard Road recycling transfer station, to be compacted and then hauled away again to the gouged, misshapen, ever-shifting landscape of the Tioga County landfill.

Carefully, the Tioga County sheriff has explained that "foul play" has not been ruled out as a possibility, though the medical examiner has determined that the "massive injuries" to the body of Hector Campos, Jr., are "compatible" with injuries that would have been caused by the trash-compacting process. A more complete autopsy may yield new information. The police investigation will continue, and the university administration will convene an investigating committee. As many as a hundred college students have been interviewed: Hector's roommates, classmates, Phi Epsilon pledges and brothers, even Hector's professors, who take care to speak of him in the neutral terms befitting one who has suffered a terrible but inexplicable—and blameless—fate. *Jesus! You have to hope that the poor bastard died right away, smashed out of his mind, diving down the trash chute into the Dumpster and breaking his neck on contact.* Only the police investigators can bring themselves to imagine that Hector Campos, Jr., may have been "compacted" while still alive.

During the strain, anxiety, and insomniac misery of the three-week search, Mrs. Campos was fierce and frantic with hope, holding prayer vigils at St. Joseph's Church. Relatives, neighbors, and parish members lit votive candles, for God is a God of mercy as well as wrath, while she hid her face in prayer. *God, let Hector return to us, send Hector back to us, Hail Mary full of grace the Lord is with thee blessed art thou among women pray for us sinners now and at the hour of our death, amen.*

Mrs. Campos would forever relive the shock of that call out of nowhere: a man, identifying himself as an assistant dean at the university, and Mrs. Campos saying, "Yes? Yes, I am Hector's mother," drawing a quick short breath. "Is something wrong?"

In weak moments, she imagined the possibility of a phone call bearing different news. The possibility of subsequent phone calls bearing different news. For it was crucial, during those days, those interminable stretches of (open-eyed, exhausted) time, to believe that Hector was alive. *Our son is alive!* She had only to shut her eyes to see him as he looked when he came home for a few days the previous month—his frowning smile, such a handsome boy. Mrs. Campos always had to tell him how handsome he was. Hector had hated his "fat face" since puberty, his "beak nose," his "ape forehead, like Dad's." Mrs. Campos winced at such words, pulled at Hector's hands when, unconsciously, he dug and picked at his nose. Any serious discussion between them had to be initiated by Mrs. Campos, and then only gingerly, for her son so quickly took offense. "Jesus, Mom, lighten up, will you? Must've missed your call—what's the big deal, this crappy cell phone you bought me." And Mrs. Campos cried, "But I love you! We love you," but her words were muffled. She was sweating and thrashing in her sleep; the nightmare had not lifted. She had to keep the flame alive those terrible days, weeks.

At Easter Sunday Mass, she shut her eyes tight, but this time saw only Hector, Jr.,'s grimace—how he'd hated going to church. In recent years he'd refused altogether, even refused midnight Mass on Christmas Eve. Mrs. Campos had been so ashamed, so hurt. Now she was kneeling at the Communion rail, hiding her hot-skinned face in her hands, her numbed lips moving rapidly in prayer. She was dazed and desperate, snatching at prayer as you'd snatch at something for balance. The tranquillizers she was taking had affected her balance, her sense of her (physical) self; there was a buzzing in her head. *Please help us, please do not abandon us in our hour of need.* She looked up as the elderly priest made his way to her, and craned her neck like a starving bird, opening her mouth to take the doughy white Communion wafer on her tongue, her dry, dry tongue. *This is my body, and this is my blood.*

She was half fainting then, in ill-chosen patent-leather pumps, staggering away from the Communion rail, into the aisle, all eyes fixed on the heavily made-up woman with so clearly dyed, dark-red hair, a middle-aged fleshiness to her face, bruiselike circles beneath her eyes, and quickly there came Mr. Campos to help the swaying woman back to the family pew, fingers gripping her arm at the elbow. Hector Campos, Sr.! Father of the missing boy! Swarthy-skinned, with dark wiry hair, a low forehead criss-crossed with lines, and large, oddly simian ears protruding from the sides of his head. There was a grim set to the man's mouth, a flush of indignation or impatience, as Mrs. Campos confusedly struggled with him as if to wrench her arm out of his grip, as if he were hurting her.

In the car driving home, Mrs. Campos dissolved into hysteria, screaming, "You don't have faith! You've given up faith, I hate you!" For it was crucial to believe, as Mrs. Campos believed, that, nearly three weeks after Hector, Jr., "disappeared," he might yet be found unharmed. He might yet call his anxious parents, after so many days of (inexplicably) not calling. He might show up to surprise his parents on Easter Sunday when they returned from St. Joseph's, might be in the kitchen, eating from the refrigerator.

Or maybe Hector had been injured and was amnesiac, or had been abducted but would escape his captor or be released. Or he had been wandering, drifting, who knew where, hitchhiking; he'd left the university without telling anyone, he was upset, had problems with a girl, a girl he'd never told his parents about, just as he'd never told them much about his personal life since sophomore year of high school, since he put on weight, grew several inches, and became so involved with weight lifting, and then with wrestling, the fanatic weight obsessions of wrestling—fasting, binge eating, fasting, binge eating. And maybe the Phi Epsilons had been putting pressure on Hector; maybe he'd been made to feel inferior among the pledges. He'd once called his mother to say how crappy he felt, never having enough money—the other guys had money, but *he* didn't. He'd told her how shitty he was made to feel, and that if the fraternity dropped him, didn't initiate him with the other pledges, he'd kill himself, he would. He swore he'd kill himself! And Mrs. Campos had pleaded, "Please don't say such terrible things! You don't mean what you're saying, you're breaking my heart."

Mrs. Campos blamed Mr. Campos for coercing Hector into engineering. Such difficult courses, who could have excelled at such difficult courses? It was no wonder that Hector had been so lonely, away from home for the first time in his life. None of his Southfield High friends were at Grand Rapids. His classes were too large; his professors scarcely knew him. Twelve thousand undergraduates at Grand Rapids. Three hundred residents in Brest Hall, an ugly high-rise where poor Hector shared a room with two other guys—Reb and Steve—who, in Hector's words, never went "out of their way" to be friendly to him.

In turn, Hector's roommates spoke vaguely of him when they were interviewed by Tioga County sheriff's deputies. *Didn't know Scoot too well, he kind of kept to himself, kind of obsessed about things, like the wrestling team last fall. He didn't make it, but the coach encouraged him to try again, so he was hopeful. It was hard to talk to him, y'know? You had to care a lot about Scoot's interests—that's all he wanted to talk about, in kind of a fast, nervous way. He'd be, like, laughing, interrupting himself laughing. Fraternity rush was a crazed time for Scoot. He was really happy when he got a bid from the Phi Eps. He was so proud of his pledge pin, and he was looking forward to living in the frat house next year if his dad O.K.'d it. Because there was some money issue, maybe. Or maybe it was Scoot's grades. He was having kind of a meltdown with Intro Electrical Engineering, also his computer course. He'd ask some of the guys on the floor for help, which was mostly O.K.—you had to feel sorry for him—but then Scoot would get kind of weird, and sarcastic, like we were trying to screw him up, telling him the wrong things. There were times Scoot wouldn't speak to us and stayed away from the room and over at the frat house. Phi Eps are known for their keg parties—they're kind of wild-party guys. There aren't many engineering majors there on the Hill, not in the Phi Ep house, anyway.*

No. 228 Pitt Street is a large, three-story Victorian house with peeling gunmetal-gray paint, moss growing in rain gutters, rotting turrets, and steep shingled roofs in need of repair. The Phi Epsilon house dates back to the early decades of the twentieth century, when the Hill was Grand Rapids' most prestigious residential neighborhood. Now the Hill is known as Fraternity Row, and Phi Epsilon exudes an air that is both derelict and defiant, its enormous metallic-silver "ΦΕ" above a listing portico. Scrub grass grows in the stunted front yard. Vehicles are parked in the cracked asphalt driveway, in the parking lot at the rear, in the weedy front yard, and at the curb. Often, the Dumpster at the rear of the house overflows and trash lies scattered at its base. It's a feature of the Phi Epsilon house that, warm weather or cold, its windows are likely to be flung open to emit high-decibel rock music, particularly at night; and that, out of the flung-open windows, begrimed and frayed curtains blow in the wind.

Inside the house there's a pervasive odor of stale beer, fried foods, and cigarette smoke. The high-ceilinged rooms are sparsely furnished with battered leather sofas and chairs, the decades-old gifts of alums. On the badly scarred hardwood floors are threadbare carpets; on the walls, torn and discolored wallpaper. Brass chandeliers have grown black with tarnish. There are rickety stairs and bannisters, gouged wood panelling, and in the dining room a long table carved with initials like fossil traces. In the basement is the enormous party room running the width of the house, with a stained linoleum floor, more battered leather furniture, leprous-green mold growing on the walls and ceiling, and more intense odors. Scattered throughout the house are filth-splotched lavatories, and in a small room beyond the party room is an ancient, rattling oil furnace.

For several years in the nineteen-nineties, Phi Epsilon fraternity was "suspended" from the university for having violated a number of campus and city ordinances: underage/illegal drinking on the premises, keg parties in the front yard, "operating a public nuisance," sexual assaults against young women and high-school-age girls, and even, during a secret initiation ceremony in 1995, against a Phi Epsilon pledge who had to be rushed to a local emergency room with "rectal hemorrhaging." Bankrupt from fines, lawsuits, and a dwindling membership, the fraternity had gone off campus until, in 1999, a group of aggressive alums, led by a Michigan state legislator, campaigned to have it reinstated. Still, by 2006 the fraternity hadn't yet regained its pre-suspension numbers—it had only twenty-six active members, one-third of whom were on academic probation.

In the rush season when Hector Campos, Jr., became a pledge, the fraternity had needed at least seventeen pledges, but only nine young men accepted bids: Zwaaf, Scherer, Tickler, Tuozzolo, Vreasy, Felbush, Herker, Krampf, and Campos. Of these, only the first three were first choices of the fraternity; the others were accepted to help fill out the membership. None of the pledges knew this, of course. Although, you know how guys are when they're drinking. It might have been, nobody can recall exactly, but it might have been the case that Herker's "big brother," who was pissed off at Scoot Campos for his falling-down-drunk belligerence and his all too frequent assholish behavior, told him that he wasn't anybody's first choice. "Fuck you, fuck-head!" the guys yelled, lurching at each other. Or maybe this never happened, or didn't happen in this way. When interviewed by the Tioga County investigators, none of the guys could remember, exactly. *First we knew Scoot was missing, it's the dean calling. Nobody here knew he was missing. Must've gone back to his dorm and something happened there, or maybe he never went back. But whatever happened to him didn't happen here.*

Mrs. Campos tried to take pride in this fact: Mr. Campos brought his family from Detroit to live in the city of Southfield, in a white, four-bedroom Colonial, and no one in Irene Campos's family had such a beautiful home—not her sisters, not her cousins—and no one in Mr. Campos's family, either. Mr. Campos's mother was living out her life on lower Dequindre, in mostly black Detroit, where for thirty-five years her husband, Cesar, worked for Gratiot Construction & Roofing—he squatted and stooped on roofs in the blazing sun and drove a truck for the company, hauling rubble from construction sites until his back gave out. He died of heart failure at the age of sixty-seven, and Irene Campos was terrified of seeing in her husband's face the defeated look of the old father, resigned always to the worst—that peasant soul, bitter in resignation—dying before his time. *He has given up, he has lost hope that we will see our son again. I will never forgive him.* Mrs. Campos continued to have faith. How many times had she called Hector, Jr.,'s cell phone, knowing that her son's cell phone was no longer in operation, that no one knew where it was. (In the vast Tioga County landfill amid tons of rubble, very likely. Where else? Hector, Jr., kept his cell phone in the back pocket of his jeans, and that part of his clothing had been torn from him.)

Mutations are the key to natural selection, Hector had learned in Intro to Biology, his science-requirement course—said to be the easiest of the science-requirement courses, though he hadn't found it so easy, had barely maintained a C average. *Natural selection is the key to evolution and survival,* he'd written in wavering ballpoint, fighting to keep his eyelids open, so very tired, still wasted from the previous night of hanging out with the guys. He was trying to concentrate, a taste of beer and pizza dough coming up on him even now, hours later. *Genes are the key to change, evolution is only possible through change, species change not by free will but blindly.* No idea what this meant, what the lecturer was saying. If words were balloons, these words were floating up to bounce against the ceiling of the windowless fluorescent-lit lecture hall, colliding with one another and drifting about, stupidly. He would've used his laptop, except his fucking laptop wasn't working right. *No purpose, just chance. The pattern of scout ants seeking food would look to a viewer like "intelligent design" but was really the result of the random, haphazard trails of ants seeking food.* Ants? No idea what the hell this guy's droning on about, like it matters. Jesus, he's so bored! And thirsty for a beer—his throat is parched.

He checks his cell and finds a text message: "PLEASE CALL MOM DARLING." His heart sinks, and with a stab of annoyance he erases the message. *What looks like "intelligent design" is merely random. Instinct, not intelligence. Any questions?* Meant to call his mother, but, Jesus, why doesn't that woman get a life of her own? It's pledge-party weekend. Scoot Campos has other priorities. The girl he'd been planning to take to the party had sent an e-mail: *Something's come up.* Bitch, he knew he couldn't trust her. A girl one of the Phi Ep guys hooked him up with last time said thanks, but she'd be out of town starting Friday. Scoot is damn disappointed, depressed. What's he going to have to do, pay for it?

Kind of earnest and boring when he was, like, sober. You got the impression Campos hadn't a clue how totally uninterested people were in the things he'd talk about — the frat house, wrestling, his opinions on his courses, girls. Me and Steve liked him O.K. at first, it's cool we got a Hispanic roommate, or what's it — Latino? — that's cool. But Campos, he's just some guy, nothing special about him you could pick on, except he wanted to hang out with the frat guys. Thought we were weird for not signing up for rush. After he pledged, he'd start coming back to the room really late, stumbling around drunk like an asshole, mess up in here, piss on the toilet seat and the floor and next day act like it's some goddam joke. That last weekend he didn't come back, truth is it was great. That poor guy, you have to feel sorry for him, but we didn't, much. It's a shitty thing to say, can't tell any adult, but we don't miss Scoot. And we're fed up answering questions about him — we told all we know. Fed up with everybody assuming we were friends of his, involved somehow, or responsible. Fuck it, we are not involved and we're not responsible! And seeing his parents, Mrs. Campos so sad and so pathetic, trying to smile at me, hugging me, and Steve, like we were Scoot's best friends. It's totally weird to realize that a guy like Scoot Campos, so pathetic, a loser, is somebody that is loved by somebody.

At the party, things are going O.K. in spite of the red-haired girl ditching him first chance she has, hooking up with one of the older guys. O.K., Scoot can live with that, but later there's some exchange of words — he's hot-faced, trying not to show he's pissed at the guys taunting him. Then he's laughing to himself, crawling — where? Upstairs, where? He can't think, his head is bombarded with deafening music, so loud you almost can't hear it. Some kind of a joke, eager to make the guys laugh to show that he isn't hurt by, who was it, that girl, blond girl, little-bitty tits, skinny little ass in jeans so tight it's all you can do not to trace the crack of her ass with your forefinger. Maybe, in fact, somebody did just that, and he's cracking up with laughter, braying belly laughter, until somebody slaps him, kicks him, and he's on his knees, on his hands and knees crawling, needing to get to a toilet, and fast. Maybe it isn't funny, or is it? Scoot Campos has fine-honed a reputation at the Phi Ep house as a joker, funniest goddam pledge. The other pledges are losers, but Scoot Campos is a wrestler, he's witty and wired. And good-looking, in that swarthy Hispanic way, with dark wavy hair, a solid jawline, and a fleshy mouth. Funny like somebody on Comedy Central, except Scoot makes it up himself, improvises. A few beers, some tequila, and Scoot isn't tongue-tied and sweating but witty and wired. By coincidence it's Newman's Day, the twenty-fourth of the month, named for the actor Paul Newman — Scoot doesn't know why, nobody knows why, and the challenge is to chug twenty-four beers in some record time, and, of course, there's tequila at the party, too. Scoot has acquired a taste for tequila! If he'd known about tequila in fucking high school, he might've had a goddam better time.

Now he's trying to remember what it was, a few weeks ago — some crappy thing one of the brothers did, humiliating, hurt his feelings, right in the middle of midterms. He'd fucked up the engineering exam, he knew, so he was drinking with some of the guys over at the frat house and (somehow) fell down the stairs somewhere. He'd been puking, and sort of passed out, and somebody had dragged him into a bathroom and turned on the shower and left him, and after a while one of the guys came back and turned off the shower, and by this time Scoot had crawled out onto the floor and flopped over onto his back. The guy kicked him — Hey, Campos. Hey, man, how ya doin'? — meaning to wake him, maybe, or turn him over, but when Scoot didn't move he left him to sleep off the drunk, soaking wet and shivering in the cold. Next morning when Scoot woke up, groggy and dazed, with a pounding headache, a taste of vomit in his mouth, and dried vomit all down his front, he'd had to admit with the cruel clarity of stone-cold sobriety: They left me here on my back to puke and choke and die, the fuckers. His friends! His fraternity brothers-to-be! And he thought, Never again. Not ever. Meaning he'd de-pledge Phi Ep, and he'd stop drinking. But, somehow, the next weekend he'd come trailing back, couldn't stay away. These guys are his friends, his only friends.

Except tonight there's some kind of bad feeling again, Scoot's feelings are bruised, but, fuck, he isn't going to show it. Of the pledge class, Scoot Campos is possibly the alums' favorite, he's been given to know. *Ethnic diversity—an idea whose time has come for Phi Epsilon.* At the top of the stairs he's out of breath, can't hold it back, God damn, is he pissing his pants? Can't help it, can't stop it. How'd this happen? If the girls downstairs learn of Scoot's accident they'll be totally grossed out, and who can blame them? The guys are going to be disgusted. It's not the first time that Scoot has been too staggering drunk to lurch to a toilet, or outside to the lawn, too confused about where he is, if he's awake or, in fact, asleep. Maybe this is a dream, one of those weird dreams, and it's O.K. to piss, nobody will scold, it's O.K. to piss into some receptacle or crack in the floor, that hot wet sensation spreading in his groin, soaking his underwear and down his legs, quickly turning cold.

A piss trail follows Scoot Campos up the stairs, soaking into the carpet, and he's laughing like a deranged little kid who's wet his diaper on purpose—hell, the carpets at the Phi Ep house are already (piss?) stained, what's the big deal? "Fuck you," he's saying, defending himself against some guy, or guys, stooping over him, calling him names. Scoot Campos is wired tonight, he's laughing in their faces, and somebody's dragging him—where? Toward a window? Through the wide-open windows the curtains are sucked outside and flapping in the rain, and there's a moon, a glaring-white moon like a beacon, some kind of crazy eye peering into Scoot Campos's soul, like, *How ya doin', Scoot? Hey, man, know what? You're O.K.*

This is God's eye, Scoot thinks. (Or maybe a street light? Outside on Pitt Avenue?) Somebody is lifting him, and he's thrashing and flailing his arms, laughing so hard that any remaining dribble of piss leaks out, and whoever it is grabs Scoot in a hammerlock. Probably one of the older guys, one of the wrestlers, built like a tank and taut-jawed and giving off heat and the pungent smell of a male body in fighting mode. He's cursing Scoot, calling him *asshole, dickhead, fuckhead,* and Scoot is being lifted, pushed into an opening in the wall—the trash chute. Or maybe the drunken pledge is crawling head first into the chute of his own volition, and one of the guys grabs his ankles to pull him back, and Scoot is kicking and yelling and laughing. At least it sounds like laughter; with this wild-wired spic anything is possible. *Hey, guys? Help me? Help me, guys?*

He's kicking like crazy, so whoever has hold of his ankles has to let go—Campos is goddam dangerous when he's been drinking—and then his thick, stocky body lurches down the trash chute. It sounds like a pig squealing, or a kid shooting down a slide in an amusement park. At the end of the pitch-black, stale-air chute there should be something soft to break his fall, except there isn't, and with the impact of a hundred and seventy-five pounds Scoot Campos strikes the edge of the trash bin and his forehead hits its sharp metal lip.

Immediately he's bleeding, dazed; his neck has been twisted, his spine, his legs are buckled weirdly beneath him. He's too dazed to be panicked, not knowing what has happened or where he is. Feebly, he pleads "Hey, guys? Help me?" amid a confusion of rich, ripe, rotting smells, something rancid. He's upside down trying to turn, to rotate his body, stunned and quivering like a mangled worm, trying to lift his head, to breathe, to open his mouth, a terrible throbbing pain in his neck, in his upper spine. Like a gasping fish he opens his mouth, but he can't make a sound, can't call for help. For sure the guys will check on Scoot, make their way downstairs shouting and laughing like hyenas. *Craziest damn thing, this drunk pledge, smashed out of his head, slid down the trash chute.* It's not the first time a drunken pledge or active at the Phi Ep house has slid down the trash chute into the Dumpster. Anyway, at some point there *was* the intention to check on the pledge in the Dumpster, but amid the party noise, the swarm of people — including heavily made-up high-school girls — and the pounding music there were too many distractions.

Later, it will be claimed that a couple of guys did, in fact, check the Dumpster but Campos wasn't there. Possibly Campos had been bleeding, but he couldn't have been seriously hurt because evidently he'd crawled out of the Dumpster and gone away, back to the dorm maybe. Anyway, nobody was in the Dumpster when they checked, they swore. Yet the guy had a weird sense of humor — everybody would testify to Scoot Campos's weird sense of humor — and he might've returned and crawled back into the Dumpster, like a little kid would do, like hide-and-seek, except he'd fallen asleep there, or he'd hurt his head and passed out, and got covered in party trash. Had to be some freak accident like that — what other explanation was there?

As Scoot's brain is bleeding, as Scoot's mouth is filling with trash, as Scoot's heart beats and lurches with a frantic stubbornness, seventy miles to the east, in Whispering Woods Estates, Southfield, Irene Campos lies awake in bed uncomfortably perspiring, hot flushes in her face and in her upper chest. Her thoughts come confused and slow, and have something to do with the moon veiled by curtains, or by high scudding clouds — the full moon is a sign of good luck and happiness, or is there something disquieting about the full moon, so whitely glaring? Or is it a neighbor's outside light? Mrs. Campos isn't fully awake, nor is she asleep, and she is planning tomorrow to insist to Mr. Campos that they drive over to Grand Rapids to visit with Hector, Jr., who hasn't been answering her calls. Beside her, Mr. Campos is sleeping fitfully on his back, twitching and thrashing in the smelly underwear that she'll sometimes find kicked beneath the bed or in a corner of Mr. Campos's closet why? Why would a man hoard soiled underwear? And socks?

Mr. Campos snores, snorts, sounds like a drowning man, and, careful not to wake him, Mrs. Campos pokes and nudges him until he rolls off his back, now grinding his teeth but facing away, at the edge of the bed. Earlier that day, Mrs. Campos sent Hector, Jr., a pleading text message: "PLEASE CALL MOM DARLING." But Hector, Jr., did not respond, and she has become seriously worried. Oh, if only that college hadn't been so aggressive about recruiting students from Southfield High, sending brochures and pamphlets, even calling on the phone — not that the university was going to offer Hector, Jr., a scholarship, not a penny, his parents would be paying full tuition. If only Hector, Jr., had decided to go to Eastern Michigan University at Ypsilanti, no more than forty miles away. There's an engineering school at Ypsilanti, too, and fraternities, and Hector, Jr., could live at home, and Mrs. Campos could take better care of him. Unconsciously caressing her left breast, holding her left breast in her right hand — how like a sac of warm water it is, or warm milk — and, on the brink of a dream of surpassing beauty and tenderness, Mrs. Campos shuts her eyes. Why does Mr. Campos never caress her breasts anymore? Why does Mr. Campos never suck her nipples anymore? Mrs. Campos runs her thumb over the large soft nipple, stirring it to hardness, like a little berry. She is driving back from the city, driving back from ugly Detroit to Whispering Woods Estates, such joy, such pride, turning into the brick-gated subdivision off Southfield Road, making her way floating along Pheasant Pass, Larkspur Drive, Bluebell Lane, and, at last, to Quail Circle, where, in the gleaming-white Colonial at No. 23, the Campos family lives.

CHRISTOPHER ROWE

Another Word for Map Is Faith

*Appropriately enough, "Another Word for Map Is Faith" was published in
the August issue of* The Magazine of Fantasy & Science Fiction. *Appropriate because this story about stories has been selected for both fantasy and science fiction best of the year volumes. With Gwenda Bond, Rowe runs a small
press,* The Fortress of Words, *which produces the annual zine,* Say . . . *His
fiction has been published in* Swan Sister: Fairy Tales Retold, Trampoline,
SCI FICTION, Realms of Fantasy, *and elsewhere. His story "The Voluntary
State" was a Hugo, Nebula, and Theodore Sturgeon Award finalist. Rowe
lives in Lexington, Kentucky.*

—K.L. & G.G.

The little drivers threw baggage down from the top of the bus and out from its
rusty undercarriage vaults. This was the last stop. The road broke just beyond
here, a hundred yards short of the creek.

With her fingertip, Sandy traced the inked ridge northeast along the map,
then rolled the soft leather into a cylinder and tucked it inside her vest. She looked
around for her pack and saw it tumbled together with the other Cartographers' luggage at the base of a catalpa tree. Lucas and the others were sorting already, trying to
lend their gear some organization, but the stop was a tumult of noise and disorder.

The high country wind shrilled against the rush of the stony creek; disembarkees
pawed for their belongings and tried to make sense of the delicate, coughing talk of
the unchurched little drivers. On the other side of the valley, across the creek, the
real ridge line—*the geology*, her father would have said disdainfully—stabbed up-
stream. By her rough estimation it had rolled perhaps two degrees off the angle of its
writ mapping. Lucas would determine the exact discrepancy later, when he extracted his instruments from their feather and wax paper wrappings.

"Third world *bullshit*," Lucas said, walking up to her. "The transit services people
from the university paid these little schemers before we ever climbed onto that death-
trap, and now they're asking for the fare." Lucas had been raised near the border, right
outside the last town the bus had stopped at, in fact, though he'd dismissed the notion
of visiting any family. His patience with the locals ran inverse to his familiarity with
them.

"Does this count as the third world?" she asked him. "Doesn't there have to be a
general for that? Rain forests and steel ruins?"

Lucas gave his half-grin—not quite a smirk—acknowledging her reduction.

Cartographers were famous for their willful ignorance of social expressions like politics and history.

"Carmen paid them, anyway," he told her as they walked towards their group. "Probably out of her own pocket, thanks be for wealthy dilettantes."

"Not fair," said Sandy. "She's as sharp as any student in the seminar, and a better hand with the plotter than most post-docs, much less grad students."

Lucas stopped. "I hate that," he said quietly. "I hate when you separate yourself; go out of your way to remind me that you're a teacher and I'm a student."

Sandy said the same thing she always did. "I hate when you forget it."

Against all odds, they were still meeting the timetable they'd drawn up back at the university, all those months ago. The bus pulled away in a cloud of noxious diesel fumes an hour before dark, leaving its passengers in a muddy camp dotted with fire rings but otherwise marked only by a hand lettered sign pointing the way to a primitive latrine.

The handful of passengers not connected with Sandy's group had melted into the forest as soon as they'd found their packages ("Salt and sugar," Lucas had said. "They're backwoods people—hedge shamans and survivalists. There's every kind of lunatic out here.") This left Sandy to stand by and pretend authority while the Forestry graduate student whose services she'd borrowed showed them all how to set up their camps.

Carmen, naturally, had convinced the young man to demonstrate tent pitching to the others using her own expensive rig as an example. The olive-skinned girl sat in a camp chair folding an onionskin scroll back on itself and writing in a wood-bound notebook while the others struggled with canvas and willow poles.

"Keeping track of our progress?" Sandy asked, easing herself onto the ground next to Carmen.

"I have determined," Carmen replied, not looking up, "that we have traveled as far from a hot water heater as is possible and still be within Christendom."

Sandy smiled, but shook her head, thinking of the most remote places she'd ever been. "Davis?" she asked, watching her student's reaction to mention of that unholy town.

Carmen, a Californian, shuddered but kept her focus. "There's a naval base in San Francisco, sí? They've got all the amenities, surely."

Sandy considered again, thinking of cold camps in old mountains, and of muddy jungle towns ten days' walk from the closest bus station.

"Cape Canaveral," she said.

With quick, precise movements, Carmen folded a tiny desktop over her chair's arm and spread her scroll out flat. She drew a pair of calipers out from her breast pocket and took measurements, pausing once to roll the scroll a few turns. Finally, she gave a satisfied smile and said, "Only 55 miles from Orlando. We're almost twice that from Louisville."

She'd made the mistake Sandy had expected of her. "But Orlando, Señorita Reyes, is Catholic. And we were speaking of Christendom."

A stricken look passed over her student's face, but Sandy calmed her with exaggerated conspiratorial looks left and right. "Some of your fellows aren't so liberal as I am, Carmen. So remember where you are. Remember *who* you are. Or who you're trying to become."

Another reminder issued, Sandy went to see to her own tent.

The Forestry student gathered their wood, brought them water to reconstitute their freeze-dried camp meals, then withdrew to his own tent far back in the trees. Sandy told him he was welcome to spend the evening around their fire—"You built it after all," she'd said—but he'd made a convincing excuse.

The young man pointed to the traveling shrine her students had erected in the center of their camp, pulling a wooden medallion from beneath his shirt. "That Christ you have over there, ma'am," he said. "He's not this one, is he?"

Sandy looked at the amulet he held, gilded and green. "What do you have there, Jesus in the Trees?" she asked, summoning all her professional courtesy to keep the amusement out of her voice. "No, that's not the Christ we keep. We'll see you in the morning."

They didn't, though, because later that night, Lucas discovered that the forest they were camped in wasn't supposed to be there at all.

He'd found an old agricultural map somewhere and packed it in with their little traveling library. Later, he admitted that he'd only pulled it out for study because he was still sulking from Sandy's clear signal he wouldn't be sharing her tent that night.

Sandy had been leading the rest of the students in some prayers and thought exercises when Lucas came up with his moldering old quarto. "Tillage," he said, not even bothering to explain himself before he'd foisted the book off on his nearest fellow. "All the acreage this side of the ridge line is supposed to be under tillage."

Sandy narrowed her eyes, more than enough to quiet any of her charges, much less Lucas. "What's he got there, Ford?" she asked the thin undergraduate who now held the book.

"Hmmmm?" said the boy; he was one of those who fell instantly and almost irretrievably into any text and didn't look up. Then, at an elbow from Carmen, he said, "Oh! This is . . ." He turned the book over in his hands, angled the spine toward one of the oil lamps and read, "This is *An Agricultural Atlas of Clark County, Kentucky*."

"'County,'" said Carmen. "*Old* book, Lucas."

"But it's *writ*," said Lucas. "There's nothing superseding the details of it and it doesn't contradict anything else we brought about the error. Hell, it even confirms the error we came to correct." Involuntarily, all of them looked up and over at the apostate ridge.

"But what's this about tillage," Sandy said, giving him the opportunity to show off his find even if it was already clear to her what it must be.

"See, these plot surveys in the appendices didn't get accounted for in the literature survey we're working from. The book's listed as a source, but only as a supplemental confirmation. It's not just the ridge that's wrong, it's the stuff growing down this side, too. We're supposed to be in grain fields of some kind down here in the flats, then it's pasturage on up to the summit line."

A minor find, sure, but Sandy would see that Lucas shared authorship on the corollary she'd file with the university. More importantly, it was an opportunity before the hard work of the days ahead.

"We can't do anything about the hillsides tonight, or any of the acreage beyond the creek," she told them. "But as for these glades here . . ."

It was a simple exercise. The fires were easily set.

In the morning, Sandy drafted a letter to the Dean of Agriculture while most of her students packed up the camp. She had detailed a few of them to sketch the corrected valley floor around them, and she'd include those visual notes with her instructions to the Dean, along with a copy of the writ map from Lucas's book.

"Read that back to me, Carmen," she said, watching as Lucas and Ford argued over yet another volume, this one slim and bound between paper boards. It was the same back country cartographer's guide she'd carried on her own first wilderness forays as a grad student. They'd need its detailed instructions on living out of doors without the Tree Jesus boy to help them.

"'By my hand,'" read Carmen, "'I have caused these letters to be writ. Blessings on the Department of Agriculture and on you, Dean. Blessings on Jesus Sower, the Christ you serve.'"

"Skip to the end, dear." Sandy had little patience for the formalities of academic correspondence, and less for the pretense at holiness the Agriculturalists made with their little fruiting Christ.

"'So, then, it is seen in these texts that Cartography has corrected the error so far as in our power, and now the burden is passed to you and your brethren to complete this holy task, and return the land to that of Jesus's vision.'" Carmen paused.

"Then you promise to remember the Dean in your prayers and all the rest of the politesse."

"Good. Everything observed. Make two copies and bring the official one to me for sealing when you're done."

Carmen turned to her work and Sandy to hers. The ashen landscape extending up the valley was still except for some ribbons twisting in a light breeze. The ribbons were wax sealed to the parchment banner her students had set at first light, the new map of the valley floor drawn in red and black against a cream background. Someone had found the blackened disc of the Forestry student's medallion and leaned it against the base of the banner's staff and Sandy wondered if it had been Carmen, prone to sentiment, or perhaps Lucas, prone to vague gestures.

By midmorning, the students had readied their gear for the march up the ridge line and Carmen had dropped Sandy's package for the university in the mailbox by the bus stop. Before they hoisted their backpacks, though, Sandy gathered them all for fellowship and prayer.

"The gymnasiums at the University have made us fit enough for this task," and here she made a playful flex with her left arm, earning rolled eyes from Lucas and a chuckle from the rest. "The libraries have given us the woodscraft we need, and the chapels have given us the sustenance of our souls."

Sandy swept her arm north to south, indicating the ridge. "When I was your age, oh so long ago—" and a pause here for another ripple of laughter, acknowledgment of her dual status as youngest tenured faculty member at the university and youngest ordained minister in the curia. "When I was your age, I was blessed with the opportunity to go to the Northeast, traveling the lands beyond the Susquehanna, searching out error."

Sandy smiled at the memory of those times—*could they be ten years gone already?* "I traveled with men and women strong in the Lord, soldiers and scholars of God. There are many errors in the Northeast."

Maps so brittle with age that they would flake away in the cold winds of the Adirondack passes, so faded that only the mightiest of prayers would reveal Jesus's true intentions for His world.

"But none here in the heartlands of the Church, right? Isn't that what our parish priests told us growing up?" The students recognized that she was beginning to teach and nodded, murmured assent.

"Christians, there *is* error here. There is error right before our eyes!" Her own students weren't a difficult congregation to hook, but she was gratified nonetheless by the gleam she caught in most of their eyes, the calls, louder now, of "Yes!" and "I see it! I see the lie!"

"I laid down my protractor, friends, I know exactly how far off north Jesus mapped this ridge line to lay," she said, sweeping her arm in a great arc, taking in the whole horizon, "And that ridge line sins by two degrees!"

"May as well be two *hundred*!" said Carmen, righteous.

Sandy raised her hand, stopped them at the cusp of celebration instead of loosing them. "Not yet," she said. "It's tonight. It's tonight we'll sing down the glory, tonight we'll make this world the way it was mapped."

The march up the ridge line did not go as smoothly as Sandy might have wished, but the delays and false starts weren't totally unexpected. She'd known Lucas—a country boy after all—would take the lead, and she'd guessed that he would dead-end them into a crumbling gully or two before he picked the right route through the brambles. If he'd been some kind of natural-born hunter he would never have found his way to the Lord, or to education.

Ford and his friends—all of them destined for lecture halls and libraries, not fieldwork—made the classic, the *predicted* mistake she'd specifically warned against in the rubric she'd distributed for the expedition. "If we're distributing 600 pounds of necessities across twenty-two packs," she asked Ford, walking easily beside him as he struggled along a game trail, "how much weight does that make each of us responsible for?"

"A little over twenty-seven pounds, ma'am," he said, wheezing out the reply.

"And did you calculate that in your head like a mathematician or did you remember it from the syllabus?" Sandy asked. She didn't press too hard, the harshness of the lesson was better imparted by the straps cutting into his shoulders than by her words.

"I remembered it," Ford said. And because he really did have the makings of a great scholar and great scholars are nothing if not owners of their own errors, he added, "It was in the same paragraph that said not to bring too many books."

"Exactly," she said, untying the leather cords at the top of his pack and pulling out a particularly heavy looking volume. She couldn't resist looking at the title page before dropping it into her own pack.

"*Unchurched Tribes of the Chiapas Highlands: A Bestiary*. Think we'll make it to Mexico on this trip, Ford?" she asked him, teasing a little.

Ford's faced reddened even more from her attention than it had from the exertions of the climb. He mumbled something about migratory patterns then leaned into the hike.

If most of the students were meeting their expectations of themselves and one another, then Carmen's sprightly, sure-footed bounding up the trail was a surprise to most. Sandy, though, had seen the girl in the gym far more frequently than the other students, most of whom barely met the minimum number of visits per week required by their advising committees. Carmen was as much an athlete as herself, and the lack of concern the girl showed about dirt and insects was refreshing.

So it was Carmen who summited first, and it was her that was looking northeast with a stunned expression on her face when Sandy and Lucas reached the top side by side. Following Carmen's gaze, Lucas cursed and called for help in taking off his heavily laden pack before he began unrolling the oilcloth cases of his instruments.

Sandy simply pursed her lips and began a mental review of her assets: the relative strengths and weaknesses of her students, the number of days worth of supplies they carried, the nature of the curia designed—instruments that Lucas exhibited a natural affinity for controlling. She began to nod. She'd marshaled more than enough strength for the simple tectonic adjustment they'd planned, she could set her own unquestionable faith against this new challenge if it revealed any deficiencies among her students. She would make a show of asking their opinions, but she already knew that this was a challenge she could meet.

Ford finally reached the top of the ridge line, not so much climbing as stumbling to the rocky area where the others were gathering. Once he looked up and around, he said, "The survey team that found the error in the ridge's orientation, they didn't come up here."

"They were specifically scouting for projects that the university could handle," said Sandy. "If they'd been up here, they would have called in the Mission Service, not us."

Spread out below them, ringed in tilled fields and dusted with a scattering of wooden fishing boats, was an unmapped lake.

Sandy set Ford and the other bookish scholars to cataloguing all of the texts they'd smuggled along so they could be integrated into her working bibliography. She hoped that one of them was currently distracted by waterways the way that Ford was distracted by fauna.

Lucas set their observation instruments on tripods in an acceptably devout semi-circle and Sandy permitted two or three of the others to begin preliminary sight-line measurements of the lake's extent.

"It turns my stomach," said Lucas, peering through the brass tube of a field glass. "I grew up seeing the worst kind of blasphemy, but I could never imagine that anyone could do something like this."

"You need to work on that," said Sandy. Lucas was talking about the landscape feature crosshaired in the glass, a clearly artificial earthworks dam, complete with a retractable spillway. "Missionaries see worse every day."

Lucas didn't react. He'd never abandoned his ambition, even after she'd laughed him down. *Our sisters and brothers in the Mission Service,* she'd said with the authority that only someone who'd left that order could muster, *make up in the pretense of zeal what they lack in scholarship and access to the divine. Anyone can move a mountain with whips and shovels.*

The sketchers showed her their work, which they annotated with Lucas's count and codification of architectural structures, fence lines, and crops. "Those are corn cribs," he said. "That's a meeting house. That's a mill."

This was the kind of thing she'd told him he should concentrate on. The best thing any of them had to offer was the overlay of their own personal ranges of unexpected expertise onto the vast body of accepted Cartography. Lucas's barbaric background, Ford's holographic memory, Carmen's cultured scribing. Her own judgment.

"They're *marmotas!*" said Ford. They all looked up at where he'd been awkwardly turning the focus wheel on one of the glasses. "Like in my book!" He wasn't one to flash a triumphal grin, which Sandy appreciated. She assented to the line of inquiry with a nod and he hurried over to the makeshift shelf that some of his friends had been using to stack books while they wrote their list.

The unchurched all looked alike to Sandy, differing only in the details of their dress, modes of transportation, and to what extent the curia allowed interaction with them. In the case of the little drivers, for example, tacit permission was given for commercial exchange because of their ancient control of the bus lines. But she'd never heard of *marmotas*, and said so.

"They're called 'rooters' around here," said Lucas. "I don't know what Ford's on about. I've never heard of them having a lake, but they've always come into the villages with their vegetables, so far as I know."

"Not always," said Carmen. "There's nothing about any unchurched lineages in the glosses of the maps we're working from. They're as new as that lake."

Sandy recognized that they were in an educable moment. "Everybody come here, let's meet. Let's have a class."

The students maneuvered themselves into the flatter ground within the horseshoe of instruments, spreading blankets and pulling out notebooks and pens. Ford lay his bestiary out, a place marked about a third of the way through with the bright yellow fan of a fallen gingko leaf.

"Carmen's brought up a good point," said Sandy, after they'd opened with a prayer. "There's no Cartographical record of these diggers, or whatever they're called, along the ridge line."

"I don't think it matters, necessarily, though," said Carmen. "There's no record of the road up to the bus stop, either, or of Lucas's village. 'Towns and roads are thin scrims, and outside our purview.'"

Sandy recognized the quote as being from the autobiography of a radical cleric intermittently popular on campus. It was far from writ, but not heretical by any stretch of the imagination and, besides, she'd had her own enthusiasms for colorful doctrinal interpretations when she was younger. She was disappointed that Carmen would let her tendency toward error show so plainly to the others but let it pass, confident that one of the more conservative students would address it.

"Road building doesn't affect landscape?" asked Lucas, on cue. "The Mapmaker *used* road builders to cut canyons all over the continent. Ford, maybe Carmen needs to see the cutlines on your contour maps of the bus routes."

Before Ford, who was looking somewhat embarrassed by the exchange, could reply, Carmen said, "I'm not talking about the Mapmaker, Lucas, I'm talking about your *family*, back in the village we passed yesterday."

"Easy, Carmen," said Sandy. "We're getting off task here. The question at hand isn't *whether* there's error. The error is clear. We can feel the moisture of it on the breeze blowing up the hill right now." Time to shift directions on them, to turn them on the right path before they could think about it.

"The question," she continued, "is how much of it we plan to correct." Not *whether* they'd correct, don't leave that option for them. The debate she'd let them have was over the degree of action they'd take, not whether they'd take any at all.

The more sophisticated among them—Ford and Carmen sure, but even Lucas, to his credit—instantly saw her tack and looked at her with eyebrows raised. Then Lucas reverted to type and actually dared to say something.

"We haven't prepared for anything like this. That lake is more than a mile across at its broadest!"

"A mile across, yes," said Sandy, dismissively. "Carmen? What scale did you draw your sketch of the valley in?"

Carmen handed her a sheaf of papers. "24K to one. Is that all right?"

"Good, good," said Sandy. She smiled at Ford. "That's a conversion even I can do in my head. So . . . if I compare the size of the *dam*—" and she knitted her eyebrows, calculating. "If I compare the dam to the ridge, I see that the ridge we came to move is about three hundred times the larger."

Everyone began talking at once and at cross purposes. A gratifying number of the students were simply impressed with her cleverness and seemed relaxed, sure that it would be a simple matter now that they'd been shown the problem in the proper perspective. But Carmen was scratching some numbers in the dirt with the knuckle of her right index finger and Ford was flipping through the appendix of one of his books and Lucas . . .

Lucas stood and looked down over the valley. He wasn't looking at the lake and the dam, though, or even at the village of the unchurched creatures who had built it. He was looking to his right, down the eastern flank of the ridge they stood on, down the fluvial valley towards where, it suddenly occurred to Sandy, he'd grown up, towards the creek side town they'd stopped in the day before.

Ford raised his voice above an argument he'd been having with two or three others. "Isn't there a question about what that much water will do to the topography downstream? I mean, I know hydrology's a pretty knotty problem, theologically speaking, but we'd have a clear hand in the erosion, wouldn't we? What if the floodwaters subside off ground that's come unwrit because of something that we did?"

"That *is* a knotty problem, Ford," said Sandy, looking Lucas straight in the eye. "What's the best way to solve a difficult knot?"

And it was Lucas who answered her, nodding. "Cut through it."

Later, while most of the students were meditating in advance of the ceremony, Sandy saw Carmen moving from glass to glass, making minute focusing adjustments and triangulating different views of the lake and the village. Every so often, she made a quick visual note in her sketchbook.

"It's not productive to spend too much time on the side effects of an error, you know," Sandy said.

Carmen moved from one instrument to the next. "I don't think it's all that easy to determine what's a side effect and what's . . . okay," she said.

Sandy had lost good students to the distraction she could see now in Carmen. She reached out and pivoted the cylinder down, so that its receiving lens pointed straight at the ground. "There's nothing to see down there, Carmen."

Carmen wouldn't meet her eye. "I thought I'd record—"

"Nothing to see, nothing to record. If you could go down and talk to them you wouldn't understand a word they say. If you looked in their little huts you wouldn't find anything redemptive; there's no cross hanging on the wall of the meeting house, no Jesus of the Digging Marmots. When the water is drained, we won't see anything along the lake bed but mud and whatever garbage they've thrown in off their docks. The lake doesn't have any secrets to give up. You know that."

"Ford's books—"

"Ford's books are by anthropologists, who are halfway to being witch doctors as far as most respectable scholars are concerned, and who keep their accreditation by dint of the fact that their field notes are good intelligence sources for the Mission Service. Ford reads them because he's got an overactive imagination and he likes stories too much—lots of students in the archive concentration have those failings. Most of them grow out of it with a little coaxing. Like Ford will, he's too smart not to. Just like *you're* too smart to backslide into your parents' religion and start looking for souls to save where there are no souls to be found."

Carmen took a deep breath and held it, closed her eyes. When she opened them, her expression had folded into acquiescence. "It is not the least of my sins that I force you to spend so much time counseling me, Reverend," she said formally.

Sandy smiled and gave the girl a friendly squeeze of the shoulder. "Curiosity and empathy are healthy, and valuable, señorita," she said. "But you need to remember that there are proper channels to focus these things into. Prayer and study are best, but drinking and carousing will do in a pinch."

Carmen gave a nervous laugh, eyes widening. Sandy could tell that the girl didn't feel entirely comfortable with the unexpected direction of the conversation, which was, of course, part of the strategy for handling backsliders. Young people in particular were easy to refocus on banal and harmless "sins" and away from thoughts that could actually be dangerous.

"Fetch the others up here, now," Sandy said. "We should set to it."

Carmen soon had all twenty of her fellow students gathered around Sandy. Lucas had been down the eastern slope far enough to gather some deadwood and now he struck it ablaze with a flint and steel from his travel kit. Sandy crumbled a handful of incense into the flames.

Ford had been named the seminar's lector by consensus, and he opened his text. "Blessed are the Mapmakers . . ." he said.

"For they hunger and thirst after righteousness," they all finished.

Then they all fell to prayer and singing. Sandy turned her back to them—congregants more than students now—and opened her heart to the land below her. She felt the effrontery of the unmapped lake like a caul over her face, a restriction on the land that prevented breath and life.

Sandy showed them how to test the prevailing winds and how to bank the censers in chevrons so that the cleansing fires would fall onto the appropriate points along the dam.

Finally, she thumbed an ashen symbol onto every wrist and forehead, including her own, and lit the oils of the censer *primorus* with a prayer. When the hungry flames began to beam outward from her censer, she softly repeated the prayer for emphasis, then nodded her assent that the rest begin.

The dam did not burst in a spectacular explosion of mud and boulders and waters. Instead, it atrophied throughout the long afternoon, wearing away under their prayers even as their voices grew hoarse. Eventually, the dammed river itself joined its voice to theirs and speeded the correction.

The unchurched in the valley tried for a few hours to pull their boats up onto the shore, but the muddy expanse between the water and their lurching docks grew too quickly. They turned their attention to bundling up the goods from their mean little houses then, and soon a line of them was snaking deeper into the mountains to the east, like a line of ants fleeing a hill beneath a looking glass.

With the ridge to its west, the valley fell into evening shadow long before the Cartographers' camp. They could still see below though, they could see that, as Sandy had promised Carmen, there were no secrets revealed by the dying water.

IRA SHER

Lionflower Hedge

Ira Sher's short fiction has appeared in The Gettysburg Review, Chicago Review, *and been featured on NPR as part of "This American Life." This story is one of two written by Sher in the anthology* ParaSpheres, *itself a great grab bag of recent and new slipstream fiction. In a very short space, Sher manages to capture the magic and strangeness of fantasy novels like C. S. Lewis's* The Lion, The Witch, and The Wardrobe. *He is the author of a novel,* Gentlemen of Space *(Free Press). He lives with his wife, the poet Rebecca Wolfe, in Hudson, NY.*

—K.L. & G.G.

That night around the fire, having recalled the threat held over us as children that we might be sent "into the Hedge," Francis was, to say the least, surprised by my suggestion we go and revisit it.

I doubt any of us had given the Hedge a moment's thought in years. And while "the Hedge" was not infrequently the final invocation of an exasperated caretaker on evenings our parents were away, and on those occasions we lay awake in our beds in the great room, quietly murmuring together about its menace, it had, naturally, found no place that weekend in our discussion of how to dispose of the estate. Joseph (had he ever *not* been a lawyer?) even went so far as to remind us that despite repeated recourse to "the Hedge" in name, none of us were ever really sent "into" it. Still, we were by then childishly drunk, sentimental with the knowledge we were to return to our separate, adult homes and families in the morning—

The Lionflower Hedge formed a wild patch in the garden, a shelter for birds and foxes. With its low arcades of branches and superannuated foliage, it seemed an ideal place for a child, and no doubt some farsighted governess had gathered the hedge within the rubric of punishment to obscure from us its pleasures, and save the trouble of washing us of its debris.

"If I remember rightly," Francis mused at one of the entries, "there was always a ruckus inside—the sound of children one would have thought." Kneeling to listen, before long the cries returned to us like a nursery rhyme: as a conch contains the sea, we heard the distant noise of boys and girls at play.

The flowers had withered and lay like gloves among the branches. The ground was soaked from afternoon showers. A cold rain started. "We'll get wet," Joseph complained; yet rather than rise and return to the house, I pushed on, into the hedge, and heard them rustle in pursuit.

At first the garden lamps shone among the leaves, the rectangles of the recently-quitted dining room showed a lattice of fronds and shoots, a sort of backlit wallpaper; but darkness quickly embraced us—though the hedge wasn't so large that shouldering through seemed foolhardy, given the alternate difficulty, having come this far, of turning around. The best we could do was get along on all fours, staying in a line of which I was the leader, grappling with low foliage, roots, and the clustered stems forming the thicket's pillars. The problem lay in the fact that it was *so* dark. I simply groped, awaiting the glow of the opposite perimeter and the halogens of the conservatory. And then, blind, I found my hands wrapped around what I can only describe as two ankles, as if someone, in the midst of everything, stood upright. A hinge creaked. A woman's silhouette loomed in a doorway.

"Here you are," she said softly, bending forward. "You're all in bed. You were good, weren't you, while I was gone?"

She brushed her hand to her lips and reached down to plant the kiss on my cheek. Then she drew back, closed the door, and we were alone in the dark.

"That was our mother," Joseph said.

"Yes," I whispered, feeling still the warm touch.

"Shh," Francis told us. "Go to sleep."

MINSOO KANG

A Fearful Symmetry

"A Fearful Symmetry," a gentle, Borges-flavored fable involving a ghost, a soldier, and the role of the reader, first appeared in Of Tales and Enigmas *(Prime Books), Minsoo Kang's varied and marvelous debut collection of almost all original short stories. Kang, currently an assistant professor of history at the University of Missouri, St. Louis, has also lived in Korea, Austria, New Zealand, Brunei, Iran, and Germany, among other places. His short stories have appeared in* Lady Churchill's Rosebud Wristlet, *while his reviews and essays have been published in* The American Historical Review, Manoa, *and* The Times Literary Supplement. *He is currently working on a history of the automaton as well as a literary novel set in Korea.*

—K.L. & G.G.

It is natural that I should have heard so many ghost stories while serving in the army of the Republic of Korea, at a base near the Demilitarized Zone, where the possibility of sudden death is a perpetual cloud hanging over everyday life. The tales ranged from the incidental (the night sentry's flashlight invariably turning off as he passes by a spot where a soldier died after stepping on a mine) to the extremely elaborate (on violated graves, wood spirits, a mad woman from a local village who disappeared into the hills after murdering her family, and headless spirits of soldiers who had slept during guard duty and were decapitated by North Koreans). The one that made the greatest impression on me is a handed-down story related to me by a corporal of a reconnaissance unit. It is but a trifle of a tale with a predictable moral, which I suspect to be a modern version of a traditional legend of local origin, yet I am drawn to the modest fable for what I might call its quality of symmetry.

Less than a month after I was promoted to private first class, I spent some time as a patient at a military hospital situated a few miles south of the corps headquarters responsible for coordinating the defense of the so-called "central corridor" in eastern Gyeongi and western Gangwon provinces. The bed next to mine was occupied by Corporal An, a former professional baseball player who was suffering from a severe case of stomach ulcer. On a particularly humid July night, we found ourselves unable to fall asleep after lights-out, so we tried to forget our pains and homesickness by exchanging scary stories like children. Since I was the junior soldier, I went first by telling him the plot of a rather good horror movie I once saw on late night television, back in Los Angeles; back in my old life as a carefree graduate student spending leisurely days on Santa Monica beach reading Darkbloom novels and dreaming up stories instead of working on my dissertation. I managed to give An a good scare with a vivid narration, and then it was his turn to play the storyteller. He took a moment to gather his thoughts before telling me about a defunct guard post back at his base.

After An had completed basic training at Nonsan, he was sent up to the recon unit at the front, one of the toughest posts in the army. Late one night, his "father" (in army lingo, a corporal assigned to a newly arrived private for orientation) woke him with a harsh slap to the forehead and told him to get ready for sentry duty. It was about ten minutes to two o'clock when they set out in the cold January night, shivering in the wind that pushed against their bodies and lashed at their exposed faces. The post they were assigned to was one of the farthest from the barracks, so they had to walk clear across the base, to an isolated corner at the southern end An had never been to before. The bunker itself was set below a low hill that looked down on a small village outside the barbed wires. After relieving the guards before them and taking up their positions behind the sandbags, An noticed a rectangular structure nearby that looked like another guard post. He wondered why there was one so close by, but he knew better than to speak to the Corporal before being spoken to.

Junior soldiers feared the hours of sentry duty at night as seniors often took advantage of the darkness and isolation to discipline them for infractions they may have committed earlier, or to harass them just to relieve boredom. A great deal of physical abuse occurred in those hours. An expected to be punished for having gotten into trouble that day with the company commander for failing to clean his rifle properly, but the Corporal, a former night-club bouncer who was given to pinching and twisting both ears until they burned, stood still and silent, seemingly preoccupied with his thoughts.

Time crawled at a maddeningly slow pace as the cold seeped into An's coat and fatigues before biting into his skin. He tried to forget the icy numbness spreading across his body by concentrating on the sound of the wind wailing through the trees. The piercing noise grated on his tired mind, but better this tedium, he told himself, than doing push-ups while being kicked in the head by his "father."

It was well into the second hour when he was startled by the Corporal suddenly stiffening and taking up his rifle before looking around the area. An himself tensed and searched for movement in the darkness but saw nothing. The invisible wind continued to howl in the night. A moment later An realized that within the sound of the wind was another noise, that of a woman weeping, coming from the other guard post.

"What is that?" he asked, his stomach tightening with the grip of fear.

"Be quiet," the Corporal hissed in a quivering voice.

It unnerved An even more to see that the tough Corporal was obviously frightened as well.

They stood stock still and listened to the uncanny lament for what seemed an eternity, until it gradually faded into the ordinary scream of the wind.

"What was that noise?" An asked again.

"I said shut up, you son of a bitch!" the Corporal spat out, embarrassed at having shown his fear.

The rest of the hour passed in fearful silence, until they were finally relieved by the next guards. They quickly made their way back to Operations where they reported to the officer on duty and returned to the barracks. After they put away their gear, the Corporal motioned for An to follow him into the bathroom. There they leaned against a radiator and smoked in silence, warming their bodies and settling down their nerves. The story the Corporal then told him had supposedly taken place several years before. When he himself had been a newly arrived private, he had heard it from a sergeant who had claimed to have known the people involved and had sworn that the tale was true.

There was a certain Sergeant Hong at the base who befriended a young woman named Miss Jin who worked as a waitress in the nearby village. It amused him to flirt with the innocent country girl who felt flattered to receive the attention of a college boy from Seoul, though he had only two months left in his service and had no intention of seeing her after he was discharged. One Sunday, he took a day pass and met the girl at a bar that evening after she got off from work. Hong got a bit drunk and asked Jin to accompany him to a motel. When she refused he became annoyed with what he took to be her coyness and pretended to walk off in a huff. The girl went after him, pleading for him to stop and let her explain. She told him that although she liked him very much she could not do as he asked because of a promise she had made to her father.

When the old widower had found out that he was dying of lung cancer, he had feared that his pretty daughter would become a prostitute like many poor and unprotected girls in the village near army bases. So on his deathbed, he had made her swear on her life that she would remain a virgin until she was married.

As Sergeant Hong still seemed upset, Miss Jin told him that she could make it up to him in another way. There was a girl she knew who had also dated a soldier at the base. Whenever her boyfriend had sentry duty at a certain post below a low hill near the village, he would give her a phone call and she would sneak over to him at the appointed hour with some rice wine and snacks. As she had told Miss Jin how to get into the place, she would do the same for Hong.

Toward the end of the following week, when Hong found out that he was assigned there, he called up Miss Jin who promised to come. Later that night, as he and a corporal named Min headed for the place, Hong told him about the girl. He was in a bad mood from having been harassed all day by the platoon commander, so he found himself getting upset all over again at her refusal to sleep with him. He told the Corporal what a teasing little bitch she was, and the conversation drifted to how the two of them would teach her a lesson that night.

Not long after they had occupied the post, Miss Jin arrived with rice wine and snacks. They did not speak much as she served them and they quickly drank down the liquor. When the two of them were sufficiently drunk they fell on her and took turns raping and beating her for the better part of an hour. When they were done, they sent the girl away, threatening that if she told anyone about what they had done they would find her and kill her. She went back to the village, to the tiny room at the back of a farmhouse where she lived. There, she cleaned herself thoroughly with ice cold water, put on her best dress and then hanged herself on a bare tree outside the house.

Three days later, soldiers standing guard at that post heard the crying of a woman in the night. One of them called out for her to identify herself but the lament continued. They then searched the area carefully but found nothing. They remained at the post for half an hour more, listening to the invisible weeper, before they finally lost their nerve and ran all the way back to Operations where they reported the incident. The same thing occurred almost every night. It got so bad that every soldier at the base was in dread of going to the place as even the most skeptical ones came back terrorized.

The regiment commander, Colonel Hwang, was visiting the base when he heard about the haunted guard post from a master sergeant of the unit. As the Colonel had a great aunt who had been a renowned shaman in Jeolla Province, he was open-minded about such stories and resolved to get to the bottom of it. That night, he and a captain accompanied the soldiers assigned to the place at the hour the crying was said to begin. They did not have to wait long before hearing the uncanny noise.

The Colonel, who had been instructed as a child on how to approach a ghost, walked alone into the night. In a calm and serious voice he asked whose spirit was there and what sorrow kept it in the living world. A moment later, the image of a young girl with a pale face and disheveled hair appeared before him, her eyes flowing with tears that streamed down to a ring of purple bruise around her neck. As he beheld the slight figure with her head bowed down and hands folded before her in a modest manner, his fear of the apparition was replaced by pity. The ghost spoke in a quiet voice without raising her head, telling him of who she had been in life. She told him of the promise she had made to her dying father, of Sergeant Hong who had befriended her, and of how he and Corporal Min had violated her, making it impossible for her to live on. When she fell silent, Colonel Hwang asked if bringing the wrongdoers to justice would satisfy her. She answered that that would allay her anger but not her sorrow, before dissolving into the darkness, the sound of her sobbing lingering in the night.

The following day, Colonel Hwang ordered an immediate investigation. Sergeant Hong and Corporal Min were quickly identified and put under arrest. Although Hong had only a month of service left, the stress from keeping the terrible secret had taken its toll on him and he confessed readily. The two of them were sent to the stockade where after three days they were found hanging in their cells.

When Corporal An finished the tale I was impressed by the neatness of the narrative but felt dissatisfied by what I initially perceived to be a flaw in its symmetry. A wrong committed was made right; a secret was brought to light; the victim's suicide by hanging led to the death of the perpetrators in the same manner; through supernatural means justice triumphed and balance was restored. The story should have ended there but it apparently did not. Soldiers continued to hear the ululation in the night, though An assured me that it was a rare occurrence now. But they still had to close down the guard post and build a new one nearby, the place where An himself heard the crying. So the ghost was still not completely at peace, returning every once in a while to the place of her violation to grieve over what had happened there.

As I considered the story further, I thought of what she had told Colonel Hwang, that bringing the wrongdoers to justice would allay her anger but not her sorrow. It occurred to me that her sorrow must be not only from her terrible end but also the life she was deprived of when she killed herself. I thought then that perhaps what she may want, what it would take for her spirit to finally rest, was for her story to be written down, so that she might take on a new life, if only as a character in a story. I am forced then to come to the disturbing conclusion that she was ultimately crying for me, with Corporal An acting as her messenger. So on this dark, desolate night I find myself trying to relieve her sorrow by giving her an existence in a world of words.

And so I become a part, the final equation in the fearful symmetry of her tale, and you as well, as I imagine the ghost of Miss Jin becoming silent at last as she is reborn in your memory.

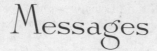 Messages

Brett Alexander Savory is the Bram Stoker Award–winning editor in chief of ChiZine: Treatments of Light and Shade in Words, is a senior editor at Scholastic Canada, writes for Rue Morgue magazine, and has had nearly fifty short stories published.

His horror-comedy novel The Distance Travelled was published in 2006 and In and Down, a dark literary novel, will be published this September.

In the works are three more novels, and a dark comic book series with artist Homeros Gilani.

When he's not writing, reading, or editing, he plays drums for the southern-tinged hard rock band Diablo Red, whose second album, A Statue of Mary with Bullhorns, was released in 2006.

"Messages" was originally published in the February issue of Realms of Fantasy.

—E.D.

This time is no different. This time is exactly the same as the last hundred, the last thousand. Since paper was invented. Maybe before. Different people, but always the same objectives.

Because some words are more important than others.

Some words have the power to change history.

Written in red. As always.

She reads the words on the piece of paper, burns it, changes into black clothes, leaves her tiny apartment quickly, and returns three hours later, shaking, with blood on her fists.

In the shower, more red as the blood washes off, swirls around the drain, vanishes.

When she steps out of the shower ten minutes later, this is written in lipstick on the bathroom mirror: "Next time, keep it clean."

She wraps a bath towel around herself, walks into her bedroom.

Yeah, keep it clean, she thinks. Like I asked the fat bastard to bleed all over me.

"Joseph—"

"Shut up."

"Joseph, listen—"

"Shut the fuck up."

The man in the dark blue suit stares hard at Joseph. Contemplates whether he can risk another interruption. Knows he cannot. Decides he doesn't care, anyway. So he just sits quietly and fiddles with a crease in his pants.

And waits.

Joseph holds a red pen in his right hand, taps it on his big wooden desk. Thinking. "How did she know?" Joseph says, his voice a cracked rock.

The man in the dark blue suit knows there is no way out of this. He knows he is going to die. In this room. Soon.

"There's no way she could have known about Jennings," he says, knowing it's a stupid thing to say. Pointless. Just going through the motions. He imagines he feels the world slowing down, its creator finished with us, no longer watching, no longer caring what happens.

Joseph nods his head, holds his breath, purses his lips. He pulls a very long knife from a sheath taped to the underside of his desk. Shows it to the man in the dark blue suit.

"That manuscript was very important," Joseph says. "Probably the most important manuscript we would ever have worked with. We've been doing this a long time, you and I. You've never fucked up like this. I don't understand it. And don't try to shift the blame. You're the one who hired Jennings."

The knife catches a flicker of light from a nearby lamp. Joseph taps it on the desk a few times, like he'd done with his pen. Breathing now. Just breathing. "And you've nothing from the brother, either? Nothing whatsoever?"

The man in the dark blue suit stays quiet. Just offers up a silent prayer to a god he has never believed in, and that he knows with absolute certainty is no longer watching.

A moment later, Joseph leans forward quickly, buries the knife to the hilt in the man's neck.

"So what's it say?"

"What's what say?"

"What do you think? The manuscript. What's it say this time? Staggering earthquake? The second coming of Hitler? Flood, drought, tidal wave, fucking plague of locusts? What?"

Emma Philson stares down at her dinner plate. Her hair is still damp from her shower.

"Don't know. Didn't read it." She looks back up. "It's not my job to read them; it's my job to steal them."

The man across from her puts his fork down on his plate, tilts his head, looks at her with disbelief.

"You've never read any of them? The fate of the world right there in your hands and you don't even sneak a bloody peek?"

Emma picks up her knife and fork, cuts into her fish. "I don't want to know."

The man still staring at her with incomprehension is Jim Leeds, her only contact in the organization. The restaurant they're eating at is a five-star in Vancouver. Neither of them is particularly enjoying the dishes they've ordered. They never do.

"So why do you bother?" Jim says, poking at his mussels.

Emma shrugs. "Your organization pays me very well."

"That's all that matters to you? The money?"

Emma says nothing. She forks a chunk of undercooked fish into her mouth and grimaces.

"I mean, don't you ever think about how important your work is? Don't you get any satisfaction from knowing that through this manuscript maneuvering—"

"I wish you'd stop calling it that," Emma interrupts, her voice rising. "We kill people and steal their writings."

Jim leans forward, looks at her hard. His fingers curl tight around the glass of red wine in his hand. "Keep. Your. Voice. *Down*."

He leans back slowly, straightens his tie, sips from his wine, then glowers at his food, pushes his plate away.

Emma stares out the window, all pretence to enjoying a lovely dinner with a colleague vanished.

"They aren't *their* writings anyway, Emma. They're not owned by anyone."

"Jim?" Emma says, leaning forward, lowering her voice to a whisper. "Listen to me, okay? I'm bored. And I'm tired of acting like this shit is somehow beneficial to the human race. Doesn't matter how many people get killed as long as we get our manuscript. As long as these documents make it into the 'right hands,' everyone's happy. Well, fuck that, *I'm* not happy."

Emma leans back, takes a deep breath.

"So what are you saying?"

"I'm saying that I don't want to do this anymore, Jim."

Jim doesn't blink, doesn't waver. "But you will, won't you." Statement. Fact.

Emma sighs, looks out the window again, at city lights, at cars, trains, people. She nods slowly.

But Emma knows something Jim doesn't. She lied; she *has* read the manuscript for which she slit the fat man's throat.

Seth Philson fidgets in his seat. Not because he is afraid of flying, not even because he has to piss so bad his teeth are floating; Seth fidgets because he is six-foot-seven and airplane seats are not made for people his height. He squirms around in his aisle seat, cursing the fact that no one with a roomier emergency-exit seat would swap with him. He tries to get comfortable first *with* his little pillow—folding and scrunching it, placing it between his knees and on the back of the seat in front of him—then without it. No dice either way. And no matter which way he tries it, the guy in the seat ahead turns around and glares at him.

Five foot fuck-all, Seth thinks. *Must be real tough to get comfortable in that seat when you're bloody well swimming in it, eh, shithead?*

More fidgeting. Deep sighing. If he could afford first-class, he'd be up there in a heartbeat, but writing jacket copy for crappy mainstream paperbacks sure isn't going to buy him a ticket up there—he's lucky he can afford this trip to Vancouver at all.

Seth needed a vacation. Seth was having very sharp, very clear images of ripping off his co-workers' heads.

Mountains. Snow. Calming white. A visit with his sister, whom he hasn't seen in . . . how many years has it been? He has no idea.

As the plane taxies up the runway, Seth closes his eyes and pictures the resort he's booked into. He inhales deeply, exhales slowly. The plane's thrumming engines help with the overall effect, blurring his thoughts, mashing his anger at short people down, down . . . until he feels the plane lift off, its nose scoop upward.

He looks out the window to his right, across the aisle. The ground slowly gives way to blue sky, dotted with little puffs of cloud.

Pure white.

He keeps his breathing steady until the plane reaches its cruising altitude, waits for the pilot's permission to operate assorted technological gadgets, and reaches down into the thin black bag at his feet.

Seth's gadget of choice is a laptop. Using its word processing program, he writes stories and essays on it that he has never let anyone see. He figures he probably never will. Not because he thinks they're bad, not because he has self-esteem issues, but because those words are his and his alone. They are not written for other people to see, and they are certainly not written for sale. He might well be able to sell his stories, but this doesn't interest him in the least.

What interests him even less is writing jacket copy for other people's shitty writing.

Seth powers up his laptop, waits for his Flying Spaghetti Monster screensaver to come up, then opens his word processor, flicks to File, then Open. Clicks on "magicians_hangnail.rtf." The title page pops up. He scrolls down to the first page, reads the three pages he wrote last night, cues up his cursor, and stares at it for the next five minutes.

Blink. Blink.

"You a writer?"

Guy next to him. Filthy bugger. Messy hair. Uneven beard the colour of burnt chestnuts. Sloppy blue eyes too big for his ruddy, round face.

"Nope," Seth says. Goes back to staring at the blinking cursor.

"So, if you don't mind my asking, what's that you're working on?"

Fake cheer: Boy, I sure want to get to know you, even though I really don't give a flying fuck what you're doing or why.

"Short story," Seth says, this time not turning his face away from the cursor.

"But I thought you just said—"

"I'm not a writer. I write things in this little computer here, but I'm not a writer. Writers sell their stories, join workshops to have their work critiqued for improvement. I do neither of those things. I do not consider myself a writer."

"Oh," the filthy guy says. Faces forward again.

Seth stares at the cursor and hopes that when he lands in Vancouver, his sister Emma won't ask him about his writing. He has told her before not to, but she persists—Emma and whatever the hell it is she does for a living. Something that requires her to travel a lot—almost more than Seth, and Seth practically lives on airplanes. Whenever he asks for more information about her job, she asks for more information about his latest short story. And that's where the conversation ends.

Though Seth is wholly unaware of it, a man in a dark blue suit sits three rows back and to the right of him. Ostensibly reading *The Vancouver Sun*, but watching. Waiting for Seth's fingers to connect with the laptop's keys.

Waiting for him to start writing.

•   •   •

"Give me the manuscript. I won't ask again."

"Fuck you, cunt."

The fat man holding the sheaf of papers reeks like a compost heap. Emma's head swims from the stench. She closes her eyes, steadies herself.

Always the same game: One side tracks the writer down, waits for the fugue to begin and end, kills the writer, makes off with the manuscript. The only difference is that the "good" side leaves the manuscript intact, the "bad" side edits it to serve its own agenda. The line between the two is blurry at best. Now, standing here in this disgusting man's shithole apartment, listening to him call her a cunt, Emma has one clear thought: *I want out. This is the last one.* A voice in her head—not her own— telling her to pack it in.

She'll bring it up with Jim tonight at dinner.

"Fuck me, huh?" Emma says, brings her gun out of her holster quickly, trains it on the fat man's face. "Hand it over, and I let you walk. Simple deal."

The man backs up, trips over a phone book on the floor behind him, but doesn't fall. He raises his free hand, warding her off, his bravado leaking out of his pores along with his sweat. "Look . . . look, please don't shoot. I'm sorry, okay?"

This is the best they have? Emma thinks. *This snivelling mound of flab?*

"I don't want apologies," she says, kicking the phone book out of the way, advancing on the enemy operative. "I want the manuscript."

Back against the wall. No more name-calling, no more false courage: a man caught without his gun. Now just the stench of garbage, sweat rolling down a fat, pimply face, wrinkles like a pitbull. Apologetic. Pathetic.

But Emma has never killed anyone with a gun; its only use for her is intimidation. She pulls a knife from a sheath behind her back. Steps forward. Slashes at the man's outstretched arm. It cuts the skin, the man cries out, drops his arm. Blood drips onto the plush beige carpet. The fat man's other hand still clenches the manuscript for a moment, then drops it as he uses this hand to try to stop the flow of blood from his arm.

When he looks down at his wound, moves his free hand over to press on it, Emma steps forward quickly, drags the blade across the man's throat and moves out of reach again in one quick motion. Emma hits an artery, takes a heartbeat's worth of spray in the face.

The fat man slumps, gurgles, drops.

Emma wipes her face with her forearm, reaches down, grabs the manuscript.

Normally, she would clean up. Carpet is a bitch, and it would take her most of the night, but normally she'd do it.

But this is the last one, she tells herself.

So she lets him bleed out.

The man in the dark blue suit should have known better than to hire that fat piece of shit Jennings, brother of one of their best. Nepotism and triple-checked referrals are the only way anyone gets in—and this blubbery fuck came highly recommended—but still, the man should have known. Just by looking at him. It wasn't in his eyes: what it takes. To kill without flinching, to kill without knowing why. Could be built like a brick shit house and talk the hardest game in town, but when it came to murdering people for nothing more than a sheaf of paper, you had to see that capability in their eyes.

The man in the dark blue suit had not seen it in Jennings' eyes, but he would have caught shit from every direction had he fought it, regardless of his experience, his years of moving manuscript.

And now he has to tell Joseph.

And Joseph will not be happy.

Leaving the clean-up crew behind him—hacking arms, legs, and head from the corpse—the man in the dark blue suit turns the incongruously fancy brass knob on the front door of Jennings' hovel, steps out into the hallway.

He does not expect to live out the next twenty-four hours.

But there is one more potential fugue writer to track before he's due back at headquarters, and that might give him something with which to placate his boss.

If he doesn't get a move on, he'll be late for his flight.

Emma sits at her kitchen table, stares at the manuscript in front of her. Black cup of coffee steaming in her right hand. Her left is shaky, fluttering, hovering over the first sheet of the 213-page manuscript.

Sometimes she looks. Most times, she doesn't bother. Not that it's boring—the direct word of God can be called many things, but hardly boring. If that's what these are, that is—writings from God, channelled through ordinary people from every nation on earth.

She thinks that's what they are, but there are other theories: Collective subconscious. Messages from aliens. Mass hallucinations. Whatever you believed, it hardly mattered. What mattered was that people dropped into some other state of mind when they wrote these manuscripts. They blipped out for minutes, hours, sometimes *days* at a time, wrote instructions, stories, parables, poetry, essays, in hundreds of languages. The occasional predictions were what made it hardest to discount the phenomenon.

Since its discovery, instructions and predictions have made up more and more of each manuscript. Less stories, less fables, less vague lessons. More hard truth, more concrete directions.

As if time were running out.

The coffee slides down Emma's throat, warms her belly, makes her sweat, quickens her pulse ever so slightly. She sets the mug down, turns the first page over, her hand still shaking, but now under relative control.

Three pots of coffee later, she has read the entire manuscript.

Shivers rack her slight frame as she gets up from the table, head spinning, full of information that, in the hands of the other side, could destroy everything. Certain things denoted authenticity, and they were incredibly hard to fake—hard, but not impossible.

The President of the United States, the Prime Ministers of Canada and Britain, leaders all over the world, they sometimes see the originals, sometimes the doctored versions—depending on who died, depending on which side got the upper hand. These world leaders, though aware of this bizarre "automatic writing" phenomenon, do not know where the manuscripts come from. They just arrive, are reviewed for authenticity by staff experts, then are hand-delivered to them.

Emma's organization has tried to warn them of the other side's efforts to tamper with these manuscripts, but their messages are never received. They are always intercepted before they reach anyone on the inside who could be trusted with the information. Or, if they *are* received, they're ignored as having come from an "unreliable source."

Sometimes, at least, the manuscripts themselves get through. Untouched, unchanged. But more often than not, they arrive skewed, tainted, adjusted to perpetuate wars and greed.

Surely these leaders think they're doing the will of their respective gods when they follow these words. Certainly they believe what they're doing is right for their people. They really have no reason to believe otherwise. An inexplicable direct line to the Big Guy in the Sky.

But this manuscript . . . this one absolutely *needs* to arrive untouched. There are too many ways to manipulate what it says, too many gaps in the physical spacing of the handwriting.

What is probably the most important document in history, Emma thinks, *is right here under my arm.* She slips on her coat, makes sure her gun is loaded (this time she *will* use it, if necessary), and heads to the airport to pick up her brother, Seth. She glances at her watch, realizes she will probably be late.

She hopes the flight is a little behind schedule.

But the most important document in history is not under Emma's arm; it is currently being written on Flight 762 to Vancouver, British Columbia.

The man in the dark blue suit watches Seth's mannerisms, knows it should hit him soon—the fugue state he has seen so many times in his career. Seth fits the profile to the proverbial "T." Certain types of personalities are more susceptible to the phenomenon: lonely drunkards, societal freaks, geeks—anti-social types, in general. Behavioral experts working for the man in the dark blue suit's organization have computers that calculate probability based on past fugue writers; they crunch numbers, input personal information about as many traceable humans on earth as possible, extrapolate the data, then tell the operatives who to watch and, subsequently—in nine cases out of ten—who to kill.

Once his name had popped up on their screens, they'd had their eye on Seth Philson for almost as long as they'd had their eye on his sister. But for very different reasons.

The man in the dark blue suit—so uncomfortable in his own skin that he often worries about having his own name pop up on his organization's computers—thinks that most times things just go to shit for no good reason at all, just the natural entropy of the universe. But tonight . . . tonight, he feels like things might just work out.

He is just about to get up and go to the bathroom when Seth's head nods.

Once.

Twice.

Drops completely, head resting on his chest.

When his head comes up again, this time very slowly, his fingers suddenly move swiftly over the keyboard, writing. Words not his own.

The man in the dark blue suit sits tight, waits to see if it's going to be one of these "flash sessions," as his organization calls them—a few brief insights into whatever power controls fugue writers. These synaptic blips usually produce indecipherable sentences—a bad connection, a cosmic wrong number.

But after fifteen full minutes of constant tapping on the keys, the man knows this one was real. He just hopes it isn't a two- or even three-day marathon, else he'll have nothing with which to assuage Joseph when he breaks the news about Jennings' monumental fuck-up.

He rises to go to the bathroom, squeezes out into the aisle.

He does not turn his head in either direction on his way; if he had done so, he would have seen, off in the distance, a bright white flash of lightning.

The first of many.

In seat 15C, Seth Philson, gripped by something unknowable, continues to write.

After dinner with Jim—and her abortive attempt to quit her job—Emma drives to the airport through sheets of rain so heavy she thinks the glass will crack, splinter, and cave in before she gets anywhere near the airport.

She calls ahead and Seth's flight is right on time, meaning she'll be late picking him up. Perfect. A great foot to get off on with her brother, whom she'd not seen in at least six years. She wonders if she'll tell him about her job this time. If ever there was a time she wanted to tell *some*one about it, get the burden off her chest, now was that time.

But she knows she won't, no matter if it would help bring Seth and her closer. Their mother dead from an early age, and their father off travelling God knew where—apathetic about their existence, as he'd always been—they'd floated off to very different lives, drifting without much thought as to what they would do next. Content to depend on no one. Be with no one.

Emma slows down as the rain turns to marble-sized chunks of hail, drumming off her car roof. The sound is deafening, and Emma feels a headache winding its way through her spine, up into her brain.

She changes lanes. Closes her eyes for a moment.

When she reopens them, the night flashes white, lightning touches down not far ahead, near the airport. Thunder cracks—the loudest she's ever heard it—and something explodes, bursts into flame.

Behind her, in the rear-view mirror, more lightning touches down, slices the dark, burns orange-blue after-images into her retinas. More thunder, more buildings on either side of her exploding, filling the night air with the smell of ozone, the crackling of fire.

Emma slows to a crawl, terrified. She sees the airport, nearly half of it engulfed in flames, rise over the horizon. She watches as a plane coming in for a landing—unable to safely pull up once the airport exploded—bursts apart, lightning cleaving it in two.

She slams on the brakes, pulls the car over to the shoulder, opens the door, steps out onto the tarmac. She hugs herself, shaking in the rain, stares at the destroyed plane in the distance, glances quickly at the flames all around her.

Where are you, Seth? she thinks, looks skyward, her brain unable to move out of shock and into an appropriate panic response.

Through the black rain, she sees a blinking light far off, glances at her watch, knows that Seth must be aboard this plane; the one that just exploded is too early to be his.

She tries to think of an explanation for the destruction around her, but is only capable of thinking one clear, useless thought: *Stay up there, Seth. Please.*

Stay up there.

When the man in the dark blue suit comes out of the bathroom, he immediately notices several passengers looking and pointing out the windows. He returns to his seat, leans across a sleeping woman next to him, peers out the window. Flashes of lightning crisp the night sky. Some of it looks pretty low to the ground, but nothing he hasn't seen before.

He shrugs, glances over at Seth—still clattering away—and settles back into his seat. The plane suddenly hits some heavy turbulence. After a few seconds of rocky riding, the captain comes over the speaker, announces that they've hit some turbulence.

Thank you, Dr. Obvious, the man in the dark blue suit thinks.

The captain goes on to say that they'll be starting their descent into Vancouver very soon, asks people to please return to their seats and fasten their seatbelts. What he does not say over the speakers is that in the cockpit there is some tension, as they've just lost radio contact with Vancouver International Airport. But the captain is confident that once they break through the heavier clouds below, radio reception will clear up.

Seth does not fasten his seatbelt. Seth continues to type.

The man watching Seth catches a glimpse of his document. Many different languages are displayed across the screen—some the man can distinguish, others he cannot. Fascinated, he unbuckles his seatbelt, goes out into the aisle, hangs back a few feet, trying not to appear nosy. He reaches up to an overhead compartment, rustles about with a few bags, hoping no one remembers that this isn't where he originally stashed his carry-on luggage. But people are either staring down at the lightning storm, or closing their eyes to catch a few more Zs while the plane descends.

A few more pecks of the laptop's keys, then Seth stops typing, drops instantly into a deep sleep, slumped over his computer. The man in the dark blue suit can only see the bottom half of the last page of the document.

The words are in English, as follows:

> *This is not, and never has been, about you. Any of you.*
> *This is not, and never has been, about good and bad.*
> *This makes no sense to you, I know.*
> *I have taken all who are worthy.*
> *There will be no further messages.*

The man in the dark blue suit slumps against one of the seats in the aisle, as if having just had the wind knocked out of him. He has never known religion, never wanted to know it, but he feels, very distinctly, something leave him just then. The word "soul" comes to mind, but he does not feel that this word fits for him.

A burly male flight attendant bustles up behind him, escorts him to his seat, tells him to buckle his seatbelt.

Just then there is a bright flash, taking a snapshot of the turmoil in the sky. A loud thud rocks the aircraft. A fire blazes on the left wing. Another strike and the engine on that side of the airplane flames out.

Seth Philson wakes up to screaming.

Below the black clouds under the plane—clouds that Flight 762 has just broken through—Vancouver International Airport burns.

Emma sits on the hood of her car, drenched, sobbing, waiting for another glimpse of the blinking light to cut through the clouds, hoping the tiny light stays up there, or carries on to another airport to land. Surely, unlike the other plane, Seth's will see the devastation below and have time to pull up.

Over the thunder and drilling rain, she hears a droning engine, searches the sky, sees a bright flash, a sharp crack, and her heart stops, kicks twice in her chest, flutters. The plane breaks through the low-lying clouds. She raises her right hand to her mouth at the same time that the fire bursts to life in the left engine: a tiny firefly weaving and bobbing far above her.

Unable to do anything but stare, Emma watches, wide-eyed, open-mouthed, as fierce winds batter the plane around in the sky for several torturous minutes. Nearly overhead, it tilts, rights itself, loses altitude, nose dipping, then straightens up again. Now directly above, another lightning strike sears its tail, temporarily blinding her.

Seth, she thinks, a strange calm coming over her. *Where are you going? I'm here, Seth. Right here below you.*

When the plane crashes into a forest about a mile away—continued lightning strikes from the overcharged air missing her by less than a hundred feet—she imagines she feels the earth shudder. Imagines she feels it ripple through her entire body.

She expects an explosion to accompany the plane crash, but there is nothing. Just silence after it disappears over the highest treetop.

She feels something inside her, some part of her, slip away, drift up into the night.

After calmly calling in the plane crash from her cell phone, Emma drives home. As soon as she's a few miles away from the crash site, the weather abruptly clears up. The rain and hail stop, the lightning peters out, the winds grow calm.

The manuscript on Emma's passenger seat—the one she thought would change the world forever if it wound up in the wrong hands—is now blank. Even as she leans over from the driver's side, incredulous, flipping through the hundreds of pages, the words fade before her eyes.

A conversation she'd had with Jim Leeds at dinner earlier that night, after she told him she wanted to quit her job, comes back to her as she drives:

"So what do you think it is?" Jim asked.

"What do I think what is?" Emma said, still annoyed that Jim was so certain she would keep doing her job, even though she hated it.

"Where do you think they're coming from? The words."

Emma was silent for nearly a full minute. She swilled wine around in her glass.

"I think they're coming from God."

Jim snorted. "God? I didn't know you believed."

"I don't. But I think that's where the words are coming from."

The next day, *The Vancouver Sun* runs a story about the disastrous crash of Flight 762, the obliteration of the airport, and the bizarrely focused lightning storm that disintegrated every building and airplane within a two-mile radius of the crash site.

There is also a smaller article about reports of disappearances throughout Vancouver. At press time, several hundred other missing-persons reports were coming in from around the world. Police, the paper said, were investigating.

Incredibly, Seth was safe. A little bruised and battered, but otherwise fine. As were all 114 of the other passengers aboard the plane. A "miracle," the *Sun* said.

Seth's laptop, however, was not so lucky; it was lost in the crash.

A week later, sitting across from his sister in her apartment, eating French toast and sipping coffee, Seth tells his sister what he remembers about the flight.

"I remember getting on the plane, and I remember some guy beside me asking if I was a writer. I told him no. Then I remember getting sleepy. That's it." Seth cuts into a piece of toast, jabs it with his fork, sops up some syrup with it, and pops it into his mouth.

"That's it? Nothing about the crash?"

"Nothing."

Emma gets up from her chair, heads for the shower. She stops at the doorway leading to the bathroom.

"You're staying for . . . a while, Seth?" she says.

Seth looks up, sees something in his sister's eyes he's never seen before. He thinks it might be loneliness. He thinks he might have some of that right now in his own eyes.

"Yeah," he says. "I'm staying for a while. As long as you need me."

Emma smiles, steps into the bathroom, closes the door quietly.

The man in the dark blue suit dials Emma Philson's number from a phone booth downtown. She sounds breathless when she answers, as if having had to run to grab the receiver before it stopped ringing.

"Hello?"

"Emma Philson?"

A pause. "Who is this?" One hand dries her hair with a towel, the other holds the phone.

"There will be more disappearances," the man says. "More reported each day. Probably millions."

"Who the *hell* is this?"

"All the work we've done—none if it mattered, none of it changed anything, Ms. Philson. Good or bad, it didn't matter at all. Judgement day has come and gone, and now we're all just walking around, already dead. Just too fucking stupid to lay down."

Perhaps having an idea who this might be, Emma says nothing. Just listens.

"Your brother. He wrote this. On the plane, just before it went down. I was there to steal his manuscript, kill him. He was a fugue writer. I'm surprised you didn't know. Just listen: 'This is not, and never has been, about you. Any of you. This is not, and never has been, about good and bad. This makes no sense to you, I know. I have taken all who are worthy. There will be no further messages.'"

Emma calls the man in the dark blue suit by his real name. Keep your friends close, but your enemies closer.

"Yes, it's me," the man says, his voice rusted, hollowed out. "You know, I thought maybe there really was something to this whole good and bad thing. I thought maybe when I called you, there would be no answer. That maybe you'd have disappeared along with the others. Taken . . . wherever." His voice trails off, and he feels the emptiness inside his chest more acutely now. It squeezes his heart. The man coughs once, looks across the street. His eyes drift up to his boss's office window.

"Hello?" Emma says tentatively. The man hears her as a dead voice in a tin can.

"I'm here," he replies. Breathes deeply, feels his chest tighten more. "There will be no more manuscripts, Emma. It's over. All of it. We were never in control. Whether we believed in them or not, there were always other, bigger forces at work. God, the Devil, or something else entirely, what does it matter in the end?"

No reply.

The man hangs up the phone.

Emma listens to the dead line hum for a long time. She is crying and has no idea why.

The man in the dark blue suit crosses the street carefully, making sure to look both ways, climbs three flights of stairs, enters Joseph's office, sits down.

"Joseph—"

"Shut up."

"Joseph, listen—"

"Shut the fuck *up*."

The man in the dark blue suit stares hard at Joseph. Contemplates whether he can risk another interruption. Knows he cannot. Decides he doesn't care, anyway. So he just sits quietly and fiddles with a crease in his pants.

And waits to die for nothing.

WILLIAM HOPE HODGSON

Ballade

My Babe, My Babe

William Hope Hodgson was born in Essex, England, in 1877. During his relatively short life he produced a large body of work, consisting mostly of short stories and novels of horror, fantasy, and science fiction. His most famous novel is The House on the Borderland. *He also wrote poetry, but few of his poems were published during his lifetime. He also attracted some notice as a photographer. He was killed by an artillery shell in 1918.*

Night Shade Books has been publishing The Collected Fiction of William Hope Hodgson *since 2003, intending to ultimately produce a five-volume set of his work.*

"Ballade" and "My Babe, My Babe" were originally published in The Lost Poetry of William Hope Hodgson, *edited by Jane Frank and copublished by PS Publishing and Tartarus Press.*

—E.D.

Ballade

Who Make Their Bed in the Deep Waters

We are dying,
　　And the sea is very still,
And some of the children are crying,
　　And some are ill,
　　　　And seven are dead
　　　　And their mothers make their bed.

We are dying,
　　Two boats just full of us,
And the little ones are lying
　　Quietly—thus and thus,

And twelve are dead
　And their mothers made their bed.

We are dying,
　Another day has gone,
And no child is crying,
　In the gloaming wan
　　They all are dead
　　And their mothers made their bed.

We are dying,
　It is just before the dawn,
The mothers all are lying
　Silent e'er the morn

　　Forlornly dead
　　And I made their bed.

We are dying,
　The evening's sun is low,
And my lover-lad is crying
　Weak in utter woe
　　O'er me dead
　　E'er he make my bed.

We are dying,
　My lover thought me gone,
In his two arms lying,
　But I saw him wan
　　Nearly dead
　　And his arms my bed.

We are silent now,
　For I reached and drew
　　My lover to me, dying,
And the glad young brow
　　Sailed against me lying
E'er he knew
　　　Quietly dead
　　　On my bosom for his bed.

My Babe, My Babe

And my babe lay dying
　And my babe lay dead
And my bones are crying, crying
　By an empty bed.

I meet my babe on that first stair
　Where early months he climbed and fell,
And pass swift by that memory's lair
　Sundered with thoughts I dare not tell.

I meet my babe without my door
   And pass him by in silence there,
My little babe who is no more
   I meet him lonely without care.

I meet my babe in that quiet room
   Where one wee cot calls through the night
An empty voice through all the gloom
   Once so strangely light.

My husband's arms are opened wide,
   But oh! my babe is crouched so near—
The babe that in my two arms died;
   My heart is dry and sere.

And when I lift the skirt I wore
   A silent shadow flits away—
My babe there nestled, as of yore—
   My babe that died on that gray day.

STEPHEN GALLAGHER

The Box

Stephen Gallagher was born in Salford, England, in 1954. He is the author of over a dozen novels, including Nightmare, with Angel; Red, Red Robin; *and* The Spirit Box. *He has numerous screenplay credits and in 1997 wrote and directed a TV adaptation of his novel* Oktober. *His short stories have been published in various magazines and anthologies including* The Magazine of Fantasy & Science Fiction, Asimov's Science Fiction, Weird Tales, Shadows, *and* The Dark; *his collection* Out of His Mind *won a British Fantasy Award in 2004.*

His latest novel is The Painted Bride *and Subterranean Press will publish a new story collection in 2007. His recently completed historical novel,* The Kingdom of Bones, *is to be published by Random House under the imprint of senior editor Shaye Areheart.*

"The Box" was originally published in Retro Pulp Tales, *an anthology of science fiction, horror, fantasy, and westerns.*

—E.D.

It was a woman who picked up the phone and I said, "Can I speak to Mr. Lavery, please?"

"May I ask what it concerns?" she said.

I gave her my name and said, "I'm calling from Wainfleet Maritime College. I'm his instructor on the helicopter safety course."

"I thought that was all done with last week."

"He didn't complete it."

"Oh." I'd surprised her. "Excuse me for one moment. Can you hold on?"

I heard her lay down the phone and move away. Then, after a few moments, there came the indistinct sounds of a far-off conversation. There was her voice and there was a man's, the two of them faint enough to be in another room. I couldn't make out anything of what was being said.

After a while, I could hear someone returning.

I was expecting to hear Lavery's voice, but it was the woman again.

She said, "I'm terribly sorry, I can't get him to speak to you." There was a note of exasperation in her tone.

"Can you give me any indication why?"

"He was quite emphatic about it," she said. The implication was that no, he'd not only given her no reason, but he also hadn't appreciated being asked. Then she lowered her voice and added, "I wasn't aware that he hadn't finished the course. He told me in so many words that he was done with it."

Which could be taken more than one way. I said, "He does know that without a safety certificate he can't take up the job?"

"He's never said anything about that." She was still keeping her voice down, making it so that Lavery—her husband, I imagined, although the woman hadn't actually identified herself—wouldn't overhear. She went on, "He's been in a bit of a funny mood all week. Did something happen?"

"That's what I was hoping he might tell me. Just ask him once more for me, will you?"

She did, and this time I heard Lavery shouting.

When she came back to the phone she said, "This is very embarrassing."

"Thank you for trying," I said. "I won't trouble you any further, Mrs. Lavery."

"It's *Miss* Lavery," she said. "James is my brother."

In 1950 the first scheduled helicopter service started up in the U.K., carrying passengers between Liverpool and Cardiff. Within a few short years helicopter travel had become an expensive, noisy, and exciting part of our lives. No vision of a future city was complete without its heliport. Children would run and dance and wave if they heard one passing over.

The aviation industry had geared up for this new era in freight and passenger transportation, and the need for various kinds of training had brought new life to many a small airfield and flight school. Wainfleet was a maritime college, but it offered new aircrew one facility that the flight schools could not.

At Wainfleet we had the dunker, also known as The Box.

We'd been running the sea rescue and safety course for almost three years, and I'd been on the staff for most of that time. Our completion record was good. I mean, you expect a few people to drop out of any training program, especially the dreamers, but our intake were experienced men with some living under their belts. Most were ex-navy or air force, and any romantic notions had been knocked out of them in a much harder theater than ours. Our scenarios were as nothing compared to the situations through which some of them had lived.

And yet, I was thinking as I looked at the various records spread across the desk in my little office, our dropouts were gradually increasing in their numbers. Could the fault lie with us? There was nothing in any of their personal histories to indicate a common cause.

I went down the corridor to Peter Taylor's office. Peter Taylor was my boss. He was sitting at his desk signing course certificates.

I said, "Don't bother signing Lavery's."

He looked up at me with eyebrows raised, and I shrugged.

"I'm no closer to explaining it," I said.

"Couldn't just be plain old funk, could it?"

"Most of these men are war heroes," I said. "Funk doesn't come into it."

He went back to his signing, but he carried on talking.

"Easy enough to be a hero when you're a boy without a serious thought in your head," he said. "Ten years of peacetime and a few responsibilities, and perhaps you get a little bit wiser."

Then he finished the last one and capped the fountain pen and looked at me.

I didn't quite know what to say. Peter Taylor had a background in the merchant marine but he'd sat out the war right here, in a reserved occupation.

"I'd better be getting on," I said.

I left the teaching block and went over to the building that housed our sea tank. It was a short walk and the sun was shining, but the wind from the ocean always cut through the gap between the structures. The wind smelled and tasted of sand and salt, and of something unpleasant that the new factories up the coast had started to dump into the estuary.

Back in its early days, Wainfleet had been a sanitorium for TB cases. Staffed by nuns, as I understood it; there were some old photographs in the mess hall. Then it had become a convalescent home for mine workers and then, finally, the maritime college it now was. We had two hundred boarding cadets for whom we had dormitories, a parade ground, and a rugby field that had a pronounced downward slope toward the cliffs. But I wasn't part of the cadet teaching staff. I was concerned only with the commercial training arm.

Our team of four safety divers was clearing up after the day's session. The tank had once been an ordinary swimming pool, added during the convalescent-home era but then deepened and reequipped for our purposes. The seawater was filtered, and in the winter it was heated by a boiler. Although if you'd been splashing around in there in December, you'd never have guessed it.

Their head diver was George "Buster" Brown. A compact and powerful-looking man, he'd lost most of his hair and had all but shaved off the rest, American GI style. With his barrel chest and his bullet head, he looked like a human missile in his dive suit. In fact, he'd actually trained on those two-man torpedoes toward the end of the war.

I said to him, "Cast your mind back to last week. Remember a trainee name of Lavery?"

"What did he look like?"

I described him, and added, "Something went wrong and he didn't complete."

"I think I know the one," Buster said. "Had a panic during the exercise and we had to extract him. He was almost throwing a fit down there. Caught Jacky Jackson a right boff on the nose."

"What was he like after you got him out?"

"Embarrassed, I think. Wouldn't explain his problem. Stamped off and we didn't see him again."

Buster couldn't think of any reason why Lavery might have reacted as he did. As far as he and his team were concerned, the exercise had gone normally in every way.

I left him to finish stowing the training gear, and went over to inspect the Box.

The Box was a stripped-down facsimile of a helicopter cabin, made of riveted aluminum panels and suspended by cable from a lifeboat davit. The davit swung the Box out and over the water before lowering it. The cabin seated four. Once immersed, an ingenious chain-belt system rotated the entire cabin until it was upside down. It was as realistic a ditching as we could make it, while retaining complete control of the situation. The safety course consisted of a morning in the classroom, followed by the afternoon spent practicing the escape drill from underwater.

The Box was in its rest position at the side of the pool. It hung with its floor about six inches clear of the tiles. I climbed aboard, and grabbed at something to keep my balance as the cabin swung around under my weight.

There had been no attempt to dress up the interior to look like the real thing;

upside down and six feet under, only the internal geography needed to be accurate. The bucket seats and harnesses were genuine, but that was as far as it went. The rest was just the bare metal, braced with aluminum struts and with open holes cut for the windows. In appearance it was like a tin Wendy House, suspended from a crane.

I'm not sure what I thought I was looking for. I put my hand on one of the seats and tugged, but the bolts were firm. I lifted part of the harness and let the webbing slide through my fingers. It was wet and heavy. Steadying myself, I used both hands to close the buckle and then tested the snap-release one-handed.

"I check those myself," Buster Brown said through the window. "Every session."

"No criticism intended, Buster," I said.

"I should hope not," he said, and then he was gone.

It happened again the very next session, only three days later.

I'd taken the files home and I'd studied all the past cases, but I'd reached no firm conclusions. If we were doing something wrong, I couldn't see what it was.

These were not inexperienced men. Most were in their thirties and, as I'd pointed out to Peter Taylor, had seen service under wartime conditions. Some had been ground crew, but many had been fliers who'd made the switch to peacetime commercial aviation. Occasionally we'd get students whose notes came marked with a particular code, and whose records had blank spaces where personal details should have been; these individuals, it was acknowledged but never said, were sent to us as part of a wider MI5 training.

In short, no sissies. Some of them were as tough as you could ask, but it wasn't meant to be a tough course. It wasn't a trial, it wasn't a test. The war was long over.

As I've said, we began every training day in the classroom. Inevitably, some of it involved telling them things they already knew. But you can't skip safety, even though some of them would have loved to; no grown man ever looks comfortable in a classroom situation.

First I talked them through the forms they had to complete. Then I collected the forms in.

And then, when they were all settled again, I started the talk.

I said, "We're not here to punish anybody. We're here to take you through a scenario so that hopefully, if you ever *do* need to ditch, you'll have a much greater chance of survival. Most fatalities don't take place when the helicopter comes down. They happen afterward, in the water."

I asked if anyone in the room had been sent to us for rebreather training, and a couple of hands were raised. This gave me a chance to note their faces.

"Right," I said. "I'm going to go over a few points and then after the break we'll head for the pool."

I ran through the routine about the various designs of flight suits and harnesses and life vests. Then the last-moment checks; glasses if you wore them, false teeth if you had them, loose objects in the cabin. Hold on to some part of the structure for orientation. Brace for impact.

One or two had questions. Two men couldn't swim. That was nothing unusual.

After tea break in the college canteen, we all went over together. Buster Brown and his men were already in the water, setting up a dinghy for the lifeboat drill that would follow the ditch. The students each found themselves a suit from the rail before disappearing into the changing room, and I went over to ready the Box.

When they came out, they lined up along the poolside. One of the divers steadied the Box and I stayed by the controls and called out, "Numbers one to four, step forward."

The Box jiggled around on its cable as the first four men climbed aboard and strapped themselves into the bucket seats. Buster Brown checked everyone's harness from the doorway, and then signaled to me before climbing in with them and securing the door from the inside. I sounded the warning Klaxon and then eased back the lever to raise the Box into the air.

In the confines of the sea tank building, the noise of the crane's motor could be deafening. Once I'd raised the payload about twelve feet in the air, I swung the crane around on its turntable to place the Box directly over the pool. It swung there, turning on its cable, and I could see the men inside through the raw holes that represented aircraft windows.

Two divers with masks and air bottles were already under the water, standing by to collect the escapees and guide them up to the surface. Buster would stay inside. This was routine for him. He'd hold his breath for the minute or so that each exercise took, and then he'd ride the Box back to the poolside to pick up the next four.

Right now he was giving everyone a quick recap of what I'd told them in the classroom. Then it was, *Brace, brace, brace for impact!* and I released the Box to drop into the water.

It was a controlled drop, not a sudden plummet, although to a first-timer it was always an adrenaline moment. The Box hit the water and then started to settle, and I could hear Buster giving out a few final reminders in the rapidly filling cabin.

Then it went under, and everything took on a kind of slow-motion tranquillity as the action transferred to below the surface. Shapes flitted from the submerged Box in all directions, like wraiths fleeing a haunted castle. They were out in seconds. As each broke the surface, a number was shouted. When all four were out, I raised the Box.

It was as fast and as straightforward as that.

The exercise was repeated until every student had been through a straightforward dunk. Then the line re-formed and we did it all again, this time with the added refinement of a cabin rotation as the Box went under. It made for a more realistic simulation, as a real helicopter was liable to invert with the weight of its engine. To take some of the anxiety out of it, I'd tell the students that I considered escape from the inverted cabin to be easier—you came out through the window opening facing the surface, which made it a lot easier to strike out for.

Again, we had no problems. The safety divers were aware of the nonswimmers and gave them some extra assistance. The Box functioned with no problems. No one panicked, no one got stuck. Within the hour, everyone was done.

At that point, we divided the party. The two men on rebreather training stayed with Buster Brown, and everyone else went to the other end of the pool for lifeboat practice. I ran the Box through its paces empty yet again, as Buster stood at the poolside with them and ran through his piece on the use of the rebreather unit.

The rebreather does pretty much what its name suggests. Consisting of an airbag incorporated into the flotation jacket with a mouthpiece and a valve, it allows you to conserve and reuse your own air. There's more unused oxygen in an expelled breath than you'd think. It's never going to replace the Aqua-lung, but the device can extend your underwater survival time by a vital minute or two.

Both men looked as if they might be old hands at this. Their names were Charnley and Briggs. Even in the borrowed flight suit, Charnley had that sleek, officer-material look. He had an Errol Flynn mustache and hair so heavily brilliantined that two dunks in the tank had barely disturbed it. Briggs, on the other hand, looked the noncommissioned man to his fingertips. His accent was broad and his hair looked as if his wife had cut it for him, probably not when in the best of moods.

Buster left them practicing with the mouthpieces and came over to pick up his mask and air bottle. I was guiding the empty Box, water cascading from every seam, back to the poolside.

"Just a thought, Buster," I said, raising my voice to be heard as I lowered the cabin to the side. "Wasn't Lavery on the rebreather when he had his little episode?"

"Now that you mention it, yes, he was."

"How many were in the Box with him?"

"Two others. Neither of them had any problem."

I didn't take it any further than that. None of our other nonfinishers had been on the rebreather when they chose to opt out, so this was hardly a pattern in the making.

The rebreather exercise was always conducted in three stages. First, the Box was lowered to sit in the water so that the level inside the cabin was around chest-height. The student would practice by leaning forward into the water, knowing that in the event of difficulty he need do no more than sit back. This confidence-building exercise would then be followed by a total immersion, spending a full minute under the water and breathing on the apparatus. Assuming all went well, the exercise would end with a complete dunk, rotate, and escape.

All went well. Until that final stage.

The others had all completed the lifeboat drill and left the pool by then. The Box hit the water and rolled over with the spectacular grinding noise that the chain belt always made. It sounded like a drawbridge coming down, and worked on a similar principle.

Then the boomy silence of the pool as the water lapped and the Box stayed under.

The minute passed, and then came the escape. One fleeting figure could be seen under the water. But only one. He broke surface and his number was called. It was Briggs. I looked toward the Box and saw Buster going in through one of the window openings. My hand was on the lever, but I waited; some injury might result if I hauled the Box out in the middle of an extraction. But then Buster came up and made an urgent signal and so I brought the cabin up out of the water, rotating it back upright as it came. Tank water came out of the window openings in gushers.

Buster came out of the pool and we reached the Box together. Charnley was still in his harness, the rebreather mouthpiece still pushing his cheeks out. He was making weak-looking gestures with his hands. I reached in to relieve him of the mouthpiece, but he swatted me aside and then spat it out.

Fending his hands away, Buster got in with him and released his harness. By then, Charnley was starting to recognize his surroundings and to act a little more rationally. He didn't calm down, though. He shoved both of us aside and clambered out.

He stood at the poolside, spitting water and tearing himself out of the flotation jacket.

"What was the problem?" I asked him.

"You want to get that bloody thing looked at," Charnley gasped.

Buster, who had a surprisingly puritan streak, said in a warning tone, "Language," and I shot him a not-now look.

"Looked at for what?" I said, but Charnley just hurled all his gear onto the deck as if it had been wrestling him and he'd finally just beaten it.

"Don't talk to me," he said, "I feel foul." And he stalked off to the changing room.

The two of us got the Box secure, and while we were doing it I asked Buster what happened. Buster could only shrug.

"I tapped his arm to tell him it was time to come out, but he didn't move," Buster said. "Just stayed there. I thought he might have passed out, but when I went in he started to thrash around and push me away."

So, what was Charnley's problem? I went to find him in the changing room. Briggs had dressed in a hurry in order to be sure of getting out in time for his bus. As he passed me in the doorway he said, "Your man's been wasting a good shepherd's pie in there."

Shepherd's pie or whatever, I could smell vomit hanging in the air around the cubicles at the back of the changing room. Charnley was out. He was standing in front of the mirror, pale as watered milk, knotting his tie. An RAF tie, I noted.

"Captain Charnley?" I said.

"What about it?"

"I just wondered if you were ready to talk about what happened."

"Nothing happened," he said.

I waited.

After a good thirty seconds or more he said, "I'm telling you nothing happened. Must have got a bad egg for breakfast. Serves me right for trusting your canteen."

I said, "I'll put you back on the list for tomorrow. You can skip the classroom session."

"Don't bother," he said, reaching for his blazer.

"Captain Charnley . . ."

He turned to me then, and fixed me with a look so stern and so urgent that it was almost threatening.

"I didn't see anything in there," he said. "Nothing. Do you understand me? I don't want you telling anyone I did."

Even though I hadn't suggested any such thing.

There was a bus stop outside the gates, but Captain Charnley had his own transport. It was a low, noisy, open-topped sports car with a racing green paint job, all dash and Castrol fumes. Off he went, scaring the birds out of the trees, swinging out onto the road, and roaring away.

I went back to my office and reviewed his form. According to his record, he'd flown Hurricanes with 249 Squadron in Yorkshire. After the war he'd entered the glass business, but he'd planned a return to flying with BEA.

Hadn't seen anything? What exactly did that mean? What was there to see anyway?

I have to admit that in a fanciful moment, when we'd first started to suspect that there might be some kind of a problem on the course, I'd investigated the Box's history. But it had none. Far from being the salvaged cabin of a wrecked machine, haunted by the ghosts of those who'd died in it, the Box had been purpose-built as an exercise by apprentices at the local aircraft factory.

It was no older than its three and a half years, and there was nothing more to it than met the eye. The bucket seats were from scrap, but they'd been salvaged from training aircraft that had been decommissioned without ever having seen combat or disaster.

When I went back to the sea tank, Buster Brown was out of his diving gear and dressed in a jacket and tie, collecting the men's clocking-off cards prior to locking up the building. The other divers had cleared away the last of their equipment and gone.

I said, "Can I ask a favor?"

He said, "As long as it doesn't involve borrowing my motor bike, my missus, or my money, ask away."

I think he knew what I was going to say. "Stay on a few minutes and operate the dunker for me? I want to sit in and see if I can work out what all the fuss is about."

"I can tell you what the fuss is about," he said. "Some can take it and some can't."

"That doesn't add up, Buster," I said. "These have all been men of proven courage."

Suddenly it was as if we were back in the Forces and he was the experienced NCO politely setting the greenhorn officer straight.

"With respect, sir," he said, "you're missing the point. Being tested doesn't diminish a man's regard for danger. I think you'll find it's rather the opposite."

We proceeded with the trial. I found a suit that fit me and changed into it. I put on a flotation jacket and rebreather gear. No safety divers, just me and Buster. Like the tattooed boys who ride the backs of dodgems at the fairground, you feel entitled to get a little cavalier with the rules you're supposed to enforce.

I strapped myself in, and signaled my readiness to Buster. Then I tensed involuntarily as the cable started moving with a jerk. As the Box rose into the air and swung out over the pool, I looked all around the interior for anything untoward. I saw nothing.

Buster followed the normal routine, lowering me straight into the water. The box landed with a slap, and immediately began to rock from side to side as it filled up and sank. It was cold and noisy when the seawater flooded into the cabin, but once you got over that first moment's shock it was bearable. I've swum in colder seas on Welsh holidays.

Just as it reached my chin, I took a deep breath and ducked under the surface. Fully submerged, I looked and felt all around me as far as I could reach, checking for anything unusual. There was nothing. I wasn't using the rebreather at this point. I touched the belt release, lifting the lever plate, and it opened easily. There was the usual slight awkwardness as I wriggled free of the harness, but it wasn't anything to worry about. I took a few more moments to explore the cabin, again finding nothing, and then I went out through a window opening without touching the sides.

I popped up no more than a couple of seconds later. When Buster saw that I was out in open water, he lifted the dunker. As I swam to the side it passed over me, streaming like a raincloud onto the heaving surface of the pool.

By the time I'd climbed up the ladder, the Box was back in its start position and ready for reboarding. I said to Buster, "So which seat was Charnley in? Wasn't it the left rear?"

"Aft seat on the port side," he said.

So that was the one I took, this second time. Might as well try to re-create the experience as closely as possible, I thought. Not that any of this seemed to be telling me anything useful. I strapped myself in and gave Buster the wave, and we were off again.

I had to run through the whole routine, just so that I could say to Peter Taylor that the check had been complete. It was second nature. In all walks of life, the survivors are the people who never assume. This time I inflated the rebreather bag while the cabin was in midair, and had the mouthpiece in by the time I hit the water. Again it came flooding in as the cabin settled, but this time there was a difference. Almost instantly the chain belt jerked into action and the cabin began to turn.

It feels strange to invert and submerge at the same time. You're falling, you're floating . . . of course people get disoriented, especially if they've never done it before. This time I determined to give myself the full minute under. Without a diver on hand to tap me when the time was up, I'd have to estimate it. But that was no big problem.

The cabin completed its turn, and stopped. All sound ended as well, apart from boomy echoes from the building above, pushing their way through several tons of water. I hung there in the harness, not breathing yet. I felt all but weightless in the straps. The seawater was beginning to make my eyes sting.

I'd forgotten how dark the cabin went when it was upside down. The tank was gloomy at this depth anyway. I'd heard that the American military went a stage further than we did, and conducted a final exercise with everyone wearing blacked-out goggles to simulate a nighttime ditching. That seemed a little extreme to me; as I'd indicated to the men in the classroom, the Box was never intended as a test of endurance. It was more a foretaste of something we hoped they'd never have to deal with.

I found myself wondering if Buster had meant anything by that remark. The one about men who'd been tested. As if he was suggesting that I wouldn't know.

I'd been too young to fight at the very beginning of the war, but I joined up when I could and in the summer of 1940 I was selected for Bomber Command. In training I'd shown aptitude as a navigator. I flew twelve missions over heavily defended Channel ports, bombing the German invasion barges being readied along the so-called Blackpool Fron.

Then Headquarters took me out and made me an instructor. My crew was peeved. It wasn't just a matter of losing their navigator; most crews were superstitious, and mine felt that their luck was being messed with. But you could understand Bomber Command's thinking. Our planes were ill-equipped for night navigation, and there was a knack to dead reckoning in a blackout. I seemed to have it, and I suppose they thought I'd be of more value passing it on to others.

My replacement was a boy of no more than my own age, also straight out of training. His name was Terriss. He, the plane, and its entire crew were lost on the next mission. I fretted out the rest of the war in one classroom or another.

And was still doing that, I supposed.

How long now? Thirty seconds, perhaps. I breathed out, and then drew warm air back in from the bag.

It tasted of rubber and canvas. A stale taste. The rebreather air was oddly unsatisfying, but its recirculation relieved the aching pressure that had been building up in my lungs.

I looked across at one of the empty seats, and the shadows in the harness looked back.

That's how it was. I'm not saying I saw an actual shape there. But the shadows fell as if playing over one. I turned my head to look at the other empty seat on that side of the cabin, and the figure in it raised its head to return my gaze.

The blood was pounding in my ears. I was forgetting the drill with the rebreather. Light glinted on the figure's flying goggles. On the edge of my vision, which was beginning to close in as the oxygen ran down, I was aware of someone in the third and last seat in the cabin right alongside me.

That was enough. I didn't stop to think. I admit it, I just panicked. All procedure was gone from my head. I just wanted to get out of there and back up to the surface.

I was not in control of the situation. I wondered if I was hallucinating, much as you can know when you're in a nightmare and not have it help.

Now I was gripping the sides of the bucket seat and trying to heave myself out of it but, of course, the harness held me in. My reaction was a stupid one. It was to try harder, over and over, slamming against resistance until the webbing cut into my shoulders and thighs. I was like a small child, angrily trying to pound a wooden peg through the wrong shape of hole.

Panic was burning up my oxygen. Lack of oxygen was making my panic worse. Somewhere in all of this I managed the one clear thought that I was never going to get out of the Box if I didn't unbuckle my harness first.

It was at this point that the nonexistent figure in the seat opposite leaned forward. In a smooth, slow move, it reached out and placed its hand over my harness release. The goggled face looked into my own. Between the flat glass lenses and the mask, no part of its flesh could be seen. For a moment I believed that it had reached over to help me out. But it kept its hand there, covering the buckle. Far from helping me, it seemed intent on preventing my escape.

I felt its touch. It wore no gloves. I'd thought that my own hand might pass through it as through a shadow, but it was as solid as yours or mine. When I tried to push it aside, it moved beneath my own as if all the bones in it had been broken. They shifted and grated like gravel inside a gelid bag.

When I tried to grab it and wrench it away, I felt its fingers dig in. I was trying with both hands now, but there was no breaking that grip. I somehow lost the re-breather mouthpiece as I blew out, and saw my precious breath go boiling away in a gout of bubbles. I wondered if Buster would see them break the surface but of course they wouldn't, they'd just collect and slide around inside the floor pan of the Box until it was righted again.

I had a fight not to suck water back into my emptied lungs. Some dead hand was on my elbow. It had to be one of the others. It felt like a solicitous touch, but it was meant to hamper me. Something else took a firm grip on my ankle. Darkness was overwhelming me now. I was being drawn downward into an unknown place.

And then, without sign or warning, it was over. The Box was revolving up into the light, and all the water was emptying out through every space and opening. As the level fell, I could see all around me. I could see the other seats, and they were as empty as when the session had begun.

I was still deaf and disoriented for a few seconds, and it lasted until I tilted my head and shook the water out of my ears. I had to blow some of it out of my nose as well, and it left me with a sensation like an ice cream headache.

My harness opened easily, but once I'd undone it I didn't try to rise. I wasn't sure I'd have the strength. I gripped the seat arms and hung on as the Box was lowered.

I was still holding on when Buster Brown looked in through one of the window holes and said, "What happened?"

"Nothing," I said.

He was not impressed. "Oh, yes?"

"Had a bit of a problem releasing the buckle. Something seemed to get in the way."

"Like what?"

"I don't know."

He looked at the unsecured harness and said, "Well, it seems to be working well enough now."

I'd thought I could brazen it through, but my patience went all at once. "Just leave it, will you?" I exploded, and shoved him aside as I climbed out.

I never did tell Buster what I'd seen. That lost me his friendship, such as it was. I went on sick leave for three weeks, and during that time I applied for a transfer to another department. My application was successful, and they moved me onto the fire-fighting course. If they hadn't, I would have resigned altogether. There was no force or duty on earth that could compel me into the tank or anywhere near the Box again.

The reason, which I gave to no one, was simple enough. I knew that if I ever went back, they would be waiting. Terriss, and all the others in my crew. Though the choice had not been mine, I had taken away their luck. Now they kept a place for me among them, there below the sea.

Wherever the sea might be found. Far from being haunted, the Box was a kind of tabula rasa. It had no history, and it held no ghosts. Each man brought his own.

My days are not so different now. As before they begin in the classroom, with forms and briefings and breathing apparatus drill. Then we go out into the grounds, first to where a soot-stained, mocked-up tube of metal stands in for a burning air-craft, and then on to a maze of connected rooms that we pump full of smoke before sending our students in to grope and stumble their way to the far exit.

They call these rooms the Rat Trap, and they are a fair approximation of the haz-ard they portray. Some of the men emerge looking frightened and subdued. When pressed, they speak of presences in the smoke, of unseen hands that catch at their sleeves and seem to entreat them to remain.

I listen to their stories. I tell them that this is common.

And then I sign their certificates and let them go.

FRANCES HARDINGE

Halfway House

Frances Hardinge's story was published in the third and final issue of Edge-wood Press's elegant and literary fantasy magazine Alchemy. *The author of an inventive and charming young adult novel,* Fly by Night, *the first of three connected novels, Hardinge studied English at Oxford University, where she was a founding member of a writers' workshop and won a magazine short story competition. She lives in England.*

—K.L. & G.G.

Would you mind holding her for just a moment? I won't be long." The baby did not cry as it was handed over. It was beyond the age of prune-faced screaming at any strange hands. Its eyes were marbles of drugged and pompous incredulity, its mouth pursed to blow tiny bubbles. Its head wobbled, and its limbs floated vaguely like an astronaut's.

Instinctively supporting its head, the boy took the child and watched the mother walk off down the carriage way, the fabric about the slit in her skirt twitching with her stride.

We're in a station, he thought. How does she know I won't run off with her baby? He let little fingers fiddle with his blazer lapel as he watched four pigeons mob a crisp packet on the platform. After two minutes the carriage juddered, and the little scuffle slid away to the left, yielding to verges of purple loosestrife and the combed gold of fields. Twenty minutes later, the mother had not returned.

So Kaiser took the baby home.

"Look what I got."

Eve looked up from sweeping the wood shavings, her long, thick pigtails swinging with the motion.

"Where'd you get it?" she asked, in her quiet man-voice.

"Someone give it to me." Kaiser sat the baby down on the cold cobbles. The nappy padded it into duck proportions, and propped it upright. Unfocused, it watched a butterfly, and dribbled at it.

"It needs better eyes. And paint." Having delivered her professional advice Eve sat and went on whittling, curls of white wood falling unregarded into her lap.

"No. She needs a name."

"Sharmadyne's got lots at the moment. He found a book on Latin names for mushrooms."

"I don't want to call her mushroom." The baby took drunken fistfuls of shavings and found it could crush them. "What's a word for something nice?"

"Forever," said Sharmadyne, from the balustrade above.

"Biscuit," said Eve.

"No. Wrong." Kaiser frowned his forehead into a crisscross, like a teacher's mark, echoing his word "wrong." "What's a word for something quiet?"

"Death," said Wolf from his easy chair, removing his hat from his face.

"Cloud," said Sharmadyne.

"Biscuit," said Eve.

"Library."

"Small rock."

"Mushrooms can be very, very quiet," said Sharmadyne, hopefully.

Wrong, said Kaiser's frown.

"What else do you get on trains?"

"Arguments and plastic foam cups."

"Horses."

"That's not trains, Eve, that was something else and they don't have them any-more."

The baby hardly heard the boom of voices. Her hand wouldn't hold the shavings properly, and the white flakes of crack and crackle went off to play with the wind and wouldn't wait for her.

They called her Ticket and left it at that.

Years went by. They installed automatic doors on the trains and little screens that scrolled luminous station names. Many of the smaller stations closed down, and signs appeared everywhere telling bombs to be alert.

The negotiations went badly in London, and Paul left his briefcase on the Circle Line. The jacket with the redundancy papers in the pocket he left on the train from Paddington to Ardenbeck. Seated now in a heat-stiffened shirt on a second train to his home in darkest Wiltshire, he had made a neat pile on the table before him of his tie, his fountain pens, and the key to his company car. While he carefully kicked off his shoes and considered getting off at the next station to walk in the fields, a wasp was noisily going about the clumsy business of dying against the window.

A little boy was lying on the floor. A mild concern that the child had been over-come by heat or succumbed to some illness pulled Paul out of his own thoughts. As he watched, an elderly woman hobbled down the aisle hugging plastic-packed sand-wiches to her chest, carefully stepped over the prone form, and continued. Paul leaned forward for a better look.

The boy wore a school uniform of sky blue and smoke gray, the tie looped and knotted into a rough cravat-bow. He lay with his head under one of the tables, tongue tip pushed out at the corner of his mouth in concentration. With a penknife he was levering at the underside of the table, working loose the cement gray wedges of aban-doned chewing gum. The family seated about the table moved their feet to let him wriggle this way and that, without a break in their conversation.

The boy squirmed out, crawling to Paul's table without a glance upward. He lifted Paul's shoes, looked them in and out, peered at the soles, then knotted the laces and slung them about his neck. Rising to his knees he cast a quick glance about, like a hare reared to watchfulness. The little pile of Paul's life apparently caught his attention. The boy glanced up at him with eyes grub gray as pencil rub-bings, seemed to make some assessment, then swept the heap into his palm and filled his pocket. As an apparent afterthought he reached across and plucked the dead wasp from beside the window.

The next stop was not listed on the neon scroll. No one looked up to note the place sign on the platform. The doors opened for the boy to step out. After a moment's hesitation, Paul found his feet and followed, the door sliding to just behind him.

The windows of the little station house were dusted dull as ice, and dandelions had insinuated their way through its lower bricks. No one stood on the platform before him, and the track behind him was empty.

To his left, a meadow was visible through the frame of a stile. Between the bars he saw the bobbing of a fair, little head, receding as if its owner were running. Paul moved to the stile, the paving stones warming him through his socks.

A ragged route had been trampled through a plain of sunflowers. Paul stumbled along it through the choke of pollen, blinded with black and gold, his mind too taken with prickle and stab of stalks in his shins and the weight of sun on his skull to notice the thousands of heads turning slowly as he passed, following his progress with hot black eyes as if facing for the sun.

The hedgerows seemed larger, the way he remembered them as a boy, and he was only a little surprised to find himself crawling through a hole in the underbelly of one, burring his clothes and running a thorn up under his thumbnail. Halfway through, the briar playfully set its teeth in his shirt and refused to release him. He strained, and twisted, and ceased, and panted, and heard.

Music there was, a breathless breath of it. It was tuneless and unseemly, like a wind chime jumble. It was ritualized and right, like birdsong. Paul reached back and loosed his clothes from the brambles.

He had forgotten the late summer stills, with their hanging menace and their eternities of blinding sky. A thousand leaves wavered and watched his clumsy progress, flashing blue-white as the sun caught their sleek. The corn stubble was striped with tree shadow like the belly of a tiger, and the wind was hot as breath. A hedge rose high as two men and beyond it windows blazed white, windows in colored capsules slung like carry cots on a great frame. With the appearance of the big wheel, the music began to phrase itself freakishly. My bonny lies over the ocean, it sang. Paul saw the pointed pinnacles of pavilions, see, pink, white, yellow, or striped like raspberry ripple. We'll meet again, sang the music. Paul found a slim stile half buried in the foliage. *Trill, tinkle, clang*, sang the music. *Clang*, sang the music. *Clang, cling, clang.*

Tarpaulin flapped on the skeleton of the big wheel, and the canvas of the pavilion tents was sun-bleached, greenish pools gathered in its folds. Some still stood erect under decades of bird trophies, while others sagged like failed cakes. A rough roof of corrugated iron rusted over the ghost train, where three peeling specters gaped from the painted wall. Four white geese huddled and gossiped nervously. In the center of the old fairground two women worked. One wore a leather apron and swung a hammer onto a great gray anvil, a hammer that sang *clang, clang, cling, clang*. The other sat cross-legged a few yards away, hands busy and head bowed low.

The standing woman was manly in proportion and motion. She had the thick neck and firm jaw of a Rossetti female. The simple, girlish cut of her patchily dyed blue dress, combined with her heavy, black pigtails, gave her the appearance of a youthful giantess. The other woman was light and slight as straw. The hair of her lowered head was a rich toffee gold and tied back in a vaguely archaic manner. Her skin was golden pale and dimly dappled, like corn as it loses its green.

"Do you like her?" The boy sat on the stile just behind Paul, rolling a gobstopper from one cheek to another. "She's mine."

"She's your sister?" Paul assumed he had misheard.

"No, she's mine. I found her."

Kaiser took the sweet out of his mouth and held it to the sun. It glowed like an emerald.

"Are you selling or buying or dying?" he asked.

Paul rose and walked forward toward the two women. The taller laid down her hammer to watch him, eyes wide, brown, and frightless. The other worked, apparently oblivious. Her pale lashes darkened toward the tips, and her fingers seemed unnaturally slender and rapid. They fashioned corn dolls, ribbon throated, who raised their fingerless hands to their invisible mouths as if blowing a kiss or smothering a scream. She wore a red ribbon about her own throat, stark as a gash of poppies in a cornfield.

Kaiser felt a certain proprietorial pride as the stranger seated himself beside Ticket and watched her work in rapt silence.

Paul put out a hand to touch one of the corn dolls, but halted at the last moment. The dolls were too much like the girl herself. Touching them casually seemed a violation. It would have been akin to handling their creator like an object for sale.

Looking at her he felt an ache of the mind, like the feather touch of a forgotten word. The word was almost palpable, it already belonged to him, it would make sense of every sentence in his life, but it was held from him by something insubstantial as a bubble-skin. He almost felt that if he touched her hand he would tear through this barrier into a rich new world, but there was a fear that if the bubble burst she would vanish with it.

Uncertainly, Paul reached across to the pile of corn at her side, and began sorting the stalks into groups of the same length for her. She picked up the four longest and started to fashion them without giving him a glance, but when she finished the doll she placed it next to Paul rather than with the pile at her feet. This doll had a twisting straw skirt, woven to look as if it had been flung out by wind or whirling motion, the hem describing slow dips and rises. As if the meshing were coming undone, the little figure started to twist on itself, the skirt's undulation shifting. As Paul watched, however, the doll twisted the other way, its crude hands seeming to drag at its ribbon collar. The pale girl's face remained calm as milk while her doll thrashed slowly to and fro, threads of torn straw jutting from its knobbed joints.

"She didn't used to be like that," remarked Kaiser. "Her head was all pink, and bald, and empty like a balloon. Then she got hair, like chick feathers, and Wolf wanted to borrow her but I said no. I let him borrow a baby bird once, and when he gave it back it wasn't the same anymore." Kaiser ceased, a shadow of a frown creasing his forehead. There was something too eager in the way the stranger watched the girl, as if he were feeding on her, as if somehow he could draw her in through his eyes and steal her away.

"She's mine," repeated Kaiser.

Wolf strolled in from trawling the spilt oil in the gutter puddles, his eyes shining like grease and his pockets full of rainbows. Wolf, whose smile went on and on like a horizon. Wolf in his great coat with the bird-skull buttons. Wolf straddled on the bar of the little roundabout, kicking the ground away and away with his cowboy boots. The stranger's defeat was in his nose, so he grinned, and watched, and waited for him to die.

"She's mine," whispered Kaiser.

"No harm in him looking, if he's here to buy." Eve propped the metal claw she had been fashioning on the anvil. It drew its nails along the metal with a screech, and felt blindly for the edge with a clatter like cutlery. "You know the rules. Everything is for trade."

"Ticket goes away now. Ticket goes away to sleep." Kaiser raised his voice slightly.

The girl stood and moved off toward the helter-skelter. The rattle of feet on the metal stairway dwindled, until a pale face appeared for an instant at the uppermost window. Then a thin hand reached out to pull across the tarpaulin like a curtain.

Paul realized suddenly that it was evening, and could not swear that he had not spent a whole day staring at the straw-fair girl, or watching her ascend her clown-painted tower. His mind told him he was alone now in the dusk, but the part of his mind that smelt the mud cooked to the crack and understood the ache in the wood pigeon's cry could hear the stir of steps, and voices that seemed to settle on his mind like dust, rather than passing through the medium of his ears. When he slept he dreamed dimly of the long-faced man who widdershinned about and about in the gray light, watching him with hot, black eyes as great as sunflowers and waiting for him to die.

Paul woke to the smell of frying bacon. A slender, little man, quick as a stoat, was stirring the contents of a great, charcoal black pan with fastidious care. His velvet waistcoat wore its black and blue ink stains like bruises.

"Still here, young man? I thought you came here to die." The older man's eyes twinkled like quartz chips in an old wall. "Gave up your shoes, didn't you? Weren't planning to go anywhere. Gave up your wallet, didn't you? It had your name in it. Shouldn't give away your name if you're still going to be using it." The tall man with the broad-brimmed hat and the many-layered coat strolled past, pulled a piece of bacon out of the hot fat, tossed it, and snapped it out of the air with his teeth. He strolled away, pulling the rind loose from the clamp of his grin. "He thinks you're his, anyway. Wolf does. Longer you stay here, the more he'll watch for you."

With slender tongs the diminutive chef drew one rasher from the pan and held it slightly raised, like someone teaching a dog to beg.

"Three words," he demanded.

"Please?" suggested Paul, perplexed.

"Please is an old word. Only new words are any use to me." Bewildered, Paul rattled off a term he had encountered in a computer manual, a makeshift word from an advertising jingle and one of the indelicate little euphemisms for redundancy he had heard used by the personnel manager the day before. A second later his hand was full of hot, greasy bacon, and the words he had just spoken were withering in his head like leaves, losing their meaning. Paul left the other man smoothing back his gray hair and repeating the new words over and over, as if he could taste them.

On the steps of the fortune-teller's hut Wolf chewed a grass stem and watched Ticket as she sewed the new patches onto his coat. Paul recognized their navy-blue fabric as that of his own jacket, which he had abandoned on the Ardenbeck train. Elsewhere the coat was padded and patched with tweed of catkin grays and greens, plastic from refuse sacks, fringed brown suede, canary-colored polyester, rayon red and great swathes of boot leather, still studded with lace holes and buckle straps.

Eve backed out of the fortune-teller's tent, ducking under the fringes of its Persian rug roof. She was rubbing at three long gashes in her forearm.

"It must be finished," she said by way of explanation. "Last night it ate all the mice." She closed the wooden slatted door behind her, carefully, drawing across the dozen or so knitting needles that served the function of bolts.

"Hullo," she said, on seeing Paul. "Kaiser said you were here to die, but you're not, are you? I'm Evening Performance. You don't have a name anymore, do you?" Ticket bit through the thread, then folded one hand in another and gazed into her palm. "What are you looking for? I do leavings soup and goose fool. I do animals too, but they tend to come out strange. What you lost? I got socks and watches and manners. I got safety pins and teaspoons and those metal things with handles that you kept under the stairs and couldn't find when you moved house. I got spirit levels and rubber bands and ambitions and bottle openers. I got lots of wedding rings." Paul crouched beside Ticket, feeling her awareness of him like sun. "You want her? Talk to Kaiser."

Kaiser at this moment was waking in his tiny bed in the baby blue carriage of the big wheel, to find that the wind had blown the wheel around and left him at the apex. This did nothing to improve his temper. Goose-feather beds were, he was assured, supposed to be the epitome of luxury, but he found that the feathers tickled his nose, and blew everywhere when he sneezed. Besides this, they pricked at him, and embedded themselves in his clothes. Shaking them like snow from his hair, he climbed from his precariously swinging cradle, and slid down the bar of the wheel to the axle, then dropped to earth, still shedding feathers like a mangled cherub.

Rising from his knees he saw Paul, still breathing, still in fascinated contemplation of the gold-white girl. Wrong, said Kaiser's frown, wrong.

"I'll buy her from you. For a day."

"Just a day?"

"A day." Paul slipped off his wristwatch and after a pause the boy took it. With adjustment to the strap it fitted his chubby wrist.

Ticket stood and lifted her eyes. They were blue-violet, and blinding. They filled the sky, and suddenly it was evening. Paul knew that they had walked alone for a whole day. She had opened her pale mouth, and he had seen the warm pink of her inner lip as she had said things that startled him immensely, and which he forgot immediately. He felt an appalled, poignant sense of loss, like a condemned man who wakes to find he has slept sweetly through his last few hours of life. Ticket lowered her eyes and drifted away in the direction of the helter-skelter. She wore a new necklace of beads that gleamed black and gold. Their pattern bothered Paul, and he suddenly recalled the trapped, frustrated battering of the wasp against its glass prison. He heard the dim clatter of her steps, like a nail being run down a metal comb.

The next day he bought breakfast from Sharmadyne with some obscure terms he had encountered in a *Times* crossword. Then he bought an afternoon with Ticket for three ballpoints and a pencil rubber. The time was sweet and melted to nothing in an instant, like candy floss. He slept with a haunting sense that she had told him things with greatest earnestness, things that had slid off his mind like water off wax.

The next day he traded a handful of nicknames for a bowlful of blackbird stew. Then he bought a few hours with Ticket for a cigarette lighter and both his socks.

All this while Wolf watched him with a taxidermist's eye.

Eve watched too, as she rolled out mouse biscuits for the thing in her tent.

"You'll have to set a final price on her, you know," she told Kaiser. "You'll get a decent price. She's becoming a Maker, and a good one."

"I think I'm going to keep her."

"It's against the rules. We don't really own anything. It just passes through our hands, and sometimes we change it, that's all. He has asked you to set a price, and you must do so."

So Kaiser set a price, and Paul agreed to hand over his dreams. Ticket saw it happen, saw the fine handful of gold, frail as corn, pass from the hand of the stranger to that of her owner and could do nothing to prevent it. She could only watch as a blind numbness spread across the stranger's face, and she felt herself vanish from his view.

Paul was woken from his brown study by the slamming of the restaurant door. The clock on the wall showed three hours were still to run before lunch. He snatched up the mop to swab the spillage from the kebab racks, dodging the waitresses and ignoring the stink of grease. He stooped to pick up the trampled litter and flung it binward. The sesame seeds got up under his fingernails.

"You're his now," laughed Kaiser. "Go where he goes! Do anything he says!" Ticket watched Paul furiously sweeping at the ashes and shavings of the fairground floor, dodging imaginary obstacles. A goose fled the thrust of his broom and turned to hiss. Paul wrinkled his nose as if he heard the hiss of rancid meat cooking in its own fat. He looked up and at her, and through her, and reflected in his eyes she saw a dowdy, introverted stranger as irrelevant to his thoughts as a window handle might be to the wasp dedicated to beating itself to death against glass.

Kaiser had a laugh like a barnful of roosters.

Wolf slept in the ghost train, coat shielding his head like a bat's wing, hat hung on the broomstick of a plastic witch. Kaiser curled like a nestling in a mass of birds' feathers, sheep's wool, and cotton scraps, rocked to slumber at the top of the Big Wheel. Sharmadyne cushioned his head with a book of birds in the souvenir stall, and dreamed of dictionaries. Ticket lay cocooned in tablecloths and curtains in her boudoir at the top of the helter-skelter. Paul slept leaning against the anvil in the yard, hugging his broom like a mate. Eve sat up in the fortune-teller's tent and made moccasins out of jacket lining.

She moved carefully about her tent to avoid waking her creations, her rounded limbs rolling to and fro slowly like peaches on a bough. The bottle opener stirred and rasped its razorbill in sleep, then settled. The spirit in the spirit level lay dormant. From the pocket of the apron of bat-wing leather Eve drew a small hammer with a broad head.

She opened a box at the back of the room, fingering the contents carefully. Two white gloves. A scarf of black silk. A folded poster of a dapper man in a top hat, with white, white teeth, and "Evening Performance" blazoned on a stylized banner above his head. A ball of glass, palm-size.

Eve muffled the globe in muslin, and carefully tapped it with the hammer until it broke. She continued tapping, crushing it to powder.

Out she crept, bearing navy-blue moccasins and a muslin bag full of dream. Paul woke when she poured the crushed glass into his opened hand. Reflexively he tried to shake it out of his palm, but she prevented him and closed his hand upon the glittering pile.

"It's all I got of dreams," she hissed. "I don't know how long it'll last you, but hold on to it as long as you can, however much it hurts." Then she cut off all his shirt buttons as payment.

Ticket was awake long before Eve reached the topmost stair of the helter-skelter. She rose, already dressed and quite composed, pulling a cloth from an object beside her. They carried it down between them, and left it upright in the yard.

Paul was dizzy and his hand hurt. With half his mind he saw the dingy lodgings that he knew to be his home, with the black beetles behind the radiator and the tiny crackling television, and with the other he saw Ticket take him by the hand and lead him through nocturnal fields, fleeing the pale stain of dawn. Desperately he clung to the latter image, even while the tiny shards of the crystal ball penetrated his skin. He clung to the early morning chill, and the stab of corn stubble through his moccasins.

The wind turned the big wheel once more, and when dawn came Kaiser awoke to find himself a mere yard from the ground. He alighted from his little cabin like a lord from a carriage, shaking the plumes out of his shorts. There lay the broom, crusted with wood shavings. Where was Paul?

"Where's the man without a name?"

"Can't have gone far." Eve was varnishing a terrapin Wolf had traded her the day before. "Got no dreams, can't see where he's going. Got no shoes, can't run anywhere. Maybe he died, and Wolf took him." A few yards away, Ticket sat in her usual place, intensely studying an object in her palm.

Wolf did not take kindly to having his sleep interrupted and most found excuses to avoid trespassing upon his territory. Kaiser was just resolving to question him later when the wind picked up. The figure of Ticket toppled, and tumbled, and was torn open by the wind as it skittered and rolled over the fairground floor. A papier-mâché mask fell loose. Bundles of stripped maple wood fingers tumbled from the sleeves. The straw gold hair was straw, and the thing in the bleach blue muslin dress was a corn doll, made to the size of life by cunning fingers.

Kaiser had a scream like a fox feast in a chicken coop.

The door of the ghost train was flung wide. Wolf gave a low growl like a lawn-mower engine and shielded his yellow eyes from the sun. Kaiser stood in the doorway, his frown like a crisscross brand on his forehead.

"Where are they?" he demanded. Things rattled down the overhead rail and dangled in the dark like malevolent puppets, leather-skinned and glass-eyed, waiting to observe their master's will. They watched his hands in the brown leather gloves, with the knuckle creases and the nails attached, for the signal to attack, but it did not come. Wolf saw Kaiser's frown and blinked like a chidden dog.

"They run through the sunflowers," he said.

Ticket heard the distant scream of rage and felt the air change. The early morning sunlight was suddenly paler, and she suddenly seemed to move through silt. The sunflowers around them ceased to thresh their heads indiscriminately in the freshening wind, and started to turn their broad, singed-looking faces to watch the passage of the pair. Wolf is awake, she thought. Wolf sees.

A bank of cloud was racing with impossible speed in their pursuit, borne by a wind that howled like a thousand little deaths. Kaiser is awake, she thought. Kaiser comes.

Paul she had to lead each step, to stop him casting a foot from the ragged path through the flowers. Sometimes he would pause, and gaze around blindly, so that it took all her effort to keep him moving. Even as she struggled to support his weight upon her slender arm, she could see behind his eyes her newfound miracle, a wounded, smoky, human mind, half-blind but blood-warmed.

All the while Ticket's own mind was in moth-wing motion, for her thoughts were as fast as her fingers. From her fosterfolk she had learned the importance of gathering up the unregarded, and so for years she had silently collected negligently cast remarks and stored them for future use.

She narrowed her eyes. The air was full of the hiss of the wind snakes. Reaching up she caught one by its tail. The tug nearly pulled her from her feet, but she hooked her toes among the sunflower roots and held on. Drawing the snake in like a rope, she forced its tail into its own mouth. The wind snake whirled about and about, trying to loose itself. Taking off her necklace, Ticket pulled loose the wasp-body beads and cast them into the little whirlwind behind her, and hurried on.

Kaiser raged onward like a forest fire with a following gale. The corn parted before him as if in fear, and the birds drew in their voices. He danced a dance of rage down the little path that zig-a-zagged like a frightened hare through the coal-faced flowers.

The whirl of the crippled wind snake caught him unaware. It spun him around so that he almost lost his footing and fell into the grip of Wolf's flowers. Then the wasp bellies struck, and stuck, and stung and stung again. Covering his face he retreated, and fled back to the fairground.

Kaiser ran to the fortune-teller's tent, hopping with fury and howling like a storm rising. Eve had hidden her great square bulk under the table and peered out fearfully as he entered, through a hole in the checkered cloth.

"I need to borrow your car," he said. Eve covered her earth brown eyes with her great hands. She heard the catches of the closet open. She heard Kaiser trill as he took the rein of the thing within. She heard the clatter of aluminum hooves and a cry like a violin being tuned.

It was bigger than Kaiser expected, and he had to pull half of Eve's tent loose from the peggings to get it out.

Ticket looked about the hill for Kaiser's railway station, but saw not a trace of it. There was a field full of pale horses with terra-cotta manes, but not an inch of brick and mortar, nor the dimmest glint of a railway line. She struggled up the hill, one hand hoisting her skirt up to stop her tripping, the other dragging Paul behind her as he complained of the rainy streets and asked to go back to his bed.

Behind her she heard the wind bring a harsh music of different noises. There was a chorus of squeaks like an orchestra of bicycle wheels, or a war of metal mice. There was a whish and hush like scythes cutting air or the slice of great wings.

At the very apex of the hill, in the place that Paul had described, Ticket found the station. She found the ravaged cassette tape with its loosened ribbon that fluttered and gleamed like a metal track as it looped about the shoebox with the clumsily drawn windows and door. A rusted toy train the size of her thumb lay nearby on its side. There was nothing else, only a tumble of litter and leavings.

Behind her the music was clearer. There was a sound like the whetting of knives. There was a long hunting call like a baby foghorn.

Ticket seated herself on the thick grass and started to work. Her fingers became a white whirl, like the churn of a moth's wings. Cans she crushed into carapaces, rending them to provide aluminum teeth. Crisp packets fluttered under her hands like wings. Corn stalks jointed into legs and clawed the air unsensingly. She drenched their wings in dew, and in the rage of patience. One after another she flung them into the air.

Kaiser's frown was black as wrought iron, like the crosses they use to stop walls bulging, and his face was red as brick. The wind snakes foamed against his reins. Behind him a wake was ravaged, and clods of earth thrown house-high. Before him hedges broke and corn scattered, torn aside by a thresh of metal and claw, and a flounder of hoof. He sounded the horn again, and the horse skull opened and screamed. The sun hid its face.

Down the hill surged Ticket's butterflies. They came upon Kaiser with a whicker and a flutter, on wings made of tinfoil and TV dinner packages, of sandwich crusts and cellophane. Their limbs swiveled in joints of chewing gum, and they stared with bottle-top eyes. With metal-gash mouths they caught and bit.

Eve's car veered crazily as its driver lost control. It floundered through thickets, snapping off bones, blades, handles, and appendages against the low-hanging boughs. The butterflies followed. A wheel spun loose, and the vehicle careered over a bracken ridge to plunge and tumble down the scarp to ruin in the hollow below. The butterflies flitted overhead, looking for Kaiser. What did they find?

A school uniform with the seams mended too many times, and a tie knotted beyond recovery. A little flesh-pink plush, and a black cross of iron. A paper bag of sweets that had glued themselves into one multicolored mass. A frog, a snail, and a furred something shorter than a finger. An empty packet of cigarettes marked "Kaiser Kingsize."

The butterflies had weakened their frail fixings by their exertions. They tumbled loose and scattered. Now there was nothing moving on the slope but a handful of litter that rolled before the wind.

Later Wolf found the pieces of Kaiser and collected them, weeping. He took them back to Eve the Maker to see if she could mend them.

Paul paused by a shop window and viewed his reflection with discontent. He yawned and rubbed at the blue of his jaw. Beyond his own image, the glass-eyed girl in the blue dress suit tried to sell him soap from a thousand screens.

The straw blond girl with the folded hands still stood beside him. Had she been saying something? He had not been listening. She took his hand again, and he let her. He should be at work, but she was so insistent in her passive, quiet way. Perhaps he should humor her—she seemed a bit touched. Perhaps it would be nice to see that almost indiscernible pucker at the corners of her straight, little mouth become a smile.

Where had she come from? Had he met her at that party last night? Had he . . . well if he had she would probably tell him sooner or later.

Damn that party! He had woken that morning on a train with the girl's head resting against his shoulder, and his hand full of broken glass. Probably crushed a pint glass with his bare hand for a dare. He had bandaged it as best he could, and picked out the pieces. Nonetheless, his palm twinged sometimes, as if tiny shards had escaped his notice, had burrowed deep beneath his skin and remained within him.

With his uninjured hand, he gave the girl's palm a squeeze. She looked up to meet his gaze with something akin to a smile.

Ticket's eyes were blue-violet and blinding. Reflected in them he saw no trace of the grub gray heaven that ceilinged his world. He saw wide mauve skies freckled with the flight of birds, and seas of corn and grass, down gray in the dusk.

DELIA SHERMAN

La Fée Verte

Delia Sherman's historical fantasy "La Fée Verte" originally appeared in Ellen Datlow and Terri Windling's anthology, Salon Fantastique. *Sherman has published four novels,* The Porcelain Dove, Through a Brazen Mirror, The Fall of the Kings *(with Ellen Kushner), and* Changeling. *Sherman is one of the founders of the Interstitial Arts Foundation and, with Theodora Goss, she recently coedited* Interfictions: An Anthology of Interstitial Writing. *Sherman makes her home in New York City.*

—K.L. & G.G.

Winter 1868

When Victorine was a young whore in the house of Mme Boulard, her most intimate friend was a girl called La Fée Verte.

Victorine was sixteen when she came to Mme Boulard's, and La Fée Verte some five years older. Men who admired the poetry of Baudelaire and Verlaine adored La Fée Verte, for she was exquisitely thin, with the bones showing at her wrist and her dark eyes huge and bruised in her narrow face. But her chief beauty was her pale, fine skin, white almost to opalescence. Embracing her was like embracing absinthe made flesh.

Every evening, Victorine and La Fée Verte would sit in Mme Boulard's elegant parlor with Madame, her little pug dog, and the other girls of the establishment, waiting. In the early part of the evening, while the clients were at dinner, there was plenty of time for card-playing, for gossip and a little apéritif, for reading aloud and lounging on a sofa with your head in your friend's lap, talking about clothes and clients and, perhaps, falling in love.

Among the other girls, La Fée Verte had the reputation of holding herself aloof, of considering herself too good for her company. She spoke to no one save her clients, and possibly Mme Boulard. Certainly no one spoke to her. The life of the brothel simply flowed around her, like water around a rock. Victorine was therefore astonished when La Fée Verte approached her one winter's evening, sat beside her on the red velvet sofa, and began to talk. Her green kimono fell open over her bony frame and her voice was low-pitched and a little rough—pleasant to hear, but subtly disturbing.

Her first words were more disturbing still.

"You were thirteen, a student at the convent when you grandmother died. She was your stepfather's mother, no blood kin of yours, but she stood between you and your stepfather's anger, and so you loved her—the more dearly for your mother's having died when you were a child. You rode to her funeral in a closed carriage with her youngest son, your stepuncle."

Victorine gaped at her, moving, with each phrase, from incredulity to fury to wonder. It was true, every word. But how could she know? Victorine had not told the story to anyone. How did she dare? Victorine had never so much as smiled at her.

La Fée Verte went on: "I smell old straw and damp, tobacco and spirits. I see your uncle's eyes—very dark and set deep as wells in a broad, bearded face. He is sweating as he looks at you, and fiddling in his lap. When you look away for shame, he put his hands upon you."

Victorine was half-poised to fly, but somehow not flying, half-inclined to object, but listening all the same, waiting to hear what La Fée Verte would say next.

"He takes your virginity hastily, as the carriage judders along the rutted lanes. He is done by the time it enters the cemetery. I see it stopping near your grandmother's grave, the coachman climbing down from his perch, opening the door. Your uncle, flushed with his exertions, straightens his frock coat and descends. He turns and offers you his hand. It is gloved in black—perfectly correct in every way, save for the glistening stains upon the tips of the fingers. I can see it at this moment, that stained glove, that careless hand."

As La Fée Verte spoke, Victorine watched her, mesmerized as her hands sketched pictures in the air and her eyes glowed like lamps. She looked like a magician conjuring up a vision of time past, unbearably sad and yet somehow unbearably beautiful. When she paused in the tale, Victorine saw that her great dark eyes were luminous with tears. Her own eyes filled in sympathy—for her own young self, certainly, but also for the wonder of hearing her story so transformed.

"You will not go to him," La Fée Verte went on. "Your uncle, impatient or ashamed, turns away, and you slip from the carriage and flee, stumbling in your thin slippers on the cemetery's stony paths, away from your grandmother's grave, from your uncle, from the convent and all you have known."

When the tale was done, La Fée Verte allowed her tears to overflow and trickle, crystalline, down her narrow cheeks. Enchanted, Victorine wiped them away and licked their bitter salt from her fingers. She was inebriated, she was enchanted. She was in love.

That night, after the last client had been waved on his way, after the gas had been extinguished and the front door locked, she lay in La Fée Verte's bed, the pair of them nested like exotic birds in down and white linen. La Fée Verte's dark head lay on Victorine's shoulder and La Fée Verte's dusky voice spun enchantment into Victorine's ear. That night, and many nights thereafter, Victorine fell asleep to the sound of her lover's stories. Sometimes La Fée Verte spoke of Victorine's childhood, sometimes of her first lover in Paris: a poet with white skin and a dirty shirt. He had poured absinthe on her thighs and licked them clean, then sent her, perfumed with sex and anise, to sell herself in cafés for the price of a ream of paper.

(There were other stories, too. La Fée Verte had at her command the life histories of all the great courtesans, past and present: La Dame aux Camellias, Cora Pearl the English whore, La Mogador, and a dozen other queens of their profession. To Victorine, these histories were like fairy-tales in which the princess does not wait passively to be saved from the witch's service, but orchestrates her own rescue, the prince [or princes] playing at most a secondary role in her adventures.)

These stories, even more than the caresses that accompanied them, simultaneously excited Victorine and laid a balm to her bruised soul. The sordid details of her past and present receded before La Fée Verte's romantic revisions. Little by little,

Victorine came to depend on them, as a drunkard depends on his spirits, to mediate between her and her life. Night after night, Victorine drank power from her lover's mouth and caressed tales of luxury from between her thighs. Her waking hours passed as if in a dream, and she submitted to her clients with a disdainful air, as if they'd paid to please her. Intrigued, they dubbed her la Reine, proud queen of whores, and courted her with silk handkerchiefs, kidskin gloves, and rare perfumes. For the first time sine she fled her uncle's carriage Victorine was happy.

Spring, 1869

That April, a new client came to Mme Boulard's, a writer of novels in the vein of M. Jules Verne. He was a handsome man with a chestnut moustache and fine, wavy hair that fell over a wide, pale brow. Bohemian though he was, he bought La Fée Verte's services—which did not come cheap—two or three evenings a week.

At first, Victorine was indifferent. This writer of novels was a client like other clients, no more threat to her dream-world than the morning sun. Then he began to occupy La Fée Verte for entire evenings, not leaving until the brothel closed at four in the morning and La Fée Verte was too exhausted to speak. Without her accustomed anodyne, Victorine grew restless, spiteful, capricious.

Her clients complained. Mme Boulard fined her a night's takings. La Fée Verte turned impatiently from her questions and then from her caresses. At last, wild with jealousy, Victorine stole to the peephole with which every room was furnished to see for herself what the novelist and La Fée Verte meant to each other.

Late as it was, the lamp beside the bed was lit. La Fée Verte was propped against the pillows with a shawl around her shoulders and a glass of opalescent liquid in her hand. The novelist lay beside her, his head dark on the pillow. An innocent enough scene. But Victorine could hear her lover's husky voice rising and falling in a familiar, seductive cadence.

"The moon is harsh and barren," La Fée Verte told the novelist, "cold rock and dust. A man walks there, armed and helmed from head to foot against its barrenness. He plants a flag in the dust, scarlet and blue and white, marching in rows of stripes and little stars. How like a man, to erect a flag, and call the moon his. I would go just to gaze upon the earth filling half the sky and the stars bright and steady—there is no air on the moon to make them twinkle—and then I'd come away and tell no-one."

The novelist murmured something, sleepily, and La Fée Verte laughed, low and amused. "I am no witch, to walk where there is no air to breathe and the heat of the sun dissipates into an infinite chill. Nevertheless I have seen it, and the vehicle that might carry a man so high. It is shaped like a spider, with delicate legs."

The novelist gave a shout of pleasure, leapt from the bed, fetched his notebook and his pen and began to scribble. Victorine returned to her cold bed and wept.

Such a state of affairs, given Victorine's nature and the spring's unseasonable warmth, could not last forever. One May night, Victorine left the salon pretending a call of nature, stole a carving knife from the kitchen, and burst into the room where La Fée Verte and her bourgeois bohemian were reaching a more conventional climax. It was a most exciting scene: the novelist heaving and grunting, La Fée Verte moaning, Victorine weeping and waving the knife, the other whores crowded at the door, shrieking bloody murder. The novelist suffered a small scratch on his buttock, La Fée Verte a slightly deeper one on the outside of her hip. In the morning she was gone, leaving blood-stained sheets and her green silk kimono with a piece of paper pinned to it bearing Victorine's name and nothing more.

Summer 1869–Winter 1870

Respectable women disappointed in love went into a decline or took poison, or at the very least wept day and night until the pain of their betrayal had been washed from their hearts. Victorine ripped the green kimono from neck to hem, broke a chamber pot and an erotic Sèvres grouping, screamed and ranted, and then, to all appearances, recovered. She did not forget her lost love or cease to yearn for her, but she was a practical woman. Pining would bring her nothing but ridicule, likely a beating, certainly a heavy fine, and she already owed Mme Boulard more than she could easily repay.

At the turn of the year, Victorine's luck changed. A young banker of solid means and stolid disposition fell under the spell of Victorine's beauty and vivacity. Charmed by his generosity, she smiled on him, and the affair prospered. By late spring, he had grown sufficiently fond to pay off Victorine's debt to Mme Boulard and install her as his mistress in a charming apartment in a building he owned on the fashionable rue Chaptal.

After the conventual life of a brothel, Victorine found freedom very sweet. Victorine's banker, who paid nothing for the apartment, could afford to be generous with clothes and furs and jewels—sapphires and emeralds, mostly to set off her blue eyes and red hair. She attended the Opera and the theatre on his arm and ate at the Café Anglais on the boulevard des Italiens. They walked in the Tuileries and drove in the Bois de Boulogne. Victorine lived like a lady that spring, and counted herself happy.

June 1870

Nemesis is as soft-footed as a cat stalking a bird, as inexorable, as unexpected. Victorine had buried all thoughts of La Fée Verte as deep in new pleasures and gowns and jewels as her banker's purse would allow. It was not so deep a grave that Victorine did not dream of her at night, or find her heart hammering at the sight of a black-haired woman with a thin, pale face. Nor could she bear to part with the torn green kimono, which she kept at the bottom of her wardrobe. But the pain was bearable, and every day Victorine told herself that it was growing less.

This fond illusion was shattered by the banker himself, who, as a treat, brought her a book, newly published, which claimed to be a true account of the appearance of the moon's surface and man's first steps upon it, to be taken far in an unspecified future. Victorine's banker read a chapter of it aloud to her after dinner, laughing over the rank absurdity of the descriptions and the extreme aridity of the subject and style. The next morning, when he'd left, Victorine gave it to her maid with instructions to burn it.

Victorine was not altogether astonished, when she was promenading down the Boulevard des Italiens some two or three weeks later, to see La Fée Verte seated in a café. It seemed inevitable, somehow: first the book, then the woman to fall into her path. All Paris was out in the cafés and bistros, taking what little air could be found in the stifling heat, drinking coffee and absinthe and cheap red wine. Why not La Fée Verte?

She had grown, if anything, more wraith-like since quitting Mme Boulard's, her skin white as salt under her smart hat, her narrow body sheathed in a tight green walking dress and her wild black hair confined in a snood. She was alone, and on the table in front of her was all the paraphernalia of absinthe: tall glass of jade green liquor, carafe of water, dish of sugar cubes, pierced silver spoon.

Victorine passed the café without pausing, but stopped at the jeweler's shop beside it and pretended an interest in the baubles displayed in the window. Her heart beat so she was almost sick with it. Having seen La Fée Verte, she must speak to her. But what would she say? Would she scold her for her faithlessness? Inquire after her lover? Admire her gown? No. It was impossible.

Having sensibly decided to let sleeping dogs lie, Victorine turned from the sparkling display and swept back to the café. While she had been hesitating, La Fée Verte had tempered her absinthe with water and sugar, and was lifting the resulting opaline liquid to her lips. There was a glass of champagne on the table, too, its surface foaming as if it had just that moment been poured.

Victorine gestured at the wine. "You are expecting someone."

"I am expecting you. Please, sit down."

Victorine sat. She could not have continued standing with that rough, sweet voice drawing ice along her nerves.

"You are sleek as a cat fed on cream," La Fée Verte said. "Your lover adores you, but you are not in love with him."

"I have been in love," Victorine said. "I found it very painful."

La Fée Verte smiled, very like the cat she'd described. "It is much better to be loved," she agreed. "Which you are, which you will always be. You are made to be loved. It is your destiny."

Victorine's temper, never very biddable, slipped from her control. "Are you setting up for a fortune-teller now?" she sneered. "It's a pity the future, as outlined in your lover's novel, appears so dull and unconvincing. I hope he still loves you, now that you've make him the laughing-stock of Paris. Your stories used to be much more artistic."

La Fée Verte made a little movement with her gloved hand, as of brushing aside an insect. "Those stories are of the past," she said. "Me, I have no past. My present is a series of photographs, stiff and without color. My future stares at me with tiger's eyes." She held Victorine's gaze until Victorine dropped her eyes, and then she said, "Go back to your banker. Forget you have seen me."

Victorine picked up her champagne and sipped it. She would have liked to throw the wine at La Fée Verte's head, or herself at La Fée Verte's narrow feet. But the past months had taught her something of self-control. She took money from her purse and laid it on the table and rose and said, "My destiny and my heart are mine to dispose of as I please. I will not forget you simply because you tell me to."

La Fée Verte smiled. "*Au revoir*, then. I fear we will meet again."

July–August 1870

La Fée Verte's prophecy did not immediately come to pass, possibly because Victorine avoided the neighborhood of the café where she'd seen La Fée Verte in case she might be living nearby. It was time, Victorine told herself, to concentrate on distracting her banker, who was much occupied with business as the General Assembly of France herded the weak-willed Emperor Napoleon III towards a war with Prussia. Kaiser Wilhelm was getting above himself, the reasoning ran, annexing here and meddling there, putting forward his own nephew as a candidate for the vacant Spanish throne.

"How stupid does he think we are?" the banker raged, pacing Victorine's charming salon and scattering cigar ashes on the Aubusson. "If Leopold becomes King of Spain, France will be surrounded by Hohenzollerns on every side and it will only be a matter of time before you'll be hearing German spoken on the Champs-Élysées."

"I hear it now," Victorine pointed out. "And Italian and a great deal of English. I prefer Italian—it is much more pleasing to the ear. Which reminds me: *La Bohème* is being sung at the Opera tonight. If you'll wait a moment while I dress, we should be in time for the third act."

Victorine was not a woman who concerned herself with politics. It was her fixed opinion that each politician was duller than the next, and none of them, save perhaps the Empress, who set the fashion, had anything to do with her. She did her best to ignore the Emperor's declaration of war on July 16 and the bellicose frenzy that followed it. When her banker spoke to her of generals and battles, she answered him with courtesans and opera-singers. When he wanted to go to the Hôtel de Ville to hear the orators, she made him go to the Eldorado to hear the divine Thérèsa singing of love. When he called her a barbarian, she laughed at him and began to think of finding herself a more amusing protector. Men admired her; several of the banker's friends had made her half-joking offers she'd half-jokingly turned aside. Any one of them would be hers for a smile and a nod. But none of them appealed to her, and the banker continued generous, so she put off choosing. She had plenty of time.

One Sunday in late August, Victorine's banker proposed a drive. Victorine put on a high-crowned hat with a cockade of feathers and they drove down the Champs-Élysées with the rest of fashionable Paris, headed towards the Bois de Boulogne, where the sky was clearer than within the city walls and the air was scented with leaves and grass.

As they entered the park, Victorine heard an unpleasant noise as of a building being torn down over the clopping of the horses' hooves. The noise grew louder, and before long the carriage drew even with a group of men wearing scarlet trousers and military kepis. They were chopping down trees.

The banker required his driver to stop. Victorine gaped at the men, sweating amid clouds of dust, and at the shambles of trampled grass, tree-trunks, and stumps they left in their wake. "Who are these men?" she demanded. "What are they doing?"

"They are volunteers for the new Mobile Guard, and they are clearing the Bois." He turned to her. "Victorine, the time has come for you to look about yourself. The Prussians are marching west. If Strasbourg falls, they will be at Paris within a month. Soon there will be soldiers quartered here, and herds of oxen and sheep. Soon every green thing you see will be taken within the walls to feed or warm Paris. If the Prussians besiege us, we will know hunger and fear, perhaps death."

Victorine raised her eyes to her lover's pink, stern face. "I cannot stop any of these things; what have they to do with me?"

He made an impatient noise. "Victorine, you are impossible. There's a time of hardship coming, a time of sacrifice. Pleasure will be forced to bow to duty, and I must say I think that France will be the better for it."

She had always known his mouth to be too small, but as he delivered this speech, it struck her for the first time as ridiculous, all pursed up like a sucking infant's under his inadequate moustache.

"I see," she said. "What do you intend to do?"

"My duty."

For all her vanity, Victorine was not a stupid woman. She had no need of La Fée Verte to foresee what was coming next. "I understand completely," she said. "And what of my apartment?"

He blinked as one awakened from a dream. "You may stay until you find a new one."

"And my furniture?"

The question, or perhaps her attitude, displeased him. "The furniture," he said tightly, "is mine."

"My clothes? My jewels? Are they yours also?"

He shrugged. "Those, you may keep. As a souvenir of happier times."

"Of happier times. Of course." Really, she could not look at his mouth any longer. Beyond him, she saw a tall chestnut tree sway and topple to the ground. It fell with a resounding crack, like thunder. The banker started; Victorine did not. "Well, that's clear enough." She put out her hand to him. "Good-bye."

He frowned. "I hadn't intended . . . I'd thought a farewell dinner, one last night together."

"With duty calling you? Surely not," Victorine said. He had not taken her hand; she patted his sweating cheek. "Adieu, my friend. Do not trouble yourself to call. I will be occupied with moving. And duty is a jealous mistress."

She climbed down from the carriage and walked briskly back along the path. She was not afraid. She was young, she was beautiful, and she had La Fée Verte's word that it was her destiny to be loved.

September, 1870

Victorine's new apartment was a little way from the grand boulevards, on the rue de la Tour, near the Montmartre abattoir. It was small—three rooms only—but still charming. When it came to the point, none of the admiring gentlemen had been willing to offer her the lease on a furnished house of her own, not with times so troubled. She had sent them all about their business, renting and furnishing the place herself on the proceeds from an emerald necklace and a sapphire brooch. She moved on September 3. When evening came, she looked about her at the chaos of half-unpacked trunks and boxes, put on her hat, and went out in search of something to eat, leaving her maid to deal with the mess alone.

Although it was dinnertime, everyone seemed to be out in the streets—grim-faced men, for the most part, too intent on their business to see her, much less make way for her. Passing a newspaper kiosk, she was jostled unmercifully, stepped upon, pushed almost into the gutter. A waving hand knocked her hat awry. Gruff voices battered at her ears.

"Have you heard? The Emperor is dead!"

"Not dead, idiot. Captured. It's bad enough."

"I heard dead, and he's the idiot, not me."

"Good riddance to him."

"The Prussians have defeated MacMahon. Strasbourg has fallen."

"Long live Trochu."

The devil take Trochu, Victorine thought, clutching purse and muff. A thick shoe came down heavily on her foot. She squealed with pain and was ignored. When she finally found a suitable restaurant, her hat was over her ear, and she was limping.

The Veau d'Or was small, twelve tables perhaps, with lace curtains at the windows and one rather elderly waiter. What made it different from a thousand other such establishments was its clientèle, which seemed to consist largely of women dressed in colors a little brighter and hats a little more daring than was quite respectable. They gossiped from table to table in an easy camaraderie that reminded Victorine at once of Mme Boulard's salon.

The conversations dropped at Victorine's entrance, and the elderly waiter moved forward, shaking his head.

"We are complete, Madame," he said.

Presented with an opportunity to vent her ill-temper, Victorine seized it with relief. "You should be grateful, Monsieur, that I am sufficiently exhausted to honor your establishment with my custom." She sent a disdainful glance around the room. "Me, I am accustomed to the company of a better class of tarts."

This speech elicited some indignant exclamations, some laughter, and an invitation from a dumpling-like blonde in electric blue to share her corner table.

"You certainly have an opinion of yourself," she said, as Victorine sat down, "for a woman wearing such a hat as that. What happened to it?"

Victorine removed the hat and examined it. The feather was broken and the ribbons crushed. "Men," she said, making the word a curse. "Beasts."

The blonde sighed agreement. "A decent woman isn't safe in the streets these days. What do you think of the news?"

Victorine looked up from the ruin of her hat. "News? Oh, the Emperor."

"The Emperor, the Prussians, the war. All of it."

"I think it is terrible," Victorine said, "if it means cutting down the Bois de Boulogne and stepping on helpless women. My foot is broken—I'm sure of it."

"One does not walk on a broken foot," the blonde said reasonably. "Don't spit at me, you little cat—I'm trying to be friends. Everyone needs friends. There's hard times ahead."

"Hard times be damned," Victorine said airily. "I don't expect they will make a difference, not to us. Men desire pleasure in hard times, too."

The blonde laughed. "Possibly; possibly not. We'll find out soon enough which of us is right." She poured some wine into Victorine's glass. "If you're not too proud for a word of advice from a common tart, I suggest you take the veal. It's the specialty of the house, and if it comes to a siege, we won't be able to get it anymore."

"Already I am bored by this siege," Victorine said.

"Agreed," said the blonde. "We will talk of men, instead."

That night, Victorine drank a glass of absinthe on her way home. It wasn't a vice she usually indulged in, finding the bitterness of the wormwood too intense and the resulting lightheadedness too unsettling. Tonight, she drank it down like medicine. When she got home, she dug the green kimono out of her wardrobe and fell into bed with it clasped in her arms, her head floating in an opalescent mist.

Her sleep was restless, her dreams both vivid and strange. Her banker appeared, his baby mouth obscene in a goat's long face, and disappeared, bloodily, into a tiger's maw. A monkey wore grey gloves, except it was not a monkey at all, but a pig, beyond whose trotters the fingers of the gloves flapped like fringe. It bowed, grinning piggily, to the dream-presence that was Victorine, who curtsied deeply in return. When she rose, the tiger blinked golden eyes at her. She laid her hand upon his striped head; he purred like the rolling of distant thunder and kneaded his great paws against her thighs. She felt only pleasure from his touch, but when she looked at her skirts, they hung in bloody rags. Then it seemed she rode the tiger through the streets of Paris, or perhaps it was an open carriage she rode, or perhaps she was gliding bodily above the pavement, trailing draperies like the swirling opalescence of water suspended in a glass of absinthe.

She slept heavily at last, and was finally awakened at noon by a group of drunks singing the Marseillaise at full voice on the street under her window. She struggled out of bed and pulled back the curtains, prepared to empty her chamber pot over them. Seeing her, they cried out "*Vive la République*," and saluted, clearly as drunk on patriotic sentiment as on wine. Victorine was not entirely without feeling for her country, so she stayed her hand.

France was a Republic again.

Victorine considered this fact as her maid dressed her and pinned up her hair. If the drunkards were anything to judge by, the change of government had not changed a man's natural reaction to the sight of a shapely woman in a nightgown. She would walk to the Tuileries, buy an ice-cream, and find someone to help her celebrate the new Republic.

It was a warm day, grey and soft as mouse fur. Victorine bought a patriotic red carnation from a flower-seller on the steps of Notre Dame de Lorette, and pinned it to her bosom. The streets were full of workers in smocks and gentlemen in top hats, waving greenery and tricolor flags with democratic zeal. Spontaneous choruses of *Vive la République!* exploded around Victorine at intervals. As she drew nearer the Tuileries, her heart beat harder, her cheeks heated; she felt the press of strange bodies around her as the most intense of pleasures. Soon she was laughing aloud and shouting with the rest: *Vive la République!*

At last, she reached the gate of the Tuileries. A man thrust a branch in her face as she passed through. "This is it!" he cried blissfully. "Down with the Emperor! *Vive la République!*"

He was a soldier, young, passably good-looking in his little round kepi and gold-braided epaulets. Victorine turned the full force of her smile at him. "*Vive la République,*" she answered, and brushed his fingers with hers as she took the branch.

He didn't seem to notice.

For the blink of an eye, Victorine was filled with a rage as absolute as it was unexpected. And then it was gone, taking her patriotic fervor with it. Suddenly, the pressure of the crowd seemed intolerable to her, the shouting an assault. She clung to the iron railings of the high fence and fanned herself with her handkerchief while she caught her breath.

All the wide promenade between railings and palace overflowed with a seething mass of humanity. Victorine's view was obstructed by top hats and cloth caps, smart hats and shabby bonnets and checked shawls. By standing on tiptoe, she could just see a stream of people swarming up the steps like revelers eager to see the latest opera. La République had moved quickly. She noticed that the "N's" and imperial wreaths had been pried from the façade or shrouded with newspapers or scarlet sheets, which gave the palace a blotched and raddled look. And above the gaping door, someone had chalked the words UNDER THE PROTECTION OF THE CITIZENS on the black marble.

The open door of the palace beckoned to Victorine, promising wonders. She put away her handkerchief, took a firm hold on her bag, and launched herself into the current that flowed, erratically but inevitably, towards the forbidden palace where the Emperor and his foreign wife had lived so long in imperial splendor.

The current bore Victorine up a flight of shallow steps, the press around her growing, if possible, even denser as the door compacted the flow. She stepped over the threshold, passing a young infantryman who held out his shako and cried out with the raucous monotony of a street vendor: "For the French wounded! For the French wounded!" Impulsively, Victorine fished a coin from her bag, dropped it into his shako, and smiled up into his sweating face. He nodded once, gravely, and then she was in the foyer of the Imperial Palace of the Tuileries.

It was every bit as magnificent as she'd imagined. Victorine, who had a taste for excess, worshipped every splendid inch of it, from the goddesses painted on the ceiling, to the scintillating lustres on the chandeliers, the mirrors and gold leaf everywhere, and the great, sweeping staircase, designed to be seen on.

There must have been a hundred people on that staircase, mounting and descending, gawking over the rail. But Victorine saw only one woman, standing still as a rock in the waterfall of sightseers. The woman's hair was dark under her green hat, and her profile, when she turned her head, was angular. Victorine's blood recognized La Fée Verte before her mind did, racing to her face and away again, so that she swayed as she stood.

A hand, beautifully gloved in grey leather, touched her arm. Victorine became aware of a gentleman in top hat and a beautifully-tailored coat, carrying a gold-headed cane. "Mademoiselle is faint?" he inquired.

Victorine shook her head and sprang up the steps so heedlessly that she caught her toe on the riser. The solicitous gentleman, who had not moved from her side, caught her as she stumbled.

"If you will permit?" he asked rhetorically. Then he slipped one arm around her waist, shouting for everyone to make way, and piloted her firmly out of the palace without paying the slightest heed to her protestations that she was very well, that she'd left a friend on the stair and wished to be reunited with her.

The solicitous gentleman was plumper than Victorine liked, and his hair, when he removed his tall glossy hat, was woefully sparse. But he bore her off to the Georges V for coffee and pastries and then he bought her a diamond aigrette and a little carnelian cat with emerald eyes and agreed that it was a great pity that an exquisite creature like herself should be in exile on the rue de la Tour. What could Victorine do? She took the luck that fate had sent her and gave the gentleman to understand that his gifts were an acceptable prelude to a more serious arrangement. A week later, she and her maid were installed in an apartment off the Champs-Élysées, with her name on the lease and furniture that was hers to keep or sell as it pleased her.

It was not a bad bargain. The solicitous gentleman wasn't as good-looking as the banker and his love-making was uninspired. But, besides being very rich, he was as devoted to amusement as even Victorine could wish.

"Why should I worry about the Prussians?" he said. "I have my days to fill. Let everyone else worry about the Prussians if it amuses them. It is of more concern to me whether M. Gaultier beats me to that charming bronze we saw yesterday."

Still, the Prussians, or rather the threat of the Prussians, was increasingly hard to ignore. Victorine and her solicitous gentleman made their way to the antiquaries and the rare bookshops through platoons of National Guardsmen marching purposefully from one place to another and ranks of newly-inducted Mobile Guards learning to turn right in unison. She could not set foot outside the door without being enthusiastically admired by the soldiers camped along the Champs, and the horses stabled there made pleasure-drives to the Bois de Boulogne (or what was left of it) all but impossible. Even the theatre wasn't what it had been, houses closing left and right as the timid fled the anticipated discomforts of a siege. The Comédie Française and the Opera remained open, though, and the public balls and the cafés-concerts were frequented by those without the means to fly. However tenuously, Paris remained Paris, even in the face of war.

One night, Victorine and her solicitous gentleman went strolling along the boulevard de Clichy. Among the faded notices of past performances that fluttered like bats' wings in the wind, crisp, new posters announced the coming night's pleasures.

"Look, *ma belle*," the gentleman exclaimed, stopping in front of a kiosk. "A mentalist! How original! And such a provocative name. We really must go see her."

Victorine looked at the poster he indicated. It was painted red and black, impossible to ignore:

The Salon du Diable presents
La Fée Verte!
The mists of time part for her. The secrets of the future are unveiled.
Séance at nine and midnight.
La Fée Verte!

Tears sprang, stinging, to Victorine's eyes. Through their sparkling veil, she saw a white bed and a room lit only by dying embers and her palm tingled as if cupped over the small, soft mound of La Fée Verte's breast. She drew a quick breath. "It sounds very silly," she said weakly. "Besides, who has ever heard of the Salon du Diable?"

"All the more reason to go. It can be an adventure, and well worth it, if this Fée Verte is any good. If she's terrible, it will make a good story."

Victorine shrugged and acquiesced. It was clearly fate that had placed that poster where her protector would notice it, and fate that he had found it appealing, just as it was fate that Victorine would once more suffer the torment of seeing La Fée Verte without being able to speak to her. Just as well, really, after the fiasco on the Champs-Élysées. At least this time, Victorine would hear her voice.

The Salon du Diable was nearly as hot as the abode of its putative owner, crowded with thirsty sinners, its only illumination a half-a-dozen gas-lights, turned down low. A waiter dressed as a devil in jacket and horns of red felt showed them to a table near the curtained platform that served as a stage. Victorine, as was her habit, asked for champagne. In honor of the entertainer, her protector ordered absinthe. When it came, she watched him balance the sugar cube on the pierced spoon and slowly pour a measure of water over it into the virulent green liquor. The sugared water swirled into the absinthe, disturbing its depths, transforming it, drop by drop, into smoky, shifting opal.

The solicitous gentleman lifted the tall glass. "La Fée Verte!" he proposed.

"La Fée Verte," Victorine echoed obediently, and as if at her call, a stout man in a red cape and horns like the waiter's appeared before the worn plush curtain and began his introduction.

La Fée Verte, he informed the audience, was the grand-daughter of one of the last known fairies in France, who had fallen in love with a mortal and given birth to a son, the father of the woman they were about to see. By virtue of her fairy blood, La Fée Verte was able to see through the impenetrable curtains of time and space as though they were clear glass. La Fée Verte was a visionary, and the stories she told—whether of past, present, or future—were as true as death.

There was an eager murmur from the audience. The devil of ceremonies stepped aside, pulling the faded plush curtain with him, and revealed a woman sitting alone on the stage. She was veiled from head to toe all in pale, gauzy green, but Victorine knew her at once.

Thin white hands emerged from the veil and cast it up and back like a green mist. Dark eyes shone upon the audience like stars at the back of a cave. Her mouth was painted scarlet and her unbound hair was a black smoke around her head and shoulders.

Silence stretched to the breaking point as La Fée Verte stared at the audience and the audience stared at her. And then, just as Victorine's strained attention was on the point of shattering, the thin red lips opened and La Fée Verte began to speak.

"I will not speak of war, or victory or defeat, suffering or glory. Visions, however ardently desired, do not come for the asking. Instead, I will speak of building.

"There's a lot of building going on in Paris these days—enough work for everyone, thanks to *le bon* Baron and his pretty plans. Not all Germans are bad, eh? The pay's pretty good, too, if it can buy a beer at the Salon du Diable. There's a builder in the audience now, a mason. There are, in fact, two masons, twice that number of carpenters, a layer of roof-slates, and a handful of floor-finishers."

The audience murmured, puzzled at the tack she'd taken. The men at the next table exchanged startled glances—the carpenters, Victorine guessed, or the floor-finishers.

"My vision, though, is for the mason. He's got stone-dust in his blood, this mason. His very bones are granite. His father was a mason, and his father's father and his father's father's father, and so on, as far back as I can see. Stand up, M. le Maçon. Don't be shy. You know I'm talking about you."

The audience peered around the room, looking to see if anyone would rise. In one corner, there was a hubbub of encouraging voices, and finally, a man stood up, his flat cap over one eye and a blue kerchief around his throat. "I am a mason, Mademoiselle," he said. "You're right enough about my pa. Don't know about *his* pa, though. He could have been a train-conductor, for all I know. He's not talked about in the family."

"That," said La Fée Verte, "was your grandmother's grief, poor woman, and your grandfather's shame."

The mason scowled. "Easy enough for you to say, Mademoiselle, not knowing a damn thing about me."

"Tell me," La Fée Verte inquired sweetly. "How are things on the rue Mouffetard? Don't worry: your little blonde's cough is not tuberculosis. She'll be better soon." The mason threw up his hands in a clear gesture of surrender and sat down. A laugh swept the audience. They were impressed. Victorine smiled to herself.

La Fée Verte folded her hands demurely in her green silk lap. "Your grandfather," she said gently, "was indeed a mason, a layer of stones like you, Monsieur. Men of your family have shaped steps and grilles, window-frames and decorations in every building in Paris. Why, men of your blood worked on Nôtre Dame, father and son growing old each in his turn in the service of Maurice de Sully."

The voice was even rougher than Victorine remembered it, the language as simple and undecorated as the story she told. La Fée Verte did not posture and gesture and lift her eyes to heaven, and yet Victorine was convinced that, were she to close her eyes, she'd see Nôtre Dame as it once was, half-built and swarming with the men who labored to complete it. But she preferred to watch La Fée Verte's thin, sensuous lips telling about it.

La Fée Verte dropped her voice to a sibylline murmur that somehow could be heard in every corner of the room. "I see a man with shoulders like a bull, dressed in long stockings and a tunic and a leather apron. The tunic might have been red once and the stockings ochre, but they're faded now with washing and stone-dust. He takes up his chisel and his hammer in his broad, hard hands flecked with scars, and he begins his daily prayer. *Tap*-tap, *tap*-tap. *Pa*-ter *Nos*-ter. A-ve *Ma*-ri-*a*. Each blow of his hammer, each chip of stone, is a bead in the rosary he tells, every hour of every working day. His prayers, unlike yours and mine, are still visible. They decorate the towers of Nôtre Dame, almost as eternal as the God they praise.

"That was your ancestor, M. le Maçon," La Fée Verte said, returning to a conversational tone. "Shall I tell you of your son?"

The mason, enchanted, nodded.

"It's not so far from now, as the march of time goes. Long enough for you to marry your blonde, and to father children and watch them grow and take up professions. Thirty years, I make it, or a little less: 1887. The president of France will decree a great Exposition to take place in 1889—like the Exposition of 1867, but far grander. Eighteen eighty-nine is the threshold of a new century, after all, and what can be grander than that? As an entrance arch, he will commission a monument like none seen before anywhere in the world. And your son, Monsieur, your son will build it.

"I see him, Monsieur, blond and slight, taking after his mother's family, with a leather harness around his waist. He climbs to his work, high above the street— higher than the towers of Nôtre Dame, higher than you can imagine. His tools are not yours: red-hot iron rivets, tin buckets, tongs, iron-headed mallets. His faith is in the engineer whose vision he executes, in the maker of his tools, his scaffolds and screens and guard-rails: in man's ingenuity, not God's mercy."

She fell silent, and it seemed to Victorine that she had finished. The mason thought so, too, and was unsatisfied. "My son, he won't be a mason, then?"

"Your son will work in iron," La Fée Verte answered. "And yet your line will not falter, nor the stone-dust leach from your blood as it flows through the ages."

Her voice rang with prophecy as she spoke, not so much loud as sonorous, like a church bell tolling. When the last echo had died away, she smiled, a sweet curve of her scarlet lips, and said, shy as a girl, "That is all I see, Monsieur. Are you answered?"

The mason wiped his hands over his eyes and, rising, bowed to her, whereupon the audience roared its approval of La Fée Verte's vision and the mason's response, indeed of the whole performance and of the Salon du Diable for having provided it. Victorine clapped until her palms stung through her tight kid gloves.

The solicitous gentleman drained his absinthe and called for another. "To La Fée Verte," he said, raising the opal liquid high. "The most accomplished fraud in Paris. She must be half-mad to invent all that guff, but damn me if I've ever heard anything like her voice."

Victorine's over-wrought nerves exploded in a surge of anger. She rose to her feet, snatched the glass from the gentleman's hand, and poured the contents over his glossy head. While he gasped and groped for his handkerchief, she gathered up her bag and her wrap and swept out of the Salon du Diable in a tempest of silks, dropping a coin into the bowl by the door as she went.

The next day, the gentleman was at Victorine's door with flowers and a blue velvet jewel-case and a note demanding that she receive him at once. The concierge sent up the note and the gifts, and Victorine sent them back again, retaining only the jewel-case as a parting souvenir. She did not send a note of her own, since there was nothing to say except that she could no longer bear the sight of him. She listened to him curse her from the foot of the stairs, and watched him storm down the street when the concierge complained of the noise. Her only regret was not having broken with him before he took her to the Salon du Diable.

In late September, the hard times foretold by the blonde in the Veau d'Or came to Paris.

A city under the threat of siege is not, Victorine discovered, a good place to find a protector. Top-hatted gentlemen still strolled the grand boulevards, but they remained stubbornly blind to Victorine's saucy hats, graceful form, and flashing eyes.

They huddled on street-corners and in cafés, talking of the impossibility of continued Prussian victory, of the threat of starvation that transformed the buying of humble canned meat into a patriotic act. Her cheeks aching from unregarded smiles, Victorine began to hate the very sound of the words "siege," "Prussian," "Republic." She began to feel that Bismarck and the displaced Emperor, along with the quarrelsome Generals Gambetta and Trochu, were personally conspiring to keep her from her livelihood. Really, among them, they were turning Paris into a dull place, where nobody had time or taste for pleasure.

A less determined woman might have retired for the duration, but not Victorine. Every day, she put on her finest toilettes and walked, head held high under the daring hats, through the military camp that Paris was fast becoming. Not only the Champs-Élysées, but all the public gardens, squares, and boulevards were transformed into military camps or stables or sections of the vast open market that had sprung up to cater to the soldiers' needs. Along streets where once only the most expensive trinkets were sold, Victorine passed makeshift stalls selling kepis and epaulets and gold braid, ramrods and powder-pouches and water-bottles, sword-canes and bayonet-proof leather chest-protectors. And everywhere were soldiers, throwing dice and playing cards among clusters of little grey tents, who called out as she passed: "Eh, sweetheart! How about a little tumble for a guy about to die for his country?"

It was very discouraging.

One day at the end of September, Victorine directed her steps towards the heights of the Trocadéro, where idle Parisians and resident foreigners had taken to airing themselves on fine days. They would train their spyglasses on the horizon and examine errant puffs of smoke and fleeing peasants like ancient Roman priests examining the entrails of a sacrifice, after which they gossiped and flirted as usual. A few days earlier, Victorine had encountered an English gentleman with a blonde moustache of whom she had great hopes. As she climbed the hill above the Champs de Mars, she heard the drums measuring the drills of the Mobile Guards.

At the summit of the hill, fashionable civilians promenaded to and fro. Not seeing her English gentleman, Victorine joined the crowd surrounding the enterprising bourgeois who sold peeps through his long brass telescope at a franc a look. A clutch of English ladies exclaimed incomprehensibly as she pushed past them; a fat gentleman in a round hat moved aside gallantly to give her room. She cast him a distracted smile, handed the enterprising bourgeois a coin, and stooped to look through the eyepiece. The distant prospect of misty landscape snapped closer, bringing into clear focus a cloud of dark smoke roiling over a stand of trees.

"That used to be a village," the enterprising bourgeois informed her. "The Prussians fired it this morning—or maybe we did, to deny the Prussians the pleasure." The telescope jerked away from the smoke. "If you're lucky, you should be able to see the refugees on their way to Paris."

A cart, piled high with furniture, a woman with her hair tied up in a kerchief struggling along beside it, lugging a bulging basket in each hand and a third strapped to her back. A couple of goats and a black dog and a child riding in a hand-cart pushed by a young boy. "Time's up," the enterprising bourgeois said.

Victorine clung to the telescope, her heart pounding. The smoke, the cart, the woman with her bundles, the children, the dog, were fleeing a real danger. Suddenly, Victorine was afraid, deathly afraid of being caught in Paris when the Prussians came. She must get out while there was still time, sell her jewels, buy a horse and carriage, travel south to Nice or Marseilles. She'd find La Fée Verte, and they could leave at once. Surely, if she went to the Place Clichy, she'd see her there, wait-ing for Victorine to rescue her. But she'd have to hurry.

As quickly as Victorine had thrust to the front of the crowd, so quickly did she thrust out again, discommoding the English ladies, who looked down their long noses at her. No doubt they thought her drunk or mad. She only thought them in the way. In her hurry, she stepped on a stone, twisted her ankle, and fell gracelessly to the ground.

The English ladies twittered. The gentleman in the round hat asked her, in vile French, how she went, and offered her his hand. She allowed him to pull her to her feet, only to collapse with a cry of pain. The ladies twittered again, on a more sym-pathetic note. Then the crowd fell back a little, and a masculine voice inquired courteously whether Mademoiselle were ill.

Victorine lifted her eyes to the new-comer, who was hunkered down beside her, his broad, open brow furrowed with polite concern. The gold braid on his sleeves proclaimed him an officer, and the gold ring on his finger suggested wealth.

"It is very silly," she said breathlessly, "but I have twisted my ankle and cannot stand."

"If Mademoiselle will allow?" He folded her skirt away from her foot, took the scarlet boot into his hand, and bent it gently back and forth. Victorine hissed through her teeth.

"Not broken, I think," he said. "Still, I'm no doctor." Without asking permission, he put one arm around her back, the other under her knees, and lifted her from the ground with a little jerk of effort. As he carried her downhill to the surgeon's tent, she studied him. Under a chestnut-brown moustache, his mouth was firm and well-shaped, and his nose was high-bridged and aristocratic. She could do worse.

He glanced down, caught her staring. Victorine smiled into his eyes (they, too, were chestnut-brown) and was gratified to see him blush. And then they were in the surgeon's tent and her scarlet boot was being cut away. It hurt terribly. The surgeon anointed her foot with arnica and bound it tightly, making silly jokes as he worked about gangrene and amputation. She bore it all with such a gallant gaiety that the officer insisted on seeing her home and carrying her to her bed, where she soon demonstrated that a sprained ankle need not prevent a woman from showing her gratitude to a man who had richly deserved it.

October, 1870

It was a strange affair, at once casual and absorbing, conducted in the interstices of siege and civil unrest. The officer was a colonel in the National Guard, a man of wealth and some influence. His great passion was military history. His natural posture—in politics, in love—was moderation. He viewed the Monarchists on the Right and the Communards on the Left with an impartial contempt. He did not pre-tend that his liaison with Victorine was a grand passion, but cheerfully paid the rent on her apartment and bought her a new pair of scarlet boots and a case of canned meat, with promises of jewels and gowns after the Prussians were defeated. He ex-plained about Trochu and Bismarck, and expected her to be interested. He told her all the military gossip and took her to ride on the peripheral railway and to see the canons installed on the hills of Paris.

The weather was extraordinarily bright. "God loves the Prussians," the officer said, rather sourly, and it certainly seemed to be true. With the sky soft and blue as June, no rain slowed the Prussian advance or clogged the wheels of their caissons or the hooves of their horses with mud. They marched until they were just out of the range of the Parisian cannons, and there they sat, enjoying the wine from the cellars of captured country houses and fighting skirmishes in the deserted streets of burned-out villages. By October 15, they had the city completely surrounded. The Siege of Paris had begun.

The Generals sent out their troops in cautious sallies, testing the Prussians but never seriously challenging them. Victorine's colonel, wild with impatience at the shilly-shallying of his superiors, had a thousand plans for sorties and full-scale counter-attacks. He detailed them to Victorine after they'd made love, all among the bed-clothes, with the sheets heaped into fortifications, a pillow representing the butte of Montmartre, and a handful of hazelnuts for soldiers.

"Paris will never stand a long siege," he explained to her. "Oh, we've food enough, but there is no organized plan to distribute it. There is nothing really organized at all. None of those blustering ninnies in charge can see beyond the end of his nose. It's all very well to speak of the honor of France and the nobility of the French, but abstractions do not win wars. Soldiers in the field, deployed by generals who are not afraid to make decisions, that's what wins wars."

He was very beautiful when he said these things, his frank, handsome face ablaze with earnestness. Watching him, Victorine very nearly loved him. At other times, she liked him very well. He was a man who knew how to live. To fight the general gloom, he gave dinner parties to which he invited military men and men of business for an evening of food, wine, and female companionship. Wives were not invited.

There was something dream-like about those dinners, eaten as the autumn wind sharpened and the citizens of Paris tightened their belts. In a patriotic gesture, the room was lit not by gas, but by branches of candles, whose golden light called gleams from the porcelain dishes, the heavy silver cutlery, the thin crystal glasses filled with citrine or ruby liquid. The gentlemen laughed and talked, their elbows on the napery, their cigars glowing red as tigers' eyes. Perched among them like exotic birds, the women, gowned in their bare-shouldered best, encouraged the gentlemen to talk with smiles and nods. On the table, a half-eaten tarte, a basket of fruit. On the sideboard, the remains of two roast chickens—two!—a dish of beans with almonds, another of potatoes. Such a scene belonged more properly to last month, last year, two years ago, when the Empire was strong and elegant pleasures as common as the rich men to buy them. Sitting at the table, slightly drunk, Victorine felt herself lost in one of La Fée Verte's visions, where past, present, and future exist as one.

Outside the colonel's private dining room, however, life was a waking nightmare. The garbage carts had nowhere to go, so that Victorine must pick her way around stinking hills of ordure on every street corner. Cholera and smallpox flourished among the poor. The plump blonde of the Veau d'Or died in the epidemic, as did the elderly waiter and a good proportion of the regulars. Food grew scarce. Worm-eaten cabbages went for three francs apiece. Rat pie appeared on the menu at Maxim's, and lapdogs went in fear of their lives. And then there were the French wounded, sitting and lying in rattling carriages and carts, muddy men held together with bloody bandages, their shocked eyes turned inwards, their pale lips closed on their pain, being carted to cobbled-together hospitals to heal or die. Victorine turned her eyes from them, glad she'd given a coin to the young infantryman that day she saw La Fée Verte in the Tuileries.

And through and over it all, the cannons roared.

French cannon, Prussian cannon, shelling St. Denis, shelling Boulogne, shelling empty fields and ravaged woodlands. As they were the nearest, the French cannon were naturally the loudest. Victorine's colonel prided himself on knowing each cannon by the timbre and resonance of its voice as it fired, its snoring or strident or dull or ear-shattering BOOM. In a flight of whimsy one stolen afternoon, lying in his arms in a rented room near the Port St. Cloud, Victorine gave them names and made up characters for them: Gigi of the light, flirtatious bark on Mortemain, Philippe of the angry bellow at the Trocadéro.

October wore on, and the siege with it. A population accustomed to a steady diet of news from the outside world and fresh food from the provinces began to understand what it was like to live without either. The lack of food was bad enough, but everyone had expected that—this was war, after all, one must expect to go hungry. But the lack of news was hard to bear. Conflicting rumors ran through the streets like warring plagues, carried by the skinny street rats who hawked newspapers on the boulevards. In the absence of news, gossip, prejudice, and flummery filled their pages. Victorine collected the most outrageous for her colonel's amusement: the Generals planned to release the poxed whores of the Hôpital St. Lazare to serve the Prussian army; the Prussian lines had been stormed by a herd of a thousand patriotic oxen.

The colonel began to speak of love. Victorine was becoming as necessary to him, he said, as food and drink. Victorine, to whom he was indeed food and drink, held his chestnut head to her white breast and allowed him to understand that she loved him in return.

Searching for a misplaced corset, her maid turned up the ripped green kimono and inquired what Mademoiselle would like done with it.

"Burn it," said Victorine. "No, don't. Mend it, if you can, and pack it away somewhere. This is not a time to waste good silk."

That evening, Victorine and her colonel strolled along the Seine together, comfortably arm in arm. The cannon had fallen to a distant Prussian rumbling, easily ignored. Waiters hurried to and fro with trays on which the glasses of absinthe glowed like emeralds. The light was failing. Victorine looked out over the water, expecting to see the blue veil of dusk drifting down over Nôtre Dame.

The veil was stained with blood.

For a moment, Victorine thought her eyes were at fault. She blinked and rubbed them with a gloved hand, but when she looked again, the evening sky was still a dirty scarlet—nothing like a sunset, nothing like anything natural Victorine had ever seen. The very air shimmered red. All along the quai came cries of awe and fear.

"The Forest of Bondy is burning," Victorine heard a man say and, "an experiment with light on Montmartre," said another, his voice trembling with the hope that his words were true. In her ear, the colonel murmured reassuringly, "Don't be afraid, my love. It's only the aurora borealis."

Victorine was not comforted. She was no longer a child to hide in pretty stories. She knew an omen when she saw one. This one, she feared, promised fire and death. She prayed it did not promise her own. Paris might survive triumphantly into a new century, and the mason and his blonde might survive to see its glories, but nothing in La Fée Verte's vision had promised that Victorine, or even La Fée Verte, would be there with them.

The red light endured for only a few hours, but some atmospheric disturbance cast a strange and transparent radiance over the next few days, so that every street, every passer-by took on the particularity of a photograph. The unnatural light troubled Victorine. She would have liked to be diverted with kisses, but her colonel was much occupied just now. He wrote her to say he did not know when he'd be able to see her again—a week or two at most, but who could tell? It was a matter of national importance—nothing less would keep him from her bed. He enclosed a pair of fine kidskin gloves, a heavy purse, a rope of pearls, and a history of Napoleon's early campaigns.

It was all very unsatisfying. Other women in Victorine's half-widowed state volunteered to nurse the French wounded, or made bandages, or had taken to their beds with Bibles and rosaries, or even a case of wine. Victorine, in whom unhappiness bred restlessness, went out and walked the streets.

From morning until far past sunset, Victorine wandered through Paris, driven by she knew not what. She walked through the tent cities, past stalls where canteen girls in tri-colored jackets ladled out soup, past shuttered butcher shops and greengrocers where women shivered on the sidewalk, waiting for a single rusty cabbage or a fist-sized piece of doubtful meat. But should she caught sight of a woman dressed in green or a woman whose skin seemed paler than normal, she always followed her for a street or two, until she saw her face.

She did not fully realize what she was doing until she found herself touching a woman on the arm so that she would turn. The woman, who was carrying a packet wrapped in butcher's paper, turned on her, frightened and furious.

"What are you doing?" she snapped. "Trying to rob me?"

"I beg your pardon," Victorine said stiffly. "I took you for a friend."

"No friend of yours, my girl. Now run away before I call a policeman."

Shaking, Victorine fled to a café, where she bought a glass of spirits and drank it down as if the thin, acid stuff would burn La Fée Verte from her mind and body. It did not. Trying not to think of her was still thinking of her; refusing to search for her was still searching.

On the morning of October 31, rumors of the fall of Metz came to Paris. The people revolted. Trochu cowered in the Hôtel de Ville while a mob gathered outside, shouting for his resignation. Victorine, blundering into the edges of the riot, turned hastily north and plunged into the winding maze of the Marais. Close behind the Banque de France, she came to a square she'd never seen before. It was a square like a thousand others, with a lady's haberdasher and a hairdresser, an apartment building and a café all facing a stone pedestal supporting the statue of a dashing mounted soldier. A crowd had gathered around the statue, men and women of the people for the most part, filthy and pinched and blue-faced with cold and hunger. Raised a little above them on the pedestal's base were a fat man in a filthy scarlet cloak and a woman, painfully thin and motionless under a long and tattered veil of green gauze.

The fat man, who was not as fat as he had been, was nearing the end of his patter. The crowd was unimpressed. There were a few catcalls. A horse turd, thrown from the edge of the crowd, splattered against the statue's granite base. Then La Fée Verte unveiled herself, and the crowd fell silent.

The weeks since Victorine had seen her on the stage of the Salon du Diable had not been kind to her. The dark eyes were sunken, the body little more than bone draped in skin and a walking-dress of muddy green wool. She looked like a mad woman: half-starved, pitiful. Victorine's eyes filled and her pulse sped. She yearned to go to her, but shyness kept her back. If she was meant to speak to La Fée Verte, she thought, there would be a sign. In the meantime, she could at least listen.

"I am a seer," La Fée Verte said, the word taking on a new and dangerous resonance in her mouth. "I see the past, the present, the future. I see things that are hidden, and I see the true meaning of things that are not. I see truth, and I see falsehoods tricked out as truth." She paused, titled her head. "Which would you like to hear?"

Puzzled, the crowd muttered to itself. A woman shouted, "We hear enough lies from Trochu. Give us the truth!"

"Look at her," a skeptic said. "She's even hungrier than I am. What's the good of a prophetess who can't foresee her next meal?"

"My next meal will be bread and milk in a Sèvres bowl," La Fée Verte answered tranquilly. "Yours, my brave one, will be potage—of a sort. The water will have a vegetable in it, at any rate."

The crowd, encouraged, laughed and called out questions.

"Is my husband coming home tonight?"

"My friend Jean, will he pay me back my three sous?"

"Will Paris fall?"

"No," said La Fée Verte. "Yes, if you remind him. As for Paris, it is not such a simple matter as yes and no. Shall I tell you what I see?"

Shouts of "No!" and "Yes!" and more horse turds, one of which spattered her green skirt. Unruffled, she went on, her husky voice somehow piercing the crowd's rowdiness.

"I see prosperity and peace," she said, "like a castle in a fairy-tale that promises that you will live happily ever after."

More grumbling from the crowd: "What's she talking about?"; "I don't understand her."; and a woman's joyful shout—"We're all going to be rich!"

"I did not say that," La Fée Verte said. "The cholera, the cold, the hunger, will all get worse before it gets better. The hard times aren't over yet."

There was angry muttering, a few catcalls: "We ain't paying to hear what we already know, bitch!"

"You ain't paying me at all," La Fée Verte answered mockingly. "Anyone may see the near future—it's all around us. No, what you want to know is the distant future. Well, as you've asked for the truth, the truth is that the road to that peaceful and prosperous castle is swarming with Germans. Germans and Germans and Germans. You'll shoot them and kill them by the thousands and for a while they'll seem to give up and go away. But then they'll rise again and come at you, again and again."

Before La Fée Verte had finished, "Dirty foreigner!" a woman shrieked, and several voices chorused, "Spy, spy! German spy!" Someone threw a stone at her. It missed La Fée Verte and bounced from the pedestal behind her with a sharp crack. La Fée Verte ignored it, just as she ignored the crowd's shouting and the fat man's clutching hands trying to pull her away.

It was the sign. Victorine waded into the melee, elbows flailing, screaming like a cannonball in flight. There was no thought in her head except to reach her love and carry her, if possible, away from this place and home, where she belonged.

"I see them in scarlet," La Fée Verte was shouting above the noise. "I see them in grey. I see them in black, with peaked caps on their heads, marching like wooden dolls, stiff-legged, inexorable, shooting shopgirls and clerks and tavernkeepers, without pity, without cause."

Victorine reached La Fée Verte at about the same time as the second stone and caught her as she staggered and fell, the blood running bright from a cut on her cheek. The weight of her, slight as it was, over-balanced them both. A stone struck Victorine in the back; she jerked and swore, and her vision sparkled and faded as though she were about to faint.

"Don't be afraid," the husky voice said in her ear. "They're only shadows. They can't hurt you."

Her back muscles sore and burning, Victorine would have disagreed. But La Fée Verte laid a bony finger across her lips. "Hush," she said. "Be still and look."

It was the same square, no doubt of that, although the café at the corner had a different name and a different front, and the boxes in the windows of the apartment opposite were bright with spring flowers. Victorine and La Fée Verte were still surrounded by a crowd, but the crowd didn't seem to be aware of the existence of the two women huddled at the statue's base. People were watching something passing in the street beyond, some procession that commanded their attention and their silence. The men looked familiar enough, in dark coats and trousers, bareheaded or with flat caps pulled over their cropped hair. But the women—ah, the women were another thing. Their dresses were the flimsy, printed cotton of a child's shirt or a summer blouse, their skirts short enough to expose their naked legs almost to the knee, their hair cut short and dressed in ugly rolls.

Wondering, Victorine looked down at La Fée Verte, who smiled at her, intimate and complicit. "You see? Help me up," she murmured. As Victorine rose, lifting the thin woman with her, she jostled a woman in a scarf with a market basket on her arm. The woman moved aside, eyes still riveted on the procession beyond, and Victorine, raised above the crowd on the statue's base, followed her gaze.

There were soldiers, as La Fée Verte had said: lines of them in dark uniforms and high, glossy boots, marching stiff-legged through the square towards the rue de Rivoli. There seemed to be no end to them, each one the mirror of the next, scarlet arm-bands flashing as they swung their left arms. A vehicle like an open carriage came into view, horseless, propelled apparently by magic, with black-coated men seated in it, proud and hard-faced under peaked caps. Over their heads, banners bearing a contorted black cross against a white and scarlet ground rippled in the wind. And then from the sky came a buzzing like a thousand hives of bees, as loud as thunder but more continuous. Victorine looked up, and saw a thing she hardly knew how to apprehend. It was like a bird, but enormously bigger, with wings that blotted out the light, and a body shaped like a cigar.

If this was vision, Victorine wanted none of it. She put her hands over her eyes, releasing La Fée Verte's hand that she had not even been aware of holding. The buzzing roar ceased as if a door had been closed, and the tramp of marching feet. She heard shouting, and a man's voice screaming with hysterical joy:

"The Republic has fallen!" he shrieked. "Long live the Commune! To the Hôtel de Ville!"

The fickle crowd took up the chant: "To the Hôtel de Ville! To the Hôtel de Ville!" And so chanting, they moved away from the statue, their voices gradually growing fainter and more confused with distance.

When Victorine dared look again, the square was all but empty. The fat man was gone, and most of the crowd, all heading, she supposed, for the Hôtel de Ville. A woman lingered, comfortingly attired in a long gray skirt, a tight brown jacket with a greasy shawl over it, and a battered black hat rammed over a straggling bun.

"Better take her out of here, dear," she said to Victorine. "I don't care, but if any of those madmen come back this way, they'll be wanting her blood."

That night, Victorine had her maid stand in line for a precious cup of milk, heated it up over her bedroom fire, and poured it over some pieces of stale bread torn up into a Sèvres bowl.

La Fée Verte, clean and wrapped in her old green kimono, accepted the dish with murmured thanks. She spooned up a bit, ate it, put the spoon back in the plate. "And your colonel?" she asked. "What will you tell him?"

"You can be my sister," Victorine said gaily. "He doesn't know I don't have one, and under the circumstances, he can hardly ask me to throw you out. You can sleep in the kitchen when he spends the night."

"Yes," La Fée Verte said after a moment. "I will sleep in the kitchen. It will not be for long. We. . . ."

"No," said Victorine forcefully. "I don't want to hear. I don't care if we're to be ruled by a republic or a commune or a king or an emperor, French or German. I don't care if the streets run with blood. All I care is that we are here together now, just at this moment, and that we will stay here together, and be happy."

She was kneeling at La Fée Verte's feet, not touching her for fear of upsetting the bread and milk, looking hopefully into the ravaged face. La Fée Verte touched her cheek very gently and smiled.

"You are right," she said. "We are together. It is enough."

She fell silent, and the tears overflowed her great, bruised eyes and trickled down her cheeks. They were no longer crystalline—they were just tears. But when Victorine licked them from her fingers, it seemed to her that they tasted sweet.

LEE BATTERSBY

Father Muerte & the Flesh

Lee Battersby lives in Perth, Western Australia, with his wife, writer Lyn Battersby, anywhere up to five children depending on the day, and as much weird stuff as the house will hold. He is the author of over fifty stories, a number of which are collected in Through Soft Air. *He has won the Aurealis, Ditmar, and Australian Shadows Awards, and his fiction has been published in markets as diverse as* Writers of the Future, *vol. 18,* Znak Sagite, *and the Australian* Woman's Day. *A tutor at Clarion South 2007, his current plans center around playing "Hunt the Agent" for his first novel. He maintains a Web site at www.battersby.com.au and a Weblog at battersblog.blogspot.com and can generally be goaded into commenting on anything.*

"Father Muerte & the Flesh," one of a series of "Father Muerte" stories, was first published in Aurealis #36.

—E.D.

There are very few completely true things in Costa Satanas. Of those that are, perhaps the truest is that it is impossible to climb to the summit of Point Arrival, the bony finger of land pointing out into the ocean at the west end of town. Or the east, depending upon where you look, and who you are when you're looking.

Any number of theories have abounded over the years to explain its isolation, from geological anomalies to one involving the body of an ancient giant and the curse of a jealous lover. That one is my favourite, possibly because it comes closest to the truth. Today, however, Point Arrival's remoteness stems from an entirely different source, one more mundane than anyone would suspect: sometimes I like to be alone.

Slightly winded by the long hike up the hillside, I laid out my picnic blanket, unwrapped a cheese and jam sandwich, and took a bite. I sat, and with my face to the ocean breeze, uncorked my thermos. The smell of Benito D'Amico's special macchiato blend rose into the air, mixing with the sea current and wafting toward the front beach. As the molecules combined, I saw the sunburn addicts wrap towels around themselves and walk up the beach to deposit sand onto Benito's suede-covered wicker chairs.

The first sip of Benito's coffee is a solemn ritual, a meaningful one despite its ordinary accoutrements. I take great pains to make sure I am never, ever interrupted. This made the woman's arrival all the more incredible, and all the more annoying.

"Whew," she said, wiping her forehead with a bandanna wrapped around one brown wrist like a sweatband. "That's some climb." She rounded the last lip of rock and planted herself opposite me as if it were the most natural thing in the world.

"It's meant to be." My cup was not yet halfway to my expectant lips. I placed it back on the blanket. "Pardon my asking, but how did you get up here?"

She favoured me with a look that questioned my sanity in a gentle way. "I walked. Don't tell me there's a bus service I could have taken?"

"No, it's just . . ." I looked around my spoiled sanctuary. "This place is private."

"Oh, I'm sorry. I didn't realize. The photographer said . . . this is yours?"

"In a manner of speaking." I sighed. "This photographer. Young man, black, carries an odd looking camera?"

"That's him." She smiled, and I decided not to notice what a lovely smile she had. "He said I'd like the view."

"I bet he did." Henri Anglomarre suffers a terminal inability to remain single. He wishes to inflict his curse upon me, one of the reasons I found myself climbing the Point more and more often in recent times. "One of these days I shall have to introduce him to the meaning of privacy."

"I'm sorry." She looked me up and down. "Hey, are you that priest everyone talks about?"

"I keep telling them I'm not a priest."

"No, you don't look like one. Is that coffee? May I? I'd kill for a good coffee."

"Here." I handed her the cup and passed the thermos behind it. "It's lost its taste."

She drew deeply on the brew then sprawled backward into the grass, a moan of pleasure escaping her parted lips. I busied myself in folding the blanket, ignoring her long legs as I slid its edge from underneath them. I left the sandwiches to the circling gulls. The intruder looked up at me as I busied myself, then slowly rose to her feet, screwed the cup back on the thermos, and handed it to me with an air of regret.

"No taste?" she said to the circling clouds. "You, sir, have been spoiled." I smiled despite my annoyance, and she stuck out a slim hand. "Bonnie Crake."

I shook it. Her skin was soft, with just a hint of callous where tools had suffered years of grip. Her shake was firm, decisive.

"Well, Miss Crake." I indicated a path she would never have found without me. "Would you care to share the journey back to town?"

We were halfway along the beach when I spied a group of children, gathered around a large, indistinct lump on the sand. I moved toward it, Bonnie in my wake.

"What is it, a body?"

The group parted as we drew near. I knelt by the slab, running my hands over the mass of matter. It was cold, despite the mid-afternoon heat, and bore no resemblance to anything I could remember having seen.

"Not a body," Bonnie said as she knelt beside me and reached out a tentative hand. "It's flesh, though."

"Yes." I kneaded a small piece between finger and thumb, while the children screwed up their faces and chorused a squeal of disgust. I pointed to one. "Kaylee, run and fetch Henri for me, will you? He'll be at Benito's."

"Yes, Papa." She set off at a self-important trot. I turned back to Bonnie.

"I'd say this is a globster."

"A whatster?"

"Globster. They float up onto beaches every now and again. Scientists think they might be pieces of giant squids attacked by sperm whales." I smiled at her over the bulbous mound of flesh. "Or might not. Henri should be able to tell us."

"He's a scientist?"

"Not quite." Henri's father had been a football manager in his native Cameroon, and a firm follower of tribal superstitions. His son had grown up with the ability to "sense" animals, a skill he'd blocked until recent events had sent it bubbling to the surface of his consciousness. I was hoping he'd identify the animal that had donated our little mystery, before we carted it away. Within a minute he was loping up the sand behind Kaylee, a smile of triumph plastered across his deliberately innocent face. I reached into my jacket pocket and removed a stick of Blackpool rock. Kaylee received it as due reward. As she skipped away, I spied Henri and Bonnie with their heads together.

"Told you so," he was saying. They straightened when they saw my glance. I frowned in puzzlement, and at the giggle Bonnie gave in return. I placed a hand on the lump.

"Any ideas?"

Henri knelt, then leaned forward and pressed his face against the cool, slippery flesh. After a minute or so, in which I ignored the pretty young woman's questioning looks, he tilted back and glanced up at me.

"Nothing. Whatever this is, it isn't animal."

"What is it, then?" Bonnie looked between us. I reached into a jacket pocket and withdrew a scalpel and test tube.

"That is what I intend to find out."

I have, over the course of what other people would consider a number of lifetimes, accumulated knowledge in a variety of areas. Some of it is more practical than others. How to use a microscope, for example. Even so, I had to triple check before I believed the evidence presented to me by the eyepiece.

"It's human."

"What?" Henri leaned forward on his stool. "Are you sure?"

"I wish I wasn't."

"But how?" Bonnie had perched upon the edge of a bench. She jumped off and elbowed me out of the way, peering into the microscope with professional ease. "That mound must be four feet long. There were no bones, no framework." She turned the focus, lapsed into silence, then, "Shit, you're right. Undeniably human." She glanced up into our inquiring stares. "Sorry, forgot to mention. Forensic pathologist."

Henri laughed. "Oh, nice one. Really nice, eh Father?"

Bonnie chuckled. To cover my consternation I lifted the slide from the microscope and carried it across to the bench I use for my more unusual investigations. I mixed together some basil, a little shaved mandrake, and some milk from a nursing white whale. I crushed the skull of a long-extinct mammal into the mix, then scooped a finger through it and spread a blob across a slice of the flesh, chanting in a language known only to myself and three monks in Tibet.

"Should he be doing stuff like that?" Bonnie whispered.

"He's not exactly a priest," Henri replied. I smiled. I might be getting through to people. I placed the sliver of flesh onto a fresh slide and slid it back under the microscope.

"So," Henri asked as I bent to the eyepiece, "is it still human?"

The mixture on the slide spelled out the owner of the flesh in a pattern I could not mistake. I stared at it, refusing to allow the shock of recognition to reach my voice.

"It's more than that," I told him. "It's someone we know."

Costa Satanas has many fascinating features, not least of which is its topography. If you can navigate a tesseract and you know where to look, you can travel the length of the entire town in little more than a few steps. I had been banging on the front door of Mama Casson's Hotel Quixote for over three minutes before Henri and Bonnie staggered round the corner at the far end of the street.

"One of these days," Henri gasped as they reached me, "you're going to have to introduce me to a map of this place."

"It's locked." I indicated the entrance. "There's no answer."

"Locked? Mama C locked the hotel door?" We exchanged worried frowns. Mama Casson never closed the Quixote. Time of day was no impediment to parting a tourist from their cash.

"If that really was her on the beach, she may not have been the one who did."

"You don't think it was her, do you?"

I stopped to consider the mass of flesh we had carried up the beach to the cooler room at Benito's.

"Mama is one of my earliest residents, and one of my oldest friends. If it is, I shall never stop taking revenge on whoever did such a thing to her."

"But it can't be. Surely."

I pulled my lock picking gear from inside my jacket. "There's only one way to find out."

"Excuse me." Bonnie moved past us and reached into her purse. She pulled out a key, inserted it, and opened the entry. "After you."

"A key?" Henri stage-whispered as we entered the darkened hallway.

"I'm as surprised as you are," I replied. I couldn't recall Mama Casson using a normal key, and I've been here longer than the town. We stopped creeping halfway down the hall, outside Mama's apartment. The door was closed. I knocked.

"Mama?"

No answer came from within. I knocked louder, and called her name once more. Still she made no reply. Henri made to grab the doorknob, and I stopped his hand.

"I wouldn't do that just yet."

Mama Casson was driven from her homeland for being a witch. She wasn't, not entirely, but her knowledge of arcane matters outstripped my own in many places. Protection charms were something she could do in her sleep. A scent in the deadened air of the corridor teased at my memory.

"Mothers?" I looked at the others in surprise. "Why would she be afraid of mothers?"

"You've obviously not met mine."

I smiled at Henri's nervous joke. "Okay, you can open it."

He turned the knob, and the door swung open on silent hinges. The air inside smelled clean, and altogether wrong for a woman who spent every spare moment huddled over pot, saucepan, and cauldron. I traded glances with Henri, moved inside, and reached for the light switch.

"What the hell?" Henri stepped past me. The last time either of us was here, the room had been scaffolded by shelving. Books and ornaments from a thousand travels leaned together in joyful chaos. Now it was all gone, and in its place . . .

"It's a shrine."

"Did she mention anything to you?"

"No." I took a step forward. "No, she didn't."

"But you're her priest."

"I keep telling you . . ." I reached the far corner and bent to examine the memorial. "Oh, no."

"What is it?" Bonnie's voice reached us from the doorway. We turned toward her, and she gestured at the room helplessly.

"Is it . . . ?"

"You can come in."

"I . . . uh, I have a son."

"Ah. Wait a moment." I pulled a medallion from a jacket pocket, walked over, and placed it round her neck. "Saint Anne," I explained. "Patron saint. You should be fine now."

I took her hand and led her inside, ignoring Henri's intentionally guileless face. Bonnie took one look at the picture forming the shrine's backdrop and gasped.

"Holy Mother," she whispered. "*Matris of templum, matris nostri fides, servo quod indulgeo nos ut vos did qui unseated quod pessum ire vos.*"

"What? What did she say?"

"I don't know," I replied.

"It's a prayer," Bonnie told us. "To the Holy Mother Joan."

"You recognize her?"

Bonnie smiled. "Catholic girls' school. We had to hero worship *somebody*."

"Anybody fancy clueing me in?" Henri raised his eyebrows in mock encouragement. I indicated the cheap print.

"It's a picture of a statue which once adorned an edicola on the Vicus Papissa in Rome."

"The whatus?"

"Street of the Woman Pope," Bonnie translated.

"Woman Pope."

"Pope Joan." As I spoke her name, the woman in the portrait turned her head and regarded me with a look both calculating and watchful. Bonnie took a step backward. I reached out a hand to stop her.

"Now would not be the time to run." She stood rigid. I did my best not to recognize the warmth beneath her trembling skin. "She reigned as Pope John the Eighth during the ninth century, disguised as a man. But she fell in love with a junior bishop on the Papal staff. When she gave birth while journeying along the Vicus Papissa they hanged her, along with her baby and lover." I regarded the print. "The likeness does not do her justice."

The picture opened its mouth, and a voice like ancient sand filled the room.

"Where is he?"

"Where is who?" Bonnie whispered.

"Where is he?" The voice became more strident, angrier. The eyes fixed upon me, and grew wide as recognition distorted its features. "You! How could you . . . ?"

"Run!" I pushed my two companions toward the exit. Ripping sounds filled the room behind us, and a scream of rage. We bundled into the hallway. I slammed the door, catching a glimpse of the ruined shrine and the creature half emerged from it as I did so.

"The medallion! Quickly!" I pointed to the ornament dangling from Bonnie's throat. She tore it off and flung it to me. I wrapped it round the doorknob and spat on it three times, murmuring a chant in Black Aramaic.

"She's a Pope," I explained as I herded them out of the building. "Mother to a whole cult. Reversing the charm might hold her for a while."

"Catholicism is hardly a cult."

"All religions are cults." I set off down the street.

"Some priest," Bonnie muttered as they fell in behind me.

"He's not a priest," Henri replied, but I was too lost in thought to take any pleasure in his denial. "So where are we going? We're not just leaving her there, surely?"

I looked back at the hotel. I had thought never to revisit the pain that suddenly encircled my throat. "No," I replied, "we're going to seek psychiatric help."

"What is all this about, Father? I'm a very busy man."

Mister Gull had an office on Jongleur Street, just below Henri's photographic studio. He was always busy, although he no longer practiced medicine, at least not upon the locals. I disregarded the speculative look he gave Bonnie and explained our problem. Gull stared at me over steepled fingers.

"Why should this concern me?"

"I need an insight into her psyche. I need someone with experience."

Bonnie snorted. "As opposed to, say, a woman?"

"Sir William was physician in ordinary to Her Majesty the Queen," I replied, not shifting my eyes from the doctor's measured gaze. "He was also the world authority on the treatment of madness in women, and the first man to accurately diagnose epilepsy, not to mention his studies into the occult. He is well placed, believe me."

Gull harrumphed, and rose from his chair, walking round the room with slow steady steps. "I no longer consult. You know that."

"I do."

"Why not?" Bonnie asked.

"Because I have no need to."

"Sir William is interested in transubstantiation." I did my best to keep my voice neutral. "Especially the transformation of female flesh into something else."

"Something *higher*, Father." Gull crossed the room to gaze up at a Walter Sickert portrait of Victoria. "Her Majesty was a remarkable woman, both mystically powerful and . . . troubled. She foresaw her death, and knew it would herald the death of the Empire. I was charged with finding a way to transform her into something higher, more permanent."

"Five prostitutes died."

"Were transubstantiated, Father. Ennobled. As was Her Majesty, in the end."

"Wait a minute!" Bonnie strode past me to confront the heavyset surgeon. "Queen Victoria? But that was . . ."

"A lifetime ago. No more."

She turned to me, throwing her arms wide in exasperation. "This is too much. It's just too much. Globsters made out of people, pictures coming to life and attacking me, now ageless doctors from a hundred and forty odd years ago?" She made for the door. "I can't take this. I came here for a holiday. Two weeks in the sun. That's all."

"Bonnie." I placed a hand on her shoulder and let a small portion of my being flow through my skin and into her. She stiffened, turning wild eyes upon me. "I understand your fear. But this is very real, and very urgent. Leave if you want to, but I cannot guarantee your safety. She has seen you."

Gull advanced upon us. Bonnie raised her head to him. I removed my hand, and she sagged against me.

"Five prostitutes," she whispered.

"Five martyrs," he replied, reaching out to wipe away the tears that sprung to her eyes. "And I have changed so very much since that time."

"You're . . ."

"I am a surgeon, young lady, nothing more." Gull contemplated the portrait for long, silent seconds. I sensed the loneliness in him, and the soundless apologies he sent toward the painting's subject. I wondered what they had to say to each other, in the evenings, when the two of them were alone and she could climb down from her frame in safety. Eventually he bowed his head, and turned back to me, his eyes full of memory.

"This woman, Father."

"Yes?"

"She seeks to reclaim someone. A male. If she has been transformed and comes back, it is because she cannot be complete without him."

"Who?"

"The baby, perhaps. Or the lover. Both, if necessary."

I looked into his steady, knowing gaze, and felt a hidden weight shift within me.

"Do you think you might know who, Father?"

"Yes," I whispered. "Yes."

There is a small room toward the back of my house, at the end of a corridor that appears only when it is absolutely unavoidable. I keep my items of pain there, all the mistakes and evils I cannot rectify, and cannot bear to keep within me. I placed my hand on the door and turned to my two companions.

"Please wait in the kitchen."

They left. I closed my eyes and opened the door, stepping into the dark interior. No light infiltrates the room. It isn't necessary. I can find what I want without illumination. Directly inside, on the top shelf, lay a pine box, exactly twenty-four inches long by eight wide. I lifted it down with both hands and made my way to my companions. The door locked itself fast behind me, as it always does, until I need it again.

"What is it?" Henri asked as I placed the box gently on the kitchen table. I prised the lid off and gazed down at the tiny figure within.

"My son," I said, allowing pain to fill me. Bonnie choked back a sob and began to whisper a prayer in Latin. Henri simply stared, his fingers turning white as they gripped the edge of the table.

"Joan was not hanged for being female," I said, reaching into the casket and gently raising the body out. "She was a good Pope. The people loved her. She was on the verge of heralding a new era of Papal responsibility, widening the Church's influence in areas that were significant in the coming Dark Ages. She was an efficient administrator, incorruptible, holy in every thought and deed."

I nestled my son against my chest, stroking his mummified brow as I talked.

"Those in power knew she was a woman, and didn't care. Joan was good for the Church. Even when she secretly wed a member of her staff and became pregnant they re-ordered their calendar to accommodate it. The mother of the Church would become the mother of a child. It was as a second coming of sorts, a symbol to unite the people under God. The perfect union of faith, humanity, and motherhood."

"But . . ." Henri choked.

"But she gave birth a month early, on her way through the streets of Rome. And she gave birth to this." I ran my fingers over my son's horns, down across the scales on his body, along the tail to its forked point. "My son."

"I don't . . . I don't get it."

"Her body rejected him, I think." I looked up from his wizened visage. "Joan was the personification of God upon earth. She had . . . *transubstantiated*. Her husband wasn't evil, but his flesh came from an evil source. She could no longer bear it inside her, so she simply . . . rejected him. This is the reason she was hanged." I held him out to them. "This is what she has come back to claim."

"But . . . that was over a thousand years ago," Bonnie gasped, her eyes fixed on the baby. "Who are you? *What* are you?" She backed away from me, stumbling as she banged into a stool. I spoke as gently as I am capable.

"I am old, and trying to be wise, and much better than I was."

"Oh God, you're . . . you're . . ."

"No," I said, reading the conclusion in her eyes. "I'm not him. He wouldn't even consider himself my father. I am a part that was lost, that is all."

"No." She retreated to the door. "No." She flung it open, running into the street.

"Bonnie!" I turned to Henri. "Follow her, please. Make sure she's okay. She'll need your protection."

Henri moved past me, turning at the door to view me with more tiredness than fear.

"What about you?" he said. "Shouldn't you go after her?"

"I have things I need to do," I replied, holding my son close.

The hallway of Mama Casson's hotel lay quiet around me as I carried my tiny burden to her apartment. The charm was still twisted round the doorknob. I placed my ear against the door but heard nothing from within.

"I'd be terrified if it wasn't for the fear," I muttered in my best Hawkeye Pearce voice, and loosened the charm. I dropped it into a jacket pocket, pushed open the door, and stepped through in one swift movement. Only once I was fully inside did I let go of the breath I was holding.

The room was dark; the rubble of Joan's frenzied attack visible only by the glow emanating from her figure, hanging in the air three feet in front of me. She glared at me from a twisted caricature of the face I once cradled in my hands, her eyes elongated slits of hatred and need. She raised her hands toward me, and they stretched into claws more avian than human. I returned the gesture, showing her the baby.

"They salted his flesh," I said. "After they took him. They quartered him, and salted him, and took the parts to four pagan countries and buried them in ground they decreed could never be consecrated."

Joan floated down and placed her claws beneath my hands. I withdrew them, and my son stayed where he was, supported by ectoplasm and his mother's desperate love.

"It took me six hundred years to find him," I whispered. "But I did, in the end."

She drew her eyes away from his body. Iridescent tears streamed down her cheeks. Her lips twitched, and she mouthed a name I have not owned in over a millennium. Then she drew the little corpse up, nestling him against her breast in an unearthly parody of a feeding embrace. With her free hand she reached out to stroke my cheek. I was surprised to find it wet.

"I'm sorry," I said. "I never wanted to . . ."

"No!"

Joan's attention snapped from me to the door. She flew back across the room with an enraged hiss.

"Get away from him!"

I turned to see Bonnie outlined in the doorway.

"Bonnie, don't!"

She stepped forward as I spoke, fists raised in the beginning stance of a Jeet-kun-do expert. As she crossed the threshold, Mama Casson's protection spell activated, lifting her and flinging her backward. She struck the wall outside the apartment with a wet thud and hung there, three feet above the floor. I moved on impulse, diving out the door, shouting an anti-spell in an effort to free her. I heard a shriek behind me. Bonnie began to slide down the wall. Joan swept past me, engulfing Bonnie's helpless form with her own.

Bonnie screamed and I joined in. I clawed at her waist, trying to pull her away from the maddened form of my former love. She turned to jelly as I watched, voice cutting off as her body transformed into a shapeless blob of flesh. It hit the floor with a soft plop. Joan spared me a single glance before swooping down the hallway and into the sky beyond, leaving me kneeling, Bonnie's cooling corpse in my arms, crying out her name until my voice gave way to helpless tears.

Henri was waiting for me when I returned to my house.

"How did it . . . what's wrong?"

"Go to Benito's," I told him, pushing past and striding into the kitchen. "I want a bottle of his best red. His best, you understand, the stuff laid down in the bomb shelter he doesn't think anyone knows about. Here," I pulled a handful of coins from my jacket pocket and threw them on the bench. "Go quickly."

"He'll take doubloons?"

"Henri." I turned my back on him and let a little anger creep into my voice. "Go now. Tell him there is another globster at Mama's for his cool room."

"Yes, Father."

The door clicked shut, and I went to work. Within an hour I was ready, and waiting for Henri's return. There was a knock, and the young photographer stepped through, a bottle of wine in his hand.

"I've got . . . what the . . . ?"

Deep in the bowels of the house I have a cabinet full of candles. Each century I make another set, imbuing them with the essence of the most potent experience of the last hundred years. If lit, they cast shadows in such a way that the memories are released and fill the room. A dozen such candles circled the kitchen. Henri stood in the gilded doorway of the private dining quarters of Pope John the Eighth, the night she and I first made love. I sat at the small dining table, my simple cassock tight and itchy across my chest.

"Thank you, Henri. Leave the bottle with me, please."

He crossed the room in amazement, circling slowly in an attempt to take everything in.

"How . . . ? I mean, what is this place? How did you . . . ?"

"She has her child now." I concentrated on the ball of calm that sits within my chest whenever I am about to reach an end that will leave me altered. "A child needs a father. A wife needs her husband."

"What are you going to do?"

"Transformations, Henri. We all need to change, to reach higher states of being. If we don't, we stand still, or worse, regress. And if we regress, we die." I reached for my jacket pocket, then remembered my simple robes and crossed to the sideboard to retrieve a corkscrew. I bent to the bottle, releasing the cork with a satisfied grunt. "She's coming. You should leave."

"I . . . yeah, okay." Henri made for the door. He opened it, and glanced back at me. "Good luck, Father."

"Goodbye, Henri."

He left, and I waited for the arrival of my lost love. I did not wait for long. She was before me within minutes, glowing blue in the dark light of the candles. She was dressed as I best remembered her, in the cotton shift she favoured in her private apartments. Her hair was tied in an uncomplicated bun, a single flower tucked behind her ear. Her neck spoiled the illusion. It twisted to one side, her head tilted at an angle only achievable by a hangman's noose. Even in death, even with her child returned to her, she could not move past that moment.

"Lady," I bowed my head toward the bottle, "will you join me?"

She floated to the chair opposite me. I poured two glasses, and pushed one in front of her.

"Your health." I raised my glass and sipped. Joan placed a ghostly hand around her own glass and it glided up toward her mouth. I watched the wine drip down her throat, as well as the stream that crossed her angled cheek to spill upon the table-cloth. I stood and moved to the sideboard. Two plates lay upon it, next to a bowl of fresh vegetables and a small cut of dark meat. I filled each plate with thin slices. I placed a plate in front of Joan, turning it so the meat was closest. Then I regained my seat, speared a slice, and brought it to my lips.

"To our son," I said, and ate. Joan acknowledged my toast, then raised a sliver to her own mouth. She chewed and swallowed. The little ball fell down her throat until it reached the hangman's bend. Then it lodged. Joan swallowed, and again, but the meat remained stuck.

"Interesting cut, don't you think?" I asked. Joan stared at me with bugged eyes, hands clawing at the obstruction. "I found it, eventually, in a box buried in a garden in the courtyard of the Emperor's Palace in Tokyo. It was guarded by a small Shinto spirit called into being for that exact purpose. It is heart, my lady. Your son's heart."

Very gently I placed my cutlery on the table, then left my seat and walked round so that I stood with my hands on the back of her chair. I leaned forward, closed my eyes, and whispered.

"A devil's choice, don't you think? The meat will poison you, spirit though you are, if you leave it there. Or you can reject it, spit it out. But you will need to become flesh to do so. Either way you will be transformed." I kissed her ear, feeling the electric tingle of her substance beneath my lips. "What shall it be, my love?"

She said nothing in response, merely stiffened as realization of her position deepened. I kept my eyes closed, trying to remember the way Bonnie smelled, the way Mama Casson's hips swayed as she walked.

The room began to grow cold. Matter is energy condensed into a slow-moving form. A spirit is a being of energy. It can become flesh again. All it takes is will, and chemical change. I stood silent in the midst of Joan's endothermic reaction; until she bucked forward and I heard choking erupt from the flesh of her newly substantial throat. I saw Bonnie's screaming face in my mind, saw the indisputable fact of Mama's transformation on the microscope slide, watched the images melt and run down into the ball of calm at my centre. Then I reached out and enclosed Joan's throat with my fingers.

"I shall never stop taking revenge."

I squeezed until my knuckles throbbed, until the last feeble struggle died away beneath my hands, and I stood alone in the room with only my own steady breathing for company.

I buried them at the top of Point Arrival. Four graves, one smaller than the rest, each marked with a single, millennium-old candle. When the task was done I sat on a rug and drank a final cup of coffee from my thermos. I overturned the rest, and let the hot fluid run into the grass. Henri was waiting for me at the bottom of the incline.

"Are you okay?"

"No."

"Are you going to be?"

"That remains to be seen." I drew a small vial of smoke from a jacket pocket, uncorked it, and spread the contents around. The language I spoke is so old the only words remembered are those of that spell, and then, only by me. Point Arrival shimmered and disappeared. By the time the smoke cleared, no sign of the spur remained. A small beach stood in its place, easily accessible to all. Henri exhaled deeply.

"One thing I don't understand."

"Yes?"

"What was Mama C doing on the beach? And why didn't anyone notice?"

I turned away from his questions. "I don't know."

"What?"

"I'm not perfect, Henri. I'm only human."

His gaze flickered down my length, the look on his face telling me all I needed to know about his opinion. Finally he shrugged, and changed the subject.

"What about Bonnie's son?"

"He'll be taken care of. I've made arrangements."

The young photographer looked past me at the new beach, then up at the spot in mid-air where four graves deserved to be.

"You frighten me sometimes, you know."

"No more than I do myself."

I walked away, and took the long way back to town.

MARGO LANAGAN

Winkie

Margo Lanagan has published three collections of speculative short stories:
White Time, Black Juice, *and, recently,* Red Spikes. *Her stories have won
two World Fantasy Awards, two Ditmar Awards, three Aurealis Awards, and
a Michael L. Printz Honor, and have been shortlisted for many other
awards, including a Nebula, a Hugo, and the James Tiptree, Jr. Award.
Lanagan taught at Clarion South in 2005 and will do so again in 2007. She
lives in Sydney, Australia, and works as a contract technical writer. She has
also published poetry, and fiction for junior readers and teenagers. She
maintains a blog at www.amongamidwhile.blogspot.com.*

"Winkie" was one of several original stories in Lanagan's collection Red
Spikes.

—E.D.

Ollyn lay awake among the snoring Keller kids. The man goggled in at her
through the window.

I will go home, she thought. Somehow. As soon as he's gone. I will run
out of here; I will run home. No matter about the new baby coming; I will
sit quiet in a corner. Only, I can't be here. I can't be here a moment longer than I
have to be. I am just not brave enough.

"Skinny little thing, aincha?" Tod Keller had said when she sidled in their
kitchen door last evening. "I never even noticed you among those rousty-boys,
your brothers."

Ma Keller had laughed, a sudden laugh that made Oll start. "Tuck her away in
the press," she said. "Pop her on the mantel for the night, couldn't we, petal?" Her
finger under Oll's chin had scraped like splintery wood.

He was too tall a man. He was extraordinarily tall. No one else she knew could
look in over the sill of an upstairs window. If it could be called "looking," when a
person's eyes swivvered left and right like that, never meeting up in the same
direction—at least as far as Oll had seen. She'd had the good sense, when an I beam
swung near, to lie limp and asleep-looking. She breathed slowly while her heart
banged like a soldiers' band.

He shifted out there in the laneway, and muttered some question to himself. He
rapped softly on the windowpane, and it was all Oll could do to not cringe at the
sound, which was spongy somehow, as well as bony.

Go away, you horror, she thought, so I can get home from here.

———

Ple-ease! Why was she like this now? She knew her ma hated it, and yet the whining came up from her deeps and she needed, needed to be pressed up against warm Ma, couldn't see why Ma would not stop a moment what she was doing and hold onto her and make things all right. Just the once would do.

Get her off me, Ma had said through her teeth.

Huvvy had peeled her off claw by claw. *Come here you little limpet, you little sticky octopoddle,* he laughed as she wailed.

Ollyn had lost her head a moment, thinking she would die of her distress.

And that was when Ma had rounded on her. *It's because of* this *you must go, silly girl! All this clinging and sooking, you're sending me mad!*

Ollyn had blinked silent at Ma's vehemence; Huvvy had stopped laughing and held her quite firm and protectingly.

But Ma had kept on. *Our baby will not come* out *with you around! It will not want to see the face that horrible noise comes out of!*

She was bent over them; Huvvy and Oll were blown back by the wind of her anger. They all three had leaned like that a moment.

Take her, Huv. Take her to Kellers'. I can't stand it any longer. And Ma turned away and spread her hands on the table and gritted her teeth there with a pain.

Get your nightgown, Huvvy had murmured in Oll's ear, and she had hurried to do so.

The man's feet, on the cobbles, slid, paused, and then slapped. His muttering moved away from the window. Oll waited, because her heart of hearts knew he might well come back to a window he had peered in before. But she could not wait too long, because she must see which direction he went in, so she could avoid him.

Up she got from between fat Anya and bony Sarra Keller, and ran lightly to the window, keeping to the shadows. She pressed her cheek to the window frame.

At first she didn't see him up the lane. Oh, she thought, maybe I only dreamed him. But I will go home anyway. Ma will protect me from my dreams.

But then a clot of shadow moved low against that door, at the top of those stairs there, and a high cry snaked down the lane, and the thing, the man, unfolded himself, the full kinked lanky height of him, with his shining round head, a few hairs streaked across it, a few others floating out sideways, bright and frizzly in the lamplight.

Watching him crane to see into that house, hearing his cry, Oll was like Mixie Dixon's doll that her pa brought from Germany, held together with stiff wires. How will I *get* home, she thought, if I cannot even move?

The man's nightgown confused her eye. It was made of the oddest shaped patches, all patterned differently. Buttons gleamed here and there. Unhemmed, it stroked his stringy calves with fraying threads. His feet—look how many cobbles his feet covered! Oll was likely to faint with it.

He swayed out from the window, back towards the Kellers' and called, in a high, reasonable voice borrowed from someone sane, someone real, "*Well* past! So far past their bedtime!" Then he loped up the steps past Draper Downs's house where there were no children, and past the House of the Indigent Aged. And around into Spire Street, to the *right*, turning *up* the hill.

Oll's wires turned to workable muscle again, and her mind cleared somewhat. Ma, she thought. Ma. She must put herself near Ma.

She did not dress. She did not take her clothes. She did not even stop for boots. In her nightdress, cool air puffing inside it, she ran noiselessly down the stairs.

The cat by the coals lifted its black head as she passed. The kitchen door was just like the one at home; she knew how to raise the latch, hold it up while she tiptoed through, and lower it silently behind her.

It was a clear, cold night, the sky thick-frosted with stars. A part of Oll quailed and quaked and covered its head inside her, while her body ran stiffly along the house-path, across the back of Kellers', and down the narrow side way. She peeped around into the lane, and there was the same view as from the upper room, the fine-cut key-stone over Draper Downs's door, the House's curly-iron sign silhouetted against the lamplit wall—except she was lower down in this view now, so much more at the mercy of things, and the night was cold, cold.

She dived down into the shadows to her left, stubbing her toe on a cobble but not stopping, not even missing a step to hop. She gasped the pain out as she ran. Her breath was the only sound, that and the slight rubbings and shiftings of her night-dress, which was soft and damp with sleep, chilling around her. Her feet made no sound on the cobbles, their soles being smooth and damp too, and Oll being so light. The row houses of Pitcher Street flew past her up the hill.

A noise in the Square, just before she reached it, made her slide to a stop; her hair swung out, and her nightdress hem, just to the house—corner exactly and no farther. The clank of the lamplighter's hook, the squeak of the lamp door. The scrape of the lamplighter's boots. His sweetish pipe smoke wisped around the corner and tickled her nose.

She ran back up Pitcher Street; it was far to the first lane. She hid, and panting peeped back down. There: he was crossing the street-end, attending to the lamp there, closing it—and moving on around the Square?

No. Oll swallowed a whimper. The lamplighter was coming up Pitcher Street. She could go to him, perhaps; she could ask him to take her home. He would have to.

But I'm not brave enough, she thought. I can't go up and talk to a man, not in the middle of the night, not after seeing that other. And she ran away along the lane.

She could have taken the back way behind the row houses, but a dog was barking somewhere down there, and the noise was too much for her all by itself in this huge night. So she ran on to Swale Street—and out into the middle of the street she ran, and down she ran in the full lamplight right alongside the drain there, so that when the tall patched shadow unkinked itself from a doorway uphill, why, there she was, clear as anything, little and live as he could wish for.

"Ooh, there's one!"

She skittered aside like a rat, under a jettied upper floor. There was nowhere to run on to, though, however much she searched; and however small she was, no cav-ity could hide her.

His great feet walked down Swale Street, treading with exaggerated care. His voice fluted up there among the stars. His nightgown—Oll was the wired-together doll again—his nightgown was made of many nightdresses, she saw now, small ones, unpicked and spread out flat, and clumsily sewn together.

His knees came down inside the nightgown-cloth like two great tree-bolls falling from a woodcutter's cart, and his fists came down like two more, either side of the jutting room.

Ollyn wilted and whimpered and shrank into a ball.

His face came down: the wide mouth with bad teeth saying, "Where can she be, the little mousette?" in that too-high voice; his nose, long and uneven and gristly-looking, with sprays of dark hairs from the nostrils; then the eyes, so big and so mis-matched, searching, searching, first this one then that.

"Ah. Ha-ha-*ha*." That was his own voice, that deep one, that rougher one. "But you can't make yourself small *enough*, can you?"

She looked from eye to eye. *Ma*, she mouthed, and tears came.

"That's what I like to see," he said.

He picked her up and brought her out and examined her, laying her flat across the palms of his big hands. She could not identify the bad smell of them.

And then she was too busy trying to breathe, because he had stopped her mouth with soft wax, tied it in with a rag. She was near dead with fright, just as a mouse or bird will die in your hand, from being so enclosed.

He held her tight and carried her out of town the misty, marshy way, the way no one walked here—but then, no one had such long legs as these; he gathered up his patchwork nightgown and stepped across the marsh's lumps and glimmers. Her feet swung out in the cold like bell-clappers, but struck noise from nothing. The man waded in among trees, where it was still misty, and then onto drier ground. He put Oll down, and pinned her with his foot while he lifted a door in the side of a mound of earth. He carried her inside, and the door closed and entombed them.

Dizzy, her eyes full of stars that weren't there, no voice to scream with and no breath to cry, Ollyn stayed limp where he had laid her, on wood as scratchy as Ma Keller's fingers. Her eyelids turned dimly red as he made a light. Such a smell!

He frightened her eyes open, speaking close. "Let's look at you." He was there with a smutchy lamp. She was on a table, and he sat down by it. The dark parts of his eyes skated about on his eyeballs. He propped her upright, took a tool, cut through the rag around her mouth and hooked the wax out. "There," he said. "Squeak to me. Squeak as loud as you like."

When she did not, he poked her in the tum. "Blink, then. Show me how you can blink."

This she did, and it delighted him. His delight was all brown teeth and spittle and spongy hands clapping.

Oll blinked some more; blinking was better than being eaten.

"Yes, that'll *do*." He smacked her so that she fell sideways on the table. "No need to be a *smarty*-britches."

He brought his face close to hers, pointed to his own staring eyes with his flat fingers. "You see these?"

She nodded, still dazed from the blows.

"Do you see blinkers? Do you see any lids?"

Ollyn shook her head.

"You know what my name is, by those that rule the world, those mums and das, those butchers and merchants and clerks and councillors?"

She shook her head again. Maybe if she did not utter, he would not harm her.

"Wee Will Winkie. 'Wee' because I am so *big*, you see. 'Winkie' because I *cannot* wink. I cannot wink, or blink, or sleep. I can barely *see* for my dry eyes and their irritations; do you see how red are these eyes?"

Oll nodded.

"I will show you," he said. He darted away, darted back. "Cannot wink, or blink, but *aahh* he can think, this one. And you shall help me."

He went off and rummaged in the shadows. "I have hid them, in case of intruders," he said in a muffled voice. "Beasts, you know, or thieves."

The lamplight did not push back much of the darkness. Boxes, she thought, were stacked in a corner. There was a heap of cloths, another heap of scrambled dark shapes—firewood, perhaps, from some twisty kind of tree. A fire snoozed in a filthy, rusted stove, the rotten smell near-smothered her.

"Here." Out of the corner the giant came. He placed—either side of the lamp so that they lit up like lamps themselves—two large finger-smudged flasks made of glass. They were nearly full with clear water. Its rocking had stirred up the fine white sediment on the bottom, which spiraled up slowly. In each flask something like a mottled pig's ear hung from gray threads that passed up through a wax-sealed hole in the flask's broad cork and trailed off across the table.

"Aren't they beautiful?" said the giant. "So much work in them."

Ollyn examined one pink-and-brown glowing shape. The work was—

"Stitches," she said, surprised into speech. It was clumsy stitches.

"Yes!" he said. "Stitches-stitches, in the softest skin! *Many* nights' work. And look along the bottom—what do you see there?"

"Uh . . . a—a *fringe*." A fringe of tiny spikes. Of hairs.

"Of real lashes." He breathed the words into her face. "Of *real* lashes! Can you believe it?"

"It's. It's. It's." She waved a hand helplessly at the flasks, thinking she might faint again, or be sick, from this smell and this sight, the fleshy patchworks hanging, glowing. She looked away, but the only other thing to look at besides the giant's face was his nightgown, which had so much the same appearance, the different colours, the seams, the recognisable shapes of arms and chests, but splayed out, spread out as if flayed from—

"I want my ma," she said to him, trying not to boo-hoo it, trying to speak as if she were one giant talking to another. Tears weaseled out of her eyes. "I want my ma and pa, and Huvvy and Daff and all my brothers. You must let me go home."

He seemed startled, but when she was unable to stifle a hiccough and a teary sniff, he relaxed again. "How about," he sing-songed, "a nice hot cup of tea, eh? And a bit of . . . cake. I have a cake."

"I don't want a cake," whispered Oll, but he went looking. She pulled her legs up under her nightgown and wept into her knees, as he moved things and dragged things and muttered.

"Was over *here*," he said. "I put the child *here*, cause it was broken, and the cake *here*. Although, maybe I have mixed that up. Maybe it is among—"

He started to rearrange the pile of twisty firewood. The bad smell was much worse all of a sudden. Oll choked into the knee-cloth of her nightgown, trying to see through her tears.

"Agh," he said. "Well, how about—these is good for a snack sometimes, after they've lain awhile."

He looked doubtfully at the pile. He had one in his hand, by its little blackened leg. As Oll watched, the leg came out of its rotten hip socket, and the rest of the baby fell back onto the pile.

The sounds of the breaking, of the falling, stayed in the air a moment.

Then, too fast to think, Oll exploded off the table. She could not be faster than him, but she beat him to the door. She was not strong enough, but she lifted the heavy wooden hatch. She was not very clever, but she ran behind the mound and flattened herself to the grass there, and when Will Winkie burst out of the hatch and stood howling towards the town she clawed a stone out of the ground, and she knelt up and threw it high into the mist, so that it splashed down into marshwater far out in front of him.

The giant plunged after it, still howling. It will not fool him long, Oll thought. He will come back and search here. And she crept down and slipped into the marsh's edge and found a place where she could crouch and rest her head against a hummock, to look like another hummock. It was shockingly cold, that water, but she must hide. And when she was hidden, if she kept very tight and still, wrapping her arms about her bent legs, there was a small amount of warmth that she could harbor there, and her feet and ankles warmed their mud socks just a tad, and she would not quite die.

She opened her eyes. She was in the Kellers' upper room.

"Did you sleep well?" said fat Anya without turning over.

"Yes, thank you," said Ollyn timidly.

But then all the Keller kids got up at once, and their faces were mud, and their nightwear was soaked with it and they trooped wetly to the stairhead, mud sliding from their hanging fingers, trailing mud behind them on the floor, and they slopped downstairs to Ma Keller who was frying something and calling them in her fluting voice.

Oll woke under the stars. It was quite warm in the water now. The shivering had stopped. She did not want to move; certainly she did not want to feel that night air on her wet skin. Besides, if she were not carried by a giant, she could not get across the marsh without drowning. She must wait for daylight and find a way, hummock to hummock, somehow.

She opened her eyes. Sparse golden leaves on black branches moved against a blue sky. She was a warm baby, at home, without thoughts or cares. Voices somewhere spoke of everyday matters, quietly so as not to disturb her, without urgency or anger.

Her eyes blinked open. The stars had tilted in the sky. Other lights, midsummer lights, flashed and moved on the marshwater. Voices spoke, the voices from her dream, nothing to be afraid of. She laid her head against the hummock again; perhaps she could sink back into that dream?

They were lifting her from the marsh—her corpse, for she was surely dead; she could do nothing with her legs and arms, only feel them hanging off her like quartersacks of grain.

"He killed me, then," she said.

"What's that, Olliepod?" Huvvy's head was huger than a giant's against the stars.

"She spoke?" said Pa somewhere.

"He threw me on the pile," Oll managed. "He . . . he cut off my eyelids for his jar, for his own."

"Ollie, are you in there?" said Huvvy, frightened. "Is our Ollie in there, or is she bewitched somehow?"

She *did* have eyelids; they drooped across her sight. She was wrapped like a baby in rough, dry cloth. She was shivering, shivering. The shivering shook her whole body and almost all her mind. She was cold against her pa. He was chafing her arm and shoulder back to life through the blanket.

"Did you go into his house?" she said through her shivering jaws. "Did you see all those babies?"

"That house there?" Pa pointed and she saw the mound fading into the moonlit mist.

"Did *you* cleave it?"

"What's that, my darling?"

"Did you break it like that, the top of it?"

"It were broken all along, Ollyn. It were rotten wrecked when we found it. And no babies inside, loved one. Nothing inside at all but earth. I saw it myself, and Huv and his lamp. Because we looked good and hard in there. Your ma said you might well be in there, buried. But we dug it apart and you weren't. Then and then only, when we were spent and giving up, did you move yourself, and make that cry in the water."

"Like a little cat," said Daff, rowing. "Miou, miou."

"I don't remember," said Oll.

"Of course not," said Huvvy. "You were just about insensible."

Ollyn and Ma scoured the pots, down by the stream. It was Ma's first outing since the baby. They were numb-fingered with scrubbing, and the wind blew unpredictably, buffeting them off-balance and twitching their hair.

"How did you know?" said Oll.

"Know what?" Ma slapped a fresh handful of sand into the rinsed stewpot.

"Where to find me that night. Where to tell Pa and Huvvy to go. And to get a boat. How'd you know about that man?"

Ma scrubbed. "Everyone knows about that man."

"Pa didn't. And 'How'd she get there?' says Huvvy. And I told them and they said, 'Ooh, sounds like Romany Tom' or someone. They would have guessed and guessed, and gone out and had someone thrown in jail, if you didn't shut them up."

Ma scrubbed on. There was a stubborn set to her.

Well, Oll could be stubborn too. "So *not* everyone knows." She was back on her heels now, not even pretending to scour. "How'd you know any of it? Pa says you woke him and told him where to go if I weren't at Kellers', where to look. Kellers didn't even know I was gone from the bed until he knocked."

Ma gave her head a little toss. With the wind, her hair clambered back into her eyes, as busy and black as duelling spiders.

"Ma?"

"What."

"Well?"

Ma lifted the wet sand and let it dribble into a turdy pile in the pot: *blat-blat-blat, blat-blot.* "All my babies," she said. "They wake in the night? I wake. I knew it were you in a minute. The way you carried on about going up to Kellers', I knew you would not stay put."

Oll laughed. "How *could* I wake you, halfway across the town?"

"I don't know." Ma bent to scrubbing again. "There must be a sound you make, your eyelids opening. It carries to my ears."

Oll watched Ma's wayward hair, her determined shoulders, her white and purple feet with the toes digging into the sand. These sights satisfied her like a solid meal in her belly. "But what about those other children, the dead ones, on the pile? Does not every mother hear that eyelid sound?"

Ma bunched up her mouth in thought. She rinsed the pot in the stream, holding it out wide where it would catch the clearer, faster water. "I don't know"—she swirled the water in the pot—"how it is for other mothers. I can only say how it is for me."

Through the fiddle and rush of the stream they heard the baby's thin cry. They sat straight to see over the bank, up to the house. Daff was carrying her down, her tiny fists and feet awheel in his awkward arms, her blanket dangling.

"Oh lord," sighed Ma. "Take her, Ollyn, while I finish here. Wrap her tight and walk her up and down. *Behind* the house, where I can't hear her noise so well."

Oll climbed the bank. The sunlight dazzled her after the shadowy stream bank; the earth was warm underfoot; the grass sprang high all up the hill and weedflowers nodded and lounged in it, yellow and red and pale purple. Daff waded through them fast with the crying baby, and Oll went to meet him, almost laughing, he looked so frightened of the tiny mewling thing.

NATHALIE ANDERSON

Tell

Nathalie Anderson's poem "Tell" was first published in the summer/autumn issue of The Journal of Mythic Arts. *She is the author of the collection* Following Fred Astaire, *and her poems have appeared in* Cimarron Review, Denver Quarterly, DoubleTake, The Paris Review, *and* Prairie Schooner, *among others. Anderson is the poet-in-residence at the Rosenbach Museum and Library and teaches at Swarthmore College.*

—K.L. & G.G.

One sees. One is enticed. One goes
or not. One pines, or not. That's all
it is. Still, every time one tells,
by hairsbreadth, hairsbreadth, on it grows.

The slant of eye. The cut of tooth.
One thinks what one describes explains.
While spouses sneer and parents strain,
sift sigh from sly, clip rune from brood.

Whatever one might think to say
one says. Despite one's innocence
strange words serve, stranger, to estrange.
Hearsay. Soothsay. Verité. Fey.
One's wooden tongue sprouts eloquence.
Oh changeling, this is how you change.

SCOTT NICHOLSON

Dog Person

Scott Nicholson is the author of six novels, including They Hunger *and* The Farm. *He's published over fifty stories in six countries, some of which are collected in* Thank You for the Flowers. *He is a journalist and screenwriter in the Southern Appalachian Mountains of North Carolina, where much of his work is set. A volunteer in the Horror Writers Association, he tends goats and an organic garden, picks obscure love songs penned for unsuspecting sweethearts, and nurtures an obsession for Batboy and Kim Possible. More is revealed at www.hauntedcomputer.com. "Dog Person" was originally published in issue 56 of* Cemetery Dance.

—E.D.

The final breakfast was scrambled eggs, crisp bacon, grits with real butter. Alison peeled four extra strips of bacon from the slab. On this morning of all mornings, she would keep the temperature of the stove eye just right. She wasn't the cook of the house, but Robert had taught her all about Southern cuisine, especially that of the Blue Ridge Mountains. Before they met, her breakfast consisted of a cup of what Robert teasingly called a "girly French coffee" and maybe a yogurt. He'd introduced her to the joys of an unhealthy start to the morning, along with plenty of other things, the best of the rest coming after sundown.

Even after two years, Alison wasn't as enthusiastic about the morning cholesterol infusion as Robert was. Or his dog. About once a week, though, she'd get up a half-hour early, drag the scarred skillet from beneath the counter, and peel those slick and marbled pieces of pig fat. The popping grease never failed to mark a red spot or two along her wrist as she wielded the spatula. But she wouldn't gripe about the pain today.

Robert would be coming down any minute. She could almost picture him upstairs, brushing his teeth without looking in the mirror. He wouldn't be able to meet his own eyes. Not with the job that awaited him.

Alison cracked six eggs in a metal bowl and tumbled them with a whisk until the yellow and white were mingled but not fully mixed. The grits bubbled and burped on the back burner. Two slices of bread stood in the sleeves of the toaster, and the coffee maker gurgled as the last of its heated water sprayed into the basket. Maxwell House, good old all-American farm coffee.

She avoided looking in the pantry, though the louvered doors were parted. The giant bag of Kennel Ration stood in a green trash can. On the shelf above was a box of Milk Bones and rows of canned dog food. Robert had a theory that hot dogs and turkey bologna were cheaper dog treats than the well-advertised merchandise lines, but he liked to keep stock on hand just in case. That was Robert, always planning ahead. But some things couldn't be planned, even when you expected them.

Robert entered the room, buttoning the cuffs on his flannel shirt. The skin beneath his eyes was puffed and lavender. "Something smells good."

She shoveled the four bacon strips from the skillet and placed them on a double layer of paper towels. "Only the best today."

"That's sweet of you."

"I wish I could do more."

"You've done plenty."

Robert moved past her without brushing against her, though the counter ran down the center of the kitchen and narrowed the floor space in front of the stove. Most mornings, he would have given her an affectionate squeeze on the rear and she would have threatened him with the spatula, grinning all the while. This morning he poured himself a cup of coffee without asking if she wanted one.

She glanced at Robert as he bent into the refrigerator to get some cream. At thirty-five, he was still in shape, the blue jeans snug around him and only the slightest bulge over his belt. His brown hair showed the faintest streaks of gray, though the lines around his eyes and mouth had grown visibly deeper in the last few months. He wore a beard but he hadn't shaved his neck in a week. He caught her looking.

Alison turned her attention back to the pan. "Do you want to talk about it?"

"Not much to say." He stirred his coffee, tapped his spoon on the cup's ceramic rim, and reached into the cabinet above the sink. He pulled the bottle of Jack Daniels into the glare of the morning sun. Beyond the window, sunlight filtered through the red and golden leaves of maple trees that were about to enter their winter sleep.

Robert never drank before noon, but Alison didn't comment as he tossed a splash into his coffee. "I made extra bacon," she said. "A special treat."

Robert nodded, his eyes shot with red lightning bolts. He had tossed all night, awakening her once at 3 a.m. when his toenails dug into her calf. He must have been dreaming of days with Sandy Ann, walking by the river, camping in the hollows of Grandfather Mountain, dropping by the animal shelter to volunteer for a couple of hours.

Alison moved the grits from the heat and set them aside. The last round of bacon was done, and she drained some of the bacon grease away and poured the eggs. The mixture lay there round and steaming like the face of a cartoon sun. She let the eggs harden a bit before she moved them around. A brown skin covered the bottom of the skillet.

"Nine years is a lot," she said. "Isn't that over seventy in people years?"

"No, it's nine in people years. Time's the same for everybody and everything."

Robert philosophy. A practical farm boy. If she had been granted the power to build her future husband in a Frankenstein laboratory, little of Robert would have been in the recipe. Maybe the eyes, brown and honest with flecks of green that brightened when he was aroused. She would have chosen other parts, though the composite wasn't bad. The thing that made Robert who he was, the spark that juiced his soul, was largely invisible but had shocked Alison from the very first exposure.

She sold casualty insurance, and Robert liked to point out she was one of the "Good Hands" people. Robert's account had been assigned to her when a senior agent retired, and during his first appointment to discuss whether to increase the limit on his homeowner's policy, she'd followed the procedure taught in business school, trying to sucker him into a whole-life policy. During the conversation, she'd learned he had no heirs, not even a wife, and she explained he couldn't legally leave his estate to Sandy Ann. One follow-up call later, to check on whether he would get a discount on his auto liability if he took the life insurance, and they were dating.

The first date was lunch in a place that was too nice and dressy for either of them to be comfortable. The next week, they went to a movie during which Robert never once tried to put his arm around her shoulder. Two days later, he called and said he was never going to get to know her at this rate so why didn't she just come out to his place for a cook-out and a beer? Heading down his long gravel drive between hardwoods and weathered outbuildings, she first met Sandy Ann, who barked at the wheels and then leapt onto the driver's side door, scratching the finish on her new Camry.

Robert laughed as he pulled the yellow Labrador retriever away so Alison could open her door. She wasn't a dog person. She'd had a couple of cats growing up but had always been too busy to make a long-term pet commitment. She had planned to travel light, though the old get-married-two-kids-house-in-the-suburbs had niggled at the base of her brain once or twice as she'd approached thirty. It turned out she ended up more rural than suburban, Robert's sperm count was too low, and marriage was the inevitable result of exposure to Robert's grill.

She plunged the toaster lever. The eggs were done and she arranged the food on the plates. Her timing was perfect. The edges of the grits had just begun to congeal. She set Robert's plate before him. The steam of his coffee carried the scent of bourbon.

"Where's the extra bacon?" he asked.

"On the counter."

"It'll get cold."

"She'll eat it."

"I reckon it won't kill her either way." Robert sometimes poured leftover bacon or hamburger grease on Sandy Ann's dry food even though the vet said it was bad for her. Robert's justification was she ate rotted squirrels she found in the woods, so what difference did a little fat make?

"We could do this at the vet," Alison said. "Maybe it would be easier for everybody, especially Sandy Ann." Though she was really thinking of Robert. And herself.

"That's not honest. I know you love her, too, but when you get down to it, she's my dog. I had her before I had you."

Sandy Ann had growled at Alison for the first few weeks, which she found so unsettling that she almost gave up on Robert. But he convinced her Sandy Ann was just slow to trust and would come around in time. Once, the dog nipped at her leg, tearing a hole in a new pair of slacks. Robert bought her a replacement pair and they spent more time at Alison's apartment than at the farm. Alison bought the groceries and let him cook, and they did the dishes together.

The first time Alison spent the night at the farm, Sandy Ann curled outside Robert's door and whined. He had to put the dog outside so they could make love. They were married four months later and Robert was prepared to take the dog with them on their honeymoon, an RV and backpacking trip through the Southwest. Only a desperate plea from Alison, stopping just short of threat, had persuaded Robert to leave Sandy Ann at a kennel.

"You got the eggs right," Robert said, chewing with his mouth open.

"Thank you."

He powdered his grits with pepper until a soft black carpet lay atop them. The dust was nearly thick enough to make Alison sneeze. He worked his fork and moved the grits to his mouth, washing the bite down with another sip of the laced coffee.

"Maybe you can wait until tomorrow," Alison said. She bit into her own bacon, which had grown cool and brittle. She didn't want to wait another day, and had waited months too long already, but she said what any wife would.

"Tomorrow's Sunday." Robert wasn't religious but he was peculiar about Sundays. It was a holdover from his upbringing as the son of a Missionary Baptist. Though Robert was a house painter by trade, he'd kept up the farming tradition. The government was buying out his tobacco allocation and cabbage was more of a hobby than a commercial crop. Robert raised a few goats and a beef steer, but they were more pets than anything. She didn't think Robert would slaughter them even if they stood between him and starvation. He wasn't a killer.

"Sunday might be a better day for it," she said.

"No." Robert nibbled a half-moon into the toast. "It's been put off long enough."

"Maybe we should let her in."

"Not while we're eating. No need to go changing habits now."

"She won't know the difference."

"No, but I will."

Alison drew her robe tighter across her body. The eggs had hardened a little, the yellow gone an obscene greenish shade.

Sandy Ann had been having kidney and liver problems and had lost fifteen pounds. The vet said they could perform an operation, which would cost $3,000, and there would still be no guarantee of recovery. Alison told Robert it would be tough coming up with the money, especially since she'd given up her own job, but she would be willing to make the necessary sacrifices. Robert said they would be selfish to keep the dog alive if it was suffering.

"Want some more grits?" she asked. Robert shook his head and finished the coffee. She looked at the fork in his hand and saw that it was quivering.

Sandy Ann ran away when Alison moved in. Robert stayed up until after midnight, going to the door and calling its name every half-hour. He'd prowled the woods with a flashlight while Alison dozed on the couch. Sandy Ann turned up three days later in the next town, and Robert said if he hadn't burned his phone number into the leather collar, the dog might have been lost forever.

Sandy Ann was mostly Lab, with a little husky mix that gave its eyes a faint gray tint in certain light. The dog had been spayed before Robert got it at the pound. Robert's mother had died that year, joining her husband in their Baptist heaven and leaving the farm to their sole heir. Sandy Ann had survived thirty-seven laying hens, two sows, a milk cow, one big mouser tomcat that haunted the barn, and a Shetland pony.

Until today.

Alison's appetite was terrible even for her. Three slices of bacon remained on her plate. She pushed them onto a soiled paper napkin for the dog.

"Four's enough," Robert said.

"I thought you could give her one piece now."

"It's not like baiting a fish. A dog will follow bacon into hell if you give it half a chance."

Robert finished his plate and took the dishes to the sink. She thought he was going to enter the cabinet for another shot of bourbon but he simply rinsed the dishes and stacked them on top of the dirty skillet. His hair seemed to have become grayer at the temples and he hunched a little, like an old man with calcium deficiency.

"I'd like to come," she said.

"We've been through that."

"We're supposed to be there for each other. You remember April eighth?"

"That was just a wedding. This is my dog."

Alison resented Sandy Ann's having the run of the house. The carpets were always muddy and no matter how often she vacuumed, dog hair seemed to snow from the ceiling. The battle had been long and subtle, but eventually Sandy Ann became an outdoor dog on all but the coldest days. The dog still had a favorite spot on the shotgun side of Robert's pick-up, the vinyl seat cover scratched and animal-smelling. Alison all but refused to ride in the truck, and they took her Camry when they were out doing "couple things."

"Do you want to talk about it?" Alison asked. She had tried to draw him out. In the early days, Robert had been forthcoming about everything, surprising her with his honesty and depth of feeling. Despite the initial attraction, she had thought him a little rough around the edges. She'd been raised in a trailer park but had attended Wake Forest University and so thought she had escaped her breeding. But Robert reveled in his.

"Nothing left to say. Maybe later."

"We can go down to the farmer's market when you get back. Maybe we can get some sweet corn for dinner. And I've been looking for a Philodendron for the living room."

"I won't feel like it."

"Robert, I know it's hard. Talk to me."

"I am talking."

"Really. Don't shut me out."

"Never have."

She slammed her fist on the table, causing her flatware to jump and clatter. "Damn it, don't be so stoic. You're allowed to grieve."

Robert wiped his hands on the kitchen towel that hung from the refrigerator handle. "Thanks for breakfast."

He went past her to the hall. She heard him open the closet door and rummage on the upper shelf. One of the snow skis banged against the door jamb. She had convinced Robert to try skiing, and they'd spent a weekend at Wintergreen in Virginia. He'd twisted his ankle on the first run. He said skiing was a rich kid's sport and it had served him right to try and escape his breeding.

Robert came back to the kitchen, the rifle tucked against his right shoulder. A single bullet made a bulge in his pocket, the shape long and mean.

"Have you decided where to bury her?" Alison had always thought of Sandy Ann as an "it," and had to consciously use the feminine pronoun. Alison wanted to show she cared, whether her husband appreciated it or not.

"She's not that heavy, or I'd do it near where I was going to bury her. I'm figuring behind the barn. She loved to lay in the shade back there."

Alison hated the back of the barn. It was full of barbed wire and blackberry vines, and once she'd seen a snake slither through the tall weeds. The garden lay beyond it, and she tended a bed of marigolds there, but she associated shadows with unseen reptiles. Sandy Ann would sometimes watch from the edge of the garden while Alison worked, but the two rarely communicated when Robert wasn't around, though Alison often left bacon for it by the back steps.

The grease from breakfast coated Alison's throat, and her chest ached. Robert went through the back door onto the porch. Alison followed him, leaving the heavy smells of the kitchen for the tart, dry October morning. The mountains were vibrant in their dying glory, umber, burgundy, ocher.

Sandy Ann was sleeping in a hollowed-out place under the steps. The dog lifted its head at the sound of their feet. It must have smelled the bacon in Robert's hand, because its nose wiggled and Sandy Ann dragged itself into the yard.

The sun glinted in the tears that ran down Robert's cheeks. "Good girl," he said, giving the dog a piece of bacon. The dog swallowed it without chewing and ran its rough tongue over its lips, ears lifting a little in anticipation of more. Robert moved the bacon to his rifle hand and scratched the dog on top of the head.

"Come on, girl, let's take a walk." He headed toward the woods.

Sandy Ann looked back at Alison, eyes dim and hiding pain, brown crust in their corners. She held out the bacon in her hand. Unlike the other pieces she had fed it, this one wasn't sprinkled with rat poison. The dog licked its lips once more, exhaled a chuffing sigh, then followed Robert, the yellow tail swinging gently like a piece of frozen rope.

Robert led the way across the yard, holding the bacon aloft so the dog could smell it. He and Sandy Ann went through a crooked gate and Robert leaned the rifle against the fence while he fastened the latch. He looked back at the porch. Alison waved and bit into her own bacon.

They started again, both of them stooped and limping. They reached the trees, Robert's boots kicking up the brittle leaves, Sandy Ann laboring by his side. The last she saw of him was his plaid flannel shirt.

She should chase them. Maybe she could hold the bacon while Robert loaded the gun. After all, she had cooked it. And, in a way, she was replacing Sandy Ann. If Robert ever got another dog, it would be Alison's home and therefore it would be the dog that would have to adjust, not the other way around. She didn't think they would get another dog, not for a while.

Sandy Ann was just a dog, and Alison wasn't a dog person. She was the practical one in the relationship. She could have driven Sandy Ann to the vet, even at the risk of getting dog hair in her car. The vet would have drawn out a nice, clean needle and Sandy Ann could drift off to sleep, dreaming of squirrel chases and chunks of cooked meat and snacks by the back porch of home.

Maybe Robert needed the catharsis of violence. Perhaps that would be his absolution, though surely he couldn't view the dog's infirmity as his fault. After all, it would have aged no matter the owner. Sandy Ann, like all of them, would die and go to whatever heaven was nearest. Robert's way might be best. One split-second and then all pain would end.

Alison went inside and poured herself a half cup of coffee and sat at the kitchen table, looking through the window. The sunlight was soft on the stubbled garden. Some of the marigolds clung to a defiant life, their edges crinkled and brown. Collard leaves swayed in the breeze like the ears of small green puppies. The shovel stood by the barn, waiting.

Her coffee mug was to her lips when the shot sounded. The report echoed off the rocky slopes and the hard, knotty trees. Alison didn't know whether to smile or pout against the ceramic rim. The house was hers.

When Robert returned, she would have tears in her eyes. She would hug him and let him sag onto her, and she would lead him to the couch. She would remind him of all the great memories, and let him talk for hours about the dog's life. She would kneel before him and remove his boots and wipe the mud from them. He would have no appetite, but she would cook for him anyway, maybe something sweet, like a pie. If he wanted, he could have some more of the Jack Daniels. She would turn on the television and they would sit together, the two of them in their house.

Her house.

Alison finished her coffee. The remaining bacon was covered with a gray film of grease but she ate it anyway, her stomach finally unclenching.

She washed dishes, a chore she loathed. She rinsed the pans with hot water. Later in the evening, she would vacuum, try to remove the last traces of Sandy Ann from the living room carpet.

Something clicked on the porch steps. She wondered if Robert had decided to come back to the house before he began digging. Either way, Alison would be there for him. She would shovel until she raised blisters if he would let her. Alison wiped her hands on her bathrobe and hurried to the door, blinking rapidly so her eyes would water.

The scratching sound was at the door now, as if Robert were wiping his boots on the welcome mat. She braced herself for Robert's crestfallen expression, the caved-in look of his eyes, the deep furrows at the corners of his mouth. She would have never brought such suffering if it weren't for the best.

Alison opened the door. On the porch, Sandy Ann stood on bowed legs, working her dry lips. The dog lifted a forlorn paw and dropped it with a click of nails. There were spatters of blood across the dog's snout.

One shot.

Robert couldn't have missed.

Not from so close.

Could he have . . . ?

No, not Robert.

But it was the kind of choice Robert would make.

His only choice.

A dog person to the end.

Alison's ribs were a fist gripping the yolk of her heart. Her legs were grits, her head popping like hot grease on a griddle. Her spine melted like butter. She sagged against her house and slid to a sitting position. Sandy Ann whimpered, limped over, and ran a papery tongue against her cheek.

The dog's breath smelled of bacon and poison.

SIMON CLARK

The Extraordinary Limits of Darkness

Simon Clark lives in Doncaster, England. Upon the sale of his first novel, Nailed by the Heart, *he banked the money and embarked upon his dream of becoming a full-time writer. His novels include* Blood Crazy, Darkness Demands, Death's Dominion, *and* The Night of the Triffids, *which continues the story of Wyndham's classic* The Day of the Triffids. *His revival of the wickedly ambulatory Triffid plants won the British Fantasy Society's August Derleth Award for best novel. His most recent book is* This Rage of Echoes.

He also created and co-presented Winter Chills *for the BBC and experiments in short films, one of which has been featured in the U.K.'s Channel 4 Short Doc series.*

He says, "I was determined NOT to write 'The Extraordinary Limits of Darkness.' I faced a tight deadline for completing a novel, but I was asked to contribute a piece to a charity fund-raising anthology. It was such a worthwhile cause I couldn't reply, 'No way!' This tale of African misadventure still haunts me and is one of the most satisfying (for me) that I've ever produced. And now I'm very glad I ignored my own self imposed 'No More Short Stories!' order and wrote it all down."

"The Extraordinary Limits of Darkness" was originally published in Shrouded by Darkness, *an anthology published to raise money for DebRA, a national charity working on behalf of people with the genetic skin blistering condition, epidermolysis bullosa. Simon's Web site is www.bbr-online.com/nailed.*

—E.D.

The offing was barred by a black bank of clouds, and the tranquil waterway leading to the uttermost ends of the earth flowed sombre under an overcast sky—seemed to lead into the heart of an immense darkness.

—*Heart of Darkness* by Joseph Conrad

Remember that afternoon on the beach when I told you about my expedition to Africa? Did I say expedition? If you wish, substitute "expedition" for the word "folly" or "frolic." I was much younger then, and having lived so many years as a seaman, I found my home town such a drab place that even when my brother sailors were retreating to their townhouses to work in offices and trim their rose gardens and cultivate their families, I felt this need for adventure. It was like a dull ache in a bad tooth. I didn't relish the adventure for adventure's sake. I simply knew that it was my lot in life to embark on yet another exploration, because even though I'd encounter hardship and loneliness, the alternative was worse. The wilds of the Congo are hell. The ivy clad villas of Essex are a deeper hell. You remember my yarn of the journey upriver by steam paddle boat to find Kurtz, and bring him back to civilisation with his mountain of ivory? We found him and his ivory after a gruelling voyage. The ivory was poor quality. Kurtz had become a murderous tyrant who fed the darkest of his appetites in ways I can't even begin to put into words. I daresay even the Emperor Caligula, who hacked off his nephew's head because of an irritating cough, would have paled at the sight of what Kurtz inflicted on the natives. On the return journey, Kurtz died. We left his body in a muddy grave by the river. But we brought his diaries back with us. And it was in one of those diaries that the seed of what was to come began to grow.

As so often with these things, there is a long, involved sequence of events that ferment away in their own, dark world before we become aware of them. But the gist of it is, that on New Year's Day, 1913, I found myself disembarking at the African port of Dakar. I was as disappointed with the place as I was with my companions on my new expedition. Some men quaff their whisky in anticipation of the riotous, laughter-filled evening ahead of them. Some drink the spirit in the joyless certainty of the crushing headache and dry throat of the hangover that waits for them, come morning. I—I'm sorry to say—am attached to the latter. Dakar is a miserable town: cheaply built houses and warehouses in the modern French style. The land is flat. There are palms, there is dust. The climate manages to inflict a burning sun combined with a cold, northerly wind. My companions in adventure hadn't been to Africa before. In fact, they hadn't been further south than their wintering quarters in Monte Carlo. They insisted on dressing in a bizarre confection of white suits with feathered hats, imagining that it is the necessity of every civilised gentleman to promenade in such a way so as to impress on the African the European's godlike stature. The French crew of the ship were so richly amused by my companions strutting down the gangplank at Dakar that many of them lapsed into helpless laughter.

There were three days of wrangling with customs officers over the fourteen cases of gin those in my expedition had brought with them (those and the rifles, pistols, blasting powder and magnesium torches)—after that, we were delivered to the train station for the five-day journey to where Kurtz had so considerately buried his riches for us to find.

And what of me? Why had I agreed to accompany these men on the expedition? I didn't know them. The offer of three percent of the net wealth of the treasure didn't really appeal. No, curse the devil on my back, it was the adventure! It was the promise of travel to Africa; it was a suggestion of sleeping in snake-infested huts in malarial swamps where hippos roared one awake in the middle of the night. That was the devil that brought me so meekly to heel in the company's British office—the one and the same company that had employed me to navigate a moribund boat into the heart of the Congo to find the despicable Kurtz. What was the alternative? Yes, yes, the alternative would be a winter at leisure in my English sitting room, with tea and buttered scones, and gleaming cutlery and spotless bedding and . . . oh, the crushing hand of boredom. Always boredom. Eternal boredom. Forever and ever without end . . .

So that is how I found myself in the company office with one of its esteemed directors, who exhibited himself behind his vast and stately galleon of a desk. There, he folded his arms so he could stroke his own elbows as he dropped the wonderful phrases into my ear. His long, gray hair fell across the rich velvet collar of his coat as he uttered those phrases—those honey-dipped phrases. "A journey to where few white men have been . . . hardships will be great but the rewards greater. Three percent of Kurtz's treasures will be yours—once the value has been assessed, of course. Sail from Portsmouth on Christmas Eve. Africa by New Year's Day. You will be in the company of three gallant gentlemen, three fellow adventurers—Dr. Lyman, Sir Anthony Winterflood, and Henry Sanders. Sanders is a solicitor, a good, solid man, dependable as the Bank of England."

On the voyage, my companions hadn't talked about the treasure we'd find. They spoke incessantly of the sport. The sport was the thing. In England there was sport, of course, but not the sport they favoured. They talked of a "grand sport" to be had in Africa. A great and wonderful sport that would enrich their lives and their memories for many a year to come. They rarely spoke to me, even though I was supposedly an equal member of the team. And they rarely mentioned the rigors of the journey to come. But sport? Yes, indeed, the talk was of the fine sport to be had on the Dark Continent.

Toward the end of that first week of the new year, with 1912 flung on the scrap heap of time, and with 1913 rearing up in front of us like an untrod mountain, we boarded the train for our journey into Africa's secret heart. The company had chartered the train specially for us. They had no doubt we would return it to the coast laden with Kurtz's fabulous treasure. Our transport consisted of one derelict-looking locomotive—the plaque on its side advertised that it had been built in Doncaster, England, in 1859. Behind the loco that was merrily spitting boiling water all over the platform was the tender heaped with more coal—although a poor, muddy coal, I noted with some misgivings. Next in line after the tender were two goods vans that would carry our treasure, then the carriage containing a cook's galley and half a dozen cabins that offered our private quarters; then at the very end of the train an elegant structure of carved timbers combined with an extravagant amount of glass. This final carriage of our treasure train was a communal lounge. Apart from the train's crew, we four would be the only passengers carried by that astonishing luxury liner of dry land.

By the time I'd unpacked my case, washed and shaved, the train had shrieked its way out of the station. As you would imagine from the nature of the iron beast, our progress was stately to say the least. At no time did we accelerate to faster than twelve miles per hour. The terrain immediately outside Dakar is flat, open land; however, within thirty minutes, thorn trees began rising from the dry earth like skeletons frozen in time. Leaves? Yes, they must have borne leaves, but all I recall of the skeletal branches are immense, dagger-like thorns, and the way the trees multiplied quite discreetly until, whereas I'd been watching a few dozen trees sliding by on an open plain, I now saw a dense thicket of thorn trees that closed in on the track until we had no more of a view than if we'd been travelling through a tunnel. I had hoped to sit on my cabin bunk and watch elephants wander across a savannah, or be entertained by monkeys leaping through their arboreal kingdom. Yet there was nothing but thorn trees. Damned thorn trees through which we moved at our twelve miles per hour. Thorn trees that appeared to be home to nothing—not even birds.

With the view being nothing, I busied myself with my papers regarding the next leg of the expedition. In three days' time, the train would reach the end of its track; from there, we would cross country on foot until we reached a lake. Waiting there would be a sailing barque, which I would skipper to an island where Kurtz had concealed his glittering hoard. There were matters concerning the transportation of provisions that I needed to discuss with my travelling companions, so I took my map to the salon in the hope of finding them there. Of the three, however, only Dr. Lyman had ventured from his cabin.

The heat in our tunnel of thorns had become formidable. Dr. Lyman was seated on a sofa of plush velvet in his black frock coat, perhaps in readiness for attracting the awe-stricken glances of any native who happened to be peeping from the thorn forest. He was a plump man with a round face and round hands that protruded from beneath starched shirt cuffs. His hair was neatly parted down the centre; the scalp revealed itself as a bright pink strip of overheated skin. His black boots were polished, as were the buttons on that frock coat. He was astonishing and wore a pink carnation in his lapel. On the little table beside him, a glass, containing gin and peppermint cordial, trembled from the vibrations induced by the twelve-mile-an-hour rush through the spiky jungle. Those same vibrations made the rifle propped up against the sofa slide sideways, so he had to steady it to prevent it falling. An action he repeated frequently during the following.

I cleared my throat. "Dr. Lyman, good morning."

He nodded, then sipped his gin and pep—he and his companions always drank gin and pep, chilled by a veritable rock of ice, so the contents of their glasses were never a mystery for me. I knew drinking liquor in a hot climate wasn't helpful to one's constitution, and so avoided it. The doctor's nod seemed to be the extent of his conversation with me. After adjusting his carnation and wiping a speck of dust from the black sleeve of his frock coat, he returned to his silent, dignified pose, while the train chack chacked at precisely twelve miles an hour. His face became very red. Yet by an effort of willpower he checked the escape of perspiration from his skin. Dr. Lyman was a man of formidable willpower. Maybe the power of his mind retarded the speed of the train. He blinked to the rhythm of the *chack . . . chack . . . chack . . .*

"Dr. Lyman . . ." I wasn't going to be cheated of this vital discussion on logistics. "Dr. Lyman. I've been checking our travel itinerary against the map . . ."

"Excellent! You have everything on the nail. The company told me that you were just the man for the job. Their words to me were, 'He'd have everything on the nail—right on the very nail!' Good work, sir."

"Thank you, but I thought we should talk about how many native bearers we'll require for—"

"Oh, as many as you need. The company told me that you'd plan everything with aplomb. They speak very highly of you. After all, you brought the papers that belonged to Kurtz back to London." He sipped his gin and pep; the little iceberg clunked against the glass. "This time, they'll reward you amply, so I'm given to understand." He nodded, satisfied that he'd granted me precious moments of his time. There you have it; this wasn't so much as an expeditionary team, rather me playing Cook's tour representative to three of my social betters who wished to see something of savage lands from the comfort of the carriage.

And what a carriage. The windows were vast. The carpet underfoot deep. The carved furniture boasted an abundance of delicate scrollwork and deep upholstery.

From the roof hung crystal chandeliers. This was the salon of a duchess that some-how had been gifted wheels and set rolling—rolling at twelve miles per hour, mind—through a thorn forest in Africa. As I witnessed later, a mere pull on a velvet bell rope would cause a French waiter dressed in a pristine white jacket to manifest himself into the carriage, where he would ask with the gravest of respect what meal or drink we required. Gin and pep—always gin and pep for my companions. And ice—plenty of ice! Meanwhile the train maintained its stately twelve miles per hour on a track that didn't seem to possess even a whisper of a bend. Nor did it venture upon a single break in our thorn-tree tunnel.

I decided to await my other travelling companions before broaching the subject of the bearers again—although I suspected they too would quickly congratulate me on my energy and organisational skill before returning to their debate about the sport. This was "the sport" they'd discussed so avidly on the ship. Oh, the rapture that blazed in their eyes. "The sport in Africa is extraordinary," they'd murmur with a disquieting intimacy to each other. "It is quite worth the trip for that alone." Their talk always made me weary and irritable. Hang their sport, I'd tell myself. I glanced across the swaying carriage with its chinking chandeliers to the round-faced, red-faced man. The rapture filled his eyes again. He was thinking about his sport. Sport filled him from his polished boots to the pink stripe of scalp that ran across the top of his head. Blast his sport. Blast his indolence. All this and a miserly twelve miles an hour.

The monotonous rhythm of the *chack . . . chack . . . chack* of iron wheels on an iron track suddenly vanished with the arrival of the other two adventurers. One, Sir Anthony, was dressed in green silk pajamas in a style best described as Chinese; his companion, the solicitor, wore an immaculate white suit. They carried repeating ri-fles, while their faces wore such expressions of joy. When they spoke, it proved this was too special a time to waste on coherent speech.

"Fine animals! Six of them." Then to me. "Open the window man . . . No! No! The one on the left." Then to the doctor, "Your rifle! Quick! Quick! Before they run into the forest! Have you opened that window yet, man! There! Stand back!"

The doctor couldn't believe their good fortune. "Sport," he insisted on repeating in a daze of pure happiness. "Is there sport? So soon? Are you sure?"

"We have our sport, gentlemen, praise be. Ready with the rifle, doctor!" The man in the pajamas cocked his rifle and poked the muzzle through the window I'd slid back to create a cavernous aperture in the side of the carriage. I smelled hot dust and the sun-scorched branches of the thorn trees. "Do you see them?" Sir Anthony's voice rose into high piping. "Ah! There they are!"

Walking along the dusty borderland between the rail track and the start of the thorn trees fifty paces away was a line. A loose, undulating line of ten figures. Five men, five women—husbands and wives. It seemed they carried bundles of every-thing they possessed on their heads. One woman carried a dozing child in a papoose on her back. The natives were an ebony black that glistened in the sunlight. All ten were very thin; their knees appeared as bulbous oddities compared with the narrow-ness of their thighs and shins. They were barefoot. All were naked. Naked, that is, apart from a belt of some red material worn around their waists.

My three companions discharged their weapons with so much fervour it was as if those long-awaited gunshots had been held in pent-up frustration all their adult lives. The powder discharged the bullets at speed. But the willpower of the three men sped the lead shot to velocities that seemed to melt the air around them. They fired again and again. The men and women fell without murmur. Maybe in some undreamed-of way, they knew this was their fate. Perhaps they'd seen it in their dreams. Maybe a witch doctor had told them to be at this place at this time to meet their destiny. They didn't cry out; they didn't flinch; they didn't react with any expression of pain or unhappiness at reaching the end of their lives on that dirt track. As the rifles discharged the tiny but swift cargoes, the natives simply knelt down in the dirt, their burdens falling from their heads, their eyes suddenly tired looking, that's all. And there they died.

"Aim for the faces," the doctor called out with a blend of urgency and delight. The last round in his magazine enlarged upon his short statement as it demonstrated most clearly the effect of such a shot to the front of a human head. The rifle bullet popped through the face—in the centre of the flared nostrils to be more precise—before bursting out through back of the skull, resulting in the entire head deflating to perhaps half its former volume. The African toppled sideways into a cluster of weeds.

The train driver continued his majestic twelve miles per hour. The thorn trees were unbroken, from the engine a rain of soot fell on the still bodies that lay on the hot earth. The doctor permitted himself to perspire a little from his beet-root face now, as he tugged on the bell rope. "Gin and peppermint," he ordered as the white-jacketed waiter appeared. "Three." He held up three fingers. "With ice—plenty of ice."

The sport . . . oh, this *sport*. The three athletes devoted soul, mind, and fibre to their sport. And as the train *chacked* along the iron rails deeper into the heart of the eternal forest, they played their hardest. By the time the sun descended into a red blaze somewhere in that empire of thorns, I sat at the dining table. There I was served my *hors d'oeuvre* of salad with grilled sole and lemon. The cutlery shone, the white cotton tablecloth was perfection, and the golden honeysuckle display in the centre was amazing.

The three athletes stood at the very end of the carriage. Sustained by gin and pep, they fired their rifles for hour after hour. Mere shards of conversation reached me.

"A full six feet he was. Took two shots to—"

"The face, I say, aim for the face."

". . . their nakedness. What comes out of 'em isn't the color of blood at all."

"Now, gentlemen. Here's another." *Bang!* "See! The face!"

"A difficult shot."

"Tricky, very tricky."

"But admirably effective. Admirable!"

"Strikes the nail right on the head it does!"

"By Jove! Good musketry, sir!"

Men, women, old, young, lame, simple, and one with a face as fair as the Christ who takes us aloft when our toil is done. They all fell to the gentlemen's rifle work. Mothers, bambinos, silver-haired patriarchs. Oh, I can see the Africans lying on the hot soil even now. The train *chacked* at twelve miles an hour. The red sunset was glorious. I picked at my fish to avoid having a bone stick in my throat; meanwhile, the doctor's bullet was a golden star that, to me, appeared to glide gracefully toward a grandma who carried a bundle of sticks on her head, and led a child by his hand. The grandma's skin was as dark as the bark of the thorn trees, her bare feet were broad from tramping over baked earth for seventy years. The golden star that was the doctor's bullet settled on the bridge of her nose, then ever so slowly melted through the skin, to continue its mysterious journey into the dreams and visions and wonders contained in her brain.

"See!" the doctor exclaimed. "Always aim for the face."

"You'll have to be quick, Sir Anthony, the child is running into the bushes!"

"Ah, got it!"

"Bad luck, Sir Anthony, you've only winged it."

Chack . . . chack . . . chack . . . twelve miles an hour . . . never more than twelve miles an hour . . .

Going into the forest was like journeying into the underworld. The thorn trees became thicker, more gnarled, more ancient looking. And they looked less like wood than stone. It was as if the trees were formed from dark rock that had been extruded from the ground. There must have been leaves, yet for the life of me, I don't recall any leaves. Only spikes that would pierce the flesh if you attempted to walk through that deadly copse. All this and twelve miles an hour. And interminable sport.

Why didn't the natives retreat into the forest when their countrymen were being noisily dispatched by the three adventurers with their repeating rifles? The fact is that those Africans walking alongside the track formed a sparse traffic indeed. Our three in their moving hide had the opportunity to enjoy their sport only every thirty minutes or so. Even though the train rumbled at a miserable twelve miles an hour, it encountered natives at intervals of at least six miles apart. So, those that were going to give their lives in order to entertain the gentlemen wouldn't have heard the earlier gunshots, let alone witnessed the stately hunt.

Twelve miles an hour. The waiter in his white jacket poured a claret for my approval.

"Very nice. Thank you."

"*Merci, Monsieur.*"

A youth with no longer a head to call his own fell into some thistles.

Next, on my fine china plate, a row of delicately roasted lamb chops, served with saffron rice and a casserole of *courgette*, tomato, spring onion, and blue-black slivers of eggplant. Twelve miles an hour. The train driver sounded the whistle to spare the life of some animal sitting on the track. I saw it safely decamp into the forest. The athletes fired on a family padding along the path in the relative cool of the evening. For the first time, a reaction. A woman with pink strips tied in her hair ran after the train. She shouted in a fabulous tongue. Shouts of rage, or grief, or gratitude at the hunters returning her loved ones to the laps of the gods. I don't know. Just it was very noisy. I found a piece of eggshell in the vegetable casserole. That annoyed me immensely. To me, discovering eggshell in food is worse than finding a fly.

The solicitor felled the shouting woman with his revolver. She'd almost reached the train as it rumbled into our heart of darkness.

"Face." The doctor's approval was heartfelt. "Dead centre of the face."

My cabin at midnight. The air was so hot it was as if you had inhaled it over a lighted stove. Still the train rumbled along at its mandatory twelve miles per hour. I lay on the bunk with the window open. There were no stars; only darkness; a colossal, overwhelming darkness. My companions must have retired to bed. Apart from the *chack* of iron wheels on iron track, there was no other sound. From time to time, I moved around my compact room with its expensive wood paneling. Many times I washed my face in my bathroom. I always avoided looking in the mirror. I didn't like what

I saw there. Then I'd return to the bunk, where I lay staring up into the darkness. At last the train began to slow. Fantastically, or so it seemed to me, our unassailable—our sacred!—twelve miles per hour dropped to ten, then to nine. Soon we crawled. Then stopped. After eighteen hours of sullen yet indefatigable progress, the train was still. All of a sudden, the iron beast that was our locomotive seemed to hold its breath. Silence! And such a silence—it was an invasive force. Ye Gods, I remember that silence to this day. I put my hands over my ears and groaned. After eighteen hours of *chack, chack, chack,* the sudden absence of mechanical noise hurt my ears. Why had we stopped? For water or wood to feed the iron beast perhaps. Then the change was wrought . . .

Our journey on the train had rendered Africa a seemingly distant place. Until then, I hadn't been able to hear the sounds of the forest, because of our locomotive grunting and clacking. This wilderness could hitherto have been a savage island glimpsed only indistinctly from the bridge of a ship. Now we were at rest, the presence—the living, breathing, palpitating, aromatic presence—of this primeval land sidled into the train. The thorn tree forest began at its regulation fifty paces from the track; that I knew; but what I sensed was entirely different. The forest crept closer. I could feel its prickling presence. Now I divined unseen forms of prodigious size lurking in the darkness beneath its branches. Even though I didn't so much as glance out of the window, I was as certain as I am of my own name that a thousand malevolent eyes had fixed on the stationary train. When we moved, nothing could destroy us. Now I had no doubt that we could be blasted to atoms by the merest flick of a lizard's tail. The window—that widely open window drew my gaze. Now a panther could leap through it. That twelve miles an hour was our magical protection. I realized that now. Without motion, we were as vulnerable as ants beneath a boy's stamping foot.

"*Marlow!*"

My cabin door bashed open. The doctor stood there in his silk dressing gown, his chest heaving, his face red in the light of the lamp he held. In the other plump fist he clutched his rifle by its barrel.

"Marlow! Quick, man! You must catch him before he gets away!"

Before I could ask what was happening, the lamp had been thrust into my hand and the doctor had bundled me out through the carriage door onto Africa's baked mud.

"There he is," hissed the doctor. 'Bring him to us!"

The train journey had seemed, to me, like a dream. When I found myself standing on the crisp soil, with the carriages at a standstill behind me and the light of the lamp revealing something of the tangle of thorn branches: that was when I reentered the world of reality.

"Hurry, man," hissed the doctor. He pointed at an abandoned rail carriage that lay on its side in that naked borderland between track and forest. "He'll get away."

"*What?*" The irritation in my voice was plain to hear.

Sir Anthony leaned out of the carriage window in his pajamas. "There's a native dressed in gold. *Flush him out.*"

The three gentlemen, the blood-thirsty beggars, were armed with rifles. With utmost indignation I approached the wreck of the carriage. In the light of the lamp, I saw it was a twin of the opulent passenger carriage that bore us in luxury through the wilderness—although it had suffered here. Windows had been broken. Insects had devoured the plush upholstery. Chandeliers lay shattered in the remains of a great deal of crockery. A stink of rot. I noticed also, growing there in the centre of the wreck, a young thorn tree.

"Hurry up, Marlow."

"Don't take all night about it."

"Flush him out. The devil's covered from head to foot in gold."

I moved around to the far side of the carriage to find our victim. Indeed there he was. A native boy of around thirteen. His dusty body was black as onyx. One foot, I noticed, was abnormally large. And he shone with gold. Gold amulets, a gold collar; he wore a cotton shirt that was decorated by oblong panels of gold. I'd never seen anyone as extraordinary. His large, round eyes regarded mine. He didn't appear afraid. He merely waited for an outcome.

"Marlow. Flush him out. Then stand back so we can get a clear shot." Rifles cocked with a loud clicking. "And for heaven's sake give us light!"

I raised the lamp to illuminate the child of gold. Then I advanced on him, waving my arms like a man might wave his arms to shoo chickens back into their coop. Still facing me, the boy moved slowly backward. The large foot, with unusually broad toes, caused him to limp. I shooed. He still retreated. As soon as he was clear of the carriage wreck, my countrymen would have their sport. I moved more to the right. I was a little closer now. I glanced away from the brown eyes that fixed on mine to the boy's golden adornments. They caught the lamplight with yellow flashes. Oh, they were splendid, all right. They were also cut from the sheets of gold foil that are used to wrap chocolate. Bless me, the youth had decorated himself with confectioners' tinfoil. I maintained a distance of perhaps ten paces from him as I shooed, slowly flapping my arms as I did so.

From behind me came annoyed shouts. "Out of the way, Marlow!"

"We can't get a clean shot."

"I can't fire until you step aside."

"Marlow . . . you fool."

I maintained my flapping gesture until the boy in his gold tinfoil had backed into the forest, where the night swallowed him. Just for a few paces, I entered the fringes of that wall of thorn. Although I no longer saw the boy in my lamplight, I beheld a man. He'd stood there silently watching what had transpired. He must have been a great age. His white eyebrows and hair were a marked contrast to the ebony skin. His arms were thin as twigs and his bare shoulders were as wrinkled as brown paper. Only there was something about his eyes . . . something shockingly wrong. What should have been the whites of the eyes were a bright yellow in colour. Almost a luminous yellow, like a candle flame placed behind amber glass. His face was expressionless. Then he stepped forward. He gripped my forearm in his right hand and my elbow in his left. For a moment, he leaned forward a shade to look into my eyes with that pair of yellow orbs. I fancy now that he muttered some words in a singsong voice, but at the time I'd have sworn he'd said nothing. But memory is not fossil. It continues to evolve. After that, he melted back into the forest.

I returned to the train and the sportsmen's jeers.

"Marlow, what the devil were you playing at?"

"You ruined a perfectly good shot."

"The face . . . had it clear as day until you stood in the way."

"And what about our gold?"

"Didn't you see how he draped himself in the stuff?"

"Where will we find gold like that again for the picking?"

In a temper I barked at them: "There is no gold!"

The train driver sounded his whistle; steam gushed through the wheels of the locomotive as the carriage shuddered. By the time I climbed back on board, we were moving once more, gradually accelerating toward our magical twelve miles per hour.

With the dawn came searing brightness. The air in my cabin grew stifling; perspiration broke through my skin if I did so much as sit upright. So all that day I lay on my bunk. Beyond the window, the unbroken thorn forest slid by. *Chack, chack, chack* . . . The three gentlemen irked me so much that I decided to keep myself absent from the salon carriage. The waiter brought meals to me along with jugs of boiled water, that being my preferred drink in a hot climate. All through that long, hot day I heard the snap of rifle shots. However, I refrained from viewing the messy results of their sport.

By the time the sun had begun to set once more, my anger at the men had increased. I found myself wrenching back the door of my cabin before dashing down into that duchess's parlour on wheels; oh, the chandeliers were tinkling merrily as the train swayed along. The flowers were fresh in their vases. Only this time, the solicitor and Sir Anthony weren't there. Instead, there was only the doctor. He sat on a plush sofa as he stared at his gin, pep, and melting pearls of ice dancing in the glass on a little walnut table.

His eyes were almost closed, but he peeped through the fleshy slits.

"You've found it!" I shouted at him. "There's no need to go any farther!"

The doctor took his time to speak. "Go rest. The journey is more arduous than I could have believed."

"Didn't you hear me?" I wanted to hit him. "You already have it. You've found Kurtz's treasure."

"Have I, by Jove?" The doctor's voice was a ghost of a sound. No more than a breath. It was a miracle I heard it at all. Not for a moment did he remove his gaze from the glass of liquor.

"Do you know what Kurtz's treasure is? It's not ivory, it's not pearls, not diamonds. What Kurtz valued most—his prize possession—was his ability to commit the most savage acts without guilt. Kurtz was the consummate torturer and violator. It invigorated him. Every death he caused had the same virtue of a conscientious man saving another penny for his future prosperity. That talent for slaughter is Kurtz's gold. You've proved you have it. So, there is no need to go farther. Take your wretched treasure home with you. See if you can invest it! See what kind of reward murder brings to you!"

"I'm going to lie down in my cabin," he whispered. Then he looked at me. The whites of his eyes had turned quite yellow. It was as if someone shone a candle through amber.

Within the hour, the sun had set. In turn I visited the cabins of each of the sportsmen—those athletes that gave so much to indulge their sport.

Sir Anthony sat on his bathroom floor with his back to the wall. When I spoke his name, he managed only by dint of great effort to look at me. His eyes—a bright yellow. It reminded me of the gold foil stitched to the boy's clothing.

The solicitor lay beneath the blankets on his bunk as if cold to his bones. I, however, found the heat stifling. He didn't say a word; instead, his tongue constantly marched back and forth across his lips. When I looked more closely into his face, his part-open eyes formed slits of an uncannily brilliant yellow.

The doctor. He sat on his bunk, his back jammed tight against the wall. He regarded the corner of his cabin with absolute terror. He was shaking violently. The fever had ransacked his body of all physical strength. When he saw me, he beckoned—such relief at being no longer alone.

"Marlow," he gasped. "Do you see who's standing there?"

I looked at his frock coat swaying on its peg.

He clutched at my shirt sleeve. "You know who that is, don't you?"

I said nothing.

"It's Kurtz, isn't it?"

"Kurtz is dead."

"Yes, he is, isn't he?" With horror, the doctor stared into the cabin wall. "And there's something extraordinary about his eyes."

They called out as I packed my bag.

"Please help me!"

"Marlow . . . water . . ."

"Marlow! Kurtz is here. He's staring at me . . . *Those eyes!* Marlow, in the name of God . . ."

The bacillus that felled the three sportsmen could, I suppose, have been in the very air. I suspect, however, it emerged from tainted water that had been used to make the ice that chilled their drinks. To make good its escape from the frigid prison, all the germ required was a little warmth.

Twelve miles an hour. That's how fast that haunted, nightmare world travelled on its track. Not fast enough to break my neck when I jumped free of it. Moments later, with both feet firmly planted on African soil, I had my long walk in front of me. Behind me, the train continued its even longer journey along that track through an entire universe of thorn trees, and I watched it dwindle into the distance—into the heart of an even greater darkness.

TIM PRATT

Cup and Table

Tim Pratt's "Cup and Table" is reprinted from Twenty Epics, *edited by David Moles and Susan Marie Groppi, one of the year's most enjoyable anthologies. Pratt is the author of two collections,* Little Gods *and* Hart & Boot & Other Stories, *as well as a novel,* The Strange Adventures of Rangergirl. *Pratt is an editor at* Locus *and, with his wife, the writer Heather Shaw, runs Tropism Press and publishes the excellent zine* Flytrap. *Pratt and Shaw live in Oakland, California.*

—K.L. & G.G.

Sigmund stepped over the New Doctor, dropping a subway token onto her devastated body. He stepped around the spreading shadow of his best friend, Carlsbad, who had died as he'd lived: inconclusively, and without fanfare. He stepped over the brutalized remains of Ray, up the steps, and kept his eyes focused on the shrine inside. This room in the temple at the top of the mountain at the top of the world was large and cold, and peer as he might back through the layers of time—visible to Sigmund as layers of gauze, translucent as sautéed onions, decade after decade peeling away under his gaze—he could not see a time when this room had not existed on this spot, bare but potent, as if only recently vacated by the God who'd created and abandoned the world.

Sigmund approached the shrine, and there it was. The cup. The prize and goal and purpose of a hundred generations of the Table. The other members of the Table were dead, the whole *world* was dead, except for Sigmund.

He did not reach for the cup. Instead, he walked to the arched window and looked out. Peering back in time he saw mountains and clouds and the passing of goats. But in the present he saw only fire, twisting and writhing, consuming rock as easily as trees, with a few mountain peaks rising as-yet-untouched from the flames. Sigmund had not loved the world much—he'd enjoyed the music of Bach, violent movies, and vast quantities of cocaine—and by and large he could have taken or left civilization. Still, knowing the world was consumed in fire made him profoundly sad.

Sigmund returned to the shrine and seized the cup—heavy, stone, more blunt object than drinking vessel—and prepared to sip.

But then, at the last moment, Sigmund didn't drink. He did something else instead.

But first:

Or, arguably, later:

Sigmund slumped in the backseat, Carlsbad lurking on the floorboards in his semi-liquid noctilescent form, Carlotta tapping her razored silver fingernails on the steering wheel, and Ray—the newest member of the Table—fiddling with the radio. He popped live scorpions from a plastic bag into his mouth. Tiny spines were rising out of Ray's skin, mostly on the nape of his neck and the back of his hands, their tips pearled with droplets of venom.

"It was a beautiful service," Sigmund said. "They sent the Old Doctor off with dignity."

Carlsbad's tarry body rippled. Ray turned around, frowning, face hard and plain as a sledgehammer, and said, "What the fuck are you talking about, junkie? We haven't even gotten to the funeral home yet."

Sigmund sank down in his seat. This was, in a way, even more embarrassing than blacking out.

"Blood and honey," Carlotta said, voice all wither and bile. "How much of that shit did you snort this morning, that you can't even remember what day it is?"

Sigmund didn't speak. They all knew he could see into the past, but none of them knew the full extent of his recent gyrations through time. Lately he'd been jerking from future to past and back again without compass or guide. Only the Old Doctor had known about that, and now that he was dead, it was better kept a secret.

They reached the funeral home, and Sigmund had to go through the ceremony all over again. Grief—unlike sex, music, and cheating at cards—was not a skill that could be honed by practice.

The Old Doctor welcomed Sigmund, twenty years old and tormented by visions, into the library at the Table's headquarters. Shelves rose everywhere like battlements, the floors were old slate, and the lights were ancient crystal-dripping chandeliers, but the Old Doctor sat in a folding chair at a card table heaped with books.

"I expected, well, something *more*," Sigmund said, thumping the rickety table with his hairy knuckles. "A big slab of mahogany or something, a table with authority."

"We had a fine table once," the Old Doctor said, eternally middle-aged and absently professorial. "But it was chopped up for firewood during a siege in the 1600s." He tapped the side of his nose. "There's a lesson in that. No asset, human or material, is important compared to the continued existence of the organization itself."

"But surely *you're* irreplaceable," Sigmund said, in an awkward attempt at job security through flattery. The room shivered and blurred at the edges of his vision, but it had not changed much in recent decades, a few books moving here and there, piles of dust shifting across the floor.

The Old Doctor shook his head. "I am the living history of the Table, but if I died, a new doctor would be sent from the archives to take over operations, and though his approach might differ from mine, his role would be the same—to protect the cup."

"The cup," Sigmund said, sensing the cusp of mysteries. "You mean the Holy Grail."

The Old Doctor ran his fingers along the spine of a dusty leatherbound book. "No. The Table predates the time of Christ. We guard a much older cup."

"The cup, is it here, in the vaults?"

"Well." The Old Doctor frowned at the book in his hands. "We don't actually know where the cup is anymore. The archives have . . . deteriorated over the centuries, and there are gaps in my knowledge. It would be accurate to say the agents of the Table now *seek* the cup, so that we may protect it properly again. That's why you're here, Sigmund. For your ability to see into the past. Though we'll have to train you to narrow your focus to the here-and-now, to peel back the gauze of time at will." He looked up from the book and met Sigmund's eyes. "As it stands, you're almost useless to me, but I've made useful tools out of things far more broken than *you* are."

Some vestigial part of Sigmund's ego bristled at being called broken, but not enough to stir him to his own defense. "But I can only look back thirty or forty years. How can that help you?"

"I have . . . a theory," the Old Doctor said. "When you were found on the streets, you were raving about gruesome murders, yes?"

Sigmund nodded. "I don't know about *raving,* but yes."

"The murders you saw took place over a hundred years ago. On that occasion, you saw back many more years than usual. Do you know why?"

Sigmund shook his head. He thought he *did* know, but shame kept him from saying.

"I suspect your unusual acuity was the result of all that speed you snorted," the Old Doctor said. "The stimulants enabled you to see deeper into the past. I have, of course, vast quantities of very fine methamphetamines at my disposal, which you can use to aid me in my researches."

Sigmund said, "Vast quantities?" His hands trembled, and he clasped them to make them stop.

"Enough to let you see *centuries* into the past," the Old Doctor said. "Though we'll work up to that, of course."

"When I agreed to join the Table, I was hoping to do field work."

The Old Doctor sniffed. "That business isn't what's important, Sigmund. Assassination, regime change, paltry corporate wars—that's just the hackwork our agents do to pay the bills. It's not worthy of your gifts."

"Still, it's what I want. I'll help with your research if you let me work in the field." Sigmund had spent a childhood in cramped apartments and hospital wards, beset by visions of the still-thrashing past. In those dark rooms he'd read comic books and dreamed of escaping the prison of circumstance—of being a superhero. But heroes like that weren't real. Anyone who put on a costume and went out on the streets to fight crime would be murdered long before morning. At some point in his teens Sigmund had graduated to spy thrillers and Cold War history, passing easily from fiction to non-fiction and back again, reading about double- and triple-agents with an interest that bordered on the fanatical. Becoming a spy—that idea had the ring of the plausible, in a way that becoming a superhero never could. Now, this close to that secret agent dream, he wouldn't let himself be shunted into a pure research position. This was his chance.

The Old Doctor sighed. "Very well."

"What's it like?" Carlotta said, the night after their first mission as a duo. She'd enthralled a Senator while Sigmund peered into the past to find out where the microfilm was hidden. Now, after, they were sitting at the counter in an all-night diner where even *they* didn't stand out from the crowd of weirdoes and freaks.

Sigmund sipped decaf coffee and looked around at the translucent figures of past customers, the crowd of nights gone by, every booth and stool occupied by ghosts. "It's like layers of gauze," he said. "Usually I just see the past distantly, shimmering, but if I concentrate I can sort of . . . shift my focus." He thumped his coffee cup and made the liquid inside ripple. "The Old Doctor taught me to keep my eyes on the here-and-now, unless I *need* to look back, and then I just sort of . . ." He gestured vaguely with his hands, trying to create a physical analogue for a psychic act, to mime the metaphysical. "I guess I sort of twitch the gauze aside, and pass through a curtain, and the present gets blurrier while the past comes into focus."

"That's a shitty description," Carlotta said, sawing away at the rare steak and eggs on her plate.

The steak, briefly, shifted in Sigmund's vision and became a living, moving part of a cow. Sigmund's eyes watered, and he looked away. He mostly ate vegetables for that very reason. "I've never seen the world any other way, so I don't know how to explain it better. I can't imagine what it's like for you, seeing just the present. It must seem very *fragile*."

"We had a guy once who could see into the future, just a little bit, a couple of minutes at most. Didn't stop him from getting killed, but he wet himself right before the axe hit him. He was a lot less boring than you are." Carlotta belched.

"Why haven't I met you before?" Sigmund shrank back against the cushions in the booth.

"I'm heavy ordnance," Carlsbad said, his voice low, a rumble felt in Sigmund's belly and bones as much as heard by his ears. "I've been with the Table since the beginning. They don't reveal secrets like me to research assistants." Carlsbad was tar-black, skin strangely reflective, face eyeless and mouthless, blank as a minimalist snowman's, human only in general outline. "But the Old Doctor says you've exceeded all expectations, so we'll be working together from time to time."

Sigmund looked into Carlsbad's past, as far as he could—which was quite far, given the cocktail of uppers singing in his blood—and Carlsbad never changed; black, placid, eternal. "What—" *What are you*, he'd nearly asked. "What do you do for the Table?"

"Whatever the Old Doctor tells me to," Carlsbad said.

Sigmund nodded. "Carlotta told me you're a fallen god of the underworld."

"That bitch lies," Carlsbad said, without disapproval. "I'm no god. I'm just, what's that line—'the evil that lurks in the hearts of men.' The Old Doctor says that as long as one evil person remains on Earth, I'll be alive."

"Well," Sigmund said. "I guess you'll be around for a while, then."

The first time Carlsbad saved his life, Sigmund lay panting in a snowbank, blood running from a ragged gash in his arm. "You could have let me die just then," Sigmund said. Then, after a moment's hesitation: "You could have benefited from my death."

Carlsbad shrugged, shockingly dark against the snow. "Yeah, I guess."

"I thought you were *evil*," Sigmund said, lightheaded from blood loss and exertion, more in the *now* than he'd ever felt before, the scent of pines and the bite of cold air immediate reminders of his miraculously ongoing life. "I mean, you're *made* of evil."

"You're made mostly of carbon atoms," Carlsbad said. "But you don't spend all your time thinking about forming long-chain molecules, do you? There's more to both of us than our raw materials."

"Thank you for saving me, Carlsbad."

"Anytime, Sigmund." His tone was laid-back but pleased, the voice of someone who'd seen it all but could still sometimes be pleasantly surprised. "You're the first Table agent in four hundred years who's treated me like something other than a weapon or a monster. I know I scare you shitless, but you *talk* to me."

Exhaustion and exhilaration waxed and waned in Sigmund. "I like you because you don't change. When I look at most people I can see them as babies, teenagers, every step of their lives superimposed, and if I look back far enough they disappear — but not you. You're the same as far back as I can see." Sigmund's eyelids were heavy. He felt light. He thought he might float away.

"Hold on," Carlsbad said. "Help is on the way. Your death might not diminish me, but I'd still like to keep you around."

Sigmund blacked out, but not before hearing the whirr of approaching helicopters coming to take him away.

"I'm the New Doctor," the New Doctor said. Willowy, brunette, young, she stood behind a podium in the briefing room, looking at the assembled Table agents — Sigmund, Carlotta, Carlsbad, and the recently-promoted Ray. They were the alpha squad, the apex of the organization, and the New Doctor had not impressed them yet. "We're going to have some changes around here. We need to get back to basics. We need to find the *cup*. These other jobs might fill our bank accounts, but they don't further our cause."

Ray popped a wasp into his mouth, chewed, swallowed, and said, "Fuck that mystic bullshit." His voice was accompanied by a deep, angry buzz, a sort of wasp-whisper in harmony with the normal workings of his voicebox. Ray got nasty and impatient when he ate wasps. "I joined up to make money and get a regular workout, not chase after some imaginary Grail." Sigmund knew Ray was lying — that he had a very specific interest in the cup — but Sigmund also understood why Ray was keeping that interest a secret. "You just stay in the library and read your books like the Old Doctor did, okay?"

The New Doctor shoved the podium over, and it fell toward Ray, who dove out of the way. While he was moving, the New Doctor came around and kicked him viciously in the ribs, her small boots wickedly pointed and probably steel-toed. Ray rolled away, panting and clutching his side.

Sigmund peered into the New Doctor's past. She looked young, but she'd looked young for *decades*.

"I'm not like the Old Doctor," she said. "He missed his old life in the archives, and was content with his books, piecing together the past. But I'm glad to be out of the archives, and under my leadership, we're going to make history, not study it."

"I'll *kill* you," Ray said. Stingers were growing out of his fingertips, and his voice was all buzz now.

"Spare me," the New Doctor said, and kicked him in the face.

By spying on their pasts and listening in on their private moments, Sigmund learned why the other agents wanted to find the cup, and see God:

Carlotta whispered to one of her lovers, the shade of a great courtesan conjured from an anteroom of Hell: "I want to castrate God, so he'll never create another world."

Ray told Carlotta, while they disposed of the body of a young archivist who'd discovered their secret past and present plans: "I want to eat God's heart and belch out words of creation."

Carlsbad, alone, staring at the night sky (a lighted void, while his own darkness was utter), had imaginary conversations with God that always came down, fundamentally, to one question: "Why did you make me?"

The New Doctor, just before she poisoned the Old Doctor (making it look like a natural death), answered his bewildered plea for mercy by saying, "No. As long as you're alive, we'll *never* find the cup, and I'll *never* see God, and I'll *never* know the answers to the ten great questions I've composed during my time in the archives."

Sigmund saw it all, every petty plan and purpose that drove his fellows, but he had no better purpose himself. The agents of the Table might succeed in finding the cup, not because they were worthy, but simply because they'd been trying for years upon years, and sometimes persistence led to success.

Sigmund knew their deepest reasons, and kept all their secrets, because past and present and cause and effect were scrambled for him. The Old Doctor's regime of meth, cocaine, and more exotic uppers had ravaged Sigmund's nasal cavities and set him adrift in time. At first, he'd only been able to *see* back in time, but sometimes taking the Old Doctor's experimental stimulants *truly* sent him back in time. Sometimes it was just his mind that traveled, sent back a few days to relive past events again in his own body, but other times, rarely, he physically traveled back, just a day or two at most, just for a little while, before being wrenched back to a present filled with headaches and nosebleeds.

On one of those rare occasions when he traveled physically back in time, Sigmund saw the Old Doctor's murder, and was snapped back to the future moments before the New Doctor could kill him, too.

Ray ate a Sherpa's brain two days out of base camp, and after that, he was able to guide them up the crags and paths toward the temple perfectly, though he was harder to converse with, his speech peppered with mountain idioms. He developed a taste for barley tea flavored with rancid yak butter, and sometimes sang lonely songs that merged with the sound of the wind.

"We're going to Hell," the New Doctor said.

"Probably," Sigmund said, edging away.

She sighed. "No, really—we're going into the underworld. Or, well, sort of a visiting room for the underworld."

"I've heard rumors about that." Hell's anteroom was where Carlotta found her ghostly lovers. "One of the Table's last remaining mystic secrets. I'm surprised they didn't lose that, too, when they lost the key to the moon and the scryer's glass and all those other wonders in the first war with the Templars."

"Much has been lost." The New Doctor pushed a shelf, which swung easily away from the wall on secret hinges, revealing an iron grate. "But that means much can be regained." She pressed a red button. "Stop fidgeting, Sigmund. I'm not going to kill you. But I do want to know, how did you get into the Old Doctor's office and see me kill him, when I *know* you were on assignment with Carlsbad in Belize at the time? And how did you disappear afterward? Bodily bilocation? Ectoplasmic projection? What?"

"Time travel," Sigmund said. "I don't just see into the past. Sometimes I travel into the past physically."

"Huh. I didn't see anything about that in the Old Doctor's notes."

"Oh, no. He kept the most important notes in his head. So why aren't you going to kill me?"

Something hummed and clattered beneath the floor.

"Because I can use you. Why haven't you turned me in?"

Sigmund hesitated. He'd liked the Old Doctor, who was the closest thing he'd ever had to a father. He hated to disrespect the old man's memory, though he knew the Old Doctor had seen him as a research tool, a sort of ambulatory microfiche machine, and nothing more. "Because I'm ready for things to change. I thought I wanted to be an operative, but I'm tired of the endless pointless round-and-round, not to mention being shot and stabbed and thrown from moving trains. Under your leadership, I think the Table might actually *achieve* something."

"We will." The grinding and humming underground intensified, and she raised her voice. "We'll find the cup, and see God, and get answers. We'll find out why he created the world, only to immediately abandon his creation, letting chaos fill his wake. But first, to Hell. Here." She tossed something glittering toward him, a few old subway tokens. "To pay the attendant."

The grinding stopped, the grate sliding open to reveal a tarnished brass elevator car operated by a man in a cloak the color of dust and spiderwebs. He held out his palm, and Sigmund and the New Doctor each dropped a token into his hand.

"Why are we going . . . down there?" Sigmund asked.

"To see the Old Doctor, and get some of that information he kept only in his head. I know where to find the cup—or where to find the map that leads to it, anyway—but I need to know what will happen once I have the cup in hand."

"Why take me?"

"Because only insane people, like Carlotta, risk going to Hell's anteroom alone. And if I took anyone else, they'd find out I was the one who killed the Old Doctor, and they might be less understanding about it than you are." She stepped into the elevator car, and Sigmund followed. He glanced into the attendant's past, almost reflexively, and the things he saw were so horrible that he threw himself back into the far corner of the tiny car; if the elevator hadn't already started moving, he would have pried open the doors and fled. The attendant turned his head to look at him, and Sigmund squeezed his eyes shut so that he didn't have to risk seeing the attendant frown, or worse, smile.

"Interesting," the New Doctor said.

After they returned from Hell, Sigmund and the New Doctor fucked furiously beneath the card table in the Old Doctor's library, because sex is an antidote to death, or at least, an adequate placebo.

"That's it, then," the New Doctor said. "We're going to the Himalayas."

"Fucking great," Ray said. "I always wanted to eat a Yeti."

"I think you're hairy enough already," Carlotta said.

Sigmund and the New Doctor sat beneath a ledge of rock, frigid wind howling across the face of the mountain. Carlsbad was out looking for Ray and Carlotta, who had stolen all the food and oxygen and gone looking for the Temple of the cup alone. They wanted to kill God, not ask him questions, so their betrayal was troublesome but not surprising. Sigmund probably should have told someone about their planned betrayal, but he felt more and more like an actor outside time—a position which, he now realized, was likely to get him killed. He needed to take a more active role.

"Ray and Carlotta don't know the prophecy," Sigmund said. "Only the Old Doctor knew, and he only told *us*. They have no idea what they're going to cause, if they reach the Temple first."

"If they reach the Temple first, we'll die along with the rest of the world." The New Doctor was weak from oxygen deficiency. "If Carlsbad doesn't find them, we're doomed." She looked older, having left the safety of the library and the archives, and the past two years had been hard. They'd traveled to the edges and underside of the Earth, gathering fragments of the map to the Temple of the cup, chasing down the obscure references the New Doctor had uncovered in the archives. First they'd gone deep into the African desert, into crumbling palaces carved from sentient rock; then they'd trekked through the Antarctic, looking for the secret entrance to the Earth's war-torn core, and finding it; they'd projected themselves, astrally and otherwise, into the mind of a sleeping demigod from the jungles of another world; and two months ago they'd descended to crush-depth in the Pacific Ocean to find the last fragment of the map in a coral temple guarded by spined, bioluminescent beings of infinite sadness. Ray had eaten one of those guardians, and ever since he'd been sweating purple ink and taking long, contemplative baths in salt water.

The New Doctor had ransacked the Table's coffers to pay for this last trip to the Himalayas, selling off long-hoarded art objects and dismissing even the poorly-paid hereditary janitorial staff to cover the expenses. And now they were on the edge of total failure, unless Sigmund did something.

Sigmund opened his pack and removed his last vial of the Old Doctor's most potent exotic upper. "Wish me bon voyage," he said, and snorted it all.

Time unspooled, and Sigmund found himself beneath the same ledge, but earlier, the ice unmarked by human passage, the weather more mild. Moving manically, driven by drugs and the need to stay warm, he piled up rocks above the trail and waited, pacing in an endless circle, until he heard Carlotta and Ray approaching, grunting under the weight of stolen supplies.

He pushed rocks down on them, and the witch and the phage were knocked down. Sigmund made his way to them, hoping they would be crushed—that the rocks would have done his work for him. Carlotta was mostly buried, but her long fingernails scraped furrows in the ice, and Sigmund gritted his teeth, cleared away enough rocks to expose her head, and finished her off with the ice axe. She did not speak, but Sigmund almost thought he saw respect in her expression before he obliterated it. Ray was only half-buried, but unmoving, his neck twisted unnaturally. Sigmund sank the point of the axe into Ray's thigh to make sure he was truly dead, and the phage did not react. Sigmund left the axe in Ray's leg. He turned his back on the dead and crouched, waiting for time to sweep him up again in its flow.

Carlsbad found Ray and Carlotta dead, and brought back the supplies. By then Sigmund was back from the past, and while the New Doctor ate and rested, he took Carlsbad aside to tell him the truth: "There's a good chance we might destroy the world."

"Hmm," Carlsbad said.

"There's a prophecy, in the deep archives of the Table, that God will only return when the world is destroyed by fire. But it's an article of faith—the *basis* of our faith—that when the contents of the cup are swallowed by an acolyte of the Table, God will return. So by approaching the cup—by *intending* to drink from it—we might collapse the probability wave in such a way that the end of the world begins, fire and all, in the moments before we even touch the cup."

"And you and the New Doctor are okay with that?"

"The New Doctor thinks she can convince God to spare the world from destruction, retroactively, if necessary."

"Huh," Carlsbad said.

"She can be very persuasive," Sigmund said.

"I'm sure," Carlsbad replied.

The fire began to fall just as they reached the temple, a structure so old it seemed part of the mountain itself. The sky went red, and great gobbets of flame cascaded down, the meteor shower to end all others. Snow flashed instantly to steam on all the surrounding mountains, though the temple peak was untouched, for now.

"That's it, then," Carlsbad said. "Only the evil in you two is keeping me alive."

"No turning back now," the New Doctor said, and started up the ancient steps to the temple.

Ray, bloodied and battered, left arm hanging broken, stepped from the shadows beside the temple. He held Sigmund's ice axe in his good hand, and he swung it at the New Doctor's head with phenomenal force, caving in her skull. She fell, and he fell upon her, bringing the axe down again and again, laying her body open. He looked up, face bruised and swollen, fur sprouting from his jaw, veins pulsing in his forehead, poison and ink and pus and hallucinogens oozing from his pores. "You can't kill me, junkie. I've eaten wolverines. I've eaten giants. I've eaten *angels*." As he said this last, he began to glow with a strange, blue-shifted light.

"Saving your life again," Carlsbad said, almost tenderly, and then he did what the Table always counted on him to do. He swelled, he stormed, he smashed, he tore Ray to pieces, and then tore up the pieces.

After that he began to melt. "Ah, shit, Sigmund," he said. "You just aren't *evil* enough." Before Sigmund could say thank you, or goodbye, all that remained of Carlsbad was a dark pool, like a slick of old axle grease on the snow.

There was nothing for Sigmund to do but go on.

"The cup holds the blood of God," the Old Doctor said. "Drink it, and God will return, and as you are made briefly divine by swallowing the substance of his body, he will treat you as an equal, and answer questions, and grant requests. For that moment, God will do whatever you ask." The Old Doctor placed his hand on Sigmund's own. "The Table exists to make sure the cup's power is not used for evil or trivial purposes. The question asked, the wish desired, has to be worth the cost, which is the world."

"What would you ask?" Sigmund said.

"I would ask why God created the world and walked away, leaving only a cupful of blood and a world of wonders behind. But that is only curiosity, and not a worthy question."

"So anyway," Sigmund said, sniffing and wiping at his nose. "When can I start doing field work?" He wished he could see the future instead of the past. He thought this was going to be a lot of fun.

The cup in Sigmund's hands held blood, liquid at the center, but dried and crusted on the cup's rim. Sigmund scraped the residue of dried blood up with his long pinky fingernail. He took a breath. Let it out. And snorted God's blood.

Time *snapped*.

Sigmund looked around the temple. It was white, bright, clean, and no longer on a mountaintop. The windows looked out on a placid sea. He was not alone.

God looked nothing like Sigmund had imagined, but at the same time, it was impossible to mistake him for anyone else. It was clear that God was on his way out, but he paused, and looked at Sigmund expectantly.

Sigmund had gone from the end of the world to the beginning. He was so high from snorting God's blood that he could see individual atoms in the air, vibrating. He knew he could be jerked back to the top of the ruined world at any moment.

Sigmund tried to think. He'd expected the New Doctor to ask the questions, to make the requests, so he didn't know what to say. God was clearly growing impatient, ready to leave his creation forever behind. If Sigmund spoke quickly, he could have anything he wanted. Anything at all.

"Hey," Sigmund said. "Don't go."

NICHOLAS ROYLE

The Churring

Nicholas Royle, born in Manchester in the northwest of England in 1963, is the author of five novels: Counterparts, Saxophone Dreams, The Matter of the Heart, The Director's Cut, *and* Antwerp—*and one short story collection,* Mortality. *A novella, "The Enigma of Departure," is forthcoming from PS Publications. Widely published as an arts journalist and book reviewer, he teaches creative writing at Manchester Metropolitan University. He is married with two children and lives in Manchester.*

"The Churring" was first published in Royle's collection Mortality.

—E.D.

Corpse fowl. Goatsucker. The nightjar is inside my head. Its ghostly, premonitory clicking. The ironic applause of its wing-beat handclap. A summer visitor, Sylvia Plath's "Devil-bird" casts its deadly shadow from May onward. I have just one bird-spotting book (I'm not a twitcher. I don't need the ticks) and it's one my father gave me when I was ten. "To Alexander," he wrote inside it, "on becoming amphibious." Underneath, in my own childish hand, I have added a key: A pencil tick indicates that I have seen a particular bird, a tick in green ballpoint means my sister has beaten me to it (I needed the ticks then, but not now). The nightjar is ticked by neither of us. The cuckoo, on the page before, has a green tick, which strikes me as unlikely. The swift, which follows the nightjar, has two entirely plausible ticks.

The book is inaccurate. The nightjar, it says, "is more often seen than heard." In fact, the reverse is widely known to be true. I wonder if the text, which appears to have been translated from the Czech (of Jaroslav Spirhanzl Duris) by a Czech (Hedda Veselá-Stránská), has been adequately checked. I do, however, like how the writer describes the nightjar's song, as "a cry like that of a sewing machine in action." I'm so used to seeing the goatsucker's song described in print as a "churring," for some reason always with inverted commas, that the sewing machine analogy always makes me hear it afresh. At first I thought it missed the mark: The sewing machine is too noisy, the whirr of the turning wheel, the rustle of the fabric. But I've ended up thinking it's actually quite a good comparison, especially when I remember that my mother's sewing machine, constantly audible on the soundtrack of my childhood, was a Singer. It's difficult to describe birdsong, but here is someone who's had a go, and maybe a Soviet-era Czech sewing machine (the book was published four years before the Prague Spring) sounds a little different than today's cutting-edge equivalent.

I close the book and notice that the head of the goldfinch on the spine has faded, its red face a pale ochre. I return the book to the shelf and go downstairs, picking up stray books and magazines as I go.

I'm in the middle of getting the house ready for the annual meeting of the Fallowfield Film Society, which falls, as it has done for the last ten years or so, on the second weekend in May. For the benefit of those group members who are parents, it has to be scheduled for after Easter and the May Day bank holiday, but before Whit Week, so that it doesn't interfere with school holidays. Childless myself, I don't object. "Child-free," I recently read in the newspaper, is preferred by some to "childless," as it accentuates the positive side of not having children, the having taken a decision not to have any, rather than suggesting the terrible lack of something, the unbearable regret. That was in a column by a young woman who never misses an opportunity to express her displeasure at children and her impatience with overindulgent parents. She comes across as chippy and vituperative. In any case, I don't have a problem with children. I like children.

The kitchen is a mess, newspapers and CDs everywhere. I collect the jewel cases together and stow them on the shelf in the alcove. I eject Bartok's nerve-jangling String Quartets from the CD player and replace them with Beethoven's more restful Piano Sonatas. As an afterthought, I check the cassette deck. It contains a very old green BASF C90. I take it out and sit down on one of the stools at the island in the middle of the kitchen. I turn the cassette over in my hands, studying it, as if it were unfamiliar to me, as if I hadn't spent long nights listening to it over and over again. Play, rewind, play, rewind, play. On the label, in my father's handwriting, I read: "Wed 28th June 1978. Cannock Chase." I move my finger tips lightly over the line of text as if reading Braille.

Unsure where the cassette case is, I slip the tape into my top pocket and start stacking the newspapers that have accumulated on the island during the week. A headline catches my eye, as it had the day I'd bought the paper it was in: "CAN YOU CATCH CANCER?"

Pretty effective. It made you stop and think. It certainly made me stop and think, although it didn't make me read the article. Not because I'm squeamish or anything, but because the question more or less contained its own answer. Can you catch cancer? What was the piece likely to go on to say? It wouldn't be a flat "no," obviously, or the headline would be a bit cheap. Hardly a resounding "yes" either, or the feature would surely be headed "YOU CAN CATCH CANCER" and everyone would read the article and it wouldn't be the lead story in the second section, either. It would be front-page news.

So, probably, the piece would weigh up some recently uncovered facts and statistics and end up saying, "Well, perhaps. Sort of. Maybe."

Responsibility for hosting the meetings rotates around the group. This year it's my turn. People start arriving on the Friday afternoon and by mid-morning on Saturday everyone is present. I make it sound like a bigger event than it is, perhaps. It's not a real film society with a projector and an audience. The invite list is basically three couples, plus children. And me. Luckily I have a big house.

If you went to university in Manchester, England, in the early 1980s and had the sense to get on the housing ladder at that time, twenty years later you could, like me, be living in a house worth half a million. That's assuming you didn't fritter away your student grant and then hit the overland trail the moment you graduated. If you lived sensibly and walked straight into a local-government job on graduation, a flat or even a small house in Fallowfield wasn't beyond your means. Sell that for a tidy profit five years later and buy a Victorian terraced in Chorlton and you were halfway there. By that stage it's hard to go wrong. Before you know it you've landed in Didsbury, owning the sort of house the estate agents in the village would be describing as a "prestige property" by the end of the next decade.

Everyone gathers in the kitchen and I make coffee and open a packet of cookies for the kids. The newspapers on the island have become unstacked again, plus there are more of them now. I make an effort to gather them up. On top, by chance, is that piece about catching cancer. Still unread. I move the papers to the alcove, where they will be out of the way and the headline won't upset anybody.

I hand a cup of strong black coffee to Iain, who is here with his partner, Steph.

"I can't remember how you take it, Steph."

"White without, please, Alex."

Steph is pretty, with a short dark bob, a severe pair of glasses, and an odd line in 1950s dresses worn over leggings and such like. All a bit 1980s, in fact. She works in advertising. She's a few years younger than Iain, who's my age, early forties. For years Iain struggled with hair loss. He didn't seem to know what to do with what he'd got, whether to grow it or crop it, whether to use gel and make a feature of it or hide it under a baseball cap. One day he shaved it all off, what was left of it, and this became his regular look. He has the overhanging brow of a Ralph Fiennes and the amused, somewhat untrustworthy glint of a Clive Owen or a Ciaran Hinds in his smile. Iain and I were on the same landing in halls of residence at Owens Park in Fallowfield and I became his friend primarily because I liked his then girlfriend, Jenny, whom I'd met through the Student Labour Club. The three of us hung out together a lot, and in our visits to the Aaben in Hulme, making full use of its four screens showing a mixture of schlock, arthouse, and new releases, lay the origins of the Fallowfield Film Society.

Iain and Jenny surprised everybody, including themselves, when Jenny became pregnant in 1986. The following year three momentous things happened: their son, Jacob, was born; Iain and Jenny got married shortly after; and within four months Jenny was diagnosed with breast cancer. She died two years later, while the Berlin Wall was being torn down. Whenever those scenes are replayed on television, which happens more often than you might think, Iain finds himself instantly catapulted back into the grieving process. It can throw him out for up to a week, which may be a little disconcerting for Steph, but it's not like she didn't know what she was getting herself into. Jacob is grown up and away doing his own thing, but Iain and Steph have a child of their own, six-year-old Thomas. I want to like him, but to be honest he's a bit precocious, which I attribute to Steph. Thomas is in the front room with the other children, where I've put on a video for them.

Nina is a beautiful, delicate-featured Indian woman. Her wavy hair is going elegantly gray, in streaks, a bit like Susan Sontag. She's wearing a blue sari. When she was going out with my best friend, Richard Salthouse, in the early 1980s, I would join them for pub crawls around Withington and film screenings at CineCity. In those days Nina wore the same as me and Richard—jeans, T-shirts, second-hand jackets. When I became friendly with Iain and Jenny, I introduced the two couples to each other and everyone got on, the five of us spending time together as a group.

The following year, investigating the social potential of the Federation of Conservative Students, I met James, who would become the sixth member of our group, which had by now been given its name.

Later, Richard started having convulsions and blackouts. They took him in for tests and found an aggressive malignant brain tumor the size of a tangerine. His condition was terminal and his decline mercifully swift; nevertheless, the shock of his disappearance from our lives was like a punch in the gut. Nina dropped out of college and withdrew from everyone who'd known her and Richard as a couple. She went to India and came back in a sari. An arranged marriage, which she'd previously resisted, followed, but it didn't last. Nine years ago she met Sunil, a lecturer in statistics at Manchester Poly. He's not very exciting, but he seems to make Nina happy, so that's fair enough. They have a boy and a girl, Vishnu and Raji, aged eight and six, respectively. Right now they're in the front room with Thomas.

"What film have you chosen for us, Alex?" asks Steph.

I smile.

"Nice try, Steph," says James with a laugh, raising his dark eyebrows above the gold glint of his round-eye frames.

James is reminding Steph that the choice of film, which is the prerogative of the host, is kept secret until the screening is ready to begin.

"Are you not bringing anyone, James?" Steph asks him. "Or has he yet to arrive?"

"You never know who's going to turn up," James says, with a little look in my direction.

"Actually, I did meet a very nice young man in Taurus last night, but I'm not sure this would be his scene."

"Not enough rubber?" Steph asks. She delights in bringing out the queen in James.

"Oh, I don't think he's into rubber, although I haven't yet got to know him *that* well."

At this point there's a clatter of wings and a loud ratcheting cry from the back garden.

"What's that?" Nina asks and I notice that Sunil looks relieved at the change of subject.

"Magpie," I say as I watch the delicate, springy branches of the cherry tree take its weight.

"What a racket!" Nina exclaims. "Alex knows all the different birds," she adds for Sunil's benefit, although he's known me long enough perhaps to know of my avian enthusiasms. "You know, when we started, we didn't meet in people's houses. After all, we didn't have houses, did we?" She looks at me and at Iain. "Remember when we went to Dorset?"

"*Five Go Mad in Dorset,*" says Iain.

"Except there were seven of us," I remind him. "You and Jenny, Nina and Richard, James and whoever he was with that weekend—and me."

"I'm trying to remember," Iain says, looking at James. "Didn't you pick someone up there?"

"No, I wasn't that bad. Well, not then," James says with a laugh. "Wasn't I with Tim then?" he adds, looking straight at me.

I kick myself for having given him the prompt. Tim was an obsessive Smiths fan who James went out with for a few weeks. He did come on the trip to Dorset. How could I forget? Quite easily, if it wasn't for what actually happened in Wareham, because in any gathering he blended into the background. I can quite imagine having him in the back of my car, so to speak, and not being aware of him, as his lips move in silent autistic repetition of Morrissey's hallowed lyrics.

"He was the Smiths fan, wasn't he?" Iain asks.

"Who wasn't in those days?" says Nina. "Richard certainly was."

I remember that Richard was. He used to try to convince me that I should listen to their albums. I told him I liked Joy Division and the Passage, that they were my Manchester bands. A Certain Ratio. The Fall. There was no room for whiny, self-obsessed losers in my record collection, I told him.

Having mentioned Richard's name, Nina gazes out of the window. I've noticed that whenever he is the subject of conversation, everything about her seems somehow to slow down. Sunil always tries to take her hand and she lets him, but there's a moment when you can see how she still misses Richard badly. How it still hurts.

"I think Tim did go to Dorset," James says. "Surely you remember, Alex?" he presses me.

I return his look.

"Why should Alex remember?" Nina asks, snapping out of her moment of sadness and withdrawing her hand from Sunil's.

"It was Alex's weekend, wasn't it?" James says, turning to face me again. "You organized it. You were in charge. Alex is a born organizer, aren't you, Alex?"

I did organize it, although it didn't take much organizing. Two cars, mine and Richard's. Iain and Jenny went in Richard's car with him and Nina, leaving James and Tim to go in my car. I remember James sitting alongside me, so Tim must have been in the back. He really was one of those forgettable people. I've certainly forgotten him. If only James could.

We drove down in convoy on a Saturday in April. The Rex in Wareham was the country's only gas-lit picture house. The cinema itself would have been worth the trip on its own, but it was playing host to a mini-festival, a horror all-nighter. According to what had already become a tradition, I didn't tell anyone where we were going, merely that it was a very long drive and we would be coming back the following day. That we didn't need accommodation was what especially intrigued everyone.

The festival opened early on Saturday evening with an irresistible splash of gore: Lucio Fulci's *Zombie Flesh Eaters*. The second film, the rather silly *Blood Beach*, was one I had already seen and I persuaded Richard and Nina to give it a miss. "You're missing nothing," I assured them. We drove the short distance to Canford Heath, north of Poole, and parked on the edge of a housing estate, then took a path on to the heath. In the twilight, away from the streetlamps and lit windows of the estate, the sky became a liquid electric blue. The trees and shrubs around us formed vaguely suggestive shapes in the gathering gloom.

"What are we looking for?" Richard asked.

"Dartford warblers, nightjars," I said. "Nightjars really. Bit late in the day, perhaps, for Dartford warblers, but it's just the right time of day and the perfect environment for nightjars. Slightly early in the season, but we might get lucky, especially this far south."

"What does a nightjar look like?" asked Nina.

"A bit like a kestrel or a cuckoo. In fact we're very unlikely to see one. More likely to hear one. It sounds like . . . It's almost more like a knocking sound than a song. Like a woodpecker, only not on wood, more, I don't know, metallic somehow. They call it a churring. Rhymes with whirring."

"We're not looking for Dartford warblers at all, are we?" said Richard.

"No, we're not. As you very well know."

Nina gave us a look.

"We're looking for nightjars," I said. "Have you not told Nina, then, Richard?"

"Told me what?"

"I would have thought couples told each other stuff like this."

"You told me it was personal," Richard said.

"It was. I just imagined . . ."

"A lot of couples share everything, but if you tell me something and tell me it's personal, it goes no further."

"Well, that's . . . nice, I suppose."

"Is someone going to tell me what's going on?" Nina asked.

"It's nothing really," I said. "Just that I'm interested in nightjars. My father had a special interest in them, so in a way they're my link to him. My only link, really."

"Your father died, didn't he?"

"Yes, he died in 1979, when I was sixteen. Lung cancer."

"That must have been very hard."

We came to a fork in the path. We split up. It was Nina's idea. She suggested she go one way and Richard the other.

"I'll go with Nina," I said.

"I can manage," she said. "You go with Richard."

In the end, it was decided that since we would have to return to the car by the same path, Nina and I would each explore one of the two forks, while Richard would wait at the point where the path divided for us to come back. The left fork, mine, led quite quickly into full forest, which I knew was the wrong terrain for nightjars, so I went back and rejoined Richard. While we were waiting for Nina, we suddenly heard a sound. It came from the open ground to the left: a steady uninterrupted clicking. We looked at each other, eyes wide, and I nodded. "That's it," I whispered. "That's a nightjar. No question."

"Are you sure?"

"A hundred per cent."

"The tape recording your father made?"

"Identical."

We strained our eyes in the dark, but there was nothing to see. No bird sat in a tree silhouetted against the sky. No hawklike shape flew past us questing for prey. The nightjar was on the ground somewhere, churring, and given that they were practically invisible by day, thanks to the superb camouflage provided by their gray-brown feathers and mottled, barred markings, what chance did we have of seeing it in the darkness?

None. But it didn't matter. We had heard it, and with the nightjar, that counted.

The churring continued for up to a minute, rising and falling in pitch. Richard and I breathed slowly and quietly, leg muscles taut from standing on tiptoe, focusing all our efforts on listening. Eventually it stopped. We waited, tense and expectant, for it to start again, but it didn't. We relaxed, let the tension flow out of our bodies. Richard bent over, pressing his hands against his knees. I rested mine on Richard's shoulder. My legs felt wobbly. It was the first time I had heard the churring in the flesh, my first actual encounter with a nightjar. Even if we hadn't seen it, I had had a clear image in my mind of its enormous black eyes and cavernous mouth, its beak edged with bristles. I pictured it on the wing, hoovering up moths and beetles like a whale shark gorging on plankton.

"It's like a Geiger counter," Richard said.

"What?" I said, keeping my eyes averted.

"It sounds like a Geiger counter."

I thought of the blasts of radiation my father had had to endure at the Christie Hospital. All for nothing.

Shortly after that, we heard Nina returning along her fork of the path. We told her about the churring, and she wanted to wait around and see if we would hear it again. We gave it ten minutes or so, but the night was as quiet as the grave, and eventually we headed back to where we'd left the car.

We got back to Wareham in time to watch child actor Mark Lester touching up Britt Ekland in the third installment in that night's program, *Night Hair Child* — and rather wished we hadn't.

Richard fell ill later that year. After he died, Nina told me how happy he had been in the days after the weekend in Wareham. Specifically it seemed to have been hearing the nightjar that had moved him so deeply. Hearing it, moreover, in my presence, because he had a pretty good idea what it meant to me.

"If you could have seen his face," she told me, "you'd have known it was worth all the effort of getting us down there."

We go for a walk in the afternoon. Fletcher Moss Gardens, with its south-facing hill-side rockeries and botanical riches, attracts a lot of birds. In the low flat meadows between the park and the River Mersey I once saw a fieldfare (slightly dubious pencil tick in the book) and more recently a small bird I thought might be a bullfinch, but which I doubt since I discovered how rare they've become.

The children run on ahead. Iain and Sunil walk together and I'm flanked by Steph and Nina. James is hanging back, making a phone call. I wonder who he's calling. I even let Steph and Nina dictate our slow pace in the hope that he might approach within earshot. James lives in an apartment in one of the big conversions in town. India House. Very much the bachelor lifestyle. The single gay man's lifestyle, to be precise. The anonymity of the corridors. Could almost be a hotel. I wonder if he ever sees Tim these days. Maybe he's calling the lad he met in Taurus, trying to persuade him to join us for tonight's screening.

"So what have we got to look forward to tonight?" Nina asks, as if reading my mind.

"You'll find out soon enough."

"More horror, I suppose," she adds, with a sigh of mock impatience.

"I don't always pick horror films," I protest. "Didn't I pick a film about birds last time?"

"Yes," says Steph. "Hitchcock's *The Birds*."

"Ah yes. Look, next time, I promise. I'll find something different. Although, don't assume you're going to hate tonight's film. It has local appeal, I'll say that much."

Nina and Sunil moved out to Cumbria, close to the M6 to facilitate Sunil's commute to the Poly, now MMU, while Steph and Iain live in north London. Steph is a big cheese at one of the ad agencies in Fitzrovia; Iain works part-time for a housing charity and does the school run.

I notice that Iain and Sunil have stopped and Sunil is pointing at a small bird in a tree.

"What is it?" he asks me when we catch up.

"A chaffinch," I say.

Sunil looks hopeful. "Are they rare?" he asks.

"No, they're very common," I say, and I wonder if it was a chaffinch I saw when I thought I'd seen a bullfinch, except there's a marked difference in size. A hawfinch, then, perhaps.

Sunil, Steph, Nina, and I are still watching the chaffinch, the UK's second commonest breeding bird, hardly deserving of our attention, when I realize Iain has left us and is walking off toward the children.

The 1987 meeting was always going to be tricky. Jacob was less than three months old, yet Iain and Jenny, to their credit, said they were not going to let the side down and would attend. There may have been one or two members slightly less excited at the prospect of a small baby joining the group, but those people kept their opinions to themselves.

It was to be Nina's first meeting since Richard's death. She was back from India but the arranged marriage was not yet in the bag, so she came on her own. James was definitely a solo act that year. (The previous year had been James's turn as host and he had taken us all to the Aaben, where we each drew lots to decide which film we saw. Somehow he and his then partner, Andrew, ended up together in screen number four, but didn't see much of the picture. I sat through Wim Wenders' *The Goalkeeper's Fear of the Penalty*, having had my request to swap with Iain, who'd landed had a double bill of *Halloween* and *Assault on Precinct 13*, turned down.)

I had hired a small farmhouse on the edge of the North York Moors. There was neither a VCR, nor even a television. On the first night Iain, James, and I went to the pub, leaving Nina and Jenny with the baby in the farmhouse. Iain and Jenny tended to give each other breaks from childcare, and Nina said she would prefer to stay behind with Jenny. I waited until we were on our second pint apiece to ask Iain and James if they felt like a walk in the forest.

"Cropton Forest," I said. "It's just up the road."

"Go on, then."

The road allowed us to drive into the forest, then turn on to a bridleway. I pulled over when it narrowed to a track and we got out and walked.

"What are we looking for?" Iain asked.

"Any cleared section," I said. "This is nightjar country. They like it where the trees have been cut down."

I told them what to listen for if we did come across any manmade clearings. Eventually we did, but if there were any goatsuckers present, they were keeping quiet about it.

On the way back to the car James asked why I was so interested in nightjars.

"No special reason, except they're extremely rare," I said, "and there's a whole mythology grown up around them. They're supposed to steal milk from goats, which of course they don't. People say they presage misfortune and even death, hence corpse fowl—another nickname. If one lands on the roof of your house, you're fucked, basically. Fortunately they don't tend to come into residential areas."

The following day we drove to Whitby and toured the Dracula sites, visiting the abbey and St. Mary's churchyard. In the afternoon there was a special screening of Terence Fisher's 1958 adaptation of Stoker's novel at Whitby Museum. This wasn't a great success, with baby Jacob screaming the place down when he woke up and trying to get out of his pushchair halfway through. As we left, Nina told me she wanted to go home to Manchester and asked me if I would drive her to York so she could catch a train. We tried to persuade her to stay another night, but she was adamant. In the end, James took her. He said he needed to get back to Manchester as well to take care of a work matter and so the two of them left that year's meeting before it was really over. A sense of anticlimax hung over the farmhouse and I asked Jenny if she wanted to go out hunting for nightjars, assuming it was Iain's turn to look after the baby.

As Jenny and I walked through the forest on a different path to the one I had taken with Iain and James the night before, we talked in low voices. I had always been close to Jenny. I think it was because I sensed in her an acceptance of me, a lack of judgment. She was constant, happy with herself, and secure in her opinions. Even having had a child didn't seem to have changed her a great deal.

"It's a bit weird, James and Nina leaving early," I said.

"I think it's been hard for Nina," Jenny said, casting sidelong glances into the darkness between the trees. "You know, it was her first meeting since losing Richard. She's been in India, getting her head straight. Probably the last thing she needed—and I'm not criticizing your choice—but maybe a Dracula weekend wasn't the ideal one to come back on."

"Oh," I said, disconsolately, "yeah."

"I think whatever it had been, even if it had been someone else's turn to choose, she would have struggled."

Jenny was being kind to me. We walked in silence for a while.

"Alex," she said after a bit, "can I ask you a question?"

"Um, of course."

"Why do you never have anyone with you on these weekends? I mean, why have you been on your own for so long? I hope you don't mind me asking, but are you gay or do you just not like girls or what?" It had come out in a rush and for a moment all either of us could hear was the sound of our feet landing on the path and the occasional crack of a broken twig.

Eventually, I opened my mouth to answer and Jenny started speaking at the same time.

"You know what?" she said. "Ignore all of that. It was a mistake. I shouldn't have said it."

"No . . . No . . . It's fine. It's . . . I . . ." I was having trouble formulating a response. "Am I gay? I don't know. I watch James, I see what he gets up to and who he gets up to it with, and I think to myself, I could do that. I see guys I like the look of. But could I really, *really* go through with it? I don't know." I thought for a moment as I looked into the forest ahead of us. There was a clearing coming up. "Why am I always alone? It's not that I want to be, but I can't seem to get my head round the alternative. I'm not sure I'm very comfortable with people. With a few exceptions. Like you. But you're taken and you have been as long as I've known you, and I'm not the kind of person who can do anything about something like that. Ssh!"

I stopped and put my hand out and Jenny held her breath alongside me. The clearing on the right was just a few yards away. We listened, but there was nothing to hear. Slowly we advanced, taking care to step lightly on the path. Then, what I'd thought I'd heard I heard again. The unmistakable churring of a nightjar. It was very close to us. No more than twenty feet away. We stood transfixed. I felt Jenny's hand take hold of mine and squeeze it. I held tight as we listened. I felt enormously privileged. I felt the very edge of something I suspected was happiness, or the possibility of happiness, but also I felt like a pauper touching the hem of the king's robes. Then I remembered the last time I had heard the churring, with Richard, and I felt a strange sensation in my stomach. It wasn't sadness or regret. It didn't make me feel wholesome. It was not unlike a caffeine high. I felt apprehensive and a little excited, and I didn't know if I liked it or not.

As we walked back, Jenny took my arm and leaned her upper body against mine. At the time I interpreted it as a caring, protective gesture. With hindsight and the knowledge that only a matter of weeks lay between that night and the diagnosis of Jenny's breast cancer, I wonder if it was the other way around and if it was that she was seeking support from me.

The night contained one further surprise. As we reached the car and separated and I walked around to the driver's side, Jenny said, "What about Tim?"

"What *about* Tim? What do you mean?" I looked over the roof of the car at Jenny. It was too dark to read her expression.

Eventually she shook her head and said, "Never mind."

On the drive back to the farmhouse a barn owl flashed across the road in front of the car, its moon-like face briefly caught in the headlamps. Jenny gasped, but neither of us spoke.

I've made chili. On our return from Fletcher Moss, I heat it up and open a couple of beers and a bottle of wine. Everyone's in the back room apart from me. I'm in the kitchen chopping up coriander to sprinkle on the chili. Nina comes through and asks if she can help. I tell her there's nothing to do and she leans back against the cooker, raising her wineglass to her lips. She asks me how my job with the council is going, am I enjoying it, am I being sufficiently stretched? Nina can be quite direct. I tell her it's fine. Then I tell her it's a bit dull, actually, and not terribly rewarding. Out of the blue I tell her I'm thinking of standing for parliament.

"To be an MP?" she asks incredulously.

"Why not?"

"No reason. I'm just surprised." She looks at me quizzically, then adds: "For which party?"

"Wherever I'll do best."

"You mean do the best work for people or have the best chance of getting in?"

"I wouldn't be going into politics in order to lose."

"Yes, but left or right? Red or blue?"

"Whichever's going to get in. It might even be yellow. It's yellow round here nowadays. Dirty tricks over Christie's. According to Labour." Nina is staring at me in apparent bafflement. "Just a thought," I said. "Will you give me a hand with these plates?"

"What if the party that stood the greatest chance of winning was the BNP? What would you do then?"

I paused, appearing to give the question serious consideration.

"Alex!"

"No, of course I wouldn't join the BNP," I said, smiling. "They're still not respectable. I need to be respectable. I *am* respectable."

"But what if they managed to make themselves respectable while still pursuing the same policies? Would you go against what you believe in merely to gain power?"

"Go against what I believe in?" I stopped serving chili for a moment and looked at her.

"That's my great strength, Nina. I don't believe in anything." I looked away as her face creased in disapproval. "That's why I quite like the idea of the Liberal Democrats."

"Skeletons in the cupboard?" Nina asks, changing tack.

"If I've got any I'll take care of them. Trust me. I'm serious."

We take the plates through.

We're ready to start the screening. I put the DVD on and no one recognizes the title that comes up on screen, *Let Sleeping Corpses Lie*.

"What's this, Alex?" Iain asks.

"That's the American title. The British title was *The Living Dead at the Manchester Morgue*."

Nina groans and Iain laughs.

"Watch these opening shots," I advise. "It's Manchester in the early '70s. Orange buses. Miserable-looking shoppers. That antique shop is right near the cathedral, just this side of Victoria station."

"Great," says James. "The Manchester everybody was glad to see consigned to the dustbin of history."

"By the IRA," adds Iain.

"I'm not sure they should take full credit," says Steph.

"The end justifies the means?" says Nina, without looking away from the screen, but I know for whose benefit she said it.

"Are we watching the film or what?" I say.

"Sorry."

"Soz."

The choice of film is a qualified success. Its unusual blend of American lead (Arthur Kennedy), Euro zombies (director Jorge Grau), and English pastoral (most of it is shot in the Lake District) was never going to make it a mainstream hit, but it works for me.

"It's a bit derivative of *Night of the Living Dead*, don't you think?" says Iain.

"Well, it's a zombie movie."

"We saw that in Wareham, didn't we?" Iain says.

"Did we?" I say.

"Some of us did," says Nina. "It was on in the early hours. I remember you and James and James's friend Tim squeezing past me to leave the cinema when it had only just started." She's watching me as she says this, as if to gauge my reaction.

"I'd seen it before," I say. "I must have needed some air."

I could do with some air right now.

"The three of you were gone for some time," Nina says.

I notice Sunil take Nina's hand.

"Well," I say. "I'm going to put some coffee on."

Iain follows me into the kitchen.

I'm filling the kettle, aware of Iain sitting down at the table next to the alcove. I hear him pick up a newspaper.

"Did you read this?" he asks.

"What's that?" I say, turning round. "Oh, that. No, I intended to, but haven't got round to it yet. So what does it say?"

"I read it the other day. It's about how cervical cancer develops from one virus and stomach cancer from another. That sort of thing. Kaposi's sarcoma from HIV. It's good news, though. That they're making these discoveries, I mean. If they know that a particular virus might cause cancer, and if they can flick a switch to stop us getting the virus, then we're less likely to get cancer. Well, that cancer, anyway."

"That's good," I say, pouring the water into the cafetière.

"Jacob's boyfriend had a scare recently."

"What?" I look up.

"Jacob's boyfriend. He had these red marks on his back, got them checked out. Harmless, thank goodness, but we were worried sick for about a week."

"Jacob's gay?" I say, putting the cafetière down.

"Yes. Didn't you know?"

"How would I know?"

"I don't know. I thought everyone knew."

"How do you feel about it?"

"How do I feel about it? Great! I mean, why wouldn't I?"

"Jenny . . ."

"Jacob was two when Jenny died. A bit young to be hanging out down Canal Street."

"It's just a shock, that's all. I mean, I had no idea," I say, sitting down at the table across from Iain.

"There are a lot of things about Jacob that Jenny never got to know. His sexuality is only one of them. It's not a problem for you, is it?"

I shake my head. "Of course not. I'm just trying to take it in."

Iain smiles and folds the newspaper.

"It's just a pity," I say, "that more fathers can't be as forgiving as you've been."

"What's to forgive?" A trace of scorn has crept into his voice. I suppose if I don't explain, he can't understand.

"Accepting, then. Not forgiving. Accepting."

"It's just the way things are. Times change."

We sit in silence for a while.

Eventually I speak. "I wish I could be more like you. More accepting. More forgiving, in my case. But I can't. I've tried and I can't."

"Forgiveness breeds forgiveness. The inability to forgive creates rancor, and that can spread like a cancer," he says equably, replacing the newspaper on the pile. "That coffee should be ready by now."

When everyone has retired for the night, I unplug the stereo from the kitchen and take it up to my bedroom. I crawl into bed and drop the green cassette into the machine, close the little door, and press play. It plays for thirty seconds and then has to be rewound and played again, over and over. The churring of a nightjar recorded at Cannock Chase, Staffordshire, on 28 June 1978.

It was the year I took my O-levels and for some reason the German and French oral exams took place about six weeks before the written papers, which we sat in June and July. The German oral was first, toward the end of April. That spring I'd been hanging out with a kid from another class. I never knew his real name, but everyone called him Faz. He had floppy blond hair that fell down low over his eyes and he was forever sweeping it out of his face like my sister. When you could see his eyes, they sparkled. We never really questioned why we'd been spending time together. We didn't have a lot in common. I collected bus numbers; he played cricket for the school. But if I look back at my diary I see that throughout March and April I spent a lot of time at his house and he at mine. The German orals took place on the Tuesday and Wednesday in the last week in April. Faz came to ours on the Saturday. Whether you blame the pressure we'd been under to get through the oral, or we just took "oral" too literally, we ended up in my bedroom on the Saturday afternoon, believing ourselves alone in the house. Maybe we were at the start, but we became too involved in what we were doing and didn't hear my father climbing the stairs. He pushed open the door—maybe he'd knocked, I don't know—and saw us, Faz sitting on the edge of the bed and me kneeling on the floor. I turned and looked at him and he looked at me and I braced myself for an assault of some kind, whether verbal or physical, but none came. He just stepped back out of the room and closed the door.

Faz is not mentioned in my diary again after that. My father never spoke to me about what he had witnessed, nor did he tell my mother, as far as I could tell. He'd always been interested in ornithology and had a special fondness for nocturnal birds, the nightjar in particular, although he had never seen or heard one. He started going on longer birdwatching trips, staying out overnight, sometimes longer. If my mother asked him for an explanation, I don't know what he said to her. One afternoon I arrived home and my father's car was standing in the drive. The Phillips cassette recorder that was his normal means of listening to tapes in the kitchen was sitting on the passenger seat. Through the little Perspex window I could see a green BASF cassette. I was peering at this equipment when my father came out of the house and approached the car. When he saw me, he stopped and looked down. He seemed almost frightened of me. I waited for a moment, but he didn't look up, and I walked past him into the house.

I dealt with the situation by focusing solely on my exams, which finished in early July. We were supposed to be going on a family holiday to Cornwall, but it was cancelled. My father had to go to Christie's for tests.

He died the following May, just as the nightjars would have been arriving from Africa.

In the morning, Iain, Steph, and Thomas set off for London straight after breakfast. Nina and Sunil are in less of a hurry, allowing Vishnu his regular Sunday morning lie-in. Raji watches DVDs while waiting for her brother to get up. James sits in the kitchen doing the cryptic crosswords in the Sunday papers, one after another. After a late lunch Nina and Sunil start packing their car. I go out to say goodbye. Nina rolls down her window to thank me for the weekend.

"It was my pleasure," I say.

She smiles and looks through the windshield, then back at me. "Were you serious about running for office?" she asks.

"Absolutely. Skeleton removal work begins today."

This makes her laugh. I laugh, too. Sunil waves and they drive off, the children's noses buried in their Gameboys.

I go back into the house. James is working on the final corner of the *Observer* crossword.

"Do you want to go for a walk later, if you're not in a hurry to get back?" I ask him.

"Sounds good," he says without looking up.

"Bit of a drive first, but it's something to do, if you're sure you don't have to be home by a particular time."

"I've got nothing on till tomorrow morning."

"Perfect."

He completes the crossword. "There!" he says, dropping the paper on the table. "Where are we going, then?"

"Cannock Chase," I say, "but there's no hurry. We can drive down on the A34, take it slowly. Find a nice little pub and have a couple of drinks, then have a walk in the forest and drive back up the M6. I'll drop you back in town."

"Whatever," he says as he sifts through the papers on the table looking for another crossword.

I sit and watch the light outside the window, waiting for the first signs of it beginning to fade.

KAARON WARREN

Dead Sea Fruit

Kaaron Warren's short story collection, The Grinding House, *won the 2006 ACT Writers' and Publishers' Fiction Award. A short film of her Aurealis Award–winning story "A Positive" will be shot this year by Bearcage Productions.*

Warren is presently based in Fiji, where the tropical storms, dense foliage, and local taboos are providing plenty of ideas for the future.

"Dead Sea Fruit" was originally published in the fourth issue of Fantasy Magazine.

—E.D.

I have a collection of baby teeth, sent to me by recovered anorexics from the ward. Their children's teeth, proof that their bodies are working.

One sent me a letter. "Dear Tooth Fairy, you saved me and my womb. My son is now six, here are his baby teeth."

They call the ward Pretty Girl Street. I don't know if the cruelty is intentional; these girls are far from pretty. Skeletal, balding, their breath reeking of hard cheese, they languish on their beds and terrify each other, when they have the strength, with tales of the Ash Mouth Man.

I did not believe the Pretty Girls. The Ash Mouth Man was just a myth to scare each other into being thin. A moral tale against promiscuity. It wouldn't surprise me to hear that the story originated with a group of protective parents, wanting to shelter their children from the disease of kissing.

"He only likes fat girls," Abby said. Her teeth were yellow when she smiled, though she rarely smiled. Abby lay in the bed next to Lori; they compared wrist thickness by stretching their fingers to measure.

"And he watches you for a long time to make sure you're the one," Lori said.

"And only girls who could be beautiful are picked," Melanie said. Her blonde hair fell out in clumps and she kept it in a little bird's nest beside her bed. "He watches you to see if you could be beautiful enough if you were thinner then he saunters over to you."

The girls laughed. "He saunters. Yes," they agreed. They trusted me; I listened to them and fixed their teeth for free.

"He didn't saunter," Jane said. I sat on her bed and leaned close to hear. "He beckoned. He did this," and she tilted back her head, miming a glass being poured into her mouth. "I nodded. I love vodka," she said. "Vodka's made of potatoes, so it's like eating."

The girls all laughed. I hate it when they laugh. I have to maintain my smile. I can't flinch in disgust at those bony girls, mouths open, shoulders shaking. All of them exhausted with the effort.

"I've got a friend in New Zealand and she's seen him," Jane said. "He kissed a friend of hers and the weight just dropped off her."

"I know someone in England who kissed him," Lori said.

"He certainly gets around," I said. They looked at each other.

"I was frightened at the thought of him at first," Abby said. "Cos' he's like a drug. One kiss and you're hooked. Once he's stuck in the tongue, you're done. You can't turn back."

They'd all heard of him before they kissed him. In their circles, even the dangerous methods of weight loss are worth considering.

I heard the rattle of the dinner trolley riding the corridor to Pretty Girl Street. They fell silent.

Lori whispered, "Kissing him fills your mouth with ash. Like you pick up a beautiful piece of fruit and bite into it. You expect the juice to drip down your chin but you bite into ashes. That's what it's like to kiss him."

Lori closed her eyes. Her dry little tongue snaked out to the corners of her mouth, looking, I guessed, for that imagined juice. I leaned over and dripped a little water on her tongue.

She screwed up her mouth.

"It's only water," I said. "It tastes of nothing."

"It tastes of ashes," she said.

"They were hoping you'd try a bite to eat today, Lori," I said. She shook her head.

"You don't understand," she said. "I can't eat. Everything tastes like ashes. Everything."

The nurse came in with the dinner trolley and fixed all the Pretty Girls' IV feeds. The girls liked to twist the tube, bend it, press an elbow or a bony buttock into it to stop the flow.

"You don't understand," Abby said. "It's like having ashes pumped directly into your blood."

They all started to moan and scream with what energy they could muster. Doctors came in, and other nurses. I didn't like this part, the physicality of the feedings, so I walked away.

I meet many Pretty Girls. Pretty Girls are the ones who will never recover, who still see themselves as ugly and fat even when they don't have the strength to defecate. These ones the doctors try to fatten up so they don't scare people when laid in their coffins.

The recovering ones never spoke of the Ash Mouth Man. And I did not believe, until Dan entered my surgery, complaining he was unable to kiss women because of the taste of his mouth. I bent close to him and smelt nothing. I found no decay, no gum disease. He turned his face away.

"What is it women say you taste like?" I said.

"They say I taste of ashes."

I blinked at him, thinking of Pretty Girl Street.

"Not cigarette smoke," the girls had all told me. "Ashes."

"I can see no decay or internal reason for any odour," I told Dan.

After work that day I found him waiting for me in his car outside the surgery.

"I'm sorry," he said. "This is ridiculous. But I wondered if you'd like to eat with me." He gestured, lifting food to his mouth. The movement shocked me. It reminded me of what Jane had said, the Ash Mouth Man gesturing a drink to her. It was non-sense and I knew it. Fairytales, any sort of fiction, annoy me. It's all so very convenient, loose ends tucked in and no mystery left unsolved. Life isn't like that. People die unable to lift an arm to wave and there is no reason for it.

I was too tired to say yes. I said, "Could we meet for dinner tomorrow?"

He nodded. "You like food?"

It was a strange question. Who didn't like food? Then the answer came to me. Someone for whom every mouthful tasted of ash.

"Yes, I like food," I said.

"Then I'll cook for you," he said.

He cooked an almost perfect meal, without fuss or mess. He arrived at the table smooth and brown. I wanted to sweep the food off and make love to him right there. "You actually like cooking," I said. "It's nothing but a chore for me. I had to feed myself from early on and I hate it."

"You don't want the responsibility," he said. "Don't worry. I'll look after you."

The vegetables were overcooked, I thought. The softness of them felt like rot.

He took a bite and rolled the food around in his mouth.

"You have a very dexterous tongue," I said. He smiled, cheeks full of food, then closed his eyes and went on chewing.

When he swallowed, over a minute later, he took a sip of water then said, "Taste has many layers. You need to work your way through each to get to the base line. Sensational."

I tried keeping food in my mouth but it turned to sludge and slipped down my throat. It was fascinating to watch him eat. Mesmerizing. We talked at the table for two hours then I started to shake.

"I'm tired," I said. "I tend to shake when I'm tired."

"Then you should go home to sleep." He packed a container of food for me to take. His domesticity surprised me; I laughed on entering his home at the sheer seductiveness of it. The masculinity masquerading as femininity. Self-help books on the shelf, their spines unbent. Vases full of plastic flowers with a fake perfume.

He walked me to my car and shook my hand, his mouth pinched shut to clearly indicate there would be no kiss.

Weeks passed. We saw each other twice more, chaste, public events that always ended abruptly. Then one Wednesday, I opened the door to my next client and there was Dan.

"It's only me," he said.

My assistant giggled. "I'll go and check the books, shall I?" she said. I nodded. Dan locked the door after her.

"I can't stop thinking about you," he said. "It's all I think about. I can't get any work done."

He stepped towards me and grabbed my shoulders. I tilted my head back to be kissed. He bent to my neck and snuffled. I pulled away.

"What are you doing?" I said. He put his finger on my mouth to shush me. I tried to kiss him but he turned away. I tried again and he twisted his body from me.

"I'm scared of what you'll taste," he said.

"Nothing. I'll taste nothing."

"I don't want to kiss you," he said softly.

Then he pushed me gently onto my dentist's chair. And he stripped me naked and touched every piece of skin, caressed, squeezed, stroked until I called out.

He climbed onto the chair astride me, and keeping his mouth well away, he unzipped his pants. He felt very good. We made too much noise. I hoped my assistant wasn't listening.

Afterwards, he said, "It'll be like that every time. I just know it." And it was. Even massaging my shoulders, he could make me turn to jelly.

I had never cared so much about kissing outside of my job before but now I needed it. It would prove Dan loved me, that I loved him. It would prove he was not the Ash Mouth Man because his mouth would taste of plums or toothpaste, or of my perfume if he had been kissing my neck.

"You know we get pleasure from kissing because our bodies think we are eating," I said, kissing his fingers.

"Trickery. It's all about trickery," he said.

"Maybe if I smoke a cigarette first. Then my breath will be ashy anyway and I won't be able to taste you."

"Just leave it." He went out, came back the next morning with his lips all bruised and swollen. I did not ask him where he'd been. I watched him outside on the balcony, his mouth open like a dog tasting the air, and I didn't want to know. I had a busy day ahead, clients all through and no time to think. My schizophrenic client tasted yeasty; they always did if they were medicated.

Then I kissed a murderer; he tasted like vegetable waste. Like the crisper in my fridge smells when I've been too busy to empty it. They used to say people who suffered from tuberculosis smelled like wet leaves; his breath was like that but rotten. He had a tooth he wanted me to fix; he'd cracked it on a walnut shell.

"My wife never shelled things properly. Lazy. She didn't care what she ate. Egg shells, olive pits, seafood when she knew I'm allergic. She'd eat anything."

He smiled at me. His teeth were white. Perfect. "And I mean anything." He paused, wanting a reaction from me. I wasn't interested in his sexual activities. I would never discuss what Dan and I did. It was private, and while it remained that way I could be wanton, abandoned.

"She used to get up at night and raid the fridge," the murderer said after he rinsed. I filled his mouth with instruments again. He didn't close his eyes. Most people do. They like to take themselves elsewhere, away from me. No matter how gentle a dentist is, the experience is not pleasant.

My assistant and I glanced at each other.

"Rinse," I said. He did, three times, then sat back. A line of saliva stretched from the bowl to his mouth.

"She was fat. Really fat. But she was always on a diet. I accused her of secretly bingeing and then I caught her at it."

I turned to place the instruments in my autoclave.

"Sleepwalking. She did it in her sleep. She'd eat anything. Raw bacon. Raw mince. Whole slabs of cheese."

People come to me because I remove the nasty taste from their mouths. I'm good at identifying the source. I can tell by the taste of them and what I see in their eyes.

He glanced at my assistant, wanting to talk but under privilege. I said to her, "Could you check our next appointment, please?" and she nodded, understanding.

I picked up a scalpel and held it close to his eye. "You see how sharp it is? So sharp you won't feel it as the blade gently separates the molecules. Sometimes a small slit in the gums releases toxins or tension. You didn't like your wife getting fat?"

"She was disgusting. You should have seen some of the crap she ate."

I looked at him, squinting a little.

"You watched her. You didn't stop her."

"I could've taken a football team in to watch her and she wouldn't have woken up."

I felt I needed a witness to his words and, knowing Dan was in the office above, I pushed the speaker phone extension to connect me to him.

"She ate cat shit. I swear. She picked it off the plate and ate it," the murderer said. I bent over to check the back of his tongue. The smell of vegetable waste turned my stomach.

"What was cat shit doing on a plate?" I asked.

He reddened a little. When I took my fingers out of his mouth he said, "I just wanted to see if she'd eat it. And she did."

"Is she seeking help?" I asked. I wondered what the breath of someone with a sleep disorder would smell like.

"She's being helped by Jesus now," he said. He lowered his eyes. "She ate a bowlful of dishwashing powder with milk. She was still holding the spoon when I found her in the morning."

There was a noise behind me as Dan came into the room. I turned to see he was wearing a white coat. His hands were thrust into the pockets.

"You didn't think to put poisons out of reach?" Dan said. The murderer looked up.

"Sometimes the taste of the mouth, the smell of it, comes from deep within," I said to the murderer. I flicked his solar plexus with my forefinger and he flinched. His smile faltered. I felt courageous.

As he left, I kissed him. I kiss all of my clients, to learn their nature from the taste of their mouths. Virgins are salty, alcoholics sweet. Addicts taste like fake orange juice, the stuff you spoon into a glass then add water.

Dan would not let me kiss him to find out if he tasted of ash.

"Now me," Dan said. He stretched over and kissed the man on the mouth, holding him by the shoulders so he couldn't get away.

The murderer recoiled. I smiled. He wiped his mouth. Scraped his teeth over his tongue.

"See you in six months' time," I said.

I had appointments with the Pretty Girls, and Dan wanted to come with me. He stopped at the ward doorway, staring in. He seemed to fill the space, a door himself.

"It's okay," I said. "You wait there."

Inside, I thought at first Jane was smiling. Her cheeks lifted and her eyes squinted closed. But there was no smile; she scraped her tongue with her teeth. It was an action I knew quite well. Clients trying to scrape the bad taste out of their mouths. They didn't spit or rinse, though, so the action made me feel queasy. I imagined all that buildup behind their teeth. All the scrapings off their tongue.

The girls were in a frenzy. Jane said, "We saw the Ash Mouth Man." But they see so few men in the ward I thought, Any man could be the Ash Mouth Man to these girls. I tended their mouths, tried to clear away the bad taste. They didn't want me to go. They were jealous of me, thinking I was going to kiss the Ash Mouth Man. Jane kept talking to make me stay longer, though it took her strength away. "My grandmother was kissed by him. She always said to watch out for handsome men, cos' their kiss could be a danger. Then she kissed him and wasted away in about five days."

The girls murmured to each other. *Five days! That's a record! No one ever goes down in five days.*

In the next ward there are Pretty Boys, but not so many of them. They are much quieter than the girls. They sit in their beds and close their eyes most of the day. The ward is thick, hushed. They don't get many visitors and they don't want me as their dentist. They didn't like me to attend them. They bit at me as if I was trying to thrust my fingers down their throats to choke them.

Outside, Dan waited, staring in.

"Do you find those girls attractive?" I said.

"Of course not. They're too skinny. They're sick. I like healthy women. Strong women. That's why I like you so much. You have the self-esteem to let me care for you. Not many women have that."

"Is that true?"

"No. I really like helpless women," he said. But he smiled.

He smelt good to me, clean, with a light flowery aftershave which could seem feminine on another man. He was tall and broad; strong. I watched him lift my car to retrieve a paper I'd rolled onto while parking.

"I could have moved the car," I said, laughing at him.

"No fun in that," he said. He picked me up and carried me indoors.

I quite enjoyed the sense of subjugation. I'd been strong all my life, sorting myself to school when my parents were too busy to care. I could not remember being carried by anyone, and the sensation was a comfort.

Dan introduced me to life outside. Before I met him, I rarely saw daylight; too busy for a frivolous thing like the sun. Home, transport, work, transport, home, all before dawn and after dusk. Dan forced me to go out into the open. He said, "Your skin glows outdoors. Your hair moves in the breeze. You couldn't be more beautiful." So we walked. I really didn't like being out. It seemed like time wasting.

He picked me up from the surgery one sunny Friday and took my hand. "Come for a picnic," he said. "It's a beautiful day."

In my doorway, a stick man was slumped.

"It's the man who killed his wife," I whispered.

The man raised his arm weakly. "Dentist," he rattled. "Dentist, wait!"

"What happened to you? Are you sleepwalking now?" I asked.

"I can't eat. Everything I bite into tastes of ash. I can't eat. I'm starving." He lisped, and I could see that many of his white teeth had fallen out.

"What did you do to me?" he whispered. He fell to his knees. Dan and I stepped around him and walked on. Dan took my hand, carrying a basket full of food between us. It banged against my legs, bruising my shins. We walked to a park and everywhere we went girls jumped at him. He kissed back, shrugging at me as if to say, "Who cares?" I watched them.

"Why do it? Just tell them to go away," I said. They annoyed me, those silly little girls.

"I can't help it. I try not to kiss them but the temptation is too strong. They're always coming after me."

I had seen this.

"Why? I know you're a beautiful looking man, but why do they forget any manners or pride to kiss you?"

I knew this was one of his secrets. One of the things he'd rather I didn't know.

"I don't know, my love. The way I smell? They like my smell."

I looked at him sidelong. "Why did you kiss him? That murderer. Why?"

Dan said nothing. I thought about how well he understood me. The meals he cooked, the massages he gave. The way he didn't flinch from the job I did.

So I didn't confront him. I let his silence sit. But I knew his face at the Pretty Girls ward. I could still feel him fucking me in the car, pulling over into a car park and taking me, after we left the Pretty Girls.

"God, I want to kiss you," he said.

I could smell him, the ash fire warmth of him and I could feel my stomach shrinking. I thought of my favourite cake, its colour leached out and its flavour making my eyes water.

"Kissing isn't everything. We can live without kissing," I said.

"Maybe you can," he said, and he leant forward, his eyes wide, the white parts smudgy, grey. He grabbed my shoulders. I usually loved his strength, the size of him, but I pulled away.

"I don't want to kiss you," I said. I tucked my head under his arm and buried my face into his side. The warm fluffy wool of his jumper tickled my nose and I smothered a sneeze.

"Bless you," he said. He held my chin and lifted my face up. He leant towards me. He was insistent.

It was a shock, even though I'd expected it. His tongue was fat and seemed to fill my cheeks, the roof of my mouth. My stomach roiled and I tried to pull away but his strong hands held my shoulders till he was done with his kiss.

Then he let me go.

I fell backwards, one step, my heels wobbling but keeping me standing. I wiped my mouth. He winked at me and leant forwards. His breath smelt sweet, like pineapple juice. His eyes were blue, clear and honest. You'd trust him if you didn't know.

The taste of ash filled my mouth.

Nothing else happened, though. I took a sip of water and it tasted fresh, clean. A look of disappointment flickered on his face before he concealed it. I thought, You like it. You like turning women that way.

I said, "Have you heard of the myth the Pretty Girls have? About the Ash Mouth Man?"

I could see him visibly lifting, growing. Feeling legendary. His cheeks reddened. His face was so expressive I knew what he meant without hearing a word. I couldn't bear to lose him but I could not allow him to make any more Pretty Girls.

I waited till he was fast asleep that night, lying back, mouth open. I sat him forward so he wouldn't choke, took up my scalpel, and with one perfect move I lifted his tongue and cut it out of his mouth.

CALEB WILSON

Directions

Caleb Wilson grew up in Vermont where he reports that there is a stock character, the old farmer by the side of the road giving unhelpfully elaborate directions, who was no doubt in the back of his mind when he wrote this story. Wilson lives in Nashville, Tennessee.

"Directions" originally appeared online in Diagram, 6.4.

—K.L. & G.G.

Some things you will need are a full tank of gas, a flashlight, an axe, a bicycle. Heading north on Route 110, turn left onto Entwhistle. The street will be paved in dark, fresh asphalt and tree-lined. The web of shadows, light dark light, will fall through the teeth of the leaves onto the windshield. Drive through four lights and beneath an iron railroad bridge.

Turn right onto Jackabash. Hold the steering wheel tightly, the car's suspension might lurch as the asphalt gives way to gravel. You'll trail behind the rear bumper a roostertail of dust. The foliage will have grown thicker, and wilder, hanging over the road, pinching the sky to a slender blue thread. You will approach a clearing on your left, in the center of which, in a field of golden grass, sits a circular stone barn. Atop it you will see a weathercock that spins furiously in the dead calm.

Jackabash dead-ends at Tuhlooloo. Tuhlooloo is sun-baked dirt, with wilted weeds cresting the ridge between the ruts. Turn right. You'll need to drive slowly, the road has but one lane and if you should meet another vehicle you might have to pull onto the shoulder. The greenery alongside will have thickened to a hedge, and will be strung with all manner of vines, creepers and stranglers that hang low with the weight of their blossoms, yellow, pink, white and pale green. A black bloom might show itself, in the shade. Passing through a glade, you will notice a sunken pond on your right, with walls of green stone, and glassily still even in the new-sprung breeze.

Turn left onto Bowlandiron, paved in moss-slippery bricks. The road will be wider here, but do not forgo caution, as the ground drops away from both shoulders into bog-land. Cheerful though they look, the hummocks, peeking from bright pools of green scum, hide quicksand and fossil flats. Roll up your windows, chemical balloons and witch fires often seep, bubble or flare from the mud and confound proper brain functions. You will approach a mangrove big as a house with thousands of roots and stems grasping at water and mud. Should the offshoots have blockaded the road, you are permitted to exit the vehicle and cut them away with your axe, although remember, hold your breath when exposed directly to the swamp air.

Past the mangrove turn right onto Shingraglia. The ground on either side will drain and rise, till the shoulders are a yard higher than the road itself, which is paved in coins. Do not bother trying to pry them free, as the states and nations which minted them no longer exist. The terrain will be hilly, with a carpet of tough grass and heather broken by lumps of stone like teeth in a gum. You'll turn a sharp corner to the left, to a sudden view of the River Vino, and onto a bridge which jumps the bank out over the red water. Look down into the river as you drive across the bridge and you'll doubtless notice that the car is being paced by elongated forms paddling just beneath the surface. Do not panic, you will meet them soon enough, at the midway point, where a fence woven of metal slats blocks the road. Stop the car, turn off the engine, open the gas tank. The Wine-men will emerge from the river, dripping red puddles from their wrinkled, glossy skins, and gather round your car. Do not be afraid, they only want to collect the toll. They will unfurl their long, tubular tongues and drink deeply from the gas tank, gorging on the gasoline within. Unless a crowd of more than five Wine-men gathers or your tank is low, you will be unharmed, otherwise, in lieu of the proper payment, they will take what they are owed in blood from your veins. Once the toll is paid, they will move the gate aside and you will be allowed to continue across. The shoulders will rise and rise until they are walls of earth, and the road narrow and narrow, coins pinging beneath the wheels, until you reach the inevitable spot where the car can no longer squeeze through. You will need to continue a short distance along Shingraglia on bicycle, keeping watch on the left for a cairn of skulls, inhabited by a swarm of bees.

The cairn of bees marks a low, pointed archway. Go through it. This is Krift. Krift is paved, or rather floored, with beams of worn oak, which will knock and clatter as you cycle over them. Hedges of yew and boxwood will line the way, and the white berries spotting the bushes will begin to glow as the darkness falls. Attach your flashlight to the handlebars and be wary of nocturnal animals, raccoons and deft marsupials, perhaps a translucent night viper, its meal of rats and insects still visible in its crystalline gullet. After some time, you'll ride through a forest of varnished pillars supporting the ossuaries erected by long-dead heretic priests. Now the shadow patterns strobe on the spokes of bicycle wheels, dark light dark, moonlight filtering through a lattice of skeletons. Listen carefully and if you hear the telltale clatter of bones from above, duck your head. This is the sign of a mischievous bone-parrot about to bombard you with crushed relic pellets stolen from a casket.

Turn right onto Xu. It will be very cold. The grinding whisper from under the tires is due to the fact that Xu is paved in fingernail clippings. You might now wish to extinguish your flashlight. The sights to the left and right are not fit to be seen by human eyes. Ride in darkness, in contemplation.

Xu dead-ends.

And there I shall wait for you.

TERRY DOWLING

La Profonde

Terry Dowling is one of Australia's most awarded, acclaimed, and best-known writers of imaginative fiction. He has had stories published in the anthologies Dreaming Down Under, Centaurus, Gathering the Bones, *and* The Dark, *and reprinted in several* Year's Best *volumes. They are collected in* Rynosseros, Blue Tyson, Twilight Beach, Wormwood, An Intimate Knowledge of the Night, Blackwater Days, The Man Who Lost Red, Antique Futures: The Best of Terry Dowling, *and, most recently,* Basic Black: Tales of Appropriate Fear.

Dowling edited Mortal Fire: Best Australian SF, The Essential Ellison, *and* The Jack Vance Treasury. *He is a musician, songwriter, and communications instructor with a doctorate in creative writing, and has been genre reviewer for* The Weekend Australian *for seventeen years.*

"La Profonde" was one of the two original stories in Basic Black: Tales of Appropriate Fear. *I highly recommend the other original in the book as well,* "Cheat Light."

—E.D.

There was no mistaking how surprised Derwent was when he saw Jay walking along the railway tracks towards him. Jay's one-time business partner was wearing sunglasses, so his eyes were hidden, but his mouth actually fell open. Then, in true Derwent fashion, his surprise and fear turned immediately to anger.

"Fuck, Jay, what is all this?" he shouted. "This 'meet me at the station' stuff?"

Jay just smiled and waved, then waited till he'd reached the end of the otherwise deserted platform, and Derwent was glowering down at him over the safety rail.

"Tell me, Dee"—Jay deliberately used the unwelcome nick-name—"do you know what a *profonde* is?"

But Derwent wasn't up for any of Jay's smart-ass questions. He was hot and sweating, clearly upset. Though only thirty-seven, two years younger than Jay, red-faced and agitated like this he looked ten years older. One well-timed email had turned Derwent's world upside-down.

Dee, we need to talk. I have documented proof of what you and Cally did to Edilo Ltd. Take the 12:55 to Morley Station on Sunday for a 1:30 pm meeting. You won't tell the others and you will come alone. This is your one chance.

Jay couldn't see Derwent's eyes, but he could easily picture the determination he'd find in them amid the rage and desperation. Dee had been threatened with having his scam exposed, the dangerous emails he'd thought he'd purged from the office systems while he and Cally were plundering Edilo in true insider fashion. Three years of enjoying the spoils; now this summons to a deserted suburban railway station on a hot Sunday afternoon. He'd had enough.

Jay hauled himself up onto the platform. Morley Station was almost as new as the housing estates going up all about them beyond the cutting, just a stretch of hot concrete between two sets of tracks, with nothing more than a modest double-sided passenger shelter, two lampposts with signs attached saying *Morley*, and a set of iron steps at one end leading up to a deserted bus-stop and a car-park, both as deserted as the station at this time of day. "A *profonde*, Derwent? Ever hear of one?"

But for Derwent there was only one issue. His sunglasses might be hiding his eyes but his other features showed the full extent of his emotion. "Three fucking years, Jay. What do you want?" Not, Jay noticed, how the hell did you find out?

Jay grinned and gestured down the platform to where the rails stretched off in the afternoon glare. "I want you to take a walk with me, Dee, that's all."

"Christine and the kids know where I am, Jay."

Jay doubted that, and ultimately it didn't matter. "So what's the harm in taking a walk so we can talk about this?"

"Talk about it here. What do you want?" It was the old Derwent, the pre-scam Derwent showing through, but it truly was a mere shadowplay of how Dee had been three years before, a bravura display from a broken puppet.

Jay squinted in the glare. He glanced up and down the quiet platform in its lonely cutting. No sunglasses for him. Never. He listened to the hot breeze pushing through the grass on the embankments, then glanced at this watch. "Derwent, I'm going to start walking north along the tracks now. If you've got any sense, any interest in saving your fat ass, you'll take that walk with me. It's up to you, buddy."

And, true to his word, Jay turned and began heading along the platform.

Derwent swore, called after him, shouted abuse, even the beginnings of threats—just the beginnings—but Jay kept walking. When he reached the end of the concrete deck he crouched and jumped down onto the railbed, then began moving north along the tracks.

There were more angry shouts from the platform behind him, but Jay didn't stop. He kept walking, smiling into the day, relishing the warm breeze on his face and the realization that this could indeed be done exactly as he had planned it.

Back at that hot quiet station Derwent would be running through his options, railing at the universe, at the insufferable turn of events. Sooner rather than later, he would accept that there was nothing else he could do but follow. He'd been caught out. He could only try to survive this. Maybe he'd blame Cally, say that *she* had persuaded *him*. That was likely.

Finally Jay heard, "Well hold on then!" But, of course, Jay didn't slow his pace. Couldn't. He'd checked his watch and it truly could remain a matter of timing. Let Derwent shed some of those happy fat-cat pounds he'd been putting on during the past three years.

It was easy to tell when Dee was gaining by the laboured breathing getting nearer, the growing thud of footsteps out of time with Jay's own. It was like someone imitating an old-style steam locomotive, exactly that.

Then Derwent was there, staggering, straining, hauling in big ragged breaths. When he could get words out, they were the expected things.

"Wasn't personal—Jay. Never—personal. Un'erstan'?" It seemed like all he could manage.

"Glad to hear it, Dee." Jay didn't look at him, just kept watching the way ahead, reading every detail of the route between the two sets of tracks. "But how exactly do you mean that? Never personal?"

Derwent stumbled along, still trying to catch his breath but probably exaggerating that, giving himself time to gather his thoughts and, hardest of all, hold back his anger. Would he blame Cally, take the easy out and blame it all on her? Difficulties for him later, certainly, but a solution now.

Jay savoured the breeze on his brow and wondered what line the other man would take. However it went, Derwent would be sensing there was hope, would believe he knew exactly how he had to play this. Maybe he'd be thinking he really could reach some private settlement here, buy himself out of trouble.

Derwent finally answered. "You were just someone, okay?" More ragged breathing. "Could've been anyone." Another pause, laboured. He truly did seem to be judging every word. "You un'erstand? It was just—the situation. An opportunity. It's not like we ever—signed on to get *you*." Derwent emphasized the last word.

Finally Jay did look across at the man trudging with him between the two sets of tracks. "Who's we?"

"Aw, hell, Jay. What does it matter? It was just something that came along, you know? Never thought about it too much."

"Enough to get away with it for a while. Ruin the company. I trusted you."

"Yeah, well, some of us aren't as trusting as you, okay? We don't light up as bright. We try, but it doesn't always happen. You made it easy."

"There was Cally. Who else?"

"Hell, Jay. It's been three years! Why this now?"

"Brian had to be in on it. Those emails make that pretty clear. And Mark, doing the accounts. You needed him. Barbara, Ashley and Hiro were mentioned."

"Christine knows where I am, Jay."

"I grew up on a railway line, did you know that, Dee?"

"How the hell would I know that?" Derwent said, thrown by the change of subject and forgetting for a moment how this had to be played.

"That was out in Leederville. As kids, friends and I would walk the tracks between Leederville and Quinton, just exploring, you know. Always loved what you found along railway lines."

"Is that right?"

"Nothing forces patterns on a landscape more than a railway. All those lines and curves. No barriers. Hills cut away, fields divided. Rivers hardly stand a chance. It's all so precise, so artificial. Then it changes. It doesn't stay like that. It's almost as if the intrusion is resented, worn away."

"Resented? That's a bit much."

"Not at all. It's the elevator effect. People get in an elevator. It's really just a little room that moves up and down over a tremendous drop and takes them to where they're going. Most people don't think of using an elevator in terms of shafts and counterweights and terrible drops. It's just a room that moves and does a job. Same with railways. People notice the trains, sure, maybe the tracks while a train is on them, but what about when a train isn't passing? The tracks are overlooked, forgotten. All that precision, that regimentation gets blurred, roughed up. Pretty soon those railside corridors become wilderness, bits of a rogue landscape. People looking out train windows always look *beyond* the corridor, have you noticed?"

"No, I haven't. Listen, Jay, this is interesting but I don't see what it has to do with our situation."

"Love that word, Dee. Situation. Tidies it up so nicely, don't you think? That's why names are so important. Finding the right handles."

"What can we do about this, Jay?"

"One thing at a time. You never answered my question."

"What question?"

"When we first met back at the station. First thing I said."

"A question? What question? Hey, look, Jay, I've had a lot on my mind. You really can't expect—"

"I would've been in your thoughts though. You would have been very much aware of me. You wouldn't have given me a thought in years, but when my email arrived the other day, ever since Thursday, I would've been in your thoughts surely."

"Well, yeah, but—I mean, I was pretty mad. Worried and all. You have to allow that—"

"You were right, what you said before about destroying Edilo. It really wasn't personal, was it?"

"That's right. That's right, Jay! It just happened."

"No, I mean in the sense that I never got to *be* a person to you with a life and interests, plans and hopes. Never got on your radar."

"Well, you were the boss. Always so earnest, you know? So remote. It just never—"

"Right. But if I'd been a *person* enough, mattered more, you wouldn't have pulled something like that. You'd have picked somebody else. If you'd liked me at all, thought I was *worth* liking, worth respecting at least, you wouldn't have used me like a mark and taken advantage."

Derwent's eyes were hidden by his sunglasses, but the way he suddenly went quiet, suddenly became fixed in his gaze while walking, let Jay know that there would be a very different look in them now.

Jay smiled and glanced at his watch again. It was 1:42 and here it was at last: the *You're a wacko!* look tucked away behind black Ray-Bans.

"Where are we going, Jay?"

"Just to the next station. You ever take this line?"

"You kidding? I'm a city boy. I never get out this far."

"Right. Well, Greenwood's just another little station like Morley back there. Brand new. They all are once you get past Belmont. Just a platform, a shelter, some steps up to a bus-stop for a feeder bus line that doesn't seem to be operating yet, not much else. Not much of a train service on a Sunday out here, not yet anyway. What's that term they use a lot nowadays: abandoned in place?"

Derwent nodded and uh-huh'd. He'd adjusted again, had worked out a new strategy, all predictable really. "You did this as a kid?" His tone was pitched to invite sharing.

"It's where we played a lot. I still love walking the tracks."

Derwent knew his cue. "We never knew stuff like that, Jay. That you had a thing for trains—"

"Not so much the trains, Dee. More the landscape you find around railway lines, the narrow strip of land they run through. Even out here where it's not too built up yet you get the same no-man's-land corridor you find in cities and the inner suburbs. The moment a line is opened up, there they are: the same lines of fences and plantings, the same cuttings, power poles, the chain-link barriers and supply sheds. Look at all this! Grass, bushes, mounds of soil. Rails and sleepers for repair work, future track development. Today I've seen an old tanker bogey left on a spur not even joined to the main track. Not even joined! Then half a dozen cattle trucks, just left out here. Go figure. That's all part of it."

Derwent didn't miss a beat. "So how far have you walked today, Jay?"

Jay knew exactly how far to the precise mile and yard, the exact metre, but he pretended to think. "Let's see. I drove out early and parked at Silverton, then caught the 9:40 back to Belmont. Now I'm walking back to the car. That's five stations so far. One more to go: Greenwood, then it's Silverton again."

"I caught the train out like you said. I'll need to get back."

Jay nodded. "I can give you a lift. I can drop you off once we settle this."

That clearly made Derwent feel better. "And just how do we settle this? Like I said, Jay. It wasn't personal. I can pay you back something if—"

"It can't be about money now, Dee," Jay said, and looked at his watch again. There was a double coming up, he was sure of it.

"Hey, you're counting!" Derwent said. He'd only just noticed.

"I am," Jay answered. "Ten more paces and I'll show you something really interesting. Here we go: six, seven, eight, nine, ten. Look over there now! Where that stanchion meets the embankment. Near that pile of earth."

"What? What am I looking at?"

"You don't see it?"

"See what?"

"To the left of the stanchion. That shimmer of light on the soil. See the light near the top? It's a hot-spot. Unfinished, but what's called a double."

"Jay, it's a hot day. Of course there's going to be heat shimmer."

"Not this. This is different. It's a double."

Derwent would have that look in his eyes again. "Okay. Then it must be something *you* can see."

"Guess so."

"Walking those tracks back then, you probably learned to notice lots of things other people don't."

"Quite likely." Jay almost made it sound sad the way he said it.

Derwent reacted to the tone. He had to be figuring that every step took them closer to Greenwood. "What about the other kids you played with back then? Did any of them see these—these doubles?"

"Sometimes. Not often. Jenny Attard did for a while. Jeff Callan did a few times, but we disagreed over details. We both wanted to name them, but we always disagreed over the names."

"Are there that many?" Derwent seemed genuinely interested, though doubtless he figured this was the best way to play it. Either way they were on the same page of the script.

"You'd be surprised. You see them more easily as kids. If you work at it, you keep the skill."

"Does this other kid—Jeff?—does he still have the skill?"

"Can't say. Haven't seen Jeff since we were kids. Guess you lose it if you don't keep at it. I put in a lot of time. Only stands to reason that I've kept the knack."

Derwent didn't overdo it, didn't say something like: "There's more to you than we ever knew, Jay," or "If only we'd known . . ." He kept it simple, kept the focus on more immediate things.

"That was a double back there, you said. Okay, tell me some other names."

"I'll point them out as we come to them. There's a clearback up on the embankment, but it's very faint and the grass is hiding it."

Derwent looked to where Jay was pointing, even removed his sunglasses to squint through the heat. "A clearback. Okay. Can't see anything." He replaced his Ray-Bans.

"You won't. I barely can. Clearbacks are common, but they come and go. There should be another one soon."

"Is there a particular one I'll be able to see, do you think?"

"That's what I'm hoping to show you before we reach Greenwood. *If* it's there. Sometimes they come and go. That's why I'm counting. This one's called a *profonde* and it's a bit of a test really. If you can see it and describe it to me, I'll forget the whole Edilo business."

"But, Jay, you said it yourself. Most people don't have the skill."

"Turn back any time you like, Dee. No one's forcing you. I tell you when we're near a *profonde*. You try to see it and describe it to me. That's the deal."

Derwent stopped walking, put his hands on his hips. "I have to describe something that no one else can see but you! That I only have your word exists in the first place! You're crazy!"

Jay didn't stop. "You should be able to manage it. It's one of the more noticeable ones."

Derwent started walking again. "Oh, fine, Jay! Just one of the more noticeable among invisible things! Great!"

"Greenwood is about ten minutes around that next bend. You'll just have to master the skill. If it's any help, there's a rather special *servante* over there to the left of that bush. Nowhere near as common. There's a prime *antesammis* near that fence there."

"You know, I was just going to say that, Jay. Yessir. That's a prime antipasto over there, whatever!"

Jay ignored the barb, just breathed in the smells of hot steel tracks, the dry grass and the heated eucalypts beyond the embankments. "There's usually at least one *profonde* before we reach Greenwood."

"And you reckon I'll see it."

"If you take off those sunglasses you might."

Derwent did so, putting them in his shirt pocket. He squinted in the glare again. "Fine. Just say when."

They walked without speaking for a while, following the lines as they began to curve through another cutting. The breeze followed them. Dry grass rustled on the embankments.

The quiet was too much for Derwent. "So we're just walking through these things right now?" he said.

"Not right here," Jay told him. "But the one we want is very close. It's usually— No, there it is! Get ready, Dee. It's not even fifteen yards away, exactly in front of us. Describe what you see!"

"What I see! I can't see anything!"

"We're heading right for it. Ten yards now, right in front. Try looking from the side. Turn your head a little."

Derwent did so. "Is it still there?"

"Right there. Two yards now. Opening and closing along its seeking edge. It's got quite a rhythm going." Jay steadied himself on the stones underfoot.

"I can't see anything, Jay. What's it like exactly? How big is it?"

"Both big *and* small. That's why it's called that. A *profonde* is a word that conjurers use."

"Conjurers? Do they?" Derwent was peering into the emptiness ahead.

"It's what magicians call the long pockets in the tails of their coats. The ones they use for making things disappear."

"Okay, so how—"

It was all he managed because Jay had pushed him hard from behind. There was a single yell, more like a squawk that ended almost as it began, and it was done. There was just the heat shimmer above the tracks, the sound of the breeze rushing in the dry grass.

Jay glanced at his watch, then stepped around the hot-spot in case it was still active, and continued walking. Another hundred yards and he rounded the final curve of the tracks and saw the small Greenwood platform in the bright afternoon light. And there was Cally, exactly on time.

Jay quickened his pace and was soon looking up at the last person on his list.

"Hey, Cally," he called, pleasantly enough. "Do you know what an *oubliette* is?"

M. RICKERT

Journey into the Kingdom

Rickert's dark fantasy from the May issue of The Magazine of Fantasy &
Science Fiction *was one of our first selections for this year's anthology. Her
stories have been a staple of* F&SF *in recent years and her first collection,*
Map of Dreams (Golden Gryphon), *is one of the best books of 2006. Novel
lovers rejoice: Rickert is currently working on not one novel, but several. She
lives in Cedarburg, Wisconsin.*

—K.L. & G.G., E.D.

T he first painting was of an egg, the pale ovoid produced with faint strokes
of pink, blue, and violet to create the illusion of white. After that there
were two apples, a pear, an avocado, and finally, an empty plate on a white
tablecloth before a window covered with gauzy curtains, a single fly nestled in a fold at the top right corner. The series was titled "Journey into the Kingdom."

On a small table beneath the avocado there was a black binder, an unevenly cut
rectangle of white paper with the words "Artist's Statement" in neat, square, handwritten letters taped to the front. Balancing the porcelain cup and saucer with one
hand, Alex picked up the binder and took it with him to a small table against the
wall toward the back of the coffee shop, where he opened it, thinking it might be interesting to read something besides the newspaper for once, though he almost abandoned the idea when he saw that the page before him was handwritten in the same
neat letters as on the cover. But the title intrigued him.

AN IMITATION LIFE

Though I always enjoyed my crayons and watercolors, I was not a particularly
artistic child. I produced the usual assortment of stick figures and houses with dripping yellow suns. I was an avid collector of seashells and sea glass and much preferred to be outdoors, throwing stones at seagulls (please, no haranguing from
animal rights activists, I have long since outgrown this) or playing with my imaginary friends to sitting quietly in the salt rooms of the keeper's house, making pictures at the big wooden kitchen table while my mother, in her black dress, kneaded
bread and sang the old French songs between her duties as lighthouse keeper,
watcher over the waves, beacon for the lost, governess of the dead.

The first ghost to come to my mother was my own father who had set out the day
previous in the small boat heading to the mainland for supplies such as string and
rice, and also bags of soil, which, in years past, we emptied into crevices between

the rocks and planted with seeds, a makeshift garden and a "brave attempt," as my father called it, referring to the barren stone we lived on.

We did not expect him for several days so my mother was surprised when he returned in a storm, dripping wet icicles from his mustache and behaving strangely, repeating over and over again, "It is lost, my dear Maggie, the garden is at the bottom of the sea."

My mother fixed him hot tea but he refused it, and she begged him to take off the wet clothes and retire with her, to their feather bed piled with quilts, but he said, "Tend the light, don't waste your time with me." So my mother, a worried expression on her face, left our little keeper's house and walked against the gale to the lighthouse, not realizing that she left me with a ghost, melting before the fire into a great puddle, which was all that was left of him upon her return. She searched frantically while I kept pointing at the puddle and insisting it was he. Eventually she tied on her cape and went out into the storm, calling his name. I thought that, surely, I would become orphaned that night.

But my mother lived, though she took to her bed and left me to tend the lamp and receive the news of the discovery of my father's wrecked boat, found on the rocky shoals, still clutching in his frozen hand a bag of soil, which was given to me, and which I brought to my mother though she would not take the offering.

For one so young, my chores were immense. I tended the lamp, and kept our own hearth fire going too. I made broth and tea for my mother, which she only gradually took, and I planted that small bag of soil by the door to our little house, savoring the rich scent, wondering if those who lived with it all the time appreciated its perfume or not.

I did not really expect anything to grow, though I hoped that the seagulls might drop some seeds or the ocean deposit some small thing. I was surprised when, only weeks later, I discovered the tiniest shoots of green, which I told my mother about. She was not impressed. By that point, she would spend part of the day sitting up in bed, mending my father's socks and moaning, "Agatha, whatever are we going to do?" I did not wish to worry her, so I told her lies about women from the mainland coming to help, men taking turns with the light. "But they are so quiet. I never hear anyone."

"No one wants to disturb you," I said. "They whisper and walk on tiptoe."

It was only when I opened the keeper's door so many uncounted weeks later, and saw, spread before me, embedded throughout the rock (even in crevices where I had planted no soil) tiny pink, purple, and white flowers, their stems shuddering in the salty wind, that I insisted my mother get out of bed.

She was resistant at first. But I begged and cajoled, promised her it would be worth her effort. "The fairies have planted flowers for us," I said, this being the only explanation or description I could think of for the infinitesimal blossoms everywhere.

Reluctantly, she followed me through the small living room and kitchen, observing that, "the ladies have done a fairly good job of keeping the place neat." She hesitated before the open door. The bright sun and salty scent of the sea, as well as the loud sound of waves washing all around us, seemed to astound her, but then she squinted, glanced at me, and stepped through the door to observe the miracle of the fairies' flowers.

Never had the rock seen such color, never had it known such bloom! My mother walked out, barefoot, and said, "Forget-me-nots, these are forget-me-nots. But where . . . ?"

I told her that I didn't understand it myself, how I had planted the small bag of soil found clutched in my father's hand but had not really expected it to come to much, and certainly not to all of this, waving my arm over the expanse, the flowers having grown in soilless crevices and cracks, covering our entire little island of stone.

My mother turned to me and said, "These are not from the fairies, they are from him." Then she started crying, a reaction I had not expected and tried to talk her out of, but she said, "No, Agatha, leave me alone."

She stood out there for quite a while, weeping as she walked amongst the flowers. Later, after she came inside and said, "Where are all the helpers today?" I shrugged and avoided more questions by going outside myself, where I discovered scarlet spots amongst the bloom. My mother had been bedridden for so long, her feet had gone soft again. For days she left tiny teardrop shapes of blood in her step, which I surreptitiously wiped up, not wanting to draw any attention to the fact, for fear it would dismay her. She picked several of the forget-me-not blossoms and pressed them between the heavy pages of her book of myths and folklore. Not long after that, a terrible storm blew in, rocking our little house, challenging our resolve, and taking with it all the flowers. Once again our rock was barren. I worried what effect this would have on my mother but she merely sighed, shrugged, and said, "They were beautiful, weren't they, Agatha?"

So passed my childhood: a great deal of solitude, the occasional life-threatening adventure, the drudgery of work, and all around me the great wide sea with its myriad secrets and reasons, the lost we saved, those we didn't. And the ghosts, brought to us by my father, though we never understood clearly his purpose, as they only stood before the fire, dripping and melting like something made of wax, bemoaning what was lost (a fine boat, a lady love, a dream of the sea, a pocketful of jewels, a wife and children, a carving on bone, a song, its lyrics forgotten). We tried to provide what comfort we could, listening, nodding; there was little else we could do, they refused tea or blankets, they seemed only to want to stand by the fire, mourning their death, as my father stood sentry beside them, melting into salty puddles that we mopped up with clean rags, wrung out into the ocean, saying what we fashioned as prayer, or reciting lines of Irish poetry.

Though I know now that this is not a usual childhood, it was usual for me, and it did not veer from this course until my mother's hair had gone quite gray and I was a young woman, when my father brought us a different sort of ghost entirely, a handsome young man, his eyes the same blue-green as summer. His hair was of indeterminate color, wet curls that hung to his shoulders. Dressed simply, like any dead sailor, he carried about him an air of being educated more by art than by water, a suspicion soon confirmed for me when he refused an offering of tea by saying, "No, I will not, cannot drink your liquid offered without first asking for a kiss, ah a kiss is all the liquid I desire, come succor me with your lips."

Naturally, I blushed and, just as naturally, when my mother went to check on the lamp, and my father had melted into a mustached puddle, I kissed him. Though I should have been warned by the icy chill, as certainly I should have been warned by the fact of my own father, a mere puddle at the hearth, it was my first kiss and it did not feel deadly to me at all, not dangerous, not spectral, most certainly not spectral, though I did experience a certain pleasant floating sensation in its wake.

My mother was surprised, upon her return, to find the lad still standing, as vigorous as any living man, beside my father's puddle. We were both surprised that he remained throughout the night, regaling us with stories of the wild sea populated by whales, mermaids, and sharks; mesmerizing us with descriptions of the "bottom of the world" as he called it, embedded with strange purple rocks, pink shells spewing pearls, and the seaweed tendrils of sea witches' hair. We were both surprised that, when the black of night turned to the gray hue of morning, he bowed to each of us (turned fully toward me, so that I could receive his wink), promised he would return, and then left, walking out the door like any regular fellow. So convincing was he that my mother and I opened the door to see where he had gone, scanning the rock and the inky sea before we accepted that, as odd as it seemed, as vigorous his demeanor, he was a ghost most certainly.

"Or something of that nature," said my mother. "Strange that he didn't melt like the others." She squinted at me and I turned away from her before she could see my blush. "We shouldn't have let him keep us up all night," she said. "We aren't dead. We need our sleep."

Sleep? Sleep? I could not sleep, feeling as I did his cool lips on mine, the power of his kiss, as though he breathed out of me some dark aspect that had weighed inside me. I told my mother that she could sleep. I would take care of everything. She protested, but using the past as reassurance (she had long since discovered that I had run the place while she convalesced after my father's death), finally agreed.

I was happy to have her tucked safely in bed. I was happy to know that her curious eyes were closed. I did all the tasks necessary to keep the place in good order. Not even then, in all my girlish giddiness, did I forget the lamp. I am embarrassed to admit, however, it was well past four o'clock before I remembered my father's puddle, which by that time had been much dissipated. I wiped up the small amount of water and wrung him out over the sea, saying only as prayer, "Father, forgive me. Oh, bring him back to me." (Meaning, alas for me, a foolish girl, the boy who kissed me and not my own dear father.)

And that night, he did come back, knocking on the door like any living man, carrying in his wet hands a bouquet of pink coral which he presented to me, and a small white stone, shaped like a star, which he gave to my mother.

"Is there no one else with you?" she asked.

"I'm sorry, there is not," he said.

My mother began to busy herself in the kitchen, leaving the two of us alone. I could hear her in there, moving things about, opening cupboards, sweeping the already swept floor. It was my own carelessness that had caused my father's absence, I was sure of that; had I sponged him up sooner, had I prayed for him more sincerely, and not just for the satisfaction of my own desire, he would be here this night. I felt terrible about this, but then I looked into his eyes, those beautiful sea-colored eyes, and I could not help it, my body thrilled at his look. Is this love? I thought. Will he kiss me twice? When it seemed as if, without even wasting time with words, he was about to do so, leaning toward me with parted lips from which exhaled the scent of salt water, my mother stepped into the room, clearing her throat, holding the broom before her, as if thinking she might use it as a weapon.

"We don't really know anything about you," she said.

To begin with, my name is Ezekiel. My mother was fond of saints and the Bible and such. She died shortly after giving birth to me, her first and only child. I was raised by my father, on the island of Murano. Perhaps you have heard of it? Murano glass? We are famous for it throughout the world. My father, himself, was a talented glassmaker. Anything imagined, he could shape into glass. Glass birds, tiny glass bees, glass seashells, even glass tears (an art he perfected while I was an infant), and what my father knew, he taught to me.

Naturally, I eventually surpassed him in skill. Forgive me, but there is no humble way to say it. At any rate, my father had taught me and encouraged my talent all my life. I did not see when his enthusiasm began to sour. I was excited and pleased at what I could produce. I thought he would feel the same for me as I had felt for him, when, as a child, I sat on the footstool in his studio and applauded each glass wing, each hard teardrop.

Alas, it was not to be. My father grew jealous of me. My own father! At night he snuck into our studio and broke my birds, my little glass cakes. In the morning he pretended dismay and instructed me further on keeping air bubbles out of my work. He did not guess that I knew the dismal truth.

I determined to leave him, to sail away to some other place to make my home. My father begged me to stay: "Whatever will you do? How will you make your way in this world?"

I told him my true intention, not being clever enough to lie. "This is not the only place in the world with fire and sand," I said. "I intend to make glass."

He promised me it would be a death sentence. At the time I took this to be only his confused, fatherly concern. I did not perceive it as a threat.

It is true that the secret to glassmaking was meant to remain on Murano. It is true that the entire populace believed this trade, and only this trade, kept them fed and clothed. Finally, it is true that they passed the law (many years before my father confronted me with it) that anyone who dared attempt to take the secret of glassmaking off the island would suffer the penalty of death. All of this is true.

But what's also true is that I was a prisoner in my own home, tortured by my own father, who pretended to be a humble, kind glassmaker, but who, night after night, broke my creations and then, each morning, denied my accusations, his sweet old face mustached and whiskered, all the expression of dismay and sorrow.

This is madness, I reasoned. How else could I survive? One of us had to leave or die. I chose the gentler course.

We had, in our possession, only a small boat, used for trips that never veered far from shore. Gathering mussels, visiting neighbors, occasionally my father liked to sit in it and smoke a pipe while watching the sun set. He'd light a lantern and come home, smelling of the sea, boil us a pot of soup, a melancholic, completely innocent air about him, only later to sneak about his breaking work.

This small boat is what I took for my voyage across the sea. I also took some fishing supplies, a rope, dried cod he'd stored for winter, a blanket, and several jugs of red wine, given to us by the baker, whose daughter, I do believe, fancied me. For you, who have lived so long on this anchored rock, my folly must be apparent. Was it folly? It was. But what else was I to do? Day after day make my perfect art only to have my father, night after night, destroy it? He would destroy me!

I left in the dark, when the ocean is like ink and the sky is black glass with thousands of air bubbles. Air bubbles, indeed. I breathed my freedom in the salty sea air. I chose stars to follow. Foolishly, I had no clear sense of my passage and had only planned my escape.

Of course, knowing what I do now about the ocean, it is a wonder I survived the first night, much less seven. It was on the eighth morning that I saw the distant sail, and, hopelessly drunk and sunburned, as well as lost, began the desperate task of rowing toward it, another folly as I'm sure you'd agree, understanding how distant the horizon is. Luckily for me, or so I thought, the ship was headed in my direction and after a few more days it was close enough that I began to believe in my life again.

Alas, this ship was owned by a rich friend of my father's, a woman who had commissioned him to create a glass castle with a glass garden and glass fountain, tiny glass swans, a glass king and queen, a baby glass princess, and glass trees with golden glass apples, all for the amusement of her granddaughter (who, it must be said, had fingers like sausages and broke half of the figurines before her next birthday). This silly woman was only too happy to let my father use her ship, she was only too pleased to pay the ship's crew, all with the air of helping my father, when, in truth, it simply amused her to be involved in such drama. She said she did it for Murano, but in truth, she did it for the story.

It wasn't until I had been rescued, and hoisted on board, that my father revealed himself to me. He spread his arms wide, all great show for the crew, hugged me and even wept, but convincing as was his act, I knew he intended to destroy me.

These are terrible choices no son should have to make, but that night, as my father slept and the ship rocked its weary way back to Murano where I would likely be hung or possibly sentenced to live with my own enemy, my father, I slit the old man's throat. Though he opened his eyes, I do not believe he saw me, but was already entering the distant kingdom.

You ladies look quite aghast. I cannot blame you. Perhaps I should have chosen my own death instead, but I was a young man, and I wanted to live. Even after everything I had gone through, I wanted life.

Alas, it was not to be. I knew there would be trouble and accusation if my father were found with his throat slit, but none at all if he just disappeared in the night, as so often happens on large ships. Many a traveler has simply fallen overboard, never to be heard from again, and my father had already displayed a lack of seafaring savvy to rival my own.

I wrapped him up in the now-bloody blanket but although he was a small man, the effect was still that of a body, so I realized I would have to bend and fold him into a rucksack. You wince, but do not worry, he was certainly dead by this time.

I will not bore you with the details of my passage, hiding and sneaking with my dismal load. Suffice it to say that it took a while for me to at last be standing shipside, and I thought then that all danger had passed.

Remember, I was already quite weakened by my days adrift, and the matter of taking care of this business with my father had only fatigued me further. Certain that I was finally at the end of my task, I grew careless. He was much heavier than he had ever appeared to be. It took all my strength to hoist the rucksack, and (to get the sad, pitiable truth over with as quickly as possible) when I heaved that rucksack, the cord became entangled on my wrist, and yes, dear ladies, I went over with it, to the bottom of the world. There I remained until your own dear father, your husband, found me and brought me to this place, where, for the first time in my life, I feel safe, and, though I am dead, blessed.

Later, after my mother had tended the lamp while Ezekiel and I shared the kisses that left me breathless, she asked him to leave, saying that I needed my sleep. I protested, of course, but she insisted. I walked my ghost to the door, just as I think any girl would do in a similar situation, and there, for the first time, he kissed me in full view of my mother, not so passionate as those kisses that had preceded it, but effective nonetheless.

But after he was gone, even as I still blushed, my mother spoke in a grim voice, "Don't encourage him, Agatha."

"Why?" I asked, my body trembling with the impact of his affection and my mother's scorn, as though the two emotions met in me and quaked there. "What don't you like about him?"

"He's dead," she said, "there's that for a start."

"What about Daddy? He's dead too, and you've been loving him all this time."

My mother shook her head. "Agatha, it isn't the same thing. Think about what this boy told you tonight. He murdered his own father."

"I can't believe you'd use that against him. You heard what he said. He was just defending himself."

"But Agatha, it isn't what's said that is always the most telling. Don't you know that? Have I really raised you to be so gullible?"

"I am not gullible. I'm in love."

"I forbid it."

Certainly no three words, spoken by a parent, can do more to solidify love than these. It was no use arguing. What would be the point? She, this woman who had loved no one but a puddle for so long, could never understand what was going through my heart. Without more argument, I went to bed, though I slept fitfully, feeling torn from my life in every way, while my mother stayed up reading, I later surmised, from her book of myths. In the morning I found her sitting at the kitchen table, the great volume before her. She looked up at me with dark circled eyes, then, without salutation, began reading, her voice, ominous.

"There are many kinds of ghosts. There are the ghosts that move things, slam doors and drawers, throw silverware about the house. There are the ghosts (usually of small children) that play in dark corners with spools of thread and frighten family pets. There are the weeping and wailing ghosts. There are the ghosts who know that they are dead, and those who do not. There are tree ghosts, those who spend their afterlife in a particular tree (a clue for such a resident might be bite marks on fallen fruit). There are ghosts trapped forever at the hour of their death (I saw one like this once, in an old movie theater bathroom, hanging from the ceiling). There are melting ghosts (we know about these, don't we?), usually victims of drowning. And there are breath-stealing ghosts. These, sometimes mistaken for the grosser vampire, sustain a sort of half-life by stealing breath from the living. They can be any age, but are usually teenagers and young adults, often at that selfish stage when they died. These ghosts greedily go about sucking the breath out of the living. This can be done by swallowing the lingered breath from unwashed cups, or, most effectively of all, through a kiss. Though these ghosts can often be quite seductively charming, they are some of the most dangerous. Each life has only a certain amount of breath within it and these ghosts are said to steal an infinite amount with each swallow. The effect is such that the ghost, while it never lives again, begins to do a fairly good imitation of life, while its victims (those whose breath it steals) edge ever closer to their own death."

My mother looked up at me triumphantly and I stormed out of the house, only to be confronted with the sea all around me, as desolate as my heart.

That night, when he came, knocking on the door, she did not answer it and forbade me to do so.

"It doesn't matter," I taunted, "he's a ghost. He doesn't need doors."

"No, you're wrong," she said, "he's taken so much of your breath that he's not entirely spectral. He can't move through walls any longer. He needs you, but he doesn't care about you at all, don't you get that, Agatha?"

"Agatha? Are you home? Agatha? Why don't you come? Agatha?"

I couldn't bear it. I began to weep.

"I know this is hard," my mother said, "but it must be done. Listen, his voice is already growing faint. We just have to get through this night."

"What about the lamp?" I said.

"What?"

But she knew what I meant. Her expression betrayed her. "Don't you need to check on the lamp?"

"Agatha? Have I done something wrong?"

My mother stared at the door, and then turned to me, the dark circles under her eyes giving her the look of a beaten woman. "The lamp is fine."

I spun on my heels and went into my small room, slammed the door behind me. My mother, a smart woman, was not used to thinking like a warden. She had forgotten about my window. By the time I hoisted myself down from it, Ezekiel was standing on the rocky shore, surveying the dark ocean before him. He had already lost some of his life-like luster, particularly below his knees where I could almost see through him. "Ezekiel," I said. He turned and I gasped at the change in his visage, the cavernous look of his eyes, the skeletal stretch at his jaw. Seeing my shocked expression, he nodded and spread his arms open, as if to say, yes, this is what has become of me. I ran into those open arms and embraced him, though he creaked like something made of old wood. He bent down, pressing his cold lips against mine until they were no longer cold but burning like a fire.

We spent that night together and I did not mind the shattering wind with its salt bite on my skin, and I did not care when the lamp went out and the sea roiled beneath a black sky, and I did not worry about the dead weeping on the rocky shore, or the lightness I felt as though I were floating beside my lover, and when morning came, revealing the dead all around us, I followed him into the water, I followed him to the bottom of the sea, where he turned to me and said, "What have you done? Are you stupid? Don't you realize? You're no good to me dead!"

So, sadly, like many a daughter, I learned that my mother had been right after all, and when I returned to her, dripping with salt water and seaweed, tiny fish corpses dropping from my hair, she embraced me. Seeing my state, weeping, she kissed me on the lips, our mouths open. I drank from her, sweet breath, until I was filled and she collapsed to the floor, my mother in her black dress, like a crushed funeral flower.

I had no time for mourning. The lamp had been out for hours. Ships had crashed and men had died. Outside the sun sparkled on the sea. People would be coming soon to find out what had happened.

I took our small boat and rowed away from there. Many hours later, I docked in a seaside town and hitchhiked to another, until eventually I was as far from my home as I could be and still be near my ocean.

I had a difficult time of it for a while. People are generally suspicious of someone with no past and little future. I lived on the street and had to beg for jobs cleaning toilets and scrubbing floors, only through time and reputation working up to my current situation, finally getting my own little apartment, small and dark, so different from when I was the lighthouse keeper's daughter and the ocean was my yard.

One day, after having passed it for months without a thought, I went into the art supply store, and bought a canvas, paint, and two paintbrushes. I paid for it with my tip money, counting it out for the clerk whose expression suggested I was placing turds in her palm instead of pennies. I went home and hammered a nail into the wall, hung the canvas on it, and began to paint. Like many a creative person I seem to have found some solace for the unfortunate happenings of my young life (and death) in art.

I live simply and virginally, never taking breath through a kiss. This is the vow I made, and I have kept it. Yes, some days I am weakened, and tempted to restore my vigor with such an easy solution, but instead I hold the empty cups to my face, I breathe in, I breathe everything, the breath of old men, breath of young, sweet breath, sour breath, breath of lipstick, breath of smoke. It is not, really, a way to live, but this is not, really, a life.

For several seconds after Alex finished reading the remarkable account, his gaze remained transfixed on the page. Finally, he looked up, blinked in the dim coffee shop light, and closed the black binder.

Several baristas stood behind the counter busily jostling around each other with porcelain cups, teapots, bags of beans. One of them, a short girl with red and green hair that spiked around her like some otherworld halo, stood by the sink, stacking dirty plates and cups. When she saw him watching, she smiled. It wasn't a true smile, not that it was mocking, but rather, the girl with the Christmas hair smiled like someone who had either forgotten happiness entirely, or never known it at all. In response, Alex nodded at her, and to his surprise, she came over, carrying a dirty rag and a spray bottle.

"Did you read all of it?" she said as she squirted the table beside him and began to wipe it with the dingy towel.

Alex winced at the unpleasant odor of the cleaning fluid, nodded, and then, seeing that the girl wasn't really paying any attention, said, "Yes." He glanced at the wall where the paintings were hung.

"So what'd you think?"

The girl stood there, grinning that sad grin, right next to him now with her noxious bottle and dirty rag, one hip jutted out in a way he found oddly sexual. He opened his mouth to speak, gestured toward the paintings, and then at the book before him. "I, I have to meet her," he said, tapping the book, "this is remarkable."

"But what do you think about the paintings?"

Once more he glanced at the wall where they hung. He shook his head. "No," he said, "it's this," tapping the book again.

She smiled, a true smile, cocked her head, and put out her hand. "Agatha," she said.

Alex felt like his head was spinning. He shook the girl's hand. It was unexpectedly tiny, like that of a child's, and he gripped it too tightly at first. Glancing at the counter, she pulled out a chair and sat down in front of him.

"I can only talk for a little while. Marnie is the manager today and she's on the rag or something all the time, but she's downstairs right now, checking in an order."

"You," he brushed the binder with the tip of his fingers, as if caressing something holy, "you wrote this?"

She nodded, bowed her head slightly, shrugged, and suddenly earnest, leaned across the table, elbowing his empty cup as she did. "Nobody bothers to read it. I've seen a few people pick it up but you're the first one to read the whole thing."

Alex leaned back, frowning.

She rolled her eyes, which, he noticed, were a lovely shade of lavender, lined darkly in black.

"See, I was trying to do something different. This is the whole point"—she jabbed at the book, and he felt immediately protective of it—"I was trying to put a story in a place where people don't usually expect one. Don't you think we've gotten awful complacent in our society about story? Like it all the time has to go a certain way and even be only in certain places. That's what this is all about. The paintings are a foil. But you get that, don't you? Do you know," she leaned so close to him, he could smell her breath, which he thought was strangely sweet, "someone actually offered to buy the fly painting?" Her mouth dropped open, she shook her head and rolled those lovely lavender eyes. "I mean, what the fuck? Doesn't he know it sucks?"

Alex wasn't sure what to do. She seemed to be leaning near to his cup. Leaning over it, Alex realized. He opened his mouth, not having any idea what to say.

Just then another barista, the one who wore scarves all the time and had an imperious air about her, as though she didn't really belong there but was doing research or something, walked past. Agatha glanced at her. "I gotta go." She stood up. "You finished with this?" she asked, touching his cup.

Though he hadn't yet had his free refill, Alex nodded.

"It was nice talking to you," she said. "Just goes to show, doesn't it?"

Alex had no idea what she was talking about. He nodded half-heartedly, hoping comprehension would follow, but when it didn't, he raised his eyebrows at her instead.

She laughed. "I mean you don't look anything like the kind of person who would understand my stuff."

"Well, you don't look much like Agatha," he said.

"But I am Agatha," she murmured as she turned away from him, picking up an empty cup and saucer from a nearby table.

Alex watched her walk to the tiny sink at the end of the counter. She set the cups and saucers down. She rinsed the saucers and placed them in the gray bucket they used for carrying dirty dishes to the back. She reached for a cup, and then looked at him.

He quickly looked down at the black binder, picked it up, pushed his chair in, and headed toward the front of the shop. He stopped to look at the paintings. They were fine, boring, but fine little paintings that had no connection to what he'd read. He didn't linger over them for long. He was almost to the door when she was beside him, saying, "I'll take that." He couldn't even fake innocence. He shrugged and handed her the binder.

"I'm flattered, really," she said. But she didn't try to continue the conversation. She set the book down on the table beneath the painting of the avocado. He watched her pick up an empty cup and bring it toward her face, breathing in the lingered breath that remained. She looked up suddenly, caught him watching, frowned, and turned away.

Alex understood. She wasn't what he'd been expecting either. But when love arrives it doesn't always appear as expected. He couldn't just ignore it. He couldn't pretend it hadn't happened. He walked out of the coffee shop into the afternoon sunshine.

Of course, there were problems, her not being alive for one. But Alex was not a man of prejudice.

He was patient besides. He stood in the art supply store for hours, pretending particular interest in the anatomical hinged figurines of sexless men and women in the front window, before she walked past, her hair glowing like a forest fire.

"Agatha," he called.

She turned, frowned, and continued walking. He had to take little running steps to catch up. "Hi," he said. He saw that she was biting her lower lip. "You just getting off work?"

She stopped walking right in front of the bank, which was closed by then, and squinted up at him.

"Alex," he said. "I was talking to you today at the coffee shop."

"I know who you are."

Her tone was angry. He couldn't understand it. Had he insulted her somehow?

"I don't have Alzheimer's. I remember you."

He nodded. This was harder than he had expected.

"What do you want?" she said.

Her tone was really downright hostile. He shrugged. "I just thought we could, you know, talk."

She shook her head. "Listen, I'm happy that you liked my story."

"I did," he said, nodding, "it was great."

"But what would we talk about? You and me?"

Alex shifted beneath her lavender gaze. He licked his lips. She wasn't even looking at him, but glancing around him and across the street. "I don't care if it does mean I'll die sooner," he said. "I want to give you a kiss."

Her mouth dropped open.

"Is something wrong?"

She turned and ran. She wore one red sneaker and one green. They matched her hair.

As Alex walked back to his car, parked in front of the coffee shop, he tried to talk himself into not feeling so bad about the way things went. He hadn't always been like this. He used to be able to talk to people. Even women. Okay, he had never been suave, he knew that, but he'd been a regular guy. Certainly no one had ever run away from him before. But after Tessie died, people changed. Of course, this made sense, initially. He was in mourning, even if he didn't cry (something the doctor told him not to worry about because one day, probably when he least expected it, the tears would fall). He was obviously in pain. People were very nice. They talked to him in hushed tones. Touched him, gently. Even men tapped him with their fingertips. All this gentle touching had been augmented by vigorous hugs. People either touched him as if he would break, or hugged him as if he had already broken and only the vigor of the embrace kept him intact.

For the longest time there had been all this activity around him. People called, sent chatty e-mails, even handwritten letters, cards with flowers on them and prayers. People brought over casseroles, and bread, Jell-O with fruit in it. (Nobody brought chocolate chip cookies, which he might have actually eaten.)

To Alex's surprise, once Tessie had died, it felt as though a great weight had been lifted from him, but instead of appreciating the feeling, the freedom of being lightened of the burden of his wife's dying body, he felt in danger of floating away or disappearing. Could it be possible, he wondered, that Tessie's body, even when she was mostly bones and barely breath, was all that kept him real? Was it possible that he would have to live like this, held to life by some strange force but never a part of it again? These questions led Alex to the brief period where he'd experimented with becoming a Hare Krishna, shaved his head, dressed in orange robes, and took up dancing in the park. Alex wasn't sure but he thought that was when people started treating him as if he were strange, and even after he grew his hair out and started wearing regular clothes again, people continued to treat him strangely.

And, Alex had to admit, as he inserted his key into the lock of his car, he'd forgotten how to behave. How to be normal, he guessed.

You just don't go read something somebody wrote and decide you love her, he scolded himself as he eased into traffic. You don't just go falling in love with breath-stealing ghosts. People don't do that.

Alex did not go to the coffee shop the next day, or the day after that, but it was the only coffee shop in town, and had the best coffee in the state. They roasted the beans right there. Freshness like that can't be faked.

It was awkward for him to see her behind the counter, over by the dirty cups, of course. But when she looked up at him, he attempted a kind smile, then looked away.

He wasn't there to bother her. He ordered French Roast in a cup to go, even though he hated to drink out of paper, paid for it, dropped the change into the tip jar, and left without any further interaction with her.

He walked to the park, where he sat on a bench and watched a woman with two small boys feed white bread to the ducks. This was illegal because the ducks would eat all the bread offered to them, they had no sense of appetite, or being full, and they would eat until their stomachs exploded. Or something like that. Alex couldn't exactly remember. He was pretty sure it killed them. But Alex couldn't decide what to do. Should he go tell that lady and those two little boys that they were killing the ducks? How would that make them feel, especially as they were now triumphantly shaking out the empty bag, the ducks crowded around them, one of the boys squealing with delight? Maybe he should just tell her, quietly. But she looked so happy. Maybe she'd been having a hard time of it. He saw those mothers on *Oprah*, saying what a hard job it was, and maybe she'd had that kind of morning, even screaming at the kids, and then she got this idea, to take them to the park and feed the ducks and now she felt good about what she'd done and maybe she was thinking that she wasn't such a bad mom after all, and if Alex told her she was killing the ducks, would it stop the ducks from dying or just stop her from feeling happiness? Alex sighed. He couldn't decide what to do. The ducks were happy, the lady was happy, and one of the boys was happy. The other one looked sort of terrified. She picked him up and they walked away together, she, carrying the boy who waved the empty bag like a balloon, the other one skipping after them, a few ducks hobbling behind.

For three days Alex ordered his coffee to go and drank it in the park. On the fourth day, Agatha wasn't anywhere that he could see and he surmised that it was her day off so he sat at his favorite table in the back. But on the fifth day, even though he didn't see her again, and it made sense that she'd have two days off in a row, he ordered his coffee to go and took it to the park. He'd grown to like sitting on the bench watching strolling park visitors, the running children, the dangerously fat ducks.

He had no idea she would be there and he felt himself blush when he saw her coming down the path that passed right in front of him. He stared deeply into his cup and fought the compulsion to run. He couldn't help it, though. Just as the toes of her red and green sneakers came into view he looked up. I'm not going to hurt you, he thought, and then, he smiled, that false smile he'd been practicing on her and, incredibly, she smiled back! Also, falsely, he assumed, but he couldn't blame her for that.

She looked down the path and he followed her gaze, seeing that, though the path around the duck pond was lined with benches every fifty feet or so, all of them were taken. She sighed. "Mind if I sit here?"

He scooted over and she sat down, slowly. He glanced at her profile. She looked worn out, he decided. Her lavender eye flickered toward him, and he looked into his cup again. It made sense that she would be tired, he thought, if she'd been off work for two days, she'd also been going that long without stealing breath from cups. "Want some?" he said, offering his.

She looked startled, pleased, and then, falsely unconcerned. She peered over the edge of his cup, shrugged, and said, "Okay, yeah, sure."

He handed it to her and politely watched the ducks so she could have some semblance of privacy with it. After a while she said thanks and handed it back to him.

He nodded and stole a look at her profile again. It pleased him that her color already looked better. His breath had done that!

"Sorry about the other day," she said, "I was just . . ."

They waited together but she didn't finish the sentence.

"It's okay," he said, "I know I'm weird."

"No, you're, well—" She smiled, glanced at him, shrugged. "It isn't that. I like weird people. I'm weird. But, I mean, I'm not dead, okay? You kind of freaked me out with that."

He nodded. "Would you like to go out with me sometime?" Inwardly, he groaned. He couldn't believe he just said that.

"Listen, Alex?"

He nodded. Stop nodding, he told himself. Stop acting like a bobblehead.

"Why don't you tell me a little about yourself?"

So he told her. How he'd been coming to the park lately, watching people over-feed the ducks, wondering if he should tell them what they were doing but they all looked so happy doing it, and the ducks looked happy too, and he wasn't sure anyway, what if he was wrong, what if he told everyone to stop feeding bread to the ducks and it turned out it did them no harm and how would he know? Would they explode like balloons, or would it be more like how it had been when his wife died, a slow painful death, eating her away inside, and how he used to come here, when he was a monk, well, not really a monk, he'd never gotten ordained or anything, but he'd been trying the idea on for a while and how he used to sing and spin in circles and how it felt a lot like what he'd remembered of happiness but he could never be sure because a remembered emotion is like a remembered taste, it's never really there. And then, one day, a real monk came and watched him spinning in circles and singing nonsense, and he just stood and watched Alex, which made him self-conscious because he didn't really know what he was doing, and the monk started laughing, which made Alex stop and the monk said, "Why'd you stop?" And Alex said, "I don't know what I'm doing." And the monk nodded, as if this was a very wise thing to say and this, just this monk with his round bald head and wire-rimmed spectacles, in his simple orange robe (not at all like the orange-dyed sheet Alex was wearing) nodding when Alex said, "I don't know what I'm doing," made Alex cry and he and the monk sat down under that tree, and the monk (whose name was Ron) told him about Kali, the goddess who is both womb and grave. Alex felt like it was the first thing anyone had said to him that made sense since Tessie died and after that he stopped coming to the park, until just recently, and let his hair grow out again and stopped wearing his robe. Before she'd died, he'd been one of the lucky ones, or so he'd thought, because he made a small fortune in a dot com, and actually got out of it before it all went belly up while so many people he knew lost everything but then Tessie came home from her doctor's appointment, not pregnant, but with cancer, and he realized he wasn't lucky at all. They met in high school and were together until she died, at home, practically blind by that time and she made him promise he wouldn't just give up on life. So he began living this sort of half-life, but he wasn't unhappy or depressed, he didn't want her to think that, he just wasn't sure. "I sort of lost confidence in life," he said. "It's like I don't believe in it anymore. Not like suicide, but I mean, like the whole thing, all of it isn't real somehow. Sometimes I feel like it's all a dream, or a long nightmare that I can never wake up from. It's made me odd, I guess."

She bit her lower lip, glanced longingly at his cup.

"Here," Alex said, "I'm done anyway."

She took it and lifted it toward her face, breathing in, he was sure of it, and only after she was finished, drinking the coffee. They sat like that in silence for a while and then they just started talking about everything, just as Alex had hoped they would. She told him how she had grown up living near the ocean, and her father had died young, and then her mother had too, and she had a boyfriend, her first love, who broke her heart, but the story she wrote was just a story, a story about her life, her dream life, the way she felt inside, like he did, as though somehow life was a dream. Even though everyone thought she was a painter (because he was the only one who read it, he was the only one who got it), she was a writer, not a painter, and stories seemed more real to her than life. At a certain point he offered to take the empty cup and throw it in the trash but she said she liked to peel off the wax, and then began doing so. Alex politely ignored the divergent ways she found to continue drinking his breath. He didn't want to embarrass her.

They finally stood up and stretched, walked through the park together and grew quiet, with the awkwardness of new friends. "You want a ride?" he said, pointing at his car.

She declined, which was a disappointment to Alex but he determined not to let it ruin his good mood. He was willing to leave it at that, to accept what had happened between them that afternoon as a moment of grace to be treasured and expect nothing more from it, when she said, "What are you doing next Tuesday?" They made a date, well, not a date, Alex reminded himself, an arrangement, to meet the following Tuesday in the park, which they did, and there followed many wonderful Tuesdays. They did not kiss. They were friends. Of course Alex still loved her. He loved her more. But he didn't bother her with all that and it was in the spirit of friendship that he suggested (after weeks of Tuesdays in the park) that the following Tuesday she come for dinner, "nothing fancy," he promised when he saw the slight hesitation on her face.

But when she said yes, he couldn't help it; he started making big plans for the night.

Naturally, things were awkward when she arrived. He offered to take her sweater, a lumpy looking thing in wild shades of orange, lime green, and purple. He should have just let her throw it across the couch, that would have been the casual non-datelike thing to do, but she handed it to him and then, wiping her hand through her hair, which, by candlelight looked like bloody grass, cased his place with those lavender eyes, deeply shadowed as though she hadn't slept for weeks.

He could see she was freaked out by the candles. He hadn't gone crazy or anything. They were just a couple of small candles, not even purchased from the store in the mall, but bought at the grocery store, unscented. "I like candles," he said, sounding defensive even to his own ears.

She smirked, as if she didn't believe him, and then spun away on the toes of her red sneaker and her green one, and plopped down on the couch. She looked absolutely exhausted. This was not a complete surprise to Alex. It had been a part of his plan, actually, but he felt bad for her just the same.

He kept dinner simple, lasagna, a green salad, chocolate cake for dessert. They didn't eat in the dining room. That would have been too formal. Instead they ate in the living room, she sitting on the couch, and he on the floor, their plates on the coffee table, watching a DVD of *I Love Lucy* episodes, a mutual like they had discovered. (Though her description of watching *I Love Lucy* reruns as a child did not gel with his picture of her in the crooked keeper's house, offering tea to melting ghosts, he didn't linger over the inconsistency.) Alex offered her plenty to drink but he wouldn't let her come into the kitchen, or get anywhere near his cup. He felt bad about this, horrible, in fact, but he tried to stay focused on the bigger picture.

After picking at her cake for a while, Agatha set the plate down, leaned back into the gray throw pillows, and closed her eyes.

Alex watched her. He didn't think about anything, he just watched her. Then he got up very quietly so as not to disturb her and went into the kitchen where he, carefully, quietly opened the drawer in which he had stored the supplies. Coming up from behind, eyeing her red and green hair, he moved quickly. She turned toward him, cursing loudly, her eyes wide and frightened, as he pressed her head to her knees, pulled her arms behind her back (to the accompaniment of a sickening crack, and her scream) pressed the wrists together and wrapped them with the rope. She struggled in spite of her weakened state, her legs flailing, kicking the coffee table. The plate with the chocolate cake flew off it and landed on the beige rug and her screams escalated into a horrible noise, unlike anything Alex had ever heard before. Luckily, Alex was prepared with the duct tape, which he slapped across her mouth. By that time he was rather exhausted himself. But she stood up and began to run, awkwardly, across the room. It broke his heart to see her this way. He grabbed her from behind. She kicked and squirmed but she was quite a small person and it was easy for him to get her legs tied.

"Is that too tight?" he asked.

She looked at him with wide eyes. As if he were the ghost.

"I don't want you to be uncomfortable."

She shook her head. Tried to speak, but only produced muffled sounds.

"I can take that off," he said, pointing at the duct tape. "But you have to promise me you won't scream. If you scream, I'll just put it on, and I won't take it off again. Though, you should know, ever since Tessie died I have these vivid dreams and nightmares, and I wake up screaming a lot. None of my neighbors has ever done anything about it. Nobody's called the police to report it, and nobody has even asked me if there's a problem. That's how it is amongst the living. Okay?"

She nodded.

He picked at the edge of the tape with his fingertips and when he got a good hold of it, he pulled fast. It made a loud ripping sound. She grunted and gasped, tears falling down her cheeks as she licked her lips.

"I'm really sorry about this," Alex said. "I just couldn't think of another way."

She began to curse, a string of expletives quickly swallowed by her weeping, until finally she managed to ask, "Alex, what are you doing?"

He sighed. "I know it's true, okay? I see the way you are, how tired you get and I know why. I know that you're a breath-stealer. I want you to understand that I know that about you, and I love you and you don't have to keep pretending with me, okay?"

She looked around the room, as if trying to find something to focus on. "Listen, Alex," she said. "Listen to me. I get tired all the time 'cause I'm sick. I didn't want to tell you, after what you told me about your wife. I thought it would be too upsetting for you. That's it. That's why I get tired all the time."

"No," he said, softly, "you're a ghost."

"I am not dead," she said, shaking her head so hard that her tears splashed his face. "I am not dead," she said over and over again, louder and louder until Alex felt forced to tape her mouth shut once more.

"I know you're afraid. Love can be frightening. Do you think I'm not scared? Of course I'm scared. Look what happened with Tessie. I know you're scared too.

You're worried I'll turn out to be like Ezekiel, but I'm not like him, okay? I'm not going to hurt you. And I even finally figured out that you're scared 'cause of what happened with your mom. Of course you are. But you have to understand. That's a risk I'm willing to take. Maybe we'll have one night together or only one hour, or a minute. I don't know. I have good genes though. My parents, both of them, are still alive, okay? Even my grandmother only died a few years ago. There's a good chance I have a lot, and I mean a lot, of breath in me. But if I don't, don't you see, I'd rather spend a short time with you, than no time at all?"

He couldn't bear it, he couldn't bear the way she looked at him as if he were a monster when he carried her to the couch. "Are you cold?"

She just stared at him.

"Do you want to watch more *I Love Lucy*? Or a movie?"

She wouldn't respond. She could be so stubborn.

He decided on *Annie Hall*. "Do you like Woody Allen?" She just stared at him, her eyes filled with accusation. "It's a love story," he said, turning away from her to insert the DVD. He turned it on for her, then placed the remote control in her lap, which he realized was a stupid thing to do, since her hands were still tied behind her back, and he was fairly certain that, had her mouth not been taped shut, she'd be giving him that slack-jawed look of hers. She wasn't making any of this very easy. He picked the dish up off the floor, and the silverware, bringing them into the kitchen, where he washed them and the pots and pans, put aluminum foil on the leftover lasagna and put it into the refrigerator. After he finished sweeping the floor, he sat and watched the movie with her. He forgot about the sad ending. He always thought of it as a romantic comedy, never remembering the sad end. He turned off the TV and said, "I think it's late enough now. I think we'll be all right." She looked at him quizzically.

First Alex went out to his car and popped the trunk, then he went back inside where he found poor Agatha squirming across the floor. Trying to escape, apparently. He walked past her, got the throw blanket from the couch and laid it on the floor beside her, rolled her into it even as she squirmed and bucked. "Agatha, just try to relax," he said, but she didn't. Stubborn, stubborn, she could be so stubborn.

He threw her over his shoulder. He was not accustomed to carrying much weight and immediately felt the stress, all the way down his back to his knees. He shut the apartment door behind him and didn't worry about locking it. He lived in a safe neighborhood.

When they got to the car, he put her into the trunk, only then taking the blanket away from her beautiful face. "Don't worry, it won't be long," he said as he closed the hood.

He looked through his CDs, trying to choose something she would like, just in case the sound carried into the trunk, but he couldn't figure out what would be appropriate so he finally decided just to drive in silence.

It took about twenty minutes to get to the beach; it was late, and there was little traffic. Still, the ride gave him an opportunity to reflect on what he was doing. By the time he pulled up next to the pier, he had reassured himself that it was the right thing to do, even though it looked like the wrong thing.

He'd made a good choice, deciding on this place. He and Tessie used to park here, and he was amazed that it had apparently remained undiscovered by others seeking dark escape.

When he got out of the car he took a deep breath of the salt air and stood, for a moment, staring at the black waves, listening to their crash and murmur. Then he went around to the back and opened up the trunk. He looked over his shoulder, just to be sure. If someone were to discover him like this, his actions would be misinterpreted. The coast was clear, however. He wanted to carry Agatha in his arms, like a bride. Every time he had pictured it, he had seen it that way, but she was struggling again so he had to throw her over his shoulder where she continued to struggle. Well, she was stubborn, but he was too, that was part of the beauty of it, really. But it made it difficult to walk, and it was windier on the pier, also wet. All in all it was a precarious, unpleasant journey to the end.

He had prepared a little speech but she struggled against him so hard, like a hooked fish, that all he could manage to say was, "I love you," barely focusing on the wild expression in her face, the wild eyes, before he threw her in and she sank, and then bobbed up like a cork, only her head above the black waves, those eyes of hers, locked on his, and they remained that way, as he turned away from the edge of the pier and walked down the long plank, feeling lighter, but not in a good way. He felt those eyes, watching him, in the car as he flipped restlessly from station to station, those eyes, watching him, when he returned home, and saw the clutter of their night together, the burned-down candles, the covers to the *I Love Lucy* and *Annie Hall* DVDs on the floor, her crazy sweater on the dining room table, those eyes, watching him, and suddenly Alex was cold, so cold his teeth were chattering and he was shivering but sweating besides. The black water rolled over those eyes and closed them and he ran to the bathroom and only just made it in time, throwing up everything he'd eaten, collapsing to the floor, weeping, *What have I done? What was I thinking?*

He would have stayed there like that, he determined, until they came for him and carted him away, but after a while he became aware of the foul taste in his mouth. He stood up, rinsed it out, brushed his teeth and tongue, changed out of his clothes, and went to bed, where, after a good deal more crying, and trying to figure out exactly what had happened to his mind, he was amazed to find himself falling into a deep darkness like the water, from which, he expected, he would never rise.

But then he was lying there, with his eyes closed, somewhere between sleep and waking, and he realized he'd been like this for some time. Though he was fairly certain he had fallen asleep, something had woken him. In this half state, he'd been listening to the sound he finally recognized as dripping water. He hated it when he didn't turn the faucet tight. He tried to ignore it, but the dripping persisted. So confused was he that he even thought he felt a splash on his hand and another on his forehead. He opened one eye, then the other.

She stood there, dripping wet, her hair plastered darkly around her face, her eyes smudged black. "I found a sharp rock at the bottom of the world," she said and she raised her arms. He thought she was going to strike him, but instead she showed him the cut rope dangling there.

He nodded. He could not speak.

She cocked her head, smiled, and said, "Okay, you were right. You were right about everything. Got any room in there?"

He nodded. She peeled off the wet T-shirt and let it drop to the floor, revealing her small breasts white as the moon, unbuttoned and unzipped her jeans, wiggling seductively out of the tight wet fabric, taking her panties off at the same time. He saw when she lifted her feet that the rope was no longer around them and she was already transparent below the knees. When she pulled back the covers he smelled the odd odor of saltwater and mud, as if she were both fresh and loamy. He scooted over, but only far enough that when she eased in beside him, he could hold her, wrap her wet cold skin in his arms, knowing that he was offering her everything, everything he had to give, and that she had come to take it.

"You took a big risk back there," she said.

He nodded.

She pressed her lips against his and he felt himself growing lighter, as if all his life he'd been weighed down by this extra breath, and her lips were cold but they grew warmer and warmer and the heat between them created a steam until she burned him and still, they kissed, all the while Alex thinking, I love you, I love you, I love you, until, finally, he could think it no more, his head was as light as his body, lying beside her, hot flesh to hot flesh, the cinder of his mind could no longer make sense of it, and he hoped, as he fell into a black place like no other he'd ever been in before, that this was really happening, that she was really here, and the suffering he'd felt for so long was finally over.

BEN FOUNTAIN

The Good Ones Are
Already Taken

Ben Fountain's story "The Good Ones Are Already Taken" comes from his debut short-story collection, Brief Encounters with Che Guevara *(Ecco). His stories have appeared in* Harper's, The Paris Review, *and* Zoetrope: All-Story. *Fountain is also the fiction editor of the* Southwest Review, *a journal we look forward to reading each year. He lives with his family in Dallas, Texas.*
—K.L. & G.G.

It was after midnight when the plane came smoking down the runway at last, the vast cyclone roar of the C-130 a fair approximation of Melissa's inner state. A cheer went up from the families strung along the fence, the kids in their pajamas and scruffy cartoon slippers, the frazzled moms trying to keep it all together in the heat, hair, makeup, manic kids; they'd parboiled for hours in the parking lot while word kept coming from the off-limits terminal, *Delay, Delay, Delay,* until Melissa thought she'd chew through the chain-link fence. It had been eight months since she'd seen her husband, and every hard-fought minute for this young wife had been the home-front equivalent of trench warfare. They'd even cheated and tacked on an extra ten weeks, *a high honor* the captain said when the rest of the team ex-filled in March, *you should be so proud.* Proud, sure, she would have been proud to nail Clinton's draft-dodging ass to the wall, but what could you do? *SF wife* read the t-shirts at the Green Beret Museum, *The toughest job in the Army,* and she supposed she was proud, or would be, once she had him back. Even among the elite Dirk had proved himself special, his surprisingly quick fluency in French and Creole earning him extra duty in the Haitian Vacation, that tar baby of a mission known to the rest of the world as Operation Uphold Democracy.

Chogee boy, she'd written in her last letter, *I'm going to screw you into a coma when you get back.* Melissa was 24, a near-newlywed of fifteen months, and his leaving had been like an amputation—for weeks afterward she'd had missing-limb sensations, her skin fizzing and prickling where her husband should have been. As every man who'd undressed her mentally or otherwise would agree, celibacy was wasted on a body like hers: she had high, pillowy breasts, the compact butt of a boy, and abs you could bounce golf balls off of, a smallish package topped with a pretty heart face and reams of wavy sorrel-brown hair. That she was also smart, sensible, and socially well-adjusted didn't save her from serial panic attacks, the fear that sex was an engine that dragged the rest of you along. A month ago she'd been having drinks with friends and found her mettle being probed by an older, handsome man with a shoebox of a jaw and rapturous muscles straining at his polo shirt. This was James, ex-paratrooper, ex-special operations, now on private contract with the DOD; his mere proximity, their casual bumping of arms and legs tripped an all-over sensual buzz in her, a Pavlovian hormone flush that felt like drowning. After that there was lunch, and friendly phone calls at work, then another Happy Hour that ended with her pressed against the fender of his cherry-red Corvette while his tongue did a soft, sweet crush inside her mouth.

The whoop of his car alarm had wrenched her out of it. She'd driven home in tears, cursing Dirk for being gone and wondering how they'd done it, all those loyal, suffering women down through the ages who'd waited out crusades and world wars, not to mention whaling voyages, jungle and polar expeditions, pointless treks to wherever just because it was there. James kept calling; Melissa resorted to cold showers and masturbation until the captain called from Bragg to say Dirk was headed home, today, now, ETA 2200 hours. She wasn't sure she believed it until he walked off the plane, his sleeves in a jungle roll, beret blocked and raked to the side, head carried with the bearing of a twelve-point buck. Like someone had died, that's how strong the moment was, all that tragic magnitude suddenly floored in reverse—she had to lean into the fence while the earth stabilized, a sob dredging the soft lower tissues of her throat. Then she lifted her head and started cheering.

They lived in a trailer off base, a modest single-wide down a sandy dirt road amid the pine and sweet-gum forest outside Fayetteville, or Fayette-*Nam* as it was known when Melissa was growing up, forty miles down the Interstate. Thanks to the mighty spending power of its military bases, Fayetteville boasted more clip joints and titty bars than any city its size in the U.S., and Melissa's first business as a married woman had been to move beyond the city's trashy outer tentacles. *Aren't you scared out there, all by yourself?* people asked her, other women usually—her mother and sisters down in Lumberton, post-menopausal aunts, friends from high school who'd settled for hometown boys. *Plenty of worse things to be scared of,* she'd answer, leaving unsaid her sense of marriage as a nearer threat than any snakes or feral dogs the woods might throw out. The threat of waking one day to find a very familiar stranger next to you in bed—she felt it sometimes in his lockjawed moods, his slides toward the brute, monosyllabic style that might drive her away in twenty years. Stranger still, and maybe funny, were the shooting sounds he made in his sleep, *pow-pow, pah-pow-pow-pow* like a kid popping off an imaginary gun. Who was he shooting in that subterranean field of dreams? But he laughed when she razzed him about it in the morning, and that was the Dirk she trusted, the sweet-natured goof who could sing the "Star-Spangled Banner" in note-perfect burps and had a thing for tonguing the backs of her ears. You had to be a little crazy for the Green Berets, hardcore warriors who could kill with their hands 37 different ways.

"Ahhhh." He grinned as he stepped inside the trailer, checking eight months of combat duty at the door. Melissa went up on her toes to smack his cheek.

"How about a shot?"

She'd already set out their supplies on the coffee table, the salt and limes, shot glasses, a bottle of tequila. The jet fuel of passion.

"Well," he laughed, blushing like a prom date, "what I've really been craving is a beer. But let me hit the head first . . ."

They went in opposite directions, he to the bathroom and she to the kitchen. The trailer funneled sound so efficiently that they could talk to each other from opposite ends.

"Everything looks great!" he called from the bathroom.

"It ought to." She opened the beers and quartered a lime while a platter of nachos spat in the microwave. "I've had nothing to do but clean house for eight months."

"Hot water!" he shouted down the hall. "Clean towels! Oh dear sweet Jesus, Dial soap! It's like I've been gone about six years."

"Tell me about it," Melissa said through clenched teeth. She stuck a lime wedge in the top of each beer. "We've got some catching up to do."

Back in the den, sitting thigh to thigh on the sofa, she let him eat a few nachos and take a couple of hits of beer before she swung herself over and straddled his lap, her skirt riding artfully high on her hips.

"So how does it feel to be home?" she asked, her face six inches from his.

"It feels pretty good."

She rocked back and had a good look at him. His skin was a coppery reddish-brown, and he was leaner, his few soft edges burned away. She'd met him three years ago in the law office where she worked; Dirk had brought in a buddy who'd snagged a DUI, and while the friend met with counsel behind closed doors Dirk sat in reception and chatted up Melissa. He talked in the slow, careful manner of a man chewing cactus—it turned out he was from Valdosta, even farther south—a buff body with soulful, syrup-brown eyes and little knots of muscle at the hinges of his jaw, but it was his smile that made her anxious in an intensely pleasurable way, the coyote guile of it, his cockiness like a knock-out drug. Straddling him now, rubbing his cropped hair and searching his face, she decided he looked mostly the same—a little dazed, maybe, and definitely older, his eyes newly creased with crow's feet. Maybe Haiti aged you in dog years? He was only 28.

"You've lost weight," she said, kneading his chest and ribs. He felt as hard as an I beam. "We're gonna have to fatten you up."

"I'm looking forward to that."

She went to work on the buttons of his uniform blouse, flicking them loose with a picklock's sure touch. Her bottom settled deeper into his lap; she could feel the loaf rising to meet her there, his maximum expression straining at his pants—it took only that much pressure to make her groan. Her mind was going slack, starting to empty out, awareness liquefying to pure sensation.

Dirk gently took her wrists and pulled her away.

"Lissa, stop. We got to talk, babe."

"Talking's for wimps," she murmured, her voice slurred as a drunk's. She came at him again.

"No, listen, I'm serious," he said, and this time he firmly slid her off of him. Her ears were hissing like a lit fuse, and she felt giddy, dizzy with passion and guilt. How did he know? He couldn't know. So how did he know—

"We can't do this tonight," he told her. One of his arms held her shoulders, sympathetic yet sterile, exuding a brotherly tenderness that scared the daylights out of her. "Tomorrow's fine, we can do it all day tomorrow and frankly there's nothing I'd rather do. But tonight I can't." He paused. "I can't make love on Saturdays."

Her lungs collapsed—there was no air, nothing inside to form a response. She found a reserve at the very tip of her mouth. "What are you saying?"

"What I'm saying is—look, it's sort of complicated. But there's one thing I wanna make clear right now, I'm still your husband who loves you more than anything."

Now she was terrified; he'd never talked this way before.

"Something happened down there," he told her, "something wonderful, in a way. And you don't have to be scared, I promise you that. Just be patient, this is going to take awhile to explain. Just trust me and everything'll be okay."

"Dirk," she wailed, "what is going *on?*"

She didn't follow any of it at first, the bizarre story he unloaded on her about poison powders and a voodoo priest and his initiation into voodoo society, then some garbled business about a ceremony, and someone named Erzulie. A person, or maybe not quite a person—a spirit? Who Dirk had married somehow? Melissa thought she might throw up.

"You're telling me you got married?"

"Well, yeah. To a god. It's not all that uncommon down there."

Melissa couldn't process the part about the god. "But you're married to *me.*"

"And that hasn't changed at all." He squeezed her hand. "I know this is a lot to be laying on you, but trust me, it's okay. We're still married, I still love you, I'm still the same Dirk."

She looked at him: He was, in fact, the same, so much so that it broke her heart.

"If nothing's changed then why can't we have sex?"

"Well, that's only on Tuesdays and Saturdays. Those are the nights I have to devote to her."

"*Devote* to her?"

"Be with her. Sleep with her."

"What do you mean, sleep with her. You mean *sleep* with her?"

"In a way. It's kind of hard to explain."

She felt as if some part of her brain had been carved out, the lobe of reason, logic, reality-based thought. All the normal tools of argument deserted her, and so she sat mostly silent for the next two hours while Dirk described his journey into Haitian voodoo, which began as part of the mission, a standard hearts-and-minds tactic of the Special Forces—contact and co-opt the local power structure. In Haiti this meant befriending the village voodoo priest, who turned out to be one Moïse Dieuseul in the remote coastal town where the team was based. Dirk's near-coherent French made him the team's point man for local liaison, and from their very first meeting Moïse showed a special affinity for the young American.

"He called me his son," Dirk told her, "he said that God had brought us together. At first I thought he was just juicing me, right? The guy's a survivor, he figured to get on the winning side. But all this weird stuff kept happening between me and him, and after a while I'm like, okay, maybe I need to think about this."

What kind of weird stuff.

Dreams, coincidences, uncanny divinations. Then Moïse proved his ultimate good faith by alerting Dirk to a plot by the local Macoutes to poison the entire Special Forces team, and after that Dirk was staying for all-night sessions, going deeper and deeper into the voodoo. Which led to initiation, revelation, the mystic marriage; the stories were blurring into a hopeless purée when Melissa looked at the clock and saw that it was 5 a.m.

"Are we talking about a real woman here?"

"This is Erzulie, Lissa, a god. A *lwa.* The voodoo goddess of love."

"But you said there was a woman in a wedding dress."

"Well, yeah, she came down and possessed a woman from the temple, that's how it works in voodoo. She used this woman's body for the ceremony."

Melissa shivered, forged ahead. "So after. After you got, married. Was there, like, sex?"

"Well, no. Yes and no. It's really hard to explain." He paused. "It's more of a spiritual thing."

Melissa sputtered, rolled her eyes—was he giving her the world's lamest line? "Dirk, dammit, for eight months I've been climbing the walls like a good Army wife and now you're telling me, you, you're telling me, uh . . ." She found herself backing up. "Did you have sex with another woman down there? I mean a live human being, an actual person. Or anything else. Or *whatever*."

"Why no, baby, it's not like that." He cupped her face in his hands, turned her toward him; she searched his eyes and found them clear amber-colored wells, her own pocket-sized reflection peering back from the bottom.

"No way," he said softly, "you're the only one. You're the only woman on earth for me."

Dawn broke, filling the windows with pale, milky light; outside the birds began singing like hundreds of small bells, their notes scattered as indiscriminately as seed. Once the sun rose Dirk was released from his promise, and in the early morning they did make love, though it wasn't the dirty movie that Melissa had been scripting in her head for months. It was, instead, as gentle as a stream washing over them, with Melissa quietly crying as Dirk poured himself out behind a sweet, knowing, mysterious smile.

It had started in dreams. Luscious, full-bodied dreams in which two beautiful women, one white and one black, were making love to him—Dirk put it down to the sexual deprivation of the field, combined with the *Penthouse*-fueled fantasies of any All-American boy. Then the team was tasked to nation-build in Bainet, and Dirk started making the rounds of the surviving power elite, the neurotic mayor, the budding Hitler of a *député*, the effeminate Catholic priest, and finally M'sieur Dieuseul, the locally renowned voodoo man. Moïse received the young sergeant like this was Schwarzkopf himself, inviting him into the shade of his thatched-roof temple where they discussed *la situation* over coffee, the stew of international politics and underground intrigue that seemed more intractable with each passing day. This was grunt-level diplomacy, basic hearts and minds; Dirk was already starting to cut his French with earthy Creole slang, and while they talked he eyed the voodoo gods painted on the walls, the horned, fish-tailed, vaguely humanoid *lwa* like creatures out of Dr. Seuss on drugs, then the snakes twined around the temple's central pole like strands of neon-laced DNA. Voodoo had already become a running joke with the team, *voodoo voodoo voodoo* their simmering code for everything that was weird and wonderful in this brave new world. Then out of the blue Moïse smiled, gave Dirk's knee a friendly pat, and said:

"Maîtresse Erzulie likes you."

And he proceeded to describe the tag team that was so vividly running amuck through Dirk's dreams—the black beauty was Erzulie Dantor, the white, Erzulie Freda, twin incarnations of the goddess of love. A week later, doing recon in the hills, Dirk and the team stopped in a village where an old woman announced that she could see the Erzulies floating around Dirk. This woman—she was a few spoons short of a full set? A wired smurf of a granny with notched earlobes and crazy African stuff draped around her neck, amulets, stoppered bottles, burlap sachets, and her mouth spraying Creole in an aerosol stream, shouting how *good* this was for Dirk, *two Erzulies*! Meaning his head was well-balanced, his person much favored. The news burned through the market in a flash fire of laughs, *blan sa-a se moun voodoo li ye!* The white guy's a voodoo man!

"So what are they like?" Melissa asked. "These dreams."

"Sometimes they're pretty hot. We're talking wet dreams here."

"*Dirk*, gross."

"Hey, it is what it is, baby, balls-to-the-wall sex. The kind with all that burning truth in it, like you and me got."

"Yeah, right. Nice try."

"Weren't we telling the truth last night?" Cocky as the day she met him, which wasn't to say he hadn't come back a changed man, a more thoughtful, thankful man with a newfound gift for patience, a slackening of the male impulse to domineer. From the first she'd always been the one who tried harder, who sacrificed her pride to his moods and whims and relieved herself with tearful rages in the bathroom, but eight months of living with the wretched of the earth had returned to her a kinder, gentler Dirk who appreciated the good love he had at home. But those dreams worried her, the sense of forces, vectors of conscience and control that she couldn't see and didn't understand. So can they read your thoughts? she wondered. Can they get inside your head?

"Anyway," Dirk added, "she'll probably start showing up in your dreams, too."

Melissa bristled. "I don't *think* so."

"Maybe not, but that's how it usually works. We're all connected now."

And James, was he connected, too? He called her at work every few days, "just checking in," he'd say, "just watching out for my girl." "You're a special little lady," he told her, "I want us always to be friends."

"Sure, James, we can be friends."

"Now you tell me if he's not treating you right. I know how tough it can be at home when a soldier comes off his tour, and if there's anything, well, I just want you to know I'm here for you."

"I appreciate that. But my husband's treating me just fine, thanks."

"Now if you ever need to talk, we could meet for lunch or a drink sometime . . ."

Wasn't going off to war supposed to screw them up? And yet she was the one brooding and holding it in, not faking, exactly, but struggling to maintain, putting a happy face on the pressure cooker inside. In their spare bedroom Dirk devised an altar out of an old mahogany cabinet, "so you can shut it when company comes," he explained, "I don't want you to be embarrassed." Inside he stuffed all manner of junk, a miniature yard sale tumbling over the shelves: trinkets, perfumes, a silver comb and brush set, candy, mini-bottles of champagne and liqueur, a plaster statue of the Virgin Mary. He taped cheap-looking prints of the Virgin inside the cupboard doors, two different Virgins, one black with scars on her cheek, the other white, with a jewel-encrusted sword through her heart. At sundown on Tuesdays and Saturdays he lit candles on the altar, sparked up some incense, and played voodoo drum cassettes on the boombox in there, the rambunctious afrobeat burbling through the walls like the world's biggest migraine headache. They'd watch TV curled together on the couch, but when Leno or Letterman started to drag Dirk would kiss her on the cheek, sweetly tell her goodnight, and go padding down the hall to the spare bedroom.

So sign me up for *Oprah*, Melissa thought, the other woman in my life is a voodoo god. The sense of a third presence grew on her like guilt, like it was the haunting of every bad thing she'd ever done. Voodoo, living right here in her house: she was enough of a lapsed Baptist to know what *they* would say. *Cast OFF that demon! Satan get THEE behind! Sur-REN-der is the key that unlocks sal-VA-shun!* Here in the buckle of the Bible Belt religious messages were available in all styles, from sugar-lipped warbling to hillbilly gibbering to the sonic stampede of call-and-response.

The susceptible could easily find themselves bombarded by signals, and Melissa was, now, for the first time in her life, though actual religion still seemed strange to her. God was out there somewhere, she believed, and beyond that everything else was up for grabs, but as Dirk told his stories those first few weeks she began to understand a little of it, how a shock to the system might trigger a bizarre religious kick. Though really, was there any other kind? *In your face* was how he summed up Haiti for her, a place where everything happened altogether all at once: food, sweat, shit, grace, god, sex, and death, the raw and the cooked of life coming at you without any of the modern veneers.

"One day we set up a checkpoint out on the highway," he told her, "we were spot-checking all the SUVs for weapons. Then this big flatbed truck comes humping along, and there in the back, piled up in this huge mound are all these cow heads, hundreds and hundreds of bloody cow heads. So after it passes we're all laughing and yelling at each other like, Hey, did you see that? Can you believe that shit? 'Cause once it was gone you weren't sure you'd really seen it."

She got it, sort of, how fluid and free your mind might become when life took on the quality of hallucination. How that might blow your coping strategies all to hell. Dirk meditated daily in the middle of the den, which Melissa took for a joke at first—Green Berets, *snake-eaters*, did not meditate, nor did anyone else she know except people from Chapel Hill. "Keeping it real" was how he explained himself; meanwhile Melissa took wary note of her dreams and watched her life fill up with nagging signs and portents. *Forbidden Fruit Creates Jams* read the message of the week on Calvary Baptist's streetside sign, which Melissa passed each day going to and from work. A few miles farther on First Methodist inquired *Eternity—Smoking or Non-Smoking?* Pondering Satan, carrying on with her nominally normal life, she didn't feel so much fear as a kind of fraught spaciness, maybe fear spread thin. Then one Tuesday evening she and Dirk were cuddled on the couch, watching a *M*A*S*H* rerun while voodoo-trance music submarined through the walls. It began as a joke, a tease, Melissa's hand crabwalking up her husband's thigh, sneaking higher and higher until it reached his lap. Dirk smiled without turning from the TV and gently set her hand aside.

Thirty seconds later she was at it again.

"Melissa."

"What?" she cooed, all floozy innocence.

"You know I can't mess around tonight."

"I'm not doing anything," she blandly protested, but she giggled and found him hard when she squeezed again.

"Melissa!" The alarm in his voice hooked something fierce in her. He was helpless, she could fuck him anytime she wanted.

"Melissa, give me a break."

"I'm not doing anything!"

"Yes, you are. And I'm asking you to stop it, please."

She jumped him with a vengeance then, scooching up on her knees and grabbing his belt, hanging on as he backpedaled down the couch. They were laughing as she pinned him against the cushions, both of them gasping in strained little bursts.

"Whoa, Lissa."

"Gimme somma that!" She'd freed enough of his belt to wank it around like a lasso.

"Melissa, stop. We can't do this."

"Give it up!" she shouted.

"Come on Melissa, stop." His voice was soupy underneath, losing tensile strength; what man didn't dream of being ravished this way? She had his pants open and was starting her dive when he shuddered and grabbed her hands, pulled her up short.

"Melissa," he said steadily, without cruelty, "enough."

"You aren't sleeping in there tonight." Her voice surprised her, the harpy venom in it—could she take it back?

"But I have to sleep in there."

"Bullshit!" When she pushed she could feel the strength in his hands, how he could snap her wrists like cheesesticks if he chose.

"I made a promise—"

"Uh, hello? I seem to recall you making a few promises to me."

"I did. And I'm not forgetting that."

"Well it sure looks like it to me."

There followed the worst argument of their married lives—the worst, anyway, for Melissa, who couldn't provoke a decent angry word from him. It was like trying to punch out a roomful of shadows, her frustration climaxing with a placid kiss from Dirk and the announcement that he was going to bed.

"You aren't sleeping in there with her!" she rowled at his back. "You aren't!" she cried as he turned the corner. "Dammit, Dirk!" One final shout before futility overtook her, the realization of how dumb, how utterly clueless you were to think you might control anything about your life. She went to the kitchen and banged pots and pans for a while, then took herself to bed in a wicked funk. After cutting off the lights she masturbated, scraping herself into a shallow, passionless clench which as an act of revenge was a total failure. Then she lay there dry-eyed and completely still, wondering if she could live with this.

Five years ago, at the end of her job interview, Mr. Bryan sat her down in his corner office and gave Melissa what she described forever after as "the talk." "This is a pretty lousy business," said her future boss, a short, cheerfully caustic man with Gucci pouches under his olive eyes and a Little Richard cloud of jet-black hair. "We get rapists, murderers, drug dealers, child-molesters, just about every bad deal you can think of walks through that door, and it's our job, it is our *sworn constitutional duty*, to work like hell to get these scumbags off. So. Think you can handle that?"

Melissa was not quite 19. She was living away from home for the first time and would have dug ditches not to go back. "Yes sir," she said, "I think I can handle it."

Fayetteville might not be the big city, but it offered all the excitement a small-town girl could reasonably want. In her first several years on the job she was flashed at her desk, had a knife pulled on her, watched a gang fight erupt in the reception area, and called social services on a hooker client who slapped her toddler three times in as many minutes. As an education she couldn't have asked for more, and the strenuous sleeping around she did those first few years, that was part of the education, maybe the main part. At the time she'd felt the truest way to live was by tunneling down to the wildness at your core, though she regularly shocked herself with what she found there. Did other women feel this way? she wondered. She suspected that she had unspeakable things inside her, a black hole of lust that might suck her past the point of no return, and she took her share of hits, pushing the limits of that—plenty of men were more than happy to abuse her sexual nature. Luckily Dirk had come along just as she'd found herself at the cusp of a premature cynicism.

"So whadda we got?" Mr. Bryan asked this morning, puffy-eyed, tie dangling loose around his neck.

"You've got your sanity hearing at ten, the guy who shot his ex's dog," she called through the door to his office. "Then you're due in Judge Hershoff's at eleven-thirty, that's your motion to suppress James Fenner's kilo. Okay, phone calls." She switched to a different pad. "You know Miss Blinn, our stripper? She called and said a hose in her car broke, she'll bring the cash over as soon as she can but it's not going to be today. Artis McClellan's mother called, she said his ankle monitor's giving him infections again. Then Roland Nash, he told me to tell you that D'Shawn Weems is a lying sack of you-know-what, and if he tells the cops what he's been telling you he's going to beat D'Shawn up and stick his head down a commode."

A sigh like dust drifted through her boss's door.

For the next two hours Melissa answered the phone, typed letters and motions, juggled the walk-ins, and tracked down shifty witnesses. If she didn't singlehandedly run the criminal justice system she kept her end of it from clogging up altogether, this in spite of feeling slightly homicidal this morning. Her emotions were skidding around on a sheet of ice, a big jacknifed trailerful of ire and angst careening through the traffic of a normal day. Dirk had still been asleep when she'd left for work, so their argument was technically still in play; *time out!* she said to herself when James called, feeling something like relief. They made small talk for a while. He called her "angel." His voice was smooth and sweet as hot buttered rum.

"What say you and me grab some lunch today, how 'bout it?"

She hesitated.

"It's just lunch, babe, come on. I want to take you someplace special."

Melissa sighed. Mainly it made her sad, what he was offering.

"I don't think I can."

"Don't think you can!" he cried, still cheerful, still glib, but she could feel his anger rising. "You have to *eat*, don't you?"

"Yes, but James . . ." She lowered her voice. "I just don't think I should see you anymore."

"Melissa."

She swallowed.

"We need to talk. That's why I'm asking you out to lunch, we need to talk about that night. Outside the bar, when we—"

"I know what we did."

"These aren't casual feelings I have for you. I think we had something special going on."

"Oh James. What we had was a makeout session in a parking lot."

"You know it was more than that. You know where it was heading, if the car alarm hadn't gone off we'd of—"

"Well it did. That's life. And my husband's back and I'm in a different place now."

He sucked in a breath. "All right. All right. But you know, I heard about you. I know some people you used to party with, they told me what a little wild-ass you were—"

Her eyes burned. *Dammitdammitdammit . . .*

"—you may be acting the good little wife now but I know what you are, *whore*, you cocksucking little cunt—"

She slammed down the phone and kicked back from her desk. She would not cry, would not cry, but with this macho bastard stalking her and two sex-crazed goddesses swarming around her husband, maybe she was entitled—or maybe she was simply getting what she deserved, an evil she'd brought down on Dirk and her both. Some dark, avid thing spilling out of herself. *Lay DOWN that sin!* the radio had howled this morning. *Warning*, the sign at Calvary Baptist read today, *Exposure to the Son May Prevent Burning*. Twenty thousand American soldiers had invaded Haiti, and this creature, this succubus, had singled out Dirk as the chosen one. Melissa knew there was someone she could call for help, someone she'd been aware of all along, but this was family, which usually made everything worse. She managed to stall for most of the rest of the morning, then finally plunked the phone book down on her desk. Dialing the number she considered the pause-giving fact that PSYCHICS was right next to PSYCHOLOGISTS in the Yellow Pages.

"Hello?" Her cousin Rhee picked up on the first ring. Melissa launched into an explanation of who she was, Margaret Poole's youngest daughter and thus Rhee's second cousin once removed—

"I know who you are," Rhee interrupted, laughing—she couldn't have been less fazed if they talked twice a day.

Melissa asked if they might meet. To discuss a small, uh, personal matter—

"How about for lunch?" Rhee suggested.

"You mean today?"

"Sure, why not?"

Melissa resisted the thought that Rhee had been expecting her call. They made plans, then Melissa asked how she would know Rhee at the restaurant. She hadn't seen her older cousin in years, and had a fuzzy recollection at best.

"Oh," Rhee laughed, "don't worry about that. I'm pretty sure you'll recognize me."

Her hair was, how to put this? If not orange, then orange-like, sort of a bonfire color. Melissa's cousin turned out to be a short, sturdy woman in her early fifties, with a doughy though pleasant face, smooth, rosy cheeks, and Wedgewood-blue eyes that were happy, direct, and shrewd. They met at the India Palace restaurant near Bragg— Rhee's suggestion, Melissa had never had Indian food but the duskiness of the place seemed suitably exotic. The twangy sitar music on the sound system reminded her of cats in heat.

"Oh *honey*," Rhee exclaimed, clamping Melissa in an eye-popping hug, "I am *so glad* to see you. And just look at you! My God what a gorgeous woman you've grown into!" Hearing her cousin's weirdly familiar mile-a-minute voice Melissa at once felt the undertow of family relations. She dearly loved her family, but after a couple of hours in Lumberton she always felt herself smothering under the ties that bind, all that tightly wound energy compacting on itself like a rubber band ball.

As she followed Rhee through the buffet line Melissa considered her cousin's history, how she'd led a life of exemplary conformity until a falling kitchen light fixture knocked her cold. After that she began acting odd, the oddness consisting, so far as Melissa had gathered, of exercising, backtalking her husband, and learning to play the drums, as well as casually mentioning to family members that she could now channel signals from the other side. Eventually she left her husband and moved to Fayetteville, where to the horror of her kin she set up shop as a psychic. One of the more successful, by all accounts: word drifted back that she was much in demand among private detectives and desperate families, and that her services were not unknown to various law enforcement agencies.

Out of nervousness Melissa loaded her plate, while Rhee took only flat bread and rice. In line they talked about their hometown kin; Melissa felt herself reverting to the mumbly torpor that family always seemed to inspire, but after they'd settled themselves in a booth and unrolled their flatware, Rhee said:

"So you got out. Congratulations."

Melissa sat up; it was like a needle in the spine.

"And you did it while you're young," Rhee went on cheerfully, "see how smart you are? Whereas it took me forty years and a whack on the head to realize Lumberton was going to be the death of me. Genius is wisdom and youth, you know who said that? Me neither but I'm sure no genius, I blew half my life doing what everybody expected me to. We have to live our own lives and that's what you're doing, I'm just so proud of you! Now tell me about yourself."

Melissa gave the expanded resumé version—home, marriage, work—while Rhee ate her rice and bread in dainty garden-club bites, a style imprint from her previous life. Melissa heard herself describing Dirk as "a wonderful guy"; children were covered by alluding to the thinking-about-it stage. She was conscious of Rhee listening with a level of attention that was gratifying, and at the same time unnerving. She seemed to absorb everything, but behind that sunny, dumpling-textured face you had no idea what the woman was thinking.

"It sounds like you've done just wonderfully for yourself," Rhee observed when Melissa ran out of things to say.

"I've been lucky."

"Yes, lucky." Rhee's smile was wry, and a little distant, as if an old boyfriend's name had come up. "And I trust you're *happy*, Melissa. Because that's what I want for you."

"Well," Melissa gave a weak laugh, "mostly?" Rhee sat there pleasantly, patiently, like a sales clerk waiting for money; after several moments Melissa realized that her cousin wasn't going to break the silence, so there was nothing left to do but spill it.

"You know," the older woman remarked after Melissa had told her about Erzulie and Dirk, "it never ceases to amaze me."

"It doesn't?"

"And yet it happens all the time, this strange and wonderful way of the world which brings a thing and its polar opposite together. Think about it, Melissa—your husband, a white man, a *southern* white man and a warrior from the most powerful nation on earth, gets connected with a *black* woman spirit from *Haiti*. The goddess of *love*, opposite of *war*. And this isn't just any old fling, they get *married*. Now what could be heavier than that?" Rhee's eyes fired a startling salvo of tears; as if overwhelmed or suddenly drowsy she slumped into the booth's high back, her features flattening into a moon-like mask that Melissa found oddly compelling. After a moment Rhee surfaced with a shake of the head.

"Okay. So how do you feel about this?"

"Well, I think it's starting to make me crazy."

Rhee nodded as if this was the sanest response imaginable. "How's Dirk been treating you since he got back?"

Melissa gazed across the restaurant, suddenly miserable. "It's never been better," she said, clearing a sob from her throat.

"But you're resisting."

"I guess I am."

"Why are you resisting?"

There was a precision to Rhee's voice, a tone of vigorous self-respect, that obliged Melissa to focus her thoughts. To decide what was real in her life, perhaps. "Well, there was a guy. While Dirk was gone." She told her cousin about James.

"So do you care for him, this man?"

"Not anymore. Probably not ever, really."

"But you were attracted to him. Sexually."

"Well, yeah. I guess I was."

"Do you think that's strange?"

"I think it's wrong."

"Did you think you were going to go your whole married life without wanting to sleep with someone else?"

"I don't know. I guess I never really thought about it."

Rhee studied her. "Have you told Dirk?"

"No, no, God no, never." Melissa paused. "Do you think I should?"

Rhee shrugged. "Dirk's not having an earthly affair, you know that. Not in the sense he's stepping out with another woman."

"No."

"And it doesn't sound like he's trying to hide anything."

"God no. He wants me to know everything. It's just . . ." She concentrated. "It scares me," she went on, wondering if fear was what it took to make something real. "I don't know what I'm dealing with, what he's brought into the house—whether he's messing around with something evil, satanic. Does that make any sense?"

Rhee's face took on a neutral thoughtfulness, every feature except her smile, which revealed nothing. "Well, based on what you've told me, this Erzulie sounds like a lot of different things. Kind of a slut, a sexpot who's also a saint and virgin mother, sort of a gorgeous guardian angel—Lord, no wonder he's got a thing for her. But is she evil?" Rhee seemed to double back on herself. "I might need a couple of days to think about this. In the meantime"—she'd caught Melissa's panicked look"—I want you to take it slow. Be nice to Dirk, let him be nice to you. I bet he's dealing with a lot, coming home from a place like that. Try to see it his way as much as you can."

"All right. But what about James?"

"What about him?"

"What if he keeps coming after me?"

"Oh Melissa, that's easy. Just call the cops."

Was there a homegrown voodoo right under her nose, a french-fried North Carolina version she'd been missing all this time? It seemed possible as she made her daily commute, staring out from her car past the orderly fields toward the brooding wall of trees in the distance, that deckle-edged veil of luminous green standing in for the less penetrable jungles of the mind. There was voodoo in Haiti, why not here? With a little prodding Dirk described the ceremonies for her, which sounded chaotic but happy, like swimming in a heavy surf. Melissa tried to picture her very Caucasian spouse dancing in the midst of a couple of hundred Haitians.

"Didn't you feel funny, the only white guy in the middle of all that?"

"It felt good," he said. "I felt like I was home." So where was the evil in all this? Evil was the mini-killing field he and his buddies discovered behind the Haitian army barracks, the twenty corpses they dug up with their trenching tools. Evil was *La Normandie*, the Macoute social club in Port-au-Prince with its snapshots of murder victims taped to the wall. Evil was the hovering presence of death everywhere, the cemeteries with their scores of tiny children's graves. At night, lying in bed after love, Melissa held Dirk's hand and listened to the stories until he drifted off to target practice. *Pow-pow-pah-pow.* His leave had ended a week ago and he was putting in eight-to-five at Bragg, ramping up for the next big thing. Colombia, Bosnia, the Middle East, or maybe Haiti Part II—the rumors mutated every couple of days. And when he left, what then—she dreaded that. At work she kept getting hangup calls, while on Saturday and again on Tuesday she accepted Dirk's goodnight kiss and sent him off to sleep with his goddess. How did normal people live? She tried to remember. Meanwhile she waited for Rhee's call as if waiting for the results of a medical test, which took more out of her than she realized—when Rhee phoned on Wednesday Melissa felt the independence she'd nurtured all these years collapse in a sorry heap. *Thank God for family.*

"I'm getting some funny vibes on this," Rhee told her. "And I was thinking it might help if I could spend a little time out at your place? I'd really like to have a look at that altar he's fixed up." They made arrangements for the following day: Rhee would meet Melissa at the office and they'd drive out to the trailer together, grabbing a bite to eat while they were there.

Just your basic lunch date, that was the tone of it. They hung up, and Melissa decided that she didn't feel crazy. It seemed, rather, that reality itself had gone mad, and she was riding her own small scrap of sanity through the cosmic whirlwind.

Thursday was hot and sluggish, the sky hazed over with a scum of cloud the color of congealed bacon grease. The air had a dense, malarial weight—there'd been a rare outbreak near Myrtle Beach, more evidence of global warming—and driving out to the trailer Melissa cranked the air conditioning so high that her spit curls jumped and spun like small tornadoes. They got on the subject of Rhee's boyfriend, a retired Delta Force sergeant who raised competition roses. "He sounds neat," Melissa said, tobacco rows flashing past like shuffled cards. "You guys serious?"

"We're seriously happy," Rhee said, "with the way things are. We've got each other and got our space and that's just fine. Neither one of us is interested in shacking up."

"I hear those Delta Force guys are pretty tough."

"Sure," Rhee answered in an offhand voice. She watched the low sandy hills roll past, the scrubby brakes of saw brier and slash pine. "Men are funny, though. I never met one yet who didn't need to be mothered at least a little bit. And I think people underestimate that side of sex, the maternal side of what goes on in bed. There's a wild thing and then there's a needing thing, but nobody ever talks about that needing thing. Makes us all feel too vulnerable, I guess."

"Sex is a swamp," Melissa said by way of agreement. She turned off the paved road onto the mashed-granola track that led to the trailer, the woods closing around them like a green fog. Poplar and pine shafted through the porous undercanopy, the arching sprays of dogwood and pin oak; Melissa believed there was something watchful about deep woods, a biding if not quite sentient presence, like a block of vacant houses. Through the tunnel of trees they could make out the clearing ahead, the light flooding the open space with a jewel-box glow. "How nice," Rhee exclaimed as they pulled into the clearing. The trailer was a long aluminum carton with flimsy black shutters, but Melissa had softened the package as best she could, with azaleas and flower beds planted along its length like piles of oversized throw pillows. Inside she showed her cousin to the spare bedroom, tensing as she opened the door. Today the altar seemed even gaudier than usual, as resistant to reason as a blaring jukebox. Rhee approached it with her hands clasped in front of her. Melissa lingered by the door, wondering what she was supposed to do.

"I guess you want to be alone?"

"Doesn't matter!" Rhee answered briskly.

But Melissa felt an urgent need to be useful. She left, quietly shutting the door behind her, and went to the kitchen to fix lunch, where she reflected on the therapeutic value of staying busy. Which might explain, it occurred to her as she spooned out chicken salad, why the women in her family were such dazzling cooks? A few minutes later she was setting the table and heard a thump down the hall, a muffled fumbling as if a sack of potatoes had hit the floor.

"Rhee?"

In the den the fake-antique clock gave three iron ticks.

"Rhee, are you all right?"

Melissa walked down the hall and tapped at the door. "Rhee, is everything okay?" Melissa cracked open the door to find her cousin spreadeagled on the shag pile, eyes closed, mouth wide to the sky, a blissed-out stoner look on her face. Melissa was to her in a second, kneeling to check her pulse and set a palm to her forehead—her pulse was even, her breathing deep and steady as the tides. Whatever was happening, Melissa decided, was a psychic, as opposed to a medical, episode, and so she sat and eased Rhee's head onto her lap, wiping the ribbon of drool from her cousin's chin. There followed a prolonged series of non-moments, an enforced though not unpleasant lull like waiting in traffic for a train to pass—Melissa sat there stroking her cousin's hair and listening to the birds outside the window, the cicadas buzzing like tiny chain saws. A luxurious sense of calm stole over her, a suspension of anxieties both large and small; suddenly the strangeness of things didn't matter so much. After a while she lost all feeling of the floor, as if she were floating, enwombed in her own sphere of weightlessness, and then she realized that she was thinking of Dirk, her rambling and not-very-focused thoughts suffused with an aura of tenderness. She did love her husband, she felt sure of that; a revelation seemed to be building from this basic point, but then Rhee's eyes were fluttering open, startled at first, then locking onto Melissa from upside-down.

"Ahhh," she said, smiling through a long sigh. "Melissa."

"Be still."

"No, it's okay, I'm fine. I saw her, Lissa, she's beautiful, she's a beautiful black sister." Rhee was grunting, hoisting herself into a sitting position like a mechanic crawling out from under a car. "I saw the white one too but she was farther back, it was the sister front and center today. Whoa," she ran a hand through her hair, "that was *strong*."

"Are you all right?"

"Sure, just got to get my head back. I'd love some water by the way, and a couple of Motrin if you got it." She was rolling to her knees, determined to stand; Melissa helped her out to the kitchen, where she accepted a chair at the table. "One gorgeous sister," she was saying, "deep, deep black skin, and beautiful braided hair right down to her butt. A killer body, oh my goodness she was something."

"Uh-huh," Melissa said, moving from sink to cabinet.

"Techy," Rhee went on, "sort of a diva, a real queen-bee type. And *old*, she's been around from the beginning. One of the ancients."

"Right." Melissa was glad for this small task to do. "So did she, ah, talk?"

Rhee thought for a moment. "Actually, no! Nothing I remember. We just stared at each other for a while. Sometimes it's like that."

"But sometimes they do. Speak, I mean." Melissa placed the Motrin and water on the table and sat.

"Not really *speak*." Rhee's eyes widened as a pill went down. "It's more like sending. Direct thoughts going back and forth."

"Oh." Melissa watched the second pill disappear. She gathered her nerve; there was really no smooth way to say this. "Is she evil, do you think?"

"Oh heavens, Melissa, how should I know? She's a power that's come into your life, a force, a source, a cause, whatever you want to call it. Nature and then some, that's how I look at it." Rhee blew out her lips with a rubbery sound. "Beyond that you've got to work it out on your own. I can help you up to a point, but whether it's good or bad, that's pretty much up to you. You're the only person who can figure that out."

For some reason Melissa was more or less expecting this, a variation on the once-familiar *grow up* theme; apparently adulthood required you to be your own best psychic as well. They ate lunch, though Rhee was logy and barely picked at her food; on the drive back into town she fell asleep. Melissa nudged her awake as they pulled into the law firm's parking lot.

"Are you okay to drive?"

"I'm fine," Rhee said. She seemed a little out of it.

"Are you sure?"

"Yes, yes, no problem!"

"Well." Melissa watched her cousin hunt around for her purse. "Thank you. I don't know how to thank you enough."

"Oh Lissa, what little I did I was happy to do. We're family! And you and I are buddies, too, sort of the wild hairs of the clan. But believe me, they all show up at my door sooner or later."

Melissa giggled; she felt relief, along with a burning need to know. "*Who?*"

"Life is so much more interesting than people think." Rhee found her purse and heaved at the door. "You'd be amazed. Take care, Lissa."

Melissa arrived home that evening to find a message from Dirk on the answering machine—he would be late, a SOC briefing was going to keep him at the base. She changed clothes and went for a run, then started on supper while the sweat wicked off her skin, leaving a sheer, gummy residue like tree sap. The dusk was deep enough to see fireflies through the windows when she noticed the silence; usually she put on music and sang while she cooked, but tonight she'd forgotten, a lapse that brought on a fit of spooky self-consciousness. She stopped what she was doing and listened, staring out the window at the trees. After a minute she began to feel afraid, the fear grounded in a near-religious conviction that James was out there in the woods, watching her. Abruptly she turned and stepped across the kitchen to the door; after locking it she stood there with her head bowed, listening, her hand resting on the deadbolt latch. After a moment she turned the latch again, unlocking it.

So if you really thought he was out there, would you do that? Are you really so brave, she asked herself. She moved down the hall checking all the rooms, and on her way back, with no real purpose in mind, she stepped into the spare bedroom. There was just enough light for her to make out the altar, the ratty flea-market jumble strewn over the shelves, the cheap comic-book colors of the Virgin prints. She approached the altar and clasped her hands as Rhee had done; the two Madonnas stared back through the muddy light with the vapid self-regard of fashion models.

Melissa stood there for a while, waiting. She became aware of her breathing, the loom of her heart inside her chest. Various aches and itches asserted themselves. Eventually it seemed necessary to speak.

"I," she said, and flinched—the word went off like a gun in the tiny room. I, what—acknowledge you? But that seemed corny, false. She took a breath and tried again. "Maybe I can live with you," she said, wondering if she'd finally lost it, "but I want you to know Dirk is *mine*. I found him first, I married him, he's already taken. And if you think I'm going to give him up . . ."

She felt a tingle, a quilled prickling running up her spine—did that mean anything?

". . . well, you've got another thing coming."

A kind of spasm, a jolt of exasperation almost made her laugh. Was something happening? She felt punchy, loose in the head, and with that came a surge of sisterly affection for this *thing*, this Erzulie who'd turned the world inside-out. Melissa began to see the possible humor in this, and even the Madonnas seemed to take on a merry look, the joke expressed in a crinkling around their eyes, the shadows bundling at the corners of their lips. What, exactly, had she been fighting? She wanted to say some agency inside herself, and she stood there for a time absorbing it, feeling in a sure but as yet inexplicable way that she'd arrived at something. Clarity, perhaps. A sense of scales balancing out. She felt older, and saw how that might be a good thing. She carried the feeling with her back to the kitchen, wondering as she flipped on the stereo if any of this meant that her life had changed.

Five minutes later Dirk was blowing through the door, leading with his pelvis as he kissed her hello. He got a beer from the refrigerator and popped the top.

"Well, babe," he said, "it's Kuwait."

Melissa screamed.

"Hey, it's not so bad. They got about three million mines laying around from the war, we're gonna show their guys how to dig 'em out."

Mines. Melissa resisted the urge to tear at her hair. "When do you go?"

"Not for six weeks." He pulled her close, snaking his hand under the waist of her shorts. "Think you can stand me that long?"

Later that night Melissa had occasion to reflect that sex smelled a lot like tossed salad, one with radishes, fennel, and fresh grated carrot, and maybe a tablespoon of scallions thrown in. The idea came to her as she lay naked in bed, making a tent out of the sheet with her folded knees. Beside her Dirk was nodding in and out while they drowsily reviewed the events of the day. Melissa mentioned that she'd had lunch with her cousin the psychic.

"Psychic," he said in a drifty voice. "I know this lady?"

"You've never met her."

"Hunh. She do voodoo?"

"Well, it's more like she's got her own thing going."

"Wanna meet her," he said, seeming to fade out.

"Sure, we'll have her over before you leave." Melissa shifted, raising peckish sparks from the sheets. "So what's it supposed to be like over there? In Kuwait."

"Hot," he muttered. "Sand. Lotsa camel jocks running around."

"Any voodoo?"

He chuckled, then murmured something she didn't understand. Maybe a minute went by. Melissa listened to a hoot-owl lowing outside. Acres of crickets jangled in perfect time like thousands of synchronized maracas.

"Though in a way I guess it's all voodoo, hunh."

"Wha?"

She hesitated, taking the measure of how she felt; after a moment she decided it felt okay. "In a way it all comes down to voodoo, I said." She didn't really get it, she told him, but she could handle it. If this was something he thought was important to his life, she would trust him, she would try to understand. Because she wanted them—

"Oh honey I love you *so much*," he blurted, his voice too drastic, almost weepy. For a second she thought he was mocking her, until he went on in that same urgent voice: "Cap'll take it, yeah, Cap's got it under control. No go no show what a bull-shitter, intel says it's solid, bro. Roger that, lock and load. Ready to rock."

So he'd slept through her big concession speech. *Pow*, he hupped in her ear, *pah-pow-pow, pow*; target practice had commenced for the night, in semi-automatic mode. Melissa sighed and straightened her legs, the sheet collapsing about them like a giant flower. So in six weeks she would be alone again. The business with James was a shadow on her mind, like some strange dark smudge in an X-ray; she dreaded Dirk's leaving, but something in her was rising to it as well, anxious to see if she could manage better this time. For a while she thought about her little drama at the altar, trying to fix in her mind the true experience of it, the tingling immanence which in retrospect had about as much zip as static cling. She didn't know what to think about any of this. Voodoo, desire, oversexed spirits, dreams channeling information like a video stream—if these were real then the business of who we were transpired mostly in the air around us. You could drive yourself crazy with it, she supposed. Some did; and some found their peace in it? But at least there was this, she thought as she rolled toward Dirk, spooning herself into his concourse of knobs and hollows. This was real, whatever else life might bring—there were, finally, no words for this. Melissa kissed her husband's shoulder, closed her eyes, and waited for sleep.

MARGO LANAGAN

A Pig's Whisper

"A Pig's Whisper" was first published in Agog! Ripping Reads, *the fourth in* Agog! Press's series of original anthologies.

—E.D.

W hen is that man coming back?" said Clarice. "The friendly one?"

"Well, *I* don't know," said Henry. "He has made us miss our dinner and our biscuits-and-milk already. I hope we don't miss our supper as well."

"The sun is going." Clarice eyed the high branches.

"Then he will be along soon," said Henry firmly.

"I think we should go back out to the road, and meet him."

"But he said! Wait here, he said. Do not move from this spot."

"But what if he has forgotten us?"

The bush was vast around them, immense above them; its frail roof of leaves was a sky within a sky.

"After all those twists and turns he took us through," said Henry, "I am not even sure where the road *is*."

Henry woke in the night with Clarice on his arm, her face patched with moonlight above him. Bright with excitement too. "What is it, Henry? Up the hill there."

He had to lift his head, which was full of sleep-fog, and to which some leaves and litter had adhered behind. He had to prop himself on his elbows to see.

Firelight made a little golden cave or cavity, a little room, away up in the forest's darkness. Shapes moved about there purposefully. Men's shapes, they must be, for those were men's voices shouting, jolly and free the way they never were with ladies around. They were roasting meat on their fire; Henry's stomach whined at the smell.

"I thought I was dreaming," said Clarice happily. "I had a long dream where they were all singing and laughing up there. And the smells, Henry! Delicious smells! Maybe they will share with us! Or maybe they will have leftovers they don't need."

She was all for running straight up there and asking.

"But what if they are bad men?" said Henry. "What if they dislike children? I think we should creep up and spy on them first, and see if they look safe. Don't you?"

So that is what they did. The darkness made their movements all velvety, so that they could move no more noisily than clouds gliding. Frond and leaf tip stroked Henry's face as he passed; insects creaked and stopped; two fruit bats crossed the leafy sky, and one silent night bird.

The camp must have been farther away than it looked, for by the time they reached it, the three men there were laid out asleep very soundly.

Henry and Clarice peeped out from behind separate trees. A gray-haired gentle-man lay on his back in his trousers and shirt by the fire, his other clothes folded and stacked next to his head, a straw boater and a cane on top of the stack, two shiny black shoes beside it. He looked as if he would lie as neatly as that all night, his hands folded on his chest. The second man was all white shirtfront; he wore a tail coat that clearly would not meet across that vast belly, and his tiny head was almost sunk away into the shirt collar, with only his beaky nose poking out. The third was a working man, sprawled out with his bushy-whiskered, white-haired head on one crooked arm. He murmured between his snores, and frowned as if he were trying to remember something.

"What is that," whispered Clarice, "that he's holding?"

Henry tried to see it under the man's big hand. "Something in a pudding-bowl?"

"A pudding!" They both said it, in identical tones of longing, as a tendril of the pudding's scent tickled their noses, as sweet and cosy as a rainy Sunday in their fa-ther's house.

"A *whole* pudding, that they've not even eaten a *piece* of!" whispered Clarice. "*Jam* pudding!"

"No, plum," said Henry. "It's a good plum-duff."

"No, look; you can see the jam. Bubbling up there—"

She gasped: the pudding—it must have been from the weight of the man's hand—had moved in the bowl, turned so that a wetter part of it slid into view, a gleaming part, furrowed like a forehead. The jam or juice bubbled against it at the rim of the bowl, and a sound, half-sigh, half-snore, escaped.

Now the smell of caramelizing jam was strong among the trees, and Henry's stomach all but cried out loud. "We could wake them and ask for a piece," he said.

"Do you think?" Clarice put her hand to her mouth. "He looks a bit shouty, that man. I think I heard him shouting in my dream. And perhaps the others . . ." She looked doubtfully from the neat gentleman to the tail-coated one.

"Perhaps we could *take* it," murmured Henry.

"Oh, Henry!" He heard her think about it. "But it must be *hot*."

"Well, *he's* holding onto it without burning."

"But he would have harder hands than you. And the bowl, that would be the hottest part—oh!" She caught his arm and gripped it hard.

"What?"

Her eyes were enormous. "The pudding! It's—*looking* at us!"

The furrows had tilted in the bowl, and a large dark mark just like an eyebrow had risen, and below it in the juicier, jammier underside there was a whiteness—

"It must be a potato," said Henry.

—with a dark mark like the color on an eyeball—

"That'll be a, a raisin."

—which moved, and the dark pudding flesh closed and opened on it, exactly like an eyelid.

Clarice drew in a breath to scream. Henry was too unnerved to try to stop her.

But something else did. The trees opposite them twitched, and two men, clutch-ing each other in terror, stumbled and sneaked into the clearing.

Shakily Clarice let out her breath.

Both the men were short and solid, one pale with big ears and the other darker and more bearish. They were what Henry's father would have called "a very common sort," all bent and furtive, in cheap, tough clothing, none too clean. They fell and crept and crawled toward the beardy man.

"Rolling home across the foam!" he suddenly sang out, which put them back on their haunches a moment. But he tossed his head and went on sleeping, and on they came. When the dark one reached the beardy man, he put out paws that looked made of the coarsest leather, and snatched the pudding from under the sleeping hand, and the two thieves tumbled away out of the clearing.

"Calamity!" The beardy man sprang to his feet. Henry and Clarice shrank behind their trees. "Thievery and trickery! Awake!"

"My dear fellow—"

"What the blazes—"

"Them low puddin'-thieves have used the cover of darkness and the sleep of the innocent to approach unapprehended and make off with our Albert!"

"Which way did they go?" said the tail-coated gentleman. "After them!"

"Of all the low-lived, carrot-nosed poltroons!" The two of them ran away into the trees. The third gentleman donned his jacket, shoes and hat, stowed his bow tie in a pocket, retrieved his cane and started after them with the greatest dispatch.

The children were left with the fire. They came forward eagerly into its comforting dancing light.

"It smells wonderful," said Clarice, bending to pick up a stick for a poker.

"Yes, look!" said Henry. "They have left all this meat roasting in the—"

Quite suddenly he turned and pushed Clarice hard in the chest.

She staggered and stared at him. "What was that for!"

"Don't go near!" he said. "Don't touch them! Don't even look!"

She tried to see over his shoulder. He pawed at her eyes as he pushed her out of the clearing.

"Henry-y! Henry! All that good meat! When we're so hungry—"

"It is not good meat! It is not!" He tore the stick from her hand, threw it into the darkness and pulled her after him back down the hill, and through the fernbrake and deeper, down to the creek where the rocks and the tree ferns hid the light of the fire. There he crouched, and shivered so hard that his teeth rattled.

Clarice watched him, afraid to speak, and angry. Her stomach growled.

Henry looked up. So did she. The smoke floated moonlit through the treetops. "Oh-h-h-h," said Henry.

"What did you see?" she whispered.

"I can still smell it." He leaped up and seized her and pressed his face to her head. "It is in your hair! You will have to wash! It is in your clothes!" He pushed her again, so that one foot and the hem of her skirt went into the creek.

She gasped at the cold. Rage gave her courage, though, and she ran at him like a little bull. "Don't you push me, Henry Clarkson!" She butted him in the belly. "What do you mean, wetting me in the middle of the night!"

She stood over him, stiff with anger. He lay like a grub, curled up on the creek bank, and put his face in his hands and sobbed.

"What is it, what is it?" She knelt by him, crying too, for if Henry wept matters must be truly terrible.

It was not long before he stopped, stupefied with crying. She sat with her hand on his side, patting now and then, wiping with the hem of her skirt at her own tears, which wormed out more slowly and miserably than Henry's had.

"I just want to sleep," he said dully.

She unfolded herself from sitting and lay on the wiry grass and the sand behind him, her arm over his waist and her damp cheek pressed into the curve of his neck. He did not complain, though she had never lain so close to him before. She listened to his breathing with her ears and chest and arms; she felt his heart right there next to her own; she closed her eyes tightly against the sight of the sky, all stars and branches and drifting smoke, and before long she slept.

It was a strange, wild feeling, waking in the bush. All the things that should have been separated from them by walls and windows—the cool, scented air, the clap and whoop of wings as birds poured caroling through the treetops, the rushing of the stream—all these things were doubly fresh, doubly loud.

They lay looking up through the curved combs of the tree-fern fronds.

"Do you think he will remember us this morning?" said Clarice.

"As soon as he wakes up," said Henry. "He will say, 'Oh, my gracious, those two wee bairns!'" And he slapped his forehead as the man would, to make Clarice laugh.

They got up and drank from the stream, and watched it for a while, because it seemed so cheerful and busy about itself.

"I suppose we should wait where he said," said Henry. "If he goes there, we might not hear him from here. He might think we have wandered off and lost ourselves."

"He would call, wouldn't he? We would hear his calling?" But Clarice followed Henry up the slope. He was in a mood now; they were both too hungry for play or laughter.

After they had sat in the fernbrake long enough to doze and wake again, she ventured to say, "Henry? That fire . . ."

"No." He hunched away as if she had smacked him.

"But maybe there is meat—"

"I said *no*!"

"Still good, though, in the coals—"

"It is *not meat*!" He was on all fours, barking into her face, barely an inch away. "It is *not meat*! It is *not for eating*!"

She crumpled like a sheet of paper thrown on a fire. "All *right*!" She put her fists to her eyes and fell to the ferns. "There is no reason to shout!"

"There is *every* reason to shout! There is *every* reason!"

"You're mad, Henry," she sobbed. "You've gone mad."

They waited in the fernbrake, taking it in turns to visit the creek and fill their bellies with water.

Night and day they waited. The man did not come; he was not going to come; he was not going to remember them.

On the day they realized this, Henry said, "Well, perhaps that meat, then." His face was very thin, but his eyelids seemed huge and heavy.

"It will all be spoiled now, in the sun," said Clarice eventually.

But the thought of roasting meat was too wonderful. It dragged them up the tangled steep nightmare of the hill, on their rubbery legs. Giant ants stood in their path and waved red pincers at them. Yellow stuff seeped from ulcers in the tree trunks they leaned against to rest, and stuck to their filthy clothing, and tried to stop them moving on.

The clearing when they reached it was full of a lively, malignant hum. Clarice, crawling now across the mat of curved gum leaves and sharp sticks, smelled the smell first, and sat back and covered her mouth and nose with her hands. Henry lowered his head and stuck out his jaw. Breathing gaspingly through his mouth, he stepped into the clearing toward the dead fire.

A black cloud sprang from the objects there. Any number of them could be charred logs, fanned twigs, wood misshapen by chopping and burning. But the big round stones that lay tipped and gaping, their teeth gleaming in the sunlight, there was nothing else those could be.

"Oh!" said Clarice. "Come away, Henry!"

Even as she turned from the clearing, she saw the heap beyond him, beyond the dead fire. She crawled away fast, but she had seen it. The flies had lifted from it and she had seen all the colors. It was a pile of burst mattresses, black mattresses, with their innards forcing out through the skin, purple and yellow and green.

She fell forward onto her shoulder and head. Grit jumped into her eye. She had not thought black people could grow so *fat*; all the ones she had seen were slender, strands of stringy bark shadow that stepped out of the bush, and looked at her, and turned back into shadow again. How ugly they were, swollen up so, all split and thrusting out of themselves!

She upped and crawled again. She tried to blink away the grit. The eye was unbearable open, unbearable closed; tears spouted up in it. She crawled and kept crawling even as she slid on the leaves; crawled along in the air, it felt, scrabbling for the ground, the whole world gone slippery and sharp and half-blind. And Henry was gone too; Henry would forever stand in that clearing, facing away from her, the air around him swooping and swaying, thick with flies.

They stayed at the creekside after that; they knew now that the man would not fetch them, and they hadn't the strength to go back and forth from the fernbrake any more. And the creek was farther from the clearing than the brake was, too, which they were glad of.

There they died, Clarice first, in the night, and Henry two days later, toward evening.

Two foster-brothers came upon them that night. Long pale streaks they were, with staring blue eyes and ragged skirts, made of dried-out gum blossoms that covered neither the dangling sex before nor the thin, grimy bottom behind. They bent above the children and made their vague noises, and straightened their wooden bowl hats.

"We were as sweet and soft as these once, do you remember?"

"Soft? These are all bones and britches," sniffed the other. "We were much more rounded. And smaller. No bigger than a gumnut." He picked up a curl of dead bracken and laid it across the children. "And pink, we were. Pink as the dawn, not nasty yellow like these."

The first brother clicked his tongue, bringing a handful of leaves and scattering them over.

They covered the children with leaves and litter and sticks, and when that was done they sat up in a tree, swinging their long legs and looking down mournfully at the mound. And then they were gone, passed on like a bird or a breeze, the branch not even rocking after them.

No one came to bury the bones in the clearing at the top of the hill. Months later a stockman rode in and moved about there, turning the dry remains with his boot toe. He picked a skull—a tiny one, clean and white—out of the pile and put it in his saddlebag, but the rest he let lie, scattered in the ashes there, heaped in the sun. He climbed back up onto his sweating mare, and kicked her into movement, and rode away from that place.

Afterword

Norman Lindsay's *The Magic Pudding* and May Gibbs's *Snugglepot and Cuddlepie*, both first published in 1918, are classic Australian children's books that are still very popular. At the end of *The Magic Pudding*'s first "slice," in which we meet Bunyip Bluegum (a koala), Bill Barnacle (a sailor), and Sam Sawnoff (a penguin), we read "After such a busy day, walking, talking, fighting, singing, and eating puddin', they were all asleep in a pig's whisper." Which is where we find them in this story, along with the dastardly puddin' thieves. Although I enjoy *The Magic Pudding* as an adult reader, I wasn't sure I liked it as a child, particularly Albert the Pudding himself, and *Snugglepot and Cuddlepie* made me uneasy with its big-eyed, naked lost children, and still doesn't really appeal to me except for the gumnut hats, the gum-blossom skirts, and the house made of stitched-together eucalypt leaves. Most of these, including the unease, I've managed to fit into "A Pig's Whisper."

31/10

Stephen Volk's short stories have appeared in the magazines All Hallows, Postscripts, Samhain, *and* Crimewave, *and in various anthologies. His first collection,* Dark Corners, *was published in 2006. His screenplays include* Ken Russell's Gothic, *a wild retelling of the Mary Shelley/Frankenstein story,* Octane, Superstition, *and several TV series including the multi–award winning paranormal drama* Afterlife, *which he created.*
  "31/10" was one of the original stories in his collection Dark Corners.

—E.D.

No. *Don't want to go back to that place. No way. No how.*
     Cut to:
     12 September, 2002.

Ruth Baumgarten telephoned me with the BBC's idea. There are certain TV producers with diaries marked in green and yellow highlighter pen, the better to anticipate upcoming anniversaries to cash in on—fiftieth anniversary of World War I, twenty-fifth anniversary of Kennedy's assassination—but Ruth, the producer of *Ghostwatch* and a friend, I can safely say, is not one of them. We had all agreed long ago that GW was a once-off, never to be revisited. However, in the wolfish hunger for so-called reality TV after three mega-successful series of *Big Brother*, it wasn't difficult to see where the Powers-that-BBC was coming from, in its Greg Dyke-driven quest for ratings.

The proposal was a simple one. Put forward, no doubt over a lunch at L'Escargot by a producer I'd never heard of, who had been thirteen at the time of the original broadcast, and who now, at twenty-three, was inexperienced enough to embody the yoof audience BBC1 desperately wanted to attract. At that stage yours truly, the writer, was not consulted, even though technically the concept was still legally my property, though the rights in the program itself rested with the Beeb. The produceress, in designer glasses way more trendy than Parkinson's in his 1992 Specsavers commercials, suggested a sequel: *Ghostwatch 2, Return to Studio One*.

The reaction was that my body went into spasm. I didn't jump at the idea. I didn't rise to the occasion, or the bait, in writing, by phone call, by e-mail. Pleading, moaning, cajoling, didn't shift me one iota. I don't know what did, in the end.

I think the fact that fear—terror, bubbling up from inside—a pure, physical, ectoplasmic surge in my gut, said, *I have you.* And I wanted to prove it wrong. I wasn't afraid. Not now. Not ten years later, for God's sake.

Almost all of the people involved in *Ghostwatch* I had lost contact with, for obvious reasons.

The aftermath of the original live program from the haunted house in Northolt is well-known and well-documented. The outrage caused ripples in Parliament as well as the hallowed halls of BBC management. The horror caused by the innocuously named "Mr. Pipes"—the malevolent ghost of cross-dressing pedophile Raymond Tunstall (or was it the older, more demonic Victorian bogey-woman Mrs. Seddons?)—had held the nation in a stranglehold that Halloween night in 1992 and given our credulity and preconceptions a good old shaking. I don't mean to sound flip. I have taken to using this kind of language. It is the equivalent of the black humor used by paramedics and policemen. It protects me from the truth.

Michael Parkinson never now talks about the events of 31 October, 1992. His agent circulated the quotes used in the newspapers the following week, in which Parkinson countered attacks of irresponsibility with the remark that "some people believe the wrestling." In fact during this time, the unflappable talk-show host was recovering in a private clinic in Buckinghamshire away from the glare of publicity, his mind and memory seared by what had happened to him in that television studio, staring into space, repeating over and over, "Round and round the garden, like a teddy bear . . ." Within weeks, ostensibly fully recovered, he reentered public life, but in the intervening years he never sought to reexperience those ninety minutes of Hell via therapy or indeed via videotape. The entire event is a blank, and if it ever existed in his memory, it has been recorded over, possibly eradicated forever.

Pamela and Kim Early moved to the U.S.A. in a strategy no less secretive than the FBI witness protection scheme. Kim is now twenty and, under a different name and with a midwestern accent, studying toward a career in biological sciences. Pamela, her mother, died in a household fire in 1995. She had since remarried, in a paradox worthy of the pages of *Fortean Times,* a fireman. It is reported that she visited many psychotherapists over the years and indeed studied and became one herself, specializing in helping people with "spiritual intrusion problems." She was in the process of writing a book about guardian angels.

The fates of both Suzanne and Sarah Greene are unknown.

It is now well-known that Sarah's transmission on Children's BBC a few days after the broadcast, reassuring younger viewers that she hadn't disappeared inside the Glory Hole, was of course recorded by a lookalike, as were a number of subsequent TV appearances on holiday programs and the like.

When the Northolt police forcibly broke into the house in Foxhill Drive and pulled the door off the Glory Hole under the stairs into which Sarah had ventured to rescue a sobbing Suzanne, they found it empty except for the smell of cats and developing fluid. And a thorough search of the house from top to bottom, to the extent of demolition, revealed nothing of their whereabouts.

Studio One at BBC TV Centre was immediately closed down. The power was cut during the poltergeist-induced chaos and the doors sealed pending an internal investigation, which, predictably, drew no conclusions. The paranormal rarely does—maybe that is its purpose and its essential nature. In the ensuing weeks, superstition was rife. Broadcasting House had proven itself a haunted house. People refused to work there. Certainly people refused to work in Studio One. It was declared out of bounds (a few tabloid photographers had tried to get inside, to no avail).

Now they wanted me, the writer, to accompany five other people to go into that studio—unused for ten years—on Halloween night, 2002, at 9:30 P.M., the exact anniversary of the transmission of *Ghostwatch.*

31 October, 2002 — 2 P.M. — BBC TV Centre, Wood Lane

"There's no such thing as ghosts," says the PA, Pippa, lacking both irony and humor. Everyone just looks up at her. She mercifully adds, "Sorry."

Cigarettes stub out in quick succession.

"All I know is," I say, "I want that bloody auto-cue out of there."

We sign our release forms, whatever they are. To whom it may concern. Pact with the Devil. I promise to pay the bearer . . . my soul. Maybe we'd done that already.

4 P.M.

Alan Demescu's beard looks a lot grayer now and he has the look of a gaunt Bosnian refugee about him, as we clammily shake hands. *Somebody for God's sake smile*, I think.

The others are: myself, poor hapless screenwriter; Emma Stableford, the viewer who first phoned in having alerted the audience — if not the studio team — to the presence of Pipes by the curtains in the girls' bedroom; Emilio Sylvestri, the CSI-COP skeptic whose acerbic appearance on GW by satellite link from New York City boosted his fame and arse-holiness no end, making him the doyen of chat shows in the United States as well as a regular on *So Graham Norton*. Sylvestri, who had made the most of his involvement in *Ghostwatch* in his catch-all debunkfest *Tales from the Script* (Prometheus Press, 1993), greeted us with a bonhomie that presumed we could ignore his past record of cheap jibes and castigations. *Wrong*.

Mike Smith declined the tactless request for him to take part. As did Uri Geller, an early short-listee who was nixed after his lack of longevity on ITV's *I'm a Celebrity Get Me out of Here*. Jade apparently had been approached but said she had been "scared shitless" by *Ghostwatch* in 1992, having watched all but the last ten minutes when her mother switched off the TV.

At the time of the TX the BBC phone lines were jammed with calls, many of them from angry and terrified viewers. One such call came from the Reverend Edmund Edward Gryffin of Mold, who berated the BBC for tampering with Satanic forces, for raising demons beyond its control, and for being in league with the Devil. In the intervening years he has no less set in his convictions, and today, joining us as spiritual guide, few of us were going to argue with him — on a metaphorical level, at least.

During the original broadcast, according to the BBC duty log, three pregnant women were so shocked that they went into labor. The good old BBC had traced one of these women, Berenice Gannon of North Berwick, Scotland, whose daughter Louise was born at ten-thirty that Halloween night, at precisely the moment of *Ghostwatch*'s final fade to black. Apparently, with the slamming of the Glory Hole door, baby Louise took her first intake of breath. Louise, or as she preferred to be called, by her second name, decided months prior to her birth — *Suzanne*.

I decide I'm going to call her Louise.

She says, "Look what I've got. Remember him?" A BBC props buyer has given her a cuddly toy rabbit, exactly the kind Kimmy had in the original *Ghostwatch* house. The one whose pin-button eyes she, or Pipes, or Mrs. Seddons, had mysteriously plucked out before drowning said toy rabbit in the kitchen sink. *Shit. Whose bright idea was that*, I wonder. "Bubby wanted to come back, didn't you, Bubby?" she says.

"What the hell . . ." I mumble, knocking back my orange juice in the green room. *I'm only the writer.*

9:25

Five minutes to lift off. I can imagine those deliberately hokey graphics, those ghost-white swimming letters, being lined up on the video playback. "Roll VT," they say in my earpiece. "All systems go."

Dr. Lin Pascoe is in there, looking at the bank of TV screens as the director cuts between them.

9:32

Very *X Files*, the flashlights cut the dark. What the producer-director Cass Buchanon-Bright had called for. We six walk inside. There are three cameramen at three studio cameras, and now the cameras raise their heads like cows in a field to look at us, framing us up. Over to the left the phone-in alcove has a layer of cobwebs over it, and I am unsure whether they are genuine or a thoughtful embellishment of the design department. My flashlight scans. It finds the bedsheet-ghost image, the painting by Gottfried Helnwein I saw many years ago in a Vienna gallery, in its frame over the *Addams Family* fireplace.

We hear the control room in our earpieces.

The Studio One door slams with sarcophagus finality.

"Take two," Emilio Sylvestri says. "This time with feeling."

"Shut the fuck up," says Demescu under his breath.

I say, "That'll be bleeped for a start."

"Language," says the director in the headphones, disembodied, invisible. "Luckily we're not gone live yet. Still rolling the intro." *Language, always the BBC's priority over sex and violence.*

Demescu murmurs "sorry" to Louise Gannon, the little girl.

Louise Gannon says, "I've heard a lot worse than that. A *lot* worse!" She wears red Kicker-type shoes and a rucksack in the form of a fluffy white seal cub. Her blond hair has a few dreadlocks in colored strands and she has talked mostly so far about Gareth Gates and Britney Spears.

"What happens now?" asks Emma Stableford.

"Who knows?" says Demescu.

"Mr. Pipes, perhaps," says Sylvestri, with a sneering intonation the equal of Ned Sherrin, fluttering his fingers in the air and rolling his eyes mock-spookily.

"Be careful what you wish for, it might just happen," says the Reverend EEG. "That was the moral of the original. Correct?"

"Only fiction can have a moral," I say. "Something that really happens can't. Fact can't. Correct?"

"Correct," says Demescu.

"Are we on yet?" asks Louise.

I study the cameras. One has a red light in the dark. I remember the red eye of Raymond Tunstall, of Pipes. Of Kimmy's drawing. "Oh yes. We're on. It's *Stars in Their Eyes*, Loo-loo. Who are you playing?"

Louise laughs. It echoes. *Christ, it echoes.* "You *know*," she says, grinning, her thumbnail twisting against her teeth and jiggling her hips from side to side, childishly bashfully but not bashful at all. Acting bashful. Bashful like bashful is what we want her to be.

9:43

It is so silent it makes you want to shout. But we don't. None of us do. We whisper. Why are we whispering. We don't even ask, *Why are we whispering? This isn't church.*

"It is," says Louise. *Echoing.* Giggling, like it's a joke. Not understanding what jokes are yet. Ten years old. Exactly ten years old, I realize. *Her birthday, of course it is.* Children understand what jokes are at ten years old, don't they? Children understand good and bad, right and wrong, don't they? Do we? Now? What are we doing? Do we even know? Ever?

9:47

Then it comes. Then I hear it. The words. I knew they would come and I knew they'd come from the child.

"When's Pipes coming?"

Quiet in the control room. I'm thinking, they love it. They're not speaking because they love it. This is peeing in the shower. This is getting drunk and falling over. This is Jade's tears. This is *minging.*

"I think we should pray," says EEG. Of us all, he is the one playing—praying—to the cameras. He's the one who is really in church now. The one who protests about obscenity is more obscene than any of us. He kneels in the middle of the television studio with tightly clasped Christian hands, corny as a Mickey Rooney movie. He is the first, then Louise kneels down beside him. Then so does Emma Stableford and so do I. The only one who remains on his feet is Emilio Sylvestri—the skeptic.

And he loves it.

9:59

One thing in common with 1992: nothing happens. Hardly anything happening at all, for a long time. *Why are people watching? Why are they interested? Why are they looking at us? What do they want to see?*

Now it is campfire-like.

Emma Stableford is telling a story from her childhood about something eerie on the Yorkshire Moors. Very friend-of-a-friend. I eye Sylvestri and he eyes me. Demescu and I talk about *Ghostwatch*, the prep, the myth, the aftermath: really replaying the many Q&A sessions we have all done over the years, ad infinitum. All Q and very few A's at the end of the day.

10:07

We are playing cards. Strip Jack Naked. And the ten-year-old thrashing us every time. Is this game supposed to be based on chance? If so, the laws of chance are staying away tonight. Maybe they don't like Halloween. Maybe Halloween doesn't like them.

We switch to Snap and, every time, Louise gets excited and yells "SNAP" and grabs the cards, irrespective of whether she is right or wrong, and laughs uproariously. "Oops, I think I've wet myself."

I say, "I don't think that's allowed on BBC-1."

"What's a baby farmer?" she asks me. "Do they plant babies in the ground and watch them grow? Is it like test tube babies and Dolly the sheep? We've got a sheep in school and he's called Dolly."

"*He's* called Dolly?" says Demescu, raising an eyebrow.

"It's just a word, two words," I tell her. "It doesn't mean anything."

"Everything means something," she says, shuffling the cards, the wisdom hanging in the air. "When is Pipes coming?"

10:10

"Scooby Scooby Doo, where are you?" sings Emilio Sylvestri to the sea of darkness all round us.

I say, "God's sake, I think we've come a little way from that, don't you?"

"I was trying to lighten the proceedings."

"Please do," says Emma Stableford.

"I'm c-cold," says Louise Gannon. "Are you? Is anybody else cold? I'm f-freezing."

"Oh," says Sylvestri, with a dip in his voice. "Fasten your psychic safety belts, people, we're in for a bumpy ride."

"What is your problem?" snaps Alan Demescu, eyes flaring but voice staying calm. "Don't tell me you don't believe what happened on 31/10—that it didn't exist—that it was all some conspiracy, some fake drama like the friggin' moon landing, that bullshit. What *do* you believe?"

"Only that people experienced some delusion on a grand scale. On a scale of eleven million viewers to be precise. But just because David Copperfield makes the Statue of Liberty disappear on ABC doesn't mean it isn't still there the next morning."

"And what about Sarah?" I say. "And what about Suzanne? Are they part of the drama? Pretty good drama to lay low for ten years. I hope they're both getting royalties."

"People have reasons to disappear. People disappear for no reason at all. It doesn't mean we have to call Mulder and Hugh Scully. It doesn't mean we scuttle into the little funk hole in the desert with the sign saying IRRATIONAL BELIEF—PLEASE HIDE HERE TILL IT'S SAFE."

"God save us from the rational mind," says Demescu, turning away and shaking his head as he walks in and out of the darkness.

"God save us from God, for that matter," says Sylvestri, pleased with himself immensely.

He walks to the center of the space, to the big reel-to-reel Revox tape recorder and presses PLAY. Its wheels turn and we hear the guttural, encaphemous voice we all heard during the *Ghostwatch* broadcast.

"Switch that off," I say. "Switch that damned thing . . ."

Demescu beats me to the OFF switch. The echo, the reverb, the memory or trace of that voice continues, I'm sure, for a second or two after the tape spools stop turning.

"Roll VT," says someone in the earpiece. "That was great, well done." Not telling us what was great, or what was well done, particularly.

I rub the back of my neck, staring at the ceiling, the nothing, the night sky of the lighting rig. *What time is it? How far are we into this? I have no idea. I listen, they talk, I don't hear. What the hell is happening out there? Jesus, when is this going to end?*

Jesus—I look at them—Jesus, are the rest of them as afraid as me?

10:13

"One minute more of VT. Stand by," says the voice in the earpiece. "When we're back on air just keep the conversation going, as naturally as possible." *Naturally. I al-*

most laugh. What the fuck is natural *about this?* This from the director who had pep-talked us with: "Don't worry about content. There is no content, just character. Just talk, and atmosphere, and the audience. À la BB, get it?"

I took a second to decipher. She meant don't do anything, they'll watch anyway. Just like *Big Brother.* Geddit?

We are back for about forty noneventful seconds, then they go to the compilation VT segment, as per the script. Viewers have been voting for a week for their favorite top ten *Ghostwatch* moments, and now they are playing clips five to three in reverse order. The Welsh bloke whose sandwich did a nose dive off the arm of his chair gets a look in. They interview him, a soundbite, ten years later. This interspersed with clips of contributors recounting what they were doing, where they were, and what they thought, on the night GW went out. Sara Cox, Johnny Vegas, Linda Robson, Ross Kemp, Christine and Neil Hamilton, John Simpson, Paul Daniels, Rolf Harris, Dr. Susan Blackmore, Dr. Raj Persaud, and Marjorie Wallace, chairperson of the mental health charity SANE.

10:19

There is no monitor in Studio One, the six of us hermetically sealed off from the outside world.

"When is Pipes coming?" asks Louise, again.

Silence. I divert the question by asking her what she wants to be when she grows up.

"An adult," she answers.

With which it's very difficult to argue. I laugh a sigh, sigh a laugh, whatever. Silence again.

I walk over and press the thin membrane separating the phone-in area from the studio proper, onto which the ghostly *Ghostwatch* logo had been projected then eerily dissolved away into the ether at the top of the show. The thin veil between fact and fiction, sanity and insanity, this world and the next. *You have a way with words, mate. You ought to be a writer.*

In the silence of the haunted studio I think of the endless media studies dissertations that *Ghostwatch* has spawned over the years. I had been told by one professor at Aberystwyth that every year without fail one of his students would put it forward as a thesis subject. Pages and pages, books upon books of analysis, observation, libraries of it. It's hard to imagine. Like the last shot of *Raiders of the Lost Ark.* My favorite, predictably Freudian, interpretation of *Ghostwatch* came from the student who made the connection that *Pipes,* when translated into French slang, meant *blow jobs.* The female adolescents were therefore appealing to the TV audience for blow jobs, and this, on an unconscious level, was what the masculine-centric audience was demanding to see.

10:21

Louise looks down at the cards, plain playing cards, laid out in front of her on the studio floor. "Happy Families." She shuffles them and deals them out in a line as if she is playing some improvised form of Solitaire. I watch her, knowing that her mother Berenice is somewhere, out in the control box, sitting next to Dr. Lyn Pascoe, watching all this. A mother who leaves her child in a haunted house with five strangers. What kind of mother is that? *Mother Seddons will get you.*

"I know what this spells," she says, looking at the row of playing cards. "S-A-R-A-H . . . Sarah . . ."

"All right, very funny," I say.

"Yes, it is."

"No, it isn't."

"Yes, it *is*. He says it is. Pipes says it is." She holds up a card. "Pipes is the King with one eye. Pipes is Camera One."

"Out of the mouths of babes and sucklings," says Sylvestri.

Then the banging starts. (Banging—there's another little Freudian double entendre.) It isn't just *similar* to the banging in the Northolt house—it is the *exact same* banging. It's like someone has switched on a tape recording and it's coming amplified from some great big stadium-sized speakers in the dark. Emma Stableford immediately holds her ears and screams and starts shaking. Everybody goes rigid, looking at each other without moving. *It's the producers*, I'm about to say, *it's a joke, like Craig Charles jumping out of the kitchen cabinet in the original. It's not happening. Not really.*

"Control room, please, stop messing around, there's a child in here," Demescu says to the air. "Stop playing silly buggers."

"What's wrong?" says Dr. Lin Pascoe in the earpiece.

"The noise, stop it, turn it off, now. It's not funny!"

A fraction of a pause from Pascoe. A tremor in the voice. "Noise, what noise? We can't hear anything. What can you hear? Tell me exactly what you can hear. Can you hear me? Can you hear what I'm saying?"

"Silly buggers," laughs Louise. "Silly buggers!"

The cards spray up into the air, like a fountain, Alice-in-Wonderland fashion. One spins sideways—changing direction in mid-air—hitting Emilio Sylvestri in the face. It cuts him like a razor blade. When he looks at the trembling fingertips he instinctively raises to his cheek, they are stained with blood—his own. "*Silly buggers, silly buggers, silly buggers . . .*" crackles in the air, not matching Louise's mouth anymore. The lip sync going wrong. The lip sync going wrong *in real life*.

"Jesus she did it Jesus how Jesus sleight of hand," Demescu is gabbling, grabbing Louise by her stick-like arms, shaking her madly, twisting her wrists behind her back like a rough LA cop. "She palmed one with an edge did you see did anybody see she she she—"

"Pipes is here, Pipes is coming! He's coming! He's coming! He's here NOW!"

Emma Stableford is standing rigidly, hyperventilating, with outstretched hands like a blind person trying to find her way, pointing into the dark. *"There! There!"* she is yelling. *"There! There! I see him! I can see him!"* The banging again, sonorous as thrashing drums, from the pipes, from Pipes, from everywhere, from inside our heads. *"I can see him again!"*

I look into the dark place and I see the shape of things not there. I see nothing and the nothing walks out. And the nothing is wearing a long black coat like a Catholic priest's soutane, pedophiles all of them like life imitating art, God help us, everywhere now, demons flying out of every tabloid. And *here*, behold. Watch, watch with Mother, Mother Seddons. Bald head, skull. Bitten and sucked face, the carrion of cats, but no longer the face of Keith Ferrari the actor who played Mr. Pipes in our program, whose first appearance was silhouetted and Harry-enhanced in the folds of the children's curtains. This face with its one bloody eye, clawed out by hungry felines in the Glory Hole, is different. This face with its staring sky blue eyes—*is Sarah Greene's*.

"It's what you wanted, isn't it? *Isn't it?*" screams Louise, in the voice of Suzanne Early.

Pipes swims toward me in the dark as if dangling from a mobile gibbet, his drippy eye becoming like a ghoulish maw. The other eye, Sarah Greene's piercing blue of a lost, lost soul, fixed on mine. And her voice, in a sing-songy lilt like a lullaby, direct to me and only me: *"Round and round the garden . . . like a teddy bear . . ."*

The words my Grandmother used to sing to me before tickling me, as Pipes takes the open palm of my hand and runs his skeletal finger round its perimeter. Now it is in my earpiece too: a MILLION—how many MILLION?—voices chanting:

> Round and round the garden
> Like a teddy bear
> *One step*
> Two step
> Tickle under there!

I feel the fingers take a double leap onto my forearm then elbow, then they bury deep into my ribs, into my heart. The muscles contract and spasm as some iron hook turns and churns and guts me out, spinning my insides like they're entwined on wire and the wire connected to a lathe and the lathe switched on.

The pain explodes in my eye. A billion cats' claws explode and tear through my brain. Every inch of my body shakes. I feel blood filling my left eye, I try to blink it away but only feel its warm piss-feel on my cheek.

Opening my eyes I can only see—nothing. Pipes is gone. Vanished.

There is only us. The six of us, participants in primetime madness. Emilio Sylvestri backing into the dark with his hand over his mouth. Emma Stableford shaking and shrieking in terror. EEG with his eyes tightly shut, going "Our Father who art in heaven hallowed be thy name." Demescu waving his arms in cross like shapes into the cameras, *switch off switch off switch off*. And Louise Gannon, the ten-year-old child of *Ghostwatch*, staring at me, and pointing at me, *directly at me*— and as I grabbed her and shook her to stop, stop, stop saying it, stop, until she did stop—"It's him, it's him, it's Pipes! He's here! He's *here!*"

Afterword

Well-remembered by many in the U.K., *Ghostwatch*, written by Stephen Volk, was a 1992 Halloween special transmitted on BBC-1 TV which purported to be a live transmission from a haunted house in London. The phone lines to Television Centre were jammed and headlines in the Sunday newspapers the next day called for "heads to roll" at the BBC. Questions were raised in Parliament and some people thought the BBC had actually raised demonic forces. Subsequently, the program achieved a kind of cult notoriety for terrifying the nation (and, dubiously, was cited in the *British Journal of Medicine* as being the first TV program to cause Post Traumatic Stress Disorder in children).

GENE WOLFE

Sob in the Silence

Gene Wolfe grew up in Houston, Texas, where he attended Edgar Allan Poe Elementary School. He graduated from the University of Houston in 1956. He and his wife, Rosemary, were married that same year; they have two sons and two daughters, three granddaughters, a step-granddaughter and a step-grandson.

Wolfe's most recent novels are The Book of the Long Sun *and* The Book of the Short Sun *plus a two-volume fantasy,* The Wizard Knight, *and the forthcoming* Pirate Freedom. *His short fiction is collected in* The Island of Doctor Death and Other Stories, Castle of Days, Endangered Species, Storeys From the Old Hotel, Strange Travelers, Innocents Aboard, *and* Starwater Strains.

His work has won two Nebula Awards, three World Fantasy Awards, the Deathrealm Award, the British Science Fiction Award, the British Fantasy Award, and others.

"Sob in the Silence" is one of two original stories published in Strange Birds, *the first of the new illustrated chapbook series. Both stories were inspired by the art of Lisa Snellings-Clark.*

—E.D.

T his," the horror writer told the family visiting him, "is beyond any question the least haunted house in the Midwest. No ghost, none at all, will come within miles of the place. So I am assured."

Robbie straightened his little glasses and mumbled, "Well, it looks haunted."

"It does, young man." After teetering between seven and eight, the horror writer decided that Robbie was about seven. "It's the filthy yellow stucco. No doubt it was a cheerful yellow once, but God only knows how long it's been up. I'm going to have it torn off, every scrap of it, and put up fresh, which I will paint white."

"Can't you just paint over?" Kiara asked. (Kiara of the all-conquering pout, of the golden hair and the tiny silver earrings.)

Looking very serious, the horror writer nodded. And licked his lips only mentally. "I've tried, believe me. That hideous color is the result of air pollution—of smoke, soot, and dirt, if you will—that has clung to the stucco. Paint over it, and it bleeds out through the new paint. Washing—"

"Water jets under high pressure." Dan was Robbie's father, and Kiara's. "You can rent the units, or buy one for a thousand or so."

"I own one," the horror writer told him. "With a strong cleaning agent added to the water, it will do the job." He paused to smile. "Unfortunately, the stucco's old and fragile. Here and there, a good jet breaks it."

"Ghosts," Charity said. Charity was Mrs. Dan, a pudgy woman with a soft, not unattractive face and a remarkable talent for dowdy hats. "Please go back to your ghosts. I find ghosts far more interesting."

"As do I." The horror writer favored her with his most dazzling smile. "I've tried repeatedly to interest psychic researchers in the old place, which has a—may I call it fascinating? History. I've been persuasive and persistent, and no less than three teams have checked this old place out as a result. All three have reported that they found nothing. No evidence whatsoever. No spoor of spooks. No cooperative specters a struggling author might use for research purposes."

"And publicity," Kiara said. "Don't forget publicity. I plan to get into public relations when I graduate."

"And publicity, you're right. By the time you're well settled in public relations, I hope to be wealthy enough to engage you. If I am, I will. That's a promise."

Charity leveled a plump forefinger. "You, on the other hand, have clearly seen or heard or felt something. You had to have something more than this big dark living-room to get the psychics in, and you had it. Tell us."

The horror writer produced a sharply bent briar that showed signs of years of use. "Will this trouble anyone? I rarely smoke in here, but if we're going to have a good long chat—well, a pipe may make things go more smoothly. Would anyone care for a drink?"

Charity was quickly equipped with white wine, Dan with Johnnie Walker-and-water, and Robbie with cola. "A lot of the kids drink beer at IVY Tech," Kiara announced in a tone that indicated she was one of them. "I don't, though."

"Not until you're twenty-one," Dan said firmly.

"You see?" She pouted.

The horror writer nodded. "I do indeed. One of the things I see is that you have good parents, parents who care about you and are zealous for your welfare." He slipped Kiara a scarcely perceptible wink. "What about a plain soda? I always find soda water over ice refreshing, myself."

Charity said, "That would be fine, if she wants it."

Kiara said she did, and he became busy behind the bar.

Robbie had been watching the dark upper corners of the old, high-ceilinged room. "I thought I saw one."

"A ghost?" The horror writer looked up, his blue eyes twinkling.

"A bat. Maybe we can catch it."

Dan said, "There's probably a belfry, too."

"I'm afraid not. Perhaps I'll add one once I get the new stucco on."

"You need one. As I've told my wife a dozen times, anybody who believes in ghosts has bats in his belfry."

"It's better, perhaps," Charity murmured, "if living things breathe and move up there. Better than just bells, rotting ropes, and dust. Tell us more about this place, please."

"It was a country house originally." With the air of one who performed a sacrament, the horror writer poured club soda into a tall frosted glass that already contained five ice cubes and (wholly concealed by his fingers) a generous two inches of vodka. "A quiet place in which a wealthy family could get away from the heat and stench of city summers. The family was ruined somehow—I don't recall the details.

I know it's usually the man who kills in murder-suicides, but in this house it was the woman. She shot her husband and her stepdaughters, and killed herself."

Charity said, "I could never bring myself to do that. I could never kill Dan. Or his children. I suppose I might kill myself. That's conceivable. But not the rest."

Straight-faced, the horror writer handed his frosted glass to Kiara. "I couldn't kill myself," he told her. "I like myself too much. Other people? Who can say?"

Robbie banged down his cola. "You're trying to scare us!"

"Of course I am. It's my trade."

Dan asked, "They all died? That's good shooting."

The horror writer resumed his chair and picked up his briar. "No. As a matter of fact they didn't. One of the three stepdaughters survived. She had been shot in the head at close range, yet she lived."

Dan said, "Happens sometime."

"It does. It did in this case. Her name was Maude Parkhurst. Maude was a popular name back around nineteen hundred, which is when her parents and sisters died. Ever hear of her?"

Dan shook his head.

"She was left penniless and scarred for life. It seems to have disordered her thinking. Or perhaps the bullet did it. In any event, she founded her own church and was its pope and prophetess. It was called—maybe it's still called, since it may still be around for all I know—the Unionists of Heaven and Earth."

Charity said, "I've heard of it. It sounded innocent enough."

The horror writer shrugged. "Today? Perhaps it is. Back then, I would say no. Decidedly no. It was, in its own fantastic fashion, about as repellent as a cult can be. May I call it a cult?"

Kiara grinned prettily over her glass. "Go right ahead. I won't object."

"A friend of mine, another Dan, once defined a cult for me. He said that if the leader gets all the women, it's a cult."

Dan nodded. "Good man. There's a lot to that."

"There is, but in the case of the UHE, as it was called, it didn't apply. Maude Parkhurst didn't want the women, or the men either. The way to get to Heaven, she told her followers, was to live like angels here on earth."

Dan snorted.

"Exactly. Any sensible person would have told them that they were not angels. That it was natural and right for angels to live like angels, but that men and women should live like human beings."

"We really know almost nothing about angels." Charity looked pensive. "Just that they carry the Lord's messages. It's Saint Paul, I think, who says that each of us has an angel who acts as our advocate in Heaven. So we know that, too. But it's really very little."

"This is about sex," Kiara said. "I smell it coming."

The horror writer nodded. "You're exactly right, and I'm beginning to wonder if you're not the most intelligent person here. It is indeed. Members of the UHE were to refrain from all forms of sexual activity. If unmarried, they were not to marry. If married, they were to separate and remain separated."

"The University of Heaven at Elysium. On a T-shirt. I can see it now."

Charity coughed, the sound of it scarcely audible in the large, dark room. "Well, Kiara, I don't see anything wrong with that if it was voluntary."

"Neither do I," the horror writer said, "but there's more. Those wishing to join underwent an initiation period of a year. At the end of that time, there was a midnight ceremony. If they had children, those children had to attend, all of them. There they watched their parents commit suicide—or that's how it looked. I don't know the details, but I know that at the end of the service they were carried out of the church, apparently lifeless and covered with blood."

Charity whispered, "Good God . . ."

"When the congregation had gone home," the horror writer continued, "the children were brought here. They were told that it was an orphanage, and it was operated like one. Before long it actually was one. Apparently there was some sort of tax advantage, so it was registered with the state as a church-run foundation, and from time to time the authorities sent actual orphans here. It was the age of orphanages, as you may know. Few children, if any, were put in foster homes. Normally, it was the orphanage for any child without parents or close relatives."

Dan said, "There used to be a comic strip about it, 'Little Orphan Annie.'"

The horror writer nodded. "Based upon a popular poem of the nineteenth century . . .

> 'Little Orphant Annie's come to our house to stay,
> An' wash the cups an' saucers up,
>   an' brush the crumbs away,
> An' shoo the chickens off the porch,
>   an' dust the hearth an' sweep,
> An' make the fire, an' bake the bread,
>   an' earn her board an' keep.
> An' all us other children,
>   when the supper things is done,
> We set around the kitchen fire an' has the mostest fun
> A-list'nin' to the witch tales 'at Annie tells about,
> An' the Gobble-uns 'at gets you
>   Ef you
>   Don't
>   Watch
>   Out!'

. . . You see," the horror writer finished, smiling, "in those days you could get an orphan girl from such an orphanage as this to be your maid of all work and baby-sitter. You fed and clothed her, gave her a place to sleep, and paid her nothing at all. Despite being showered with that sort of kindness, those girls picked up enough of the monstrosity and lonely emptiness of the universe to become the first practitioners of my art, the oral recounters of horrific tales whose efforts preceded all horror writing."

"Was it really so bad for them?" Kiara asked.

"Here? Worse. I haven't told you the worst yet, you see. Indeed, I haven't even touched upon it." The horror writer turned to Dan. "Perhaps you'd like to send Robbie out. That might be advisable."

Dan shrugged. "He watches TV. I doubt that anything you'll say will frighten him."

Charity pursed her lips but said nothing.

The horror writer had taken advantage of the pause to light his pipe. "You don't have to stay, Robbie." He puffed fragrant white smoke, and watched it begin its slow climb to the ceiling. "You know where your room is, and you may go anywhere in the house unless you meet with a locked door."

Kiara smiled. "Secrets! We're in Bluebeard's cashel—castle. I knew it!"

"No secrets," the horror writer told her, "just a very dangerous cellar stair—steep, shaky, and innocent of any sort of railing."

Robbie whispered, "I'm not going."

"So I see. From time to time, Robbie, one of the children would learn or guess that his parents were not in fact dead. When that happened, he or she might try to get away and return home. I've made every effort to learn just how often that happened, but the sources are contradictory on the point. Some say three and some five, and one says more than twenty. I should add that we who perform this type of research soon learn to be wary of the number three. It's the favorite of those who don't know the real number. There are several places on the grounds that may once of have been graves—unmarked graves long since emptied by the authorities. But—"

Charity leaned toward him, her face tense. "Do you mean to say that those children were killed?"

The horror writer nodded. "I do. Those who were returned here by their parents were. That is the most horrible fact attached to this really quite awful old house. Or at least, it is the worst we know of—perhaps the worst that occurred."

He drew on his pipe, letting smoke trickle from his nostrils. "A special midnight service was held here, in this room in which we sit. At that service the church members are said to have flown. To have fluttered about this room like so many strange birds. No doubt they ran and waved their arms, as children sometimes do. Very possibly they thought they flew. The members of medieval witch cults seem really to have believed that they flew to the gatherings of their covens, although no sane person supposes they actually did."

Charity asked, "But you say they killed the children?"

The horror writer nodded. "Yes, at the end of the ceremony. Call it the children's hour, a term that some authorities say they used themselves. They shot them as Maude Parkhurst's father and sisters had been shot. The executioner was chosen by lot. Maude is said to have hoped aloud that it would fall to her, as it seems to have done more than once. Twice at least."

Dan said, "It's hard to believe anybody would really do that."

"Perhaps it is, although news broadcasts have told me of things every bit as bad. Or worse."

The horror writer drew on his pipe again, and the room had grown dark enough that the red glow from its bowl lit his face from below. "The children were asleep by that time, as Maude, her father, and her sisters had been. The lucky winner crept into the child's bedroom, accompanied by at least one other member who carried a candle. The moment the shot was fired, the candle was blown out. The noise would've awakened any other children who had been sleeping in that room, of course; but they awakened only to darkness and the smell of gun smoke."

Dan said, "Angels!" There was a world of contempt in the word.

"There are angels in Hell," the horror writer told him, "not just in Heaven. Indeed, the angels of Hell may be the more numerous."

Charity pretended to yawn while nodding her reluctant agreement. "I think it's time we all went up bed. Don't you?"

Dan said, "I certainly do. I drove one hell of a long way today."

Kiara lingered when the others had gone. "Ish really nice meeting you." She swayed as she spoke, though only slightly. "Don' forget I get to be your public relations agent. You promised."

"You have my word." The horror writer smiled, knowing how much his word was worth.

For a lingering moment they clasped hands. "Ish hard to believe," she said, "that you were Dad's roommate. You sheem—seem—so much younger."

He thanked her and watched her climb the wide curved staircase that had been the pride of the Parkhursts long ago, wondering all the while whether she knew that he was watching. Whether she knew or not, watching Kiara climb stairs was too great a pleasure to surrender.

On the floor above, Charity was getting Robbie ready for bed. "You're a brave boy, I know. Aren't you a brave boy, darling? Say it, please. It always helps to say it."

"I'm a brave boy," Robbie told her dutifully.

"You are. I know you are. You won't let that silly man downstairs fool you. You'll stay in your own bed, in your own room, and get a good night's sleep. We'll do some sight-seeing tomorrow, forests and lakes and rugged hills where the worked-out mines hide."

Charity hesitated, gnawing with small white teeth at her full lower lip. "There's no nightlight in here, I'm afraid, but I've got a little flashlight in my purse. I could lend you that. Would you like it?"

Robbie nodded, and clasped Charity's little plastic flashlight tightly as he watched her leave. Her hand—the one without rings—reached up to the light switch. Her fingers found it.

There was darkness.

He located the switch again with the watery beam of the disposable flashlight, knowing that he would be scolded (perhaps even spanked) if he switched the solitary overhead light back on but wanting to know exactly where that switch was, just in case.

At last he turned Charity's flashlight off and lay down. It was hot in the too-large, too-empty room. Hot and silent.

He sat up again, and aimed the flashlight toward the window. It was indeed open, but open only the width of his hand, He got out of bed, dropped the flashlight into the shirt pocket of his pajamas, and tried to raise the window farther. No effort he could put forth would budge it.

At last he lay down again, and the room felt hotter than ever.

When he had looked out through the window, it had seemed terribly high. How many flights of stairs had they climbed to get up here? He could remember only one, wide carpeted stairs that had curved as they climbed; but that one had been a long, long stair. From the window he had seen the tops of trees.

Treetops and stars. The moon had been out, lighting the lawn below and showing him the dark leaves of the treetops, although the moon itself had not been in sight from the window.

"It walks across the sky," he told himself. Dan, his father, had said that once.

"You could walk . . ." The voice seemed near, but faint and thin.

Robbie switched the flashlight back on. There was no one there.

Under the bed, he thought. They're under the bed.

But he dared not leave the bed to look, and lay down once more. An older person would have tried to persuade himself that he had imagined the voice, or would have left the bed to investigate. Robbie did neither. His line between palpable and imagined things was blurred and faint, and he had not the slightest desire to see the speaker, whether that speaker was real or make-believe.

There were no other windows that might be opened. He thought of going out. The hall would be dark, but Dan and Charity were sleeping in a room not very far away. The door of their room might be locked, though. They did that sometimes.

He would scolded in any event. Scolded and perhaps spanked, too. It was not the pain he feared, but the humiliation. "I'll have to go back here," he whispered to himself. "Even if they don't spank me, I'll have to go back."

"You could walk away . . ." A girl's voice, very faint. From the ceiling? No, Robbie decided, from the side toward the door.

"No," he said. "They'd be mad."

"You'll die . . ."

"Like us . . ."

Robbie sat up, shaking.

Outside, the horror writer was hiking toward the old, rented truck he had parked more than a mile away. The ground was soft after yesterday's storm, and it was essential—absolutely essential—that there be tracks left by a strange vehicle.

A turn onto a side road, a walk of a hundred yards, and the beam of his big electric lantern picked out the truck among the trees. When he could set the lantern on its hood, he put on latex gloves. Soon, very soon, the clock would strike the children's hour and Edith with the golden hair would be his. Beautiful Kiara would be his. As for laughing Allegra, he neither knew nor cared who she might be.

"Wa' ish?" Kiara's voice was thick with vodka and sleep.

"It's only me," Robbie told her, and slipped under the covers. "I'm scared."

She put a protective arm around him.

"There are other kids in here. There are! They're gone when you turn on the light, but they come back. They do!"

"Uh huh." She hugged him tighter and went back to sleep.

In Scales Mound, the horror writer parked the truck and walked three blocks to his car. He had paid two weeks rent on the truck, he reminded himself. Had paid that rent only three days ago. It would be eleven days at least before the rental agency began to worry about it, and he could return it or send another check before then.

His gun, the only gun he owned, had been concealed in a piece of nondescript luggage and locked in the car. He took it out and made sure the safety was on before starting the engine. It was only a long-barreled twenty-two; but it looked sinister, and should be sufficient to make Kiara obey if the threat of force were needed.

Once she was down there . . . Once she was down there, she might scream all she liked. It would not matter. As he drove back to the house, he tried to decide whether he should hold it or put it into one of the big side pockets of his barn coat.

Robbie, having escaped Kiara's warm embrace, decided that her room was cooler than his. For one thing, she had two windows. For another, both were open wider than his one window had been. Besides, it was just cooler. He pulled the sheet up, hoping she would not mind.

"Run . . ." whispered the faint, thin voices.

"Run . . . Run . . ."

"Get away while you can . . ."

"Go . . ."

Robbie shook his head and shut his eyes.

Outside Kiara's bedroom, the horror writer patted the long-barreled pistol he had pushed into his belt. His coat pockets held rags, two short lengths of quarter-inch rope, a small roll of duct tape, and a large folding knife. He hoped to need none of them.

There was no provision for locking Kiara's door. He had been careful to see to that. No key for the quaint old lock, no interior bolt; and yet she might have blocked it with a chair. He opened it slowly, finding no obstruction.

The old oak doors were thick and solid, the old walls thicker and solider still. If Dan and his wife were sleeping soundly, it would take a great deal of commotion in here to wake them.

Behind him, the door swung shut on well-oiled hinges. The click of the latch was the only sound.

Moonlight coming through the windows rendered the penlight in his shirt pocket unnecessary. She was there, lying on her side and sound asleep, her lovely face turned toward him.

As he moved toward her, Robbie sat up, his mouth a dark circle, his pale face a mask of terror. The horror writer pushed him down again.

The muzzle of his pistol was tight against Robbie's head; this though the horror writer could not have said how it came to be there. His index finger squeezed even as he realized it was on the trigger.

There was a muffled bang, like the sound of a large book dropped. Something jerked under the horror writer's hand, and he whispered, "Die like my father. Like Alice and June. Die like me." He whispered it, but did not understand what he intended by it.

Kiara's eyes were open. He struck her with the barrel, reversed the pistol, and struck her again and again with the butt, stopping only when he realized he did not know how many times he had hit her already or where his blows had landed.

After pushing up the safety, he put the pistol back into his belt and stood listening. The room next to that in which he stood had been Robbie's. Presumably, there was no one there to hear.

The room beyond that one—the room nearest the front stair—was Dan's and Charity's. He would stand behind the door if they came in, shoot them both, run. Mexico. South America.

They did not.

The house was silent save for his own rapid breathing and Kiara's slow, labored breaths; beyond the open windows, the night-wind sobbed in the trees. Any other sound would have come, almost, as a relief.

There was none.

He had broken the cellar window, left tracks with the worn old shoes he had gotten from a recycle store, left tire tracks with the old truck. He smiled faintly when he recalled its mismatched tires. Let them work on that one.

He picked up Kiara and slung her over his shoulder, finding her soft, warm, and heavier than he had expected.

The back stairs were narrow and in poor repair; they creaked beneath his feet, but they were farther—much farther—from the room in which Dan and Charity slept. He descended them slowly, holding Kiara with his right arm while his left hand grasped the rail.

She stirred and moaned. He wondered whether he would have to hit her again, and decided he would not unless she screamed. If she screamed, he would drop her and do what had to be done.

She did not.

The grounds were extensive, and included a wood from which (long ago) firewood had been cut. It had grown back now, a tangle of larches and alders, firs and red cedars. Toward the back, not far from the property line, he had by merest chance stumbled upon the old well. There had been a cabin there once. No doubt it had burned. A cow or a child might have fallen into the abandoned well, and so some prudent person had covered it with a slab of limestone. Leaves and twigs on that stone had turned, in time, to soil. He had moved the stone away, leaving the soil on it largely undisturbed.

When he reached the abandoned well at last, panting and sweating, he laid Kiara down. His penlight showed that her eyes were open. Her bloodstained face seemed to him a mask of fear; seeing it, he felt himself stand straighter and grow stronger.

"You may listen to me or not," he told her. "What you do really doesn't matter, but I thought I ought to do you the kindness of explaining just what has happened and what will happen. What I plan, and your place in my plans."

She made an inarticulate sound that might have been a word or a moan.

"You're listening. Good. There's an old well here. Only I know that it exists. At the bottom—shall we say twelve feet down? At the bottom there's mud and a little water. You'll get dirty, in other words, but you won't die of thirst. There you will wait for me for as long as the police actively investigate. From time to time I may, or may not, come here and toss down a sandwich."

He smiled. "It won't hurt you in the least, my dear, to lose a little weight. When things have quieted down, I'll come and pull you out. You'll be grateful—oh, very grateful—for your rescue. Soiled and starved, but very grateful. Together we'll walk back to my home. You may need help, and if you do I'll provide it."

He bent and picked her up. "I'll bathe you, feed you, and nurse you."

Three strides brought him to the dark mouth of the well. "After that, you'll obey me in everything. Or you had better. And in time, perhaps, you'll come to like it."

He let her fall, smiled, and turned away.

There remained only the problem of the gun. Bullets could be matched to barrels, and there was an ejected shell somewhere. The gun would have to be destroyed; it was blued steel; running water should do the job, and do it swiftly.

Still smiling, he set off for the creek.

It was after four o'clock the following afternoon when Captain Barlowe of the Sheriff's Department explained the crime. Captain Barlowe was a middle-aged and heavy-limbed. He had a thick mustache. "What happened in this house last night is becoming pretty clear." His tone was weighty. "Why it happened . . ." He shook his head.

The horror writer said, "I know my house was broken into. One of your men showed me that. I know poor little Robbie's dead, and I know Kiara's missing. But that's all I know."

"Exactly." Captain Barlowe clasped his big hands and unclasped them. "It's pretty much all I know, too, sir. Other than that, all I can do is supply details. The gun that killed the boy was a twenty-two semi-automatic. It could have been a pistol or a rifle. It could even have been a saw-off rifle. There's no more common caliber in the world."

The horror writer nodded.

"He was killed with one shot, a contact shot to the head, and he was probably killed for being in a room in which he had no business being. He'd left his own bed and crawled into his big sister's. Not for sex, sir. I could see what you were thinking. He was too young for that. He was just a little kid alone in a strange house. He got lonely and was murdered for it."

Captain Barlowe paused to clear his throat. "You told my men that there had been no cars in your driveway since the rain except your own and the boy's parents'. Is that right?"

The horror writer nodded. "I've wracked my brain trying to think of somebody else, and come up empty. Dan and I are old friends. You ought to know that."

Captain Barlowe nodded. "I do, sir. He told me."

"We get together when we can, usually that's once or twice a year. This year he and Charity decided to vacation in this area. He's a golfer and a fisherman."

Captain Barlowe nodded again. "He should love our part of the state."

"That's what I thought, Captain. I don't play golf, but I checked out some of the courses here. I fish a bit, and I told him about that. He said he was coming, and I told him I had plenty of room. They were only going to stay for two nights."

"You kept your cellar door locked?"

"Usually? No. I locked it when I heard they were coming. The cellar's dirty and the steps are dangerous. You know how small boys are."

"Yes, sir. I used to be one. The killer jimmied it open."

The horror writer nodded. "I saw that."

"You sleep on the ground floor. You didn't hear anything?"

"No. I'm a sound sleeper."

"I understand. Here's my problem, sir, and I hope you can help me with it. Crime requires three things. They're motive, means, and opportunity. Know those, and you know a lot. I've got a murder case here. It's the murder of a kid. I hate the bastards who kill kids, and I've never had a case I wanted to solve more."

"I understand," the horror writer said.

"Means is no problem. He had a gun, a car, and tools. Maybe gloves, because we haven't found any fresh prints we can't identify. His motive may have been robbery, but it was probably of a sexual nature. Here's a young girl, a blonde. Very good-looking to judge by the only picture we've seen so far."

"She is." The horror writer nodded his agreement.

"He must have seen her somewhere. And not just that. He must have known that she was going to be in this house last night. Where did he see her? How did he know where she was going to be? If I can find the answers to those questions we'll get him."

"I wish I could help you." The horror writer's smile was inward only.

"You've had no visitors since your guests arrived?"

He shook his head. "None."

"Delivery men? A guy to fix the furnace? Something like that?"

"No, nobody. They got here late yesterday afternoon, Captain."

"I understand. Now think about this, please. I want to know everybody—and I mean everybody, no matter who it was—you told that they were coming."

"I've thought about it. I've thought about it a great deal, Captain. And I didn't tell anyone. When I went around to the golf courses, I told people I was expecting guests and they'd want to play golf. But I never said who those guests were. There was no reason to."

"That settles it." Captain Barlowe rose, looking grim. "It's somebody they told. The father's given us the names of three people and he's trying to come up with more. There may be more. He admits that. His wife . . ."

"Hadn't she told anyone?"

"That just it, sir. She did. She seems to have told quite a few people and says she can't remember them all. She's lying because she doesn't want her friends bothered. Well by God they're going to be bothered. My problem—one of my problems—is that all these people are out of state. I can't go after them myself, and I'd like to. I want to have a good look at them. I want to see their faces change when they're asked certain questions."

He breathed deep, expanding a chest notably capacious, and let it out. "On the plus side, we're after a stranger. Some of the local people may have seen him and noticed him. He may—I said *may*—be driving a car with out-of-state plates."

"Couldn't he have rented a car at the airport?" the horror writer asked.

"Yes, sir. He could, and I hope to God he did. If he did, we'll get him sure. But his car had worn tires, and that's not characteristic of rentals."

"I see."

"If he did rent his car, it'll have bloodstains in it, and the rental people will notice. She was bleeding when she was carried out of her bedroom."

"I didn't know that."

"Not much, but some. We found blood in the hall and more on the back stairs. The bad thing is that if he flew in and plans to fly back out, he can't take her with him. He'll kill her. He may have killed her already."

Captain Barlowe left, Dan and Charity moved into a motel, and the day ended in quiet triumph. The experts who had visited the crime scene earlier reappeared and took more photographs and blood samples. The horror writer asked them no questions, and they volunteered nothing.

He drove to town the next morning and shopped at several stores. So far as he could judge, he was not followed. That afternoon he got out the binoculars he had acquired years before for bird-watching and scanned the surrounding woods and fields, seeing no one.

At sunrise the next morning he rescanned them, paying particular attention to areas he thought he might have slighted before. Selecting an apple from the previous day's purchases, he made his way through grass still wet with dew to the well and tossed it in.

He had hoped that she would thank him and plead for release; if she did either her voice was too faint for him to catch her words, this though it seemed to him there was a sound of some sort from the well, a faint, high humming. As he tramped back to the house, he decided that it had probably been an echo of the wind.

The rest of that day he spent preparing her cellar room.

He slept well that night and woke refreshed twenty minutes before his clock radio would have roused him. The three-eighths inch rope he had brought two days earlier awaited him in the kitchen; he knotted it as soon as he had finished breakfast, spacing the knots about a foot apart.

When he had wound it around his waist and tied it securely, he discovered bloodstains—small but noticeable—on the back of his barn coat. Eventually it would have to be burned, but a fire at this season would be suspicious in itself; a long soak in a strong bleach solution would have to do the job—for the present, if not permanently. Pulled out, his shirt hid the rope, although not well.

When he reached the well, he tied one end of the rope to a convenient branch and called softly.

There was no reply.

A louder "Kiara!" brought no reply either. She was still asleep, the horror writer decided. Asleep or, just possibly, unconscious. He dropped the free end of the rope into the well, swung over the edge, and began the climb down.

He had expected the length of his rope to exceed the depth of the well by three feet at least; but there came a time when his feet could find no more rope below him—or find the muddy bottom either.

His pen light revealed it, eight inches, perhaps, below the soles of his shoes. Another knot down—this knot almost the last—brought his feet into contact with the mud.

He released the rope.

He had expected to sink into the mud, but had thought to sink to a depth of no more than three or four inches; he found himself floundering, instead, in mud up to his knees. It was difficult to retain his footing; bracing one hand against the stone side of the well, he managed to do it.

At the first step he attempted, the mud sucked his shoe from his foot. Groping the mud for it got his hands thoroughly filthy, but failed to locate it. Attempting a second step cost him his other shoe as well.

This time, however, his groping fingers found a large, soft thing in the mud. His pen light winked on—but in the space of twenty seconds or a little less its always-faint beam faded to darkness. His fingers told him of hair matted with mud, of an ear, and then of a small earring. When he took his hand from it, he stood among corpses, shadowy child-sized bodies his fingers could not locate. Shuddering, he looked up.

Above him, far above him, a small circle of blue was bisected by the dark limb to which he had tied his rope. The rope itself swayed gently in the air, its lower end not quite out of reach.

He caught it and tried to pull himself up; his hands were slippery with mud, and it escaped them.

Desperately, almost frantically, he strove to catch it again, but his struggles caused him to sink deeper into the mud.

He tried to climb the wall of the well; at his depth its rough stones were thick with slime.

At last he recalled Kiara's body, and by a struggle that seemed to him long managed to get both feet on it. With its support, his fingertips once more brushed the dangling end of the rope. Bracing his right foot on what felt like the head, he made a final all-out effort.

And caught the rope, grasping it a finger's breadth from its frayed end. The slight tension he exerted on it straightened it, and perhaps stretched it a trifle. Bent the limb above by a fraction of an inch. With his right arm straining almost out of its socket and his feet pressing hard against Kiara's corpse, the fingers of his left hand could just touch the final knot.

Something took hold of his right foot, pinning toes and transverse arch in jaws that might have been those of a trap.

The horror writer struggled then, and screamed again and again as he was drawn under—screamed and shrieked and begged until the stinking almost liquid mud stopped his mouth.

JOSH BELL

Yep, I Said Camel

"Yep, I Said Camel" was published in the journal Ninth Letter, *vol. 3, no.1. Bell is the author of a collection of poetry,* No Planets Strike. *He holds degrees from Southern Illinois University and the Iowa Writers' Workshop, where he was a Paul Engle Fellow. Bell's poems have appeared in such magazines as* Boston Review, Fence, Triquarterly, Verse, *and* Volt.

—K.L. & G.G.

In the wanted poster, the famous sunflower rises,
from her cowboy hat, like a periscope. By then,
its roots had tapped into her frontal lobe, drew
her thoughts as nutrients and paid her back
with visions. Through this sunflower eye
she dreamed an endless, lurid H of train tracks,
foretold the scumbag frequency of sheep. And to
my shame, she eavesdropped while the Indians
searched my saddlebags and found the dress
I took from her. Boys, I wore it only once, tucked
the gingham into my gunbelt, rode that fucking
camel back to Taos. Whatever I said there, I said
to her, as her. If you like my dress, then keep
your bullets. Keep your bullets. They're no good here.

PAUL DI FILIPPO

Femaville 29

We took Paul Di Filippo's "Femaville 29" from Ellen Datlow and Terri Win-dling's all-original anthology Salon Fantastique. *Di Filippo is a prolific short-story writer, as well as a novelist, whose collections include* The Steampunk Trilogy, Ribofunk, Fractal Paisleys, Lost Pages, Little Door *and* Shuteye for the Timebroker. *Di Filippo lives in Providence, Rhode Island.*

—K.L. & G.G.

La Palma is a tiny mote in the Canary Islands, a mote that had certainly never intruded into my awareness before one fateful day. On La Palma, five hundred billion tons of rock in the form of an unstable coastal plateau awaited a nudge, which they received when the Cumbre Vieja volcano erupted. Into the sea a good portion of the plateau plunged, a frightful hammer of the gods.

The peeling off of the face of the island was a smaller magnitude event than had been feared; but it was a larger magnitude event than anyone was prepared for.

The resulting tsunami raced across the Atlantic.

My city had gotten just twelve hours warning. The surreal chaos of the partial evacuation was like living through the most vivid nightmare or disaster film imaginable. Still, the efforts of the authorities and volunteers and good samaritans ensured that hundreds of thousands of people escaped with their lives.

Leaving other hundreds of thousands to face the wave.

Their only recourse was to find the tallest, strongest buildings and huddle.

I was on the seventh floor of an insurance company when the wave arrived. Posters in the reception area informed me that I was in good hands. I had a view of the harbor, half a mile away.

The tsunami looked like a liquid mountain mounted on a rocket sled.

When the wave hit, the building shuddered and bellowed like a steer in an abbatoir euthanized with a nail-gun. Every window popped out of its frame, and spray lashed even my level.

But the real fight for survival had not yet begun.

The next several days were a sleepless blur of crawling from the wreckage and helping others do likewise.

But not everyone was on the same side. Looters arose like some old biological paradigm of spontaneous generation from the muck.

Their presence demanded mine on the front lines.

I was a cop.

I had arrested several bad guys without any need for excessive force. But then came a shootout at a jewelry store where the display cases were incongrously draped with drying kelp. I ended up taking the perps down okay. But the firefight left my weary brain and trembling gut hypersensitive to any threat.

Some indeterminate time afterwards—marked by a succession of candy-bar meals, digging under the floodlights powered by chuffing generators, and endless slogging through slimed streets—I was working my way through the upper floors of an apartment complex, looking for survivors. I shut off my flashlight when I saw a glow around a corner. Someone stepped between me and the light source, casting the shadow of a man with a gun. I yelled, "Police! Drop it!" then crouched and dashed toward the gunman. The figure stepped forward, still holding the weapon, and I fired.

The boy was twelve, his weapon a water pistol.

His mother trailed him by a few feet—not far enough to escape getting splattered with her son's blood.

Later I learned neither of them spoke a word of English.

One minute I was cradling the boy, and the next I was lying on a cot in a field hospital. Three days had gotten lost somewhere. Three days in which the whole world had learned of my mistake.

They let me get up the next day, ostensibly healthy and sane enough, even though my pistol hand, my left, still exhibited a bad tremor. I tried to report to the police command, but found that I had earned a temporary medical discharge. Any legal fallout from my actions awaited an end to the crisis.

I tried being a civilian volunteer for another day or two amidst the ruins, but my heart wasn't in it. So I took the offer of evacuation to Femaville 29.

The first week after the disaster actually manifested aspects of an odd, enforced vacation. Or rather, the atmosphere often felt more like an open-ended New Year's Eve, the portal to some as-yet undefined millennium where all our good resolutions would come to pass. Once we victims emerged from the shock of losing everything we owned, including our shared identity as citizens of a large East Coast city, my fellow refugees and I began to exhibit a near-manic optimism in the face of the massive slate-cleaning.

The uplift was not to last. But while it prevailed, it was as if some secret imperative in the depths of our souls—a wish to be unburdened of all our draggy pasts—had been fulfilled by cosmic fiat, without our having to lift a finger.

We had been given a chance to start all over, remake our lives afresh, and we were, for the most part, eager to grasp the offered personal remodeling.

Everyone in the swiftly erected encampment of a thousand men, women and children was healthy. The truly injured had all been airlifted to hospitals around the state and nation. Families had been reunited, even down to pets. The tents we were inhabiting were spacious, weather-tight and wired for electricity and entertainment. Meals were plentiful, albeit uninspired, served promptly in three shifts, thrice daily, in a large communal pavilion.

True, the lavatories and showers were also communal, and the lack of privacy grated a bit right from the start. Trudging through the chilly dark in the middle of the night to take a leak held limited appeal, even when you pretended you were camping. And winter, with its more challenging conditions, loomed only a few months away. Moreover, enforced idleness chafed those of us who were used to steady work. Lack of proper schooling for the scores of kids in the camp worried many parents.

But taken all in all, the atmosphere at the camp—christened with no more imaginative bureaucratic name than Femaville Number 29—was suffused with potential that first week.

My own interview with the FEMA intake authorities in the first days of the relocation was typical.

The late September sunlight warmed the interview tent so much that the canvas sides had been rolled up to admit fresh air scented with faint, not unpleasant maritime odors of decay. Even though Femaville 29 was located far inland—or what used to be far inland before the tsunami—the wrack left behind by the disaster lay not many miles away.

For a moment, I pictured exotic fish swimming through the streets and subways of my old city, weaving their paths among cars, couches and corpses. The imagery unsettled me, and I tried to focus on the more hopeful present.

The long tent hosted ranks of paired folding chairs, each chair facing its mate. The FEMA workers, armed with laptop computers, occupied one seat of each pair, while an interviewee sat in the other. The subdued mass interrogation and the clicking of keys raised a surprisingly dense net of sound that overlaid the noises from outside the tent: children roistering, adults gossiping, birds chattering. Outside the tent, multiple lines of refugees stretched away, awaiting their turns.

The official seated across from me was a pretty young African-American woman whose name-badge proclaimed her HANNAH LAWES. Unfortunately, she reminded me of my ex-wife, Calley, hard in the same places Calley was hard. I tried to suppress an immediate dislike of her. As soon as I sat down, Hannah Lawes expressed rote sympathy for my plight, a commiseration worn featureless by its hundredth repetition. Then she got down to business.

"Name?"

"Parrish Hedges."

"Any relatives in the disaster zone?"

"No, ma'am."

"What was your job back in the city?"

I felt my face heat up. But I had no choice, except to answer truthfully.

"I was a police officer, ma'am."

That answer gave Hannah Lawes pause. Finally, she asked in an accusatory fashion, "Shouldn't you still be on duty then? Helping with security in the ruins?"

My left hand started to quiver a bit, but I suppressed it so that I didn't think she noticed.

"Medical exemption, ma'am."

Hannah Lawes frowned slightly and said, "I hope you don't mind if I take a moment to confirm that, Mr. Hedges."

Her slim, manicured fingers danced over her keyboard, dragging my data down the airwaves. I studied the plywood floor of the tent while she read my file.

When I looked up, her face had gone disdainful.

"This explains much, Mr. Hedges."

"Can we move on, please?"

As if I ever could.

Hannah Lawes resumed her programmed spiel. "All right, let's talk about your options now . . ."

For the next few minutes, she outlined the various programs and handouts and incentives that the government and private charities and NGO's had lined up for the victims of the disaster. Somehow, none of the choices really matched my dreams and expectations engendered by the all-consuming catastrophe. All of them involved relocating to some other part of the country, leaving behind the shattered chaos of the East Coast. And that was something I just wasn't ready for yet, inevitable as such a move was.

And besides, choosing any one particular path would have meant foregoing all the others. Leaving this indeterminate interzone of infinite possibility would lock me into a new life that might be better than my old one, but would still be fixed, crystallized, frozen into place.

"Do I have to decide right now?"

"No, no, of course not."

I stood up to go, and Hannah Lawes added, "But you realize, naturally, that this camp was never intended as a long-term residence. It's only transitional, and will be closed down at some point not too far in the future."

"Yeah, sure," I said. "We're all just passing through. I get it."

I left then and made way for the next person waiting in line.

The tents of Femaville 29 were arranged along five main dirt avenues, each as wide as a city boulevard. Expressing the same ingenuity that had dubbed our whole encampment, the avenues were labeled A, B, C, D and E. Every three tents, a numbered cross-street occurred. The tents of one avenue backed up against the tents of the adjacent avenue, so that a cross-block was two tents wide. The land where Femaville 29 was pitched was flat and treeless and covered in newly mowed weeds and grasses. Beyond the borders of our village stretched a mix of forest, scrubby fields and swamp, eventually giving way to rolling hills. The nearest real town was about ten miles away, and there was no regular transportation there other than by foot.

As I walked up Avenue D toward my tent (D-30), I encountered dozens of my fellow refugees who were finished with the intake process. Only two days had passed since the majority of us had been ferried here in commandeered school buses. People—the adults, anyhow—were still busy exchanging their stories—thrilling, horrific or mundane—about how they had escaped the tsunami or dealt with the aftermath.

I didn't have any interest in repeating my tale, so I didn't join in any such conversations.

As for the children, they seemed mostly to have flexibly put behind them all the trauma they must have witnessed. Reveling in their present freedom from boring routine, they raced up and down the avenues in squealing packs.

Already, the seasonally withered grass of the avenues was becoming dusty ruts. Just days old, this temporary village, I could feel, was already beginning to lose its freshness and ambiance of novelty.

Under the unseasonably warm sun, I began to sweat. A cold beer would have tasted good right now. But the rules of Femaville 29 prohibited alcohol.

I reached my tent and went inside.

My randomly assigned roommate lay on his bunk. Given how the disaster had shattered and stirred the neighborhoods of the city, it was amazing that I actually knew the fellow from before. I had encountered no one else yet in the camp who was familiar to me. And out of all my old friends and acquaintances and co-workers, Ethan Duplessix would have been my last choice to be reunited with.

Ethan was a fat, bristled slob with a long criminal record of petty theft, fraud and advanced mopery. His personal grooming habits were so atrocious that he had emerged from the disaster more or less in the same condition he entered it, unlike the rest of the survivors who had gone from well-groomed to uncommonly bedraggled and smelly.

Ethan and I had crossed paths often, and I had locked him up more times than I could count. (When the tsunami sturck, he had been amazingly free of outstanding charges.) But the new circumstances of our lives, including Ethan's knowledge of how I had "retired" from the force, placed us now on a different footing.

"Hey, Hedges, how'd it go? They got you a new job yet? Maybe security guard at a kindergarten!"

I didn't bother replying, but just flopped down on my bunk. Ethan chuckled meanly at his own paltry wit for a while, but when I didn't respond, he eventually fell silent, his attentions taken up by a tattered copy of *Maxim*.

I closed my eyes and drowsed for a while, until I got hungry. Then I got up and went to the refectory.

That day they were serving hamburgers and fries for the third day in a row. Mickey Dee's seemed to have gotten a lock on the contract to supply the camp. I took mine to an empty table. Head bowed, halfway through my meal, I sensed someone standing beside me.

The woman's curly black hair descended to her shoulders in a tumbled mass. Her face resembled a cameo in its alabaster fineness.

"Mind if I sit here?" she said.

"Sure. I mean, go for it."

The simple but primordial movements of her legs swinging over the bench seat and her ass settling down awakened emotions in me that had been absent since Calley's abrupt leave-taking.

"Nia Horsley. Used to live over on Garden Parkway."

"Nice district."

Nia snorted, a surprisingly enjoyable sound. "Yeah, once."

"I never got over there much. Worked in East Grove. Had an apartment on Oakeshott."

"And what would the name on your doorbell have been?"

"Oh, sorry. Parrish Hedges."

"Pleased to meet you, Parrish."

We shook hands. Hers was small but strong, enshelled in mine like a pearl.

For the next two hours, through two more shifts of diners coming and going, we talked, exchanging condensed life stories, right up to the day of disaster and down to our arrival at Femaville 29. Maybe the accounts were edited for maximum appeal, but I intuitively felt she and I were being honest nonetheless. When the refectory workers finally shooed us out in order to clean up for supper, I felt as if I had known Nia for two weeks, two months, two years—

She must have felt the same. As we strolled away down Avenue B, she held my hand.

"I don't have a roomie in my tent."

"Oh?"

"It's just me and my daughter. Luck of the draw, I guess."

"I like kids. Never had any, but I like 'em."

"Her name's Izzy. Short for Isabel. You'll get to meet her. But maybe not just yet."

"How come?"

"She's made a lot of new friends. They stay out all day, playing on the edge of the camp. Some kind of weird new game they invented."

"We could go check up on her, and I could say hello."

Nia squeezed my hand. "Maybe not right this minute."

I got to meet Izzy the day after Nia and I slept together. I suppose I could've hung around till Izzy came home for supper, but the intimacy with Nia, after such a desert of personal isolation, left me feeling a little disoriented and pressured. So I made a polite excuse for my departure, which Nia accepted with good grace, and arranged to meet mother and daughter for breakfast.

Izzy bounced into the refectory ahead of her mother. She was seven or eight, long-limbed and fair-haired in contrast to her mother's compact, raven-haired paleness, but sharing Nia's high-cheeked bone structure. I conjectured backward to a gangly blond father.

The little girl zeroed in on me somehow out of the whole busy dining hall, racing up to where I sat, only to slam on the brakes with alarming precipitousness.

"You're Mr. Hedges!" she informed me and the world.

"Yes, I am. And you're Izzy."

I was ready to shake her hand in a formal adult manner. But then she exclaimed, "You made my Mom all smiley!" and launched herself into my awkward embrace.

Before I could really respond, she was gone, heading for the self-service cereal line.

I looked at Nia, who was grinning.

"And this," I asked, "is her baseline?"

"Precisely. When she's really excited—"

"I'll wear one of those padded suits we used for training the K-9 squad."

Nia's expression altered to one of seriousness and sympathy, and I instantly knew what was coming. I cringed inside, if not where it showed. She sat down next to me and put a hand on my arm.

"Parrish, I admit I did a little Googling on you after we split yesterday, over at the online tent. I know about why you aren't a cop anymore. And I just want to say that—"

Before she could finish, Izzy materialized out of nowhere, bearing a tray holding two bowls of technicolor puffs swimming in chocolate milk, and slipped herself between us slick as a greased eel.

"They're almost out of food! You better hurry!" With a plastic knife, Izzy began slicing a peeled banana into chunks thick as oreos that plopped with alarming splashes into her bowls.

I stood up gratefully. "I'll get us something, Nia. Eggs and bacon and toast okay?"

She gave me a look which said that she could wait to talk. "Sure."

During breakfast, Nia and I mostly listened to Izzy's chatter.

"—and then Vonique's all like, 'But the way I remember it is the towers were next to the harbor, not near the zoo.' And Eddie goes, 'Na-huh, they were right where the park started.' And they couldn't agree and they were gonna start a fight, until I figured out that they were talking about two differents places! Vonique meant the Goblin Towers, and Eddie meant the Towers of Bone! So I straightened them out, and now the map of Djamala is like almost half done!"

"That's wonderful, honey."

"It's a real skill, being a peacemaker like that."

Izzy cocked her head and regarded me quizzically. "But that's just what I've always been forever."

In the next instant she was up and kissing her mother, then out the hall and

raising puffs of dust as she ran toward where I could see other kids seemingly waiting for her.

Nia and I spent the morning wandering around the camp, talking about anything
and everything—except my ancient, recent disgrace. We watched a pickup soccer
game for an hour or so, the players expending the bottled energy that would have
gone to work and home before the disaster, then ended up back at her tent around
three.

Today was as warm as yesterday, and we raised a pretty good sweat. Nia dropped
off to sleep right after, but I couldn't.

Eleven days after the flood, and it was all I could dream about.

Ethan was really starting to get on my nerves. He had seen me hanging out with Nia
and Izzy, and used the new knowledge to taunt me.

"What's up with you and the little girl, Hedges? Thinking of keeping your hand
in with some target practice?"

I stood quivering over his bunk before I even realized I had moved. My fists were
bunched at my hips, ready to strike. But both Ethan and I knew I wouldn't.

The penalty for fighting at any of the Femavilles was instant expulsion, and an
end to government charity. I couldn't risk losing Nia now that I had found her. Even
if we managed to stay in touch while apart, who was to say that the fluid milieu of
the post-disaster environment would not conspire to supplant our relationship with
another.

So I stalked out and went to see Hannah Lawes.

One complex of tents hosted the bureaucrats. Lawes sat at a folding table with
her omnipresent laptop. Hooked to a printer, the machine was churning out travel
vouchers branded with official glyphs of authenticity.

"Mr. Hedges. What can I do for you? Have you decided to take up one of the host
offerings? There's a farming community in Nebraska—"

I shook my head in the negative. Trying to imagine myself relocated to the
prairies was so disorienting that I almost forgot why I had come here.

Hannah Lawes seemed disappointed by my refusal of her proposal, but realistic
about the odds that I would've accepted. "I can't say I'm surprised. Not many people
are leaping at what I can offer. I've only gotten three takers so far. And I can't figure
out why. They're all generous, sensible berths."

"Yeah, sure. That's the problem."

"What do you mean?"

"No one wants 'sensible' after what they've been through. We all want to be reborn as phoenixes—not drayhorses. That's all that would justify our sufferings."

Hannah Lawes said nothing for a moment, and only the minor whine of the
printer filigreed the bubble of silence around us. When she spoke, her voice was utterly neutral.

"You could die here before you achieve that dream, Mr. Hedges. Now, how can I
help you, if not with a permanent relocation?"

"If I arrange different living quarters with the consent of everyone involved, is
there any regulation stopping me from switching tents?"

"No, not at all."

"Good. I'll be back."

I tracked down Nia and found her using a piece of exercise equipment donated
by a local gym. She hopped off and hugged me.

"Have to do something about my weight. I'm not used to all this lolling around."

Nia had been a waitress back in the city, physically active eight or more hours daily. My own routines, at least since Calley left me, had involved more couch-potato time than mountain climbing, and the sloth of camp life sat easier on me.

We hugged, her body sweaty in my arms, and I explained my problem.

"I realize we haven't known each other very long, Nia, but do you think—"

"I'd like it if you moved in with Izzy and me, Parrish. One thing the tsunami taught us—life's too short to dither. And I'd feel safer."

"No one's been bothering you, have they?"

"No, but there's just too many weird noises out here in the country. Every time a branch creaks, I think someone's climbing my steps."

I hugged her again, harder, in wordless thanks.

We both went back to Lawes and arranged the new tent assignments.

When I went to collect my few possessions, Ethan sneered at me.

"Knew you'd run, Hedges. Without your badge, you're nothing."

As I left, I wondered what I had been even with my badge.

Living with Nia and Izzy, I naturally became more involved in the young girl's activities.

And that's when I learned about Djamala.

By the end of the second week in Femaville 29, the atmosphere had begun to sour. The false exuberance engendered by sheer survival amidst so much death—and the accompanying sense of newly opened horizons—had dissipated. In place of these emotions came anomie, irritability, anger, despair and a host of other negative feelings. The immutable, unchanging confines of the unfenced camp assumed the proportions of a stalag. The food, objectively unchanged in quality or quantity, met with disgust, simply because we had no control over its creation. The shared privies assumed a stink no amount of bleach could dispel.

Mere conversation and gossip had paled, replaced with disproportionate arguments over inconsequentials. Sports gave way to various games of chance, played with the odd pair of dice or deck of cards, with bets denominated in sex or clothing or desserts.

One or two serious fights resulted in the promised expulsions, and, chastened but surly, combatants restrained themselves to shoving matches and catcalls.

A few refugees, eager for stimulation and a sense of normality, made the long trek into town—and found themselves returned courtesy of local police cars.

The bureaucrats managing the camp—Hannah Lawes and her peers—were not immune to the shifting psychic tenor of Femaville 29. From models of optimism and can-do effectiveness, the officials began to slide into terse minimalist responses.

"I don't know what more we can do," Hannah Lawes told me. "If our best efforts to reintegrate everyone as functioning and productive members of society are not appreciated, then—"

She left the consequences unstated, merely shaking her head ruefully at our ingratitude and sloth.

The one exception to this general malaise were the children.

Out of a thousand people in Femaville 29, approximately two hundred were children younger than twelve. Although sometimes their numbers seemed larger, as they raced through the camp's streets and avenues in boisterous packs. Seemingly unaffected by the unease and dissatisfaction exhibited by their guardians and parents, the kids continued to enjoy their pastoral interlude. School, curfews, piano lessons—all shed in a return to a prelapsarian existence as hunter-gatherers of the twenty-first century.

When they weren't involved in traditional games, they massed on the outskirts of the camp for an utterly novel undertaking.

There, I discovered, they were building a new city to replace the one they had lost.

Or, perhaps, simply mapping one that already existed.

And Izzy Horsley, I soon learned (with actually very little surprise), was one of the prime movers of this jovial, juvenile enterprise.

With no tools other than their feet and hands, the children had cleared a space almost as big as a football field of all vegetation, leaving behind a dusty canvas on which to construct their representation of an imaginary city.

Three weeks into its construction, the map-cum-model had assumed impressive dimensions, despite the rudimentary nature of its materials.

I came for the first time to the site one afternoon when I grew tired of continuously keeping Nia company in the exercise tent. Her own angst about ensuring the best future for herself and loved ones had manifested as an obsession with "keeping fit" that I couldn't force myself to share. With my mind drifting, a sudden curiosity about where Izzy was spending so much of her time stole over me, and I ambled over to investigate.

Past the ultimate tents, I came upon what could have been a construction site reimagined for the underage cast of *Sesame Street*.

The youngest children were busy assembling stockpiles of stones and twigs and leaves. The stones were quarried from the immediate vicinity, emerging still wet with loam, while sticks and leaves came from a nearby copse in long disorderly caravans.

Older children were engaged in two different kinds of tasks. One chore involved using long pointed sticks to gouge lines in the dirt: lines that plainly marked streets, natural features and the outlines of buildings. The second set of workers was elaborating these outlines with the organic materials from the stockpiles. The map was mostly flat, but occasionally a structure, teepee or cairn, rose up a few inches.

The last, smallest subset of workers were the architects: the designers, engineers, imagineers of the city. They stood off to one side, consulting, arguing, issuing orders, and sometimes venturing right into the map to correct the placement of lines or ornamentation.

Izzy was one of these elite.

Deep in discussion with a cornrowed black girl and a pudgy white boy wearing smudged glasses, Izzy failed to note my approach, and so I was able to overhear their talk. Izzy was holding forth at the moment.

"—Sprankle Hall covers two whole blocks, not just one! C'mon, you gotta remember that! Remember when we went there for a concert, and after we wanted to go around back to the door where the musicians were coming out, and how long it took us to get there?"

The black girl frowned, then said, "Yeah, right, we had to walk like forever. But if Sprankle Hall goes from Cleverly Street all the way to Khush Lane, then how does Pinemarten Avenue run without a break?"

The fat boy spoke with assurance. "It's the Redondo Tunnel. Goes under Sprankle Hall."

Izzy and the black girl grinned broadly. "Of course! I remember when that was built!"

I must have made some noise then, for the children finally noticed me. Izzy rushed over and gave me a quick embrace.

"Hey, Parrish! What're you doing here?"

"I came to see what was keeping you guys so busy. What's going on here?"

Izzy's voice expressed no adult embarrassment, doubt, irony or blasé dismissal of a temporary time-killing project. "We're building a city! Djamala! It's someplace wonderful!"

The black girl nodded solemnly. I recalled the name Vonique from Izzy's earlier conversation, and the name seemed suddenly inextricably linked to this child.

"Well," said Vonique, "it *will* be wonderful, once we finish it. But right now it's still a *mess*."

"This city—Djamala? How did it come to be? Who invented it?"

"Nobody *invented* it!" Izzy exclaimed. "It's always been there. We just couldn't remember it until the wave."

The boy—Eddie?—said, "That's right, sir. The tsunami made it rise up."

"Rise up? Out of the waters, like Atlantis? A new continent?"

Eddie pushed his glasses farther up his nose. "Not out of the ocean. Out of our minds."

My expression must have betrayed disbelief. Izzy grabbed one of my hands with both of hers. "Parrish, please! This is really important for everyone. You gotta believe in Djamala! Really!"

"Well, I don't know if I *can* believe in it the same way you kids can. But what if I promise just not to *dis*believe yet? Would that be good enough?"

Vonique puffed air past her lips in a semi-contemptuous manner. "Huh! I suppose that's as good as we're gonna·get from anyone, until we can show them something they can't ignore."

Izzy gazed up at me with imploring eyes. "Parrish? You're not gonna let us down, are you?"

What could I say? "No, no, of course not. If I can watch and learn, maybe I can start to understand."

Izzy, Vonique and Eddie had to confer with several other pint-sized architects before they could grant me observer's status, but eventually they did confer that honor on me.

So for the next several days I spent most of my time with the children as they constructed their imaginary metropolis.

At first, I was convinced that the whole process was merely some over-elaborated coping strategy for dealing with the disaster that had upended their young lives.

But at the end of a week, I was not so certain.

So long as I did not get in the way of construction, I was allowed to venture down the outlined HO-scale streets, given a tour of the city's extensive features and history by whatever young engineer was least in demand at the moment. The story of Djamala's ancient founding, its history and contemporary life, struck me as remarkably coherent and consistent at the time, although I did not pay as much attention as I should have to the information. I theorized then that the children were merely re-sorting a thousand borrowed bits and pieces from televsion, films and video games. Now, I can barely recall a few salient details. The Crypt of the Thousand Martyrs, the Bluepoint Aerial Tramway, Penton Park, Winkelreed Slough, Mid-winter Festival, the Squid Club—these proper names, delivered in the pure, piping voices of Izzy and her peers, are all that remain to me.

I wished I could get an aerial perspective on the diagram of Djamala. It seemed impossibly refined and balanced to have been plotted out solely from a ground-level perspective. Like the South American drawings at Nazca, its complex lineaments seemed to demand a superior view from some impossible, more-than-mortal vantage point.

After a week spent observing the children—a week during which a light evening rain shower did much damage to Djamala, damage which the children industriously and cheerfully began repairing—a curious visual hallucination overtook me.

Late afternoon sunlight slanted across the map of Djamala as the children began to tidy up in preparation for quitting. Sitting on a borrowed folding chair, I watched their small forms, dusted in gold, move along eccentric paths. My mind commenced to drift amidst wordless regions. The burden of my own body seemed to fall away.

At that moment, the city of Djamala began to assume a ghostly reality, translucent buildings rearing skyward. Ghostly minarets, stadia, pylons—

I jumped up, heart thumping to escape my chest, frightened to my core.

Memory of a rubbish-filled, clammy, partially illuminated hallway, and the shadow of a gunman, pierced me.

My senses had betrayed me fatally once before. How could I ever fully trust them again?

Djamala vanished then, and I was relieved.

A herd of government-drafted school buses materialized one Thursday on the outskirts of Femaville 29, on the opposite side of the camp from Djamala, squatting like empty-eyed yellow elephants, and I knew that the end of the encampment was imminent. But exactly how soon would we be expelled to more permanent quarters not of our choosing? I went to see Hannah Lawes.

I tracked down the social worker in the kitchen of the camp. She was efficiently taking inventory of cases of canned goods.

"Ms. Lawes, can I talk to you?"

A small hard smile quirked one corner of her lips. "Mr. Hedges. Have you had a sudden revelation about your future?"

"Yes, in a way. Those buses—"

"Are not scheduled for immediate use. FEMA believes in proper advance staging of resources."

"But when—"

"Who can say? I assure you that I don't personally make such command decisions. But I will pass along any new directives as soon as I am permitted."

Unsatisfied, I left her tallying creamed corn and green beans.

Everyone in the camp, of course, had seen the buses, and speculation about the fate of Femaville 29 was rampant. Were we to be dispersed to public housing in various host cities? Was the camp to be merged with others into a larger concentration of refugees for economy of scale? Maybe we'd all be put to work restoring our mortally wounded drowned city. Every possibility looked equally likely.

I expected Nia's anxiety to be keyed up by the threat of dissolution of our hard-won small share of stability, this island of improvised family life we had forged. But instead, she surprised me by expressing complete confidence in the future.

"I can't worry about what's coming, Parrish. We're together now, with a roof over our heads, and that's all that counts. Besides, just lately I've gotten a good feeling about the days ahead."

"Based on what?"

Nia shrugged with a smile. "Who knows?"

The children, however, Izzy included, were not quite as sanguine as Nia. The coming of the buses had goaded them to greater activity. No longer did they divide the day into periods of conventional playtime and construction of their city of dreams. Instead, they labored at the construction full-time.

The ant-like trains of bearers ferried vaster quantities of sticks and leaves, practically denuding the nearby copse. The grubbers-up of pebbles broke their nails uncomplainingly in the soil. The scribers of lines ploughed empty square footage into new districts like the most rapacious of suburban developers. The ornamentation crew thatched and laid mosaics furiously. And the elite squad overseeing all the activity wore themselves out like military strategists overseeing an invasion.

"What do we build today?"

"The docks at Kannuckaden."

"But we haven't even put down the Mocambo River yet!"

"Then do the river first! But we have to fill in the Great Northeastern Range before tomorrow!"

"What about Gopher Gulch?"

"That'll be next."

Befriending some kitchen help secured me access to surplus cartons of pre-packaged treats. I took to bringing the snacks to the hard-working children, and they seemed to appreciate it. Although truthfully, they spared little enough attention to me or any other adult, lost in their make-believe, laboring blank-eyed or with feverish intensity.

The increased activity naturally attracted the notice of the adults. Many heretofore-oblivious parents showed up at last to see what their kids were doing. The consensus was that such behavior, while a little weird, was generally harmless enough, and actually positive, insofar as it kept the children from boredom and any concomitant pestering of parents. After a few days of intermittent parental visits, the site was generally clear of adults once more.

One exception to this rule was Ethan Duplessix.

At first, I believed, he began hanging around Djamala solely because he saw me there. Peeved by how I had escaped his taunts, he looked for some new angle from which to attack me, relishing the helplessness of his old nemesis.

But as I continued to ignore the slobby criminal slacker, failing to give him any satisfaction, his frustrated focus turned naturally to what the children were actually doing. My lack of standing as any kind of legal guardian to anyone except, at even the widest stretch of the term, Izzy, meant that I could not prevent the children from talking to him.

They answered Ethan's questions respectfully and completely at first, and I could see interest building in his self-serving brain, as he rotated the facts this way and that, seeking some advantage for himself. But then the children grew tired of his gawking and cut him off.

"We have too much work to do. You've got to go now."

"Please, Mr. Duplessix, just leave us alone."

I watched Ethan's expression change from greedy curiosity to anger. He actually threatened the children.

"You damn kids! You need to share! Or else someone'll just take what you've got!"

I was surprised at the fervor of Ethan's interest in Djamala. Maybe something about the dream project had actually touched a decent, imaginative part of his soul. But whatever the case, his threats gave me a valid excuse to hustle him off.

"You can't keep me away, Hedges! I'll be back!"

Izzy stood by my side, watching Ethan's retreat.

"Don't worry about him," I said.

"I'm not worried, Parrish. Djamala can protect itself."

The sleeping arrangements in the tent Nia, Izzy and I shared involved a hanging blanket down the middle of the tent, to give both Izzy and us adults some privacy. Nia and I had pushed two cots together on our side and lashed them together to make a double bed. But even with a folded blanket atop the wooden bar down the middle of the makeshift bed, I woke up several times a night, as I instinctively tried to snuggle Nia and encountered the hard obstacle. Nia, smaller, slept fine on her side of the double cots.

The night after the incident with Ethan, I woke up as usual in the small hours of the morning. Something urged me to get up. I left the cot and stepped around the hanging barrier to check on Izzy.

Her cot was empty, only blankets holding a ghostly imprint of her small form.

I was just on the point of mounting a general alarm when she slipped back into the tent, clad in pajamas and dew-wet sneakers.

My presence startled her, but she quickly recovered, and smiled guiltlessly.

"Bathroom call?" I whispered.

Izzy never lied. "No. Just checking on Djamala. It's safe now. Today we finished the Iron Grotto. Just in time."

"That's good. Back to sleep now."

Ethan Duplessix had never missed a meal in his life. But the morning after Izzy's nocturnal inspection of Djamala, he was nowhere to be seen at any of the three breakfast shifts. Likewise for lunch. When he failed to show at supper, I went to D-30.

Ethan's sparse possessions remained behind, but the man himself was not there. I reported his absence to Hannah Lawes.

"Please don't concern yourself unnecessarily, Mr. Hedges. I'm sure Mr. Duplessix will turn up soon. He probably spent the night in intimate circumstances with someone."

"Ethan? I didn't realize the camp boasted any female trolls."

"Now, now, Mr. Hedges, that's most ungenerous of you."

Ethan did not surface the next day, or the day after that, and was eventually marked a runaway.

The third week of October brought the dreaded announcement. Lulled by the gentle autumnal weather, the unvarying routines of the camp, and by the lack of any foreshadowings, the citizens of Femaville 29 were completely unprepared for the impact.

A general order to assemble outside by the buses greeted every diner at breakfast. Shortly before noon, a thousand refugees, clad in their donated coats and sweaters and jackets, shuffled their feet on the field that doubled as parking lot, breath pluming in the October chill. The ranks of buses remained as before, save for one unwelcome difference.

The motors of the buses were all idling, drivers behind their steering wheels.

The bureaucrats had assembled on a small raised platform. I saw Hannah Lawes in the front, holding a loud-hailer. Her booming voice assailed us.

"It's time now for your relocation. You've had a fair and lawful amount of time to choose your destination, but have failed to take advantage of this opportunity. Now your government has done so for you. Please board the buses in an orderly fashion. Your possessions will follow later."

"Where are we going?" someone called out.

Imperious, Hannah Lawes answered, "You'll find out when you arrive."

Indignation and confusion bloomed in the crowd. A contradictory babble began to mount heavenward. Hannah Lawes said nothing more immediately. I assumed she was waiting for the chaotic reaction to burn itself out, leaving the refugees sheepishly ready to obey.

But she hadn't counted on the children intervening.

A massed juvenile shriek brought silence in its wake. There was nothing wrong with the children gathered on the edges of the crowd, as evidenced by their nervous smiles. But their tactic had certainly succeeded in drawing everyone's attention.

Izzy was up front of her peers, and she shouted now, her young voice proud and confident.

"Follow us! We've made a new home for everyone!"

The children turned as one and began trotting away toward Djamala.

For a frozen moment, none of the adults made a move. Then, a man and woman—Vonique's parents—set out after the children.

Their departure catalyzed a mad general desperate rush, toward a great impossible unknown that could only be better than the certainty offered by FEMA.

Nia had been standing by my side, but she was swept away. I caught a last glimpse of her smiling, shining face as she looked back for a moment over her shoulder. Then the crowd carried her off.

I found myself hesitating. How could I face the inevitable crushing disappointment of the children, myself and everyone else when their desperate hopes were met by a metropolis of sticks and stones and pebbles? Being there when it happened, seeing all the hurt, crestfallen faces at the instant they were forced to acknowledge defeat, would be sheer torture. Why not just wait here for their predestined return, when we could pretend the mass insanity had never happened, mount the buses and roll off, chastised and broken, to whatever average future was being offered to us?

Hannah Lawes had sidled up to me, loud-hailer held by her side.

"I'm glad to see at least one sensible person here, Mr. Hedges. Congratulations for being a realist."

Her words, her barely concealed glee and schadenfreude, instantly flipped a switch inside me from off to on, and I sped after my fellow refugees.

Halfway through the encampment, I glanced up to see Djamala looming ahead.

The splendors I had seen in ghostly fashion weeks ago were now magnified and recomplicated across acres of space. A city woven of childish imagination stretched impossibly to the horizon and beyond, its towers and monuments sparkling in the sun.

I left the last tents behind me in time to see the final stragglers entering the streets of Djamala. I heard water splash from fountains, shoes tapping on shale sidewalks, laughter echoing down wide boulevards.

But at the same time, I could see only a memory of myself in a ruined building, gun in hand, confronting a shadow assassin.

Which was reality?

I faltered to a stop.

Djamala vanished in a blink.

And I fell insensible to the ground.

I awoke in the tent that served as the infirmary for Femaville 29. Hannah Lawes was stitting by my bedside.

"Feeling better, Mr. Hedges? You nearly disrupted the exodus."

"What—what do you mean?"

"Your fellow refugees. They've all been bussed to their next station in life."

I sat up on my cot. "What are you trying to tell me? Didn't you see the city, Djamala? Didn't you see it materialize where the children built it? Didn't you see all the refugees flood in?"

Hannah Lawes's cocoa skin drained of vitality as she sought to master what were evidently strong emotions in conflict.

"What I saw doesn't matter, Mr. Hedges. It's what the government has determined to have happened that matters. And the government has marked all your fellow refugees from Femaville 29 as settled elsewhere in the normal fashion. Case closed. Only you remain behind to be dealt with. Your fate is separate from theirs now. You certainly won't be seeing any of your temporary neighbors again for some time—if ever."

I recalled the spires and lakes, the pavilions and theaters of Djamala. I pictured Ethan Duplessix rattling the bars of the Iron Grotto. I was sure he'd reform, and be set free eventually. I pictured Nia and Izzy, swanning about in festive apartments, happy and safe, with Izzy enjoying the fruits of her labors.

And myself the lame child left behind by the Pied Piper.

"No," I replied, "I don't suppose I will see them again soon."

Hannah Lawes smiled at my acceptance of her dictates, but only for a moment, until I spoke again.

"But then, you can never be sure."

BENJAMIN ROSENBAUM

A Siege of Cranes

Benjamin Rosenbaum switches so easily between genres that his stories are just as likely to appear in a Year's Best SF *as in this volume. "A Siege of Cranes" is a traditional fantasy tale that appeared in the broad-ranging, loosely-themed anthology,* Twenty Epics, *edited by David Moles and Susan Marie Groppi. Rosenbaum's stories have appeared in* Harper's, McSweeney's, All Star Zeppelin Adventure Stories, Strange Horizons, *and elsewhere. He is a computer programmer by day and lives with his family in the Washington, D.C., area.*

—K.L. & G.G.

The land around Marish was full of the green stalks of sunflowers: tall as men, with bold yellow faces. Their broad leaves were stained black with blood.

The rustling came again, and Marish squatted down on aching legs to watch. A hedgehog pushed its nose through the stalks. It sniffed in both directions.

Hunger dug at Marish's stomach like the point of a stick. He hadn't eaten for three days, not since returning to the crushed and blackened ruins of his house.

The hedgehog bustled through the stalks onto the trail, across the ash, across the trampled corpses of flowers. Marish waited until it was well clear of the stalks before he jumped. He landed with one foot before its nose and one foot behind its tail. The hedgehog, as hedgehogs will, rolled itself into a ball, spines out.

His house: crushed like an egg, smoking, the straw floor soaked with blood. He'd stood there with a trapped rabbit in his hand, alone in the awful silence. Forced himself to call for his wife Temur and his daughter Asza, his voice too loud and too flat. He'd dropped the rabbit somewhere in his haste, running to follow the blackened trail of devastation.

Running for three days, drinking from puddles, sleeping in the sunflowers when he couldn't stay awake.

Marish held his knifepoint above the hedgehog. They gave wishes, sometimes, in tales. "Speak, if you can," he said, "and bid me don't kill you. Grant me a wish! Elsewise, I'll have you for a dinner."

Nothing from the hedgehog, or perhaps a twitch.

Marish drove his knife through it and it thrashed, spraying more blood on the bloodstained flowers.

Too tired to light a fire, he ate it raw.

On that trail of tortured earth, wide enough for twenty horses, among the burnt and flattened flowers, Marish found a little doll of rags, the size of a child's hand.

It was one of the ones Maghd the mad girl made, and offered up, begging for stew meat, or wheedling for old bread behind Lezur's bakery. He'd given her a coin for one, once.

"Wherecome you're giving that sow our good coins?" Temur had cried, her bright eyes flashing, her soft lips pulled into a sneer. None in Ilmak Dale would let a mad girl come near a hearth, and some spit when they passed her. "Bag-Maghd's good for holding one thing only," Fazt would call out and they'd laugh their way into the ale-house. Marish laughing too, stopping only when he looked back at her.

Temur had softened, when she saw how Asza took to the doll, holding it, and singing to it, and smearing gruel on its rag-mouth with her fingers to feed it. They called her "little life-light," and heard her saying it to the doll, "il-ife-ight," rocking it in her arms.

He pressed his nose into the doll, trying to smell Asza's baby smell on it, like milk and forest soil and some sweet spice. But he only smelled the acrid stench of burnt cloth.

When he forced his wet eyes open, he saw a blurry figure coming toward him. Cursing himself for a fool, he tossed the doll away and pulled out his knife, holding it at his side. He wiped his face on his sleeve, and stood up straight, to show the man coming down the trail that the folk of Ilmak Dale did no obeisance. Then his mouth went dry and his hair stood up, for the man coming down the trail was no man at all.

It was a little taller than a man, and had the body of a man, though covered with a dark gray fur; but its head was the head of a jackal. It wore armor of bronze and leather, all straps and discs with curious engravings, and carried a great black spear with a vicious point at each end.

Marish had heard that there were all sorts of strange folk in the world, but he had never seen anything like this.

"May you die with great suffering," the creature said in what seemed to be a calm, friendly tone.

"May *you* die as soon as may be!" Marish cried, not liking to be threatened.

The creature nodded solemnly. "I am Kadath-Naan of the Empty City," it announced. "I wonder if I might ask your assistance in a small matter."

Marish didn't know what to say to this. The creature waited.

Marish said, "You can ask."

"I must speak with . . ." It frowned. "I am not sure how to put this. I do not wish to offend."

"Then why," Marish asked before he could stop himself, "did you menace me on a painful death?"

"Menace?" the creature said. "I only greeted you."

"You said, 'May you die with great suffering.' That like to be a threat or a curse, and I truly don't thank you for it."

The creature frowned. "No, it is a blessing. Or it is from a blessing: 'May you die with great suffering, and come to know holy dread and divine terror, stripping away your vain thoughts and fancies until you are fit to meet the Bone-White Fathers face to face; and may you be buried in honor and your name sung until it is forgotten.' That is the whole passage."

"Oh," said Marish. "Well, that sound a bit better, I reckon."

"We learn that blessing as pups," said the creature in a wondering tone. "Have you never heard it?"

"No indeed," said Marish, and put his knife away. "Now what do you need? I can't think to be much help to you—I don't know this land here."

"Excuse my bluntness, but I must speak with an embalmer, or a sepulchrist, or someone of that sort."

"I've no notion what those are," said Marish.

The creature's eyes widened. It looked, as much as the face of a jackal could, like someone whose darkest suspicions were in the process of being confirmed.

"What do your people do with the dead?" it said.

"We put them in the ground."

"With what preparation? With what rites and monuments?" said the thing.

"In a wood box for them as can afford it, and a piece of linen for them as can't; and we say a prayer to the west wind. We put the stone in with them, what has their soul kept in it." Marish thought a bit, though he didn't much like the topic. He rubbed his nose on his sleeve. "Sometime we'll put a pile of stones on the grave, if it were someone famous."

The jackal-headed man sat heavily on the ground. It put its head in its hands. After a long moment it said, "Perhaps I should kill you now, that I might bury you properly."

"Now you just try that," said Marish, taking out his knife again.

"Would you like me to?" said the creature, looking up.

Its face was serene. Marish found he had to look away, and his eyes fell upon the scorched rags of the doll, twisted up in the stalks.

"Forgive me," said Kadath-Naan of the Empty City. "I should not be so rude as to tempt you. I see that you have duties to fulfill, just as I do, before you are permitted the descent into emptiness. Tell me which way your village lies, and I will see for myself what is done."

"My village—" Marish felt a heavy pressure behind his eyes, in his throat, wanting to push through into a sob. He held it back. "My village is gone. Something come and crushed it. I were off hunting, and when I come back, it were all burning, and full of the stink of blood. Whatever did it made this trail through the flowers. I think it went quick; I don't think I'll likely catch it. But I hope to." He knew he sounded absurd: a peasant chasing a demon. He gritted his teeth against it.

"I see," said the monster. "And where did this something come from? Did the trail come from the north?"

"It didn't come from nowhere. Just the village torn to pieces and this trail leading out."

"And the bodies of the dead," said Kadath-Naan carefully. "You buried them in—wooden boxes?"

"There weren't no bodies," Marish said. "Not of people. Just blood, and a few pieces of bone and gristle, and pigs' and horses' bodies all charred up. That's why I'm following." He looked down. "I mean to find them if I can."

Kadath-Naan frowned. "Does this happen often?"

Despite himself, Marish laughed. "Not that I ever heard before."

The jackal-headed creature seemed agitated. "Then you do not know if the bodies received . . . even what you would consider proper burial."

"I have a feeling they ain't received it," Marish said.

Kadath-Naan looked off in the distance towards Marish's village, then in the direction Marish was heading. It seemed to come to a decision. "I wonder if you would accept my company in your travels," it said. "I was on a different errand, but this matter seems to . . . outweigh it."

Marish looked at the creature's spear and said, "You'd be welcome." He held out the fingers of his hand. "Marish of Ilmak Dale."

The trail ran through the blackened devastation of another village, drenched with blood but empty of human bodies. The timbers of the houses were crushed to kindling; Marish saw a blacksmith's anvil twisted like a lock of hair, and plows that had been melted by enormous heat into a pool of iron. They camped beyond the village, in the shade of a twisted hawthorn tree. A wild autumn wind stroked the meadows around them, carrying dandelion seeds and wisps of smoke and the stink of putrefying cattle.

The following evening they reached a hill overlooking a great town curled around a river. Marish had never seen so many houses—almost too many to count. Most were timber and mud like those of his village, but some were great structures of stone, towering three or four stories into the air. House built upon house, with ladders reaching up to the doors of the ones on top. Around the town, fields full of wheat rustled gold in the evening light. Men and women were reaping in the fields, singing work songs as they swung their scythes.

The path of destruction curved around the town, as if avoiding it.

"Perhaps it was too well defended," said Kadath-Naan.

"May be," said Marish, but he remembered the pool of iron and the crushed timbers, and doubted. "I think that like to be Nabuz. I never come this far south before, but traders heading this way from the fair at Halde were always going to Nabuz to buy."

"They will know more of our adversary," said Kadath-Naan.

"I'll go," said Marish. "You might cause a stir; I don't reckon many of your sort visit Nabuz. You keep to the path."

"Perhaps I might ask of you . . ."

"If they are friendly there, I'll ask how they bury their dead," Marish said.

Kadath-Naan nodded somberly. "Go to duty and to death," he said.

Marish thought it must be a blessing, but he shivered all the same.

The light was dimming in the sky. The reapers heaped the sheaves high on the wagon, their songs slow and low, and the city gates swung open for them.

The city wall was stone, mud and timber, twice as tall as a man, and the great gates were iron. But the wall was not well kept. Marish crept among the stalks to a place where the wall was lower and trash and rubble were heaped high against it.

He heard the creak of the wagon rolling through the gates, the last work song fading away, the men of Nabuz calling out to each other as they made their way home. Then all was still.

Marish scrambled out of the field into a dead run, scrambled up the rubble, leapt atop the wall and lay on its broad top. He peeked over, hoping he had not been seen.

The cobbled street was empty. More than that, the town itself was silent. Even in Ilmak Dale, the evenings had been full of dogs barking, swine grunting, men arguing in the streets and women gossiping and calling the children in. Nabuz was supposed to be a great capital of whoring, drinking and fighting; the traders at Halde had always moaned over the delights that awaited them in the south if they could cheat the villagers well enough. But Marish heard no donkey braying, no baby crying, no cough, no whisper: nothing pierced the night silence.

He dropped over, landed on his feet quiet as he could and crept along the street's edge. Before he had gone ten steps, he noticed the lights.

The windows of the houses flickered, but not with candlelight or the light of fires. The light was cold and blue.

He dragged a crate under the high window of the nearest house and clambered up to see.

There was a portly man with a rough beard, perhaps a potter after his day's work; there was his stout young wife, and a skinny boy of nine or ten. They sat on their low wooden bench, their dinner finished and put to the side (Marish could smell the fresh bread and his stomach cursed him). They were breathing, but their faces were slack, their eyes wide and staring, their lips gently moving. They were bathed in blue light. The potter's wife was rocking her arms gently as if she were cradling a newborn babe—but the swaddling blankets she held were empty.

And now Marish could hear a low inhuman voice, just at the edge of hearing, like a thought of his own. It whispered in time to the flicker of the blue light, and Marish felt himself drawn by its caress. Why not sit with the potter's family on the bench? They would take him in. He could stay here, the whispering promised: forget his village, forget his grief. Fresh bread on the hearth, a warm bed next to the coals of the fire. Work the clay, mix the slip for the potter, eat a dinner of bread and cheese, then listen to the blue light and do what it told him. Forget the mud roads of Ilmak Dale, the laughing roar of Perdan and Thin Deri and Chibar and the others in its alehouse, the harsh cough and crow of its roosters at dawn. Forget willowy Temur, her hair smooth as a river and bright as a sheaf of wheat, her proud shoulders and her slender waist, Temur turning her satin cheek away when he tried to kiss it. Forget the creak and splash of the mill, and the soft rushes on the floor of Maghd's hovel. The potter of Nabuz had a young and willing neice who needed a husband, and the blue light held laughter and love enough for all. Forget the heat and clanging of Fat Deri's smithy; forget the green stone that held Pa's soul, that he'd laid upon his shroud. Forget Asza, little Asza whose tiny body he'd held to his heart . . .

Marish thought of Asza and he saw the potter's wife's empty arms and with one flex of his legs, he kicked himself away from the wall, knocking over the crate and landing sprawled among rolling apples.

He sprang to his feet. There was no sound around him. He stuffed five apples in his pack, and hurried towards the center of Nabuz.

The sun had set, and the moon washed the streets in silver. From every window streamed the cold blue light.

Out of the corner of his eye he thought he saw a shadow dart behind him, and he turned and took out his knife. But he saw nothing, and though his good sense told him five apples and no answers was as much as he should expect from Nabuz, he kept on.

He came to a great square full of shadows, and at first he thought of trees. But it was tall iron frames, and men and women bolted to them upside down. The bolts went through their bodies, crusty with dried blood.

One man nearby was live enough to moan. Marish poured a little water into the man's mouth, and held his head up, but the man could not swallow; he coughed and spluttered, and the water ran down his face and over the bloody holes where his eyes had been.

"But the babies," the man rasped, "how could you let her have the babies?"

"Let who?" said Marish.

"The White Witch!" the man roared in a whisper. "The White Witch, you bastards! If you'd but let us fight her—"

"Why . . ." Marish began.

"Lie again, say the babies will live forever—lie again, you cowardly blue-blood maggots in the corpse of Nabuz . . ." He coughed and blood ran over his face.

The bolts were fast into the frame. "I'll get a tool," Marish said, "you won't—"

From behind him came an awful scream.

He turned and saw the shadow that had followed him: it was a white cat with fine soft fur and green eyes that blazed in the darkness. It shrieked, its fur standing on end, its tail high, staring at him, and his good sense told him it was raising an alarm.

Marish ran, and the cat ran after him, shrieking. Nabuz was a vast pile of looming shadows. As he passed through the empty city gates he heard a grinding sound and a whinny As he raced into the moonlit dusk of open land, down the road to where Kadath-Naan's shadow crossed the demon's path, he heard hoofbeats galloping behind him.

Kadath-Naan had just reached a field of tall barley. He turned to look back at the sound of the hoofbeats and the shrieking of the devil cat. "Into the grain!" Marish yelled. "Hide in the grain!" He passed Kadath-Naan and dived into the barley, the cat racing behind him.

Suddenly he spun and dropped and grabbed the white cat, meaning to get one hand on it and get his knife with the other and shut it up by killing it. But the cat fought like a devil and it was all he could do to hold onto it with both hands. And he saw, behind him on the trail, Kadath-Naan standing calmly, his hand on his spear, facing three knights armored every inch in white, galloping towards them on great chargers.

"You damned dog-man," Marish screamed. "I know you want to die, but get into the grain!"

Kadath-Naan stood perfectly still. The first knight bore down on him, and the moon flashed from the knight's sword. The blade was no more than a handsbreadth from Kadath-Naan's neck when he sprang to the side of it, into the path of the second charger.

As the first knight's charge carried him past, Kadath-Naan knelt, and drove the base of his great spear into the ground. Too late, the second knight made a desperate yank on the horse's reins, but the great beast's momentum carried him into the pike. It tore through the neck of the horse and through the armored chest of the knight riding him, and the two of them reared up and thrashed once like a dying centaur, then crashed to the ground.

The first knight wheeled around. The third met Kadath-Naan. The beast-man stood barehanded, the muscles of his shoulders and chest relaxed. He cocked his jackal head to one side, as if wondering: is it here at last? The moment when I am granted release?

But Marish finally had the cat by its tail, and flung that wild white thing, that frenzy of claws and spit and hissing, into the face of the third knight's steed.

The horse reared and threw its rider; the knight let go of his sword as he crashed to the ground. Quick as a hummingbird, Kadath-Naan leapt and caught it in midair. He spun to face the last rider.

Marish drew his knife and charged through the barley. He was on the fallen knight just as he got to his knees.

The crash against armor took Marish's wind away. The man was twice as strong as Marish was, and his arm went around Marish's chest like a crushing band of iron. But Marish had both hands free, and with a twist of the knight's helmet he exposed a bit of neck, and in Marish's knife went, and then the man's hot blood was spurting out.

The knight convulsed as he died and grabbed Marish in a desperate embrace, coating him with blood, and sobbing once: and Marish held him, for the voice of his heart told him it was a shame to have to die such a way. Marish was shocked at this, for the man was a murderous slave of the White Witch: but still he held the quaking body in his arms, until it moved no more.

Then Marish, soaked with salty blood, staggered to his feet and remembered the last knight with a start: but of course Kadath-Naan had killed him in the meantime. Three knights' bodies lay on the ruined ground, and two living horses snorted and pawed the dirt like awkward mourners. Kadath-Naan freed his spear with a great yank from the horse and man it had transfixed. The devil cat was a sodden blur of white fur and blood: a falling horse had crushed it.

Marish caught the reins of the nearest steed, a huge fine creature, and gentled it with a hand behind its ears. When he had his breath again, Marish said, "We got horses now. Can you ride?"

Kadath-Naan nodded.

"Let's go then; there like to be more coming."

Kadath-Naan frowned a deep frown. He gestured to the bodies.

"What?" said Marish.

"We have no embalmer or sepulchrist, it is true; yet I am trained in the funereal rites for military expeditions and emergencies. I have the necessary tools; in a matter of a day I can raise small monuments. At least they died aware and with suffering; this must compensate for the rudimentary nature of the rites."

"You can't be in earnest," said Marish. "And what of the White Witch?"

"Who is the White Witch?" Kadath-Naan asked.

"The demon; turns out she's somebody what's called the White Witch. She spared Nabuz, for they said they'd serve her, and give her their babies."

"We will follow her afterwards," said Kadath-Naan.

"She's ahead of us as it is! We leave now on horseback, we might have a chance. There be whole lot more bodies with her unburied or buried wrong, less I mistake."

Kadath-Naan leaned on his spear. "Marish of Ilmak Dale," he said, "here we must part ways. I cannot steel myself to follow such logic as you declare, abandoning these three burials before me now for the chance of others elsewhere, if we can catch and defeat a witch. My duty does not lie that way." He searched Marish's face. "You do not have the words for it, but if these men are left unburied, they are *tanzadi*. If I bury them with what little honor I can provide, they are *tazrash*. They spent only a little while alive, but they will be *tanzadi* or *tazrash* forever."

"And if more slaves of the White Witch come along to pay you back for killing these?"

But try as he might, Marish could not dissuade him, and at last he mounted one of the chargers and rode onwards, towards the cold white moon, away from the whispering city.

The flowers were gone, the fields were gone. The ashy light of the horizon framed the ferns and stunted trees of a black fen full of buzzing flies. The trail was wider:

thirty horses could have passed side by side over the blasted ground. But the marshy ground was treacherous, and Marish's mount sank to its fetlocks with each careful step.

A siege of cranes launched themselves from the marsh into the moon-abandoned sky. Marish had never seen so many. Bone-white, fragile, soundless, they ascended like snowflakes seeking the cold womb of heaven. Or a river of souls. None looked back at him. The voice of doubt told him: you will never know what became of Asza and Temur.

The apples were long gone, and Marish was growing light-headed from hunger. He reined the horse in and dismounted; he would have to hunt off the trail. In the bracken, he tied the charger to a great black fern as tall as a house. In a drier spot near its base was the footprint of a rabbit. He felt the indentation. it was fresh. He followed the rabbit deeper into the fen.

He was thinking of Temur and her caresses. The nights she'd turn away from him, back straight as a spear, and the space of rushes between them would be like a frozen desert, and he'd huddle unsleeping beneath skins and woolen blankets, stiff from cold, arguing silently with her in his spirit; and the nights when she'd turn to him, her soft skin hot and alive against his, seeking him silently, almost vengefully, as if showing him—See? This is what you can have. This is what I am.

And then the image of those rushes charred and brown with blood and covered with chips of broken stone and mortar came to him, and he forced himself to think of nothing: breathing his thoughts out to the west wind, forcing his mind clear as a spring stream. And he stepped forward in the marsh.

And stood in a street of blue and purple tile, in a fantastic city.

He stood for a moment wondering, and then he carefully took a step back.

And he was in a black swamp with croaking toads and nothing to eat.

The voice of doubt told him he was mad from hunger; the voice of hope told him he would find the White Witch here and kill her; and thinking a thousand things, he stepped forward again and found himself still in the swamp.

Marish thought for a while, and then he stepped back, and, thinking of nothing, stepped forward.

The tiles of the street were a wild mosaic—some had glittering jewels; some had writing in a strange flowing script; some seemed to have tiny windows into tiny rooms. Houses, tiled with the same profusion, towered like columns, bulged like mushrooms, melted like wax. Some danced. He heard soft murmurs of conversation, footfalls and the rush of a river.

In the street, dressed in feathers or gold plates or swirls of shadow, blue-skinned people passed. One such creature, dressed in fine silk, was just passing Marish.

"Your pardon," said Marish, "what place be this here?"

The man looked at Marish slowly. He had a red jewel in the center of his forehead, and it flickered as he talked. "That depends on how you enter it," he said, "and who you are, but for you, catarrhine, its name is Zimzarkanthitrugenia-fenstok, not least because that is easy for you to pronounce. And now I have given you one thing free, as you are a guest of the city."

"How many free things do I get?" said Marish.

"Three. And now I have given you two."

Marish thought about this for a moment. "I'd favor something to eat," he said.

The man looked surprised. He led Marish into a building that looked like a blur of spinning triangles, through a dark room lit by candles, to a table piled with capon and custard and razor-thin slices of ham and lamb's foot jelly and candied apricots and goatsmilk yogurt and hard cheese and yams and turnips and olives and fish cured in strange spices; and those were just the things Marish recognized.

"I don't reckon I ought to eat fairy food," said Marish, though he could hardly speak from all the spit that was suddenly in his mouth.

"That is true, but from the food of the djinn you have nothing to fear. And now I have given you three things," said the djinn, and he bowed and made as if to leave.

"Hold on," said Marish, as he followed some candied apricots down his gullet with a fistful of cured fish. "That be all the free things, but say I got something to sell?"

The djinn was silent.

"I need to kill the White Witch," Marish said, eating an olive. The voice of doubt asked him why he was telling the truth, if this city might also serve her; but he told it to hush up. "Have you got aught to help me?"

The djinn still said nothing, but he cocked an eyebrow.

"I've got a horse, a real fighting horse," Marish said, around a piece of cheese.

"What is its name?" said the djinn. "You cannot sell anything to a djinn unless you know its name."

Marish wanted to lie about the name, but he found he could not. He swallowed. "I don't know its name," he admitted.

"Well then," said the djinn.

"I killed the fellow what was on it," Marish said, by way of explanation.

"Who," said the djinn.

"Who what?" said Marish.

"Who was on it," said the djinn.

"I don't know his name either," said Marish, picking up a yam.

"No, I am not asking that," said the djinn crossly, "I am telling you to say, 'I killed the fellow who was on it.'"

Marish set the yam back on the table. "Now that's enough," Marish said. "I thank you for the fine food and I thank you for the three free things, but I do not thank you for telling me how to talk. How I talk is how we talk in Ilmak Dale, or how we did talk when there were an Ilmak Dale, and just because the White Witch blasted Ilmak Dale to splinters don't mean I am going to talk like folk do in some magic city."

"I will buy that from you," said the djinn.

"What?" said Marish, and wondered so much at this that he forgot to pick up another thing to eat.

"The way you talked in Ilmak Dale," the djinn said.

"All right," Marish said, "and for it, I crave to know the thing what will help me mostways, for killing the White Witch."

"I have a carpet that flies faster than the wind," said the djinn. "I think it is the only way you can catch the Witch, and unless you catch her, you cannot kill her."

"Wonderful," Marish cried with glee. "And you'll trade me that carpet for how we talk in Ilmak Dale?"

"No," said the djinn, "I told you which thing would help you most, and in return for that, I took the way you talked in Ilmak Dale and put it in the Great Library."

Marish frowned. "All right, what do you want for the carpet?"

The djinn was silent.

"I'll give you the White Witch for it," Marish said.

"You must possess the thing you sell," the djinn said.

"Oh, I'll get her," Marish said. "You can be sure of that." His hand had found a boiled egg, and the shell crunched in his palm as he said it.

The djinn looked at Marish carefully, and then he said, "The use of the carpet, for three days, in return for the White Witch, if you can conquer her."

"Agreed," said Marish.

They had to bind the horse's eyes; otherwise it would rear and kick, when the carpet rose into the air. Horse, man, djinn: all perched on a span of cloth. As they sped back to Nabuz like a mad wind, Marish tried not to watch the solid fields flying beneath, and regretted the candied apricots.

The voice of doubt told him that his companion must be slain by now, but his heart wanted to see Kadath-Naan again: but for the jackal-man, Marish was friendless.

Among the barley stalks, three man-high plinths of black stone, painted with white glyphs, marked three graves. Kadath-Naan had only traveled a little ways beyond them before the ambush. How long the emissary of the Empty City had been fighting, Marish could not tell; but he staggered and weaved like a man drunk with wine or exhaustion. His gray fur was matted with blood and sweat.

An army of children in white armor surrounded Kadath-Naan. As the carpet swung closer, Marish could see their gray faces and blank eyes. Some crawled, some tottered: none seemed to have lived more than six years of mortal life. They held daggers. One clung to the jackal-man's back, digging canals of blood.

Two of the babies were impaled on the point of the great black spear. Hand over hand, daggers held in their mouths, they dragged themselves down the shaft towards Kadath-Naan's hands. Hundreds more surrounded him, closing in.

Kadath-Naan swung his spear, knocking the slack-eyed creatures back. He struck with enough force to shatter human skulls, but the horrors only rolled, and scampered giggling back to stab his legs. With each swing, the spear was slower. Kadath-Naan's eyes rolled back into their sockets. His great frame shuddered from weariness and pain.

The carpet swung low over the battle, and Marish lay on his belly, dangling his arms down to the jackal-headed warrior. He shouted: "Jump! Kadath-Naan, jump!"

Kadath-Naan looked up and, gripping his spear in both hands, he tensed his legs to jump. But the pause gave the tiny servitors of the White Witch their chance; they swarmed over his body, stabbing with their daggers, and he collapsed under the writhing mass of his enemies.

"Down further! We can haul him aboard!" yelled Marish.

"I sold you the use of my carpet, not the destruction of it," said the djinn.

With a snarl of rage, and before the voice of his good sense could speak, Marish leapt from the carpet. He landed amidst the fray, and began tearing the small bodies from Kadath-Naan and flinging them into the fields. Then daggers found his calves, and small bodies crashed into his sides, and he tumbled, covered with the white-armored hell-children. The carpet sailed up lazily into the summer sky.

Marish thrashed, but soon he was pinned under a mass of small bodies. Their daggers probed his sides, drawing blood, and he gritted his teeth against a scream; they pulled at his hair and ears and pulled open his mouth to look inside. As if they were playing. One gray-skinned suckling child, its scalp peeled half away to reveal the white bone of its skull, nuzzled at his neck, seeking the nipple it would never find again.

So had Asza nuzzled against him. So had been her heft, then, light and snug as five apples in a bag. But her live eyes saw the world, took it in and made it better than it was. In those eyes he was a hero, a giant to lift her, honest and gentle and brave. When Temur looked into those otter-brown, mischievous eyes, her mouth softened from its hard line, and she sang fairy songs.

A dagger split the skin of his forehead, bathing him in blood. Another dug between his ribs, another popped the skin of his thigh. Another pushed against his gut, but hadn't broken through. He closed his eyes. They weighed heavier on him now; his throat tensed to scream, but he could not catch his breath.

Marish's arms ached for Asza and Temur—ached that he would die here, without them. Wasn't it right, though, that they be taken from him? The little girl who ran to him across the fields of an evening, a funny hopping run, her arms flung wide, waving that rag doll; no trace of doubt in her. And the beautiful wife who stiffened when she saw him, but smiled one-edged, despite herself, as he lifted apple-smelling Asza in his arms. He had not deserved them.

His face, his skin were hot and slick with salty blood. He saw, not felt, the daggers digging deeper—arcs of light across a great darkness. He wished he could comfort Asza one last time, across that darkness. As when she would awaken in the night, afraid of witches: now a witch had come.

He found breath, he forced his mouth open and he sang through sobs to Asza, his song to lull her back to sleep:

Now sleep, my love, now sleep—
The moon is in the sky—
The clouds have fled like sheep—
You're in your papa's eye.
Sleep now, my love, sleep now—
The bitter wind is gone—
The calf sleeps with the cow—
Now sleep my love 'til dawn.

He freed his left hand from the press of bodies. He wiped blood and tears from his eyes. He pushed his head up, dizzy, flowers of light still exploding across his vision. The small bodies were still. Carefully, he eased them to the ground.

The carpet descended, and Marish hauled Kadath-Naan onto it. Then he forced himself to turn, swaying, and look at each of the gray-skinned babies sleeping peacefully on the ground. None of them was Asza.

He took one of the smallest and swaddled it with rags and bridle leather. His blood made his fingers slick, an the noon sun seemed as gray as a stone. When he was sure the creature could not move, he put it in his pack and slung the pack upon his back. Then he fell onto the carpet. He felt it lift up under him, and like a cradled child, he slept.

He awoke to see clouds sailing above him. The pain was gone. He sat up and looked at his arms: they were whole and unscarred. Even the old scar from Thin Deri's careless scythe was gone.

"You taught us how to defeat the Children of Despair," said the djinn. "That required recompense. I have treated your wounds and those of your companion. Is the debt clear?"

"Answer me one question," Marish said.

"And the debt will be clear?" said the djinn.

"Yes, may the west wind take you, it'll be clear!"

The djinn blinked in assent.

"Can they be brought back?" Marish asked. "Can they be made into living children again?"

"They cannot," said the djinn. "They can neither live nor die, nor be harmed at all unless they will it. Their hearts have been replaced with sand."

They flew in silence, and Marish's pack seemed heavier.

The land flew by beneath them as fast as a cracking whip; Marish stared as green fields gave way to swamp, swamp to marsh, marsh to rough pastureland. The devastation left by the White Witch seemed gradually newer; the trail here was still smoking, and Marish thought it might be too hot to walk on. They passed many a blasted village, and each time Marish looked away.

At last they began to hear a sound on the wind, a sound that chilled Marish's heart. It was not a wail, it was not a grinding, it was not a shriek of pain, nor the wet crunch of breaking bones, nor was it an obscene grunting; but it had something of all of these. The jackal-man's ears were perked, and his gray fur stood on end.

The path was now truly still burning; they flew high above it, and the rolling smoke underneath was like a fog over the land. But there ahead they saw the monstrous thing that was leaving the trail; and Marish could hardly think any thought at all as they approached, but only stare, bile burning his throat.

It was a great chariot, perhaps eight times the height of a man, as wide as the trail, constructed of parts of living human bodies welded together in an obscene tangle. A thousand legs and arms pawed the ground; a thousand more beat the trail with whips and scythes, or clawed the air. A thick skein of hearts, livers and stomachs pulsed through the center of the thing, and a great assemblage of lungs breathed at its core. Heads rolled like wheels at the bottom of the chariot, or were stuck here and there along the surface of the thing as slack-eyed, gibbering ornaments. A thousand spines and torsos built a great chamber at the top of the chariot, shielded with webs of skin and hair; there perhaps hid the White Witch. From the pinnacle of the monstrous thing flew a great flag made of writhing tongues. Before the awful chariot rode a company of ten knights in white armor, with visored helms.

At the very peak sat a great headless hulking beast, larger than a bear, with the skin of a lizard, great yellow globes of eyes set on its shoulders and a wide mouth in its belly. As they watched, it vomited a gout of flame that set the path behind the chariot ablaze. Then it noticed them, and lifted the great plume of flame in their direction. At a swift word from the djinn, the carpet veered, but it was a close enough thing that Marish felt an oven's blast of heat on his skin. He grabbed the horse by its reins as it made to rear, and whispered soothing sounds in its ear.

"Abomination!" cried Kadath-Naan. "Djinn, will you send word to the Empty City? You will be well rewarded."

The djinn nodded.

"It is Kadath-Naan, lesser scout of the Endless Inquiry, who speaks. Let Bars-Kardereth, Commander of the Silent Legion, be told to hasten here. Here is an obscenity beyond compass, far more horrible than the innocent errors of savages; here Chaos blocks the descent into the Darkness entirely, and a whole land may fall to corruption."

The jewel in the djinn's forehead flashed once. "It is done," he said.

Kadath-Naan turned to Marish. "From the Empty City to this place is four days' travel for a Ghomlu Legion; let us find a place in their path where we can wait to join them."

Marish forced himself to close his eyes. But still he saw it—hands, tongues, guts, skin, woven into a moving mountain. He still heard the squelching, grinding, snapping sounds, the sea-roar of the thousand lungs. What had he imagined? Asza and Temur in a prison somewhere, waiting to be freed? Fool. "All right," he said.

Then he opened his eyes, and saw something that made him say, "No."

Before them, not ten minutes' ride from the awful chariot of the White Witch, was a whitewashed village, peaceful in the afternoon sun. Arrayed before it were a score of its men and young women. A few had proper swords or spears; one of the women carried a bow. The others had hoes, scythes and staves. One woman sat astride a horse; the rest were on foot. From their perch in the air, Marish could see distant figures—families, stooped grandmothers, children in their mothers' arms— crawling like beetles up the faces of hills.

"Down," said Marish, and they landed before the village's defenders, who raised their weapons.

"You've got to run," he said, "you can make it to the hills. You haven't seen that thing—you haven't any chance against it."

A dark man spat on the ground. "We tried that in Gravenge."

"It splits up," said a black-bearded man. "Sends littler horrors, and they tear folks up and make them part of it, and you see your fellow's limbs come after you as part of the thing. And they're fast. Too fast for us."

"We just busy it a while," another man said, "our folk can get far enough away." But he had a wild look in his eye: the voice of doubt was in him.

"We stop it here," said the woman on horseback.

Marish led the horse off the carpet, took its blinders off and mounted it. "I'll stand with you," he said.

"And welcome," said the woman on horseback, and her plain face broke into a nervous smile. It was almost pretty that way.

Kadath-Naan stepped off the carpet, and the villagers shied back, readying their weapons.

"This is Kadath-Naan, and you'll be damned glad you have him," said Marish.

"Where's your manners?" snapped the woman on horseback to her people. "I'm Asza," she said.

No, Marish thought, staring at her. No, but you could have been. He looked away, and after a while they left him alone.

The carpet rose silently off into the air, and soon there was smoke on the horizon, and the knights rode at them, and the chariot rose behind.

"Here we are," said Asza of the rocky lands, "now make a good accounting of yourselves."

An arrow sang; a white knight's horse collapsed. Marish cried "Ha!" and his mount surged forward. The villagers charged, but Kadath-Naan outpaced them all, springing between a pair of knights. He shattered the forelegs of one horse with his spear's shaft, drove its point through the side of the other rider. Villagers fell on the fallen knight with their scythes.

It was a heady wild thing for Marish, to be galloping on such a horse, a far finer horse than ever Redlegs had been, for all Pa's proud and vain attention to her. The warmth of its flanks, the rhythm of posting into its stride. Marish of Ilmak Dale, riding into a charge of knights: miserable addle-witted fool.

Asza flicked her whip at the eyes of a knight's horse, veering away. The knight wheeled to follow her, and Marish came on after him. He heard the hooves of another knight pounding the plain behind him in turn.

Ahead the first knight gained on Asza of the rocky plains. Marish took his knife in one hand, and bent his head to his horse's ear, and whispered to it in wordless murmurs: fine creature, give me everything. And his horse pulled even with Asza's knight.

Marish swung down, hanging from his pommel—the ground flew by beneath him. He reached across and slipped his knife under the girth that held the knight's saddle. The knight swiveled, raising his blade to strike—then the girth parted, and he flew from his mount.

Marish struggled up into the saddle, and the second knight was there, armor blazing in the sun. This time Marish was on the sword-arm's side, and his horse had slowed, and that blade swung up and it could strike Marish's head from his neck like snapping off a sunflower; time for the peasant to die.

Asza's whip lashed around the knight's sword-arm. The knight seized the whip in his other hand. Marish sprang from the saddle. He struck a wall of chain mail and fell with the knight.

The ground was an anvil, the knight a hammer, Marish a rag doll sewn by a poor mad girl and mistaken for a horseshoe. He couldn't breathe; the world was a ringing blur. The knight found his throat with one mailed glove, and hissed with rage, and pulling himself up drew a dagger from his belt. Marish tried to lift his arms.

Then he saw Asza's hands fitting a leather noose around the knight's neck. The knight turned his visored head to see, and Asza yelled, "Yah!" An armored knee cracked against Marish's head, and then the knight was gone, dragged off over the rocky plains behind Asza's galloping mare.

Asza of the rocky lands helped Marish to his feet. She had a wild smile, and she hugged him to her breast; pain shot through him, as did the shock of her soft body. Then she pulled away, grinning, and looked over his shoulder back towards the village. And then the grin was gone.

Marish turned. He saw the man with the beard torn apart by a hundred grasping arms and legs. Two bending arms covered with eyes watched carefully as his organs were woven into the chariot. The village burned. A knight leaned from his saddle to cut a fleeing woman down, harvesting her like a stalk of wheat.

"No!" shrieked Asza, and ran towards the village.

Marish tried to run, but he could only hobble, gasping, pain tearing through his side. Asza snatched a spear from the ground and swung up onto a horse. Her hair was like Temur's, flowing gold. My Asza, my Temur, he thought. I must protect her.

Marish fell; he hit the ground and held onto it like a lover, as if he might fall into the sky. Fool, fool, said the voice of his good sense. That is not your Asza, or your Temur either. She is not yours at all.

He heaved himself up again and lurched on, as Asza of the rocky plains reached the chariot. From above, a lazy plume of flame expanded. The horse reared. The cloud of fire enveloped the woman, the horse, and then was sucked away; the blackened corpses fell to the ground steaming.

Marish stopped running.

The headless creature of fire fell from the chariot—Kadath-Naan was there at the summit of the horror, his spear sunk in its flesh as a lever. But the fire-beast turned as it toppled, and a pillar of fire engulfed the jackal-man. The molten iron of his spear and armor coated his body, and he fell into the grasping arms of the chariot.

Marish lay down on his belly in the grass.

Maybe they will not find me here, said the voice of hope. But it was like listening to idiot words spoken by the wind blowing through a forest. Marish lay on the ground and he hurt. The hurt was a song, and it sang him. Everything was lost and far away. No Asza, no Temur, no Maghd; no quest, no hero, no trickster, no hunter, no father, no groom. The wind came down from the mountains and stirred the grass beside Marish's nose, where beetles walked.

There was a rustling in the short grass, and a hedgehog came out of it and stood nose to nose with Marish.

"Speak if you can," Marish whispered, "and grant me a wish."

The hedgehog snorted. "I'll not do *you* any favors, after what you did to Teodor!"

Marish swallowed. "The hedgehog in the sunflowers?"

"Obviously. Murderer."

"I'm sorry! I didn't know he was magic! I thought he was just a hedgehog!"

"Just a hedgehog! Just a hedgehog!" It narrowed its eyes, and its prickers stood on end. "Be careful what you call things, Marish of Ilmak Dale. When you name a thing, you say what it is in the world. Names mean more than you know."

Marish was silent.

"Teodor didn't like threats, that's all . . . the stubborn old idiot."

"I'm sorry about Teodor," said Marish.

"Yes, well," said the hedgehog. "I'll help you, but it will cost you dear."

"What do you want?"

"How about your soul?" said the hedgehog.

"I'd do that, sure," said Marish. "It's not like I need it. But I don't have it."

The hedgehog narrowed its eyes again. From the village, a few thin screams and the soft crackle of flames. It smelled like autumn, and butchering hogs.

"It's true," said Marish. "The priest of Ilmak Dale took all our souls and put them in little stones, and hid them. He didn't want us making bargains like these."

"Wise man," said the hedgehog. "But I'll have to have something. What have you got in you, besides a soul?"

"What do you mean, like, my wits? But I'll need those."

"Yes, you will," said the hedgehog.

"Hope? Not much of that left, though."

"Not to my taste anyway," said the hedgehog. " '*Hope is foolish, doubts are wise.*' "

"Doubts?" said Marish.

"That'll do," said the hedgehog. "But I want them all."

"All . . . all right," said Marish. "And now you're going to help me against the White Witch?"

"I already have," said the hedgehog.

"You have? Have I got some magic power or other now?" asked Marish. He sat up. The screaming was over: he heard nothing but the fire, and the crunching and squelching and slithering and grinding of the chariot.

"Certainly not," said the hedgehog. "I haven't done anything you didn't see or didn't hear. But perhaps you weren't listening." And it waddled off into the green blades of the grass.

Marish stood and looked after it. He picked at his teeth with a thumbnail, and thought, but he had no idea what the hedgehog meant. But he had no doubts, either, so he started toward the village.

Halfway there, he noticed the dead baby in his pack wriggling, so he took it out and held it in his arms.

As he came into the burning village, he found himself just behind the great fire-spouting lizard-skinned headless thing. It turned and took a breath to burn him alive, and he tossed the baby down its throat. There was a choking sound, and the huge thing shuddered and twitched, and Marish walked on by it.

The great chariot saw him and it swung toward him, a vast mountain of writhing, humming, stinking flesh, a hundred arms reaching. Fists grabbed his shirt, his hair, his trousers, and they lifted him into the air.

He looked at the hand closed around his collar. It was a woman's hand, fine and fair, and it was wearing the copper ring he'd bought at Halde.

"Temur!" he said in shock.

The arm twitched and slackened; it went white. It reached out: the fingers spread wide; it caressed his cheek gently. And then it dropped from the chariot and lay on the ground beneath.

He knew the hands pulling him aloft. "Lezur the baker!" he whispered, and a pair of doughy hands dropped from the chariot. "Silbon and Felbon!" he cried. "Ter the blind! Sela the blue-eyed!" Marish's lips trembled to say the names, and the hands slackened and fell to the ground, and away on other parts of the chariot the other parts fell off too; he saw a blue eye roll down from above him and fall to the ground.

"Perdan! Mardid! Pilg and his old mother! Fazt—oh Fazt, you'll tell no more jokes! Chibar and his wife, the pretty foreign one!" His face was wet; with every name, a bubble popped open in Marish's chest, and his throat was thick with some strange feeling. "Pizdar the priest! Fat Deri, far from your smithy! Thin Deri!" When all the hands and arms of Ilmak Dale had fallen off, he was left standing free. He looked at the strange hands coming toward him. "You were a potter," he said to hands with clay under the nails, and they fell off the chariot. "And you were a butcher," he said to bloody ones, and they fell too. "A fat farmer, a beautiful young girl, a grandmother, a harlot, a brawler," he said, and enough hands and feet and heads and organs had slid off the chariot now that it sagged in the middle and pieces of it strove with each other blindly. "Men and women of Eckdale," Marish said, "men and women of Halde, of Gravenge, of the fields and the swamps and the rocky plains."

The chariot fell to pieces; some lay silent and still, others which Marish had not named had lost their purchase and thrashed on the ground.

The skin of the great chamber atop the chariot peeled away and the White Witch leapt into the sky. She was three times as tall as any woman; her skin was bone white; one eye was blood red and the other emerald green; her mouth was full of black fangs, and her hair of snakes and lizards. Her hands were full of lightning, and she sailed onto Marish with her fangs wide open.

And around her neck, on a leather thong, she wore a little doll of rags, the size of a child's hand.

"Maghd of Ilmak Dale," Marish said, and she was also a young woman with muddy hair and an uncertain smile, and that's how she landed before Marish.

"Well done, Marish," said Maghd, and pulled at a muddy lock of her hair, and laughed, and looked at the ground. "Well done! Oh, I'm glad. I'm glad you've come."

"Why did you do it, Maghd?" Marish said. "Oh, why?"

She looked up and her lips twitched and her jaw set. "Can you ask me that? You, Marish?"

She reached across, slowly, and took his hand. She pulled him, and he took a step toward her. She put the back of his hand against her cheek.

"You'd gone out hunting," she said. "And that Temur of yours"—she said the name as if it tasted of vinegar—"she seen me back of Lezur's, and for one time I didn't look down. I looked at her eyes, and she named me a foul witch. And then they were all crowding round—" She shrugged. "And I don't like that. Fussing and crowding and one against the other." She let go his hand and stooped to pick up a clot of earth, and she crumbled it in her hands. "So I knit them all together. All one thing. They did like it. And they were so fine and great and happy, I forgave them. Even Temur."

The limbs lay unmoving on the ground; the guts were piled in soft unbreathing hills, like drifts of snow. Maghd's hands were coated with black crumbs of dirt.

"I reckon they're done of playing now," Maghd said, and sighed.

"How?" Marish said. "How'd you do it? Maghd, what *are* you?"

"Don't fool so! I'm Maghd, same as ever. I found the souls, that's all. Dug them up from Pizdar's garden, sold them to the Spirit of Unwinding Things." She brushed the dirt from her hands.

"And . . . the children, then? Maghd, the babes?"

She took his hand again, but she didn't look at him. She lay her cheek against her shoulder and watched the ground. "Babes shouldn't grow," she said. "No call to be big and hateful." She swallowed. "I made them perfect. That's all."

Marish's chest tightened. "And what now?"

She looked at him, and a slow grin crept across her face. "Well now," she said. "That's on you, ain't it, Marish? I got plenty of tricks yet, if you want to keep fighting." She stepped close to him, and rested her cheek on his chest. Her hair smelled like home: rushes and fire smoke, cold mornings and sheep's milk. "Or we can gather close. No one to shame us now." She wrapped her arms around his waist. "It's all new, Marish, but it ain't all bad."

A shadow drifted over them, and Marish looked up to see the djinn on his carpet, peering down. Marish cleared his throat. "Well . . . I suppose we're all we have left, aren't we?"

"That's so," Maghd breathed softly.

He took her hands in his, and drew back to look at her. "Will you be mine, Maghd?" he said.

"Oh yes," said Maghd, and smiled the biggest smile of her life.

"Very good," Marish said, and looked up. "You can take her now."

The djinn opened the little bottle that was in his hand and Maghd the White Witch flew into it, and he put the cap on. He bowed to Marish, and then he flew away.

Behind Marish the fire beast exploded with a dull boom.

Marish walked out of the village a little ways and sat, and after sitting a while he slept. And then he woke and sat, and then he slept some more. Perhaps he ate as well; he wasn't sure what. Mostly he looked at his hands; they were rough and callused, with dirt under the nails. He watched the wind painting waves in the short grass, around the rocks and bodies lying there.

―――――――

One morning he woke, and the ruined village was full of jackal-headed men in armor made of discs who were mounted on great red cats with pointed ears, and jackal-headed men in black robes who were measuring for monuments, and jackal-headed men dressed only in loincloths who were digging in the ground.

Marish went to the ones in loincloths and said, "I want to help bury them," and they gave him a shovel.

JEANNE MARIE BEAUMONT

Is Rain My Bearskin?

Jeanne Marie Beaumont is the author of two collections of poetry, Placebo Effects, *a winner in the National Poetry Series, and* Curious Conduct. *Her poems have appeared in* The Norton Introduction to Literature, Double Take, Harper's, New American Writing, *and* Poetry, *and her poem "Afraid So" was made into a short film by award-winning filmmaker Jay Rosenblatt. She holds an MFA in writing from Columbia University and teaches at the Unterberg Poetry Center of the 92nd Street Y in New York City. With Claudia Carlson, Beaumont co-edited the anthology* The Poets' Grimm: Twentieth Century Poems from Grimm Fairy Tales, *which we picked as one of the best books of the year in the seventeenth volume of this series, calling it "an anthology to savor, and to read aloud." "Is Rain My Bearskin?" appeared in the Green Issue of* The Fairy Tale Review.*

—K.L. & G.G.

Pssst.
              I'm the blonde in the shower
water too hot   water too cold
              ahhh
                          No one gave me
                              the key
I picked the locks and made myself
              at home in the pantry

My belly's distended   worn
          one moment on fire   one moment on ice
I emptied the honey pot
                          cooked up all the spam
spit it out
                  had to eat a box
of nice cookies to kill the taste
          of the chowder I chowed down
                          once I'd found
a proper porringer   the right-sized spoon
a chair that
would bear
my heft

without crashing
       (it only grumbled a bit)

I'm the freeloader   thief who stole day from night
          one too dark   one too light
Look
    I've used up the sham-
poo scouring my fur   for the final act
              I crack
                  the safe
run off into the pelting rain
         counting the gold that clangs in the satchel
            wrong   wrong
Grrrrr   who am I in the story
                  I'm just right
This time the car is waiting
        I get away with everything

YSABEAU S. WILCE

The Lineaments of
Gratified Desire

Ysabeau S. Wilce's novella "The Lineaments of Gratified Desire" was published in the July issue of The Magazine of Fantasy & Science Fiction. *"Lineaments" is her third published story and, like "Metal More Attractive" (also in* The Magazine of Fantasy & Science Fiction), *is set in the same world as her excellent and recent debut young adult novel,* Flora Segunda, Being the Magickal Mishaps of a Girl of Spirit, Her Glass-Gazing Sidekick, Two Ominous Butlers (One Blue), A House with Eleven Thousand Rooms and a Red Dog. *A historian by training and a fabulist by inclination, Wilce lives in Chicago.*
—K.L. & G.G.
—E.D.

Abstinence sows sand all over
The ruddy limbs & flowing hair
But Desire Gratified
Plants fruit of life & beauty there.

—William Blake

I: Stage Fright

Here is Hardhands up on the stage, and he's cheery cherry, sparking fire, he's as fast as a fox-trotter, stepping high. Sweaty blood dribbles his brow, bloody sweat stipples his torso, and behind him the Vortex buzzsaw whines, its whirling outer edge black enough to cut glass. The razor in his hand flashes like a heliograph as he motions the final Gesture of the invocation. The Eye of the Vortex flutters, but its perimeter remains firmly within the structure of Hardhands' Will and does not expand. He ululates a Command, and the Eye begins to open, like a pupil dilating in sunlight, and from its vivid yellowness comes a glimpse of scales and horns, struggling not to be born. Someone tugs at Hardhands' foot. His concentration wavers. Someone yanks on the hem of his kilt. His concentration wiggles, and the Vortex wobbles slightly like a run-down top. Someone tugs on his kilt-hem, and his concentration collapses completely, and so does the Vortex, sucking into itself like water down a drain. There goes the Working for which Hardhands has been preparing for the last two weeks, and there goes the Tygers of Wrath's new drummer, and there goes their boot-kicking show.

Hardhands throws off the grasp with a hard shake, and looking down, prepares to smite. His lover is shouting upward at him, words that Hardhands can hardly hear, words he hopes he can hardly hear, words he surely did not hear a-right. The interior of the club is toweringly loud, noisy enough to make the ears bleed, but suddenly the thump of his heart, already driven hard by the strength of his magickal invocation, is louder.

Relais, pale as paper, repeats the shout. This time there is no mistaking what he says, much as Hardhands would like to mistake it, much as he would like to hear something else, something sweet and charming, something like: you are the prettiest thing ever born, or the Goddess grants wishes in your name, or they are killing themselves in the streets because the show is sold right out. Alas, Relais is shouting nothing quite so sweet.

"What do you mean you can not find Tiny Doom?" Hardhands shouts back. He looks wildly around the congested club, but it's dark and there are so many of them, and most of them have huge big hair and huger bigger boots. A tiny purple girl-child and her stuffy pink pig have no hope in this throng; they'd be trampled under foot in a second. That is exactly what Hardhands had told the Pontifexa earlier that day; no babysitter, he, other business, other pleasures, no time to take care of small children, not on this night of all nights: The Tygers of Wrath's biggest show of the year. Find someone else.

Well, talkers are no good doers, they say, and talking had done no good, all the yapping growling barking howling in the world had not changed the Pontifexa's mind: it's Paimon's night off, darling, and she'll be safe with you, Banastre, I can trust my heir with no one else, my sweet boy, do your teeny grandmamma this small favor and how happy I shall be, and here, kiss-kiss, I must run, I'm late, have a wonderful evening, good luck with the show, be careful with your invocation, cheerie-bye my darling.

And now see:

Hardhands roars: "I told you to keep an eye on her, Relais!"

He had too, he couldn't exactly watch over Tiny Doom (so called because she is the first in stature and the second in fate), while he was invoking the drummer, and with no drummer, there's no show (no show damn it!) and anyway if he's learned anything as the grandson of the Pontifexa of Califa, it's how to delegate.

Relais shouts back garbled defense. His eyes are whirling pie-plates. He doesn't mention that he stopped at the bar on his way to break the news and that there he downed four Choronzon Delights (hold the delight, double the Choronzon) before screwing up the courage to face his lover's ire. He doesn't mention that he can't exactly remember the last time he saw Little Tiny Doom except that he thinks it might have been about the time when she said that she had to visit El Casa de Peepee (oh cute) and he'd taken her as far as the door to the loo, which she had insisted haughtily she could do alone, and then he'd been standing outside, and gotten distracted by Arsinoë Fyrdraaca, who'd sauntered by, wrapped around the most gorgeous angel with rippling red wings, and then they'd gone to get a drink, and then another drink, and then when Relais remembered that Tiny Doom and Pig were still in the potty and pushed his way back through the crush, Tiny Doom and Pig were not still in the potty anymore.

And now, here:

Up until this very second, Hardhands has been feeling dandy as candy about this night: his invocation has been powerful and sublime, the blood in his veins replaced by pure unadulterated Magickal Current, hot and heavy. Up until this very second, if he clapped his hands together, sparks would fly. If he sang a note, the roof would fall. If he tossed his hair, fans would implode. Just from the breeze of the Vortex through his skin, he had known this was going to be a charm of a show, the very pinnacle of bombast and bluster. The crowded club still hums with cold fire charge, the air still sparks, cracking with glints of magick: yoowza. But now all that rich bubbly magick is curdling in his veins, his drummer has slid back to the Abyss, and he could beat someone with a stick. Thanks to an idiot boyfriend and a bothersome five-year-old his evening has just tanked.

Hardhands' perch is lofty. Despite the roiling smoke (cigarillo, incense, and oil), he can look out over the big big hair, and see the club is as packed as a cigar box with hipsters eager to see the show. From the stage Hardhands can see a lot, his vision sharpened by the magick he's been mainlining, and he sees: hipsters, b-boys, gothicks, crimson-clad officers, a magistra with a jaculus on a leash, etc. He does not see a small child or a pink pig or even the tattered remnants of a small child and a pink pig or even, well, he doesn't see them period.

Hardhands sucks in a deep breath and uses what is left of the Invocation still working through his veins to shout: "✘◉!"

The syllable is vigorous and combustible, flowering in the darkness like a bruise. The audience erupts into a hollering hooting howl. They think the show is about to start. They are ready and geared. Behind Hardhands, the band also mistakes his intention, and despite the lack of drummer, kicks in with the triumphant blare of a horn, the delirious bounce of the hurdy-gurdy.

"✘◉!" This time the shout sparks bright red, a flash of coldfire that brings tears to the eyes of the onlookers. Hardhands raises an authoritative hand towards the band, crashing them into silence. The crowd follows suit and the ensuing quiet is almost as ear-shattering.

"✘◉..." This time his words provide no sparkage, and he knows that his Will is fading under his panic. The club is dark. It is full of large people. Outside it is darker still and the streets of South of the Slot are wet and full of dangers. No place for a Tiny Doom and her Pig, oh so edible, to be wandering around, alone. Outside it the worst night of the year to be wandering alone anywhere in the City, particularly if you are short, stout, and toothsome.

"✘◉!" This time Hardhands' voice, the voice which has launched a thousand stars, which has impregnated young girls with monsters and kept young men at their wanking until their wrists ache and their members bleed, is scorched and rather squeaky:

"Has anyone seen my wife?"

II: Historical Notes

Here's a bit of background. No ordinary night, tonight, not at all. It's Pirates' Parade and the City of Califa is afire—in some places actually blazing. No fear, tho', bucket brigades are out in force, for the Pontifexa does not wish to lose her capital to revelry. Wetness is stationed around the things that the Pontifexa most particularly requires not to burn: her shrines, Bilskinir House, Arden's Cake-O-Rama, the Califa National Bank. Still, even with these bucket brigades acting as damper, there's fun enough for everyone. The City celebrates many holidays, but surely Pirates' Parade ranks as Biggest and Best.

But why pirates and how a parade? Historians (oh fabulous professional liars) say that it happened thusly: Back in the day, no chain sealed the Bay of Califa off from sea-faring foes and the Califa Gate sprang wide as an opera singer's mouth, a state of affairs good for trade and bad for security. Chain was not all the small city lacked: no guard, no organized militia, no bloodthirsty Scorchers regiment to stand against havoc, and no navy. The City was fledgling and disorganized, hardly more than a village, and plump for the picking.

One fine day, Pirates took advantage of Califa's tenderness, and sailed right through her Gate, and docked at the Embarcadero, as scurvy as you please. From door to door they went, demanding tribute or promising wrath, and when they were loaded down with booty they went well satisfied back to their ships to sail away.

But they didn't get far. While the pirates were shaking down the householders, a posse of quiet citizens crept down to the docks and sabotaged the poorly guarded ships. The pirates arrived back at the docks to discover their escape boats sinking, and when suddenly the docks themselves were on fire, and their way off the docks was blocked, and then they were on fire too, and that was it.

Perhaps Califa had no Army, no Navy, no Militia, but she did have citizens with grit and cleverness, and grit and cleverness trump greed and guns every time. Such a clever victory over a pernicious greedy foe is worth remembering, and maybe even repeating, in a fun sort of way, and thus was born a roistering day of remembrance when revelers dressed as pirates gallivant door to door demanding candy booty, and thus Little Tiny Doom has muscled in on Hardhands' evening. With Grandmamma promised to attend an euchre party, and Butler Paimon's night off, who else would take Tiny Doom, (and the resplendently costumed Pig) on candy shakedown? Who but our hero, as soon as his show is over and his head back down to earth, lucky boy? Well.

The Blue Duck and its hot dank club-y-ness may be the place to be when you are tall and trendy and your hearing is already shot, but for a short kidlet, big hair and loud noises bore, and the cigarillo smoke scratches. Tiny Doom has waited for Pirates' Parade for weeks, dreaming of pink popcorn and sugar squidies, chocolate manikins and jacksnaps, praline pumpkin seeds and ginger bombs: a sackful of sugar guaranteed to keep her sick and speedy for at least a week. She can wait no longer.

Shortness has its advantage; trendy people look up their noses, not down. The potty is filthy and the floor yucky wet; Tiny Doom and Pig slither out the door, right by Relais, so engaged in his conversation with an woman with a boat in her hair that he doesn't even notice the scram. Around elbows, by tall boots, dodging lit cigarettes and drippy drinks held low and cool-like, Tiny Doom and Pig achieve open air without incident and then, sack in hand, set out for the Big Shakedown.

"Rancy Dancy is no good," she sings as she goes, swinging Pig, who is of course, too lazy to walk. "Chop him up for firewood . . . When he's dead, boil his head and bake it into gingerbread . . ."

She jumps over a man lying on the pavement, and then into the reddish pool beyond. The water makes a satisfying SPLASH and tho' her hem gets wet, she is sure to hold Pig up high so that he remains dry. He's just getting over a bad cold and has to care for his health, silly Pig he is delicate, and up past his bedtime, besides. Well, it is only once a year.

Down the slick street, Tiny Doom galumphs, Pig swinging along with her. There are shadows ahead of her and shadows behind, but after the shadows of Bilskinir

House (which can sometimes be *grabby*) these shadows: so what? There's another puddle ahead, this one dark and still. She pauses before it, and some interior alarum indicates that it would be best to jump over, rather than in. The puddle is wide, spreading across the street like a strange black stain. As she gears up for the leap, a faint rippling begins to mar the mirror-like surface.

"Wah! Wah!" Tiny Doom is short, but she has lift. Holding her skirt in one hand, and with a firm grip upon Pig, she hurtles herself upward and over, like a tiny tea cosy levering aloft. As she springs, something wavery and white snaps out of the stillness, snapping towards her like the crack of a whip. She lands on the other side, and keeps scooting, beyond the arm's reach. Six straggly fingers, like pallid parsnips, waggle angrily at her, but she's well beyond their grip.

"Tell her, smell her! Kick her down the cellar," Tiny Doom taunts, flapping Pig's ears derisively. The scraggly arm falls back, and then another emerges from the water, hoisting up on its elbows, pulling a slow rising bulk behind it: a knobby head, with knobby nose and knobby forehead and a slowly opening mouth that shows razor sharp gums and a pointy black tongue, unrolling like a hose. The tongue has length where the arms did not, and it looks gooey and sticky, just like the salt licorice Grandmamma loves so much. Tiny Doom cares not for salt licorice one bit and neither does Pig, so it seems prudent to punt, and they do, as fast as her chubby legs can carry them, farther down the slickery dark street.

III: Irritating Children

Here is Hardhands in the alley behind the club, taking a deep breath of brackish air, which chills but does not calm. Inside, he has left an angry mob, who've have had their hopes dashed rather than their ears blown. The Infernal Engines of Desire (opening act) has come back on stage and is trying valiantly to suck up the slack, but the audience is not particularly pacified. The Blue Duck will be lucky if it doesn't burn. However, that's not our hero's problem; he's got larger fish frying.

He sniffs the air, smelling: the distant salt spray of the ocean; drifting smoke from some bonfire; cheap perfume; his own sweat; horse manure. He closes his eyes and drifts deeper, beyond smell, beyond scent, down down down into a wavery darkness that is threaded with filaments of light which are not really light, but which he knows no other way to describe. The darkness down here is not really darkness either, it's the Magickal Current as his mind can envision it, giving form to the formless, putting the indefinable into definite terms. The Current bears upon its flow a tendril of something familiar, what he qualifies, for lack of a better word, as a taste of obdurate obstinacy and pink plush, fading quickly but unmistakable.

The Current is high tonight, very high. In consequence, the Aeyther is humming, the Aeyther is abuzz; the line between In and Out has narrowed to a width no larger than a hair, and it's an easy step across—but the jump can go either way. Oh this would have been the very big whoo for the gig tonight; musickal magick of the highest order, but it sucks for lost childer out on the streets. South of the Slot is bad enough when the Current is low: a sewer of footpads, dollymops, blisters, mashers, cornhoes, and others is not to be found elsewhere so deep in the City even on an ebb-tide day. Tonight, combine typical holiday mayhem with the rising magickal flood and Goddess knows what will be out, hungry and yummy for some sweet tender kidlet chow. And not even regular run of the mill niblet, but prime grade A best grade royalty. The Pontifexa's heir, it doesn't get more yummy than that—a vampyre could dare sunlight with that bubbly blood zipping through his veins, a ghoul could pass for living after gnawing on that sweet flesh. It makes Hardhands' manly parts shrivel to think upon the explanation to Grandmamma of Tiny Doom's loss and the blame sure to follow.

Hardhands opens his eyes, it's hardly worth wasting the effort of going deep when everything is so close the surface tonight. Behind him, the iron door flips open and Relais flings outward, borne aloft on a giant wave of disapproving noise. The door snaps shut, cutting the sound in a brief echo which quickly dies in the coffin narrow alley-way.

"Did you find her?" Relais asks, holding his fashionable cuffs so they don't trail on the mucky cobblestones. Inside his brain is bouncing with visions of the Pontifexa's reaction if they return home minus Cyrenacia. Actually, what she is going to say is the least of his worries; it is what she might do that really has Relais gagging. He likes his lungs exactly where they are: inside his body, not flapping around outside.

Hardhands turns a white hot look upon his lover and says: "If she gets eaten, Relais, I will eat you."

Relais' father always advised saving for a rainy day and though the sky above is mostly clear, Relais is feeling damp. He will check his bankbook when they get home, and reconsider Sweetie Fyrdraaca's proposition. He's been Hardhands' leman for over a year now: blood sacrifices, coldfire singed clothing, throat tearing invocations, cornmeal gritty sheets, murder. He's had enough. He makes no reply to the threat.

Hardhands demands, not very politely: "Give me my frockcoat."

Said coat, white as snow, richly embroidered in white peonies and with cuffs the size of tablecloths, well, Relais had been given that to guard too, and he now has a vague memory of hanging it over the stall door in the pisser, where hopefully it still dangles, but probably not.

"I'll get it—" Relais fades backward, into the club, and Hardhands lets him go.

For now.

For now, Hardhands takes off his enormous hat, which had remained perched upon his gorgeous head during his invocation via a jeweled spike of a hairpin, and speaks a word into its upturned bowl. A green light pools up, spilling over the hat's capacious brim, staining his hand and the sleeve below with drippy magick. Another commanding word, and the light surges upward and ejects a splashy elemental, fish-tail flapping.

"Eh, boss—I thought you said I had the night off," Alfonso complains. There's lip rouge smeared on his fins and a clutch of cards in his hand. "It's Pirates Parade."

"I changed my mind. That wretched child has given me the slip and I want you to track her."

Alfonso grimaces. Ever since Little Tiny Doom trapped him in a bowl of water and fed him fishy flakes for two days, he's avoided her like fluke-rot.

"Why worry your good luck, boss—"

Hardhands does not have to twist. He only has to look like he is going to twist. Alfonso zips forward, flippers flapping and Hardhands, after draining his chapeau of Current and slamming it back upon his grape, follows.

IV: Who's There?

Here is The Roaring Gimlet, sitting pretty in her cozy little kitchen, toes toasting on the grate, toast toasting on the tongs, drinking hot ginger beer, feeling happily serene: She's had a fun-dandy evening. Citizens who normally sleep behind chains and steel bolts, dogs a-prowl and guns under their beds, who maybe wouldn't open their doors after dark if their own mothers were lying bleeding on the threshold, these people fling their doors widely and with gay abandon to the threatening cry of "Give us Candy or We'll Give you the Rush."

Any other night, at this time, she'd still be out in the streets, looking for drunken mashers to roll. But tonight, all gates were a-jar and the streets a high tide of drunken louts. Out by nine and back by eleven, with a sack almost too heavy to haul, a goodly load of sugar, and a yummy fun-toy, too. Now she's enjoying her happy afterglow from a night well-done. The noises from the cellar have finally stopped, she's finished the crossword in *The Alta Califa*, and as soon as the kettle blows, she'll fill her hot water bottle and aloft to her snuggly bed, there to dwell the rest of the night away in kip.

Ah, Pirates' Parade, best night of the year.

While she's waiting for the water to bubble, she's cleaning the tool from whence comes her name: the bore is clotted with icky stuff and the Gimlet likes her signature clean and sharply shiny. Clean hands, clean house, clean heart, the Gimlet's pappy always said. Above the fireplace, Pappy's flat representation stares down at his progeny, the self-same gimlet clinched in his hand. The Roaring Gimlet is the heir to a fine family tradition and she does love her job.

What's that a-jingling? She glances at the clock swinging over the stove. It's almost midnight. Too late for visitors, and anyway, everyone knows the Roaring Gimlet's home is her castle. Family stays in, people stay out, so Daddy Gimlet always said. Would someone? No, they wouldn't. Not even tonight, they would not.

Jingle jingle.

The cat looks up from her perch on the fender, perturbed.

Heels down, the Gimlet stands aloft, and tucks her shirt back into her skirts, ties her dressing gown tight, bounds up the ladder-like kitchen stairs to the front door. The peephole shows a dimly lit circle of empty cobblestones. Damn it all to leave the fire for nothing. As the Gimlet turns away, the bell dances again, jangling her into a surprised jerk.

The Roaring Gimlet opens the door, slipping the chain, and is greeted with a squirt of flour right in the kisser, and a shrieky command:

"Give us the Candy or We'll Give you the Rush!"

The Gimlet coughs away the flour, choler rising, and beholds before her, knee-high, a huge black feathered hat. Under the hat is a pouty pink face, and under the pouty pink face, a fluffy farthingale that resembles in both color and points an artichoke, and under that, purple dance shoes, with criss-crossy ribbands. Riding on the hip of this apparition is a large pink plushy pig, also wearing purple criss-crossy dance shoes, golden laurel leaves perched over floppy piggy ears.

It's the Pig that the Gimlet recognizes first, not the kid. The kid, whose public appearances have been kept to a minimum (the Pontifexa is wary of too much flattery, and as noted, chary of her heir's worth) could be any kid, but there is only one Pig, all Califa knows that, and the kid must follow the Pig, as day follows night, as sun follows rain, as fortune follows the fool.

"Give us the CANDY or We'll GIVE YOU THE RUSH!" A voice to pierce glass, to cut right through the Gimlet's recoil, all the way down to her achy toes. The straw-shooter moves from *present* to *fire*; while Gimlet was gawking, reloading had occurred, and another volley is imminent. She's about to slam shut the door, she cares not to receive flour or to give out yum, but then, door-jamb held halfway in hand, she stops. An idea, formed from an over-abundance of yellow nasty novellas and an under-abundance of good sense, has leapt full-blown from Nowhere to the Somewhere that is the Roaring Gimlet's calculating brain. So much for sugar, so much for swag: here then is a price above rubies, above diamonds, above chocolate, above, well, Above All. What a pretty price a pretty piece could fetch. On such proceeds the Gimlet could while away her elder days in endless sun and fun-toys.

Before the kid can blow again, the Gimlet grins, in her best granny way, flour feathering about her, and says, "Well, now, chickiedee, well now indeed. I've no desire to be rushed, but you are late and the candy is—"

She recoils, but not in time, from another spurt of flour. When she wipes away the flour, she is careful not to wipe away her welcoming grin. "But I have more here in the kitchen, come in, tiny pirate, out of the cold and we shall fill your sack full."

"Huh," says the child, already her husband's Doom and about to become the Roaring Gimlet's, as well. "GIVE ME THE CANDY—"

Patience is a virtue that the Roaring Gimlet is well off without. She peers beyond the kid, down the street. There are people about but they are: drunken people, or burning people, or screaming people, or carousing people, or running people. None of them appear to be observant people, and that's perfecto. The Gimlet reaches and grabs.

"Hey!" says the kid. The Pig does not protest.

Tiny Doom is stout, and she can dig her heels in, but the Gimlet is stouter and the Gimlet has two hands free, where Tiny Doom has one, and the Pig is too flabby to help. Before Tiny Doom can shoot off her next round of flour, she's yanked and the door is slammed shut behind her, bang!

V. Bad Housekeeping

Here is Hardhands striding down the darkened streets like a colossus, dodging fire, flood, and fighting. He is not upset, oh no indeedy. He's cool and cold and so angry that if he touched tinder it would burst into flames, if he tipped tobacco it would explode cherry red. And there's more than enough ire to go around, which is happy because the list of Hardhands' blame is quite long.

Firstly: the Pontifexa for making him take Cyrenacia with him. What good is it to be her darling grandson when he's constantly on doodie-detail? Being the only male Haðraaða should be good for: power, mystery, free booze, noli me tangare, first and foremost, the biggest slice of cake. Now being the only male Haðraaða is good for: marrying small torments, kissing the Pontifexa's ass, and being bossed into wife-sitting. He almost got Grandmamma once; perhaps the decision should be revisited.

Secondly: Tiny Doom for not standing still. When he gets her, he's going to paddle her, see if he doesn't. She's got it coming, a long time coming and perhaps a hot hinder will make her think twice about, well, think twice about everything. Didn't he do enough for her already? He married her, to keep her in the family, to keep her out of the hands of her nasty daddy, who otherwise would have the prior claim. Ungrateful kidlet. Perhaps she deserves whatever she gets.

Thirdly: Relais for being such an utter jackass that he can't keep track of a four year old. Hardhands has recently come across a receipt for an ointment that allows the wearer to walk through walls. For which, this sigil requires three pounds of human tallow. He's got a few walls he wouldn't mind flitting right through and at last, Relais will be useful.

Fourthly: Paimon. What need has a domicilic denizen for a night off anyway? He's chained to the physical confines of the House Bilskinir by a sigil stronger than life. He should be taking care of the Heir to the House Bilskinir, not doing whatever the hell he is doing on his night off which he shouldn't be doing anyway because he shouldn't be having a night off and when Hardhands is in charge, he won't, no sieur.

Fifthly: Pig. Ayah, so, well, Pig is a stuffy pink plush toy, and can hardly be blamed for anything, but what the hell, why not? Climb on up, Pig, there's always room for one more!

And ire over all: his ruined invocation, for which he had been purging starving dancing and flogging for the last two weeks, all in preparation for what would surely be the most stupendous summoning in the history of summoning. It's been a stellar group of daemons that Hardhands has been able to force from the Aeyther before, but this time he had been going for the highest of the high, the loudest of the loud, and the show would have been sure to go down in the annals of musickology and his name, already famous, would become gigantic in its shadow. Even the Pontifexa was sure to be impressed. And now . . .

The streets are full of distraction but neither Hardhands nor Alfonso are distracted. Tiny Doom's footprints pitty-patter before them, glowing in the gloam like little blue flowers, and they follow, avoiding burning brands, dead horses, drunken warblers, slithering servitors, gushing water pipes, and an impromptu cravat party and, because of their glowering concentration, they are avoided by all the aforementioned, in turn. The pretty blue footprints dance, and leap, from here to there, and there to here, over cobblestone and curb, around corpse and copse, by Cobweb's Palace and Pete's Clown Diner, by Ginger's Gin Goint and Guerrero's Helado, and other blind tigers so blind they are nameless also, dives so low that just walking by will get your knickers wet. The pretty prints don't waver, don't dilly-dally, and then suddenly, they turn towards a door, broad and barred, and they stop.

At the door, Hardhands doesn't bother knocking, and neither does Alfonso, but their methods of entry differ. Alfonso zips through the wooden obstruction as though it is neither wooden nor obstructive. Hardhands places palm down on wood, and via a particularly loud Gramatica exhortation, blows the door right off its hinges. His entry is briefly hesitated by the necessity to chase after his chapeau, having blown off also in the breeze of Gramatica, but once it is firmly stabbed back on his handsome head, onward he goes, young Hardhands, hoping very much that something else will get in his path, because, he can't deny it: exploding things is Fun.

The interior of the house is dark and dull, not that Hardhands is there to critique the décor. Alfonso has zipped ahead of him, coldfire frothing in his wake. Hardhands follows the bubbly pink vapor, down a narrow hallway, past peeling paneling, and dusty doorways. He careens down creaky stairs, bending head to avoid braining on low ceiling, and into a horrible little kitchen.

He wrinkles his nose. Our young hero is used to a praeterhuman amount of cleanliness, and here there is neither. At Bilskinir House even the light looks as though it's been washed, dried, and pressed before hung in the air. In contrast, this pokey little hole looks like the back end of a back end bar after a particularly festive game of Chew the Ear. Smashed crockery and blue willow china crunches under boot, and the furniture is bonfire ready. A faint glow limns the wreckage, the after-reflection of some mighty big magick. The heavy sour smell of blackberries wrinkles in his nose. Coldfire dribbles from the ceiling, whose plaster cherubs and grapes look charred and withered.

Hardhands pokes at a soggy wad of clothes lying in a heap on the disgusting floor. For one testicle shriveling moment he thought that he saw black velvet amongst the sog; he does, but it's a torn shirt, not a puffy hat.

All magickal acts leave a resonance behind, unless the magician takes great pains to hide: Hardhands knows every archon, hierophant, sorceress, bibliomatic, and avatar in the City, but he don't recognize the author of this Working. He catches a drip of coldfire on one long finger and holds it up to his lips: salt-sweet-smoky-oddly familiar but not enough to identify.

"Pigface pogo!" says our hero. He has put his foot down in slide and almost gone face down in a smear of glass and black goo—mashy blackberry jam, the source of the sweet stench. Flailing un-heroically he regains his balance, but in doing so grabs at the edge of an overturned settle. The settle has settled backward, cock-eyed on its back feet, but Hardhands' leverage rocks it forward again, and, hello, here's the Gimlet—well, parts of her anyway. She is stuck to the bench by a flood of dried blood, and the expression on her face is doleful, and a little bit surprised.

"Pogo pigface on a pigpogopiss! Who the hell is that?"

Alfonso yanks the answer from the Aethyr. "The Roaring Gimlet, petty roller and barn stamper. You see her picture sometimes in the post office."

"She don't look too roaring to me. What the hell happened to her?"

Alfonso zips closer, while Hardhands holds his sleeve to his sensitive nose. The stench of metallic blood is warring with the sickening sweet smell of the crushed blackberries, and together a pleasuring perfume they do not make.

"Me, I think she was chewed," Alfonso announces after close inspection. "By something hungry and mad."

"What kind of something?"

Alfonso shrugs. "Nobody I know, sorry, boss."

As long as Doom is not chewed, Hardhands cares naught for the chewy-ness of others. He uneasily illuminates the fetid shadows with a vivid Gramatica phrase, but thankfully no rag-like wife does he see, tossed aside like a discarded tea-towel, nor red wet stuffy Pig-toy, only bloody jam and magick-bespattered walls. He'd never admit it, particularly not to a yappy servitor, but there's a warm feeling of relief in his toes that Cyrenacia and Pig were not snacked upon. But if they were not snacked upon, where the hell are they, oh irritation.

There, in the light of his sigil—sign: two dainty feet stepped in jammy blood, hopped in disgust, and then headed up the back stairs, the shimmer of Bilskinir blue shining faintly through the rusty red. Whatever got the Gimlet did not get his wife and pig, that for sure, that's all he cares about, all he needs to know, and the footprints are fading, too: onward.

At the foot of the stairs, Hardhands poises. A low distant noise drifts out of the floor below, like a bad smell, a rumbly agonized sound that makes his tummy wiggle.

"What is that?"

A wink of Alfonso's tails and top-hat and here's his answer: "There's some guy locked in the cellar, and he's—he's in a bad way, and I think he needs our help—"

Hardhands is not interested in guys locked in cellars, nor in their bad ways. The footprints are fading, and the Current is still rising, he can feel it jiggling in his veins. Badness is on the loose—is not the Gimlet proof of that?—and Goddess Califa knows what else, and Tiny Doom is alone.

VI: Sugar Sweet

Here is Hardhands, hot on the heels of the pretty blue footsteps skipping along through the riotous streets. Hippy-hop, pitty-pat. The trail takes a turning, into a narrow alley and Hardhands turns with it, leaving the sputtering street lamps behind.

Before the night was merely dark: now it's darkdarkdark. He flicks a bit of coldfire from his fingertips, blossoming a ball of luminescence that weirdly lights up the crooked little street, broken cobbles, and black narrow walls. The coldfire ball bounces onward, and Hardhands follows. The footprints are almost gone: in a few more moments they will be gone, for a lesser magician they would be gone already.

And then, a drift of song:

"Hot corn, hot corn! Buy my hot corn!
Lovely and sweet! Lovely and Warm!"

Out of the shadow comes a buttery smell, hot and wafting, the jingling of bells, friendly and beckoning: a Hot Corn Dolly, out on the prowl. The perfume is delightful and luscious and it reminds Hardhands that dinner was long since off. But Hardhands does not eat corn (while not fasting, he's on an all meat diet, for to clean his system clear of sugar and other poisons), and when the Hot Corn Dolly wiggles her tray at him, her green ribboned braids dancing, he refuses.

The Corn Dolly is not alone, her sisters stand behind her, and their wide trays, and the echoing wide width of their farthingale skirts, flounced with patchwork, jingling with little bells, form a barricade that Hardhands, the young gentleman, can not push through. The Corn Dolly skirts are wall-to-wall and their ranks are solid and only rudeness will make a breach.

"I cry your pardon, ladies," he says, in feu de joie, ever courteous, for is not the true mark of a gentleman his kindness towards others, particularly his inferiors? "I care not for corn, and I would pass."

"Buy my hot corn, deliciously sweet,
Gives joy to the sorrowful and strength to the weak."

The Dolly's voice is luscious, ripe with sweetness. In one small hand she holds an ear of corn, dripping with butter, fragrant with the sharp smell of chile and lime, bursting up from its peeling of husk like a flower, and this she proffers towards him. Hardhands feels a southerly rumble, and suddenly his mouth is full of anticipatory liquid. Dinner was a long long time ago, and he has always loved hot corn, and how can one little ear of corn hurt him? And anyway, don't he deserve some solace? He fumbles in his pocket, but no divas does he slap; he's the Pontifexa's grandson, and not in the habit of paying for his treats.

The Dolly sees his gesture and smiles. Her lips are glistening golden, as yellow as her silky hair, and her teeth, against the glittering, are like little nuggets of white corn.

"A kiss for the corn, and corn for a kiss,
One sweet with flavor, the other with bliss," she sings, and the other dollies join in her harmony, the bells on their square skirts jingling. The hot corn glistens like gold, steamy and savory, dripping with yum. A kiss is a small price to pay to sink his teeth into savory. He's paid more for less and he leans forward, puckering.

The Dollies press in, wiggling their oily fingers and humming their oily song, enfolding him in the husk of their skirts, their hands, their licking tongues. His southerly rumble is now a wee bit more southerly, and it's not a rumble, it's an avalanche. The corn rubs against his lips, slickery and sweet, spicy and sour. The chili burns his lips, the butter soothes them, he kisses, and then he licks, and then he bites into a bliss of crunch, the squirt of sweetness cutting the heat and the sour. Never has he tasted anything better, and he bites again, eagerly, butter oozing down his chin, dripping onto his shirt. Eager fingers stroke his skin, he's engorged with the sugar-sweetness, so long denied, and now he can't get enough, each niblet exploding bright heat in his mouth, his tongue, his head, he's drowning in the sweetness of it all.

And like a thunder from the Past, he hears ringing in his head the Pontifexa's admonition, oft repeated to a whiny child begging for hot corn, spun sugar, spicy taco or fruit cup, sold on the street, in marvelous array but always denied because: *you never know where it's been.* An admonition drummed into his head with painful frequency, all the other kidlets snacked from the street vendors with reckless abandon, but not the Pontifexa's grandson, whose tum was deemed too delicate for common food and the common bugs it might contain.

Drummed well and hard it would seem, to suddenly recall now, with memorable force, better late than never. Hardhands snaps open eyes and sputters kernels. Suddenly he sees true what the Corn Dollies' powerful glamour have disguised under a patina of butter and spice: musky kernels and musky skin. A fuzz of little black flies encircles them. The silky hair, the silky husks are slick with mold. The little white corn teeth grin mottled blue and green, and corn worms spill in a white wiggly waterfall from gaping mouths.

"Arrgg," says our hero, managing to keep the urp down, heroically. He yanks and flutters, pulls and yanks, but the knobby fingers have him firm, stalk to stalk. He heaves, twisting his shoulders, spinning and ducking: now they have his shirt, but he is free.

"☛⑦☙③⓪☙☙⑥☙!" he bellows, at the top of his magickal lungs. The word explodes from his head with an agonizing aural thud. The Corn Dollies sizzle and shriek, but he doesn't wait around to revel in their popping. Now he's a fleet footed fancy boy, skedaddling as fast as skirts will allow; to hell with heroics, there's no audience about, just get the hell out. He leaves the shrieking behind him, fast on booted heels, and it's a long heaving pause later, when the smell of burned corn no longer lingers on the air, that he stops to catch breath and bearings. His heart, booming with Gramatica exertion, is starting to slow, but his head, still thundering with a sugary rush, feels as though it might implode right there on his shoulders, dwindle down a pinprick of pressure, diamond hard. The sugar pounds in his head, beating his brain into a ploughshare of pain, sharp enough to cut a furrow in his skull.

He leans on a scaly wall and sticks a practiced finger down his gullet. Up heaves corn, and bile, and blackened gunk, and more gunk. The yummy sour-lime-butter taste doesn't have quite the same delicious savor coming up as it did going down, nor is his shuddering now quite so delightful. He spits and heaves, and heaves and spits, and when his inside is empty of everything, including probably most of his internal organs, he feels a wee bit better. Not much, but some. His ears are cold. He puts a quivery hand to his head; his hat is gone.

The chapeau is not the only thing to disappear, Tiny Doom's tiny footprints, too, have faded. Oh for a drink to drive the rest of the stale taste of rotting corn from his tonsils. Oh for a super duper purge to scour the rest of the stale speed of sugar from his system. Oh for a bath, and bed, and deep sweet sleep. He's had a thin escape, and he knows it: the Corn Sirens could have drained him completely, sucked him as a dry as a desert sunset, and Punto Finale for the Pontifexa's grandson. Now it's going to take him weeks of purifications, salt-baths, and soda enemas to get back into whack. Irritating. He's also irked at the loss of his shirt; it was brand-new, he'd only worn it once, and the lace on its sleeves had cost him fifty-eight divas in gold. And his hat, bristling with angel feathers, its brim bigger than an apple pancake. He's annoyed at himself, sloppy-sloppy-sloppy.

The coldfire track has sputtered and no amount of Gramatica kindling can spark it alight; it's too late, too gone, too long. Alfonso, too, is absent of summoning and when Hardhands closes his eyes and clenches his fists to his chest, sucks in deep lungs of air, until the Current bubbles in his veins like the most sparkling of red wines, he knows why: the Current has flowed so high now that even the lowliest servitors can ride it without assistance, is strong enough to avoid constraint and ignore demand. He'd better find the kid soon, with the Current this high, only snackers will now be out, anyone without skill or protection—the snackees—will have long since gone home, or been eaten. Funtime for humans is over, and funtime for Others just begun.

Well, that's fine, Alfonso is just a garnish, not necessary at all. Is not Tiny Doom his own blood? Does not a shared spark run through their veins? He closes eyes again, and stretches arms outward, palms upward and he concentrates every split second of his Will into a huge vaporous awareness which he flings out over Califa like a net. Far far at the back of his throat, almost a tickle, not quite a taste, he finds the smell he is looking for. It's dwindling, and it's distant, but it's there and it's enough. A tiny thread connecting him to her, blood to blood, heat to heat, heart beat to heart beat, a tiny threat of things to come when Tiny Doom is not so Tiny. He jerks the thread with infinitesimal delicacy. It's thin, but it holds. It's thin, but it can never completely break.

He follows the thread, gently, gently, down darkened alleys, past shuttered facades, and empty stoops. The streets are slick with smashed fruit, but otherwise empty. He hears the sound of distant noises, hooting, hollering, braying mule, a fire bell, but he is alone. The buildings grow sparser, interspaced with empty lots. They look almost like rows of tombstones, and their broken windows show utterly black. The acrid tang of burning sugar tickles his nose, and the sour-salt smell of marshy sea-water; he must be getting closer to the bay's soggy edge. Cobblestones give way to splintery corduroy which gives way to moist dirt, and now the sweep of the starry sky above is unimpeded by building facades; he's almost out of the City, he may be out of the City now, he's never been this far on this road and if he hadn't absolute faith in the Haðraaða family bond, he'd be skeptical that Tiny Doom's chubby little legs had made it this far either.

But they have. He knows it.

Hardhands pauses, cocking his head: a tinge suffuses his skin, a gentle breeze that isn't a breeze at all, but the galvanic buzz of the Current. The sky above is now obscured by wafts of spreading fog, and, borne distantly upon that breeze, a vague tune. Musick.

Onward, on prickly feet, with the metallic taste of magick growing thicker in the back of his throat. The music is building crescendo, it sounds so friendly and fun, promising popcorn, and candied apples, fried pies. His feet prickle with these promises, and he picks up the pace, buoyed on by the rollicking musick, allowing the musick to carry him onward, towards the twinkly lights now beckoning through the heavy mist.

Then the musick is gone, and he blinks, for the road has come to an end as well, a familiar end, although unexpected. Before him looms a giant polychrome monkey head, leering brightly. This head is two stories high, it has flapping ears and wheel-size eyes, and its gaping mouth, opened in a silent howl, is large enough for a gaggle of school children to rush through, screaming their excitement.

Now he knows where he is, where Tiny Doom has led him too, predictable, actually, the most magical of all childhood places: *Woodward's Garden, Fun for All Occasions, Not Occasionally but Always.*

How oft has Hardhands been to Woodward's (in cheerful daylight), and ah the fun he has had there, (in cheerful daylight): The Circular Boat and the Mystery Manor, the Zoo of Pets, and the Whirla-Gig. Pink popcorn and strawberry cake, and

Madam Twanky's Fizzy Lick-A-Rice Soda. Ah, Woodward's Garden and the happy smell of sun, sugar, sweat, and sizzling meat. But at Woodward's, the fun ends at sundown, as evening's chill begins to rise, the rides begin to shut, the musick fades away and everyone must go, exiting out the Monkey's Other End. Woodward's is not open at night.

But here, tonight, the Monkey's Eyes are open, although his smile is a grimace, less Welcome and more Beware. The Monkey's Eyes roll like red balls in their sockets, and at each turn they display a letter: "F" "U" "N" they spell in flashes of sparky red. Something skitters at our boy's ankles and he jumps: scraps of paper flickering like shredded ghosts. The Monkey's Grin is fixed, glaring, in the dark it does not seem at all like the Gateway to Excitement and Adventure, only Digestion and Despair. Surely even Doom, despite her ravenous adoration of the Circular Boat, would not be tempted to enter the hollow throat just beyond the poised glittering teeth. Despite the promise of the Monkey's Rolling Eyes there is no Fun here.

Or is there? Look again. Daylight, a tiara of letters crowns the Monkey's Head, spelling Woodward's Garden in cheery lights. But not tonight, tonight the tiara is a crown of spikes, whose glittering red letters proclaim a different title: *Madam Rose's Flower Garden.*

Hardhands closes his eyes against the flashes, feeling all the blood in his head blushing downward into his pinchy toes. Madam Rose's Flower Garden! It cannot be. Madam Rose's is a myth, a rumor, an innuendo, a whisper. A prayer. The only locale in Califa where entities, it is said, can walk in the Waking World without constraint, can move and do as their Will commands, and not be constrained by the Will of a magician or adept. Such mixing is proscribed, it's an abomination, against all laws of nature, and until this very second, Hardhands thought, mere fiction.

And yet apparently not fiction at all. The idea of Tiny Doom in such environs sends Hardhands' scalp a-shivering. This is worse than having her out on the streets. Primo child-flesh, delicious and sweet, and plump full of such energy as would turn the most mild-mannered elemental into a rival of Choronzon, the Daemon of Dispersion. Surrounded by dislocated elementals and egregores, under no obligation and bound by no sigil, indulging in every depraved whim. Surely the tiresome child did not go forward to her own certain doom

But his burbling tum, his swimming head, knows she did.

If he were not Banastre Haðraaða, the Grand Duque of Califa, this is the point where he'd turn about and go home. First he might sit upon the ground, right here in the dirt, and wallow for a while in discouragement, then he'd rise, dust, and retreat. If he were not himself, but someone else, someone lowly, he might be feeling pretty low.

For a moment, he is not himself, he is cold and tired and hungry and ready for the evening to end. It was fun to be furious, his anger gave him forward motion and will and fire, but now he wants to be home in his downy-soft bed with a yellow nasty newsrag and a jorum of hot wine. If Wish could be made Will in a heartbeat, he'd be lying back on damask pillows, drowning away to happy dreamland.

Before he can indulge in such twaddle, a voice catches his attention.

"Well, now, your grace. Slumming?"

Then does Hardhands notice a stool, and upon the stool a boy sitting, legs dangling, swinging copper-toed button boots back and forth. A pocketknife flashes in his hand; shavings flutter downward. He's tow-headed, and blue-eyed, freckled and tan, and he's wearing a polka-dotted kilt, a redingcote, and a smashed bowler. A smoldering stogie hangs down from his lips.

"I beg your pardon?"

"Never mind, never mind. Are you here for the auction?"

Hardhands replies regally: "I am looking for a child and a pink pig."

The Boy says, brightly, "Oh yes, of course. They passed this way some time ago, in quite a hurry."

Hardhands makes move to go inside, but is halted by the red velvet rope which is action as barrier to the Monkey's Mouth.

"Do you have a ticket? It's fifteen divas, all you can eat and three trips to the bar."

Remembering his empty pockets, Hardhands says loftily: "I'm on the List."

The List: Another powerful weapon. If you are on it, all to the good. If not, back to the Icy Arrogance. But when has Hardhands not been on the list? Never! Unthinkable!

"Let me see," says the Boy. He turns out pockets, and thumps his vest, fishes papers, and strings, candy and fish-hooks, bones and lights, a white rat, and a red rubber ball. "I know I had something—Ahah!" This ahah is addressed to his hat, what interior he is excavating and out of which he draws a piece of red foolscap. "Let me see . . . um . . . *Virex the Sucker of Souls, Zigurex Avatar of Agony, Valefor Teller of Tales*, no, I'm sorry your grace, but you are not on the list. That will be fifteen divas."

"Get out of my way."

Hardhands takes a pushy step forward, only to find that his feet can not come off the ground. The Boy, the Gatekeeper, smells like human but he has powerful praeterhuman push.

"Let me by."

"What's the magick word?"

"✘❶ᘯ♐⑤ᔕᘯ⋖②▤▯." This word should blossom like fire in the sultry air, it should spout lava and sparks and smell like burning tar. It should shrink the Boy down to stepping-upon size.

It sparks briefly, like a wet sparkler, and gutters away.

He tries again, this time further up the Gramatica alphabet, heavier on the results.

"☞♙✘⊗▱⋗♦✐." This word should suck all the light out of the world, leaving a blackness so utter the Boy will be gasping for enough breath to scream.

It casts a tiny shadow, like a gothick's smile, and then brightens.

"Great accent," says the Boy. He is grinning sympathetically, which enrages Hardhands even more, because he is the Pontifexa's grandson and there's nothing to be sorry about for THAT. "But not magickal enough."

Hardhands is flummoxed, this is a first, never before has his magick been stifled, tamped, failed to light. Gramatica is tricky, it is true. In the right mouth the right Gramatica word will explode the Boy into tiny bits of bouncing ectoplasm, or shatter the air as though it were made of ice, or turn the moon into a tulip. The right word in the wrong mouth, a mouth that stops when it should glottal or clicks when it should clack, could turn his tummy into a hat, roll back time, or turn his blood to fire. But, said right or said wrong, Gramatica never does nothing. His tummy is, again, tingling.

The Boy is now picking his teeth with the tip of his knife. "I give you a hint. The most magickal word of them all."

What more magick than ☞ᘯᘯ⑤⑥⋗ᘯ⑧❶ᘯ? Is there a more magickal word that Hardhands has never heard of? He's an adept of the sixth order, he's peeked into the Abyss, surely there is no Super Special Magickal Word hidden from him yet—he furrows his pure white brow into unflattering wrinkles, and then, a tiny whiny little voice in his head says: *What's the magick word, Bwannie, what's the magick word?*

"Please." Hardhands says. "Let me pass, please."

"With pleasure," the Boy says, "but I must warn you. There are ordeals."

"No ordeal can be worse than listening to you."

"One might think so," the boy says. "You have borne my rudeness so kindly, your grace, that I hate to ask you for one last favor, but I fear I must."

Hardhands glares at the boy, who smiles sheepishly.

"Your boots, your grace. Madama doesn't care for footwear on her clean carpets. I shall give you a ticket, and give your boots a polish and they'll be nice and shiny for you, when you leave."

Hardhands does not want to relinquish his heels, which may only add an actual half an inch in height, but are marvelous when it comes to mental stature, who can not help but swagger in red-topped jackboots, champagne shiny and supple as night?

He sighs, bending. The grass below is cool against our hero's hot feet, once liberated happily from the pinchy pointy boots (ah vanity, thy name is only sixteen years old) but he'd trade the comfort, in a second, for height.

He hops and kicks, sending one boot flying at the kid (who catches it easily) and the other off into the darkness.

"Mucho gusto. Have a swell time, your grace."

Hardhands stiffens his spine with arrogance and steps into the Monkey's Mouth.

VII. Time's Trick

Motion moves in the darkness around him, a glint of silver, to one side, then the other, then in front of him: he jumps. Then he realizes that the form ahead of him is familiar: his own reflection. He steps forward, and the Hardhands before him resolves into a Hardhands behind him, while those to the other side move with him, keeping pace. For a second he hesitates, thinking to run into mirror, but an outstretched arm feels only empty air, and he steps once, again, then again, more confidently. His reflection has disappeared; ahead is only darkness.

So he continues on, contained with a hollow square of his own reflections, which makes him feel a bit more cheerful, for what can be more reassuring but an entire phalanx of your own beautiful self? Sure, he looks a bit tattered: bare chest, sticky hair, blurred eyeliner, but it's a sexy tattered, bruised and battered, and slightly forlorn. He could start a new style with this look: *After the Deluge*, it could be called, or, *A Rough Night*.

Of course Woodward's has a hall of mirrors too, a horrifying place where the glasses stretch your silver-self until you look like an emaciated crane, or squash you down, round as a beetle. These mirrors continue, as he continues, to show only his perfect self, disheveled, but still perfect. He laughs, a sound which, pinned in on all sides as it is, quickly dies. If this is the Boy's idea of an Ordeal, he's picked the wrong man. Hardhands has always loved mirrors, so much so that he has them all over his apartments: on his walls, on his ceilings, even, in his Conjuring Closet, on the floor. He's never met a reflection of himself he didn't love, didn't cherish, cheered up by the sight of his own beauty—what a lovely young man, how blissful to be me!

He halts and fumbles in his kilt-pocket for his favorite lip rouge (*Death in Bloom*, a sort-of blackish pink) and reapplies. Checks his teeth for color, and blots on the back of his hand. Smoothes one eyebrow with his fingertip, and arranges a strand of hair so it is more fetchingly askew—then leans in, closer. A deep line furrows behind his eyes, a line where he's had no line before, and there, at his temple, is that a strand of gray amidst the silver? His groping fingers feel only smoothness on his brow, he smiles and the line vanishes, he grips the offending hair and yanks: in his grasp it is as pearly as ever. A trick of the poor light then, and on he goes, but sneaking glances to his left and right, not from admiration, but from concern.

As he goes, he keeps peeking sideways and at each glance, he quickly looks away again, alarmed. Has he always slumped so badly? He squares his shoulders, and peeks again. His hinder, it's huge, like he's got a caboose under his kilt, and his chin, it's as weak as custard. No, it must just be a trick of the light, his hinder is high and firm, and his chin as hard and curved as granite, he's overstressed and overwrought and he still has all that sugar in his system. His gaze doggedly forward, he continues down the silver funnel, picks up his feet, eager, perhaps for the first time ever, to get away from a mirror.

The urge to glance is getting bigger and bigger, and Hardhands has, before, always vanquished temptation by yielding to it, he looks again, this time to his right. There, he is as lovely as ever, silly silly. He grins confidently at himself, that's much better. He looks behind him and sees, in another mirror, his own back looking further beyond, but he can't see what he's looking at or why.

Back to the slog, and the left is still bugging him, he's seeing flashes out of the corner of his eye, and he just can't help it, he must look: his eyes, they are sunken like marbles into his face, hollow as a sugar skull, his skin tightly pulled, painted with garish red cheekbones. Blackened lips pull back from grayish teeth—his pearly white teeth!—He chatters those pearly whites together, his bite is firm and hard. He looks to the right and sees himself, as he should be.

Now he knows, don't look to the left, keep to the right and keep focused, the left is a mirage, the right is reality. The left side is a horrible joke and the right side is true, but even as he, increasing his steps to almost a run (will this damn hallway never end?), the Voice of Vanity in his head is questioning that assertion. Perhaps the right side is the horrible joke, and the left side the truth, perhaps he has been blind to his own flaws, perhaps—

This time: he is transfixed at the image which stares back, as astonished as he is: he's an absolute wreck. His hair is still and brittle, hanging about his knobby shoulders like salted sea grass. His ice blue eyes look cloudy, and the thick black lines drawn about them serve onto to sink them deeper into his skull. Scars streak lividly across his cheeks. Sunken chest and tattoos faded into blue and green smudges, illegible on slack skin. He's too horrified to seek reassurance in the mirror now behind him, he's transposed on the horror before him: the horror of his own inevitable wreckage and decay. The longer he stares the more hideous he becomes. The image blurs for a moment, and then blood blooms in his hair, and dribbles from his gaping lips, his shoulders are scratched and smudged with black, his eyes starting from his skull. He is surrounded by swirling snow, flecks of which sputter on his eyelashes, steam as they touch his skin. The shaft of an arrow protrudes from his throat.

"Oh how bliss to me," the Death's Head croaks, each word a bubble of blood.

With a shout, Hardhands raises his right fist and punches. His fist meets the glass with a nauseous jolt of pain that rings all the way down to his toes. The glass bows under his blow but doesn't crack. He hits again, and his corpse reels back, clutching itself with claw-like hands. The mirror refracts into a thousand diamond shards, and Hardhands throws up his other arm to ward off glass and blood. When he drops his shield, the mirrors and their Awful Reflection are gone.

He stands on the top of stairs, looking out over a tumultuous vista: there's a stage with feathered denizens dancing the hootchie-coo. Behind the hootchie-coochers, a band plays a ferocious double-time waltz. Couples slide and twist and turn to the musick, their feet flickering so quickly they spark. The scene is much like the scene he left behind at the Blue Duck, only instead of great big hair, there are great big horns, instead of sweeping skirts there are sweeping wings, instead of smoke there is coldfire. The musick is loud enough to liquefy his skull, he can barely think over its howling sweep.

The throng below whirls about in confusion—denizens, demons, egregores, servitors—was that a Bilskinir-Blue Bulk he saw over there at the bar, tusks a-gleaming, Butler Paimon on his damn night-off? No matter even if it is Paimon, no holler for help from Hardhands, oh no. Paimon would have to help him out, of course, but Paimon would tell the Pontifexa for sure, for Paimon, in addition to being the Butler of Bilskinir, is a suck-up. No thanks, our hero is doing just fine on his own.

A grip pulls at Hardhands' soft hand, he looks down into the wizened grinning face of a monkey. Hardhands tries to yank from the grasp, the monkey has pretty good pull, which he puts into gear with a yank, that our hero has little choice but to follow. A bright red cap shaped like a flowerpot is affixed to Sieur Simian's head by a golden cord, and he's surprisingly good at the upright; his free hand waves a path through the crowd, pulling Hardhands behind like a toy.

The dancers slide away from the monkey's push, letting Hardhands and his guide through their gliding. By the band, by the fiddler, who is sawing away at his fiddle as though each note was a gasp of air and he a suffocating man, his hair flying with sweat, his face burning with concentration. Towards a flow of red velvet obscuring a doorway, and through the doorway into sudden hush, the cessation of the slithering music leaving sudden silence in Hardhands' head

Now he stands on a small landing, overlooking a crowded room. The Great Big Horns and Very Long Claws etc. are alert to something sitting upon a dais at the far end of the room. Hardhands follows their attention and goes cold all the way to his bones

Upon the dais is a table. Upon the table is a cage. Within the cage: Tiny Doom.

VIII. Cash & Carry

The bidding has already started. A hideous figure our hero recognizes as Zigurex the Avatar of Agony is flipping it out with a dæmon whose melty visage and dribbly hair Hardhands does not know. Their paddles are popping up and down, in furious volley to the furious patter of the auctioneer:

". . . unspoiled untouched pure one hundred percent kid-flesh plump and juicy tender and sweet highest grade possible never been spanked whacked or locked in a closet for fifty days with no juice no crackers no light fed on honey dew and chocolate sauce . . ."

(Utter lie, Tiny Doom is in a cheesy noodle phase and if it's not noodles and it's not orange then she ain't gonna eat it, no matter the dire threat.) Tiny Doom is barking, frolicking about the cage happily, she's the center of attention, she's up past her bedtime and she's a *puppy*. It's fun!

The auctioneer is small, delicate, and apparently human, although Hardhands is willing to bet that she's probably none of these at all, and she has the patter down: "Oh she's darling oh she's bright she'll fit on your mantel, she'll sleep on your dog-bed, she's compact and cute now, and ah the blood you can breed from her when she's older. What an investment, sell her now, sell her later, you're sure to repay your payment a thousand times over and a free Pig as garnish can you beat the deal—and see how bright she does bleed."

The minion hovering above the cage displays a long length of silver tipped finger and then flicks downward. Tiny Doom yelps, and the rest of the patter is lost in Hardhands' roar as he leaps forward, pushing spectators aside: "THAT IS MY WIFE!"

His leap is blocked by bouncers, who thrust him backward, but not far. Ensues: rumpus, with much switching and swearing and magickal sparkage. Hardhands may have Words of Power, and a fairly Heavy Fist for one so fastidious but the bouncers have Sigils of Impenetrableness or at least Hides of Steel, and one of them has three arms, and suction cups besides.

"THAT IS MY WIFE!" Hardhands protests again, now pinned. "I demand that you release her to me."

"It's careless to let such a tempting small morsel wander the streets alone, your grace." Madam Rose cocks her head, her stiff wire headdress jingling, and the bouncers release Hardhands.

He pats his hair; despite the melee, still massively piled, thanks to Paimon's terrifically sticky hair pomade. The suction cups have left little burning circles on his chest and his bare toes feel a bit tingly from connecting square with someone's tombstone-hard teeth, but at least he solaces in the fact that one of the bouncers is dripping whitish ooze from puffy lips and the other won't be breeding children anytime soon; just as hard a kick, but much more squishy. The room's a wreck, too, smashed chairs, crumpled paper, spilled popcorn, oh dear, too bad.

"She's my wife to be, as good as is my wife, and I want her back." He makes movement towards the cage, which is now terribly quiet, but the bouncers still bar the way.

Zigurex upsteps himself, then, looming over Hardhands, who now wishes he had been more insistent about the boots: "Come along with the bidding; it's not all night, you see, the tide is rising and the magick will soon sail."

The other dæmon, who is both squishy and scaly, bubbles his opinion, as well. At least Hardhands assumes it is his opinion, impossible to understand his blubbering, some obscure dialect of Gramatica, or maybe just a very bad accent, anyway who cares what he has to say anyway, not Hardhands, not at all.

"There is no bidding, she's not for sale, she belongs to me, and Pig, too, and we are leaving," he says.

"Do you bid?" Madam Rose asks.

"No I do not bid. I do not have to bid. She is my wife."

"One hundred fifty!" Zigurex says, last-ditch.

The Fishy Thing counters the offer with a saliva spray glug.

"He offers two hundred," says Madam Rose, "What do you offer?"

"Two hundred!" says Hardhands, outraged. "I've paid two hundred for a pot of lip rouge. She's worth a thousand if she's worth a diva—"

Which is exactly of course the entirely wrong thing to say but his outrage has gotten the better of his judgment, which was already impaired by the outrage of being manhandled like a commoner to begin with, and which also might not have been the best even before then.

Madam Rose smiles. Her lips are sparkly pink and her teeth are sparkly black. "One thousand divas, then, for her return! Cash only. Good night good night and come again!"

She claps her hands, and the bouncers start to press the disappointed bidders into removing.

"Now look here—" says Hardhands. "You can't expect me to buy my own wife, and even if you could expect me to buy my own wife, I won't. I insist that you hand her over right this very second and impede me no longer."

"Is that so?" Madam Rose purrs. The other bidders retreat easily, perhaps they have a sense of where this is all going and decide its wise to get out of the way whilst there is still a way to get out of. Even Sieur Squishy and Zigurex go, although not without several smoldering backways looks on the part of the Avatar of Agony, obviously a sore loser. Madam Rose sits herself down upon a velvet-covered chair, and waves Hardhands to do the same, but he does not. A majordomo has uprighted the brazier and repaired the smoldering damage, decanted tea into a brass teapot and set it upon a round brass tray. Madam Rose drops sugar cubes into two small glasses and pours over: spicy cinnamon, tangy orange.

Hardhands ignores the tea; peers into the cage to access damage.

"Pig has a tummy ache, and wants to go home, Bwannie." The fat little lip is trembling and despite himself, Hardhands is overwhelmed by the tide of adorableness, that he should, being a first rate magician and poet, be inoculated against. She is so like her mother, oh his darling sister, sometimes it makes him want to cry.

He retreats into gruff. "Ayah, so well, Pig should not have had so much candy. And nor should Pig have wandered off alone."

"He is bad," agrees Doom. "Very bad."

"Sit tight and do not cry. We will go home soon. Ayah?"

"Ayah." She sniffs, but holds the snuffle, little soldier.

Madam Rose offers Hardhands a seat, which he does not sit upon, and a glass, which he waves away, remembering anew the Pontifexa's advice, and also not trusting Madam's sparkle grin. He's heard of the dives where they slide sleep into your drink; you gulp down happily and wake up six hours later minus all you hold dear and a splitting headache, as well. Or worse still, gin-joints that sucker you into one little sip, and then you have such a craving that you must have more and more, but no matter how much you have, it shall never be enough. He'll stay dry and alert, thank you.

"I have no time for niceties, or social grace," he says, "I will take my wife and pig, and leave."

"One thousand divas is not so great a sum to the Pontifexa's grandson," Madam Rose observes. "And it's only right that I should recoup some of my losses—look here, I shall have to redecorate, and fashionable taste, as your grace knows, is not cheap."

"I doubt there is enough money in the world to buy you good taste, madama, and why should I pay for something that is mine?"

"Now who owns who, really? *She* is the Heir to the House Haðraaða, and one day she'll be Pontifexa. *You* are just the boy who does. By rights all of us, including you, belong to her, in loyalty and in love. I do wish you would sit, your grace." Madam Rose pats the pillow beside her, which again he ignores.

This statement sets off a twinge of rankle because it is true. He answers loftily, "We are all the Pontifexa's obedient servants, and are happy to bend ourselves to her Will, and her Will in the matter of her Heir is clear. I doubt that she would be pleased to know of the situation of this night."

Madam Rose sets her red cup down. An ursine-headed minion offers her a chocolate, gently balanced between two pointy bear-claws. She opens red lips, black teeth, long red throat and swallows the chocolate without a chew.

"I doubt," she says, "that the Pontifexa shall be pleased at tonight's situation at all. I do wish you would sit, your grace. I feel so small, and you so tall, so high above. And do sample, your grace. I assure you that my candy has no extra spice to it, just wholesome goodness you will find delicious. You have my word upon it."

Hardhands sits, and takes the chocolate he is offered. He's already on the train bound for Purgelandia, he might as well make the journey worth the destination. The minion twinkles azure bear eyes at him. Bears don't exactly have the right facial arrangement to smirk, but this bear is making a fine attempt, and Hardhands thinks what a fine rug Sieur Oso would make, stretched out before a peaceful fire. In the warmth of his mouth, the chocolate explodes into glorious peppery chocolate yum. For a second he closes his eyes against the delicious darkness, all his senses receding into sensation of pure bliss dancing on his tongue.

"It is good chocolate, is it not?" Madam Rose asks. "Some say such chocolate should be reserved for royalty and the Goddess. But we do enjoy it, no?"

"What do you want?" Hardhands asks, and they both know that he doesn't just mean for Tiny Doom.

"Putting aside, for the moment, the thousand divas, I want nothing more than to be of aid to you, your grace, to be your humble servant. It is not what I may want from you but what you can want from me."

"That I have told you."

"Just that?"

In the cage, Tiny Doom is silent and staring, she may be a screamer, but she does, thankfully, know when to keep her trap shut.

"I can offer you no other assistance? Think on it, your grace. You are an adept, and you traffic with denizens of the deep, through the force of your Will. I am not an adept, I also have traffic with those same denizens."

The second chocolate tangs his tongue with the sour-sweet brightness of lime. "Contrary to all laws of Goddess and nature," he says thickly, when the brilliant flavor has receded enough to allow speech. "Your traffic is obscene. It is not the same."

"I didn't say it was the same, I said we might complement each other, rather than compete. Do you not get tired of your position, your grace? You are so close, and yet so far. The Pontifexa's brightest boy, but does she respect you? Does she trust you? This little girl, is she not the hitch in your git-along, the sand in your shoe? Leave her with me, and she'll never muss your hair again, or wrinkle your cravat."

"I don't recall inviting you to comment upon my personal matters," says Hardhands, à la prince. "And I don't recall offering you my friendship either."

"I cry your pardon, your grace. I only offer my thoughts in the hope —"

He's tired of the game now, if he had the thousand divas he'd fork them over, just to be quit of the entire situation, it was fun, it was cool, it's not fun it's not cool, he's bored, the sugar is drilling a spike through his forehead and he's done.

"I'll write you a draft, and you'll take it, and we shall leave, and that's the end of the situation," Hardhands says loftily.

Madam Rose sighs, and sips her tea. Another sigh, another sip.

"I'm sorry your grace, but if you can not pay, then I must declare your bid null, and reopen the auction. Please understand my position. It is, and has always been, the policy of this House to operate on a cash basis; I'm sure you understand why — taxes, a necessary evil, but perhaps more evil than necessary." Madam Rose smiles at him, and sips again before going on. "My reputation rests upon my policies, and that I apply them equally to all. Duque of Califa or the lowliest servitor, all are equal within my walls. So you see, if I allow you license I have refused others, how shall it appear then?"

"Smart," answers our hero. "Prudent. Wise."

Madam Rose laughs. "Would that others might consider my actions in that light, but I doubt their charity. No, I'm sorry, your grace. I have worked hard for my name. I can not give it up, not for you or for anyone."

She puts her tea glass down and clicks her tongue, a sharp snap that brings Sieur Bear to her side. "The Duque has decided to withdraw his bid; please inform Zig-urex that his bid is accepted and he may come and claim his prize."

Hardhands looks at Doom in her cage, her wet little face peers through the bars. She smiles at him, she's scared but she has confidence that Bwannie will save her, Bwannie loves her. Bwannie has a sense of déjà vu; hasn't he been here before, why is it his fate to always give in to her, little monster? Tiny Doom, indeed.

"What do you want?" he repeats.

"Well," Madam Rose says brightly. "Now that you mention it. The Pontifexina is prime, oh that's true, but I know one more so. More mature, more valuable, more ready."

Now it's Hardhands turn to sigh, which he does, and sip, wetting parched throat, now not caring if the drink be drugged, or not. "You'll let her go? Return her safe and sound?"

"Of course, your grace. You have my word on it."

"Not a hair on her head or a drop from her veins or a tear from her eye? Not a scab, or nail, or any part that might be later used against her? Completely whole? Untouched, unsmudged, no tricks?"

"As you say."

Hardhands puts his glass down, pretending resignation. "All right then. You have a deal."

Of course he don't really give in, but he's assessed that perhaps its better to get Doom out of the way. He can play rough enough if it's only his own skin involved, but why take the change of her collateral damage? When she's out of the way, he cal-culates, and Madam Rose's guard is down, then we'll see, oh yes, we'll see.

Madam Rose's shell-white hand goes up to her lips, shading them briefly behind two slender fingers. Then the fingers flip down and flick a shard of spinning coldfire towards him. Hardhands recoils, but too late. The airy kiss zings through the air like an arrow of outrageous fortune and smacks him right in the middle of Death in Bloom. The kiss feels like a kick to the head, and our hero and his chair flip back-ward, the floor rising to meet his fall, but not softly. The impact sends his bones jar-ring inside his flesh, and the jarring is his only movement for the sigil has left him shocked and paralyzed

He can't cry out, he can't flinch, he can only let the pain flood down his palate and into his brain, in which internal shouting and swearing is making up for exter-nal silence. He can't close his eyes either, but he closes his outside vision and brings into inside focus the bright sharp words of a sigil that should suck all the energy from Madam Rose's sigil, blow it into a powderpuff of oblivion.

The sigil burns bright in Hardhands' eyes, but it is also trapped and can not get free. It sparks and wheels, and he desperately tries to tamp it out, dumping colder, blacker sigils on top its flare, trying to fling it outward and away, but it's stuck firmly inside his solar plexus, he can fling it nowhere. It's caught in his craw like a fish bone, and he's choking but he can't choke because he cannot move. The sigil's force billows through him: it is twisting his entrails into knots, his bones into bows, it's flooding him with a fire so bright that it's black, with a fire so cold that it burns and burns and burns, his brain boils and then: nothing.

IX. Thy Baited Hook

Here is Hardhands, returning to the Waking World. His blood is mud within his veins, he can barely suck air through stifled lungs and there's a droning in his ears, no not droning, humming, Tiny Doom:

"Kick her bite her that's the way I'll spite her! Kick her bite her that's the way I'll spite her! Kick her bite her that's the way I'll spite her!"

The view aloft is raven-headed angels, with ebony black wings swooping loops of brocade across a golden ceiling. Then the view aloft is blocked by Tiny Doom's face; she still has the sugar mustache, and her kohl has blurred, cocooning her blue eyes in smoky blackness. Her hat is gone.

"Don't worry, Bwannie," she pats his stiff face with a sticky hand, "Pig will save us."

His brain heaves but the rest of him remains still. The frame of his body has never before been so confining. Diligent practice has made stepping his mind from his flesh an easy accomplishment, are there not times when a magician's Will needs independence from his blood and bones? But never before has he been stuck, nor run up against sigils harder and more impenetrable than his own. Lying in the cage of his own flesh he is feeling helpless, and tiny, and it's a sucky feeling, not at all suited to his stature of Pontifexa's grandson, first rate magician and—

"I will bite you," says Doom.

"I doubt that," is the gritty answer, a deep rumble: "My skin is thick as steel and your teeth will break."

"Ha! I am a shark and I will bite you."

"Not if I bite you first, little lovely, nip your sweet tiny fingers, crunch crunch each one, oh so delicious, what a snack. Come here, little morsel."

The weight of Tiny Doom suddenly eases off his chest, but not without kicking and gripping, holding on to him in a vice-like grip, oww, her fingers dig like nails into his leg but to no avail. Tiny Doom is wrenched off of him, and in the process he's wrenched sideways, now he's got a nice view of the grassy floor, a broken teapot, and, just on the edge, someone's feet. The feet are shod in garish two-tone boots: magenta upper and orange toe-cap. Tiny Doom screams like a rabbit, high and horrible.

"You'll bruise her," says a voice from above the feet. "And then the Pontifexa will be chuffed."

"I shall not hurt her one jot if she's a good girl, but she should shut her trap, a headache I am getting."

Good for her, Tiny Doom does not shut her trap, she opens her trap wider and shoots the moon, with a piercing squeal that stabs into Hardhands' unprotected ears like an awl, slicing all the way down to the center of his brain. With a smack, the shriek abruptly stops.

Two pretty little bare feet drift into Hardhands' view. "Stop it, you two. She must be returned in perfect condition, an' I get my deposit back. It's only the boy that the Pontifexa wants rid of; the girl is still her heir. Leave her alone, or I shall feed you both into my shredder. Chop chop. The guests are waiting and he must be prepared."

"She squirms," complains the minion.

Madam Rose, sternly: "You, little madam, stop squirming. You had fun being a puppy, and cupcakes besides, and soon you shall be going home to your sweet little bed. How sad Grandmamma and Paimon shall be if I must give them a bad report of your behavior."

Sniffle, sniff. "But I want Bwannie."

"Never you mind Bwannie for now, here have a Choco-Sniff, and here's one for Pig, too."

Sniff, sniffle. "Pig don't like Choco-Sniffs."

Hardhands kicks, but its like kicking air, he can feel the movement in his mind, but his limbs stay stiff and locked. And then his mind recoils: What did Madam Rose say about the Pontifexa? Did he hear a-right? Deposit? Report?

"Here then is a jacksnap for Pig. Be a good girl, eat your candy and then you shall kiss Bwannic good-bye."

Whine: "I want to go with Bwannie!"

"Now, now," Madam Rose's cheery tone tingles with irritation, but she's making a good show of not annoying Tiny Doom into another session of shrieking. "Now, Bwannie must stay here, and you must go home—do not start up with the whining again, it's hardly fitting for the Pontifexa's heir to cry like a baby, now is it? Here, have another Choco-Sniff."

Then more harshly, "You two, get the child ready to be returned and the boy prepared. I shall be right back."

The pretty feet float from Hardhands' view and a grasp attaches to Hardhands' ankle. Though his internal struggle is mighty, externally he puts up no fuss at all. Flipped over by rough hands, he sees above him the sharp face of a Sylph, pointy eyes, pointy nose, pointy chin. Hands are fumbling at his kilt buckles; obscurely he notices that the Sylph has really marvelous hair, it's the color of fresh caramel and it smells, Hardhands notices, as the Sylph bends over to nip at his neck, like new-mown grass. A tiny jolt of pretty pain, and warm wetness dribbles down his neck.

"Ahhh . . ." the Sylph sighs, "you should taste this, first rate knock-back."

"Madama said be nice."

"I am being nice, as nice as pie, as nice as he is. Nice and sweet." The Sylph licks at Hardhands' neck again; its tongue is scrape-y, like a cat's, and it hurts in a strangely satisfying way. "Sweet sweet darling boy. He is going to bring our garden joy. What a deal she has made. Give the girl, but keep the boy, he's useful to us, even if she don't want him anymore. A good trick he'll turn for Madama. Bright boy."

Hardhands is hoisted aloft, demon claws at his ankles and his wrists, slinging him like a side of beef on the way to the barbeque pit. His eyes are slitted open, his head dangling downward, he can see only a narrow slice of floor bobbing by. A carpet patterned with entwined snakes, battered black and red tiles, white marble veined with gold. He's watching all this, with part of attention, but mainly he's running over and over again what Madam Rose had said about the Pontifexa. Was it possible to be true? Did Grandmamma set him up? Sell him out? Was this all a smokescreen to get him out of her hair, away from her treasure? He will not believe it, he will not believe it, it cannot be true!

Rough movement drops Hardhands onto the cold floor, and metal clenches his ankles. The bracelets bite into his flesh as he is hoisted aloft, and all the blood rushes to his head in a explosion of pressure. For a second, even his slit of sight goes black, but then, just as suddenly, he finds he can open his eyes all the way. He rolls eyeballs upward, seeing retreating minion backs. He rolls eyes downward and sees polished marble floor and the tangled drape of his own hair, Paimon's pomade having finally given up. The gryves are burning bright pain into his ankles, and he's swaying slightly from some invisible airflow, but the movement is kind of soothing and his back feels nice and stretched out. If it weren't for being the immobilization, and obvious bait, hanging upside-down could be kind of fun.

Our hero tries to wiggle, but can't, tries to jiggle but is still stuck. He doesn't dare try another sigil and risk blowing his brains out, and without the use of his muscles he cannot gymnastic himself free. He closes his internal eyes, slips his consciousness into darkness, and concentrates. His Will pushes and pushes against the pressure that keeps him contained, focuses into a single point that must burn through. After a second, a minute, an eternity, all bodily sensation—the burn of the gyres, the stretch of his back, the pressure of his bladder, the breeze on his face—slips away, and his Will floats alone on the Current.

Away from the strictures of his body, Hardhands' consciousness can take any form that he cares to mold it to, or form at all, a spark of himself drifting on the Currents of Elsewhere. But such is his fondness for his own form, even Elsewhere, that when he steps lightly from the flesh hanging like a side of beef, he coalesces into a representation of himself, in every way identical to his corporeal form, although with lip rouge that will not smudge, and spectacularly elevated hair.

On Elsewhere feet, Hardhands' fetch turns to face its meaty shell, and is rather pleased with the view; even dangling upside down, he looks pretty darn good. Elsewhere, the sigil that has caged Hardhands' motion is clearly visible as a pulsating net of green and gold, interwoven at the interstices with splotches of pink. A Coarctation Sigil, under normal circumstances no stronger than pie, but given magnitude by the height of the Current, and Hardhands' starchy condition. The fetch, however, is not limited by starch, and the Current just feeds its strength. Dismantling the constraint is the work of a matter of seconds, and after the fetch slides back into its shell, it's a mere bagatelle to contort himself down and free.

Casting free of the gyres with a splashy Gramatica command, Hardhands rubs his ankles, and then stands on tingly feet. Now that he has the leisure to inspect the furnishings, he sees there are no furnishings to inspect because the room, while sumptuously paneled in gorgeous tiger-eye maple, is empty other than a curvy red velvet chaise. The only ornamentations are the jingly chains dangling from the ceiling. The floor is bare stone, cold beneath his bare feet. And now, he notices that the flooring directly under the dangle is dark and stained, with something that he suspects is a combination of blood, sweat, and tears.

Places to go and praterhuman entities to fry, no time to linger to discover the truth of his suspicions. Hardhands turns to make his exit through the sole door, only to find that the door is gone, and in its place, a roiling black Vortex, as black and sharp as the Vortex that he himself had cut out of the Aeyther, only hours before. He is pushed back by the force of the Vortex, which is spiraling outward, not inward, thus indicating that Something is coming, rather than trying to make him go.

The edges of the Vortex glow hot-black, the wind that the Vortex is creating burns his skin; he shields his eyes with his hand, and tries to stand upright, but his tingly feet can not hold against the force, and he falls. The Vortex widens, like a surprised eye, and a slit of light appears pupil-like in its darkness. The pupil widens, becomes a pupa, a cocoon, a shell, an acorn, an egg, growing larger and larger and larger until it fills the room with unbelievable brightness, with a scorching heat that is hotter than the sun, bright enough to burn through Hardhands' shielding hand. Hardhands feels his skin pucker, his eyes shrivel, his hair start to smolder, and then just as he is sure he is about to burst into flames, the light shatters like an eggshell, and Something has arrived.

Recently, Hardhands' Invocations have grown quite bold, and, after some bitter tooth and nails, he's pulled a few large fish into his circle. But those are as like to This as a fragment of beer bottle is to a faceted diamond. He knows, from the top of his pulsating head to the tips of his quivering toes that this is no servitor, no denizen, no elemental. Nothing this spectacular can be called, corralled, or compelled. This apparition can be nothing but the highest of the high, the blessed of the blessed: the Goddess Califa herself.

How to describe what Hardhands sees? Words are too simple, they cannot do justice to Her infinite complexity, She's Everything and Nothing, both fractured and whole. His impressions are blurred and confused, but here's a try. Her hair is ruffled black feathers, it is slickery green snakes, it is as fluffy and lofty as frosting. Her eyes—one, two, three, four, maybe five—are as round and polished as green apples, are long tapered crimson slits, they are as flat white as sugar. She's as narrow as nightfall, She's as round as winter, She's as tall as moonrise, She's shorter than love. Her feet do not crush the little flowers, She is divine, She is fantastic.

She simply is.

Hardhands has found his footing only to lose it again, falling to his knees before Her, Her fresh red smile as strong as a kick to the head, to the heart. Hardhands is smitten, no not smitten, he's smote, from the tingly tingly top of his reeling head to the very tippy tip of his tingling toes. He's freezing and burning, he's alive, he's dying, he's dead. He's hypmooootized. He gapes at the Goddess, slack-jawed and tight-handed, wanting nothing more than to reach out and grasp at Her perfection, bury himself in the ruffle of Her feathers. Surely a touch of Her hand would spark such fire in him that he would catch alight and perish in a blaze of exquisite agony but it would be worth it, oh it would be worth every cinder.

The Goddess's mouth opens, with a flicker of a velvet tongue and the glitter of a double row of white teeth. The Gramatica that flows from Her mouth in a sparkly ribband is as crisp and sweet as a summer wine, it slithers over Hardhands' flushed skin, sliding into his mouth, his eyes, his ears, and filling him with a dark sweet rumble.

"Georgiana's toy," the Goddess purrs. He didn't see Her move but now She is poured over the chaise like silk, and the bear-head minion is offering bowls of snacks, ice cream sundaes, and magazines. "Chewable and sweet, ah lovely darling yum."

Hardhands has forgotten Georgiana, he's forgotten Tiny Doom, he's forgotten Madam Rose, he's forgotten himself, he's forgotten his exquisite manners—no not entirely, even the Goddess's splendor can not expunge good breeding. He toddles up onto sweaty feet, and sweeps the floor with his curtsy.

"I am your obedient servant, your grace," he croaks.

The Goddess undulates a languid finger and he finds himself following Her beckon, not that he needs to be beckoned, he can barely hold himself aloof, wants nothing more than to throw himself forward and be swallowed alive. The Goddess spreads Her wings, Her arms, Her legs, and he falls into Her embrace, the prickle of the feathers closing over his bare skin, electric and hot.

X. Doom Acts

Here is Tiny Doom howling like a banshee, a high pitched shriek that usually results in immediate attention to whatever need she is screaming for: more pudding, longer story, hotter bath, bubbles. The minion whose arm she is slung under must be pitch deaf because her shrieks have not the slightest impact upon him. He continues galumphing along, whistling slightly, or perhaps that is just the breeze of his going, which is a rapid clip.

She tries teeth, her fall-back weapon and always effective, even on Paimon whose blue skin is surprisingly delicate. The minion's hide is as chewy as rubber and it tastes like salt licorice. Spitting and coughing, Tiny Doom gives up on the bite. Kicking has no effect other than to bruise her toes and her arms are too pinned for hitting, and, down the stairs they go, bump bump, Bwannie getting farther and farther away. Pig is jolting behind them, she's got a grip on one dangly ear, but that's all, and his bottom is hitting each downward stump, but he's too soft to thump.

An outside observer might think that Doom is wailing for more candy, or perhaps is just over-tired and up past her bedtime. Madam Rose certainly thought that her commotion was based in over-tiredness, plus a surfeit of sugar, and the bouncer thinks it's based in spoiled-ness, plus a surfeit of sugar, but they are both wrong. Sugar is Doom's drug of choice, she's not allowed it officially, but unofficially she has her ways (she knows exactly in what drawer the Pontifexa's secretary keeps his stash of Crumbly Crem-O's and Jiffy-Ju's, and if that drawer is empty, Relais can be relied upon to have a box of bon-bons hidden from Hardhands in the bottom of his wardrobe), and so her system can tolerate massive quantities of the stuff before hyper-activity and urpyness sets in.

No. She is wailing because every night, at tuck-in time, after the Pontifexa has kissed her, and kissed Pig and together they have said their prayers, then Paimon sits on the edge of Tiny Doom's big white frilly bed and tells her a story. It's a different story every night, Paimon's supply of fabulosity being apparently endless, but always with the same basic theme:

Kid is told what To Do.

Kid does Not Do what Kid is told To Do.

Kid gets into Bad Trouble with various Monsters.

Kid gets Eaten.

The End, yes you may have one more drink of water, and then no more excuses and it's lights out, and to sleep. Now.

Tiny Doom loves these stories, whose Directives and Troubles are always end-lessly inventively different, but which always turn out the same way: with a Giant Monstrous Burp. She knows that Paimon's little yarns are for fun only, that Kids do not really get eaten when they do not do what they are told, for she does not do what she is told all the time, and she's never been eaten. Of course, no one would dare eat her anyway, she's the Heir to the Pontifexa, and has Paimon and Pig besides. Pai-mon's stories are just stories, made to deliciously shiver her skin, so that afterward she lies in the haze of the nightlight, cuddled tight to Pig's squishiness, and knows that she is safe.

But now, tonight, she's seen the gleam in Madam Rose's eye and seen the look she gave her minions and Tiny Doom knew instantly that Bwannie is in Big Trou-ble. This is not bedtime, there is no Paimon, and no nightlight, and no drink of wa-ter. This is all true Big Trouble and Tiny Doom knows exactly where Big Trouble ends. Now she is scared, for Bwannie and for herself, and even for Pig, who would make a perfect squishy demon dessert.

Thus, shrieking.

"Bwaaaaaaaaaaaaaaaaaaaaaaaanie!" Doom cries, "Bwaaaaaaaaaaaaanie!"

They jump the last step, Tiny Doom jolting bony hip, oww, and then round a corner. Doom sucks in the last useless shriek. Her top half is hanging half over the servitor's shoulder and her dangling down head is starting to feel tight, plus the shrieking has left her breathless, so for a few seconds she gulps in air. Gulping, her nose running yucky yuck. She wiggles, whispers, and lets go of Pig.

He plops down onto the dirty floor, hinder up and snout down, and then they round another corner and he's gone.

She lifts her head, twisting her neck, and there's the hairy interior of a pointy ear. She shouts: "Hey, minion!"

"I ain't listening," says the minion. "You can shout all you want, but I ain't listening. Madam told me not to listen and I ain't."

"I gotta pee!"

"You gotta wait," the minion says, "you be home soon and then you can pee in your own pot. And you ain't gotta shout in my ear. You make my brain hurt, you loudness little bit, you."

"I gotta pee right now!" Doom, still shouting, anyway, just in case there are noises behind them. "I'M GONNA PEE NOW!"

The minion stops and shifts Tiny Doom around like a sack full of flour, and breathes into her face. "You don't pee on me, loudness."

Like Paimon, the minion has tusks and pointy teeth but Paimon's tusks are polished white and his teeth sparkle like sunlight, and his breath smells always of cloves. The minion's tusks are rubbed and worn, his teeth yucky yellow, and he's got bits of someone caught between them.

Doom wrinkles her nose and holds her breath and says in a whine: "I can't help it, I have to go, my hot chocolate is all done." Her feet are dangling and she tries to turn the wiggle into a kick, but she can't quite reach the minion's soft bits, and her purple slippers wiggle at empty air.

"You pee on me and I snack you up, nasty baby." The minion crunches spiny fangs together, clashing sparks. "Delish!"

"You don't dare!" says Tiny Doom stoutly. "I am the Pontifexina and my grandmamma would have your knobby hide if you munch me!"

"An' I care, little princess, if you piss me wet, I munch you dry—"

"☞☜☞ᴰ✗☜ᴰ✗" whispers Tiny Doom and spits. She's got a good wad going, and it hits the minion right on the snout.

The minion howls and drops her. She lands on stingy sleepy feet, falls over, and then scrambles up, stamping. The minion is also stamping, and holding his hairy hands to his face; under his clawing fingers smoke is steaming. He careens this way and that, Doom dodging around his staggers, and then she scoots by him, and back the way they had just come.

Tiny Doom runs as fast as her fat little legs will run, her heart pounding because she is now in Big Trouble, and she knows if the minion quits dancing and starts chasing, she's going to be Eaten too. The hot word she spit burned her tongue and that hurts too, and where's Pig? She goes around another corner, thinking she'll see the stairs that they came down, but she doesn't, she sees another long hallway. She turns around to go back, and then the minion blunders towards her, his face a melt-y mess, and she reverses, speedily.

"I dance around in a ring and suppose and the secret sits in the middle and knows." She sings very quietly to herself as she runs.

Carpet silent under her feet; a brief glimpse of another running Doom reflected off a glass curio cabinet; by a closed door, the knob turns but the door will not open. She can feel the wind of closing in beating against her back, but she keeps going. The demon is shouting mean things at her, but she keeps going.

"You dance around in a ring and suppose and the secret sits in the middle and knows."

A door opens and a were-flamingo trips out, stretching its longneck out; Doom dodges around its spindly legs, ignoring yelps. Ahead, more stairs, and there she aims, having no other options, can't go back and there's no where to go sideways.

At the top of the stairs, Doom pauses and finally looks behind. The minion has wiped most of his melt off, livid red flares burn in his eye sockets and he looks pretty mad. The were-flamingo has halted him, and they are wrangling, flapping wings against flapping ears. The minion is bigger but the were-flamingo has a sharp beak—rapid fire pecking at the minion's head. The minion punches one humongous fist and down the flamingo goes, in a flutter of pink feathers.

"I snack you, spitty baby!" the minion howls and other things too mean for Doom to hear.

"We dance around in a ring and suppose and the secret sits in the middle and knows."

Doom hoists herself up on the banister, squeezing her tummy against the rail. The banister on the Stairs of Infinite Demonstration, Bilskinir's main staircase, is fully sixty feet long. Many is the time that Doom has swooped down its super-polished length, flying miles through the air, at the end to be received by Paimon's perfect catch. This rail is much shorter, and there's no Paimon waiting, but here we go!

She flings her legs over, and slides off. Down she goes, lickety-split, bumping over splinters, but still getting up a pretty good whoosh. Here comes the demon, waving angry arms, he's too big to slide, so he galumphs down the stairs, clumpty clump, getting closer. Doom hits the end of the banister and soars onward another five feet or so, then ooph, hits the ground, owww. She bounces back upward, and darts through the foyer and into the mudroom beyond, pulling open her pockets as she goes.

Choco-sniffs and jack-snaps skitter across the parquet floor, rattling and rolling. Sugarbunnies and beady-eyes, jimjoos and honeybuttons scatter like shot. Good-bye crappy candy, good-bye yummy candy, good-bye.

"I DANCE AROUND A RING AND SUPPOSE AND THE SECRET SITS IN THE MIDDLE AND KNOWS."

Ahead, a big red door, well barred and bolted, but surely leading Out. The bottom bolt snaps back under her tiny fingers, but the chains are too high and tippy-toe, hopping, jumping will not reach them. The demon is down the stairs, he's still shouting and steaming, and the smell of charred flesh is stinky indeed.

A wall rack hangs by the door, and from it coats and cloaks dangle like discarded skins; Doom dives into the folds of cloth and becomes very small and silent. She's a good hider, Tiny Doom, she's learned against the best (Paimon).

Her heart pounds thunder in her ears, and she swallows her panting. When Paimon makes discovery (*if* he makes discovery), it means only bath-time, or mushy peas, or toenail clipping. If the demon finds her, Pontifexina or not, it's snicky snack time for sure. She really did have to potty too, pretty bad. She crosses her ankles and jiggles her feet, holding.

In the other room, out of sight, comes yelling, shouting, roaring and then a heavy thud that seems to shake the very walls. The thud reverberates and then fades away.

Silence.

Stillness.

Tiny Doom peeks between the folds. Through the archway she sees rolling candy and part of a sprawled bulk. Then the bulk heaves, hooves kicking. The demon's lungs have re-inflated and he lets out a mighty horrible roar—the nastiest swear word that Tiny Doom has ever heard. Doom, who had poked her head all the way out for a better view, yanks back, just in time. The Word, roiling like mercury, howls by her, trailing sparks and smelling of shit.

A second roar is gulped off in mid-growl, and turns into a shriek, which is then muffled in thumping and slurping, ripping, and chomping. Doom peeks again: the demon's legs are writhing, wiggling, and kicking. A thick stain spreads through the archway, gooey and green. Tiny Doom wiggles her way out of the velvet and runs happily towards the slurping sound.

XI. Desire Gratified

Inside the Goddess's embrace, Hardhands is dying, he's crying, he's screaming with pleasure, with joy, crying his broken heart out. He's womb-enclosed, hot and smothering, and reduced to his pure essence. He has collapsed to a single piercing pulsing point of pleasure. He has lost himself, but he has found everything else.

And then his ecstasy is interrupted by another piercing sensation: pain. Not the exquisite pain of a well placed needle, or perfectly laid lash, but an ugly pain that gnaws into his pleasurable non-existence in an urgent painful way. He wiggles, tossing, but the pain will not go away, it only gnaws deeper, and with each razor nibble it slices away at his ecstasy. And as he is torn away from the Goddess's pleasure, he is forced back into himself, and the wiggly body-bound part of himself realizes that the Goddess is sucking him out of life. The love-torn spirit part of him does not care. He struggles, trying to dive down deeper into the bottomless divine love, but that gnawing pain is tethering him to the Waking World, and he can't kick it free.

Then the Goddess's attention lifts from him, like a blanket torn away. He lies on the ground, the stones slick and cold against his bare skin. The echo of his loss pounds in his head, farrier-like, stunning him. A shrill noise pierces his agony, cuts through the thunder, a familiar high pitched whine:

"Ya! Ya! Ya!"

His eyes are filled with sand; it takes a moment of effort before his nerveless hands can find his face, and knuckle his vision clear. Immediately he sees: Tiny Doom, dancing with the bear-headed minion. Sieur Oso is doing the Mazorca, a dance which requires a great deal of jumping and stamping, and he's got the perfect boots to make the noise, each one as big as horse's head. Tiny Doom is doing the Ronde-loo, weaving round and round Sieur Oso her circular motion too sick-making for Hardhands to follow.

Then he realizes: no, they are not dancing, Sieur Oso is trying to squash Tiny Doom like a bug, and she, rather than run like a sensible child, is actually taunting him on. Oh Haðraaða!

Dimly Tiny Doom's husband sparks the thought that perhaps he should help her, and he's trying to figure out where his feet are, so as to arise to this duty, when his attention is caught by a whirl, not a whirl, a Vortex the likes of which he has never before seen, a Vortex as black as ink, but streaked hot pink, and furious furious. Though he can see nothing but the cutting blur of the spin, he can feel the force of the fight within; the Goddess is battling it out with something, something strong enough to give Her a run for Her divas, something tenacious and tough.

"Bwannie! Bwannie!" cries Doom. She is still spinning, and the minion is starting to look tuckered, his stomps not so stompy anymore, and his jeers turned to huffy puffs. Foam is dribbling from his muzzle, like whipped cream.

Hardhands ignores Tiny Doom.

"◖✓◗◊✐" Hardhands grates, trying to through a Word of encouragement into the mix, to come to his darling's aid. The Word is a strong one, even in his weakened state, but it bounces off the Vortex, harmless, spurned, just as he has been spurned. The Goddess cares nothing for Hardhands' love, for his desire, he chokes back tears, and staggers to his feet, determined to help somehow, even if he must cast himself into the fire to do so.

Before he can do anything so drastic, there is the enormous sound of suction sucking in. For a split second, Hardhands feels himself go as flat as paper, his lungs suck against his chest, his bones slap into ribands, his flesh becomes as thin as jerky. The Current pops like a cork, the world re-inflates, and Hardhands is round and substantial again, although now truly bereft. The Goddess is gone.

The Vortex has blushed pink now, and its spin is slowing, slower, slower, until it is no longer a Vortex, but a little pink blur, balanced on pointy toes, ears flopping— what the hell? Pig?

He has gone insane, or blind, or both? In one dainty pirouette Pig has soared across the room and latched himself to the minion's scraggly throat. Suddenly invigorated, Sieur Oso does a pirouette of his own, upward, gurgling.

"What is going on—!" Madam Rose's voice raises high above the mayhem-noises, then it chokes. She has stalled in the doorway, more minions peering from behind her safety. Tiny Doom has now attached to Sieur Oso's hairy ankle and her grip—hands and teeth—are not dislodged by his antic kicking, though whether the minion is now dancing because Tiny Doom is gnawing on his ankle or because his throat is a massive chewy-mess, it's hard to say. Pig disengages from Sieur Oso and leaps to Madam Rose, who clutches him to her bosom in a maternal way, but jerkily, as though she wants less of his love, not more. Her other slaveys have scarpered, and now that the Goddess is gone, Hardhands sees no particular reason to linger either.

He flings one very hard Gramatica word edgewise at the antic bear. Sieur Oso jerks upward, and his surprised head sails backward, tears through the tent wall, and is gone. Coldfire founts up from the stump of his neck, sizzling and sparky. Hardhands grabs Tiny Doom away from the minion's forward fall, and she grasps onto him monkey-wise, clinging to his shoulders.

"Pig!" she screams, "Pig!"

Madam Rose manages to disentangle Pig, and flings him towards Hardhands and Tiny Doom. Pig sails through the air, his ears like wings, and hits Hardhands' chest with a soggy thud and then tumbles downward. Madam Rose staggers, she is clutching her throat, her hair has fallen down, drippy red. Above her, the tent ceiling is flickering with tendrils of coldfire, it pours down around her like fireworks falling from the sky, sheathing her bones in glittering flickering flesh. The coldfire has spread to the ceiling now, scorching the raven angels, and the whole place is going to go: coldfire doesn't burn like non-magickal fire, but it is hungry and does consume, and Hardhands has had enough consumption for tonight. Hefting Tiny Doom up higher on his shoulder, he turns about to retreat (run away).

"Pig! Pig!" Tiny Doom beats at his head as he ducks under the now flickering threshold, "PIG!"

The coldfire has raced across the roof beyond him and the antechamber before him is a heaving weaving maelstrom of magick, the Current bubbling and sucking, oh it's a shame to let such yummy power go to waste, but now is perhaps not the time to further test his control. Madam Rose staggers out of the flames, the very air around her is bubbling and cracking, spitting Abyss through cracks in the Current, black tendrils that coil and smoke.

Tiny Doom, still screaming: "Pig!"

Hardhands jumps and weaves through the tentacles of flame, flinging banishings as he goes, and the tendrils snap away. He's not going to stop for Pig, Pig is on his own, Hardhands can feel the Current boiling, in a moment there will be too much magick for the space to contain, there is going to be a giant implosion and he's had enough implosions for one night, too. Through the dining room they run, scattering cheese platters, waiters, cocktails and conservationists, crunching crackers under-foot, knocking down a minion—there—open veranda doors, and beyond those doors, the sparkle of hurdy-gurdy lights. Doom clinging to his head like a pinchy hat, he leaps over the bar, through breaking bottles and scattered ice, and through the doors, into blessed cool air. There ahead—the back of the Monkey's Head—keeping running, through gasps and a pain in his side.

Through the dark throat—for a second Hardhands thinks that for sure the Grin will snap shut, and they will be swallowed forever, but no, he leaps the tombstone teeth and they are clear. The sky above turns sheet white, and the ground shifts be-neath his feet in a sudden bass roll. He sits down hard in the springy grass, lungs gasping. Tiny Doom collapses from his grasp and rolls like a little barrel across the springy turf. The stars wink back in, as though a veil has been drawn back, and sud-denly Hardhands is limp with exhaustion. The Current is gone. The Monkey's Grin still grins, but his glittering letter halo is gone, and his eyes are dim. Madam Rose's is gone, as well.

Well, good riddance, good-bye, adios, farewell. From the Monkey's Grin, Pig tippy-dances, pirouetting towards Doom, who receives him with happy cries of joy.

Hardhands lies on the grass and stares upward at the starry sky, and he moves his head back and forth, drums his feet upon the ground, wiggles his fingers just be-cause he can. He feels drained and empty, and sore as hell. The grass is crispy cool beneath his bare sweaty back, and he could just lie there forever. Behind the relief of freedom, however, there's a sour sour taste.

He was set up. The whole evening was nothing but a gag. His grandmother, his darling sweet grandmother whom he did not kill out of love, respect, and honor, whom he pulled back from the brink of assassination because he held her so dear, his grandmamma sold him to Madam Rose.

Him, Hardhands, sold!

The Pontifexa has played them masterfully: Relais' incompetence, Tiny Doom's greed, Madam Rose's cunning, and his own sense of duty and loyalty. He'd gone blindly in to save Tiny Doom and she was the bait and he the stupid stupid prey, all along.

He, Hardhands, expendable! Can he believe it?

Tiny Doom is ignored but she is also insistent: "Bwannie—get up! Pig wants to go home!"

For a second our hero is wracked with sorrow, he takes a deep breath that judders his bones, and closes his eyes. The darkness is sparked with stars, flares of light caused by the pressure of holding the tears back. But under the surface of his sorrow, he feels an immense longing, longing not for the Pontifexa, or hot water, or for Re-lais' comforting embrace, or even for waffles. Compared to this longing, the rest of his feelings—anger, sorrow, guilt, love—are nothing. He should be already plotting his revenge, his payback, his turn-about-is-fair-play, but instead he is alive with thoughts of sweeping black wings, and spiraling hair, and the unutterable blissful agony of Desire.

"Pig wants a waffle, Bwannie! And I must potty, I gotta potty now!"

Hardhands opens his eyes to a dangly pink snout. Pig's eyes are small black beads, and his cotton stitched mouth is a bit red around the edges, as though he's smeared his lipstick. He smells of salty-iron blood and the peachy whiff of stale cold-fire. He looks satisfied.

"Would you please get Pig out of my face?" Hardhands says wearily. The mystery of how Pig fought and defeated a goddess is beyond him right now; he'll consider that later.

Tiny Doom pokes him. She is jiggling and bobbing, with her free hand tightly pressed. She has desires ungratified of her own; her bladder may be full, but her candy sack is empty. "Pig wants you to get up. He says Get Up Now, Banastre!"

Hardhands, thinking of desire gratified, gets up.

Raphael

Stephen Graham Jones is the author of The Fast Red Road: A Plainsong, *which won the Independent Publisher Book Award for Multicultural Fiction;* All the Beautiful Sinners, *a Texas Monthly Book Club selection;* The Bird Is Gone, *for which he was awarded a literature fellowship from the National Endowment for the Arts;* Bleed into Me, *which won the Texas Institute of Letters Jesse Jones Award for Fiction; and, most recently, the horror novel* Demon Theory. *He's published nearly a hundred short stories in nearly as many places, including textbooks and anthologies.*

An associate professor of English at Texas Tech University, Jones is a member of the Blackfeet Nation.

"Raphael" was originally published in issue 55 of Cemetery Dance *magazine.*

—E.D.

By the time we were twelve, the four of us were already ghosts, invisible in the back of our homerooms, at the cafeteria, at the pep-rallies where the girls all wore spirit ribbons the boys were supposed to buy. There was Alex in his cousin's handed-down clothes—his cousin in the sixth grade with us—Rodge, who insisted that *d* was actually in his name, Melanie, hiding behind the hair her mother wouldn't let her cut, and me, with my laminated list of allergies and the inhaler my mother had written my phone number on in black marker. Three boys who knew they didn't matter and one girl that each of us fell in love with every morning with first bell, watching her race across the wet grass to make the school doors by 8:00.

"We're the only ones who can see us," Rodge said to me once, watching Melanie run.

I nodded, and Alex fell in. When Melanie burst through the doors we each pretended not to have been watching her.

It was true, though, that we were the only ones who could see us. And there was a power in it. It let us live in a space where no one could see what we did. The rules didn't apply to us. Maybe that freedom was supposed to balance out our invisibility somehow, even. The world trying to make up for what it had failed to give us. We used it like that, anyway: not as if it were a gift, but like it was something we deserved, something we were going to prove was ours by using it all up, by pushing it farther and farther, daring it to fail us as well.

Or maybe we pushed it just because we'd been let down so many times already, we had no choice but to distrust our invisibility, our friendship. Anything this good, after everything else, had to be the opening lines of some complicated joke. We were just waiting for the punch line. By pushing what we had farther and farther each day, testing each other, we were maybe even trying to fast-forward to that punch line.

But, too, God, it just felt so good to be part of something, finally, and then act casual, like it was nothing. Even if it was the rejects club, the ghost squad. Because maybe that was where it started, right? Then, next, weeks and weeks later—homecoming—maybe one of us would understand in some small but perfect way what it felt like at the pep rally, to give a girl a spirit ribbon then watch her pin it onto her shirt, smooth it down for too long because suddenly eye contact has become an awkward thing. Or, maybe one of us would be that girl. Or, just get swept away for once in the band's music. Believe in the team, that if they can just win Friday night, then the world is going to be good and right.

More than anything, I guess, we wanted to be seen, given a chance. Not on the outside anymore. That's probably what it came down to.

And the first step towards getting seen is of course being loud, doing what the other kids won't, or are too scared to.

The days, though, they just kept turning into each other.

Nobody was noticing us, what we were doing. Even when we talked about it loud in the cafeteria, in the hall.

It would have taken so little, too.

A lift of the chin, a narrowing of the eyes.

Somebody asking where we were going after school.

If we just could have gotten that one nod of interest, maybe Alex would still be alive. Maybe Rodge wouldn't have killed himself as a fifteenth birthday present to himself. Maybe Melanie wouldn't have had to run away.

Even if whoever saw us didn't want to go with us, but just had a ribbon, maybe. For Melanie. Because she really was beautiful. The other three, then, we would have faded back into the steel-grey lockers that lined the halls, and we wouldn't have gone any farther, ever.

But we were invisible, invulnerable.

Nobody saw us walking away after final bell. We were going to the lake. It was where we always went.

In a plastic cake pan with a sealable lid, buried in the mat of leaves that Rodge said was just above where the waves the ski boats made crashed, was Alex's book. It was one of a series off a television commercial; his mom had bought it then forgot about it. And we didn't hide it because we thought it was a Satan's Bible or Anarchist's Cookbook or anything—because it was powerful—we hid it simply because we didn't want it to get wet. If my mother ever missed her cake pan, she never said anything.

"Where were we?" Melanie said, not sitting down but lowering herself so the seat of her pants hovered over the damp leaves. She balanced by hugging her knees with her arms. She'd told us once that her father had made her take ballet and gymnastics both until the third grade, when he left, and the way she moved, I believed it. We were all invisible, but she was the only one with enough throw-away grace that you never heard her feet fall.

Sitting back on her heels like that, her hair fell over her arms to the ground.

The rest of us didn't care about our clothes. Just the book.

What we were doing was trying to scare ourselves. With alien abductions, with unexplained disappearances. Ghost ships, werewolves, prophecies, spontaneous human combustion.

The person reading would read in monotone. That was one of the rules. And no eye contact either.

The first entry that day was about a man sitting in his own living room when the television suddenly goes static. He reaches for the mute button, can't find it, but then the screen clears up all at once. Only it's not his show anymore, but an aerial view of . . . he's not sure what. And then he is: his house, his own house. Ambulances pulling up. He opens his mouth, stands, his beer foaming into the carpet, and then doesn't go to work the next day, or the next, and finally starts getting his checks from disability.

"That's it?" Alex said, when Rodge was through.

"What's the question?" Melanie said.

Part of the format of the book was that the editors would ask questions in italics after each entry.

"Was he stealing his cable?" I offered, my voice spooky.

Alex laughed, not scared either.

"Was it a warning?" Rodge read, following his index finger. "Was T.J. Bentworth given that day a prophecy of his own death, and the opportunity to avoid it? And, if so, who sent that warning?"

Melanie threaded a strand of hair behind her ear, shook her head, disgusted.

The test now—and we'd sworn honesty, to not at any cost lie about it—was whether or not, that night, alone, we'd think twice with our hands on the remote control. If we thought, even for a microsecond, that that next station was going to be us.

Melanie shrugged, looked away, across the water.

"This is crap," she said. "We need a new book."

I nodded, agreeing.

Alex took the book from Rodge, buried his nose in it, determined to prove to us that this book *was* scary.

I left him to it, was prepared to go to Rodge's house, raid his pantry before his brother got home from practice, but then Alex looked up, said it: "We should tell our own stories, think?"

Rodge looked down, as if focusing into the ground.

"Like, make them up?" he said.

Alex shrugged whatever, smiled, and clapped the book shut.

He was three hours from a Buick that was coming to kill him.

The story I told was one that I'd already tried hard enough to forget that I never would. It was one of my dad's stories. I was in it.

The first thing I told Alex and Rodge and Melanie was that this one was true.

Alex nodded, said to Rodge that this was how they all start.

"It should be dark," Melanie said, swinging some of her hair around behind her. There were leaf fragments in the tip-ends. I looked past her, to the wall of trees. It *was* night, in a way. Not dark, but still, with the sun behind the clouds, the only light we had was gray. It was enough. I nodded to myself, started.

"I was like ten months old," I said.

"You *remember*?" Alex interrupted.

Rodge told him to shut up.

"My dad," I went on. "He was like, I don't know. In the bedroom. I think I was on the floor in the living room or something." I shrugged my shoulder up to rub my right ear, stalling. Not to be sure I had it right, but that my voice wasn't going to crack. The first time I'd heard my father tell this, I'd cried and not been able to stop. I couldn't even explain why, really. Just that, you look at enough pictures of yourself as a baby and you imagine that everything was normal. That it doesn't matter, it was just part of what got you to where you are now.

But then my dad took that away.

The story I told the three of them that last afternoon we were all together was that I was just sleeping there on the floor, my dad in his refrigerator in the garage, getting another beer or something, my mom asleep in their room. The television was the only light in the room. It was wrestling—the reason my mom had gone to bed early. Anyway, there's my dad, coming back from the garage, one beer open, another between his forearm and chest, when he feels more than sees that something's wrong in the living room. That there's an extra shadow.

"What?" Melanie said, her eyes locked right on me.

I looked away, down. Swallowed.

"He said that—that—" and then I started crying anyway. Twelve years old with my friends and crying like a baby.

Melanie took my hand in hers.

"You have to finish now," Alex said.

Rodge had his hand over his mouth, wasn't saying anything.

When I could, I told them: my dad, standing there in the doorless doorway between the kitchen and the living room, looking down into our living room, past the couch, the coffee table, to me, on my stomach on the floor.

Squatted down beside me, blond like nobody in our family, a boy, a fourth-grader maybe, his palm stroking my hair down to my scalp.

My father doesn't drop his beer, doesn't call for my mom, can't do anything.

"What—?" he tries to say, and the boy just keeps stroking my hair down, looks across the living room to my father, and says "I'm just patting him," then stands, walks out the other doorway in the living room, the one that goes to the front door.

". . . only it never opens," Alex finished, grinning.

I nodded as if caught, pressed my palms into my eyes and stretched my chin up as high as I could, so the lump in my throat wouldn't push through the skin.

"Good," Melanie said, "nice," and, when I could control my face again, I smiled, pointed to Rodge, his hair straw yellow, and lied, said that it was him patting me, somehow.

Rodge opened his mouth once, twice, shaking his head no, please, but, when he couldn't get out whatever he had, Alex clapped three times, slowly, and then opened his hand to Melanie, said, "Ladies first."

"Guess I'll have to wait then," she said back, flaring her eyes, but then shrugged, wrapped a coil of hair around her index finger like she was always doing, then walked her hand up the strands, each coil taking in one more finger until she didn't have any more left.

It was one of the things Alex and Rodge and I never talked about then, but each loved about her—how she was so unconscious of the small things she could do. How she took so much for granted, and, because of that, because she didn't draw attention to the magic acrobatics of her fingers, to the strength of her hair, she got to keep it.

We didn't so much love her like a girl, desire her, though that was starting, for sure. It was more like we saw in her a completeness missing in ourselves. A completeness coupled with a kind of disregard that was almost flagrant. But maybe that's what desire is, really. In the end, it didn't matter; none of us would ever hold her hand at a pep rally, or tell her anything real. It wasn't because of her story, either, but that's more or less where it starts.

"Four kids," she said, looking to each of us in turn, "sixth graders, just like us," and Alex groaned as if about to vomit, held his stomach in mock-pain.

Rodge smiled, and I did too, on the inside.

A safe story. That was exactly what we needed.

"The girl's name was . . . *Melody,*" Melanie said, arching her eyebrows for us to call her on it. When we didn't, she went on, and almost immediately the comfort level dropped. Alex flashed a look to me and I shrugged my cheeks as best I could, didn't know. What Melanie was telling us was the part *before* the story, the part we didn't want and would have never asked for, because we all already knew: the thing between her and her stepdad. What they did. Only, to amp it up for us, maybe, make it worse, Melanie added to the nightly visitations Melody's mother, standing in the doorway, watching. Mad at Melody for stealing her husband.

Desperate to not be hearing this, I latched onto that doorway as hard as I could, remembered it from my own story, and nodded to myself: all Melanie was doing was reordering the stuff I'd already laid out there. Using it again, because it was already charged—we already *knew* that bad things followed parents standing in doorways.

Or maybe it was a door I had opened, somehow, by telling a real story in the first place.

After the one rape that was supposed to stand in for the rest, Melanie nodded, said, "And then there was . . . *Hodge* . . ." at which point Rodge started shaking his head no, no, please.

"We only have an hour," Alex chimed, tapping the face of his watch.

Melanie turned her face to him and raised her eyebrows, waiting for him to back off. Finally, he did. As punishment, his character didn't even get a name. Mine was *Raphael,* what Melanie considered to be a version of *Gabriel,* I guess. But Gabe, I was just Gabe.

I couldn't interrupt her, though. Even when her story had the four of us walking away from school, to play our little "scare" game.

But this one was different.

In the Lakeview of Melanie's story, Lake*ridge,* there wasn't a book buried in a thirteen-by-nine tupperware dish, but an overgrown cemetery. It was just past the football field.

Over the past week, she told us, her face straight, the dares had been on the order of lying face-up on a grave for ninety seconds, or tracing each carved letter of the oldest headstone, or putting your hand in the water of the birdbath and saying your own name backwards sixty-six times.

"They were running out of stuff, though," she added.

"I *get* it," Alex said, holding his mother's book closer to his chest.

Melanie smiled, pulled a black line of hair across her mouth and spoke through it: "But then *Raphael* had an idea," she said, looking to me.

"What?" I said, looking behind me for no real reason.

Melanie smiled, let the silence build—she had to have done this before, I thought, before she moved here, or seen it done—and told us that *Raphael's* great idea was to take some of the pecans from the tree over in the corner, the tree that

(her voice spooking up) "had its roots down with the dead people, in their eye sockets and rib cages."

"Take them and what?" Rodge said, worried.

"Look at you," Alex said to him.

"And what?" I asked, at a whisper.

"Take them to one of your basements," she said. "Then put them in a bowl with
water for six days, then come back, with the lights off, and each eat one."

The lump was back in my throat. I thought it might be a pecan.

"That it?" Alex said, overdoing his shrug.

"Six days . . ." Melanie said, ignoring him, drawing air in through her teeth, "and
the four of them collect back in the basement, turn all the lights off except one candle,
and then, that too."

"At midnight," Alex added.

"At midnight," Melanie agreed, as if she'd been going to say that anyway, and
then drew out for us the cracking of the shells in the darkness, how they were soggy
enough to feel like the skin of dead people. Then she placed the pecan meat first on
the Alex stand-in's tongue—he throws up—then on the Hodge-character, who swallows it, gets stomach cancer two days later, then it's Raphael's turn. All he can do
though is chew and chew, the meat getting bigger in his mouth until he realizes
that, in the darkness, he's peeled his own finger, eaten *that* meat.

I laugh, liking it.

And then it's Melody's turn to eat.

With her thin, beautiful fingers, Melanie acts it out for us in a way so we can all
see Melody through the darkness of the basement, not so much cracking her pecan
as peeling it, then setting the tender meat on the back of her tongue, only to gag
when it moves.

In the darkness, we all hear the splat, then, unmistakably, something rising, trying to breathe. Not able to.

The lights come on immediately, and running down Melody's chin is blood, only
some of it's transparent, like yolk, like the pecan was an egg, and—

"C'mon . . ." Alex said. "You don't try to outgore the gore of Gabe here eating his
own *finger*, Mel."

"I'd expect that from you," Melanie said, smiling through her hair, "it was you
who was born from that dead pecan," at which point Alex hooked his head to one
side, as if not believing she would say that, then he was pushing up out of the leaves,
tackling her back into them, and we were smiling again, and I finally breathed.

When Rodge wouldn't take his turn, saying he didn't know what to say, Alex went.
Instead of telling a ghost story, though, he opened his mother's book again.

"Alex . . ." I said.

"Wait," he said, "I was just looking at this one the other . . ." and then he was
gone, hunched all the way over into the book.

I lifted my face to Melanie, said, "Where'd you hear that piece of crap?" and she
pursed her lips into a smile, said, flaring her eyes around it, "You listened."

". . . I heard it with a walnut," Alex said, turning pages, only half with us.

"A walnut?" Melanie said, crinkling her nose, "nobody plants a walnut tree in a
graveyard . . ."

Looking back, now, I can hear it—how she'd used *cemetery* in the story, *graveyard*
to Alex—but right then it didn't matter. What I was really doing anyway was thank-
ing her for it.

"You heard it at Dunbar?" I said.

Dunbar was her old school.

She opened her mouth to answer but then stopped, seemed to be fascinated by something out on the lake.

I followed where she was looking.

"What?"

"I don't know where I heard it," she said, shrugging, still not looking at me, but out over the lake. "Somewhere, I guess."

"No, what are you looking at?" I said, pointing with my chin out to the lake, and she came back to me, said it back: "What?"

"Nothing."

We were twelve years old, going to live forever.

When Alex finally got the book open to the right place, it was about witch trials all through history. Salem, the Spanish Inquisition, tribesman in Africa. A whole subsection of a chapter, with pictures of the devices used to torture confessions, pointy, Halloween hats, all of it.

"I'm shaking," I said to him.

"Can it," he said back to me, following his finger to the next page.

It was one of the blue boxes framed with scrollwork. The stuff that was supposed to be footnotes, maybe, but was too important.

"How to test for a witch," Alex read.

I leaned back, shaking my head.

"This is scary?" I said to him.

Already, one of the blue boxes from two weeks ago had given us a list on how to become werewolves: roll in the sand by water under a full moon; drink from the same water wolves have been drinking from; get bitten by a werewolf; and on and on. Our assignments that night had been to try to become werewolves. It didn't work.

"Weigh her against a *bible*?" Melanie read, incredulous.

"Her," Alex said, quieter, an intensity in his voice I knew, and knew better than to argue with.

By this time, Rodge was rocking back and forth, looking up to the road each time a car passed. When the noise got steady enough, that would mean it was 5:00, and this would be over. On a day the sun was shining, the sound of cars would slowly be replaced by the sound of boat motors, but that day, if there even was a boat, then Melanie had been the only one to see it. If she'd seen anything.

"Her," Melanie repeated, not letting it pass.

Alex smiled one side of his face, looked up to her. "How do we know?" he said.

"I'm a witch," Melanie said, "yeah."

Alex shrugged.

Melanie shook her head without letting her eyes leave him, said, "What do you want to do, then?"

Alex looked down to the blue box and read aloud, muttering: ". . . devil's mark . . . kiss of—do you, if I cut you, or stick you with a needle, will you, y'know, bleed?"

Melanie just stared at him.

"C'mon," I said, standing, pulling her up behind me. She didn't let go of my hand. Alex saw, looked from me to her, and, even though I was just twelve, still I understood in my dim way what he was doing here—*why*: he wanted to be the one holding her hand. And, if not him, then, at least for this afternoon, nobody.

"Do you?" he said, again. "If I stick you with a pin, will you bleed?"

"Do you have a pin?" she said back.

Alex scanned the ground as if looking for one, as if trying to remember a jack knife or hypodermic one of us had in a pocket.

He shook his head no.

Melanie blew air out and then held the sleeve of her right arm up, cocked her elbow out to him. It was the wide scab she'd got three days ago, when, to scare ourselves after reading about the jogger who disappeared mid-stride, we'd each had to run one hundred yards down the road, blindfolded.

Alex curled his lip up.

"What?" he said.

"You asked," she said. "It's blood. Want me to peel it?"

"But that's not—scary," he said.

Melanie lowered her elbow, let her sleeve fall back down.

Ten seconds later, Alex raised his face from the book. He was smiling.

"How about this?" he said, and I stepped around, read behind his finger.

"We can't," I said. "It's too cold."

Alex shrugged, let his voice get spooky, said, "Maybe we have to, for her own sake . . ."

"What?" Melanie said, her arms crossed now.

"Tie your hands and feet," Rodge said, from below, where he was still sitting. "Tie your hands and feet and throw you in the water."

"Bingo," Alex said, shooting him with his fingergun then blowing the smoke off, the thing the football players had all been doing during class lately, because it made no real noise.

"What?" Melanie said, to Rodge.

"He's been reading it after we leave," I said. "Right, Rodge?"

Rodge nodded. I'd caught him doing it early on. It wasn't because he wanted to know, to be more scared, but because, if he'd already read it *once*, then hearing it again wouldn't scare him so much. He'd made me promise not to tell. In return, I'd walked to what had been my spot in the leaves that day, dug my inhaler out, held it up to him like Scout's Honor.

"Well?" Alex said.

"It's cold," Melanie said.

"More like you just know you'll float," Alex said back, daring her with his eyebrows.

Melanie shook her head, blew a clump of hair from her mouth.

"Just tie my feet then," she said, and already, even then, I had a vision of her like she would have been in 1640 or whenever: bound at the wrists and ankles, sinking into the grey water. Not a witch but dying anyway.

Because we didn't have any rope like the blue box said we should, Alex sacrificed one of his shoe-laces. Melanie tied it around her ankles herself.

"It's only twenty-four inches out there," Rodge said.

He was standing now, facing the water. A defeat in his voice I would come to know over the next three years.

"Then I won't sink far, I guess," Melanie said, to Alex.

"Then we can tie your hands," he said back.

Melanie shook her head with wonder, maybe, and took the challenge, offered Alex her wrists.

"Not too tight," I told him.

He told me not to worry.

"This gets me out of homework for two weeks," she said, having to sling her head hard now to get the hair out of her face, then lean back the other way to keep from falling over.

"Three," I said back.

"A month," Rodge said.

Alex didn't say anything. Just, to Melanie, "You ready?"

She was. Alex should have asked me though, or Rodge.

All the same, he couldn't lift her all by himself.

"C'mon," he said, stepping in up to the tops of his lace-less shoes. The water sucked one of them off, kept it.

"Cold?" Melanie said.

"Bathwater," he said back, grimacing, then, because her feet were tied together, gave her his hand.

"Thanks," she said.

"It's in the book," he said, smiling.

He was on one side of her, me on the other, both of us trying to pull her along, not dunk her yet. Rodge still on the bank.

"Not *too* deep," I said, but Melanie jumped ahead of us, splashing me more than I wanted. Said, "It has to be a little deep. I don't want to hit bottom, right?"

Right. I just thought it, didn't say, because I knew she'd hear it in my voice: that this didn't feel like a game anymore. It wasn't like rolling in the sand under a full moon or running blindfolded down a part of the road that had one of us standing at each end, to watch for cars.

Something could really happen, here.

It was too late to stop it, though, too.

We followed her out until the water was at our thighs, and then Alex nodded, and she turned sideways between us, so one of us could take her feet, the other her shoulders. She leaned back into me and I held her as much as I could, but she was already wet, her hair in the water so heavy.

"If she's —" I started, taking her weight, trying not to hurt her, and when Alex looked up to me I started over: "She walked out here, I mean. Like us. Didn't float."

Alex refocused his eyes on the water and silt we'd just disturbed—all *three* of us.

"Doesn't matter," he said, "it wasn't a test, then."

"But you know she's not—"

"On three . . ." he interrupted, starting the motion, setting his teeth with the effort, and I shook my head no but had to follow too, like swinging a jump rope.

If I could go back, now, I would count to three in my head and never look away from Melanie, I think. But I didn't know. Instead of watching her the whole time, I kept looking up for boats, for somebody to catch us. Meaning all I have left of swinging her is a mental snapshot of her face, all of it for once, her hair pulled back, wet, inky, her skin so pale in contrast it was almost translucent. And then we let her go, arced her up maybe two feet if we were lucky, and four feet out. Not even high enough or far enough for her hair to pull up out of the water.

It was enough.

Without thinking *not* to, I raised my right arm, to shield my face from the splash, but then—then.

Then the world we had known was no more.

Instead of splashing into the water, Melanie rested for an instant on the surface in the fetal, cannonball position, eyes shut, all her weight on the small of her back, her hair the only thing under, and then she felt it too—that she wasn't sinking—and opened her eyes too wide, arched her back away from it, her mouth in the shape of a scream, and flipped over as fast as a cat. Once, twice, three times, until she was out over the deep water, where the gradual bank dropped off into the cold water. She was still just on the surface, writhing, screaming, whatever part of her that had been twelve years old dying. Finally, still twisting away, she lowered her mouth to the laces at her wrists, then her hands to the laces at her ankles, and then she tried to stand but fell forward, catching herself on the heels of her hands, her hair a black shroud around her.

She looked across the water at us, her eyes the only thing human on her anymore, pleading with me it seemed, and then whipped around, started running over the surface on all fours, across the mile and a half the lake was wide there, leaving us standing knee-deep in the rest of our lives.

Thirty-two years later, now, the two hours after Melanie ran away are still lost. There's an image of Alex, falling back into the water on one arm, of Rodge, just standing there, limp, and then it's trees, maybe, and roads. The red-brick buildings of town; an adult guiding my inhaler down to my mouth. Alex running up the side of the highway to meet his Buick.

At his funeral, Rodge held my hand, and I let him, but then I couldn't hold on tight enough, I guess. Three years later, on his birthday, he bungee-corded car batteries to his work boots, stepped off a stolen boat into the middle of the lake.

Leaving just me.

Geographically, I moved as far away from Lakeview as possible. There are no bodies of water for fifty miles, and my children, Reneé and Miller, each got through their twelfth years unscathed somehow. Probably because I stood guard in their doorways while they slept. Because I only allowed history and political books into the house. Because, finally, they were each popular in their classes, unaware of the kids standing at the back walls of all the rooms they were in, their faces a combination of expectance and fatalism, ready to break into a smile if somebody looked their way, *at* them instead of through them, but knowing too that that was never going to happen. I didn't tell them that that kid was me. The day Reneé came home with a ribbon on her sweater—SKIN THE BOBCATS—I almost cried. When she forgot about it, the ribbon, I took it from the dash of her car. It's in my sock-drawer, now. One Saturday morning I woke to find my wife, Sharon, studying it, but then she just put it back, patting it in place it seemed, as if putting it to bed, and I pretended not to have been awake. It's a good life. One I don't deserve, one I'm stealing, but still, mine. Last Sunday I dropped Miller off at basketball camp two towns over, then, on the way home, bought Reneé some of the custom film she said she needed for the intro to photography course she's taking at the local community college.

Three nights after that, a Wednesday, I took her to the carnival. Because she's seventeen, and I won't get many more chances. I even broke out the Bobcats ribbon; she remembered it, held it to her mouth, cried. At the carnival she took picture after picture, washing the place in silver light—clowns, camels, the carousel—and at the end of the night put her hand over mine on the shifter of my car, told me thanks.

Like I said, I don't deserve any of this.

When I was twelve years old, I helped kill a girl. Or, according to the doctors, helped her kill herself, punish herself for what her step-father had been doing to her. I never told them about the dead pecans though, or about how her hands had been tied. Just that we'd been daring each other farther and farther out into the water, until her hair snagged a Christmas tree or something. At first, I'd tried telling them the truth, but it wouldn't fit into words. And then I realized that it didn't have to, that, with Rodge clammed up, catatonic, I could say whatever I wanted. That I'd tried to save her, even. That something like I thought I'd seen just couldn't happen, was impossible, was what any twelve-year-old kid would insist he'd seen, rather than a drowning. Especially a twelve-year-old kid already in a "scare" club, a book buried in a cake pan under the leaves that nobody ever found, that's probably still there.

I told it enough like that that sometimes I almost believed it.

But then I'd see her again, running on the surface of the water, and would have to sit up in bed and force the sheets into my mouth until I gagged.

When I finally told my wife about her—the girl I'd had a crush on who I'd seen drown when I was in the sixth grade—I'd even called her Melody, I think, and then not corrected myself. The main thing I remembered was her hair. The sheets I stuffed into my mouth were supposed to be it, I think, her hair. An apology of sorts. Love. The way your lip trembles when your best friend from elementary tells you he's moving away forever. Or your mother tells you they found him out on the highway, crammed up into the wheel well of a Buick.

The story I told myself for years was that her body was still down there, really tangled up in a Christmas tree or a trotline. That Rodge was down there now for all of us, trying to free her, but his hands are so waterlogged that the skin of his fingers keeps peeling off. Above him, a mass of fish backlit by the wavering sun, feeding on the scraps of flesh.

"Keep her there," I'd tell him, out loud, at odd moments.

"Excuse me?" Sharon would say, from her side of the bed, or table, or car.

Nothing.

The other story I told myself was that I could make up for it all. That I could be the exact opposite of whatever Melanie's step-father had been—could be kind enough to Reneé that it would cancel out all the bad that had happened to Melanie, and that Melanie would somehow *see* this, forgive me.

So I go behind Sharon's back, buy her film she's supposed to buy herself. I take her to the carnival and hold her hand. I sneak into her room the morning after and—a gift—palm the film canister off her dresser, so I can pay for the developing as well, then can't wait twenty-four hours for it so go back and pay for one hour, leave the prints on her dresser without looking at them but then have to, when she leaves for a date. Like Rodge, reading the book in secret, I'm preparing myself, cataloging points to appreciate when she finally shows them to me, proud: the angle she got the man on stilts from; the flag on top of the main tent, caught mid-flap; the carousel, its lights smearing unevenly across the frame. The . . . the *tinted* or heat-sensitive lens or whatever she had on her camera, to distort the carnival. And the shutter-speed— it's like she has it jammed up against how fast the film is, so that they have to work against each other. Like she's *trying* to mess up the shots, or—this has to be it—as if it might be possible to twist the image enough that it would become just another suburban neighborhood. Maybe it's part of the project, though. They're good, all of them. She's my daughter.

Saturday, deep in the afternoon, Sharon gone to get Miller from camp, I walk into the living room and Reneé's there. On the glass coffee table, she has all the prints out, the table lamp shadeless, lying on its side under the glass, making the table into the kind of tray I associate with negatives, or slides. I see why she's done it, though: it filters out some of the purple tint in the prints, and makes everything sharper.

She's in sweats and a T-shirt, her hair pulled back to keep the oils off her face. No shoes, her feet curled under her on the couch.

"Date?" I say.

She nods without looking up.

I'm standing on the other side of the coffee table from her. Say, "These them?"

Again, she nods.

"They're—wrong," she says, shrugging about them, narrowing her eyes.

I lower myself to one knee, focus through my reading glasses, pretend to be seeing them for the first time.

"What do you mean?" I say.

"Daddy . . ." she says, as if I'm transparent here.

"They're . . . purple?" I say.

"Not that," she says, and points to one of the carousel shots that, with her lens/shutter speed trick, she's made look time-lapsed. I lift it delicately by the edge, hold it up to the light, my back old-man stiff.

"See?" she says.

I don't answer, don't remember this one from when I flipped through them the first time. It's just one of the carousel shots, though, when she was figuring out how to move her camera with the horses. The effect is to keep them in focus, more or less. Not the children—their movements are too unpredictable to compensate for—but the horses, anyway. And some of the parents standing by the horses, holding their children in place.

I shrug.

"*Look*," she says.

I shrug, try, and then see it maybe, from the corner of my eye, as I'm giving up: what's been waiting for me for thirty-two years. I relax for what feels like the first time. Don't drop the picture.

"Right?" Renée says.

I make myself look again. Tell myself it's just a trick of the light. The special *film*. It was a carnival, for Chrissake. I even manage a laugh.

What Reneé captured and the drugstore developed—maybe *that's* where the mistake was: an errant chemical, swirling in the pan—is two almost-paisley tendrils of iridescent purple breath curling up from one of the wooden horse's nostrils, the horse's eyes flared wide, as if in pain.

Somebody with a cigarette, maybe, I say, standing *behind* the carousel. Cotton candy under neon light. But then I follow the high, royal arch of the horse's neck, to the crisp outline of a perfect little child sitting on its back, holding the pole with both hands.

Standing beside him, out of focus, is his mother, her hand to the horse's neck. Patting it.

All I can see of her is her hair, spilling down the side of her legs.

This time I do drop the picture.

After she's gone on her date, her mouth moving, telling me her plans but no sound making it to me, I take the flashlight into the backyard.

Buried under what Sharon insists will be a compost pile someday is a cake pan I bought at the discount store. In it, a book. Not the same series, not the same publisher, but the same genre: an encyclopedia of the unexplained.

The carousel horse isn't going to be in there, I know. Because it was an accident. But Melanie.

That's the only page I read.

Her entry is in the chapter of disappearances. The woman jogger who disappeared is on the opposite page from her, like an old friend. The title she gets, because of a later sighting, is "Green Lady Gone."

The title of Melanie's entry is "Roger's Story." They forgot the *d*; for the thousandth time, I smile about it, then close my eyes, lower my forehead to the book the way Alex used to, in class. It was a joke: by then we both knew enough about Edgar Cayce that we wanted too to be able to just lay our heads on a book, absorb it.

Like everytime, though, it doesn't work. Or, now, this book is already in my head. All closing my eyes to it does is bring Melanie back. Not as she was on the water, but as she was running for the last bell at 7:59 in the morning, fighting to keep her hair out of her face.

Did she even leave tracks in the dew?

If she hadn't, and if we'd noticed, it would have just been because of her ballet training, her gymnastics. That she was made of something better, something that didn't interact with common stuff like grass and water.

The horse, breathing.

The mother I always imagined she would be, this is the kind of gift she would give her child, I know. If she could. If it wasn't just a trick of the light.

Rodger's story is what he left as a birthday card to himself. Not word-for-word—edited into the voice of the rest of the entries—but still, I can hear him through it. It starts just like Melanie's, with four social outcasts, creating their own little society. One in which they matter. How none of the four of us knew what we were doing, really. How we're so, so sorry. We never meant for . . . for—

Rodger places us by the lake. The reason I've never been able to stop reading his version is the same reason I was never able to forget my father's story about me as a baby, sleeping on the floor: because I'm in it, just from a different angle.

Rodger was just watching us, not as if he knew what was going to happen, but as if, in retelling it, reliving it, he had become unable to pretend that the him watching hadn't been through it a hundred times already. The way he watches us, he knows about the Buick coming for Alex, about Melanie, writhing on the surface of the lake. How a car battery changes the way a boat sits in the water.

Maybe the gases that escape from the cells of the battery on the way down are iridescent, are the last thing you see, before the strings of moss become hair, smother you.

According to Rodger, Melanie asked us to tie her hands and feet, throw her in the lake. I shake my head: he's protecting Alex. Protecting me. And then our stories synch up, more or less, the viewpoint just off a bit: instead of an image of Melanie's face just as I let her go, I see her rising from the shore, slipping out of mine and Alex's hands the way a magician might let go ten doves at once.

And then she hisses, throws up something black, and crawls across the lake, her hip joints no longer human. Her body never recovered.

The question after the entry is *What was Melanie Parker?*

I close the book, set it on the island in the middle of the kitchen, then look down the hall when the noise starts, but don't go to it.

It's the bathtub. It's filling.

I raise my chin, stretching my throat tight, and rub my larynx, trying to keep whatever's in me down, then am clawing through Sharon's cabinets in the kitchen, spice jars and sifters raining down onto the counter.

Finally I find what I know she has: the three tins of nuts, from Christmas.

The first is walnuts, the second two pecans, still in their paper shells.

I raise the blackest one up against the light, to see if I can see through it. When I can't, I feel my chest tightening the way it used to—the asthma I've outgrown—and know what I have to do. My head wobbles on my neck in denial, though.

But it's the only way.

I place the pecan on my tongue, shell and all, afraid of what might be inside, then work it over between the molars of my right side, close my eyes and jaw at once. Make myself swallow it all. Fall coughing to the floor, have to dig out one of Miller's old inhalers, from when he had asthma too.

The mist slams into my chest again and again, my eyes hot, burning.

At the end of Rodger's birthday card to himself, which the editors chose to encase in their version of the blue-box, are the words *She's still down there*.

I envy him that.

When I was twelve, I helped kill a girl I thought I loved, helped give birth to something else, something she didn't even know about. Something that saw me before crawling away. What makes it real, maybe, undeniable, is the way, that last time she looked up, she spit out the piece of Alex's shoe lace she had in her mouth. Had to shake it away from her lip.

Her tongue was any color. Maybe the same it had always been.

Because I don't know what else to do, I sit with my back against the wall, behind my chair, every light in the living room on, random muscles in my shoulder and right leg twitching, as if going through the sensory details of letting Melanie go that day, above the water. Remembering without me. My lap warms with urine and I just sway back and forth on the balls of my feet, hugging my knees to my chest, Miller's inhaler curled under my index finger.

An hour later, 11:00, 12:00, something, I try to tell the story to the end, name the out-of-focus kid on the carousel Hodge. Give him a good life. And then the front door swings in all at once and I know I'm dying, that this is what death is, and have to bite the knuckle of middle finger to keep from screaming.

From behind the chair, all I can see is the top of the door. It closes and my vision blurs, a grin spreading from my eyes to my mouth—that this will finally be over, after so long—but then a sound intrudes: keys, jangling into a brass bowl. The one on the stand by the coat rack.

Reneé.

She swishes past me in slow motion, for the mess the kitchen is. Never sees me.

I stand in the doorway behind her, my slacks dark enough that she won't see the stain maybe.

Instead of putting stuff back into the cabinets, she's looking through the book I left out. Opening it to the place I have marked—marked with a spirit ribbon.

Slowly, she cocks her head to the side, studying the ribbon, then holds it to her mouth again, breathes it in.

"Yeah," I say, to announce myself.

She sucks air in, pulls the book hard to her chest. Turns to me, leading with her eyes.

"*Daddy . . .*"

"I know," I say, breathing too hard.

She looks at me for too long it feels like, then past me, to the living room, so bright.

"You okay?"

I nod, make myself smile.

"How'd it go?" I ask—the date.

"You know," she says, opening the book again. "Sandy and his music."

I nod, remember: Sandy's the one with the custom stereo.

"What is this?" she says, about the book.

"Just—nothing," I tell her. "Old."

"Hm," she says, leafing through, wowing her eyes up at the more sensational stuff. Aliens, maybe. God.

"She did it to herself," I say, all at once.

Reneé holds her place in the book, looks up to me.

"She was . . . she was sad," I say. "Sad little girl."

Reneé nods, humoring me I think. I rub my mouth, look away, to all Sharon's cooking utensils, spilling onto the floor. When I don't look away fast enough, Reneé has to say something about it: "A surprise?"

"Surprise?" I say back, trying to make sense of the word.

"Reorganizing for her?" she tries, holding her eyebrows up.

I nod, make myself grin, feel something rising in my throat again, have to raise my shoulders to keep it down. Close my eyes.

When I open them again, Reneé's sitting on the island, the book closed beside her. Just watching me.

"I could have stayed home tonight," she says, an offering of sorts, but I wave the idea away.

"You need—need to go out," I tell her. "It's good. What you should be doing."

In reply she just shrugs, the heels of her hands on the edge of the countertop.

"Okay," she says, finally, "I guess—" but then, sliding the book back so she won't take it with her when she jumps down, her hand catches on the stiff, upper part of the spirit ribbon, pulls it from the book. "Oops," she says, doing her mouth in the shape of mock-disaster, "lost your place."

I shake my head no, it's all right, I *know* where my place is, but then she has the ribbon again, is smiling, excited.

We were ghosts, I want to tell her, smiling too. And then all of it.

Instead, I watch as she pulls the stick pin from the head of the ribbon.

"Stacy showed me this," she says, holding her right arm out, belly-up, in a way that I have to see Melanie's again, waiting for Alex to tie his shoe-lace around it.

"No," I say, taking her hand in mine, but she steps back, says, "It's all right, Daddy."

What she's doing is placing the pin in the crook of her elbow, the part of her arm that folds in.

I shake my head no again, reach for her again, but it's too late, she's already making her hand into a fist, drawing it slowly up to her shoulder.

I feel my eyes get hot, my mouth open.

When she unfolds her arm, the pin slides out of her skin like magic. No blood.

"That's—" I say, having to try hard to make the words, "in a blue box, that's the—Devil's Mark."

She looks up to me, not following.

I smile, touch her arm. Say, "You didn't bleed," and then I'm crying, trying to swallow it all back, but it's too late: the pecan is coming up.

I step back from her and throw up between us, and was right: it's not just a pecan, but bits of shell and meat and blood. Not red blood, like the movies, but darker. Real.

Reneé steps back, raising one of her shoes, to keep it clean maybe, and I look up to her, wipe the blood from my lips with the back of my forearm.

"Daddy?" she says, and I nod, sad that it's come to this, but there's nothing I can do anymore. With trembling hands I pin the ribbon to the chest of her shirt, through her skin maybe, I don't know. It makes her pull back anyway, look up to me, her eyebrows drawing together in question.

"Skin the Bobcats," I whisper to her, unable not to smile, then, when I pick her up in my arms like a little girl, say it at last—that I'm not a good person, that I've done bad things. She doesn't fight, doesn't know to. Doesn't know that we're going down the hall to the bathtub, which is already full.

Afterwards, my shirt wet like my pants, I stand again in the kitchen, hardly recognize it. Have to go outside, onto the balcony, my face flushing warm now like my eyes, my teeth chattering against each other.

Standing at the wood railing, then, I feel it: the tip ends of hair, silky long hair, lifted on the wind, trailing down from the roof.

She's up there I know, one knee to the shingles, her long fingers curled around the eave.

"Reneé?" I say weakly, unable to look around, up, and it's not so much a question as a prayer. That this isn't real. That it's Reneé on the roof, maybe. Trying to scare me.

But then Melanie speaks back in the breathy, adult voice I knew she was going to have someday: *No, Raphael.*

I nod, see my shadow stretching out over the gravel drive, how it's split, doubling from two sources of light, and I know that this is all *right*, finally, and then Sharon pulls in under me, my son in the passenger seat, and I'm invisible again. Able to do anything.

GLEN HIRSHBERG

The Muldoon

Glen Hirshberg's most recent collection, American Morons, *was published in 2006.* The Two Sams, *his first collection, won the International Horror Guild Award and was named one of the best books of 2003 by* Publishers Weekly *and* Locus. *Hirshberg is also the author of a novel,* The Snowman's Children.

With Dennis Etchison and Peter Atkins, he cofounded the Rolling Darkness Revue, a traveling ghost story performance troupe that tours the West Coast of the United States each October. His fiction has appeared in numerous magazines and anthologies, including multiple appearances in The Year's Best Fantasy and Horror *and* The Mammoth Book of Best New Horror, The Dark, Trampoline, Cemetery Dance, *and* Dark Terrors Six, *as well as online at* SCI FICTION. *He lives in southern California with his wife and children.*

"The Muldoon" first appeared in Hirshberg's collection American Morons.

—E.D.

He found that he could not even concentrate for more than an instant on Skeffington's death, for Skeffington, alive, in multiple guises, kept getting in the way.

—John O'Hara

That night, like every night we spent in our grandfather's house, my older brother Martin and I stayed up late to listen. Sometimes, we heard murmuring in the white, circular vent high up the cracking plaster wall over our heads. The voices were our parents', we assumed, their conversation captured but also muffled by the pipes in the downstairs guest room ceiling. In summer, when the wind went still between thunderstorms, we could almost make out words. Sometimes, especially in August, when the Baltimore heat strangled even the thunderclouds, we heard cicadas bowing wildly in the grass out our window and twenty feet down.

On the dead-still September night after my grandfather's *shiva*, though, when all of the more than two thousand well-wishers we'd hosted that week had finally filed through the house and told their stories and left, all Martin and I heard was the clock. *Tuk, tuk, tuk*, like a prison guard's footsteps. I could almost see it out there, hulking over the foyer below, nine feet of carved oak and that bizarre, glassed-in face, brass hands on black velvet with brass fittings. Even though the carvings all the way up the casing were just wiggles and flourishes, and even though the velvet never resembled anything but a blank, square space, the whole thing had always reminded me more of a totem pole than a clock, and it scared me, some.

"Miriam," my brother whispered. "Awake?"

I hesitated until after the next *tuk*. It had always seemed bad luck to start a sentence in rhythm with that clock. "Think they're asleep?"

He sat up. Instinctively, my glance slipped out our open door to the far hallway wall. My grandfather had died right out there, felled at last by the heart attack his physician had warned him for decades was coming if he refused to drop fifty pounds. It seemed impossible that his enormous body had left not the slightest trace in the threadbare hallway carpet. What had he even been doing up here? In the past four years or so, I'd never once seen him more than two steps off the ground floor.

The only thing I could see in the hallway now was the mirror. Like every other mirror in the house, it had been soaped for the *shiva*, and so, instead of the half-reassuring, half-terrifying blur of movement I usually glimpsed there, I saw only darkness, barely penetrated by the single butterfly nightlight plugged in beneath it.

Reaching over the edge of the bed, I found my sweatpants and pulled them on under my nightgown. Then I sat up, too.

"Why do they soap the mirrors?"

"Because the Angel of Death might still be lurking. You don't want him catching sight of you." Martin turned his head my way, and a tiny ray of light glinted off his thick owl-glasses.

"That isn't why," I whispered.

"You make the ball?"

"Duh."

With a quick smile that trapped moonlight in his braces, my brother slid out of bed. I flipped my own covers back but waited until he reached the door, poked his head out, and peered downstairs. Overhead, the vent pushed a useless puff of cold air into the heat that had pooled around us. In the foyer, the clock *tuk*-ed.

"*Voices,*" I hissed, and Martin scampered fast back to bed. His glasses tilted toward the vent. I grinned. "Ha. We're even."

Now I could see his eyes, dark brown, with huge irises, as though bulging with all the amazing things he knew. One day, I thought, if Martin kept reading like he did, badgered my parents into taking him to enough museums, just stood there and *watched* the way he could sometimes, he'd literally pop himself like an over-inflated balloon.

"For what?" he snapped.

"That Angel of Death thing."

"That's what Roz told me."

"She would."

He grinned back. "You're right."

From under my pillow, I drew out the sock-ball I'd made and flipped it to him. He turned it in his hands as though completing an inspection. Part of the ritual. Once or twice, he'd even torn balls apart and made me redo them. The dayglow-yellow stripes my mother hoped looked just a little athletic on his spindle-legs had to curve just so, like stitching on a baseball. And the weight had to be right. Three, maybe four socks, depending on how worn they were and what brand mom had bought. Five, and the thing just wouldn't arc properly.

"You really think we should play tonight?"

Martin glanced up, as though he hadn't even considered that. Then he shrugged. "Grandpa would've."

I knew that he'd considered it plenty. And that gave me my first conscious inkling of just how much our grandfather had meant to my brother.

This time, I followed right behind Martin to the door, and we edged together onto the balcony. Below us, hooded in shadow, stood the grandfather clock and the double-doored glass case where Roz, the tall, orange-skinned, sour-faced woman Grandpa had married right after I was born, kept her porcelain poodles and her milky blue oriental vases. Neither Martin nor I thought of Roz as our grandma, exactly, though she was the only one we'd known, and our mother had ordered us to call her that. Beyond the foyer, I could just see the straightened rows of chairs we'd set up for the week's last mourner's *kaddish*, the final chanting of words that seemed to have channeled a permanent groove on my tongue. The older you get, my mother had told me, the more familiar they become. *Yit-barah, v'yish-tabah, v'yit-pa-ar, v'yit-roman, v'yit-na-sey* . . .

"You can throw first," my brother said, as though granting me a favor.

"Don't you want to?" I teased. "To honor him?" Very quietly, I began to make chicken clucks.

"Cut it out," Martin mumbled, but made no move toward the stairs. I clucked some more, and he shot out his hand so fast I thought he was trying to hit me. But he was only flapping in that nervous, spastic wave my parents had been waiting for him to outgrow since he was three. "*Shush*. Look."

"I am look . . ." I started, then realized he wasn't peering over the balcony at the downstairs hall from which Roz would emerge to scream at us if she heard movement. He was looking over his shoulder toward the mirror. "Not funny," I said.

"Weird," said Martin. Not until he took a step across the landing did I realize what he meant.

The doors to the hags' rooms were open. Not much. I couldn't see anything of either room. But both had been pushed just slightly back from their usual positions. Clamminess flowed from my fingertips up the peach fuzz on my arms.

Naturally, halfway across the landing, Martin stopped. If I didn't take the lead, he'd never move another step. The clammy sensation spread to my shoulders, down my back. I went to my brother anyway. We stood, right in the spot where the mirror should have reflected us. Right where Grandpa died. In the butterfly-light, Martin's face looked wet and waxy, the way it did when he had a fever.

"You really want to go through those doors?" I whispered.

"Just trying to remember."

I nodded first toward Mrs. Gold's room, then Sophie's. "Pink. Blue." The shiver I'd been fighting for the past half-minute snaked across my ribs.

Martin shook his head. "I mean the last time we saw them open. Either one."

But he already knew that. So did I. We'd last glimpsed those rooms the week before the hags had died. Four years—almost half my life—ago.

"Let's not," I said, and Martin shuffled to the right, toward Mrs. Gold's. "Martin, come on, let's play. I'm going downstairs."

But I stayed put, amazed, as he scuttled forward with his eyes darting everywhere, like a little ghost-shrimp racing across an exposed patch of sea bottom. *He'll never do it*, I thought, *not without me*. I tried chicken-clucking again, but my tongue had dried out. Martin stretched out his hand and shoved.

The door made no sound as it glided back, revealing more shadows, the dark humps of four-poster bed and dresser, a square of moonlight through almost-drawn curtains. A split second before, if someone had asked me to sketch Mrs. Gold's room, I would have made a big, pink smear with a crayon. But now, even from across the hall, I recognized that everything was just the way I'd last seen it.

"Coming?" Martin asked.

More than anything else, it was the plea in his voice that pulled me forward. I didn't bother stopping, because I knew I'd be the one going in first anyway. But I did glance at my brother's face as I passed. His skin looked even waxier than before, as though it might melt right off.

Stopping on the threshold, I reached into Mrs. Gold's room with my arm, then jerked it back.

"*What?*" my brother snapped.

I stared at the goose bumps dimpling the skin above my wrist like bubbles in boiling water. But the air in Mrs. Gold's room wasn't boiling. It was freezing cold. "I think we found this house's only unclogged vent," I said.

"Just flick on the lights."

I reached in again. It really was freezing. My hand danced along the wall. I was imagining fat, pink spiders lurking right above my fingers, waiting while I stretched just that last bit closer . . .

"Oh, *fudder*," I mumbled, stepped straight into the room, and switched on the dresser lamp. The furniture leapt from its shadows into familiar formation, *surprise!* But there was nothing surprising. How was it that I remembered this so perfectly, having spent a maximum of twenty hours in here in my entire life, none of them after the age of six?

There it all was, where it had always been: the bed with its crinoline curtain and beige sheets that always looked too heavy and scratchy to me, something to make drapes out of, not sleep in; the pink wallpaper; the row of perfect pink powder puffs laid atop closed pink clam-lids full of powder or God-knows-what, next to dark pink bottles of lotion; the silver picture frame with the side-by-side posed portraits of two men in old army uniforms. Brothers? Husbands? Sons? I'd been too young to ask. Mrs. Gold was Roz's mother, but neither of them had ever explained about the photographs, at least not in my hearing. I'm not sure even my mother knew.

As Martin came in behind me, the circular vent over the bed gushed frigid air. I clutched my arms tight against myself and closed my eyes and was surprised to find tears between my lashes. Just a few. Every visit to Baltimore for the first six years of my life, for one hour per day, my parents would drag chairs in here and plop us down by this bed to *chat* with Mrs. Gold. That was my mother's word for it. Mostly, what we did was sit in the chairs or—when I was a baby—crawl over the carpet and make silent faces at each other while Mrs. Gold prattled endlessly, senselessly, about horses or people we didn't know with names like Ruby and Selma, gobbling the Berger cookies we brought her and scattering crumbs all over those scratchy sheets. My mother would nod and smile and wipe the crumbs away. Mrs. Gold would nod and smile, and strands of her poofy white hair would blow in the wind from the vent. As far as I could tell, Mrs. Gold had no idea who any of us were. All those hours in here, and really, we'd never even met her.

Martin had slipped past me, and now he touched the fold of the sheet at the head of the bed. I was amazed again. He'd done the same thing at the funeral home, stunning my mother by sticking his hand into the coffin during the visitation and gently, with one extended finger, touching my grandfather's lapel. Not typical timid Martin behavior.

"Remember her hands?" he said.

Like shed snakeskin. So dry no lotion on earth, no matter how pink, would soften them.

"She seemed nice," I said, feeling sad again. For Grandpa, mostly, not Mrs. Gold. After all, we'd never known her when she was . . . whoever she was. "I bet she was nice."

Martin took his finger off the bed and glanced at me. "Unlike the one we were actually related to." And he walked straight past me into the hall.

"Martin, no." I paused only to switch out the dresser lamp. As I did, the clock in the foyer *tuk*-ed, and the dark seemed to pounce on the bed, the powder puffs, and the pathetic picture frame. I hurried into the hall, conscious of my clumping steps. Was I *trying* to wake Roz?

Martin stood before Sophie's door, hand out, but he hadn't touched it. When he turned to me, he had a grin on his face I'd never seen before. "*Momzer*," he drawled.

My mouth dropped open. He sounded exactly like her. "Stop it."

"*Come to Gehenna. Suffer with me.*"

"Martin, *shut up!*"

He flinched, bumped Sophie's door with his shoulder and then stumbled back in my direction. The door swung open, and we both held still and stared.

Balding carpet, yellow-white where the butterfly light barely touched it. Everything else stayed shadowed. The curtains in there had been drawn completely. When was the last time light had touched this room?

"Why did you say that?" I asked.

"It's what she said. To Grandpa, every time he dragged himself up here. Remember?"

"What's *momzer*?"

Martin shook his head. "Aunt Paulina slapped me once for saying it."

"What's *henna*?"

"*Gehenna*. One sixtieth of Eden."

Prying my eyes from Sophie's doorway, I glared at my brother. "What does that mean?"

"It's like Hell. Jew Hell."

"Jews don't believe in Hell. Do we?"

"Somewhere wicked people go. They can get out, though. After they suffer enough."

"Can we play our game now?" I made a flipping motion with my hand, cupping it as though around a sock-ball.

"Let's . . . take one look. Pay our respects."

"Why?"

Martin looked at the floor, and his arms gave one of their half-flaps. "Grandpa did. Every day she was alive, no matter what she called him. If we don't, no one ever will again."

He strode forward, pushed the door all the way back, and actually stepped partway over the threshold. The shadows leaned toward him, and I made myself move, thinking I might need to catch him if he fainted. With a flick of his wrist, Martin switched on the lights.

For a second, I thought the bulbs had blown, because the shadows glowed rather than dissipated, and the plain, boxy bed in there seemed to take slow shape, as though reassembling itself. Then I remembered. Sophie's room wasn't blue because of wallpaper or bed coverings or curtain fabric. She'd liked dark blue light, barely enough to see by, just enough to read if you were right under the lamp. She'd lain in that light all day, curled beneath her covers with just her thin, knife-shaped head sticking out like a moray eel's.

Martin's hand had found mine and, after a few seconds, his touch distracted me enough to glance away, momentarily, from the bed, the bare dresser, the otherwise utterly empty room. I stared down at our palms. *"Your brother's only going to love a few people,"* my mother had told me once, after he'd slammed the door to his room in my face for the thousandth time so he could do experiments with his chemistry set or read Ovid aloud to himself without me bothering him. *"You'll be one of them."*

"How'd they die?" I asked.

Martin seemed transfixed by the room, or his memories of it, which had to be more defined than mine. Our parents had never made us come in here. But Martin had accompanied Grandpa, at least some of the time. When Sophie wasn't screaming, or calling everyone names. He took a long time answering. "They were old."

"Yeah. But didn't they like die on the same day or something?"

"Same week, I think. Dad says that happens a lot to old people. They're barely still in their bodies, you know? Then someone they love goes, and it's like unbuckling the last straps holding them in. They just slip out."

"But Sophie and Mrs. Gold hated each other."

Martin shook his head. "Mrs. Gold didn't even know who Sophie was, I bet. And Sophie hated everything. You know, Mom says she was a really good person until she got sick. Super smart, too. She used to give lectures at the synagogue."

"Lectures about what?"

"Hey," said Martin, let go of my hand, and took two shuffling steps into Sophie's room. Blue light washed across his shoulders, darkening him. On the far wall, something twitched. Then it rose off the plaster. I gasped, lunged forward to grab Martin, and a second something joined the first, and I understood.

"No one's been in here," I whispered. The air was not cold, although the circular vent I could just make out over the bed coughed right as I said that. Another thought wriggled behind my eyes, but I shook it away. "Martin, the mirror."

Glancing up, he saw what I meant. The glass on Sophie's wall—the wall facing the hall, not the bed, she'd never wanted to see herself—stood unsoaped, pulling the dimness in rather than reflecting it, like a black hole. In that light, we were just shapes, our faces featureless. Even for Grandpa's *shiva*, no one had bothered to prepare this room.

Martin turned from our reflections to me, his pointy nose and glasses familiar and reassuring, but only until he spoke.

"Miriam, look at this."

Along the left-hand wall ran a long closet with sliding wooden doors. The farthest door had been pulled almost all the way open and tipped off its runners, so that it hung half-sideways like a dangling tooth.

"Remember the dresses?"

I had no idea what he was talking about now. I also couldn't resist another glance in the mirror, but then quickly pulled my eyes away. There were no pictures on Sophie's bureau, just a heavy, wooden gavel. My grandfather's, of course. He must have given it to her when he retired.

"This whole closet used to be stuffed with them. Fifty, sixty, maybe more, in plastic cleaners bags. I don't think she ever wore them after she moved here. I can't even remember her getting dressed."

"She never left the room," I muttered.

"Except to sneak into Mrs. Gold's."

I closed my eyes as the clock *tuk*-ed and the vent rasped.

It had only happened once while we were in the house. But Grandpa said she did it all the time. Whenever Sophie got bored of accusing her son of kidnapping her from her own house and penning her up here, or whenever her ravaged, rotting lungs allowed her enough breath, she'd rouse herself from this bed, inch out the door in her bare feet with the blue veins popping out of the tops like rooster crests, and sneak into Mrs. Gold's room. There she'd sit, murmuring God knew what, until Mrs. Gold started screaming.

"It always creeped me out," Martin said. "I never liked looking over at this closet. But the dresses blocked *that*."

"Blocked wh—" I started, and my breath caught in my teeth. Waist-high on the back inside closet wall, all but covered by a rough square of wood that had been leaned against it rather than fitted over it, there was an opening. A door. "Martin, if Roz catches us in here—"

Hostility flared in his voice like a lick of flame. "Roz hardly ever catches us playing the balcony ball game right outside her room. Anyway, in case you haven't noticed, she *never* comes in here."

"What's with you?" I snapped. Nothing about my brother made sense tonight.

"What? Nothing. It's just . . . Grandpa brings Roz's mother here, even though she needs constant care, can't even feed herself unless she's eating Berger cookies, probably has no idea where she is. Grandpa takes care of her, like he took care of everyone. But when it comes to *his* mother, Roz won't even bring food in here. She makes him do everything. And after they die, Roz leaves her own mother's room exactly like it was, but she cleans out every trace of Sophie, right down to the closet."

"Sophie was mean."

"She was sick. And ninety-two."

"And mean."

"I'm going in there," Martin said, gesturing or flapping, I couldn't tell which. "I want to see Grandpa's stuff. Don't you? I bet it's all stored in there."

"I'm going to bed. Goodnight, Martin."

In an instant, the hostility left him, and his expression turned small, almost panicked.

"I'm going to bed," I said again.

"You don't want to see Grandpa?"

This time, the violence in my own voice surprised me. "Not in there." I was thinking of the way he'd looked in his coffin. His dead face had barely even resembled his real one. His living one. His whole head had been transformed by the embalming into a shiny, vaguely Grandpa-shaped *bulge* balanced atop his bulgy, overweight body, like the top of a snowman.

"Please," Martin said, and something moved downstairs.

"Shit," I mouthed, going completely still.

Clock tick. Clock tick. Footsteps. *Had I left the lights on in Mrs. Gold's room?* I couldn't remember. If Roz wasn't looking, she might not see Sophie's blue light from downstairs. Somehow, I knew she didn't want us in here.

I couldn't help glancing behind me, and then my shoulders clenched. The door had swung almost all the way shut.

Which wasn't so strange, was it? How far had we even opened it?

Footsteps. Clock tick. Clock tick. Clock tick. Clock tick. When I turned back to Martin, he was on his hands and knees, scuttling for the closet.

"Martin, *no*," I hissed. Then I was on my knees too, hurrying after him. When I drew up alongside him, our heads just inside the closet, he looked my way and grinned, tentatively.

"Sssh," he whispered.

"What do you think you'll find in there?"

The grin slid from his face. "Him." With a nod, he pulled the square of wood off the opening. Then he swore and dropped it. His right hand rose to his mouth, and I saw the sliver sticking out of the bottom of his thumb like a porcupine quill.

Taking his wrist, I leaned over, trying to see. In that murky, useless light, the wood seemed to have stabbed straight through the webbing into his palm. It almost looked like a new ridge forming along his lifeline. "Hold still," I murmured, grabbed the splinter as low down as I could, and yanked.

Martin sucked in breath, staring at his hand. "Did you get it all?"

"Come where it's light and I'll see."

"No." He pulled his hand from me, and without another word crawled through the opening. For one moment, as his butt hovered in front of me and his torso disappeared, I had to stifle another urge to drag him out, splinters be damned. Then he was through. For a few seconds, I heard only his breathing, saw only his bare feet through the hole. The rest of him was in shadow.

"Miriam, get in here," he said.

In I went. I had to shove Martin forward to get through, and I did so harder than I had to. He made no protest. I tried lifting my knees instead of sliding them to keep the splinters off. When I straightened, I was surprised to find most of the space in front of us bathed in moonlight.

"What window is that?" I whispered.

"Must be on the side."

"I've never seen it."

"How much time have you spent on the side?"

None, in truth. No one did. The space between my grandfather's house and the ancient gray wooden fence that bordered his property had been overrun by spiders even when our mom was young. I'd glimpsed an old bike back there once, completely draped in webs like furniture in a dead man's room.

"Probably a billion spiders in here too, you know," I said.

But Martin wasn't paying attention, and neither was I, really. We were too busy staring. All around us, stacked from floor to four-foot ceiling all the way down the length of the half-finished space, cardboard boxes had been stacked, sometimes atop each other, sometimes atop old white suitcases or trunks with their key-coverings dangling like the tongues on strangled things. With his shoulder, Martin nudged one of the nearest stacks, which tipped dangerously but slid back a bit. Reaching underneath a lid flap, Martin stuck his hand in the bottom-most box. I bit my cheek and held still and marveled, for the hundredth time in the last fifteen minutes, at my brother's behavior. When he pulled out a *Playboy*, I started to laugh, and stopped because of the look on Martin's face.

He held the magazine open and flat across both hands, looking terrified to drop it, almost in awe of it, as though it were a Torah scroll. It would be a long time, I thought, before Martin started dating.

"You said you wanted to see Grandpa's stuff," I couldn't resist teasing.

"This wasn't his."

Now I did laugh. "Maybe it was Mrs. Gold's."

I slid the magazine off his hands, and that seemed to relieve him, some. The page to which it had fallen open showed a woman with waist-length brown hair and strangely pointed feet poised naked atop the gnarled roots of an oak tree, as though she'd just climbed out of the branches. The woman wasn't smiling, and I didn't like the picture at all. I closed the magazine and laid it face down on the floor.

Edging forward, Martin began to reach randomly into other boxes. I did the same. Mostly, though, I watched my brother. The moonlight seemed to pour over him in layers, coating him, so that with each passing moment he grew paler. Other than Martin's scuttling as he moved down the row on his knees, I heard nothing, not even the clock. That should have been a comfort. But the silence in that not-quite-room was worse.

To distract myself, I began to run my fingers over the boxes on my right. Their cardboard skin had sticky damp patches, bulged outward in places but sank into itself in others. From one box, I drew an unpleasantly damp, battered, black rectangular case I thought might be for pens, but when I opened it, I found four pearls strung on a broken chain, pressed deep into their own impressions in the velvet lining like little eyes in sockets. My real grandmother's, I realized. Roz liked showier jewelry.

I'd never met my mother's mother. She'd died three months before Martin was born. Dad had liked her a lot. I was still gazing at the pearls when the first gush of icy air poured over me.

Martin grunted, and I caught his wrist. We crouched and waited for the torrent to sigh itself out. Eventually, it did. Martin started to speak, and I tightened my grasp and shut him up.

Just at the end, as the gush had died . . .

"Martin," I whispered.

"It's the air-conditioning, Miriam. See?"

"Martin, did you hear it?"

"Duh. Look at—"

"Martin. The vents."

He wasn't listening, didn't understand. Dazed, I let him disengage, watched him crab-walk to the next stack of boxes and begin digging. I almost started screaming at him. If I did, I now knew, the sound would pour out of the walls above our bed, and from the circular space above Mrs. Gold's window, and from Sophie's closet. Because these vents didn't connect to the downstairs guest room where our parents were, like we'd always thought. They connected the upstairs rooms and this room. And so the murmuring we'd always heard—that we'd heard as recently as twenty minutes ago—hadn't come from our parents at all. It had come from right—

"Jackpot," Martin muttered.

Ahead, wedged between the last boxes and the wall, something stirred. Flapped. Plastic. Maybe.

"Martin . . ."

"Hi, Grandpa."

I spun so fast I almost knocked Martin over, banging my arms instead on the plaque he was wiping free of mold and dust with the sleeve of his pajamas. Frozen air roared over us again. Up ahead, whatever it was flapped some more.

"Watch *out*," Martin snapped. He wasn't worried about me, of course. He didn't want anything happening to the plaque.

"We have to get out of here," I said.

Wordlessly, he held up his treasure. Black granite, with words engraved in it, clearly legible despite the fuzzy smear of grime across the surface. *To the Big Judge, who takes care of his own. A muldoon, and no mistake. From his friends, the Knights of Labor.*

"The Knights of Labor?"

"He knew everyone," Martin said. "They all loved him. The whole city."

This was who my grandfather was to my brother, I realized. Someone as smart and weird and defiant and solitary as he was, except that our grandfather had somehow figured out people enough to wind up a judge, a civil rights activist, a bloated and beloved public figure. Slowly, like a snake stirring, another shudder slipped down my back.

"What's a muldoon?"

"Says right here, stupid." Martin nodded at the plaque. "He took care of his own."

"We should go, Martin. Now."

"What are you talking about?"

As the house unleashed another frigid breath, he tucked the plaque lovingly against his chest and moved deeper into the attic. The plastic at the end of the row was rippling now, flattening itself. It reminded me of an octopus I'd seen in the Baltimore Aquarium once, completely changing shape to slip between two rocks.

"There," I barked suddenly, as the air expired. "Hear it?"

But Martin was busy wedging open box lids, prying out cufflinks in little boxes, a ceremonial silver shovel marking some sort of groundbreaking, a photograph of Grandpa with Earl Weaver and two grinning grounds-crew guys in the Orioles dugout. The last thing he pulled out before I moved was a book. Old, blue binding, stiff and jacketless. Martin flipped through it once, mumbled, "Hebrew," and dumped it behind him. Embossed on the cover, staring straight up at the ceiling over my brother's head, I saw a single, lidless eye.

Martin kept going, almost to the end now. The plastic had gone still, the air-conditioning and the murmurs that rode it temporarily silent. I almost left him there. If I'd been sure he'd follow—as, on almost any other occasion, he would have—that's exactly what I would have done. Instead, I edged forward myself, my hand stretching for the book. As much to get that eye hidden again as from any curiosity, I picked the thing up and opened it. Something in the binding snapped, and a single page slipped free and fluttered away like a dried butterfly I'd let loose.

"*Ayin Harah,*" I read slowly, sounding out the Hebrew letters on the title page. But it wasn't the words that set me shuddering again, if only because I wasn't positive what they implied; I knew they meant "Evil Eye." But our Aunt Pauline had told us that was a protective thing, mostly. Instead, my gaze locked on my great-grandmother's signature, lurking like a blue spider in the top left-hand corner of the inside cover. Then my head lifted, and I was staring at the box from which the book had come.

Not my grandfather's stuff in there. Not my grandmother's, or Roz's, either. That box—and maybe that one alone—was *hers*.

Sophie's.

I have no explanation for what happened next. I knew better. That is, I knew already. Thought I did. I didn't want to be in the attic even one second longer, and I was scared, not curious. I crept forward and stuck my hand between the flaps anyway.

For a moment, I thought the box was empty. My hand kept sliding deeper, all the way to my elbow before I touched cloth and closed my fist over it. Beneath whatever I'd grabbed was plastic, wrapped around some kind of heavy fabric. The plastic rustled and stuck slightly to my hand like an anemone's tentacles, though everything in that box was completely dry. I pulled, and the boxes balanced atop the one I'd reached into tipped back and bumped against the wall of the attic, and my hands came out, holding the thing I'd grasped, which fell open as it touched the air.

"Grandpa with two presidents, look," Martin said from down the row, waving a picture frame without lifting his head from whatever box he was looting.

Cradled in my palms lay what could have been a *matzoh* covering, maybe for holding the *afikomen* at a seder. When I spread out the folds, though, I found dark, rust-colored circular stains in the white fabric. Again I thought of the seder, the ritual of dipping a finger in wine and then touching it to a plate or napkin as everyone chanted plagues God had inflicted upon the Egyptians. In modern Hagadahs, the ritual is explained as a symbol of Jewish regret that the Egyptian people had to bear the brunt of their ruler's refusal to free the slaves. But none of the actual ceremonial instructions say that. They just order us to chant the words. *Dam. Tzfar de'ah. Kinim. Arbeh.*

Inside the fold where *matzoh* might have been tucked, I found only a gritty, black residue. It could have been dust from the attic, or split spider sacs, or tiny dead things. But it smelled, faintly, on my fingers. An old and rotten smell, with just a hint of something else. Something worse.

Or maybe not *worse. Familiar.* I had no idea what it was. But Sophie had smelled like this.

"Martin, please," I heard myself say. But he wasn't listening. Instead, he was leaning almost *into* the last box in the row. The plastic jammed against the wall had gone utterly still. At any moment, I expected it to hump up like a wave and crash down on my brother's back. I didn't even realize my hands had slipped back inside Sophie's box until I touched wrapping again.

Gasping, I dragged my hands away, but my fingers had curled, and the plastic and the heavy fabric it swaddled came up clutched between them.

A *dress*, I thought, panicking, shoving backward. *From her closet.* I stared at the lump of faded material, draped half out of the box now, the plastic covering rising slightly in the stirring air.

Except it wasn't a dress. It was two dresses, plainly visible through the plastic. One was gauzy and pink, barely there, with wispy flowers stitched up the sleeves. The other, dull white and heavy, had folded itself inside the pink one, the long sleeves encircling the waist. Long, black smears spread across the back of the white dress like finger-marks. *Like fingers dipped in Sophie's residue . . .*

I don't think I had any idea, at first, that I'd started shouting. I was too busy scuttling backwards on my hands, banging against boxes on either side as I scrambled for the opening behind us. The air-conditioning triggered, blasting me with its breath, which didn't stink, just froze the hairs to the skin of my arms and legs. Martin had leapt to his feet, banging his head against the attic ceiling, and now he was waving his hands, trying to quiet me. But the sight of him panicked me more. The dresses on the ground between us shivered, almost rolled over, and the plastic behind him rippled madly, popping and straining against the weight that held it, all but free. My hand touched down on the *Playboy*. I imagined the well-woman climbing out of the magazine on her pointy feet, and finally fell hard half out of the attic opening, screaming now, banging my spine on the wood and bruising it badly.

Then there were hands on my shoulder, hard and horny and orange-ish, yanking me out of the hole and dragging me across the floor. Yellow eyes flashing fury, Roz leaned past me and ducked her head through the hole, screeching at Martin to get out. Then she stalked away, snarling *"Out"* and *"Come on."*

Never had I known her to be this angry. I'd also never been happier to see her pinched, glaring, unhappy face, the color of an overripe orange thanks to the liquid tan she poured all over herself before her daily mah-jongg games at the club where she sometimes took us swimming. Flipping over and standing, I hurried after her, the rattle of the ridiculous twin rows of bracelets that ran halfway up her arms sweet and welcome in my ears as the tolling of a dinner bell. I waited at the lip of the closet until Martin's head appeared, then fled Sophie's room.

A few seconds later, my brother emerged, the *Knights of Labor* plaque clutched against his chest, glaring bloody murder at me. But Roz took him by the shoulders, guided him back to his bed in my mother's old room, and sat him down. I followed, and fell onto my own bed. For a minute, maybe more, she stood above us and glowed even more than usual, as though she might burst into flame. Then, for the first time in all my experience of her, she crossed her legs and sat down between our beds on the filthy floor.

"Oh, kids," she sighed. "What were you doing in there?"

"Where are mom and dad?" Martin demanded. The shrillness in his tone made me cringe even farther back against the white wall behind me. Pushing with my feet, I dug myself under the covers and lay my head on my pillow.

"Out," Roz said, in the same weary voice. "They're on a walk. They've been cooped up here, same as the rest of us, for an entire week."

"Cooped up?" Martin's voice rose still more, and even Roz's leathery face registered surprise. "As in, sitting *shiva*? Paying tribute to Grandpa?"

After a long pause, she nodded. "Exactly that, Martin."

From the other room, I swore I could hear the sound of plastic sliding over threadbare carpet. My eyes darted to the doorway, the lit landing, the streaks of soap in the mirror, the floor.

"How'd they die?" I blurted.

Roz's lizard eyes darted back and forth between Martin and me. "What's with you two tonight?"

"Mrs. Gold and Sophie. Please, please, please. Grandma." I didn't often call her that. She scowled even harder.

"What are you babbling about?" Martin said to me. "Roz, Miriam's been really—"

"Badly, Miriam," Roz said, and Martin went quiet. "They died badly."

Despite what she'd said, her words had a surprising, almost comforting effect on me. "Please tell me."

"Your parents wouldn't want me to."

"Please."

Settling back, Roz eyed me, then the vent overhead. I kept glancing into the hall. But I didn't hear anything now. And after a while, I only watched her. She crossed her arms over her knees, and her bracelets clanked.

"It was an accident. A horrible accident. It really was. You have to understand . . . you have no idea how awful those days were. May you never have such days."

"What was so awful?" Martin asked. There was still a trace of petulance in his tone. But Roz's attitude appeared to be having the same weirdly soothing effect on him as on me.

She shrugged. "In the pink room, you've got my mother. Only she's not my mother anymore. She's this sweet, stupid, chattering houseplant."

I gaped. Martin did, too, and Roz laughed, kind of, without humor or joy.

"Every single day, usually more than once, she shit all over the bed. The rest of the time, she sat there and babbled mostly nice things about cookies or owls or whatever.

Places she'd never been. People she may have known, but I didn't. She never mentioned me, or my father, or my brother, or anything about our lives. It was like she'd led some completely different life, without me in it."

Roz held her knees a while. Finally, she went on. "And in the blue room, there was Sophie, who remembered everything. How it had felt to walk to the market, or lecture a roomful of professors about the *Kabbalah* or whatever other weird stuff she knew. How it had been to live completely by herself, with her books, in her own world, the way she had for twenty-two years after your great-grandfather died. Best years of her life, I think. And then, just like that, her body gave out on her. She couldn't move well. Couldn't drive. She couldn't really see. She broke her hip twice. When your grandpa brought her here, she was so angry, kids. So angry. She didn't want to die. She didn't want to be dependent. It made her mean. That's pretty much your choices, I think. Getting old—getting *that* old, anyway—makes you mean, or sick, or stupid, or lonely. Take your pick. Only you don't get to pick. And sometimes, you wind up all four."

Rustling, from the vent. The faintest hint. Or had it come from the hallway?

"Grandma, what happened?"

"An accident, Miriam. Like I said. Your goddamn grandfather . . ."

"You can't—" Martin started, and Roz rode him down.

"Your goddamn grandfather wouldn't put them in homes. Either one. '*Your mother's your mother.*'" When she said that, she rumbled, and sounded just like Grandpa. " '*She's no trouble. And as for my mother . . . it'd kill her.*'"

"But having them here, kids . . . it was killing us. Poisoning every single day. Wrecking every relationship we had, even with each other."

Grandma looked up from her knees and straight at us. "Anyway," she said. "We had a home care service. A private nurse. Mrs. Gertzen. She came one night a week, and a couple weekends a year when we just couldn't take it and had to get away. When we wanted to go, we called Mrs. Gertzen, left the dates, and she came and took care of both our mothers while we were gone. Well, the last time . . . when they died . . . your grandfather called her, same as always. Sophie liked Mrs. Gertzen, was probably nicer to her than anyone else. Grandpa left instructions, and we headed off to the Delaware shore for five days of peace. But Mrs. Gertzen had a heart attack that first afternoon and never even made it to the house. And no one else on earth had any idea that my mother and Sophie were up here."

"Oh my God," I heard myself whisper, as the vent above me rasped pathetically. For the first time in what seemed hours, I became aware of the clock, *tuk*-ing away. I was imagining being trapped in this bed, hearing that sound. The metered pulse of the living world, just downstairs, plainly audible. And—for my great-grandmother and Mrs. Gold—utterly out of reach.

When I looked at Roz again, I was amazed to find tears leaking out of her eyes. She made no move to wipe them. "It must have been worse for Sophie," she half-whispered.

My mouth fell open. Martin had gone completely still as well as silent.

"I mean, I doubt my mother even knew what was happening. She probably prattled all the way to the end. If there *is* an Angel of Death, I bet she offered him a Berger cookie."

"You're . . ." *nicer than I thought*, I was going to say, but that wasn't quite right. *Different than I thought.*

"But Sophie. Can you imagine how horrible? How infuriating? To realize—she must have known by dinner time—that no one was coming? She couldn't make it downstairs. We'd had to carry her to the bathroom, the last few weeks. All she'd done that past month was light candles and read her *Zohar* and mutter to herself. I'm sure she knew she'd never make it to the kitchen. I'm sure that's why she didn't try. But I think she came back to herself at the end, you know? Turned back into the person she must have been. The woman who raised your grandfather, made him who he was or at least *let* him be. Because somehow she dragged herself into my mother's room one last time. They died with their arms around each other."

The dresses, I thought. *Had they been arranged like that on purpose? Tucked together, as a memory or a monument?* Then I was shivering, sobbing, and my brother was, too. Roz sat silently between us, staring at the floor.

"I shouldn't have told you," she mumbled. "Your parents will be furious."

Seconds later, the front door opened, and our mom and dad came hurtling up the stairs, filling our doorway with their flushed, exhausted, everyday faces.

"What are you doing up?" my mother asked, moving forward fast and stretching one arm toward each of us, though we were too far apart to be gathered that way.

"I'm afraid I—" Roz started.

"Grandpa," I said, and felt Roz look at me. "We were feeling bad about Grandpa."

My mother's mouth twisted, and her eyes closed. "I know," she said. "Me, too."

I crawled over to Martin's bed. My mother held us a long time, while my father stood above her, his hands sliding from her back to our shoulders to our heads. At some point, Roz slipped silently from the room. I didn't see her go.

For half an hour, maybe more, our parents stayed. Martin showed them the plaque he'd found, and my mother seemed startled mostly by the realization of where we'd been.

"You know I forgot that room was there?" she said. "Your cousins and I used to hide in it all the time. Before the hags came."

"You shouldn't call them that," Martin said, and my mother straightened, eyes narrowed. Eventually, she nodded, and her shoulders sagged.

"You're right. And I don't think of them that way. It's just, at the end . . . Good-night, kids."

After they'd gone, switching out all the lights except the butterfly in the hall, I thought I might sleep. But every time I closed my eyes, I swore I felt something pawing at the covers, as though trying to draw them back, so that whatever it was could crawl in with me. Opening my eyes, I found the dark room, the moon outside, the spider shadows in the corners. Several times, I glanced toward my brother's bed. He was lying on his back with the plaque he'd rescued on his chest and his head turned toward the wall, so that I couldn't see whether his eyes were open. I listened to the clock ticking and the vents rasping and muttering. A *Muldoon, and no mistake*, I found myself mouthing. *Who takes care of his own.* When I tried again to close my eyes, it seemed the vent was chanting with me. *No mistake. No mistake.* My heart twisted in its socket, and its beating bounced on the rhythm of the clock's tick like a skipped stone. I think I moaned, and Martin rolled over.

"Now let's play," he said.

Immediately, I was up, grabbing the sock-ball off the table where I'd left it. I wasn't anywhere near sleep, and I wasn't scared of Roz anymore. I wanted to be moving, doing anything. And my brother still wanted me with him.

I didn't wait for Martin this time, just marched straight out to the landing, casting a single, held-breath glance at Sophie's door. Someone had pulled it almost closed again, and I wondered if the wooden covering over the opening to the attic had also been replaced. Mrs. Gold's door, I noticed, had been left open. *Pushed open?*

Squelching that thought with a shake of my head, I started down the stairs. But Martin galloped up beside me, pushed me against the wall, took the sock-ball out of my hands, and hurried ahead.

"My ups," he said.

"Your funeral," I answered, and he stopped three steps down and turned and grinned. A flicker of butterfly light danced in his glasses, which made it look as though something reflective and transparent had moved behind me. I didn't turn around, couldn't turn around, *turned* and found the landing empty.

"She's asleep," Martin said, and for one awful moment, I didn't know whom he meant.

Then I did, and grinned weakly back. "If you say so." Retreating upstairs, I circled around the balcony into position.

The rules of Martin-Miriam Balcony Ball were simple. The person in the foyer below tried to lob the sock-ball over the railing and have it hit the carpet anywhere on the L-shaped landing. The person on the landing tried to catch the sock and slam it to the tile down in the foyer, triggering an innings change in which both players tried to bump each other off balance as they passed on the steps, thereby gaining an advantage for the first throw of the next round. Play ended when someone had landed ten throws on the balcony, or when Roz came and roared us back to bed, or when any small porcelain animal or *tuk*-ing grandfather clock or crystal chandelier got smashed. In the five year history of the game, that latter ending had only occurred once. The casualty had been a poodle left out atop the cabinet. This night's game lasted exactly one throw.

In retrospect, I think the hour or so between the moment our parents left and my brother's invitation to play were no more restful for Martin than they had been for me. He'd lain more still, but that had just compressed the energy the evening had given him, and now he was fizzing like a shaken pop bottle. I watched him glance toward Roz's hallway, crouch into himself as though expecting a hail of gunfire, and scurry into the center of the foyer. He looked skeletal and small, like some kind of armored beetle, and the ache that prickled up under my skin was at least partially defensive of him. He would never fill space the way our grandfather had. No one would. That ability to love people in general more than the people closest to you was a rare and only partly desirable thing. Martin, I already knew, didn't have it.

He must have been kneading the sock-ball all the way down the stairs, because as soon as he reared back and threw, one of the socks slipped free of the knot I'd made and dangled like the tail of a comet. Worse, Martin had somehow aimed straight up, so that instead of arching over the balcony, the sock-comet shot between the arms of the chandelier, knocked crystals together as it reached its apex, and then draped itself, almost casually, over the arm nearest the steps. After that, it just hung.

The chandelier swung gently left, then right. The clock *tuk*-ed like a clucking tongue.

"Shit," Martin said, and something rustled.

"*Sssh.*" I resisted yet another urge to jerk my head around. I turned slowly instead, saw Sophie's almost-closed door, Mrs. Gold's wide-open one, the butterfly light. Our room. Nothing else. If the sound I'd just heard had come from downstairs, then Roz was awake. "Get up here," I said, and Martin came, fast.

By the time he reached me, all that fizzing energy seemed to have evaporated. His shoulders had rounded, and his glasses had clouded over with his exertion. He looked at me through his own fog.

"Mir, what are we going to do?"

"What do you think we're going to do, we're going to go get it. *You're* going to go get it."

Martin wiped his glasses on his shirt, eyeing the distance between the landing where we stood and the chandelier. "We need a broom." His eyes flicked hopefully to mine. He was Martin again, alright.

I glanced downstairs to the hallway I'd have to cross to get to the broom closet. "Feel free."

"Come on, Miriam."

"You threw it."

"You're braver."

Abruptly, the naked woman from the tree in the magazine flashed in front of my eyes. I could almost see—almost *hear*—her stepping out of the photograph, balancing on those pointed feet. Tiptoeing over the splinter-riddled floor toward those wrapped-together dresses, slipping them over her shoulders.

"What?" Martin said.

"I can't."

For the second time that night, Martin took my hand. Before the last couple hours, Martin had last held my hand when I was six years old, and my mother had made him do it whenever we crossed a street—for his protection more than mine, since he was usually thinking about something random instead of paying attention.

"I have a better idea," he whispered, and pulled me toward the top of the staircase.

As soon as he laid himself flat on the top step, I knew what he was going to do. "You can't," I whispered, but what I really meant was that I didn't believe he'd dare. There he was, though, tilting onto his side, wriggling his head through the railings. His shoulders followed. Within seconds he was resting one elbow in the dust atop the grandfather clock.

Kneeling, I watched his shirt pulse with each *tuk*, as though a second, stronger heart had taken root inside him. *Too* strong, I thought, *it could throb him to pieces.*

"Grab me," he said. "Don't let go."

Even at age ten, my fingers could touch when wrapped around the tops of his ankles. He slid out farther, and the clock came off its back legs and leaned with him. "*Fuck!*" he blurted, wiggling back as I gripped tight. The clock tipped back toward us and banged its top against the railings and rang them.

Letting go of Martin, I scrambled to my feet, ready to sprint for our beds as I awaited the tell-tale bloom of lights in Roz's hallway. Martin lay flat, breath heaving, either resigned to his fate or too freaked out to care. It seemed impossible that Roz hadn't heard what we'd just done, and anyway, she had a sort of lateral line for this kind of thing, sensing movement in her foyer the way Martin said sharks discerned twitching fish.

But this time, miraculously, no one came. Nothing moved. And after a minute or so, without even waiting for me to hold his legs, Martin slithered forward once more. I dropped down next to him, held tighter. He kept his spine straight, dropping as little of his weight as possible atop the clock. I watched his waist wedge briefly in the railings, then slip through as his arms stretched out. It was like feeding him to something. Worse than the clock's *tuk* was the groan from its base as it started to lean again. My hands went sweaty, and my teeth clamped down on my tongue, almost startling me into letting go. I had no idea whether the tears in my eyes were fear or exhaustion or sadness for my grandfather or the first acknowledgement that I'd just heard rustling, right behind me.

"Ow," Martin said as my nails dug into his skin. But he kept sliding forward. My eyes had jammed themselves shut, so I felt rather than saw him grab the chandelier, felt it swing slightly away from him, felt his ribs hit the top of the clock and the clock start to tip.

I opened my eyes—not looking back, *not behind*, it was only the vents, had to be—and saw Roz step out of her hallway.

Incredibly, insanely, she didn't see us at first. She had her head down, bracelets jangling, hands jammed in the pockets of her shiny silver robe, and she didn't even look up until she was dead center under the chandelier, under my brother stretched full-length in mid-air twenty feet over her head with a sock in his hands. Then the clock's legs groaned under Martin's suspended weight, and the chandelier swung out, and Roz froze. For that one split second, none of us so much as breathed. And that's how I knew, even before she finally lifted her eyes. This time, I really had heard it.

"Get back," Roz said, and burst into tears.

It made no sense. I started babbling, overwhelmed by guilt I wasn't even sure was mine. "Grandma, I'm sorry. Sorry, sorry—"

"BACK!" she screamed. "*Get away! Get away from them.*" With startling speed, she spun and darted up the steps, still shouting.

Them. Meaning *us.* Which meant she wasn't talking to us.

The rest happened all in one motion. As I turned, my hands came off Martin's legs. Instantly, he was gone, tipping, the clock rocking forward and over. He didn't scream, maybe didn't have time, but his body flew face-first and smacked into the floor below just as Roz hurtled past and my parents emerged shouting from the guest bedroom and saw their son and the clock smashing and splintering around and atop him and I got my single glimpse of the thing on the landing.

Its feet weren't pointed, but bare and pale and swollen with veins. It wore some kind of pink, ruffled something, and its hair was white and flying. I couldn't see its face. But its movements . . . The arms all out of rhythm with the feet, out of order, as if they were being jerked from somewhere else on invisible strings. And the legs, the way they moved . . . not Mrs. Gold's mindless, surprisingly energetic glide . . . more of a tilting, trembling lurch. Like Sophie's.

Rooted in place, mouth open, I watched it stagger past the blacked out mirror, headed from the pink room to the blue one.

"*Takes care of his own,*" I found myself chanting, helpless to stop. "*Takes care of his own. And no mistake. No mistake.*" There had been no mistake.

Roz was waving her hands in front of her, snarling, stomping her feet as though scolding a dog. *Had she already known it was here? Or just understood, immediately?* In seconds, she and the lurching thing were in the blue room, and Sophie's door slammed shut.

"*No mistake,*" I murmured, tears pouring down my face.

The door flew open again, and out Roz came. My voice wavered, sank into silence as my eyes met hers and locked. Downstairs, my father was shouting frantically into the phone for an ambulance. Roz walked, jangling, to the step above me, sat down hard, put her head on her knees and one of her hands in my hair. Then she started to weep.

Martin had fractured his spine, broken one cheekbone, his collarbone, and both legs, and he has never completely forgiven me. Sometimes I think my parents haven't either. Certainly, they drew away from me for a long time after that, forming themselves into a sort of protective cocoon around my brother. My family traded phone calls with Roz for years. But we never went back to Baltimore, and she never came to see us.

So many times, I've lunged awake, still seeing the Sophie-Mrs. Gold creature lurching at random into my dreams. If I'd ever had the chance, I would have asked Roz only one thing: how much danger had Martin and I really been in? Would it really have hurt us? Was it inherently malevolent, a monster devouring everything it could reach? Or was it just a peculiarly Jewish sort of ghost, clinging to every last vestige of life, no matter how painful or beset by betrayal, because only in life—*this* life—is there any possibility of pleasure or fulfillment or even release?

I can't ask anyone else, because Roz is the only one other than me who knows. I have never talked about it, certainly not to Martin, who keeps the plaque he lifted from the attic that night nailed to his bedroom wall.

But I know. And sometimes, I just want to scream at all of them, make them see what's staring them right in the face, has been obvious from the moment it happened. My grandfather, the Muldoon who took care of his own, during the whole weekend he was away with Roz, never once called his mother? Never called home? Never checked in with Mrs. Gertzen, just to see how everyone was? And Mrs. Gertzen had no family? Had left no indication to the service that employed her of what jobs she might have been engaged in?

My grandfather had called Mrs. Gertzen's house before leaving for Delaware, alright. He'd learned about Mrs. Gertzen's heart attack. Then he'd weighed his shattering second marriage, his straining relationships with his children, his scant remaining healthy days, maybe even his own mother's misery.

And he'd made his decision. Taken care of his own, and no mistake. And in the end—the way they always do, whether you take care of them or not—his own had come back for him.

Honorable Mentions: 2006

Abidi, Azhar, "The Secret History of the Flying Carpet," *Southwest Review*, vol. 91, issue 1.

Ackerson, Duane, "Instructions for a Safe Transit" (poem), *The Magazine of Speculative Poetry*, spring.

——, "Taking Back the Moon" (poem), *Strange Horizons*, May 1.

Adams, Danny, "After the Circus," *Paradox*, winter.

Adobe, Agnes, "Mother Goose" (poem), *Stand*, vol. 6, number 3.

Agarwal, Dev, "Queen of Engines," *Albedo One* 31.

Akers, Tim, "The Song," *Interzone* 204.

——, "A Walking of Crows," *Electric Velocipede* 10.

Albrecht, Aaron, "The Night and Its Shadow," Science Fiction Writers of Earth, Web site.

Alexander, William, "Divination," *Zahir* 11.

Alfar, Dean Francis, "Six From Downtown," *Philippine Speculative Fiction*, vol. 2.

Allen, Mike, "Petting the Time Shark" (poem), *Strange Wisdoms of the Dead*.

——, "finale" (poem), Ibid.

——, "saecula saeculorum" (poem), Ibid.

——, "that strange man with the green petunias" (poem), Ibid.

——, "The Music of Bremen Farm," *Cabinet des Fées*.

——, "The Psychic Above Burritoville" (poem), *Jabberwocky*.

Alspaugh, Brandon, "The Love of Children," *Dark Doorways*.

Ang, Arlene, "A Glimpse of Sirens" (poem), *Star*Line* 29/6.

Antieau, Kim, "Storm Poet," *Asimov's Science Fiction*, Jan.

Aramata, Hiroshi, "The Road," *Straight to Darkness*.

Arnott, Marion, "The Little Drummer Boy," *Extended Play*.

Arnzen, Michael A., "The Dead Lantern," *Poe's Lighthouse*.

Atkins, Peter, "Between the Cold Moon and the Earth," *Rolling Darkness Review*, 2006.

Attebery, Brian, "The Cubist's Attorney," *Cemetery Dance* 56.

——, "Fairest," *Strange Horizons*, Sep. 11.

Aul, Billie, "Dead Man's Tale," *Realms of Fantasy*, Oct.

Ayres, Neil, "Kissing Cousins," *Apex*, fall.

Bach, Mischa, "Full Moon," *Ellery Queen's Mystery Magazine*, Jan.

Bacigalupi, Paolo, "Pop Squad," *The Magazine of Fantasy & Science Fiction*, Oct./Nov.

Baker, James Ireland, "Monkey Lot 9," *Cemetery Dance* 54.

Baker, Kage, "Calamari Curls," *Dark Mondays*.

——, "Oh, False Young Man!" Ibid.

——, "So This Guy Walks into a Lighthouse," *Poe's Lighthouse*.

——, "The Maid on the Shore" (novella), *Dark Mondays.*
Ballantine, Tony, "The Exchange," *Postscripts* 7.
Barker, Trey "Here's a Thing," *Dead Cat's Traveling Circus of Wonders.*
——, "In Articulo Mortis," *Evermore.*
Barzak, Christopher, "Dead Letters," *Realms of Fantasy*, Feb.
Barrett, Neal, Jr., "Getting Dark," *Subterranean* 5.
Barrette, Elizabeth, "The Selkie Thief" (poem), *Not One of Us* 35.
Barron, Laird, "Hallucigenia" (novella), *F & SF*, June.
Batchelor, David, "Bob," *The Alpine Fantasy of Victor B and Other Stories.*
Battersby, Lee, "Dark Ages," *Through Soft Air.*
——, "Elyse," Ibid.
Baumer, Jennifer Rachel, "Fishing Line, Feathers and Waffles," *Not One of Us* 36.
——, "Scare Tactics," *Talebones* 33.
Beagle, Peter S., "Chandail," *Salon Fantastique.*
—— "El Regalo," *The Line Between.*
——, "Salt Wine," *Fantasy Magazine* 3.
Bear, Elizabeth, "Los Empujadores Furiosos," *On Spec*, winter 2006.
——, "Love Among the Talus," *Strange Horizons*, Dec. 11.
——, "Wane," *Interzone* 203.
Beatty, Greg, "Why I Pray at Potholes" (poem), *On Our Way to Battle.*
Bechtel, Greg, "Blackbird Shuffle (The Major Arcana)," *Tesseracts Ten.*
Beliaeva, Maria, "Owls," *Cabinet des Fées.*
Bell, David, "Marcum's Teeth," *Shadow Regions.*
Bell, Helena, "Bluebeard's Second Wife" (poem), *Mythic* 2.
Bell, Kara Kellar, "The Bride," *Lady Churchill's Rosebud Wristlet* 19.
Bell, Peter, "Resurrection," *All Hallows* 41.
Bellamy, Lisa, "Howling Boy" (poem), *Skidrow Penthouse*, spring.
Bennett, Daniel, "You Will be Wearing Green," *Crimewave* 9.
Bennett, Renee, "The Cold Drake," *Realms of Fantasy*, Aug.
Benz, Stephen, "La Mendiga," *All Hallows* 41.
Berry, Jedediah, "To Measure the Earth," *Salon Fantastique.*
Biancotti, Deborah, "Stealing Free," *Agog! Ripping Reads.*
——, "Surrender 1: Rope Artist," *Shadowed Realms* 9.
Bisson, Terry, "Billy and the Fairy," *F & SF*, May.
Blake, John Southern, "The Exterminator," *On Spec*, summer.
Bloch, Robert, "Maternal Instinct," *Mondo Zombie.*
Bobet, Leah, "Deer's Heart," *ChiZine* 30.
——, "The Girl with the Heart of Stone," *Strange Horizons*, Jan. 9.
——, "And Its Noise as the Noise in a Dream . . ." *On Spec*, fall.
——, "Lost Wax," *Realms of Fantasy*, Dec.
——, "To Her Mother" (poem), *Strange Horizons*, Aug. 14.
Bolen, William, "Harris Valley Reclamation," *Trabuco Road*, Nov.
Boston, Bruce, "I Build Engines" (poem), *Lone Star Stories*, Feb.
——, "In the Coarse Morn" (poem), *Shades Fantastic.*
——, "Reach of the Mutant Rain Forest" (poem), *ChiZine* 27.
Bowes, Richard, "Dust Devil on a Quiet Street," *Salon Fantastique.*
Bowker, John, "A Bit of the True Material," *On Spec*, fall.
Bradbury, Ray, "The Beautiful Shave," *Masques* V.
Bramlett, Terry, "Accident Prone," *DeathGrip: Exit Laughing.*
——, "So the Story Ends," *Dark Wisdom*, winter.

Braum, Daniel, "Across the Darien Gap," *Cemetery Dance* 55.
Braunbeck, Gary A., "The Ballad of Road Mama and Daddy Bliss," *Destinations Unknown*.
——, "Congestion," *Destinations Unknown*.
——, "Fisherman's Delight," *Poe's Lighthouse*.
——, "In a Hand or a Face," *Masques V*.
——, "Our Things," chapbook.
——, "You Must Remember This," *Shadow Regions*.
Breedlove, Bill, "Drowning in the Sea of Love," *Candy in the Dumpsters*.
Brenchley, Chaz, "Every Day a Little Death," *British Fantasy Society: A Celebration*.
Brennan, Marie, "The Wood, the Bridge, the House," *Dark Wisdom*, spring.
Brenner, Wendy, "The Predicament," *Fairy Tale Review*, green issue.
Brite, Poppy Z., "Wandering the Borderlands," *Masques V*.
Broaddus, Maurice, "Family Business," *Weird Tales* 338.
Brosa, Ernesto, "Tea for Three," *Paradox* 9.
Brown, Eric, "The Memory of Joy," *Choices*.
Brown, Simon, "Tarans," *Andromeda Spaceways Inflight Magazine* 24.
——, "The Cup of Nestor," *Troy*.
Bruce, Colin, "Death in the East End," *Ghosts in Baker Street*.
Bucher-Jones, Simon, "Some Thoughts on the Problem of Order," *Hardboiled Cthulhu*.
Buckner, M.M., "Babble," *Apex* 8.
Bull, Emma, "What Used to Be Good Still Is," *Firebirds Rising*.
Bunn, Austin, "The Ledge," *One Story* 68.
Burke, Kealan Patrick, "Symbols," *Brimstone Turnpike Preview*.
Burrage, Nathan, "The Sidpa Bardo," *Shadowed Realms* 10.
Busick, Jennifer, "The Thief," *Thou Shalt Not . . .*
Butcher, Jim, "Something Borrowed," *My Big Fat Supernatural Wedding*.
Cacek, P.D., "Campfire Story," *Night Visions* 12.
——, "Forced Perspective" (novella), Ibid.
——, "The Monster," *Lords of the Razor*.
Cadnum, Michael, "Give Him the Eye," *Can't Catch Me and Other Twice-Told Tales*.
——, "Hungry," Ibid.
Cain, James R., "The Thing in the Park," *Dark Wisdom* 8.
Caine, Rachel, "Dead Man's Chest," *My Big Fat Supernatural Wedding*.
Cambias, James L., "Parsifal (Prix Fixe)," *F & SF*, Feb.
Campbell, Marlissa, "Promise Them Aught," *Apex* 7.
Campbell, Ramsey, "The Decorations," chapbook.
——, "The Place of Revelation," *Read by Dawn*.
Campbell, Tyree, "Generation Gap," *Dark Wisdom* 8.
Campbell-Wise, Alison, "After Midnight," *Fantasy Magazine* 4.
Campisi, Stephanie, "Why the Balloon Man Floats Away," Ibid.
Cardin, Matt and McLaughlin, Mark, "Nightmares, Imported and Domestic," *Dark Arts*.
Carlisi, Cathy, "Fragile" (poem), *Gargoyle* 51.
Carroll, Monica, "Sacrifice for the Nation," *The Outcast*.
Carter, Scott William, "Last Stop on Dowling Street," *Crimewave* 9.
——, "The Grand Mal Reaper," *Realms of Fantasy*, Aug.
——, "Happy Time," *Postscripts* 8.
Caselberg, Jay, "Early," *Dark Wisdom* 10.
——, "Empties," *Aurealis* 36.
Casil, Amy Sterling, "Perfect Stranger," *F & SF*, Sept.
Castle, Mort, "FYI," *Masques V*.

Cave, Hugh B., "Brief Stay in a Small Town," *Lords of the Razor.*
Chadbourn, Mark, "The Ones We Leave Behind," *Dark Horizons* 47.
——, "Whisper Lane," *British Fantasy Society: A Celebration.*
Chambers, James, "The Roaches in the Walls," *Hardboiled Cthulhu.*
Chapman, Maile, "Bit Forgive," *A Public Space* 2.
Chappell, Fred, "The White Cat," *Evermore.*
Chen, E.L., "Wayfaring Girls," *Strange Horizons*, Mar. 27.
Choo, Mary, "Jig" (poem), *ChiZine* 30.
Chrywenstrom, Lily, "Ghosts of 1930," *Borderlands* 6.
Clark, Simon, "Frankenstein, Victor," *Night Visions* 12.
——, "Poe, Lovecraft, Jackson," Ibid.
——, "She Loves Monsters" (novella), chapbook.
Clarke, Susanna, "John Uskglass and the Cumbrian Charcoal Burner," *F & SF*, Dec.
Cleary, David Ira, "The Kewlist Thing of All," *Asimov's*, March.
Clegg, Douglas, "The American," *Wild Things.*
——, "The Wolf," Ibid.
Cline, Emma, "Perseids," *Tin House*, vol. 7, issue 4.
Conlon, Christopher, "Bathing the Bones," *Thundershowers at Dusk.*
——, "Darkness, and She Was Alone," *Poe's Lighthouse.*
——, "Ghosts in Autumn," *Masques V.*
——, "Thundershowers at Dusk," *Thundershowers at Dusk.*
Cooper, Constance, "The Tongueless Bell" (poem), *Jabberwocky* 2.
Cooper, James, "A Frailty of Moths," Hub 1.
——, "You are the Fly," *Dark Doorways.*
Copley-Woods, Haddayr, "Cows, Water, Whiskey," *Flytrap* 5.
Cortese, Katie, "Hovering," *Zahir* 10.
Costa, Shelley, "Blue Morpho," *Crimewave* 9.
Cowdrey, Albert E., "Animal Magnetism," *F & SF*, June.
Crider, Bill, "Zekiel Saw the Wheel," *Retro Pulp Tales.*
Crooks, Christina, "The Seat," *Chimeraworld* 4.
Crow, Jennifer, "A House-Ghost" (poem), *Not One of Us* 35.
——, "Icehcart" (poem), *Illumen*, autumn.
——, "The Music of the Dead" (poem), *Jabberwocky* 2.
——, "The Secret Names of Angels"(poem), *Mag. of Spec. Poetry*, spring.
Cummings, Shane Jiraiya, "Genesis Six," *Apex* 8.
——, "Prescience," *Borderlands* 8.
Cupp, Scott A., "One Fang," *Cross Plains Universe.*
Curran, Tim, "Pumpkin Witch," *Shivers IV.*
D, Romola, "The Next Corpse Collector," *Green Mountain Review*, new series XIX.
Davenport, Tristan, "Terminus," *ChiZine* 27.
Day, R. W., "Hell and Half of Georgia," *Damned Nation.*
Dean, Pamela, "Cousins," *Firebirds Rising.*
De Bernières, Louis, "A Walberswick Goodnight Story" (poem), chapbook.
De Bodard, Aliette, "Through the Obsidian Gates," *Shimmer*, autumn.
De La Rosa, Becca, "Nine Lives," *Ideomancer*, Dec.
——, "This Is the Train the Queen Rides On," *Lady Churchill's Rosebud Wristlet* 18.
de Lint, Charles, "Old Man Crow," *Christmas Chapbook.*
de Long, Aaron, "The Concentrator," *Zahir* 9.
Deal, Ef, "Czesko," *F & SF*, Mar.
Decker, Sherry, "Gifts from the North Wind," *Hook House and Other Horrors.*

Dedman, Stephen, "The Dead of Winter," *Weird Tales* 339.

DeNiro, Alan, "Meet the Elms," *The Journal of Mythic Arts*, spring.

——, "Quiver," *Skinny Dipping in the Lake of the Dead.*

Denton, Bradley, "Blackburn and the Blade" (novella), *Lords of the Razor.*

Dermatis, Dayle A., "Hell's Belles," *DeathGrip: Exit Laughing.*

Devereaux, Robert, "God's Madmen," *Farthing* 4.

——, "Holy Fast, Holy Feast," *Mondo Zombie.*

Di Filippo, Paul, "Billy Budd," *Shuteye for the Timebroker.*

Disch, Thomas M., "The Kiss" (poem), Disch weblog.

Dolton, Brian, "The Man Who Was Never Afraid," *Abyss & Apex* 20.

Donahoe, Erin, "Gaki" (poem), *ChiZine* 29.

Done, Becky, "Tremolando," *Extended Play.*

Dowling, Terry, "Cheat Light," *Basic Black: Tales of Appropriate Fear.*

Downum, Amanda, "Dogtown," *Strange Horizons*, June 12.

——, "Smoke & Mirrors," *Strange Horizons*, Nov. 20.

——, "Snake Charmer," *Realms of Fantasy*, Oct.

Dray, Stephanie, "Somewhere, Sometime on the Nile," *Paradox* 9.

Duane, Diane, "The Fix," *The Magic Toybox.*

Dugan, Grace, "The Conqueror," *Eidolon* 1.

Duncan, Julia, "Steeling Little Girls," *Dreams of Decadence* 19.

Duncan, Hal, "The Angel of Gamblers," *Eidolon* 1.

Dutcher, Roger, "The Mummy's Task" (poem), *Talebones* 32.

Edric, Robert, "The Empty Pool, *Postscripts* 8.

Edwards, Paul, "Painting Blind Circles," *Dark Doorways.*

Emar, Juan, "The Green Bird," *Web Conjunctions.*

Emshwiller, Carol, "Killers," *F & SF*, Oct.

——, "The Seducer," *Asimov's*, Oct./Nov.

Evans, S., "Water, Fire, and Faith," *Strange Horizons*, Jan. 2.

Everson, Karen, "The What-Not Doll," *The Magic Toybox.*

Every, Gary, "Tarahumara Chiles" (poem), *Mythic Delirium* 15.

Ewert, Marcus, "Choose Your Own Epic Adventure," *Twenty Epics.*

Ezzo, Joseph A., "Just Beyond the Middle of the Journey," *Alone on the Darkside.*

Farland, David, "The Mooncalfe," *Intergalactic Medicine Show* 2.

Faulkner, Ian R., "A Handful of Dust," *Crimewave* 9.

Feld, Lisa Batya, "Problem, Child," *Farthing* 3.

Ferguson, Andrew, "Drums and Drums," *Ten Plagues.*

Files, Gemma, "Heart's Hole," *In the Dark: Stories from the Supernatural.*

——, "Heart-Dust," *Horror Carousel* 4.

——, "Jack-Knife," *Shivers IV.*

——, "Landscape with Maps and Legends," *Suspect Thoughts* 17.

——, "Spectral Evidence 1" *ChiZine* 30.

Finch, Paul, "Elderly Lady, Lives Alone," *Bare Bone* 9.

——, "Kid," *Choices.*

——, "Of the Wild and Berserk Prince Drakula," *Shrouded by Darkness.*

——, "The Old North Road," *Alone on the Darkside.*

Finlay, Charles Coleman, "Hail, Conductor," *Talebones* 32.

——, "Passing Through," *F & SF*, May.

Fisher, Christopher, "Tattletale," *Thou Shalt Not . . .*

Fishler, Karen D., "Among the Living," *Interzone* 203.

Flinthart, Dirk, "One Night Stand," *Agog! Ripping Reads.*

Flynn, Michael F., "Dawn, and Sunset, and the Colors of the Earth," *Asimov's*, Oct./Nov.
Ford, Jeffrey, "Botch Town" (novella), *The Empire of Ice Cream*.
——, "The Way He Does It," *Electric Velocipede* 10.
Foster, Eugie, "The Son that Pain Made," *Aberrant Dreams* 6.
Fowler, Christopher, "The Luxury of Harm," *Postscripts* 10.
Fredericks, Deby, "Bonewood Forest," *Andromeda Spaceways* 25.
Fredsti, Dana, "You'll Never Be Lunch in This Town Again," *Mondo Zombie*.
Friedman, C.S., "Terms of Engagement," *F & SF*, June.
Fritz, Sandra, "Achieving Absolution" (poem), *Dark Wisdom* 10.
Frost, Gregory, "So Coldly Sweet, So Deadly Fair," *Weird Tales* 339.
Fry, Gary, "Going Back," *Midnight Street* 7.
——, "Kiss and Tell," *The Impelled and Other Head Trips*.
——, "Now and Then," Ibid.
——, "School of Fought," *When Graveyards Yawn*.
——, "The Sunken Garden," *The Impelled and Other Head Trips*.
——, "Unmoored," Ibid.
——, "What Goes Around . . . ," *Midnight Street* 7.
Fuhrman, Joanna, "Architecture Moraine," *Moraine*.
Gagliani, William D., "The Great Belzoni and the Gait of Anubis," *Amazon Shorts*.
Gaiman, Neil, "How to Talk to Girls at Parties," *Fragile Things*.
Gallagher, Stephen, "The Butterfly Garden," *Lords of the Razor*.
——, "The Plot," *Subterranean* 5.
Garcia, R.S., "Douen Mother," *Abyss & Apex* 17.
Garrott, Lila, "Une Conte de Fée," *Cabinet des Fées*.
Gaskin, John, "Rigor Mortis," *The Long Retreating Day*.
——, "St John's Wood," Ibid.
——, "Tapiola," Ibid.
Geronimo, Russell Stanley Q., "The Sign of the Cross," *Philippine Speculative Fiction 2*.
Gibson, Stephen, "At Mazar-E Sharif," *Gargoyle* 51.
Gilman, Greer, "Down the Wall," *Salon Fantastique*.
Godwin, Parke, "My Sister's House," *Weird Tales* 338.
Goldberg, D.G.K., "The Cheerleaders, the Geek, and the Lonesome Piney Woods," *Alone on the Darkside*.
—— and Hicks, WIlliam D., "Time and Tide," *DeathGrip: Exit Laughing*.
Golden, Christopher, "The Art of the Deal," *Lords of the Razor*.
—— and Moore, James A., "Bloodstained Oz," chapbook.
Goldman, Ken, "Poe 103," *Evermore*.
Goodfellow, Cody, "To Skin a Dead Man," *Hardboiled Cthulhu*.
Goodrich, John, "Arkham Rain," *Arkham Tales*.
Goodwin, Geoffrey H., "Release the Bats," *Rabid Transit: Long Voyages, Great Lies*.
Gordon, D.M., "Sliding," *Lady Churchill's Rosebud Wristlet* 19.
Gorman, Ed, "Beauty," *Cemetery Dance* 55.
Goss, Theodora, "Arachne," *Jabberwocky* 1.
——, "Bal Macabre," *Mythic Delirium* 15.
——, "Beauty to the Beast," *Mythic* 1.
——, "Conrad," *In the Forest of Forgetting*.
——, "Lessons with Miss Gray," *Fantasy Magazine* 2.
——, "Letters From Budapest," *Alchemy* 3.
Graham, Brenna Yovanoff, "The Virgin Butcher," *ChiZine* 30.
Gramlich, Charles, "Rotted Angels," *Star*Line*, May/June.

Grant, Helen, "Purslane the Witch," *Supernatural Tales* 10.

Gray, Robert, "Breathing a Fine Stone Mist," *Alfred Hitchcock's Mystery Magazine*, June.

Greco, Ralph Jr., "Twitter," *Cthulhu Sex* 24.

Gregory, Daryl, "Damascus," *F & SF*, Dec.

Gregory, Eric, "The Redaction of Flight 5766," *Sybil's Garage* 3.

Grice, Gordon, "Hide," *ChiZine* 27.

Grimsley, Jim, "Wendy," *Subterranean* 5.

——, "Unbending Eye," *Asimov's*, Feb.

Groff, Lauren, "Lucky Chow Fun," *Ploughshares*, fall.

Haines, John Paul, "Burning from the Inside," *Doorways for the Dispossessed.*

——, "Lifelike and Josephine," *Agog! Ripping Reads.*

——, "Mnemphonic," *Doorways for the Dispossessed.*

——, "Ten With a Flag," *Interzone* 203.

Haire, Durant, "Scarecrow," *Dark Wisdom* 10.

Hall, Rayne, "Burning," *Byzarium*, Jan.

——, "The Bridge Chamber," *Read by Dawn.*

Hall, Wheeler Joseph, "Will You Hold My Hand . . . ," *Outer Darkness* 33.

Hamilton, Laurell K., "Here Be Dragons," *Strange Candy.*

Hammond, Chris, "The Alpine Fantasy of Victor B," *The Alpine Fantasy of Victor B and Other Stories.*

Hand, Elizabeth, "The Saffron Gatherers," *Saffron and Brimstone: Strange Stories.*

Hansen, Jon, "The Goblin Party," *Flytrap* 6.

Hanson, Robert, "The Ogress," *Zahir* 11.

Harland, Richard, "Domestic Arrangements," *C0ck.*

——, "On the Way to Habassau," *The Outcast.*

Harn, Darby, "The Switch," *Jigsaw Nation.*

Harvard, Katie, "Renaissance," *Surrounded* 1.

Hautala, Rick, "Blood Ledge," *Four Octobers.*

——, "Tin Can Telephone," Ibid.

Hazen, Elizabeth Brooke, "Why I Love Zombie Woman #6," *Gargoyle* 51.

Healy, Jeremiah, "Hitch-Hunting," *AHMM*, July/Aug.

Hemmingson, Michael, "Hardboiled Stiff," *Badass Horror.*

Henderson, C.J., "The Idea of Fear," *Arkham Tales.*

Henderson, Samantha, "Girl with the Lute," *ChiZine* 28.

——, "Histories," *Lone Star Stories* 18.

——, "Route Nine," *Shimmer*, winter.

——, "Triptych: Three Views of the Capture of the City of Bisanthe," *Lone Star Stories* 15.

Hiebert, Michael, "Dust," *Hags, Sirens, and Other Bad Girls of Fantasy.*

Higgins, Peter, "Monadnock & Bramble Jam," *Zahir* 11.

——, "The Original Word for Rain," Ibid.

Hikmet, Nazim, "Girl," (translated by Amy Grupp) *Atlanta Review*, spring/summer.

Hines, Jim C., "Sister of the Hedge," *Realms of Fantasy*, June.

Hirshberg, Glen, "Devil's Smile," *Alone on the Darkside/American Morons.*

——, "Millwell," *Rolling Darkness Review* 2006.

——, "Transitway," *Cemetery Dance* 56/*American Morons.*

Hobson, M.K., "Discovery's Wake," *Flytrap* 6.

Hodge, Brian, "And Our Turn Too, Will One Day Come," *Alone on the . . .*

Hoffman, Nina Kiriki, "To Grandmother's House," *Weird Tales* 338.

——, "The Weight of Wishes," *Children of Magic.*

Hoffmeister, Curtis, "Wet Work," Desdmona.com.

Holder, Nancy, "The Winter of Our Discontent," *Children of Magic*.

Hollander, John, "Ghosts," *Georgia Review*, spring.

Hood, Daniel, "Pavel Petrovich," *Realms of Fantasy*, June.

Hood, Martha A., "Missing Piece," *Tales of the Unanticipated* 27.

Hopkinson, Elizabeth, "A Short History of the Dream Library," *Interzone* 204.

Horrocks, Caitlin, "Embodied," *The Cincinnati Review*, spring.

Horsley, Ron, "In the Empty Country," *Masques V*.

Houarner, Gerard, "The Alchemy from the Towers of Silence," *Damned Nation*.

——, "The Chrysalis King," *Inhuman* 3.

——, "The Hellbound Kid," *Dead Cat's Traveling Circus* . . .

——, "Topsy the Elephant," *Ibid*.

Humfrey, Michael, "In the Picture," *Zahir* 9.

Humphrey, Andrew, "Last Song," *Extended Play*.

——, "Out of Area," *In the Dark: Stories from the Supernatural*.

Hurley, Kameron, "The Women of Our Occupation," *Strange Horizons*, July 31.

——, "Wonder Maul Doll," *From the Trenches*.

Hutchins, Blake, "The Sword from the Sea," *Writers of the Future XXII*.

Hutchinson, David, "The Sutherland King," *Read by Dawn*.

Ireland, Davin, "The Essences," *Badass Horror*.

——, "Something Bad," *Dark Doorways*.

Irvine, Alex, "New Game in Town," *Retro Pulp Tales*.

Ison, Sunshine, "And If They Are Not Dead, They May Be Living Still," *Lady Churchill's* . . . 18.

Jacob, Charlee, "And Where Thy Footstep Gleams," *Geek Poems*.

——, "Geek Poems," *Ibid*.

——, "The Mist Machine," *Dark Arts*.

——, "Night Writing," *Evermore*.

——, "Yeah, Yeah, Dog Gone South," *Geek Poems*.

Jacobson, Jeff, "Last Day on the Job," *Read by Dawn*.

Jamieson, Trent, "Persuasion," *Reserved for Travelling Shows*.

Jennings, A.H., "This Is Mars," *Damned Nation*.

Jeter, K.W., "Ninja Two-Fifty," *Postscripts* 8.

Johnson, Alaya Dawn, "Among Their Bright Eyes," *Fantasy Magazine* 5.

Jones, Jeff P., "Agony of the Forgotten," *Zahir* 10.

Johnson, Jeffrey D., "The Tamale God," *On Spec*, spring.

Jones, Diana Wynne, "I'll Give You My Word," *Firebirds Rising*.

Jones, Jaida, "The Relationship between Lovers and Words," *Jabberwocky* 2.

Jones, William, "Through the Eye of a Needle," *Thou Shalt Not* . . .

Justice, Mark, "The Whispered Sighs of Grateful Souls," *Bare Bone* 9.

Kaftan, Vylar, "Keybones," *ChiZine* 29.

——, "Lydia's Body," *Clarkesworld*, Nov.

Kane, David J., "Very Like a Whale," *Agog! Ripping Reads*.

Kang, Minsoo, "Four Tales and an Enigma," *Of Tales and Enigmas*.

——, "The Infinite City," *Ibid*.

——, "The Ghost Child," *Ibid*.

——, "The Lost Pictures," *Ibid*.

Kaysen, Daniel, "Clocks," *Interzone* 207.

Keane, Erin, "Angels' Share," *Full Unit Hookup* 8.

Keene, Brian, "An Appointment Kept," *For Fear of* . . .

——, "Take the Long Way Home," chapbook.

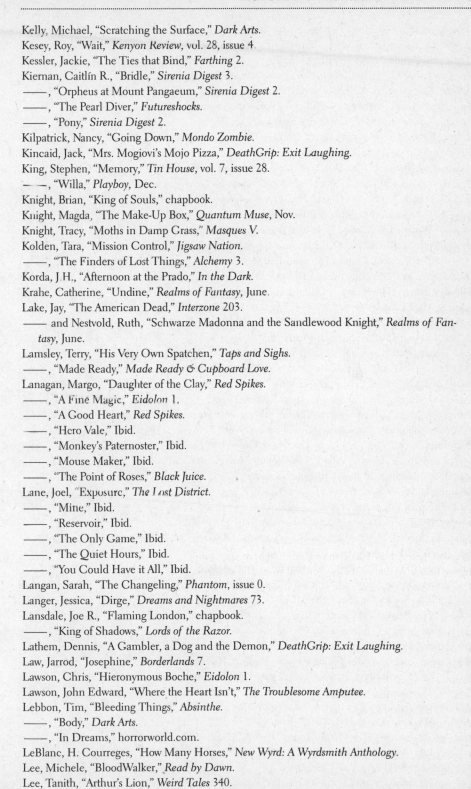

Kelly, Michael, "Scratching the Surface," *Dark Arts.*

Kesey, Roy, "Wait," *Kenyon Review*, vol. 28, issue 4.

Kessler, Jackie, "The Ties that Bind," *Farthing* 2.

Kiernan, Caitlín R., "Bridle," *Sirenia Digest* 3.

———, "Orpheus at Mount Pangaeum," *Sirenia Digest* 2.

———, "The Pearl Diver," *Futureshocks.*

———, "Pony," *Sirenia Digest* 2.

Kilpatrick, Nancy, "Going Down," *Mondo Zombie.*

Kincaid, Jack, "Mrs. Mogiovi's Mojo Pizza," *DeathGrip: Exit Laughing.*

King, Stephen, "Memory," *Tin House*, vol. 7, issue 28.

———, "Willa," *Playboy*, Dec.

Knight, Brian, "King of Souls," chapbook.

Knight, Magda, "The Make-Up Box," *Quantum Muse*, Nov.

Knight, Tracy, "Moths in Damp Grass," *Masques V.*

Kolden, Tara, "Mission Control," *Jigsaw Nation.*

———, "The Finders of Lost Things," *Alchemy* 3.

Korda, J.H., "Afternoon at the Prado," *In the Dark.*

Krahe, Catherine, "Undine," *Realms of Fantasy*, June.

Lake, Jay, "The American Dead," *Interzone* 203.

——— and Nestvold, Ruth, "Schwarze Madonna and the Sandlewood Knight," *Realms of Fantasy*, June.

Lamsley, Terry, "His Very Own Spatchen," *Taps and Sighs.*

———, "Made Ready," *Made Ready & Cupboard Love.*

Lanagan, Margo, "Daughter of the Clay," *Red Spikes.*

———, "A Fine Magic," *Eidolon* 1.

———, "A Good Heart," *Red Spikes.*

———, "Hero Vale," Ibid.

———, "Monkey's Paternoster," Ibid.

———, "Mouse Maker," Ibid.

———, "The Point of Roses," *Black Juice.*

Lane, Joel, "Exposure," *The Lost District.*

———, "Mine," Ibid.

———, "Reservoir," Ibid.

———, "The Only Game," Ibid.

———, "The Quiet Hours," Ibid.

———, "You Could Have it All," Ibid.

Langan, Sarah, "The Changeling," *Phantom*, issue 0.

Langer, Jessica, "Dirge," *Dreams and Nightmares* 73.

Lansdale, Joe R., "Flaming London," chapbook.

———, "King of Shadows," *Lords of the Razor.*

Lathem, Dennis, "A Gambler, a Dog and the Demon," *DeathGrip: Exit Laughing.*

Law, Jarrod, "Josephine," *Borderlands* 7.

Lawson, Chris, "Hieronymous Boche," *Eidolon* 1.

Lawson, John Edward, "Where the Heart Isn't," *The Troublesome Amputee.*

Lebbon, Tim, "Bleeding Things," *Absinthe.*

———, "Body," *Dark Arts.*

———, "In Dreams," horrorworld.com.

LeBlanc, H. Courreges, "How Many Horses," *New Wyrd: A Wyrdsmith Anthology.*

Lee, Michele, "BloodWalker," *Read by Dawn.*

Lee, Tanith, "Arthur's Lion," *Weird Tales* 340.

McKillip, Patricia A., "Jack O'Lantern," *Firebirds Rising*.

McLane, Maureen N., "White Girl," *ParaSpheres*.

McMahon, Gary, "Day of the Mask," *Gods and Monsters*.

——, "I See a Darkness," *Lighthouse VI*.

McMahon, Paul, "Killing Puffball," *Damned Nation*.

McMullen, Sean, "The Measure of Eternity," *Interzone* 205.

McNair, Wesley, "The Side," *Pleiades* 26:1.

McNew, Pam, "Distant Stars," *Lone Star Stories* 17.

Meikle, William, "The Mouth," *Hardboiled Cthulhu*.

Melling, Stephen, "Epilogue," *Whispers of Wickedness* 12.

Mellon, Michelle, "The Good Life," *Thou Shalt Not . . .*

Meltzer, Kat, "Change of Life," *Asimov's*, Feb.

Menge, Elaine, "Boxes of Hell," *AHMM*, Oct.

——, "Perpetual Care," *AHMM*, Mar.

Menon, Amil, "Harris on the Pig: Practical Advice for the Pig Farmer," *From the Trenches*.

Mercure, Bonnie, "Teapot in the Well," *Shadow Regions*.

Merriam, Joanne, "Cherries for Buttons," *Strange Horizons*, Feb. 27.

Messinger, Megan, "Branson Rebellion," *Fantasy Magazine* 4.

——, "The Dark Lady," *Jabberwocky* 2.

Minnion, Keith, "Up in the Boneyard," *Shivers IV*.

Mitchell, David, "Acknowledgments," *A Public Space* 2.

Mitchell, Karen Anne, "Light of the Moon," *Fantasy Magazine* 2.

Monette, Sarah, "Draco Campestris," *Strange Horizons*, Aug. 7.

—— "A Night in Electric Squidland," *Lone Star Stories*, Feb.

—— "Katabasis: Seraphic Trains," *Tales of the Unanticipated* 27.

—— "The Séance at Chisholm End," *Alchemy* 3.

Monk, Devon, "Ducks in a Row," *Realms of Fantasy*, Apr.

Monteleone, Thomas F., "How Sweet It Was," *Masques V*.

Moorcock, Michael, "The Third Jungle Book: A Mowgli Story," *ParaSpheres*.

Moore, Marlowe, "Ashes of Love, Flame Burned Out," *Zahir* 10.

Moore, Ralph Robert, "Fleeing, on a Bicycle . . ." *Midnight Street* 7.

——, "The Little Girl Who Lives in the Woods," *Read by Dawn*.

Morgan, Terry, and Morgan, Christopher, "Zaambi," *Mondo Zombie*.

Morlan, A.R., "Chiaroscuro," *Cemetery Dance* 54.

Morrell, David, "They," *Amazon Shorts*.

Morris, Jan, "Hav of the Myrmidons," *Last Letters from Hav*.

Morris, Mark, "What Nature Abhors," *Night Visions* 12.

Moser, Elise, "Citrine: A Fable," *Room of One's Own* 29:2.

Moyer, Jaime Lee, "Eldest Daughter" (poem), *Star*Line*, July/Aug.

Muir, Brian, "With Mine Own Hands This Grave I Dig," *AHMM*, Dec.

Mundt, Martin, "Babies Is Smart," *Candy in the Dumpster*.

——, "Freedom," *The Dark Underbelly of Hymns*.

——, "Penis in Furs," Ibid.

——, "Nothing Good Ever Came . . ." Ibid.

Munroe, Emma, "Spare Parts," *Borderlands* 6.

Murakami, Haruki, "A Shinagawa Monkey," *The New Yorker*, Feb. 13 & 20.

Murphy, Joe, "The Doom that Came to Smallmouth," *Aeon* 7.

Muslim, Kristine Ong, "Cold Earth" (poem), *Oddities*.

——, "Family Secrets" (poem), *Poe Little Thing* 5.

Nagle, Pati, "Dawn's Early Light," *From the Trenches*.

Nestvold, Ruth, "Feather and Ring," *Asimov's*, Sept.

Nethercott, Michael, "The Banjo House," *Gods and Monsters*.

Newman, Kim, "Clubland Heroes," *Retro Pulp Tales*.

——, "The Man Who Got off the Ghost Train" (novella), *The Man from the Diogenes Club*.

Nicholls, Mark, "A Family Communion," *All Hallows* 41.

Nicholson, Scott, "She Climbs a Winding Stair," *Dark Wisdom* 9.

Nickels, Tim, "Fight Music," *Extended Play*.

Nickle, David, "The Delilah Party," *Cemetery Dance* 56.

Ó Guilín, Peadar, "Hurdy Gurdy," *Dark Arts*.

O'Brien, Kevin L., "We Deliver," *Nightscapes*.

O'Driscoll, Mike, "Evelyn Is Not Real," *Unbecoming*.

O'Keefe, Claudia, "The Moment of Joy Before," *F & SF*, Apr.

O'Rourke, Monica, "One Breath," *Cthulhu Sex* 24.

Oakes, Rita, "Lupercalia," *Aeon* 7.

Oates, Joyce Carol, "Babysitter," *EQMM*, June.

Ochse, Weston, "The Secret Lives of Heroes," *Horror Garage* 11.

Ochsner, Gina, "Song of the Selkie," *Tin House* 29.

Odom, Mel, "The Affair of the Wooden Boy," *The Magic Toybox*.

Odom, Scott K., "Bone Dance" (poem), *Pleiades* 26:1.

Ogletree, Wade, "The Sphinx and Ernest Hemingway," *Fantasy Magazine* 2.

Oldknow, Antony, "After the Party," *The Passion Play and Other Ghost Stories*.

——, "From the North Window," Ibid.

——, "Harrow," Ibid.

——, "The Wanderer," Ibid.

Oosterman, André, "The Navel of the Universe," *Electric Velocipede* 10.

Padgett, Abigail, "The Dancer," *Zahir* 9.

Palmer, M.E., "Hungry Ghosts," *Fantasy Magazine* 3.

Park, John, "Oubliette" (poem), *ChiZine* 28.

Parker, Steve, "Starfish," *Apex* 5.

Parks, Richard, "A Garden in Hell," *Fantasy Magazine* 5.

——, "Brillig," *Jabberwocky* 2.

——, "Moon Viewing at Shijo Bridge," *Realms of Fantasy*, Apr.

Partridge, Norman, "Carrion," *Retro Pulp Tales*.

——, "Dark Harvest" (novella), chapbook.

——, "The Fourth Stair up from the Landing," *Subterranean* 3.

Peek, Ben, "theleeharveyoswaldband," *Polyphony* 6.

——, "Under the Red Sun," *Fantasy Magazine* 4.

Pelan, John, "For Art's Sake," *Dark Arts*.

Pelland, Jennifer, "Captive Girl," *Helix*, Oct.

Pendergrass, Tom, "Sell Your Soul to the Devil Blues," *Shimmer*, winter.

Person, Lawrence, "The Toughest Jew in the West," *Cross Plains Universe*.

Peters, Shawn, "Ticker Hounds," *On Spec*, winter 2005.

Petty, J.T., "Grapefruit Spoons," *Cemetery Dance* 55.

Pflug, Ursula, "Isolde, Shea, and the Donkey Brea," *Strange Horizons*, Dec. 4.

Phillips, Holly, "Gin," *Eidolon* 1.

Phillips-Sears, Cassandra, "Love Story," *Jabberwocky* 2.

Piccirilli, Tom, "Thin Skin of the Soul Worn Away," *In Delirium*.

Pierce, Tamora, "Huntress," *Firebirds Rising*.

Pineau, Gisele, "The Woman in Flames," (translated by C. Dickson), *Ninth Letter*.

Pinn, Paul, "Stench Man Killer Boy," *Chimeraworld* 3.

Pirie, Steven, "Mrs. Mathews Is Afraid of Cricket Bats," *Dark Doorways*.

Ponto, Michelle, "The Soul Hunter," *When Graveyards Yawn*.

Porter, Karen R., "The Visitor" (poem), *Not One of Us* 36.

Powers, Tim, "A Soul in a Bottle," chapbook.

Prater, Lon, "Even at the End, There Was Gridlock," *Florida Horror*.

Pratt, Tim, "The Crawlspace of the World," *Polyphony* 6.

——, The Third-Quarter King, *Eidolon* 1.

Prentiss, Norman, "In the Best Stories . . ." *Shivers IV*.

——, "The Everywhere Man," *Damned Nation*.

Priest, Cherie, "The Immigrant," *Mythic* 2.

——, "The October Devotion," *Subterranean* 3.

Prill, David, "The Star System," *Subterranean* 3.

Prineas, Sarah, "Hekaba's Demon," *Lone Star Stories* 14.

——, "Jane: A Story of Magic, Manners, and Romance," *Realms of Fantasy*, Apr.

Probert, John Llewellyn, "The Kreutzenberg Sonata," *The Faculty of Terror*.

——, "The States of the Art," Ibid.

Prufer, Kevin, "Apocalypse" (poem), *Ploughshares*, vol. 31, issue 4.

Pugmire, W.H., "Oh, Baleful Theophany," *The Fungal Stain*.

——, "Past the Gate of Deepest Slumber," Ibid.

——, "The Saprophytic Fungi," Ibid.

Rabinowitz, Rosanne, "In the Pines" (novella), *Extended Play*.

Rambo, Cat, "Magnificent Pigs," *Strange Horizons*, Nov. 27.

Rainey, Stephen Mark, "The Lake of Shadows," *Dark Wisdom* 10.

——, "LZ-116: Das Fliegenschloss," *Shivers IV*.

——, "Sky of Thunder, Island of Blood," *Amazon Shorts*.

Rath, Tony, and Rath, Tina, "Aftermath," *Weird Tales* 341.

Read, Nigel, and Battersby, Lee, "Instinct," *Andromeda Space . . .* 23.

Reed, Kit, "Biodad," *Asimov's*, Oct./Nov.

Reed, Robert, "Intolerance," *F & SF*, Mar.

——, "Rwanda," *Asimov's*, Mar.

——, "Show Me Yours," *F & SF*, May.

Reents, Stephanie, "Trespassers," *Pleiades* 26:1.

Reisman, Jessica, "Two Hearts in Zamora," *Cross Plains Universe*.

Rennie, Alistair, "Il Duca di Cesena," *Electric Velocipede* 10.

Reynolds, Joshua, "The Screaming Gun," *Hell's Hangmen*.

Richards, Kim, "Beauty Is," *Surreal*, vol. 1, issue 4.

Richards, Tony, "Alsiso," *Postscripts* 8.

——, "Hanako From Miyazaki," *Cemetery Dance* 55.

——, "Nine Rocks in a Row," *Cemetery Dance* 54.

——, "A Night in Tunisia," *Extended Play*.

Richardson, Robert Burke, "The Girl with the Half-Moon Eyes," *On Spec*, spring.

Richerson, Carrie, "With/By Good Intentions," *F & SF*, Oct./Nov.

Rickert, M., "Map of Dreams" (novella), *Map of Dreams*.

——, "The Christmas Witch," *F & SF*, Dec.

——, "You Have Never Been Here," *Feeling Very Strange*.

Roberts, Tansy Rayner, "Rosebuds," *Agog! Ripping Reads*.

Riley, Barry, "The Overcoat," *Dark Animus* 9.

Ringler, Chris, "The Third Horseman," *Bare Bone* 9.

Roessner, Michaela, "Horse-Year Women," *F & SF*, Jan.

Rogers, Mark D., "Mr. Whiteneck's Aviary," *Horror Carousel* 4.

Roggie, Deborah, "Swansdown," *Realms of Fantasy*, Feb.
Rohrig, Judi, "Flesh to Bone," *Furry Fantastic*.
——, "A Thousand Words," *Masques V*.
Rollins, James, "Kowalski's in Love," *Thriller*.
Ronald, Margaret, "Bear Lake," *Fantasy Magazine* 5.
——, "Sparking Anger," *Fantasy Magazine* 2.
Rose, Rhea, "Summer Silk," *Tesseracts Ten*.
Rosenman, John B., "The Death Technique," *Dark Arts*.
Rowe, Christopher, "The League of Last Girls," *Aegri Somnia*.
Royle, Nicholas, "Continuity Error," *London: City of Disappearances*.
Rubis, Jason, "Beauty Thrasher," *Garden of the Perverse: Fairy Tales for Twisted Adults*.
Rucker, Lynda E., "The Last Reel," *Supernatural Tales* 10.
Rusch, Kristine Kathryn, "Dark Corners," *Polyphony* 6.
——, "Except the Music," *Asimov's*, Mar.
Russo, Patricia, "Lemon Filled," *Not One of Us* 36.
——, "The Ogre's Wife," *Tales of the Unanticipated* 27.
Sailors, Susan M., "In Deepest Shadow" (poem), *Horror Carousel* 4.
Sakmyster, David, "The Red Envelope," *Writers of the Future XXII*.
Sammons, Brian M., "Disconnected," *Arkham Tales*.
Samuels, Mark, "The Face of Twilight" (novella), chapbook.
SanGiovanni, Mary, "Kins," *Postscripts* 9.
Saplak, Charles, "Cemetery Seven," *Mythic* 1.
Sarrantonio, Al, "Summer," *Retro Pulp Tales*.
——, "The Man in the Other Car," *Shivers IV*.
Savile, Steve, "Temple" (novella), *Apex* 5–8.
——, "Mens Rea," *Aegri Somnia*.
Scalise, Michelle, "The Disinterment of Ophelia," *Dark Arts*.
Schanoes, Veronica, "Sir Walter Raleigh in Guiana" (poem), *Jabberwocky* 2.
Schow, David J., "Obsequy," *Subterranean* 3.
——, "Scoop vs. the Leadman" (novella), *Havoc Swims Jaded*.
——, "What Happened with Margaret," Ibid.
——, "What Scares You," Ibid.
Schwader, Ann K., "Blood Rosetta" (poem), *Star*Line*, Sept./Oct.
——, "Whitechapel Autumn, 1888" (poem), *Jabberwocky* 2.
Schwaeble, Hank, "Mugwumps," *Alone on the Darkside*.
Schwartz, David J., "Five Hundred and Forty Doors," *Twenty Epics*.
——, "Grandma Charlie and the Wolves," *Flytrap* 6.
——, "Shackles," *Rabid Transit: Long Voyages, Great Lies*.
Schwartz, Jason, "Preamble," *Web Conjunctions*.
Sedia, Ekaterina, "Simargl and the Rowan Tree," *Mythic* 2.
Seeger, Jerry, "Memory of a Thing That Never Was," *F & SF*, July.
Selengut, Zoe, "Smitten," *Twenty Epics*.
Shan, Darren, "Life's a Beach," *Shrouded by Darkness*.
Shannon, Lorelei, "Kodachrome," *Dark Arts*.
Sharp, Jonathan, "White Mountains," *Hardboiled Cthulhu*.
Shaw, Heather, "Mountain, Man," *Rabid Transit: Long Voyages, Great Lies*.
Shaw, Melissa Lee, "Foster," *Asimov's*, Oct./Nov.
Sheldon, Anne, "The Duke of Bedford Prays for His Brother's Soul," *Paradox* 10.
Shepard, Lucius, "The Lepidopterist," *Salon Fantastique*.
Shiel, Julie, "Transformation" (poem), *Mythic Delirium* 15.

Shirley, John, "Blind Eye," *Poe's Lighthouse.*

——, "TechnoTriptych: Panel 1: Call Girl, Echoed," *Dark Wisdom* 8.

Shiro, Sano, "Horror Special" (novella), *Straight to Darkness.*

Shugart, Stephen, "Making Faces," *ParaSpheres.*

Sigrist, Brandon, "Life on the Voodoo Driving Range," *Writers of the Future XXII.*

Simms, Chris, "Baba's Bites," *EQMM*, May.

Simon, Marge, "Tapestry" (poem), www.southernroseproductions.net.

Singer, Sean, "Franz Kafka—Serious about Your Safety" (poem), *Salmagundi*, spring/summer.

Sinha-Morey, Bobbi, "Eye of the Lynx" (poem), *Sybil's Garage* 3.

Slatter, Angela, "Bluebeard," *Shimmer*, summer.

——, "The Angel Wood," *Shimmer*, autumn.

——, "The Little Match Girl," *Shimmer*, spring.

Smith, Douglas, "Memories of the Dead Man," *On Spec*, winter 2005.

Smith, Neil, "Bang Crunch," *Fiddlehead* 223.

Snyder, Jena, "Heart of Ice," *Realms of Fantasy*, Apr.

Sofian, Terry, "Blackwater Ghosts," *Weird Tales* 341.

Sparks, Cat, "Blue Stars for All Savior's Day," *The Outcast.*

Speegle, Darren, "Exposure," *Fantasy Magazine* 4.

——, "Secrets and Silken Threads," *Cemetery Dance* 55.

Spindler, Cara, and Nelson, David Erik, "You Were Neither Hot Nor Cold But Lukewarm, and So I Spit You Out," *LCRW* 19.

Stableford, Brian, "The Elixir of Youth," *Weird Tales* 341.

Stanger, Vaughan, "Touching Distance," *Postscripts* 7.

Steinwachs, Joanne, "Recognition," *Talebones* 32.

Strantzas, Simon, "Off the Hook," *Supernatural Tales* 10.

Stratton, Margaret, "The Traveler's Wiles," *Lies and Limericks.*

Sturgill, Alyssa, "Chokecherryblack," *Bare Bone* 9.

Summer-Smith, Karina, "The Voices of the Snakes," *Fantasy Magazine* 2.

Sunseri, John, "A Little Job in Arkham," *Hardboiled Cthulhu.*

Sutton, David A., "The Holidaymakers," *Clinically Dead.*

——, "Zulu's War," *When Graveyards Yawn.*

Swanwick, Michael, "An Episode of Stardust," *Asimov's*, Jan.

——, Lord Weary's Empire, *Asimov's*, Dec.

Sword, Joanna, "Ghosting," *In the Dark: Stories from the Supernatural.*

Taaffe, Sonya, "Bar Golem," *Electric Velocipede* 9.

——, "Beneath the Garden of Proserpine" (poem), *Dreams and Nightmares* 74.

——, "Chez Vous Soon," *Not One of Us* 35.

——, "Countries of the Sun" (poem), *Jabberwocky* 2.

——, "Exorcisms," *Mythic* 1.

——, "Homecoming," *Mythic* 2.

——, "Like the Stars and the Sand," *Alchemy* 3.

——, "Profundis" (poem), *Star*Line*, Jan./Feb.

——, "Sea-Changes," *Change.*

Tambour, Anna, "See Here, See There," *Agog! Ripping Reads.*

——, "The Cat Story," *Andromeda Spaceways Inflight* 24.

Tate, James, "Police Slumbering" (poem), *Paris Review* 177.

Tarr, P.G., "Forest for the Souls," *In the Dark: Stories from the Supernatural.*

Taylor, Lucy, "Linkage," *Alone on the Darkside.*

Tem, Steve Rasnic, "The Disease Artist," *Dark Arts.*

—— and Tem, Melanie, "Pit's Edge," *Mondo Zombie.*

Tentchoff, Marcie Lynn, "Jacky" (poem), *Star*Line*, Sept./Oct.

Terceira, Ayne, "Nomenculture," *Andromeda Spaceways Inflight* 25.

Tham, Hilary, "The Seventh Day," *Poe's Lighthouse.*

Thomas, Jeffrey, "Close Enough," *Thirteen Specimens.*

——, "The Mask Play of Hahoe Byeolsin Exorcism"(novella), *Punktown: Shades of Grey.*

——, "Merciful Universe," Ibid.

——, "Monster," *Thirteen Specimens.*

——, "Pulse," *Punktown: Shades of Grey.*

——, "Sweaty Betty, Termite Queen of the Danged," Ibid.

——, "Sweet Oblivion," *Dead Cat's Traveling Circus of Wonders.*

——, "Under the Cherub," *Punktown: Shades of Grey.*

——, "The Young of the Old Ones," *Unholy Dimensions.*

Thomas, M., "The Great Conviction," *Lone Star Stories* 16.

Thomas, Scott, and Thomas, Jeffrey, "Apples and Oranges," *In Delirium.*

Thomas, Sheree Renee, "Fallen" (poem), *Strange Horizons*, May 8.

Tidhar, Lavie, "304, Adolph Hitler Strasse," *Clarkesworld Magazine*, Oct.

——, "Children of the Revolution," *Fantasy Magazine* 2.

——, "Eine Kleine Nachtmusik (1943)," *Read by Dawn.*

——, "Letters From Weirdside," *Aegri Somnia.*

Tobler, E. Catherine, "Ticket to Ride," *Fantasy Magazine* 4.

Totton, Sarah, "The Bone Fisher's Apprentice," *Writers of the Future XXII.*

——, "The Undoing," *Tesseracts Ten.*

Tremblay, Paul G., "Feeding the Machine," *Phantom*, issue 0.

——, "It's against the Law to Feed the Ducks," *Fantasy Magazine* 2.

Trimm, Mikal, "Still Born," *Book of Shadows, vol.* 1.

——, "Urban Renewal" (poem), *Star*Line*, Jan./Feb.

——, "Vera Lynn Sings for the Boys," *From the Trenches: An Anthology of Speculative War Stories.*

——, "Veteran of the Last War" (poem), *On Our Way to Battle.*

Tumasonis, Don, "Thrown," *New Genre* 4.

——, "www.thedead.hades.com," *Supernatural Tales* 10.

Uppal, Priscila, "Mycosis," *In the Dark.*

Valente, Catherynne M., "The Cook's Wife" (poem), *Star*Line*, Jan./Feb.

——, "The Descent of the Corn-Queen of the Midwest" (poem), *Mythic Delirium* 14.

——, "The Eight Legs of Grandmother Spider" (poem), *Mythic* 1.

——, "Helen in the Underworld" (poem), *Lone Star Stories*, Aug.

——, "Milk and Apples," *Electric Velocipede* 11.

——, "Suttee" (poem), *Jabberwocky* 2.

——, "Urchins, while Swimming," *Clarkesworld Magazine*, Dec.

Vanderhooft, JoSelle, "The River in Winter," *Cabinet des Fées.*

——, "The Tale of the Desert in the Rain" (poem), *Sybil's Garage* 3.

——, "The Tale of the Desert That Vanished Inside Her"(poem), *Mythic* 2.

——, "Two Rivers" (poem), *Mythic Delirium* 15.

VanderMeer, Jeff, "The Secret Paths of Rajan Khanna," *ParaSpheres.*

Vande Velde, Vivian, "Holding On," *All Hallows Eve.*

——, "My Real Mother," Ibid.

——, "Pretending," Ibid.

van Eekhout, Greg, "The Osteomancer's Son," *Asimov's*, Apr./May.

Velichansky, Michail, "Games on the Children's Ward," *Writers of the Future XXII.*

Vernon, Steve, "Under the Skin, Under the Bones," *From the Trenches.*

Villegas, Halli, "Hair Wreath," *In the Dark: Stories from the Supernatural.*
Volk, Stephen, "The Best in the Business," *Dark Corners.*
——, "Little H," Ibid.
——, "No Harm Done," Ibid.
——, "A Paper Tissue," *Postscripts* 7.
——, "A Whisper to a Grey," *All Hallows* 41.
Vukcevich, Ray, "Tubs," *Lady Churchill's Rosebud Wristlet* 19.
Waggoner, Tim, "Waters Dark and Deep," *Masques V.*
Waldrop, Howard, "Thin, on the Ground," *Cross Plains Universe.*
Walker, Aimee, "The Error," *The Paris Review*, fall.
Walker, Leslie Claire, "The Truth According to Margot Williams," *Fantasy Magazine*, 5.
Wallin, Myna, "The Closet," *In the Dark: Stories from the Supernatural.*
Warburton, Geoffrey, "The Wainwright Glass," *All Hallows* 41.
Ward, C.E., "The Guardian," *Supernatural Tales* 10.
Ward, Kyla, "The Bat's Boudoir," *Shadowed Realms* 9.
Wardle, Susan, "Iron Shirt," *Ticonderoga Online*, summer.
Warren, Kaaron, "The Gibbet Bell," *Borderlands* 8.
——, "Woman Train," *Outcast.*
Webb, Don, "Souvenirs from a Damnation," *When They Came.*
——, "The Collector," Ibid.
Weekes, Carol, "Burial" (poem), *Poe Little Thing* 4.
Wells, Martha, "Wolf Night," *Lone Star Stories*, Aug.
Wentworth, K.D., "The Rose War," *Twenty Epics.*
——, "True North," *Realms of Fantasy*, Aug.
West, Julian, "My Marriage," *Albedo One* 31.
West, Michelle, "Shahira," *Children of Magic.*
Wexler, Robert Freeman, "The Adventures of Philip Schuyler and the Dapper Marionette in the City of the Limbless Octopi," *Polyphony* 6.
White, James Michael, "Bliss," *Talebones* 33.
White, Mike, "Tentacled Motherfucker" (poem), *Pleiades* 26:1.
Whittier, Dave, "Coming Back to Kabul," *On Spec*, summer.
Whyte, Ewan, "Whelan's Ghost," *In the Dark . . .*
Wick, Jessica Paige, "Lullabye to a Selkie's Child" (poem), *Star*Line*, May/June.
Williams, Conrad, "The Veteran," *Postscripts* 6.
Williams, Liz, "The Age of Ice," *Asimov's*, Apr./May.
——, "Tiger, Tiger," *Electric Velocipede* 9.
Williams, Sean, and Brown, Simon, "Dying for Air," *Andromeda Spaceways* 23.
Williams, Timothy, "The Hollows," *Alchemy* 3.
Williamson, Neil, "The Codsman and His Willing Shag," *The Ephemera.*
——, "The Gubbins," *Dark Horizons* 49.
Willrich, Chris, "Penultima Thule," *F & SF*, Aug.
Wilson, F. Paul, "Sex Slaves of the Dragon Tong," *Retro Pulp Tales.*
Witteveen, David, "Ache," *Hardboiled Cthulhu.*
Wodzinski, Beth, "The Minotaur's Rabbit," *Apex* 7.
Wolfe, Gene, "Bea and Her Bird Brother," *F & SF*, May.
——, "Christmas Inn," *Christmas Inn.*
——, "On a Vacant Face a Bruise," *Strange Birds.*
Wood, Simon, "Acceptable Losses," *Dark Wisdom* 9.
Wright, T.M., "I Am the Bird" (novella), chapbook.
——, "Tomato as Metaphor," *Postscripts* 7.

Yaniv, Nir, "A Wizard on the Road," (translated by Lavie Tidhar) *Shimmer*, autumn.

YellowBoy, Erzebet, "A Remedy for Sorry," *Not One of Us* 36.

——, "Moonstone," *Mythic* 2.

Yohalem, Mark, "Mercy in the Lazaretto," *Ten Plagues*.

Zebrowski, George, "Black Pockets" (novella), *Black Pockets*.

Zirbel, Mark, "Bags," *DeathGrip: Exit Laughing*.

The People Behind the Book

Ellen Datlow was editor of *SCI FICTION*, the multi award-winning fiction area of scifi.com for six years, editor of *Event Horizon: Science Fiction and Fantasy* for one-and-a-half years, and fiction editor of *OMNI* and *OMNI* Online. She continues to edit anthologies for adults, young adults, and children.

Her most recent anthologies are *The Dark*, *The Faery Reel*, *Salon Fantastique*, and *The Coyote Road*, (the latter three with Terri Windling). Her horror anthology, *Inferno*, will be out in December. She's been coediting *The Year's Best Fantasy and Horror* for over twenty years. Datlow has won multiple World Fantasy Awards, Bram Stoker Awards, Hugo Awards, Locus Awards, and the International Horror Guild Award, for her editing. She lives in New York City. For more information and lots of photos see www.datlow.com.

Kelly Link and **Gavin J. Grant** started Small Beer Press in 2000. They have published the zine *Lady Churchill's Rosebud Wristlet* ("Tiny, but celebrated"—*Washington Post*) for ten years. An anthology, *The Best of Lady Churchill's Rosebud Wristlet*, will be published this autumn. With Ellen Datlow they have won the Bram Stoker Award and the Locus Award for editing *The Year's Best Fantasy and Horror*. Link and Grant live in Northampton, Massachusetts.

Kelly Link is the author of two collections, *Stranger Things Happen* and *Magic For Beginners* (one of *Time Magazine*'s Best Books of the Year). She edited the anthology *Trampoline*. Stories from her collections have won the Nebula, Hugo, World Fantasy, Tiptree, and Locus awards, and her work has appeared in *A Public Space*, *Firebirds Rising*, and *Best American Short Stories 2005*.

Originally from Scotland, **Gavin J. Grant** regularly reviews fantasy and science fiction. He cohosts the Fantastic Fiction Reading Series with Ellen Datlow at KGB Bar in New York City. Publications where his work has appeared include the *Los Angeles Times*, *BookPage*, *SCI FICTION*, *Strange Horizons*, and *Salon Fantastique*.

Media critic **Edward Bryant** is an award-winning author of science fiction, fantasy, and horror, having published short fiction in countless anthologies and magazines. He's won the Nebula Award for his science fiction, and other works of his short fiction have been nominated for many other awards. He's also written for television. He lives in Denver, Colorado.

Jeff VanderMeer is a two-time winner of the World Fantasy Award, and has made the year's best lists of *Publishers Weekly*, the *San Francisco Chronicle*, the *Los Angeles Weekly*, *Publishers' News*, and amazon.com. His fiction has been shortlisted for *Best American Short Stories* and appeared in several years' best anthologies. Books by VanderMeer are forthcoming from Bantam, Pan Macmillan, and Tor.

Music critic **Charles de Lint** is a full-time writer and musician who presently makes his home in Ottawa, Canada, with his wife MaryAnn Harris, an artist and musician. His most recent novels are *Little (Grrl) Lost, The Blue Girl,* and *Widdershins.* Other recent publications include the chapbook *Old Man Crow* and the collections *Triskell Tales 2* and *The Hour before Dawn.* For more information about his work, visit his Web site at www.charlesdelint.com.

Series jacket artist **Thomas Canty** has won the World Fantasy Award for Best Artist. He has painted and/or designed covers for many books and has art-directed many other covers in a career that spans more than twenty years. He lives outside Boston, Massachusetts.

Packager **James Frenkel**, a book editor since 1971, has been an editor for Tor Books since 1983, and is currently a senior editor. He has also edited various anthologies, including *True Names and the Opening of the Cyberspace Frontier, Technohorror,* and *Bangs and Whimpers.* He lives in Madison, Wisconsin.